NOV
VENERATIO, DEDECUS ET BELLUM

L R WOLLACOTT

2007

NOVO ROMA

Copyright © 2007 L R WOLLACOTT
All rights reserved.
ISBN: 1-4196-2516-0
ISBN-13: 978-1419625169
Library of Congress Control Number: 2001012345

Visit www.booksurge.com to order additional copies.

NOVO ROMA

CONTENTS

PART ONE	CAESAR	1
PART TWO	REBELLION	35
PART THREE	AN AMBUSH AND A FORT	69
PART FOUR	A BRIEF REST	111
PART FIVE	TRIBUTARY SKIRMISH	141
PART SIX	COUNCIL OF LORD AARUN	163
PART SEVEN	AZAR-KAD	205
PART EIGHT	BATTLE OF THE RIVER	241
PART NINE	A NEW ALLIANCE	281
PART TEN	A JOURNEY SOUTH	311
PART ELEVEN	HOLVIDAR	355
PART TWELVE	VALENUS	399
PART THIRTEEN	REUNIONS	427
PART FOURTEEN	DIVINE INTERVENTION	471
PART FIFTEEN	RETURN OF THE GODS	519
Index of main characters and locations		579

THE WORLD OF TANNIS (NORTHERN HEMISPHERE)
Lord Khazumar's sketch for Marcellus

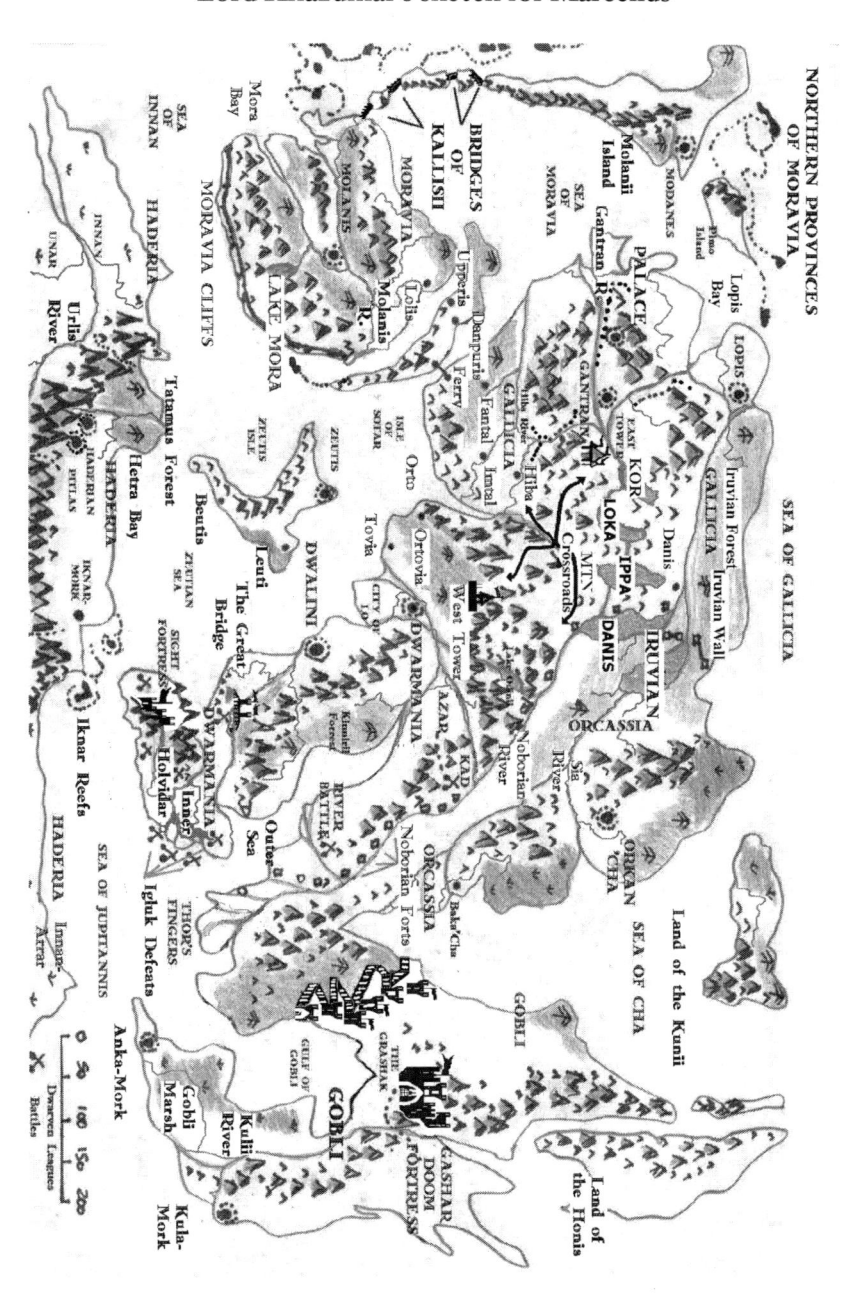

In memory of my Grandfather Thomas Frederick Harris and my mother Janet Silvia Curtis Wollacott whose memory will never fade.

A special thanks also to my Grandmother Mary Harris.

Additional thanks to all those who helped to complete a dream, especially Miriam, Mary and Parvez, I am also extremely grateful to Bridget, John and Alison for their professional support.

You have all made this book a reality.

PART ONE

CAESAR

The fundamental problems that have confronted armies and their commanders over the years have never really changed from one century to the next. The difficulties of supply and demand encompassed a large proportion of any person's time in relation to the very real dangers of combat. The supply of troops at the critical point of conflict, to meet the demand of those threatened, was normally the real issue when dealing with political negotiations that had degenerated into a state of warfare.

In the spring of 58 BC, this very problem was handed to a prominent politician in the hope that he would fail, but it rebounded in turn on the original political plotters, with unexpected results. The man in question was by no stretch of the imagination a commonplace person with an ordinary destiny, but even for him what transpired was hardly expected.

All this man needed at first was to secure a safe base of operation. Next came food for the army in the field, the provision of trained manpower, and the creation of the correct political climate, which had to date served this particular individual well, timing being all-important when dealing with slippery politicians. Having successfully manipulated his position within the Senate of Roma, the true power of the Roman Republic, he now recognised the perfect opportunity to achieve his greater ambitions, while his enemies viewed this singular chance in a very different light. At first he was advised to wait, but they all knew this would be to no avail. This man had not defeated the Phoenecian and Illyricum pirates by hesitating.

No...All he needed was the right people to follow in his shadow, and to be sacrificed when necessary, and the world would be subdued. In terms of status and success, his name was sufficient to cause many brave men to falter and hesitate in their own political and military aspirations, to seize power in the fickle baths and halls of Roma.

Many had sought his destruction and failed, and he knew that many more would try again, but this did not deter him from a task that could lead the Republic to an even greater degree of world domination. *His* domination! He had not helped to deny Pro-consul Crassus his triumph only for the victory over Spartacus to be set aside, while those such as Gnais Pompeius Magna rose to new heights of power. His success was paramount!

This man was none other than *Gaius Julius Caesar*!

To some, Caesar was an unknown politician of some military experience in recent campaigns against the Lusitanian barbarians in Hispania, where many battles had been fought. However, most others agreed that in this new province not all the rumours were true, leaving an air of uncertainty as to what precisely could be believed, as he had, most suspiciously, written all the senatorial reports personally. A trait he was never to delegate to any hand other than his own. To those of greater ambitions and less scruples he was the backdoor aspect in the halls of power, but not a man to trust.

To cross this man might not induce an immediate rebuke, indeed decorum demanded no such lack of manners, but rest assured that when Caesar's mind finally decided it was time to repay any unkindness then the best option was to leave Roma for a very long time. Decisions having been made and orders issued, all the backbiting and character assassination seemed to fade into the background. For those who rode with Julius Caesar during those early eight days, from Roma to the Rhodanus River in the Transalpine Gallia province, there was nothing to indicate that their futures would lead them to the very brink of war, indeed to the very brink of existence.

Caesar knew, as far as any mortal could know, but like all great men he saw little profit in sharing this information with his colleagues. For each of them, the objective was to seek adventure and vast amounts of monetary gains, cattle, lands, slaves and, just as important,...maidens.

All of these men saw in Caesar a man of destiny and future wealth. But to Caesar they represented only a means to an end. If only they could have known? Loyalty was always rewarded by Caesar, but not by too much and not too soon. He was a shrewd man indeed. It was enough to keep the strings tight, while allowing the greed to fester and create the desire for more. As oft as not he would smile to himself as he recollected that his own gold reserves were practically gone.

They did not know this either, but it did not matter in those heady eight days as they rode north along the Via Cassia, the new road constructed to speed up the legion's march north. Now they used it for their own personal use, making sure the local magistrates were informed of their journey, as indeed all travellers were required by law to do.

Power, wealth and control of the Republic now rested in the firm grip of the Triumvirate created by Caesar himself, Gnais Pompeius Magna and Marcus Lucinius Crassus of the eastern provinces. Politically Pompeius Magna held the balance of power, being situated in Roma and controlling Hispania, while Crassus maintained control over the eastern territories and Scythia. Caesar initially only controlled the northern peninsular of Italia, but clearly intended to add Gallia to his domain.

Where Pompeius Magna had some loyalty to Caesar and visa versa, Crassus was barely loyal and they both knew, due to their friendship and Pompeius being married to Caesar's daughter, that sooner or later war with the eastern power block was as inevitable as the rising of the sun. Caesar's real influence had in actuality not yet come into existence. He was, as before, still in the shadow of Pompeius Magna. Most annoying!

Now, as they continued north, Caesar recalled the legitimate, and the underhanded, methods that had been necessary to elevate his influence within the Senate. Day by day cajoling of individual senators who were as greedy as the sky is red at dusk. Money was borrowed and painstakingly paid back at the right moments, to ensure certain votes in the senatorial debates. At first Pompeius Magna had stood to oppose, but when he could not fathom the real purpose he had lost interest and slowly the steps began to create a stairway to an opening. Then, and suddenly, the greatest event so far in Caesar's life had occurred, when the Helvetii tribesmen attacked the settlements north of Corunna.

Peace followed quickly, but this was not what Caesar desired. He needed the crisis to continue. He had to prevent the local administration from dealing with such a minor irritation and therefore sent orders for two of the three legions guarding the border to be moved to rest at Placentia and Genoa, leaving only the elite tenth legion on station in the border forts. He later added orders for all crossings to be held by at least half a cohort of legionaries, thus dissipating even further this force's ability to stop the raids. As a result, the killing continued until it became necessary to resolve the matter in person. Pompeius Magna had other responsibilities and plans to travel to Hispania so it was that he became the natural person to send. It all seemed so simple now as they crossed a bridge and descended the hills towards Arretium.

Now, as always, Caesar's mind switched to his greater purpose and became ever more engrossed with the problem of seizing the remainder of the Gallic peninsular without openly invading and declaring war on the indigenous tribes. By this time he had been advised that the combined tribes could field an army of over half a million warriors. Even a mind as mighty as his could see the impossibility of fighting such a horde. No, open war was not the way, but a localised war that began to escalate was a different policy altogether.

The Helvetii problem had now given him the opportunity to focus the border difficulties onto one group of tribes alone, thus increasing his influence over those tribes that were sympathetic to his views and further isolating those who opposed him. They themselves feared invasion by the Helvetii, and he began to draw them ever closer to Roma, and sent hundreds of merchants and their families to secure this continued friendship through whatever form of bribery was deemed fit for the purpose. It was a drain on his resources, but a necessary one if he was to add the loyal tribes' cavalry to his small army.

Roma could not furnish sufficient men to invade central Gallia, there were simply too many tribes to resist their will, but a series of separate enterprises might enable Caesar to slowly usurp power from under the population's eyes, before they perceived his true intentions of a permanent occupation.

The campaigns in Lusitania had given Caesar a reputation for bravery on the battlefield, which helped with the marshalling of the troops; and with his spectacular ability as an orator, the immense personality was more than capable of seizing any such opportunities as they arose. Add to this a love of art, statues, poetry and strong masculine features, and we can paint a picture of a man of destiny to whom so many had affiliated their loyalties.

Where Marcus Lucinius Crassus was idle, Gaius Julius Caesar never slept. Where Gnais Pompeius Magna would offer gifts to maintain loyalty, Caesar rewarded only those who had earned such gratitude, but always maintained the desire for more. Failure did not necessarily mean execution, but few dared to report such failings until Caesar's mood encouraged such news. Success was the key to his good favour. Failure would, in time, sooner or later, be the end of you, irrespective of your political support in Roma, or the loyalty of the legion. The legions obeyed Caesar and even within the Roma contingent this was apparent to Pompeius Magna and must have been a constant irritation.

Nowhere within the entire Republic was a man more loved and feared simultaneously than Caesar, who now rode into Pistoriae without any disturbance or announcements and with only a ten-man escort of friends. Such trust in the population was the main reason for the continued loyalty of the Roma mob, the people of the suburbs.

He was loved for the glory he brought to Roma, and feared by his enemies, who breathed a sigh of relief as news reached them of his later arrival at Pisae. Some believed that he would never return. Others were not so optimistic and saw a different outcome to this new adventure in the annals of Caesar. The latter were correct, but perhaps our truth will alter the recorded history.

Either way, friend or foe, most agreed *Caesar must go*!

To those who joined him at the small feast in Genoa, none of this was apparent. The Senate had blessed their arms to victory and sanctioned the raising of new legions to defeat the barbarians. Indeed, almost two months previously, Caesar had ordered that two more be created and ready to move, long before the border disputes had escalated to the possibility of a conflict. Everything was planned down to the very month that he expected the Helvetii to switch from peaceful talks to more aggressive border raids. There was nothing that escaped his attention.

He had, on arrival in the northern provinces, sacked the two Legates that had commanded the legions and that had, earlier that year, mysteriously decided on a training march away from their border duties. In their place he promptly promoted two loyal Caesareans to support his new policies, anticipating senatorial approval by seven days: what miraculous forethought, they all agreed. The new legion commanders promptly destroyed Caesar's written orders of only a few months earlier for them to move the legions in the first place, but his ploy would remain a closely guarded secret until no longer of value.

They had no reason to ignore the rumours regarding Pompeius Magna's true intentions of eventually ruling alone. To be honest, it seemed odd that such a man of power did not seek more, it was certainly within Caesar's policy, otherwise why join him? Previous campaigns had been profitable and they saw no reason to see the border situation as anything else. Caesar's new appointment as the pro-consul of Gallia was a blessing from the Gods themselves and all of them saw two avenues open to them.

As military officers in Caesar's legion, they could achieve power beyond most men's dreams. Or as rich senators, when the twelve months compulsory tour of duty had been completed, they could perhaps reach the prestigious heights of the consulship, then a pro-consular post and eventual retirement in a villa made of gold. Either route had its pitfalls and advantages, but for now Caesar offered the greater probability of success.

As military tribunes they held their posts with the authority of the Senate, through political appointments that could not be refused by the pro-consul. The decision as to where they would then serve, however, remained with Caesar, but they could not be returned to Roma until they had completed the compulsory service. To those who had served in Hispania during the Lusitanian campaign the next step had always been a distasteful one.

On completion of service, they would then be obliged to return to Roma to begin their careers as political representatives. All of them had to do this service to obtain the crowd's respect, if indeed the consulship was their ambition. If they were to rule, they must be seen to be above the average citizen. Most of those who travelled with Caesar eventually preferred to remain with the army.

This was unusual in a time when betrayal, plots and assassins were part of everyday life. Kill Caesar and you could usurp his power, but in truth the loyalty of his attendants had made this practically impossible. So in the legions they remained! Some died, of battle wounds or disease. Some refused to return to Roma and thus enrolled for twenty-five years; others maintained a happy existence within the local militia assignments, commanding the auxiliary regiments throughout the Republic.

The lure of greater things attracted these men to Caesar. His ability to tear victory from almost certain defeat had been clearly demonstrated in Hispania, where several battles had been won through his personal intervention. This trend alone had created a strong bond with a few of these men, while the others had been persuaded by the stories of the wealth divided and the spoils of victory. He was unique and they knew it only too well!

The provincial difficulties that they now travelled towards had not developed overnight. Indeed they knew of Caesar's continued review of the information on the raids as they came in from his spies and client states' kings within Gallia. Each report of twenty raiders became two hundred when forwarded to the forum. A few lives lost or a local merchant's home burnt down became an entire suburb of the local settlements. After an entire year in the consulship Caesar had learnt a new level of ruthlessness, and exploiting the Helvetii was hardly worth any loss of sleep.

This had surprised several of his most loyal friends who openly foresaw disaster from a military point of view, as only senatorial legates could predict. They quoted openly in debate the great Marius who had managed to forestall the sacking of Roma, daring to add their own quotes in his absence, about how Caesar hardly matched these military skills after fighting in Hispania! The floating voters, on hearing of the local demands from merchants for another senatorial appointment, had also switched to direct support of Pompeius Magna, as more and more money was lavishly furnished; and even stories of Caesar's death on the road north had been circulated, to wrest away support for his endeavours.

It failed due to the population's support. The people and *not* the Senate supported Caesar and the citizenry of Roma was a difficult creature to pin down at the best of times. Recent bread riots had hardly diminished Caesar's popularity. He had personally taken food to the masses, even to the point of shaking their diseased hands and breathing the same air. He had known the risks but even now, as he rode north, every soul knew of its worth, as the people eagerly retained their interest in Caesar's activities in his absence, demanding daily reviews at the auditoriums.

In a modern sense, he had become irreplaceable, a rising star. For Pompeius Magna, at this time, there was little to concern his elevated status in the senate after Marcus Lucinius Crassus had left for the eastern provinces, so the adoration was permitted in the knowledge that Caesar would be forgotten within the year. Had he known of Caesar's plans for Gallia would he have opened his eyes just that little bit more? Caesar had no intention of being forgotten! He had every intention of seeing the Rubicon once more!

To Caesar, however, war was what he expected to encounter, because he had engineered the current rivalry between the tribes on their northern borders. Decrees forbidding trade with any faction of the Helvetii while increasing trade with the Germanic tribes added to this precarious situation. He had learnt only days before of a great battle that had taken place between them, as the Germanic peoples sought to expand their territory by destroying the Helvetii. They had failed, but the increasing pressure on the agricultural status of the Helvetii people and the added military threat, both of Roma and from the Germanic people, left few avenues for the Helvetii to alleviate their suffering. It was not the Germanic people who needed more land!

He set his mind to developing this situation accordingly. In their arrogance the Senate continued to refuse to believe that another invasion would take place after the massacre at the battle of Aquae Sextiae, forty years before. Eighty thousand barbarians had paid with their lives for the invasion of Transalpine Gallia and Narbonensis. Caesar, however, believed otherwise, and was not prone to such a lack of understanding of people, as were the higher classes of the Roman civilian population. Although he excelled in such public outcries for peace and prosperity, he knew in his heart that the Helvetii would attack. The alternative was starvation, and Caesar related their situation to what he would have done, had the roles been reversed.

He therefore journeyed north with an open mind, and a clear determination to delay the inevitable and to hopefully change the cards that fate had dealt into a winning hand. It would not be difficult, but should success be achieved then the laurels would be his alone, even if he were responsible for causing them in the first place. Then, by the Gods, they would all crawl and prostrate themselves before his exalted feet! If they thought his consulship was harsh, then they were in for a serious shock when his plans came to fruition. His mind was set on the destruction of the Republic, not just the acquisition of power! His ambition knew no limits.

For the moment though, as he dismounted for the night at a small inn, he took time to recap the plight on the border. For many years the Helvetii and the local tribes had approached Roma, either to obtain a treaty of trade or to seek permission to migrate to more fertile lands within the Republic. As already stated, these trade routes had already been deliberately cut by Caesar as, individually, the tribes represented no serious threat.

This failure had therefore led them to create an alliance of their own with other smaller tribes who had also been attacked by the Germanic peoples, whom Roma seemingly supported. Further attempts at a political approach having failed, the Helvetii then approached their allies for more active solutions and they all agreed to close their borders to Roma's merchants, although this put more strain on their resources than on the Senate.

They found that they all faced a common ground, the dire circumstances in which they struggled against the same weapons of ignorance and malice that denied them even the basic fundamentals such as food. Roma and the Germanic tribes had little to gain from supporting one another directly in force, but they knew a starving animal when they saw one and neither saw fit to raise a helping hand. That would have been too easy. Discussions, of which Caesar was well aware, had begun as early as the autumn of the previous year, but continued hostilities between some of the minor tribes had prevented any joint efforts regarding the proposed alliance. The policy therefore failed miserably and starvation was the only reward for their peoples.

With the winter that starvation came, and within a few weeks of the New Year the entire local population had sought out the Helvetii council of elders, to act as their spokesmen in yet another final effort to find food. In quick succession, the Tulingi, Latabrogi and Boii all signed the agreements to act as a single entity. Only the Rauraci disputed the place of the leading members of the proposed new council. Caesar immediately sent supplies to the Rauraci to imply that their allegiance was not solid, and the result was a further delay in the council's actions.

By the time Caesar was aware of this new situation, the local populace had risen up in defiance of the uncivilised barbarians, fuelled of course by local politicians who saw as much profit in Gallia as did Caesar. Trade by the barbarians with Roma had been extremely beneficial until two years before and the more ambitious souls were beginning to feel the pinch. It was time to put the barbarians in their place and remind them of the power of Roma.

It was then that Caesar accepted the new post and rode north with his small entourage, determined to avoid another winter of struggle for the citizens of Cisalpine and the bordering provinces. He was, after all, the conquering saviour that each group of civilians he met cheered on, while the bands of slaves nearby said nothing. The memories of Spartacus were still fresh in their memories.

The slaves of course sympathised with the Helvetii and understood their plight. All they wanted was food, which this Republic could afford, with little loss on its part. However, the greedy merchants saw only more slaves, more land and more wealth. The barbarian suffering did not enter their equation. However, the Helvetii alone did not raise the alarm, but the combined tribes left many a mother terrified to walk alone at night, and so the call for the military to help was heard as clear as a crying child.

Previously they had faced a large enemy, but now they faced an alliance that literally doubled the barbarian ability to wage war. They too sought victory, but their error lay in the fact that they first sought this through peaceful measures. Caesar had no such inhibitions. He saw a weakened enemy and had no hesitation in increasing that discomfort.

As the victor of any border conflict, the spoils would be his and be more advantageous than on the Eastern, Pro-Consul Crassus, or African, Pro-Consul Marcellus, borders, where various conflicts had now been temporarily resolved. His only purpose now was to subdue the Helvetii alliance and prevent their continued incursions across the border, which so far had amounted to no more than an exaggerated irritation. To this end, he had sent his most trusted aide ahead with an understanding of the military difficulties; long before he himself had left Roma.

He had issued orders to the border commander Titus Labienus to create specific fortifications at certain points along the Rhodanus River, even before the other two local legates had been replaced by Caesareans. Now was the time for his policy of dispersal to be reversed, and very rapidly too! When ordering the consolidation of the other provincial legions against any unknown developments north and south, he added two new legions that had been created in Narbonensis.

He had not even set foot within Labienus' command tent, and yet he had already changed the military situation to one of certain stability. Previously, the legion had remained on station opposite the northern lake and maintained a constant patrol along the river settlements. Before the winter, it had been an adequate force, but now the enemy had shown a greater level of activity and larger bands crossed the river regularly. Caesar's deliberate positioning of local camps along the river, thus leaving Labienus with little more than a few cohorts at any time to deal with any specific incursion, had worked perfectly. Labienus had had to deal with furious merchants terrified of losing everything.

The Hevetii council, not knowing of Caesar's impending arrival, also followed a policy of seeking out the local men of power, to continue their pleas for a peaceful migration to the sea. At first there seemed to have been some good progress, as local citizens temporarily demanded that the people be allowed to walk through Narbonensis to the sea. It was actually this development that had prompted Caesar's swift departure from Roma.

However, a local tribal leader had taken it upon himself to massacre a caravan of traders, of close to one hundred unarmed people, to steal their food, and Roma could not have asked for a better excuse to end any further discussions. All attempts now failed. Further attempts ended abruptly when Caesar arrived and immediately arrested all the dignitaries sent by the barbarian council. There would be no more discussions. His only concern related to a bridge recently constructed for easier access across the Rhodanus. Roma's only weakness that needed to be rectified.

Caesar had arrived to accomplish that task!

"I will succeed in bringing the Helvetii tribes to peace and to the understanding of the right of Roma to protect its borders for the glory of Roma," he instructed his second in command and trusted friend Tulla. "Success, however, will depend on the capture of the Rhodanus Bridge or at a minimum its immediate destruction. Send a message to Labienus immediately that he is to seize the initiative personally."

The order, as always, had been blunt and to the point, with the intention of striking while the heat of battle was close to ignition. Tulla also knew that the bridge was of vital importance and did not really need reminding, but such aggressive tactics had always served Caesar well and there was no reason to alter the approach, especially as he anticipated that the prospect of starvation would be his strongest ally.

"I will see to it, noble Caesar." Tulla replied, respectfully, but at the tent exit suddenly turned.

"Yes?"

It was unusual for Tulla to hesitate.

"My honour bids me to obey, mighty Caesar, but should we not have kept our legions combined before we provoke a battle? Labienus' men will be hard pressed to hold the river. If they fail..."

"I am not aware that I requested a debate from you, Tulla. Because it is you, I will relent on this one occasion, but be warned: there is little room in my patience for those who hesitate. I do not lecture you on how you treat your slaves, so do not repeat this lack of trust again. If the river is held against them they will have no choice but to move through Gallia and I intend to have my army there to end any further migration. If Labienus fails then they will be executed," Caesar finished, with a nonchalant shrug of the shoulders, provoking a satisfying look of surprise from Tulla who was well aware of Caesar's policy of dispersal. "However, your point is perhaps well made, Tulla. So I will leave this task to you. If the local commander proves to be inadequate, I give you leave to assume command and do as I have bidden. You accept?"

"I do, noble Caesar. But I am sure Labienus will not fail."

"See to it that he does not, my friend, or you will join him and take your chances in the decimation that I *will* order should you fail. Now go, we have wasted enough time. I must rest."

Tulla raised a clenched fist to thump his left breast in salute then left, returning to the tent exit in order to organise his victuals for the journey. Caesar would remain to finalise the organisation and concentration points of the army, which was at that time spread all across the northern provinces. Labienus would need to buy them time. Time was all they required.

Caesar initially began to apply his mind to the widespread formations that would join to create his intended army, but it was not long before he was sidetracked into resolving the minor issues still remaining from the day's travel. Of these only one truly preoccupied his mind. Local centurions and tribunes had efficiently resolved everything else and so, for the first time since leaving Roma, he was free to relax and he decided to do so with his entourage. The task was to decide which posts his tribunes would occupy during the coming campaign. More important, which ones could he trust?

By the usual protocols he had received a list of those very tribunes who would accompany him north. These he would need to choose carefully, to avoid any obvious spies planted by Pompeius Magna or Marcus Crassus, to report back on his failures. He had of course forgotten Marcellus in Africa, but that fat fool was hardly a true contender, as he was only the consular legate and not a member of the Triumvirate. As the evening proceeded, Caesar relaxed more and for a moment or two held onto his suspicions, but eventually he accepted that none here would betray him. He quickly marked against each name a specific command post, and also added several of his more trusted aides to ride with each one. He was not above using spies and assassins himself, and he would watch them all very closely. Amongst these officers he trusted only one man completely, Marcus Antoninus, to him he gave a sweeping freedom to act on his behalf in his absence, just to reinforce the sense of being observed.

This task completed he then retired, satisfied temporarily. He dozed for a moment on the silken pillows. When this did not alleviate his tension he moved over to a divan and finally found the comfort to sleep. It was not to last very long.

With a jolt he jerked back to full wakefulness, reaching instinctively for the dagger he always carried, even in bed. His head ached and he fought for a few seconds to regain his vision. Once recovered he contemplated informing the herbalist, but he deemed that this would be taken as a bad omen, so he slowly lay back on the comfortable divan. He could not remember the dream that had caused such anguish, but as his mind became fully aware he knew that it had not involved him. The omen had been for the tenth legion alone.

It took another two hours to find sleep again. In the meantime he deliberated about the ill fortune his dreams heralded. He could not see the future and did not wish to raise the alarm with futile enquiries, but the dream nevertheless continued to taunt him: a black cloud hovering over the silent form of a legionary who knelt in obedience. What could this possibly mean?

He realised that he could not find the answer, but he would hold sacrifices at dawn and see what could be confirmed, knowing only too well that the result would be a good omen. If the priests valued their heads! As he considered which sacrifices would be required, sheer exhaustion began to take its toll and he finally found the comfort of a heavy sleep that involved no further disturbances.

It was a sleep many others also watched with an interested gaze, of malevolence and protection in equal proportions. He did not know of his own true destiny, but sought to achieve what he believed to be the fate of the world: to be ruled by one government of Roma, ordained by the Gods no less. He could only hope that they were in agreement.

Others of course had a different itinerary. Just as Caesar had no sympathy for those he used for his own purposes, so others had no empathy for him. He was not alone in the whirlpool of ambition.

⁘⁛⁘

Caesar rode through the camp as faces turned to see who had descended upon them at such an early hour. It had taken three days to reach Labienus' camp from Genoa, and as they rode forward, having navigated the guards at the southern gate, confusion reigned. His gait made it was clear he was a dignitary of some sort, but none of them could place the face. None of these legionaries and camp followers had been to the capital for over five years, and during that time this person had been in Lusitania, hence the lack of recognition.

Of course a few tribunes had been sent forward to warn of his approach, but only those who needed to know. The order to form ranks had been given only thirty minutes earlier. It did not of course help them at all to have their mild day disturbed by a sudden onrush of activity. They were hardened professionals, but they held fast to the old liberties of a soldier and they grumbled profusely at having a day of rest disturbed.

Now they suspected that a long day of trudging in thick sandals and building another camp twenty leagues away, in whatever direction, would be ordered before much longer. Whoever this stranger was, it foretold imminent danger and it also meant that some, if not all of them, might not return or even reach the new destination. They were all more than aware of the barbarian uprising!

In times of peace, Caesar had seen many attributes to a show of force, and the necessity of pomp and aplomb to impress those that could support his cause or oppose from other powers or provinces. However, in times of impending war he saw little point in advertising his whereabouts to any host intent on interception. Now was the time for action, not for procrastinating over minor social issues such as administrators and military honour guards. Back in Roma he had determined that no such entourage was required. He would hardly change his mind now.

He watched as the troops began to form ranks on either side of him, most of them still extremely dishevelled. He smiled secretly, as he knew they had been taken by surprise. The last person they had expected to see was a full blown senatorial pro-consul riding nonchalantly along the central road in their camp, clearly intent on causing mischief. It mattered little to them in the real scheme of their lives, but each man expected a little rest, and the sudden arrival of government officials hardly implied that he had travelled so far to bring good news.

Caesar shifted his cloak irritably and blinked as the sun's rays suddenly caught the breastplate, blinding him momentarily. After adjusting the approach to the central compound, where all sorts of weaponry had been stored, the rising sun found other objects to glitter from, giving the scene an absence of reality. This would not last as the sun was rising quickly, but the confusion continued, or so it seemed; but already numerous maniples had linked together and some order could be discerned in the activity all around.

Caesar noted that the provost guard had been alerted to his presence and that the local cavalry commander had despatched patrols to link up with him and to secure his safe arrival. How that person had known of his exact whereabouts had momentarily stunned them all into inactivity, and had impressed Caesar immensely. Perhaps a word of thanks would be beneficial to the praefectus equitum, the senior cavalry officer in this province.

"Who is the praefectus equitum of this province, Attilus?" he asked his aide, as they rode up the main central approach to the command tent.

Attilus was a young man who had originally been the herder with the legions in Lusitania. However, during a raid he had personally defeated ten warriors who had been intent on stealing a portion of the cattle herd. His bravery had saved one month's supply of meat, and such was Caesar's gratitude that the slave had suddenly found a place among his personal entourage. He now served as a personal encyclopaedia, and his high intelligence soon made clear that the decision to promote him had been right.

It was of course a promotion that had been opposed from the beginning due to the slave's origins. However, Julius had never been one to restrict his ambitions by taking seriously society's ridiculous laws of discrimination. He saw bravery beyond the normal edicts and he rewarded as he saw fit. It was perhaps one of the more openly recited reasons why many in the Senate had such a high disregard for him, but that was hardly an issue while on campaign. There or in Gallia!

"I believe his name is Lentulus, noble Caesar," Attilus replied, jostling gently with his horse, which had suddenly spied a mare that drew its interest. The bout of neighing certainly left them in no doubt, but to Attilus the sudden movement was a cause for concern, as he had never been an especially good rider.

"That name is familiar to me. Has this man served with me previously?"

"I am not aware that he served in Lusitania, but I will make enquiries when we have stabled and fed the horses. There were many junior officers that I did not know during the campaign, noble Caesar, but it will not take too long to determine the facts."

Caesar squinted, then turned to face Attilus. The sun was as radiant as it was painful to the eyes, and the relief from its glare made the pro-consul sigh deeply. Of course to Attilus the sigh could only mean one thing, and the irritation of Caesar was not a good idea. He alone recognised his good fortune far more than all the detractors of his promotion.

"That will not be necessary. When we reach the command tent, order the senior officers present to attend a staff meeting. I require an update of the military situation. I see no reason to delay here longer than is necessary to confirm what needs to be done. Our place is at that bridge."

"As you command, noble Caesar, so shall it be done."

Caesar smiled at that, he had always liked the way Attilus spoke and offered such niceties that left no room for barbarity on his part. Not that he found the slave a burden. He would of course execute him without a second thought, but why let Attilus know? He was after all rather useful.

"Good," he replied finally, looking ahead, to where he assumed the main command tent would be.

They rode on through the confusion about them. It was unusual to see so many men idle, but clearly the order given must have been to mobilise only a portion of the men in this camp. Caesar should have left them in no doubt as to the grave danger they all faced. He had not campaigned with Titus Labienus before this day, but had received several reports indicating that this man was of exceptional ability.

He had noted this in his journals several months before and then secretly had this legion transferred from the Danubian front months earlier. It was not the normal procedure for a Legate to remain in command of any specific legion for any length of time. Indeed it was often the case that the command staff would ride with the relevant senatorial pro-consul, and assign a legion only in the event of battle. To Caesar this had seemed too cumbersome, and the one thing he knew for certain was that he was not the only one who could identify a good commander. The men were just as capable of recognising who were the soldiers on his staff, and who were the politicians.

They invariably fought better when led by an experienced commander, and he had tried to implement a new way whereby a legion would retain its current commander until he decided otherwise or they came into disfavour. It created a much more efficient military formation.

However, his first impression was of men of little value entertaining themselves, while the officers were nowhere to be seen. Except for the few maniples so far aroused, at least two thirds had remained ensconced in their activities with barely a glance at the new arrival. It was not a good start. Even if Labienus had ordered a day of rest, Caesar's presence countermanded all previous instructions.

A few minutes later they caught sight of the main line of tents in the central area and slowed the horses to a walk. Drawing his horse to a stop outside the main tent that served as headquarters, Caesar waited patiently for Labienus to appear. Presently the man did so and brought his staff, holding a map, a table and numerous wineskins with a bowl of fruit. Without even glancing towards Caesar, Labienus motioned for the table to be brought forward and quickly laid the map out for everyone's perusal.

Caesar remained mounted and for the moment saw no point in wasting time with unnecessary reprimands, as he deemed none necessary. He had after all arrived without the normal entourage and therefore he could hardly have expected a regal welcoming carpet and niceties. So many people, especially military officers, spent too much time seeking faults in a person. The purpose of this was to find a weapon to either implicate the commanding legate in any failures encountered, or to use the information to bribe them into reporting their *greater* involvement in the victory to the Senate.

To Caesar such things increased the negative employment of the forces around him. Besides he and he alone wrote the reports to the Senate and he had no plans to allow anyone other than himself to receive the admiration of the people. Before, as now, he had admired strength of will. His opinion of Labienus was already beginning to change. Not much, but it was at least a little better than before. Perhaps he could after all use this man for his purposes? We shall see, he thought, we shall see.

As he sat on his horse Caesar quickly flicked through what he knew of this man and tried to determine how best to utilise his personality. Born of a powerful family in Roma, Labienus had a high regard for poetry and read numerous books written in Greek as well as Latin, which naturally indicated an above average intelligence. He had a love for statues and had to date collected numerous masterpieces to adorn his villa on the outskirts of Roma. It was not uncommon to become wealthy while on campaign.

But what of the real man?

With a rounded face and solid military build, he stood just a few inches shorter than Caesar. Yet to many he actually resembled the great man himself. The familiarity in looks, however, disappeared in his tendency to lack initiative, a point raised by Tulla, which Caesar had attributed to jealousy, as the facts did not indicate a lack of aggression on Labienus' part. Once given instructions, he moved with speed and efficiently employed logic to encompass the task at hand. In battle he was cold and calculating in his approach, but singularly lacked Caesar's nervous activity, which saw him continually travelling the length of the battlefield to shout encouragement to those who might falter.

This too was not uncommon, as many would expect junior officers, not the legion commander, to be in the line to encourage a greater level of effort to attain victory. Caesar was unique in this respect. So, all in all, this was a very capable man who could be trusted to a certain extent, but at critical moments it would serve him better to be present to ensure success.

Nothing new there then, he scoffed, descended to the ground and walked to the table to look at the map that now occupied everyone's attention.

"Pro-consul," Labienus said quietly, with a curt nod, but did not formally salute. "If you will join me I will proceed with the report as regards my dispositions."

With a nod the two locked eyes and a test of wills commenced. None of the others dared move or interfere. However, Labienus had to secure a future, while Caesar needed to affirm who commanded. It was, of course, Labienus who broke the gaze, while Caesar looked to either side to indicate that they should all move closer, but then extended his gaze further, as if searching for someone. Turning back to the table he nodded to Labienus to begin his report.

"Tulla is not at this camp, noble Caesar," offered Labienus, guessing the reason for Caesar's searching gaze. "I requested his assistance in maintaining control of this predicament and he now commands our centre. I hope this meets with your approval?"

"You will be made aware when it does not, Labienus," responded Caesar brutally. "As will your centurions of this camp, if your men are not posted immediately to march north, where I anticipate the Helvetii will try to force a crossing. Have these men in formation immediately!"

Caesar waited, the tension immediate, but it did not matter to him what personal etiquette he was now trampling over. He needed results and he needed them quickly and he could ill afford to have one man idle, never mind two cohorts. The reaction was just as prompt and he noted that only Labienus showed no outward sign of disapproval of his tone. Yes, he could indeed use such a man.

"Colidius," Labienus said, calmly. "Have the cohorts form for an immediate march. Inform the questor that all impedimenta will be transported at the best speed and will be protected by one century from each cohort. Is that clear?"

"As you command," replied Colidius, who raised his fist in salute to Caesar, before moving away to make preparations for the march.

For a few moments silence continued to reign as seats materialised as if by magic. Then, Labienus briefly introduced his staff and Caesar politely thanked Lentulus for the cavalry escort that had met him five leagues from the camp. With a nod Lentulus acknowledged the thanks and they all returned to the serious business at hand.

"What dispositions have you ordered?"

"As requested by yourself, Caesar, I moved my cohorts forward from their camps to secure the known crossing places of the Rhodanus..."

"Known?" interrupted Caesar.

"I have it on good authority that there are seven main avenues of approach to the river," continued Lentulus, on behalf of his commander, having acknowledged the nod of approval from Labienus. It had been his cavalry that had initially mapped the crossings during the spring of the year before, although the legion had supplied the muscle and expertise to sketch the maps requested.

"My men moved swiftly to secure several known fording points that were not covered by a fortification previously raised. Although the forts located at Cologny, Charnay, Avully, Cartigny and Aire all needed additional work, that has now been implemented as per your instructions, Caesar. While this work proceeded my men undertook aggressive patrols over the river to pin the barbarian activities, since the end of the winter and the beginning of spring."

"Your decision, Lentulus?" asked Caesar, who now made a mental note to include this man in all future campaigns for the subjugation of Gallia. He also noted the look of derision Lentulus sent sideways at Labienus, clearly indicating either professional jealously or just plain hatred.

Caesar noted the reaction for future use and then promptly ignored the expression, seemingly embroiled in the details on the map.

"We have no time for political or social differences, Lentulus. I encourage anyone to speak their mind at my staff gatherings and I suggest you accustom yourself to my approach or you will be removed."

"Yes...of course, noble Caesar. The decision was that of Titus Labienus. I did nothing more than my duty to Roma."

"Which is only to be expected, is it not?"

"Yes, noble Caesar, I offer my apologies."

For a few seconds silence again descended on this small group of officers who stood, or sat, around a rectangular table high in the Cisalpine hills, with a spring wind gently ruffling the legion eagle that stood to one side. Now they saw the true measure of Caesar. Fair, but firm. All of Labienus' staff had noted the change in him as the almost irrelevant exchange had occurred. From abject silence to irritation within seconds, and yet he had listened quietly to Lentulus and nodded in agreement to his statement that patrolling on the far side of the river had definitely delayed the Helvetii intervention on the river fortifications. Even though the aggrandisement of the task was hardly necessary.

This personality trend was to cause many men a great deal of difficulty, but just as Caesar ignored Lentulus' small-minded attitude, so too did Labienus ignore Caesar's reproach, almost.

"To continue, Pro-consul," he said, pouring himself some wine from a container to his left, and offering the same to Caesar. "We moved as quickly as our cohorts could to seize each of the points mentioned as well as the lower and upper traditional fords, both of which are now fortified. We encountered little resistance at most of the locations except Aire. Here a large horde of barbarians surged across to attack the small fort and thus prevent more castella being built. Tribune Achium commanded here and with customary skill turned the enemy back with heavy losses, securing over one hundred prisoners..."

"Have they been interrogated?" Caesar asked while reaching to pour a goblet of wine, but a servant quickly moved to do this before he had raised his hand more than a few inches.

"Yes, they were interrogated, even executed, but they refused to inform us of their movements. This compelled us to send further patrols over the river in force but, before we could action this, a large group struck in the rear of Cartigny, causing considerable confusion. Although Tribune Sullasi easily repulsed this attack due to our legion engineers being present, twenty of our men allowed themselves to be captured."

Caesar stopped in mid-flow of taking another mouthful of wine and replaced the goblet on the table. No words needed to be spoken on the fate of these men.

"We found them a few days later, after Lentulus again clashed with the Helvetii across the river opposite Charnay. They had been nailed to trees with spikes and used for spear practice. We did not even have sufficient time to recover the bodies, and Domitius' men have reported the foul stench of rotting flesh from across the border. Revenge for this has become their paramount purpose."

Caesar sighed heavily and took the wine that he had momentarily refused. Such tactics were not uncommon in his own campaigns, as such brutality as oft as not stopped new recruits from joining the enemy. When it was their own men, in turn, the act itself became a significant propaganda tool to barbarianise an enemy that some might still view as a civilised people simply trying to survive. That was a type of sympathy he could ill afford when he was outnumbered almost ten to one.

"What are the overall dispositions of your legion, Labienus? I need to know if you can hold this river line against the Helvetii, while I move our main force through Provence to block the road to the sea."

"At first sight, numerically, I would say no, Caesar. I have approximately seven thousand of all arms, including the baggage escort, facing a minimum of seventy thousand enemies. That was before the alliance was formed and, as far as our intelligence can ascertain, they have increased their numbers to over one hundred thousand. To date losses have been minor on both sides.

"However, I am not prone to defeatism, and I am sure, as you are yourself, that if we can secure the bridge the Helvetii homeland will be permanently under threat of attack. If it is destroyed, then they will try to pour across a more convenient crossing point. For this purpose I have placed one cohort at each location. The forces here act as my main reserve to hold any breakthrough. To the north, I have despatched the First Cohort with auxiliaries with my most trusted and experienced subordinate in command, Tribune Scipio. He will then command the right, Tulla the centre and Domitius the left."

Caesar nodded his approval. With a swift motion of the arm he finished his refreshment and stood so quickly that several of the officers present were taken momentarily off guard.

"You have served me well, Labienus. You all have and I thank you for your duty done. Now I must ask more of you, perhaps more than any other Roman has been called upon to achieve. I believe you can hold this line, and the longer you do so the more vital it will be for the Helvetii to seek victuals elsewhere. If they move, then you will have no alternative but to follow, and I will make it clear when this is essential. Until then it is critical that you hold this river line against anyone sent against you. As for me, I will be raising a force of five legions to march when necessary to cut any access to our southern provinces and the sea. My purpose is to resolve this situation one way or another. Labienus, have your men march swiftly to support Scipio. Lentulus..."

"Pro-consul."

"Have your cavalry ready to move within the hour."

"We will be ready in half that time."

"Good...good. Well, we seem to have sufficiently covered the situation for the moment."

"What do you think the barbarians will do?" Labienus asked pensively.

"The barbarians have been left a choice of three." Caesar motioned away a platter of fruit. "Stay where they are and watch half their population begin to starve to death. Attack Roma and defeat us and force a way through to the sea, and therefore defend any new lands they take in Provence or Narbonensis. Or move through these provinces to the coast and build a fleet to travel to another shore, which is the least likely of the three, as the fleet alone would take ten years to build. I believe they will march onto Gallic lands if we hold this river line, and that will give us the allegiance of the southern tribes.

"If they comply with this action, then I can move to secure stronger relations with the threatened tribes that they will meet. It is our purpose to keep these barbarians where they are and failure is not an option. I thank the Gods that the Germanic peoples are so predictable in their aggressive attitude towards the Helvetii. Even after numerous defeats they still try to attack the mountain forts of the Helvetii. It is this continued pressure that will decide the final choice."

With that ultimate statement, he turned and threw a leg high to re-mount his horse and joined Lentulus during his preparations to move out to join Scipio. Behind him Labienus frowned openly and looked on in despair. What he had just experienced was only a foretaste of what was to come, and he wondered if his pride would allow it to continue for long. For the moment he had no choice, but perhaps after the campaign in Gallia matters would take a different course? He would wait and see.

As Caesar rode along at a slow pace, next to Lentulus, the men about him also stopped to gaze at their new consular commander, appointed by the Senate. Word had spread swiftly through the camp when a few new arrivals had recognised the face from the coinage of the realm. To these men this was just another senatorial puppet, but to some he represented a whole new change. Already many had heard of his new approach to warfare. That he only punished the extremists and on occasion had even permitted acts of treason to go unpunished. For the moment he was an enigma that most knew very little about, and the others saw just as many dangers from this man, as glories blinded the vainglorious.

Only time would tell whether any of them would survive to enjoy the spoils of victory and Time, an entity that could not be controlled by anyone in the higher plains of existence, would help nobody but itself!

The rain fell in torrents, drenching everything that had even the slightest degree of absorbency. Heavy clouds, the half-light and the prospect of a full morning's march were all that they could hope for as the column marched west. None of them knew why they had had to break camp so early during this spring shower, but that was the normal approach. Few, if any, ever questioned the centenate on what the urgency entailed.

For the most part the legionaries felt that tomorrow would have been soon enough, but as always the officers decided otherwise. Rain was for some unknown reason as much of a nuisance as the barbarians. It lowered morale and drove a few to desert, although it could be argued that the first cohort had experienced very few such cases. To many of the new recruits the weather had been a shock, after the normal sunny conditions of the peninsular. Here, however, spring meant the odd shower mixed in with cloudy days and intermittent moments of glorious sunshine. They had never even met a barbarian as their ranks were filled entirely with Roman citizens, although many argued that some did not hold this status because of their origins, but through the political ramblings of the

Senate. Either way in recent weeks they had certainly become very well acquainted with the rain!

They marched in numerical order, with the senior formations well ahead of the main force, commanded by a man to whom most of them accorded a certain level of respect, but definitely not their trust. Tribune Titanus Scipio was in truth regarded with a certain degree of fear due to his uncertain temperament, which swayed from abject ignorance to outward arrogance and a tendency to brutalise the objects of his displeasure. Punishment was commonplace although a strong undercurrent had seeped into the ranks of legionaries for a movement to change such unnecessary barbarity. It was of course acceptable for them to enact such cruelty on the heathens outside of the borders of the Republic, but for their own people to do so to Roman citizenry now seemed improper.

As was to be expected, this more confrontational approach to individuality naturally led to numerous challenges to any high ranking official and many, such as Scipio, sought to destroy such sentiments before the army they knew and loved vanished forever. The fact that nobody else felt the same did little to sway their resolve, and crucifixions had become a routine method adopted by many senior officers. Discipline was accepted as essential, while brutality and executions for minor offences were fast becoming an intolerable spectacle.

It was an explosive arena in which to command and, if anything, Scipio failed abysmally when dealing with the soldiers' issues of morale, sustenance and the spoils of victory, preferring to demand obedience on pain of death rather than through loyalty.

As the column entered yet another group of trees bordering a gigantic forest, the attempts to discern what lay ahead of them remained apparent, although these efforts were also coupled with hesitation and fear. Ahead of the main column, the light auxiliaries had expressed a nervous mistrust of Scipio's abilities, and strode well ahead of the column with the purpose of exposing any ambushes, but never straying so far ahead that they could not return at speed if necessary. It was hardly the approach of an all-conquering army, but everyone still prayed that they would be successful in dissuading any barbarian attacks, as recent news of ambushes on small Roman patrols had become well known in these woods.

To one man in particular the future was of even less interest, as he did not expect to have much time left. His history contained even less honour and chivalry, but plenty of bitter struggles fighting the dreaded barbarian. To this man survival was the only topic worthy of his time. Too many people within the ranks continually dreamed of attaining vast levels of wealth while on campaign. It was a fantastic way to obtain new recruits, which was unarguable, but it left them with a false idea of the true life of a legionary. It was always harder than they thought possible and some did not make the grade, while others died quickly as they sought the perfect pot of gold. The remainder continued, but they soon realised that the best they could hope for was occasional cattle and the rarity of partial payment of their wages once every six months. Hardly something to bleed or die for, but if you were the right kind of man this way of life offered many great wonders. If not, you generally died very quickly.

Optio Marius Capparticus had a feeling of foreboding, which had dominated his sleep for the last two weeks. Fatalism was a concept beyond his understanding as he was without doubt a legionary's man, but for an unknown reason certain members of the maniple to which he belonged gave rise to severe misgivings. He was not entirely a man heavily disposed towards the Gods, preferring abject obedience to the more direct worship of the superstitious. In truth he could not foretell the future and so he continued to move blindly, step by tiring step, towards a destiny that he had for some time openly feared.

He could not alter that destiny, and many would have said that a prayer to the Gods would have been the answer. He had only laughed and walked on, but why, after almost twenty years of fighting all over the world, should fear now decide to poison his heart? It was a feeling he was not prone to and he did not consider it an honourable disposition for a legionary; and anything that was so judged should be placed to one side and ignored. If only that was possible, he thought, as the downpour suddenly increased.

Honour, he spat, deluging a small plant, not that it needed an additional downpour, mind you. The third rainstorm that morning alone! Wiping the rain out of his eyes he looked once more at the sky. It was as black as the night and so dark he wondered if the dawn had actually passed them by. He did not like this at all.

What is honour anyway? His family honour vanished with the dishonour his grandfather had brought upon the family, which in turn had led him to shorten his family surname to *Cappa* to avoid inquiries into his past. Had he done anything else his papers would have been incorrect, and there would then have been problems with his citizenship. Twenty years ago, however, the conscription rules had been considerably more lax than today. Nevertheless, he was not even sure if the commanding centurions knew his first name, as they always referred to him as plain Cappa. This was a fact that he was in no hurry to alter.

It was not even his grandfather's actions that influenced his opinions about honour. His own father had done little to impress the concept into the child's mind. He had conspired with Dalmatian pirates to sack Brundisium, an enormous seaport in the southern peninsular. The grandfather had conspired with the barbarians to defeat Legate Marius, forty years ago, but it was his father's shame that was more potently remembered and the greater threat. Marius had triumphed, eventually, but sustaining a high level of loss and with the destruction of several villages by the barbarians. If they had known his real origins there would have been nothing but trouble. Trouble that he could do well without!

It was at the age of five, while his father was being hunted by the Senate, that the young Marius, named after such a great man of Roma, ran away from his mother and changed his name in a childish attempt to avoid the inevitable social backlash.

He was of course caught within a few days, but the shame forced them both to move, and the mother soon adopted his way of thinking as regards their family name. From this early age a strong personality developed within the youth and at the age of sixteen, with the natural death of his mother, the youthful Marius Cappa of Brundisium joined the auxiliaries. Too young to join the legions, he worked as a groom for the cavalry until eighteen and then joined the army. He could not have joined at a better time.

When he finished training, two years later, the Mithradatic War was on the verge of exploding and in it he learnt the trade, as well as in several other places that he was soon to frequent. It was also here that he earned a reputation amongst the legion as a whole. He had never looked back since, and every day he thanked his mother for the opportunity to eradicate the dishonour of his predecessors. He did retain one irritating personality trait, his continual refusal to accept absolute authority, which had left him unable to accept promotion beyond his current status. It brought him into conflict with just about everyone, but not a soul disputed his skills as a soldier of Roma, and in truth he should by now have been a Primus Pilum, first spear, within this legion or another. He was the epitome of just how good a legionary could truly be...but also an enigma that few could understand.

"By Hades, this rain is unnatural," Cappa grumbled, pulling his cloak tighter about his shoulders and frowning at the nearest legionary, Cornelius Porta.

"I never could swim, but I can now," Porta replied.

Cappa could only nod, as his bones felt weary.

Another man shouted from behind, "This is spring and yet the weather closed over yesterday, as if we had marched to the top of Mount Vesuvius!"

"Where?"

"Vesuvius, you fool! What are you, an idiot?"

Porta looked over his shoulder and grinned. "Why, Marcellus Sabinus, my friend, do I detect a note of sarcasm in your voice? Not all of us have had the rich life of a teacher. Or was it as a village square orator or clown? I am easily confused. Telling so many merry stories as you do."

"If you don't shut it, Porta, I'll show you just how much of an education I have had with my Gladius!"

A ripple of laughter rolled across the lines of marching men and for a brief moment the stamp of their feet drifted into the background. Such conditions were to be expected but they always reserved the right to moan, even if they continued on regardless. The merriment did not last long.

"If I had wished to command a group of childish women I would not have joined the legion," shouted the Centurion on horseback. "Silence in the ranks. I will inform you when you have permission to speak."

A few grumbles sounded off as a reply across the front ranks, but as with all disciplined men this dissipated quickly as Centurion Atia Valenus turned to seek a culprit for the grumbles.

Only Porta dared to respond...

"That Valenus," he grunted vehemently. "Someday I will..."

"Shut your mouth, Porta," interrupted Cappa. "For once in your life can we just reach our destination without that fool placing us on the fossa or digging our latrines?"

The fossa was a wide ditch that had to be dug around the night camp every evening while in a compromised province. The latrines, I suspect, need no explanation. Until now every man had willingly participated, as it was to their benefit and that of the others to do so, while moving through a potential battlefield. However, in recent weeks the Centurion in command of their particular maniple of the cohort had shown a growing mistrust of them.

This had led to a strong lack of confidence, and to compensate this man had taken to volunteering regularly for the most dangerous tasks. Primarily due to Porta's continual flow of sarcastic comments, which did little to endear them to their superiors, Cappa knew that his feelings were just as much the fault of this man as of the overall situation. Perhaps he was just getting too old for this kind of life? Perhaps Porta would sign his own death warrant? It was already a miracle that the fool had lasted five years, and he also knew that the others had set up a small fund for whoever guessed the day of his demise.

It was, as usual, too late and Valenus noted to whom the latrine duty would again be assigned.

The result was for them to be singled out to dig their portion of the ditch, as well as many others' fair share. This invariably led to tension amongst the individual century of legionaries, and it came close to exploding with the latrine digging. In their case they numbered one hundred and twenty, as their cohort was double the size of the normal complement. Each century normally numbered eighty men but all five, minus desertions, stood at the same number as them. Independent rivalry was strong, but not so enthusiastic as to cause injury. Cappa was now of the opinion that the abuse was close to changing from verbal to physical. He had to avoid that at all costs. Having them digging latrines continually did not help in this quest.

The tendency to transfer anyone of reasonable skill to the other centuries, and replace them with the scum of the cohort, did not help matters either. Even this so-called elite formation had a very small, dissatisfied band of customers, and it seemed as though Cappa had the lot in one unhappy barrel.

The digging and physical exertions involved were considerable when added to a march of twenty leagues or more, and were not entirely welcomed by everyone. Indeed not everyone found Porta particularly amusing, which by itself was a sore point that added to the consternation as Cappa fought to control the low morale so inherent in this band of misfits.

In reality Cappa's rank was not much higher than the legionaries' were, but it was commonplace for many of the optio to be held in high regard by their respective cohorts. Above them stood the centenate, centurions dominated by a senior Centurion called the Primus Pilum. Finally there was the tribune, Scipio. It was if anything a long way to the top, but to Cappa it was also a long way back down to the bottom. He ruled with a rod of iron and Porta knew better than to push his luck that morning, even though the damage had already been done.

With no further disobedience, they all breathed a sigh of relief as Valenus rode ahead to join another Centurion at the vanguard. For a few hours they continued quietly trampling the weeds on the dirt road that many had been told would be dug up soon and replaced with a permanent road. It would certainly have made the walking easier, but for now the rumours made no difference.

On returning, the Centurion mercilessly ordered the pace to be quickened, and they now proceeded at the double to race ahead of the main column and reach the agreed camp-site prior to all and sundry. With no cavalry and very few auxiliaries this was an act of pure stupidity in the opinion of just about all of them and many in the column began to voice their opinions. One hundred men would not last long against a hostile country that, to their knowledge, was occupied by an entire army of barbarians that numbered in the thousands, if not tens of thousands. Morale suffered yet another blow and Cappa frowned inwardly while desperately striving to hold his tongue.

The experienced soldiers from the rank and file had little respect for this new type of military man, promoted due to their political connections and money. Even other officers shunned their company, unless of course their contacts rode high within the senatorial house in Roma. Then it was prudent to remain on their good side for obvious reasons. Cappa never moved in such circles, and spent most of his free time either alone or with the troops he commanded within the formation. For this, the other officers arbitrarily shunned him in turn, except for a few who rose above the superiority complex bred into many of the higher ranks. He could recall only one man he would call a friend...the Primus Pilum, Atronius Sulla.

Now, as always as they approached the chosen campsite for this day, Valenus rode ahead and surveyed the area with great aplomb, only to be curtly sent back with his tail between his legs by the senior Centurion, who invariably located the site and then planned the entire construction. It was a daily routine that amused even the newest recruits and helped to stave off the desire to lie down and relax.

"This is worth all the fossa digging in the last week!" triumphed Porta, grinning.

"Not to mention the latrines we dug yesterday," added Constantine Palignusea, a youthful recruit who had so far shown a great deal of promise.

Once again a ripple of annoyance ran through the ranks. This is not good, Cappa thought. This is not good at all. Latrines or not he began to sense trouble.

The thought mulled inside his head as the deflated Valenus rode back to them with the clear intent of finding them something to do while they awaited the main column. A decent man would have ordered a rest and then posted sentries to cover the survey team. However, they all knew by his facial expression that it was more likely that a few more latrines would be required. There would be little rest this day.

Before this could occur, however, two things happened in such swift succession that Cappa and the other optio were momentarily lost for words.

First, a messenger rode up to Valenus and, with little respect, saluted and rendered a brief message for all to see.

"Centurion, I have been ordered to attend your presence to forward an order from your commander, the noble Tribune Scipio. Had you been in formation as previously ordered my journey would not have been necessary. Nevertheless, you are ordered to move further ahead to scout the approaches north, as the entire cohort will be moving on from tonight's camp at first light. I require neither confirmation nor your seal of approval. Shall I inform the Tribune that you have proceeded with the orders?"

"You may," responded Valenus, between pursed lips, the obvious signs of discourtesy clear for all to see. This messenger, as far as they could see, held no rank. He was obviously a close intimate of the Tribune, or perhaps one of the other senior centurions?

"Then so be it," came the reply.

The rider turned and sped off back towards the column, which still stood a good two hours away. This in itself was not really unusual as Valenus continued on his campaign to impress the Tribune, who showed nothing more than contempt. To everyone present it seemed that, for the sake of their officer's vanity, they would from now on be offered several ways to die for his glorification. Yet again Cappa watched in dismay, as several men broke ranks and sat on the roadside to rest, a blatant act of disregard for discipline and contempt for the Centurion, who was not slow to respond with a gaze of acknowledged power and hatred.

"You there!" Valenus screamed. "Return to the ranks before I have you crucified as an example to the others!"

"Come on!" added Cappa, a little bemused and gesticulating profusely. "Back in line!"

Valenus rode a little closer and dangerously drew his blade, pointing threateningly at Constantine, who quickly returned to the ranks. Cappa sighed. Had he not done so it was almost a certainty that Cappa and the other junior officers would have found it impossible to avoid further signs of rebellion. He had seen it a few times before, and Romans had fought Romans in a brief skirmish that had normally ended with the execution of the officers involved. Thankfully he had not been connected to any such rebellion in the last twenty years, and it now looked as if his reward was to be Valenus.

By Jupiter and Mars, if he did not change soon then just about all of these men would rebel, and then they would all suffer!

They marched off a few minutes later and moved through to the other side of the forest. Here Valenus ordered a bracken fort to be constructed for an immediate resumption the following morning. Piling the brambles high they then set guards, and almost as soon as the tents had been raised most of the men fell fast asleep. That day they had marched well over twenty leagues and continued for ten hours non-stop. Most of them benefited from such exertions but it was not this that caused rebellious actions: the singular lack of trust in Valenus worried them all. In just two months, this man had reduced a well-trained faction of experienced legionaries into a nervous group of people tentatively awaiting disaster.

To achieve that took skill, and a method of buying into certain circles of officialdom, a fact that Cappa had not noticed before, as Porta had generally kept spirits as light as possible. However, as mentioned, his comments had not helped to diffuse the growing resentment and he wondered whether he should apply for a transfer.

Shaking his head he knew that such an act was tantamount to deserting the few friends that he still retained. Of course he would remain, but he was not sure just how much longer these men would tolerate the ridiculous fact that an inexperienced political puppet was leading them. Even if he was only a lowly centurion, Valenus was, by his decisions, the door to survival or death, and the future did not bode well for any of them. Ordinarily the men would vote in their centurion. In the case of Valenus that had not occurred, and that alone was a breach of their most basic rights as legionaries, in the first place. To also have to put up with a useless bungler was altogether too much.

Caesar had indeed arrived, but then so had Optio Marius Cappa! What tomorrow would bring was anyone's guess...

PART TWO

REBELLION

The Tribune lay sprawled on the couch that his servants had faithfully transported along with the normal impedimenta of the cohort. With one arm over the side and the other preoccupied with raising a wineglass to his parched lips, he gave the impression of boredom. The new orders from the legate had promised at least some possibility of excitement, but so far it had involved no more than additional marching and camping. Hardly the kind of victory to build a reputation for glory in a world dominated by this very concept.

Raising one eyebrow, Scipio glanced in turn at each side of the line of tents and viewed the officers, who stood like statues and dutifully kept silent. To the left stood Lepidus, an unassuming Centurion of little character or initiative, while to the right stood the Primus Pilum, Atronius Sulla, a totally different breed: a man of honour, or so it was rumoured.

Scipio sighed, pursing his lips.

"My mind is becoming docile," he said to no one in particular, flexing his toes in a languid stretch. "Is this war with the barbarians never to produce any opportunities for victory?"

The question did not receive an answer, as neither Lepidus nor Atronius had yet come off duty from the night watch. Their exhaustion had dampened their ardour, as regards bolstering Scipio's flagging ego. Both men shuffled their feet irritably as Valenus, another man despised by both of them and Scipio, joined them after seemingly completing the dawn rounds along each palisade of the camp.

"I suppose you are about to tell me that there is no sign of the barbarians who dare to threaten Roma and that all is well, Centurion?" Scipio barked, determined to find an argument this morning.

"The guards have assured me, noble Tribune, that there have been no signs of the enemy during the night."

"Good. Good, but rather tedious."

The four men fell into an almost forced silence, as the atmosphere between them had already given rise to numerous disagreements. It was commonly known that Atronius was without doubt the most experienced officer in the legion, while Scipio should have retired ten years ago. This had led to a division of loyalties in the officer's camp, which for the moment was in Scipio's favour. However, the overall effect on the men had been a lowering of morale, but an outward expression of high regard for Atronius. To them he was a legionary and no different from them as individuals, while the others had come from the same stock but openly sought to distance themselves from that fact. They were therefore more loyal to Atronius, but they all recognised that the power remained with Scipio! Duty demanded obedience and for now no legionary would dare to question his right to command.

On a smaller scale, Cappa feared a rebellion by his own men on a daily basis, but Atronius feared the same by the entire cohort. Never before had he seen so much hatred towards a commanding officer as he now experienced. It did not help him to sleep, for one, and, second, they represented the best men within the Tenth Legion of Roma, but it did not feel as though the men believed this, even if Scipio did. The situation was not pleasant.

Having risen at the first sign of light, with barely any sleep after night duty, Atronius had already been awake longer than most of the officers and had also supervised the camp arousal. Contrary to Valenus' optimistic report, several barbarians had been seen during the night, but no attacks had been made on the palisades. The report was therefore incorrect, but this was nothing new from a man that none could understand. If you had political connections why in the name of Jupiter or Mars would you become a centurion? Surely you would try for a more senior rank as far away from the battle lines as possible? Valenus if nothing else created a different kind of anxiety in Atronius. Valenus was eager for glory and Scipio knew this only too well. It made him nervous, very nervous!

As the light increased, Scipio had, finally, made an appearance and the others had followed, save for Fabius who was known to always oversleep, and Crassus, who had remained on duty even though he too had been awake all night. Scipio rose irritably and both Lepidus and Valenus moved forward to offer supporting arms. By Jupiter and Mars, Atronius thought, we'll be wiping his backside before long!

"Daylight and yet we have no word from the legion or from the river fort," Scipio said abjectly. "Perhaps we should send a few scouts ahead to determine whether we should continue? It seems rather pointless if they are already dead!"

"A noble suggestion, Tribune," responded Lepidus, bowing so low that his face nearly struck a nearby table. "Perhaps we could send word to the cavalry..."

"What cavalry?" interrupted Atronius, irritably. "We have only one decurion and thirty cavalry as it is, to scout ahead of the main column. I suppose we should now disperse what mobility we have to confirm what we already know?"

"Which is?" Scipio asked, turning on Atronius coldly.

"That the barbarians have already compromised the Rhodanus and that our initial objective must be to secure all the crossing points. To disperse our resources would be foolish. Labienus..."

"...Is not here, Primus, a fact that you will do well to remember," snapped Scipio, swinging his legs over the side of his throne, his eyes glaring into Atronius' face. "I command here and not Labienus or you. But I think you are right about the cavalry, we need to keep them as close to us as possible. Perhaps we should send you with a few legionaries of choice to perform such an important task?"

Valenus smiled openly as the rebuke made Atronius redden with anger. He was about to add another comment to further increase the discomfort when a commotion on the far side of the camp drew everyone's attention.

"What is this?" Scipio scowled, again finding it all too easy to increase his bad mood. "Lepidus, find out what is going on! If it is not important I will have the guards flogged!"

"As you wish, noble Tribune," Lepidus replied, with another of his monumental bows.

He was gone no more than a few minutes before returning at a fast pace to enlighten them all.

"As far as can be determined," reported Lepidus, now a little short of breath, "Two hundred or more enemy horsemen have crossed the river and have attacked several baggage trains and ambushed a mounted patrol not more than five leagues from here. The local decurion has pulled his cavalry back to regroup with the main column, while these men became separated and seemed rather pleased that our camp is here and not a few leagues further away.

They felt that their horses were blown and the pursuing barbarians would catch them."

"Is this cowardice?" ranted Scipio. "I will not have them remain within these palisades if they have deserted their command. Send them away, Lepidus, tell them we are in no need of additional mouths to feed. Tell them the main column is fifty leagues that way."

To which end, Scipio raised a hand and pointed in between bouts of laughter. None could understand why such news caused such merriment.

"Has the local commander thought to order any support or reported this situation to the legion?" Atronius asked, stepping forward and ending the amusement.

"I did not ask. It was not my place to ask," retorted Lepidus coldly. "I am not in the habit of conversing with the common cavalry."

"Common cavalry," Atronius declared incredulously. "What in the name of Jupiter has that to do with this predicament? Where are these raiders? In which direction are they travelling? Where did the last ambush take place? Has their true number been established as being two hundred? Is this camp in danger? What kind of officer...!"

"Enough!" interrupted Scipio, raising one hand. "You are giving me a headache with all your questions. If this issue concerns you so much, Primus, take some legionaries and find the answers yourself! I had already suggested as much earlier."

The challenge was obvious for all to see. Not as before, where the odd callous comment had been thrown in the direction of the Pilum, who had taken it as verbal rebuke. This comment had been a challenge to the pride of Atronius and to back down would be seen as cowardice. Yet to proceed would be suicide. A fact that showed on Lepidus' face as blatantly as his flat nose.

"Heavy infantry would have little chance against a mobile force. If you will permit the use of the decurion's men and our own then perhaps..."

"Just now you stated that we should keep them together, not disperse them to the wind, Primus," shouted Lepidus, happy to again cross swords with a man he despised. "Besides, as you indicated, there are only thirty. What difference will ten more make?"

Atronius fumed and fought desperately to keep control of his temper, which today had been tested to breaking point, and for the moment he managed to remain silent. All he needed now was for Fabius to arrive to complete the opposition to everything he had to say, and life would be perfect. This was similar to discussing tactics with a group of five-year olds!

"Perhaps I could complete the task for the Tribune, if our Primus is a little timid today," boasted Valenus. "I am sure my men will be more than capable of dealing with any barbarians, mounted or otherwise."

Lepidus smiled approvingly while Scipio rose from his seat with an evil smirk that distorted his features in the diminishing shadows of the dawn. "You would take on this task for me, Centurion? Yes, why not. It is about time that you saw true experience of how to deal with these poor excuses for men. They deserve nothing better than death at the hands of their betters, and sympathy is not a prerequisite. I have yet to lose a battle against them and I am sure you will succeed and bring honour to the legion. Take your men immediately and locate the enemy and destroy them, Valenus. May the Gods bless you with victory."

Atronius stood amazed as Valenus saluted and turned to leave. All earlier attempts to remain silent now evaporated.

"This is madness, noble Tribune. These men will not have the mobility to deal with enemy cavalry that fight as well on foot as mounted. We need cavalry support and light troops to act as scouts. If you send them out alone they will be caught in the open and cut to pieces. At least send the entire cohort! Two hundred would never dare to attack such a large formation."

"Correction, Primus," mocked Valenus grandly. "You would need that support, I do not. In fact I believe that I will only need half of my command. I will take only eighty men and I will destroy these raiders!"

"Shut up you idiotic oaf!" Atronius shouted in response, glaring viciously towards a man who would see so many perish for the vanity of his own glory. "I am not interested in your childish boasts. This is the real world, Valenus! I am more concerned for those men than I am for your pathetic hide!"

The statement hit the Centurion as though an arrow had pierced his heart and for a moment the vanity of the man almost led him to act, by attacking the Primus. However, Scipio laughed openly for the umpteenth time, and with a smile he turned once more and signalled for his aide.

"Tribune," protested Atronius, " you cannot allow this!"

"Why?"

"Those men will not stand a chance if they are ambushed in the woods. This terrain is too wooded to allow the correct tactics for use against cavalry. Even when in close formation they will be outnumbered two to one and unable to move effectively!"

"I feel that sufficient attention has been given to this raid. If you are concerned then send a messenger back to headquarters and trouble me no longer on this matter. If Valenus is ambushed we will use his men as bait and draw these heathens out for destruction. Now leave me, I am tired of this constant bickering."

Scipio waved a dismissal and both Atronius and Lepidus saluted and took their leave of their illustrious leader. Almost immediately Lepidus headed back towards where Valenus had now mounted a handsome white stallion. Atronius quickly moved in the opposite direction, having noticed Crassus on the other side of the camp track.

"Crassus, my friend," he greeted warmly, "I require a favour from you."

"You have only to ask, Primus. You know of my loyalty."

"Go now and find the decurion who commands our tauma and tell him to arouse his men. Then tell him to send a messenger to the main camp for reinforcements. I believe Lentulus' entire regiment is assigned to the legion for our occupation of the province."

"What is going on?"

"I'll explain later, my friend. Right now I require prompt action."

"Consider it done."

Crassus moved with a speed that surprised even Atronius, as the man had not slept for twenty-four hours. He knew his exhaustion had caused the outburst earlier, and that he should not have allowed himself such a rash and stupid act, but somehow he did not care.

Turning, he spotted a legionary cleaning his armour and promptly told the man to locate Optio Cappa. By the Gods, he thought, Cappa had already warned him of the morale in the maniple and it now seemed unavoidable that Valenus would drive them to rebellion. This act of bravado might come to nothing as they might never find the enemy, but for some reason he found this hard to believe. This day would end in disaster. More important, it would end in the dishonour of the cohort!

All four men stood in abject silence as Valenus announced the task assigned. At first no reaction could be discerned, but slowly one or two people began to show outward signs of doubt. They knew any protest would be ignored and therefore pointless, as it was their duty to obey without question. This did not of course diminish the immediate concerns.

The camp began to show signs of activity. Those remaining in their slumber and not disturbed by the optios had only just heard the single note of the dawn rising from the cornicen horn blower. Normally a camp would be ready to march within one or two hours, but only the day before today had been marked as a day of rest. Now, finally, the urgency of the matter had fallen on their heads like a thunderclap. The journey to the river had taken on a more serious undertone far beyond their earlier expectations.

As they deliberated quietly amongst themselves, the legionaries began to ready their equipment and do a quick swipe with the cleaning rag on the gladius, while beyond the camp eyes sat and watched in anticipation. They had observed the cavalry enter the Roman camp and it was a safe assumption that, once news of their raid had been delivered, someone would come back out to find them. It was their task to report precisely who filled the latter role, how many and in what direction they initially began the search. A task of little difficulty under the circumstances, hidden as they were in a perfect place to see most of the activity of the Romans!

Meanwhile, within the palisades, where rank and privilege were the fount of all knowledge, Valenus now made a charade of listening silently to two juniors requesting more details on their assigned duty. Only Cappa and Olivius, the two most experienced Optio in the century, added their own presence to the doubts voiced by their colleagues and the validity of the orders given. The vocal partnership of Optio Cassius Evictus and Optio Aulus Palligeo, both of whom saw little benefit in selling their lives cheaply, had initially attracted their attention.

Cowardice? No, never in a million lifetimes could either be guilty of this, but a mind alert to any excuse to avoid a fight? Now that was certainly nearer the truth. Both Cappa and Olivius knew without a doubt that Evictus and Palligeo would abandon each other, never mind a fellow legionary, without hesitation, to save their own lives.

Cassius Evictus was often referred to as the "*Black Cassius*" because of his obsession with the dark Underworld arts of incantation and magic, which to Jupiter-fearing Roman citizens was a blasphemy, punishable by the utmost severity, death. Entailing of course the usual walk and your struggle to carry your own cross for crucifixion! To many this was enough to ward off even the slightest interest. But to Cassius it was nothing more than a continuation of his father's beliefs, and perhaps also of his grandfather's.

His reasoning was that the clouds and bad weather were all ill omens, and that the Republic should withdraw from its expansionistic policies and retire to its original boundaries within the peninsular. According to him, the rain and the cold they now experienced were the result of the Gods informing them that the soothsayers were wrong, and that death and destruction awaited all those who dared to cross the Rhodanus River, little more than ten leagues away.

Of course they all scoffed at these arguments, none more so than Cappa and Olivius, but today was a day to take a friend, and he was temporarily willing to accept any ally in an argument against Valenus. It was as though this man had learnt nothing in the last three months from those who had shown little more than hatred, mistrust and doubts. The legionaries' loyalty was to the optios, but Valenus continued to blindly ignore all reasonable suggestions.

The man was mad! His hunger for power insatiable!

To take these men into a forest with no cavalry or auxiliary support was tantamount to murder. Even at a minimum, the entire cohort should march, remembering Atronius' argument earlier, and should they encounter the raiders then so be it. This course of action was just giving the barbarians the perfect target, and Palligeo had already backed down when fully confronted with the prospect of being dragged to see the Tribune. Cappa needed to know at least who would support them if they ran into trouble. If they were to be the bait then that was his duty, and he accepted it willingly, but to send such a small force to curtail a larger, more mobile force was quite beyond his understanding.

"We must have support of some kind," Cappa continued to argue, stepping forward to stand beside Cassius. "It is unwise for the glorious Tribune to ask us to deal with an entire raiding party without cavalry! It is just an error, Centurion. I am sure if you spoke to him again…"

"Spoke to him again, you say? Do you question my right to command, Optio?" Valenus retorted, his face already contorted and turning bright crimson.

"No, noble Centurion. But I only question the lack of support for your efforts. I seek only to avoid any dishonour to your family name and to the cohort."

"Then you would do well to remember that my father has friends in high places in the senatorial house in Roma. I am not only able to deal with your disobedience, but I will add your family to my discomfort. This is an opportunity to gain that promotion I was promised when I joined this scum-infested century. The sooner we succeed the sooner we will see the back of each other, Cappa! I assume that meets with everyone's approval? Yes, I thought it might. Now join your sections and cease this irritable whining."

"I meant no ill feeling, noble Centurion, but surely the Primus Pilum would…"

"Atronius!" Valenus bellowed airily, riding so close to Cappa that his nose almost touched that of the white stallion. It would have been laughable had the Centurion not drawn his gladius to strike downwards should further disruption occur. "Why is it you always call for that foul-tempered old woman whenever we have a job for men only to do, Cappa? Your tent a little cold at night is it? Need some company? *No*, then proceed to organise your men before I decide to reduce our numbers by three. I will inform the Tribune that we will march within the hour. When I return be prepared to move at a moment's notice."

Cappa opened his mouth to reply but Valenus did not wait, bitterly turning his horse's head to ride away at an extended trot. His pace gave none the opportunity to respond and it was now Cappa's turn to blaze with frustrated anger. Beside him Cassius's expression was pure hatred.

"He will be the death of us all!" Cappa stated coldly. "And that insult I will remember until a more suitable time to respond!"

"Agreed," Cassius said loftily, throwing Cappa a look of disdain, something that Cappa found difficult to ignore. "But under the circumstances it would seem foolish to bring down the wrath of the centenate onto our shoulders. I guess we will have no choice but to obey, as indeed we are both trained to do. Something tells me that we are not going to enjoy this day."

"It seems that the Gods have abandoned us this morning and that's a fact," Cappa agreed. But he was totally unprepared for the reaction his words created.

The normally placid, albeit disliked, Cassius suddenly turned on Cappa with a wild look in his eyes, making even Olivius take an involuntary step backwards. "You are of the brotherhood?" He then asked incredulously.

"Brotherhood?"

"The Brotherhood of Vulcan. We seek to control our destiny and to bring forward the true powers of the Gods and to benefit from their benevolence."

"Power and women, you mean?"

"If that is their wish. We simply believe that our destiny is to have one power rule over everyone else. We pray openly for the destruction of all the usurpers of power and seek to bring back the pits of Tatamus for all to bathe in the glory of the underworld."

Both Cappa and Olivius smiled at the absolute belief embodied in the speech, whilst squinting at Cassius due to the position of the sun. "Shall we concern ourselves with the Gods after we have survived this preposterous patrol? I have a feeling we will need our mutual support to see this day through in one piece, whatever the Gods have intended for us."

Cassius nodded to placate his two companions, but the comment alone brought forth an anger that swelled to proportions sufficient to blur his vision, completely overreacting to a simple comment. As Cappa walked away the hatred shown to Valenus' back flashed mercilessly across his face, aimed squarely at Cappa. A loathing so strong caught hold of him, as the desire for bitter revenge for such sacrilege to his beliefs coursed through his veins, bringing with it a picture of each man's death.

Cassius had foolishly exclaimed his own membership in the Brotherhood and he immediately regretted such an act of bravado. However, his desire to find other members had forced his hand.

He would have to watch both Cappa and Olivius very carefully: if they betrayed his beliefs to the Tribune, he could be executed. They would have to die.

Not now of course, now would be too soon and obvious. These were times of stealth when dealing with the black magic, but he would this very evening hold a gathering and add a few prayers to see them both rotting corpses in a field for the carrion.

He watched them walk a little ahead of him and smiled to think that they had never even imagined how much power his gathering wielded. The almost overpowering urge to draw his sword and plunge forward on a rampage of destruction against all the non-believers in this world looked to any passer-by like an expression of utter madness. Indeed any sane person would have made it their business to avoid such a man. However, like father like son, he never acted but only prayed and used the occasional maiden sacrifice, which kept him in favour with his God, but maintained a low profile: slaves were rarely missed. In this way, he avoided the attentions of others beyond the prying eyes that kept a distance, and he intended to keep it that way for the moment.

From birth, his father, a founding member of the brotherhood, had told him that he had been born with the mark of the Gods. It was a small circle with two sharp arrowheads pointing towards his heart, but so far there had been little to confirm that his future, his destiny, was to rise above the puny people of this world. He knew that faith must be absolute, but for now the time was not right. He, like Cappa, had a very strong ill feeling about this new assignment at the Rhodanus. He needed a sign in order to act. He needed...

For a few seconds his body suddenly went taut, every muscle ached with the will to move, but nothing happened. The wind disappeared and the visual image of the camp dimmed. There was to be no warning, no explanation, only a sense of absolute domination. As an ant is to a man, life or death was held in another's hand. Then, just as swiftly, the vision returned, leaving Cassius with a distinct feeling that something inside his mind was missing. His head swam for a moment and he knelt for a few seconds to gather his thoughts.

There was nothing missing from his anatomy...but...yes, it was from his very soul! He knew this as suddenly as lightning striking. "What did this mean?" he babbled incoherently under his breath, as he slowly rose and began to search for a way to avoid the duty he had only moments earlier discussed with Cappa. He needed to think. He had to think! He would feign an injury, anything to find a moment alone to understand what had just happened. As he moved towards the healers he could not contain his excitement and joy. Perhaps his father had been right after all!

Had he looked up at any time during his walk he would have seen a small black cloud hovering barely ten feet higher. Cappa or Olivius would not have noticed such a phenomenon, but to Cassius a flurry of incantations would have been the first reaction. To the two former colleagues the cloud was unseen, as indeed was Cassius' walk towards the healers' tents, where he intended to stay for the duration of the patrol. He would feign an illness and the others would moan and swear, but that was of no importance. All that mattered now was this sensation of enlightenment. For the first time he began to believe that his father's premonition was coming *true*!

For everyone else, however, the energetic Valenus swiftly returned to Cappa to find the agreed eighty men, minus the sick Cassius, in column formation ready to march in light order. This meant they would carry only the light pilums, shield and gladius. Some had been ordered to drop their body armour and take the place of the auxiliaries that had been told not to participate in this patrol. The almighty Valenus did not require their assistance. Cappa frowned. Only the Gods could help them now.

With just one look of disdain, the Centurion rode out through the gate and proceeded to ride to a small hill that stood a hundred paces or so beyond the palisade. From here he ordered Cappa by hand signal to bring them out and watched with pride as several men gathered to watch them leave. Then, as if this was not sufficient, several loud horns signalled the exit of the troops, and probably warned everyone within five leagues that a Roman camp existed nearby.

Indeed the barbarian scouts smiled laconically as they watched the procession begin. This was going to be good sport, if nothing else.

At the command tent Scipio smiled coldly, as yet again Atronius arrived to argue the rash decisions made earlier. However, he, like Valenus, did not consider two hundred barbarians a threat to an entire formation of legionaries. The matter was again dropped reluctantly by Atronius, but it was plain to see the bitterness in his eyes about such stupidity. Not satisfied, the Pilum immediately sought out Crassus to determine whether his instructions had been carried out.

"They have, Pilum, just as requested."

"Good. Now find as many horses as you can, then put on them as many men with experience as you can. When ready, return to me. We are going out on patrol..."

"...Whilst also accidentally on purpose following the same route as that fool Valenus," finished Crassus with a grin.

"You have read my mind. I guess there is no fooling you, my friend."

Crassus shrugged. "Care for some wine?" he asked, as the topic of discussion was greedily consumed.

Atronius smiled. He could not remember the last time that he had seen his friend without a wineskin attached to his belt. It was sometimes a wonder he ever rose in the morning, but for many years he had done just that and more. Where he managed to obtain so much wine and store it was another mystery altogether.

"No. Perhaps after the patrol I will partake, but we need to move quickly, Crassus. Maybe later?"

The two grinned knowingly and clasped forearms as Crassus swallowed heavily on the wine, almost as a farewell gesture. With a nod they both then turned to complete their separate tasks, words seemingly unimportant.

Barely a league away, the legionaries in light order had already identified the scout on horseback in the undergrowth ahead. As predictable as ever, Valenus refused to stop and call forward any support. Cappa's mood was not improving.

Back at the camp, in a secluded corner, Cassius knelt in the undergrowth with several of his brotherhood on either side, having decided to avoid further inspection by the medical staff. He had decided that a prayer to his God and fulfilling his beliefs was required, in order to discern just what had happened earlier. When he obtained no reply he considered the possibility of it having been only a fit. Perhaps he was more exhausted than he thought?

With a hand on his heart, he began a chant that for centuries unknown had been handed down from one disillusioned sect to another, and would have continued had the small cloud not followed, perhaps summoned by the incantation? On this day, however, the prophecies *would* be fulfilled, for the cloud was the very essence of a God. Which God is not too important for now, suffice to say that this was to be a day of regret in many different ways.

To Cassius nothing had perceptibly changed. To the God the blackness in Cassius' soul had finally opened a doorway back to *this* world. The dimensions could finally be traversed once more! He had found the key and now all he needed was to find the door. Then he would give freedom to his people, his servants who had for millennia been locked in total darkness. They would all be free!

"Yes...yes, I have much need of your soul, mortal. Yes, indeed, you will serve my purpose perfectly. Most perfectly."

The laughter was like a faint echo that made them all stand and look about, as if they had been discovered offering their secret prayers, but they perceived no onlookers. A few shrugs and the odd arrogant grin dissuaded any further reaction, except for Cassius who remained kneeling. For him the future had most definitely changed... Now all he had to find out was how. For the Gods had come to Roma and it was now his duty to fulfil their bidding...

The sound of battle was all the incentive that Atronius required to launch forward with the men at his side. The earlier task of finding experienced riders had resulted in a little over fifty men being mounted. While he charged through the trees with half of them, the decurion took the other half around the woods in an effort to block any escape. Although it became clear that this would be little more than a ruse, as they approached they saw that the enemy outnumbered them considerably. The only chance now was for them to make as much noise as possible, to make the enemy believe that many more than fifty were moving to reinforce Cappa. If the enemy suspected their real strength for even a second, then they would just be adding themselves to the list of casualties.

By the time Atronius rode through the thickets into the clearing directly ahead, the enemy had thankfully begun to retire in good order. They had left behind none of their wounded, but did not waste time taking back the dead. It was symbolic, as they must have considered him the reinforcement in a trap of some sort, and determined that a retirement was necessary. The ruse had for one reason or another worked in their favour, but there was no telling how long this could last, or indeed if the barbarian leader would suddenly decide to renew the conflict. They would have to act swiftly to make use of this brief window of opportunity.

Waving forward those that had remained close enough to command to perpetuate the ruse, he began to survey the surrounding area. He had not managed to talk to Cappa prior to leaving, and now momentarily feared for his life. He was not particularly fond of this junior officer, but respected the fact that twenty years of service made any man a superb soldier. Ordinarily friendship was not a term he used lightly, mutual admiration being nearer the mark. No matter what the circumstances or the situation, Cappa's survival instincts far surpassed those of any other man he had ever known. Even himself!

What was his first name, he suddenly wondered, then shook his head in disbelief that such an inconsequential matter should cloud his thoughts. He surveyed the immediate undergrowth again, and at the edge of the trees the familiar features could be seen crouching over a prone body. Kicking the flanks of his horse, Atronius covered the distance in a short breath and hesitated momentarily, as the prone figure was none other than Valenus.

"Report!" he demanded curtly, giving the Optio no opportunity to withdraw into the background, as was oft his desire.

Cappa snapped to attention even though it was clear to see that exhaustion was fast beginning to take its toll.

"I am perhaps not the correct person to forward any report. I respectfully..."

"It was not forwarded with a choice, Optio. I will take your report *now*!"

Cappa frowned, in a way that others noted to be more angry than normal, but eventually shook his head in a resigned way.

"Everything was fine until we approached this belt of trees about an hour ago. We had no idea what lay within the trees and all attempts to organise scouts met the obstruction of Valenus. God help us all if he is the future of this army!"

"Confine yourself to the facts, Optio. I am not in need of your opinion on the leadership skills of a centurion."

Cappa's frown deepened, but his sense of duty was far too engrained for him to defy the Primus, so he continued in the hope that it would do some good. "As stated, we did not even have scouts ahead, but finally the Centurion agreed to see sense and Optio Olivius was sent forward with ten men. At first there was no real reason to feel uneasy. We had all seen the scout this morning, but that did not mean any others had remained behind with him. No, it was not until we suddenly came across this village."

"What happened to the scouts?" Atronius asked, perturbed.

"We do not know. They should have been ahead of us, but they were nowhere to be seen. The villagers had gone and, believing the scouts to have passed through to the far side of the clearing, we continued forward. There was no reason to suspect anything, although a few had mentioned the odd disappearance of Olivius. They hit us from three sides at once. It was utter desperation from the start and Valenus ordered us into line against the horsemen. They simply charged the front and the dismounted attacked the flanks. We had to form a square or *die*. Valenus refused, chanting about charging the cavalry on foot! It has been done before, I've seen it, but that was with men trained for such tactics. These men were not."

"What happened next?"

"Some ran. Some died. Some dropped from wounds. Some panicked, but I managed to keep them in formation. Then everything became worse."

"Worse?" Atronius said, as he dismounted and indicated to Cappa to sit on a nearby log.

"We fought like lions, Pilum. We knew that the enemy would not give us any mercy, but it was useless. I ordered the men to give ground and spread out. Valenus turned on me and looked as though he had finally snapped. He babbled something unintelligible and lunged at me. His blow did not land. As he took the first step Julius, one of the younger legionaries, brought him down with the boss on his shield and we carried him back to these trees. Here the enemy charged several times, but they could not advance effectively between the trees. They did not have any archers and this one fact saved our lives, plus your arrival of course. The Centurion will no doubt claim that we rebelled, as most of the men refused to obey his orders. But that truly was not the case."

Atronius looked away as he rose to pat his horse's neck. "You should have your wounds tended to, Optio. Then pull your survivors together and bring them back to camp. We will sort this mess out once and for all. If we are lucky, perhaps we might even shed ourselves of that fat-scum Scipio. We can only hope! Do you know the loss figure yet?"

"Twenty-five dead with the same in wounded, five critical."

"I will speak with you again at the camp."

Cappa snapped to attention and saluted. Behind him Porta laughed.

"They'll sort it out alright, by decimating all rebellious survivors."

Decimation was a random choice from a line of offenders. Each man chosen would simply be battered to death by those remaining. It was a strict disciplinarian approach, but even Cappa had ordered it once and it was certainly a possibility after this fiasco.

"We do not know that," Cappa eventually replied, as a herbalist wrapped his forearm.

"Yes we do. Oh, yes we do. How else can the discipline of the cohort be retained? Sooner or later that Scipio will have us all executed. There is something seriously wrong with his head, if you ask me."

"I did not and neither did these young ones. So why don't you move along before I decide on a decimation of my own!"

Porta walked away chuckling quietly, already resigned to his fate and impervious to Cappa's empty threat. Cappa could not believe that they would be held responsible, but he could. Cappa was a fool, but still a man to be trusted for now, so he accepted that they would march back to camp and find out.

If he was right, then perhaps this life as a legionary would not be too harsh after all, but the woods more than ever seemed very inviting. In their undergrowth he could vanish easily, but in truth where would he go?

If he was wrong, then they would all die very quickly indeed. What a choice! Crucifixion, decimation or become a desperate vagabond in the Transalpine mountains, an enemy of the barbarians and of Roma.

Porta was of course correct, and Cappa should really have seen this long before the guards removed their weapons. Within ten minutes of returning, they had been shepherded to the far side of the compound under heavy guard. Many were not arrested and were allowed to go free, but for those singled out by the now conscious

Valenus there would be no reprieve. Cappa had looked for the Primus, hoping that he would defy the Tribune, but he later learnt that he had been sent on ahead with the cavalry to report on whether the fort still held out at the river. There would be no guardian angel.

Now they sat in a tight huddle, watching the sun fall slowly over the hills to the west. For them the prospect of a beautiful spring evening was supplanted by their anguish to survive. To them things looked extremely bleak. This day might be their last on this earth, or so they thought. Fortunately for them the powers of life and death had other plans that day. For them the Gods had chosen a different fate, just as they had already chosen a new fate for Cassius, who had mysteriously disappeared within the compound, in yet another mystery on a day full of unbelievable occurrences that it was hard to understand. Would they be executed on the morrow or would the Primus arrive back in time to help?

Cappa had served on every frontier and, at one time or another, had fought against most of the barbarians who had bordered the Republic and declared themselves an enemy of Roma. It was this level of experience that caused most of the guards to retain a discreet distance as, to a man, they recognised him as the most dangerous amongst the fugitives. To them it seemed odd how the fickle hand of fate could deliver a man to respectability, or cast him to the bottom of a pit of despair.

Cappa felt the hand grip his shoulder and followed the finger indicating movement in the dying light, as Constantine pointed to the command tent. Scipio could be seen exiting and then looking over to where Valenus had stood for almost an hour, awaiting the outcome of Scipio's internal tribunal, with witnesses of his choosing.

Behind Constantine, Marcellus Sabinus, an educated and intelligent man who often wrote and recited poetry, also looked at the two men. To him Scipio was a snake of the most depraved variety, a man who would kill his own mother to gain greater riches. Now that his age was catching up with him and retirement loomed over his pathetic hide, he had no guarantees of any continued good health, while Valenus was well known as undependable and better suited to the life of a slave. Perhaps even as a sex-slave, as he doted on Scipio so openly it made them physically sick! Of slim build with a face that reminded many a man of a rat, his oily persona begged the Tribune for favours. What he received was anyone's guess.

That was well known to them all and was the real reason for this current state of affairs. Who would believe a legionary over the centenate? Without some kind of outside help, the wily teacher could see no avenue for them to escape the fate decided by Valenus' lies. By the Gods! Valenus, he thought, rolling his eyes to the heavens. How could such a man be given authority? *How?*

Marcellus smiled then at the futility of the day. As always he pondered why he had joined the army. It was not long before the memory of watching his father starve to death in Illyricum reaffirmed these reasons. Survival for his entire family had now depended on him, as it did for many people who saw the army as a steady employment with the possibility of gaining enormous riches in the spoils of victory. Meanwhile the pride of the family soared and they had food on the table. It was enough.

Now, together, Cappa, Julius, Marcellus, Constantine, Java and Porta watched as Scipio approached. Each deep in their own thoughts, but all resigned to the fact that what Cappa ordered had not been cowardice or rebellion, but a sound tactical decision made by someone who was capable of cohesive command. Now they would see whether justice would prevail!

The cornicen sounded once, twice, three times to alert the camp to prepare for the early march ordered the night before by Labienus. One by one each man began to prepare individual equipment to comply with the order to supply light provisions for a rapid march to the Rhodanus River Bridge. The noise of preparation carried for a considerable distance, and needed to be covered by scout parties whose sole purpose was to prevent enemy spies from reporting the sudden activity within the Roman camp. The Helvetii could not ignore Labienus' intentions as each suitable river crossing had now been fortified against their passage. Including the bridge!

Anger and frustration had already led to several confrontations with local patrols. In brief, no Roman formation had crossed the river since the beginning of spring. Several raids had tried unsuccessfully to contest the river crossings, while other barbarian groups had somehow crossed at unknown locations. This left the uneasy feeling that these warriors were actually swimming the rapid river, which made those sent out on patrol extremely nervous. Having split the cohesion of his command, Labienus then saw fit to assign his best troops to the task ordered by Julius Caesar and conferred on him personally by Tulla, regarding the vital bridge.

Along the river, his experience had indicated seven realistic places that the Helvetii could use to cross in force, and compel him to fight at a numerical disadvantage. On receiving the initial order from Caesar to fortify and secure each of these points, his speed of command had left little room for the barbarians to seize any initiatives. With seven chances of securing a bridgehead over this vital river, the Helvetii failed to succeed at every point.

Initially this was due to their genuine intention to peacefully traverse the Roman province of Transalpine Gallia in search of a greater level of sustenance for the three hundred thousand souls who faced starvation in the bare mountains. Although in truth little could be done to help these people, it was equally ridiculous for Roma to permit such a massive migration, which would literally have left every region stripped of supplies necessary for their own population.

Not that Caesar even slowed for a moment to consider this unduly.

Here as always the military situation was hardly one to make Labienus feel secure in any thoughts of his ultimate victory. The discussion with Caesar only yesterday evening had hardly reassured him. Having altered his dispositions to comply with Caesar's wishes, each of the seven places known to him was now held by one cohort, which in turn was commanded by one of his tribunes. With only *five thousand* legionnaires, two thousand auxiliaries and five hundred cavalry, he faced over seventy thousand Helvetii warriors, plus all the lesser tribes.

While he had only seven hundred men at any of the seven points, the Helvetii could employ ten thousand warriors, giving them an overwhelming advantage in numbers. This fact alone left Labienus with little room to take the initiatives that Caesar had ordered the day before. If he received reinforcements to the level of additional legions they could, he believed, move on to the offensive and secure the Jura mountain, while also closing off the Rhodanus Road north of the river itself, which was now the enemy's main source of movement.

Initially Tulla naturally refused permission for Labienus to summon additional troops to assist his present situation, and Caesar confirmed the reason for this, when he advised that the concentration of the main force would be to the south. The best that could be done was to send the archer formation at Cularo as a temporary addition to the troops available. To say the least, the local commanders saw little chance of holding their specific positions, should a determined attack be made.

In particular, Scipio stated that his orders seemed beyond his present ability given the very nature of the ground chosen for his attempt to seize the bridge. His minor, but firm, statement had continued to keep him in favour with the legate even when many now considered Scipio a liability. Here he could place just over one thousand men plus auxiliaries on any given field, and the command staff of twenty.

As Labienus' own camp rose with the first light, so too did Scipio's, many leagues to the northwest. The former's thoughts were full of anticipation of an imminent battle near the bridge, where his force would not be able to assist. The latter's were full of nothing short of contempt for Labienus, the barbarians and anyone else who stood in the way of his achieving glory.

Scipio's dilemma was literally more critical than that of the other commanders', simply because the greatest number of Helvetii stood beyond the bridge, ready to pour across and force a battle, to win direct access to the Cisalpine plains beyond. From the seaports, they could then travel to new lands in which to settle. Although duty demanded obedience, most of the officers at the council had tried to undermine Scipio's influence, and advised Labienus to keep the legion together to fight a delaying action. Labienus listened patiently and then quietly repeated the orders handed to him by Tulla. The policy of dissecting the legion was a military error, but after the protests had been recited no further delays ensued, with the sentence that Caesar had now personally endorsed the plan.

This brief discussion with Labienus and Tulla a few days before lay heavily on Scipio's mind that very morning, as he watched his own camp come to life. Each Centurion moved with a deliberate purpose, directing and cajoling the legionaries into a semblance of order, as individuals collected and put on the impedimenta of war. At first light the cornicen sounded with a clarity that most of these men had heard a million times before. They represented the elite troops in the legion and within their ranks resided the highest level of experience and pride, but even amongst these veterans there was a certain degree of poor quality: the poorly and the sick in mind that had been given to Valenus.

They now sat opposite him on ground still wet from the night's downpour. These men had retained their lives because of their ability to fight and so far Scipio had as yet to decide precisely what to do with them. Other commanders would have put them to death as a means of keeping the mass under control, rather than keeping such men for the mission he had now been assigned. It was a rather difficult quandary, as he had finally come to recognise that all was not well within the cohort. Further executions might not help morale, but rather cause irretrievable damage. He needed another solution...but what?

As the first century, the remainder of Valenus' legionaries and the half that had remained in camp, began to file out the northern gate, his eyes drifted to the far side of the camp to look at the culprits of this dilemma. Here sat Cappa and the few others named by Valenus as the ringleaders of the supposed rebellion in the wood. He doubted whether this minor officer had even been rebellious, but had in fact acted only to preserve the lives of his colleagues. However, it would not do to allow such blatant disregard for authority to go unpunished.

If he could only bring the irascible Cappa onto his side...

They had all had a single chance yesterday to put forward their view of events. As was to be expected, there were inconsistencies in both testimonies and he had a difficult decision to make this morning.

By Jupiter, he found Cappa impossible, quick to temper and totally biased against any kind of discipline, although he was not loath to flog a man if he stole weapons or food from his colleagues! However, Scipio had to execute some kind of discipline against those who deserved punishment, or it would be his own hands and feet being nailed to a cross by Labienus. There was more to this ridiculous attitude towards the centenate than Cappa had allowed them to know, but for now his reasons would have to remain unknown.

Scipio knew that there was a reason for Cappa's refusal to accept promotion, even when the legionaries had voted in approval of his rise to centurion: something in Cappa's past that he had already begun to make enquiries about. He had begun to ask questions, but so far no answers had arrived, but it should not be much longer, he need only be a little more patient.

With eyes as black as the pit and a stare that could look into your very soul, Cappa was to be feared. This man was a formidable sight to behold, but rarely did he openly show aggression. It was almost as though it was written in his eyes, rather than his actions. Broad in build, he measured no more than five foot three, and yet what he lacked in size he more than made up for in presence and force of personality. With his over twenty years of experience, the entire legion looked upon him as one of the unique members of the legion, and he could always be found with the small group of legionaries he referred to as friends. Scipio's abhorrence of him was well documented.

They were in brief the precise opposite of each other and were therefore completely incompatible in such a profession. Cappa despised those who abused their rank, and sought every opportunity to offer disobedience and to encourage others to follow his example. Or so it seemed to the disciplinarian.

In short, he knew of no Centurion in the entire cohort, save perhaps Atronius, who accepted this man willingly. Indeed on more than one occasion he had himself almost fallen to temptation and ordered his execution, in order to rid himself of the very irritation he now faced.

To men of rank he was an example of a soldier who undermined the discipline of the legion. Although he believed in discipline, he found that the continual execution of disobedient men caused only a continued hatred of the centenate. The loyalty issue was primarily a factor of how much could be gained on campaigns in terms of spoils, rather than by an undying loyalty to Roma and their commanding officer.

Those days had gone some time ago, although in his youth he recalled the many skirmishes he had fought in, subsequently winning promotion to his present rank. Needless to say the Tribune acknowledged the resentment of the men, but was equally aware of the lack of necessity their friendship represented. He issued orders and they obeyed, or chose to face the consequences, even if the punishments had become less fatal in recent years. Now he sought an alternative, but he would not hesitate to use other methods if necessary.

He knew that Cappa, born a son of a minor aristocrat in Brundisium, did not have the political status or support from a family of the Senate to raise his position further. None achieved the status of a legate in command of a legion without direct authorisation from the Senate, which in turn would be endorsed by the pro-consul of the province, except in times of war. Then the consul could elevate his status and might approve him for his acts of bravery, which in turn would be linked to victories—a sort of field promotion on the battlefield.

Now, at the age of forty-two, however, this particular border incident might well be Scipio's last opportunity. Already his enemies in the legion had proposed his transfer to the auxiliaries. He had no intention of allowing this to happen, and he had to plan carefully for his secured future. Perhaps if he used these fools effectively, he could sidestep blame for the loss of morale and efficiency of the cohort and place it on them. It was after all his duty to weed out any undesirable elements that sought to undermine the power of Roma.

Cappa and his companions would become a pressure valve! They all wanted a physical target for their frustrations, so he would give them this fool and a few others that were just as much of a pain in his posterior, ordering them to act as scouts. On foot of course, as a supplement to the auxiliaries with little armour and daily exposure to the threat of an ambush, they would have a short life expectancy, but their current situation required desperate measures because of their lack of cavalry.

He could of course send back for reinforcements from Lentulus, but that would prevent his current plan from developing, i.e., ridding himself of every member of the cohort who had so far opposed his authority. As with all plans there was an element of risk. For example, Julius Galienus might well be killed, but this too could be placed on the shoulders of Cappa and his cronies. Of course Scipio was the only one in the entire cohort who knew of Julius' real family connections, and he had plans to exploit this information mercilessly. He would remain aloof and blameless, but reap the enormous benefits, if he rolled his die just right.

They knew, the legionaries, as did Scipio, that most of them would not have the nerve or inclination to defy their officers, but they saw in Cappa a natural leader, a man who would dare to stand in defiance; but one that they would also be just as unlikely to support in open rebellion.

This had happened in the eastern provinces when two legions had executed their officers and stood in rebellion, proclaiming their Imperator the new leader of the Republic, carefully avoiding the use of the term "king," a word abhorrent to any true Roman. It had lasted no more than a year, then a new army was created and the rebels destroyed utterly. For such a situation to be actually developing with the main provinces was unthinkable, tantamount to the dissolution of the Republic itself!

No, he would use this fool as much as was needed to restore discipline and order. He could then use their deaths as an example of true Roman sacrifice, and give Cappa his martyrdom. He began to like the idea more and more. They were after all short of auxiliaries and cavalry, so why not use the experience of the best legionary to pave their path with security?

Scipio began to walk towards the group of prisoners and guards, finding himself amused at his own intellectual remedy. Why execute well-trained men, he thought to himself? Why not use them in a capacity that would be highly dangerous with a higher than normal death ratio? Not only for the possibility of success but also to avoid any loss of morale that an execution might cause. Oh, yes, he would allow Cappa his insolence, but at a price!

Pausing briefly to confirm that his personal bodyguard had kept pace with his movements, Scipio glanced across the camp to watch the second century march through the gate with several auxiliary troops close behind, before finishing his brisk walk to join Cappa. Now, as always, he surveyed the scene in a glance, absorbing the information necessary to stay alive. Perceiving no threat, he moved on at a slow pace keeping the guards in close proximity. An arrogant and minuscule tactician he might be but no fool wore his sandals.

Ahead stood Valenus, temporarily absent from his command. To his left and right stood the centubernia assigned as guards to the band of fugitives marked for execution, according to the information given to them as yet, of course. Of these, Cappa stood at the centre and his demeanour made plain that his eyes continued to roam, as if seeking a way in which to change his circumstances. Or, more to the point, to simply escape alive! His eyes never stopped moving, even when Scipio stood only five paces away.

By Jupiter, this man seemed more lethal at close range, Scipio judged coldly. Now he understood why so many spoke so highly of him, and also why the centenate despised his open defiance. Even now, in this situation, even with the accusations being nothing more than speculation, he knew it would take only a hand signal for them all to be put to death. Yet, here he stood without fear and, if anything, more willing than ever to express his disapproving view of the false accusations.

Scipio was reminded of a story related to him by a friend about one of their consuls, Julius Caesar. During a sea journey he had been captured and ransomed by some pirates who treated him well, but ignored his threat to return and execute them all. In short, Caesar had kept the promise but due to his respect for their fighting spirit, he had relented on sentencing them to a slow death by crucifixion, and had had their throats slit instead, to speed their end. This Caesar had been magnanimous to a fault.

Looking further afield he tried to identify some of the others, but of the men before him he knew only three names. In fact, of the three he knew, there was little to say. Then he saw the man that he really sought...Julius Galienus!

It was true, he thought, his mind racing. The nephew of a senator of Roma *was* in this group for execution. Now the chance to rise in rank loomed before him and drowned any lasting feelings of guilt. Here was the opportunity for his brother to use this information to blackmail Senator Atia Flavius, Julius' uncle, a leading politician in the Democratic political party, which surprisingly enough was the political group run by Caesar's family.

The blackmail was of course to force him into forwarding his name for promotion to command a legion. It was of no importance which legion he rose to command. In fact, it was not even necessary for him to remain in command for more than a few years, at which point he could happily retire in the knowledge that his wealth would be assured. He could not allow a lapse of concentration or let any compassion influence his plans. He was not going to allow this opportunity to pass!

It was ironic how so many issues in his life now seemed to emanate from the new pro-consul, Julius Caesar. He had met the man briefly during a brief respite in Illyricum, and had not really considered him anything other than the usual family lackey. He did, as a matter of common sense, follow his endeavours with some interest, as there was always an atmosphere whenever the pro-consul entered a room. It was not exactly fear, more a feeling of uncertainty. Not a single person, politician or legate, was able to fathom exactly how far this man intended to take the Republic in his dealings with the Senate. Politics could never be described as a black and white issue anyway, but Julius Caesar defied everyone with his lack of decorum and his belief in supporting the people of Roma directly.

Scipio stopped abruptly five or six paces from the group of condemned men.

"You," he said, firmly. "Step forward."

All eyes passed to Julius. Everyone expected the summary order of *"Have this man crucified immediately"* to follow the summons, causing a pause in breath. Surprisingly, it did not come, so they breathed again. For now it would seem they had received a stay of execution. Cappa and Marcellus exchanged worried looks, the word *why* being mouthed but not spoken by the latter.

Instead Julius was led to one side almost with unfamiliar kindness. Now more than ever the condemned men felt despair sweep through them. Kindness was not an emotion shown too often and when it was it normally meant even more trouble than before. Even more transparent was this expressionism from Scipio.

For Julius, the sense of impending danger reached a new height, as he walked slowly beside a man that he had previously only observed from a distance. Of slender build, Julius was well over the normal height, almost six feet, with brown hair and blue eyes, and he towered over Scipio, who now stood less than two feet off to his left. Had his decision to rise through the ranks and not accept his uncle's bribery been a mistake? "*Yes*," began to resound amusingly in his ears, in his uncle's tone of voice.

Like a caged animal, Julius, like Cappa, had been in the service too long to allow his guard to be lowered by Scipio's apparent kindness, and he continued to look for any avenue of escape. His was the ultimate crime and he knew it. If he lived, then there was hope for all and his mind never forgot this fact. You see, his crime had been to strike Centurion Valenus on the patrol near the river, where they had supposedly rebelled. This was a crime punishable by immediate death, and one it was not unusual for the officer to undertake on the spot, to maintain discipline in the troops who remained. Had Valenus been conscious this would have been a certainty!

Now, like himself, Valenus watched bewildered as the very man, through whose hands and feet he looked forward to hammering the spikes during crucifixion, was calmly led away by the cohort commander. He stood in momentary shock.

"You are probably wondering why I have drawn you away from the others, yes?" began Scipio, moving ever closer to the confused legionary.

Silence greeted his opening statement.

"You have my permission to speak freely to me, legionary. We are both soldiers here, are we not?" He tried again.

Still silence.

The walking stopped. Abruptly, so abruptly in fact that one of the guards continued walking straight into the back of one of his companions. Not unusual, except that the perpetrator had decided to carry his pilum horizontally with the point facing forward.

A brief scuffle, a high-pitched yell and the guard in front dropped to one knee, blood pouring from a wound in the gluteus maximus. He would not be riding for quite some time! The resultant confusion was understandable, if brief, but it lasted long enough.

Scipio spun around, his face reddening in anger. However, the man had reacted through shock more than anything else, but for a split second everyone's attention drifted away from the very reason why the guard had been told to keep pace. Even as the others smiled, and one actually jeered at the unfortunate man, Julius silently stepped forward and rammed his shoulder cleanly into one man's chest, sending him sprawling. With another step he spun inside and reached for Scipio's short sword, and with practised ease drew the blade to place the tip against the Tribune's throat.

Pandemonium resulted. Valenus panicked and ordered half of his guards to immediately assist the tribune. Perhaps a logical approach to the problem, but this offered the very chance that Cappa had sought, and with exceptional speed he and a few others quickly overpowered the remaining men.

The distraction was enough, the last troops had withdrawn from the camp and barely thirty men had been left as guards. Of these, ten had already been disarmed and not only Scipio, but also Valenus, now stood captives of the very men who only a few moments before had faced almost certain death. Or rather, from their point of view they had no alternative but to act!

"Stop! Stop this madness!" screamed Scipio, looking directly at Julius, who had not moved an inch. "This is treason. I will have you all crucified! I intended only to discuss issues with you, but if you proceed with this course of action I will be left with no other alternative, but to order the decimation I wish to avoid!"

Julius allowed a grin to curl the edges of his mouth. Not one of warmth, but one of mockery: trust was hardly a word to associate with the man before him, whether standing on the tips of his toes or not. So he moved the blade forward and upwards a fraction, his smile broadening.

"How so, Scipio?" He then said, through clenched teeth, "You intended this fate for us anyway. How will surrendering change your decision? Valenus has already lied to save his own skin. What do any of us have to gain by allowing you to live?"

"Kill him!" came a shout from behind.

"By Jupiter and Mars, kill that scum Valenus as well! I lost my brother on the patrol!" another shouted.

"Who in hell's name sends such a small force to deal with a mobile enemy in wooded terrain. I vote that we slit their throats and dance in their blood, we fight here and now!" suggested Porta.

"What do you say to the suggestion of dancing in your blood, Tribune?" Cappa then asked mockingly, adjusting the angle of the sword that he held to Valenus' throat. A slight movement by his hand sent a small trickle of blood running across the Centurion's throat and a small yelp escaped the mouth. Cappa's smile was now as broad as Julius' grin.

"There are only a few of you. Already a messenger will have been sent to the column, but even so you see around you over thirty men who will descend upon you with or without my orders," answered Scipio calmly, while the condemned watched as the said thirty slowly closed around them.

Cappa grimaced as he recognised some of the men in that thirty. He knew that to avoid joining the condemned, the *damnati*, they would without hesitation strike them all down. Them against such experienced legionaries did not bode too well for the prospect of escape, but then, in reality, did they really believe they could escape?

His initial shock having diminished, Scipio continued unperturbed. He now saw little difference in his position, other than that he would now have to make public his reasons public regarding their immediate future. He did however wish that this fool would lower the blade at his throat: he had had it sharpened that very morning and even the slightest slip would slit his trachea. Well, for now, shall we try and calm a few hotheads?

"You all know that we have been ordered to seize or destroy the Rhodanus Bridge before the Helvetii can swarm across. To do this we need a sizeable force of cavalry, which we do not have. Those we do have will be employed as scouts, but we need to use additional foot scouts, as well, who will march well ahead of the column. We need information and you men have experience in such matters, and I intended to delay your punishment pending your performance in this task," he quickly explained.

"We have auxiliaries to do this already, why speak of this to us?" Cappa asked.

"The morale of these auxiliaries is far from acceptable, Optio. In addition, they are not numerous enough to effectively guard our path. Your experience will add force to their purpose and make our progress less open to exploitation by our enemy."

"So you want us to volunteer to roam well ahead of any support, and even these auxiliaries, to find an enemy that already outnumbers us beyond our wildest dreams? Hardly worth troubling with the execution!" mocked Cappa warily, because he could see an odd expression on the Tribune's face that caused a momentary hesitation. To lie would be to die, so perhaps on this day Scipio could be trusted, but something in that expression made him falter. That expression told him of a hidden purpose, which would hardly be to their benefit. He felt the hairs on his neck begin to rise.

"More to the point, why draw Julius off to one side, then?" shouted Marcellus, who now stood a yard or so behind the youth. "Why the special attention to the youngest member of our group, save Constantine of course?"

"He is the nephew of Senator Flavius in Roma, you fool. Do you think I could have you and him executed under my command? I intended to allow you to retain your status in a new formation that

I am creating, which will wear heavier garments than the usual worn by the auxiliaries, but be armed *as* the auxiliaries. It would hardly be in my interest to kill him, as it would only have led to my own execution!"

"Is he telling the truth?" Cappa asked Julius with a certain amount of disbelief.

Slowly Julius lowered the short sword to allow Scipio to stand easier, and with a nod he answered Cappa.

The lack of recent communication with his uncle was due to the senator's annoyance at Julius' forceful personality and demands for independence. It was also due to his family having dismissed him from their villa outside Verona. Family debts and the lack of a good wine crop had led to his enlistment and the eventual necessity of sending all his spoils back to the family. Flavius was the only member who still sent his family victuals. However, he had endeavoured to keep his uncle a secret, yet the truth will out no matter how hard you try to stop it. He did not trust the man before him, but what choice did they have?

"Our actions yesterday would not harm his reputation and neither will it damage my father's. We acted out of necessity and they would have done the same thing, you may take my word on that, Tribune. But what of my uncle, how would your being generous help me or him?" Julius demanded.

"That is obvious," Marcellus offered pompously. "If he holds you in his command, then he has a hold over your uncle, Julius. No doubt a little blackmail might well have achieved more than we can imagine. Your uncle may be a senator, but what is happening in Roma is more important than the status that anyone holds. It seems we have an advantage that we should use. Do you not think so, Cappa?"

"Maybe," Cappa replied as he also followed Julius' example and lowered his gladius to allow Valenus to stand easier.

To either side of him the others had moved away from their own captors, but none of them relinquished their weapons to the imploring guards who, realising this, quickly withdrew out of striking range. The *damnati* had now released their prisoners and the next few seconds would seal their fate. Of Valenus nothing could be seen other than the dust kicked up by his heels as he rapidly withdrew to a safe distance.

"Why should we trust you?" Cappa asked, as he slowly moved towards Julius, who although standing easy had not fully lowered the tip of his blade from Scipio's throat. "As soon as Julius releases you these men will kill us anyway. You know as well as we that our actions this day are enough to seal our fate. This defiance today is but a final straw. Even should we agree, who will guarantee to you that we will remain in service once we reach open ground?"

"You have my word as a soldier of Roma, as the first Tribune of the Tenth Legion of Roma, that no retribution will be sought against any of you men, *if* you again take up arms against the Helvetii. We need every man we can find. Already Julius Caesar is on his way to join our legion on this border, and we need to complete our mission immediately! He may already be with Labienus," Scipio replied, noting the reaction caused by the mere mention of Caesar's name. "As regards your loyalty, I will leave that to you Cappa, and to the nephew of a senator of Roma.

"Caesar rewards only bravery, nothing more. At the river a few days ago you showed an enormous diversity of skills in seeking the enemy, identifying them and then accurately reporting their strengths. We lost good men that day due to the slow reactions of the officers, but we need men of your experience. I say that you can still serve Roma and the Republic. I say that you should accept the new task in order for us to move forward, Cappa, or I suggest you cut my throat now!"

For a moment silence reigned within the camp. Eyes flirted from one face to another seeking a resolution set in stone, but all they found was an unerring fear that they were all about to start killing and dying. The scene had slowly deflated, and one by one people began to resume their duties, as the tents and campsite had to be collected and stored on the mules for transportation. After a brief nod from Scipio to a nearby officer, whom Cappa did not immediately recognise, the process quickly increased. It was not an envious position to be in, a compromised province with only a pony to protect you, and all of them wished to catch up with the cohort.

Julius finally lowered the blade and slipped it into his own scabbard, making a note of the gold plated handle, while Scipio gently patted his throat, glad to see it still in one piece.

High above them all Cappa heard the cry of a hawk and wondered whether this was a good omen. Such things had never before concerned him and yet now that very thought seemed so important. They needed all the help they could obtain and any good omen, large or small, was welcome.

"That man knows how to defend a lost position, Cappa!" laughed Porta, who stood as always at Cappa's side.

"Yes, he does, but can he be trusted?"

"I think so."

"If Julius *is* the nephew of Senator Flavius," Marcellus added, "Caesar would not be pleased if the task set is not done, and the Democratic Party in Roma will surely lose face if one of their senator's nephews is executed for treason, distant relative or not. For the moment we will be safe, but I think young Julius will be the key to our survival, Cappa. We will need to keep him as safe as we keep our own genitals!"

"Then we had better take special care of him," agreed Cappa, turning to thank Marcellus with a nod. When he turned back towards Scipio, however, his face was a cold, blank stare with eyes burning with hatred. "You have your foot scouts, Tribune, but do not expect our thanks. We are aware of the circumstances we face. Even Caesar would not have tolerated what has taken place here today, but we will serve you loyally for the trust that you have shown us. One sign of betrayal, however, will set us to marching to Labienus and we shall see how he will reward the truth as regards this cohort."

Scipio nodded, then slowly turned his back on Julius, half expecting to feel the sharp bite of his own sword in his back. When this did not happen he knew he had won.

His hatred of Cappa had developed a much deeper emotional meaning, but his plan had worked out in his favour at least to some degree. He would have his revenge on the *damnati*, but for the moment they were more useful alive. Meanwhile he would use them mercilessly to extract all the information he could about the Helvetii movements, and also send a request to Labienus to send him more cavalry. On their arrival he could then have them all summarily executed, but for the moment they remained useful.

As he walked he shouted over his shoulder to Cappa.

"Have your men armed, Cappa, and then move out. You will report directly to Atronius at the head of the column. I suggest you do not waste too much time as your purpose is to be ahead of the column, not behind!"

"Consider it done, *noble* Tribune," Cappa responded, his years of service creating an instinctive reaction to the order, but in his eyes flashed the fire of defiance. He knew Scipio could not be trusted, but what other choice did he have?

As Scipio walked away he smiled once more, for the situation, although it had not taken the course he had expected, had been resolved in his favour. Walking over to his personal tent he ordered a slave to have his horse prepared, and within twenty minutes he was riding to join Atronius, who had by now travelled two leagues beyond the camp exit.

He then rode forward to a destiny he believed to have been set by the Gods. If this was true, then it was a Roman key that would secure any success and open his doors to future wealth through blackmail. With the key travelling under the name of Julius Galienus.

Another set of eyes also watched Cappa's preparation with a different kind of loathing. Cassius had already changed and to him the scene that had been played out before him would help none. He alone held the key. He alone conversed with the Gods. He alone knew the truth and he laughed to think Scipio or Cappa believed they could have any influence on what was to transpire. He laughed so hard and long that blood seeped from his mouth, but he did not care. He knew the truth, the whole truth and nothing *but* the truth!

He did not bother to ask *whose* truth he now knew.

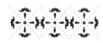

PART THREE

AN AMBUSH AND A FORT

Black clouds began to form over Jura Mountain. Cappa had watched them develop, acknowledged the low grey haze of rain beneath them and assumed that soon the downpour would cover their approach, drenching their garments. He watched transfixed, as the clouds seemed to roll and fluctuate as though they had a divine purpose and a life of their own.

Perhaps they did, he pondered, for the spring weather had as yet to stabilise and for the moment every Roman soldier breathed a sigh of relief. It had been a hard day's march and all of them were aware that their feet ached terribly.

Now, as they paused, each delved into their inner thoughts and the predicament so profanely described by Scipio. Serve and survive and their only reward would be to return to the legion. Failure meant death and for most of them this was only prevented by the whim of a man only a fool would trust.

Cappa looked sadly at the youth Constantine and watched as he rubbed his ankles feverishly. He knew that, over the next few days, they would require all their skills to assist them in the desire to live. But how much did the youth understand? He simply followed loyally, even when the prospects were not good and the weather made even the sharpest eye dull when viewing from a distance. Good weather for an ambush!

With orders to approach the small fort at the river held by auxiliaries, he had decided that a direct approach would be foolish. Not only would they have been completely exposed to attack, but their arrival, even in such small numbers, might have presaged an immediate Helvetii attack. Having traversed this region several times, and with the particular assistance of Olivius Genuas, who had commanded many a patrol here, they had diverted off the main approach road into the hills far to the left of the wood, directly south of the known position of the fort. Here the height would enable them to see not only the main Helvetii settlement to the north, but also the area surrounding the bridge.

Now, as the group sat on the fringe of the wood at the crest of the hill, the valley before them stretched as far as the eye could see. To the right, in the far distance, stood the bridge, beyond that the barbarians loitered, and far off to the left stood Jura Mountain. Although panoramic and breathtaking, this view was not the real cause for the temporary halt. All eyes rested uneasily on a large wood to their left, which stood directly in front of the far bank of the Rhodanus. This in itself was not unusual in the topography of this region, except that a large dip in the far bank raised many an awkward question. The first was where the hell had it come from? At first glance, it looked as though several hundred paces of the riverbank had collapsed into the river, but on such a scale this seemed too difficult to accept.

Cappa and many of the men with him had been here several weeks before to relieve the men in the small fort, and no such change on the far bank had been noted then. So how could such an incline suddenly topple and vanish? Additionally, how could it occur at just the right position for the wood to cover any crossings in strength? On either side of him stood twenty-three men who now looked to him for answers, and there did not seem any straightforward reply to their searching gazes.

Now armed to the teeth with short swords, pilum and daggers, they did not seem to have much choice about how to find out either.

"Porta?"

"Here."

"Can you see anything moving in that wood off to our left?" he asked, knowing that although he might be considered the clown of the group, Porta was also known to many as the *Eagle*. His eyesight was just about the only helpful thing about the scruffy lunatic!

As always, however, whether clown or hunting bird, Porta was swift to respond once directed to act. Like a snake, he slid forward into the grass ahead of the small group, causing a flurry of derisive comments. Behind him many men scowled, looked at one another and indicated their disgust at his approach. Only moments before several men had refused to kneel at the edge of the wood where the group now sheltered. It had taken a sharp order from Cappa to force them to conform. Sometimes the pride of the legion was ill-placed, if secrecy was to be their ally.

Now, as Porta reached the waist-high grass, their uneasiness started again. Bloody arrogant shits, that was what Scipio had given to him for this particular task, and Cappa could not help wondering whether these legionaries needed to worry about the barbarians. If they annoyed him much more, he would kill them himself!

As they had marched further northwest they had all taken the opportunity to discuss the predicament they now faced. They knew that for the moment Scipio could be trusted, but for how long? It was a certainty that he had other plans for Julius, and they hardly expected to be involved, if indeed they were still alive to even have such a dilemma. They all expected this particular assignment to be extremely hazardous, and as Porta crept forward the prospects of imminent danger seemed high.

To most of the *damnati*, as they had become known, the order to seek cover within the wood had seemed the logical approach, in the light of the fact that over twenty thousand Helvetii warriors, if not more, resided just across the river. It had not helped, however, that during the trudge to the wood no word had been received from the fort in seven days.

To Cappa the only real comfort was that most of them stood over six feet tall and were built like senatorial shit-houses. In fact he felt relatively dwarfed by the men assigned, even if he did try to determine who would be loyal and who was almost certainly the viper in their bosom. When at the edge of the wood though, Cappa agreed with the sense in Marcellus' good wisdom, and hid behind a tree. Or perhaps two, as Constantine's example on the far right indicated, much to Porta's amusement.

Now, with all thoughts extinguished, all eyes rested firmly on the prone figure ahead of them in the grass. Yard by painstaking yard he moved closer to the crest of the hill. He was not finding much to laugh about at the moment and could be seen continually adjusting his garments. Marcellus lightly commented that the grass was irritating not only his legs, and a few chuckled under their breath, afraid to make too much noise in case of discovery.

It was a feeling that Cappa especially recognised, as he was certain that beyond this place in the smaller wood there could be seen people moving about. Porta could be clearly heard cursing with

Godly insults, although they were certain that the wind was blowing towards them, thus concealing any sound, or so they hoped. In this misty air the noise carried several paces in all directions and nothing could be taken for granted.

Their uneasiness began to grow.

Reaching the lip of the crest, Porta slowly raised his head above the grass and took a long look towards the woods while one hand brushed aside the irritating grass, which had no business tickling him there! As he took in the mild slope on the far side of the small valley, the stream at its bottom and the damp atmosphere beyond, his instincts suddenly caused him to duck, his head darting from one direction to the next through a parting in the grass.

First upstream, then downstream where the stream angled ahead of him, then to the left, right and once more ahead. Years of training had toughened his body into a lean, muscular weapon, but it was the five years of soldiering with Cappa that had truly developed his keen sense of danger. Even before he saw the men, the tingling feeling on the back of his neck was all the warning he needed, as his eyes saw something that he had not completely recognised straight away.

They stood nonchalantly on the far side of the stream and began to relieve themselves while laughing and gesticulating in the direction of the fort. There did not seem to be too many, but there was the impression of a general build-up. If the fort had not been attacked yet, it looked as though it would be in the near future.

Back at the tree line, Cappa watched as Porta dropped his head below the line of the grass, turning to either side and motioning for everyone to move back into the foliage. It would have been a miracle for any man to see them from the wood below, but he had not lived this long by taking unnecessary risks.

Presently Porta returned. He had not gone any further down the slope for a closer look, perhaps realising that, in that direction, only enemy warriors and almost certain death awaited him. Instead he had lowered his head and come jogging back through the grass to join them.

"Well," asked Cappa impatiently, as he realised it took a lot to make this man turn tail.

"From what I saw, there are at least twenty men in the far wood facing the fort on the other side of the small stream. They are lightly armed and not carrying shields, so I can assume they are auxiliaries looking to check the defences before the main strike force crosses the river. My guess is that they will report back and that the incline must be another fording point for the river."

"That is impossible!" rejected Olivius. "I took part in the mapping of all the crossing points of the Rhodanus last winter, and this is not one of them. The water would be even higher now and this is the only suitable place to cross."

Porta shrugged. "It makes no difference to me, Optio. All I am stating are the facts as I see them. It is unlikely that only twenty men are in that wood acting as a guard on the fort. There would be absolutely no point. No, their purpose is to scout forward of the main body that must already be crossing, more than likely at the dip in the ridge over there. They may be using boats of some description, but in truth how could they have found so many? Another method I have seen was to lay enormous boulders across the river under the surface. In this way the deep river can be made temporarily fordable."

"Hence the loss of riverbank on the far side of the river," suggested Cappa.

"That would be my guess, but without a closer look it would be impossible to confirm. If we could move closer, but..."

With a raised finger Porta indicated the point where the far bank of the river suddenly ascended to below the tree line. To take a closer look they would have to leave the protection of this wood. Also, from this angle they could not see beyond the crest of the hill that they occupied, and the ridge on the far side of the river could easily be masking a large force. If they intended to cross at night for a dawn attack on the fort, which seemed feasible, why choose such a clumsy route, when the bridge offered a much easier crossing point? Had the bridge been destroyed? If so, then perhaps this crossing did make sense after all? Cappa knelt shaking his head in disbelief. This seemed a long way to approach the problem of removing just two hundred auxiliary troops occupying the fort, which surely it was their objective to secure or burn.

"Why send them out on the flanks, though?" he finally asked. "They have sufficient men to crush the fort without too much delay. It simply does not make sense!"

A few nodded. Others frowned. It all seemed superfluous, as the main column of the cohort would soon be here and the reasons, one way or another, would be resolved then. Why worry about it now?

It was only a few hours after sun-up and, at the latest, the Tribune would be here by midday, with over one thousand legionaries, and that would end any Helvetii intentions, whatever they might be! But that was not enough for some of them. It was their job to find out why they were there. It was these few who now looked to Cappa again. Not all of them were happy to be members of the *damnati* and they hoped to prove their worth and leave as soon as possible!

Having served in the valley for over a year, Cappa had dealt with the Helvetii peacefully on several occasions. He had not found them to be foolish or in want of tactical forethought. No, there was a reason for those men to be in that wood and, apart from a surprise raid on the fort, he could not at this time decide on the exact reason. He remembered Olivius' comments. No matter how much he detested at times the arrogance of his companion, he did have a great deal of experience that could alter what Cappa decided to do next. With only twenty-four of them it seemed foolish to move down the hill, cross the stream and engage those scouts or capture one for interrogation.

He needed more information in order to act, but how could he obtain this information without mounted men or a stronger force at his disposal. Maybe if...Cappa froze as the branch snapped so clearly in the morning mist that everyone instinctively drew their gladius and dropped to a lower, prone position. He had wanted information and it looked as though it had come looking for him, in person.

The high-pitched yell of the Helvetii warrior reached his ears, almost as the image of the barbarian came into view down the left-hand side of the slope, slowly walking along the line of the trees. His posture, stooped due to the incline, left Cappa in no doubt that they had not been seen and the yell was, if anything, a signal for others to follow. Without a word all of them quickly closed together for mutual support, using the trees to bolster their flanks and keep access from behind them restricted.

The formation was small, but much more flexible than the cylindrical one used by any of the larger Roman army formations. It would facilitate individual participation in the fight to come, while still allowing the efficient gladius to do its deadly work. This would not be a training camp fight, as they were all trained to fight in the open in the cylindrical formations with the standard three paces between each man. Here personal skills would be the deciding factor, as the trees would prevent concentrated support. This was going to be close infighting, as the barbarians had silently walked completely around their rear and now stood between them and the main column to the southeast.

To Cappa's far right, Porta clicked his tongue lightly and pointed with the tip of his short sword off to his far right, now that they had all turned around. Cappa noted with disgust that he had again refused to put his helmet on, preferring to fight with his head unprotected. Why was that son of a whore so obstinate? Shaking his head, Cappa looked where Porta had indicated and, raising his own sword, circled the tip tightly to order everyone to close around.

Again no word was spoken, each man knowing exactly what to do. Now more than ever their lives were in his hands and, as always before a fight, Cappa hesitated for a few seconds to collect his thoughts. Now was not the time to act rashly.

At first he had thought that the battle cry had been the signal for an ambush. As the small band of warriors came into view, their lack of discipline and lazy march made it clear that no such attack was intended. Or ever would be by these men. Moving forward in a loose group they had not only failed to set flankers, which Cappa noted he had also failed to do, but they moved through unknown enemy territory without even drawing their long, broad swords. Either way, Cappa had received a warning along with his new information and now had no choice other than to act, and with deadly intent!

Freedom now meant taking out these arrogant fools, and to perform the task he had with him some of the most experienced men in the legion…Kill or be killed. All those with him had a discipline black mark against their service to the legion, but in fighting he could not have wished for a more brutal gathering, armed with pilum, short sword, shield and two daggers per man. Cappa quickly indicated to Julius and Porta to join him. Porta's assessment of the situation earlier had once again been perfection itself and Cappa showed his approval, while frowning at the absence of his helmet.

"Helmet!" he snapped, raising his short sword threateningly.

"It itches my head when I sweat. Besides I can see and fight better without it…"

"I do not have time for this. Helmet. Now!"

For a moment they held their breath, as the last few words had been spoken a little too loudly for their comfort. Eventually Porta gritted his teeth, slowly moved back to where he had dropped the offending equipment on the first sign of trouble, and placed it on his head. He knew that at the first chance he would throw it aside, but for the moment it would be suicidal to argue with Cappa, especially when his blood was up for a fight. It was not the brightest of decisions even when he was in a good mood, never mind now, when they stood behind an enemy formation of unknown strength and location. Not a pretty picture! Much safer to just do as ordered, then worry about any consequences later, when Cappa realised he had again discarded Republican property.

On his return, Cappa quickly outlined what he intended to do to get them back to the main column.

"Porta, take five men, the best knife throwers, and hit the scum to the front. Julius, take five more and seek out a place where we can hit any following group with surprise. Try and use as much of the fallen tree trunks and foliage as possible to build a barricade near where this ravine opens out above the tributary. Move it!"

Their task set, the men did indeed move, and with consummate speed. Porta ran east, tapping five men on the shoulder as he moved. He knew full well who amongst them had the knife-throwing skills required for his task, as one and all habitually gambled on the skills within the cohort. He watched the enemy, numbering perhaps twenty counted in one hasty glance, follow the small ravine that cut almost right across the hill they now traversed, which Cappa had mentioned. He stopped to allow his companions to catch up, then watched as Julius' group ran past him to locate another place of ambush. Now as always, he drew his daggers and relished the thought of sinking the blades into the breast of an enemy. He ran his tongue in joyous anticipation along one blade's groove, which made it easier to retrieve from the corpse.

It had been a few weeks since they had practised with these short daggers, and he recalled winning quite a few bets that day, but as he flipped the blade in his hand the tingling sensation confirmed that his skill had not diminished. Ahead the unsuspecting barbarians continued along the ravine and only on the signal from Cappa, who stood a hundred paces to Porta's right, ready to launch the twelve remaining men on a flank assault, did he raise his first dagger. He took aim and, with a yell that fair shook the very earth, launched the first blade in a tight arc towards a man wearing a heavy green cloak.

The effect was instantaneous. The leading man momentarily stood still, as if shocked to find the dagger embedded in his chest. Realisation dawned as the life force ebbed from his legs and he keeled forward with a soft grunt. Two more men fell in the same manner, before their companions reacted in any way. Shields were then raised and the group moved away to try and identify their attackers.

Watching from above, Cappa raised his sword. Everyone still with him kept their eyes on him and waited, as the confusion in the ravine increased. Another man dropped, a dagger in his throat. No scream emanated from him, but the splattering of blood from the cut carotid artery sent several others into a panic.

They ran like the wind, and only ten now remained. They had been given the task of checking these woods and had anticipated no interference. Now they saw the attackers for the first time, and recognition fuelled the hatred of the few who still had the courage to stand in the ravine.

"Romans! It is the Romans who assail us! Forward! Let us avenge our brothers!"

Now that their enemy had a form, and was identified as the most hated, honour now demanded retribution. With a scream that echoed and bounced off the trees throughout the wood, giving all but the Gods a warning, these last few charged forward with weapons drawn and a facial expression that defied mercy. With only six men to face them, Porta shouted to his group to close ranks in a small clearing in the tiny ravine, then advanced forward to meet the onslaught. Still Cappa waited.

Not yet, he thought. Wait just a few seconds more.

Let them go beyond the point of safe return.

He *must* know if any others were near enough to support those fighting. Wait...Wait...

Cappa knew it might still be more prudent to drop any notions of honour and retire as best they could, save as many lives as possible, but somehow he felt that this was not required just yet. He currently had no idea how many they might, eventually, have to resist.

The clash of steel sang in the air and sparks flew in all directions. By sheer strength Porta held the warriors at bay, but one man failed to keep his balance. He was forced backwards and his shield was thrown from his grasp, as if he had intended to let go deliberately. Nothing could have been further from Constantine's mind, as he rolled backwards then swung back up onto his feet with his short sword thrust forward to protect his body.

Cappa watched for a minute or so as Porta's group fought desperately against the enormous barbarians. Then, with an almighty yell, just as Constantine was sent sprawling a second time, he lowered his sword and with the shield in one hand, gladius in the other, launched himself down the side of the ravine, effectively cutting off any possibility of retreat for the enemy. Before they even knew of his presence and entry into the fray, three more barbarians were slain.

Their arrival saw the arena devolve into individual combative contests, the prize being your own life. One man targeted Cappa and raised an arm to drop the enormous, preferred broadsword onto his head. Helmet or not, this would have sliced him open like a melon and spilt his brains out over this wood's carpet of foliage, a prospect that did little to improve his temperament.

With practised ease Cappa ducked to his left, keeping his shield to his front and high to avoid any possibility of being struck, and drove his short sword forwards and upwards. The sticky resistance of flesh confirmed that no body armour was worn, an expression of grim satisfaction flashed across his face as he pushed again, ripping the cutting edge backwards and forwards, as if he was gutting a fish for the evening meal.

A groan reached his ears as the weight of his opponent began to fall forwards. Taking a step backwards, he yanked hard to remove his weapon from the man's stomach and, with the blood lust in his eyes, watched as the man tried desperately to keep his intestines inside his abdomen, failing abysmally, the bluish, grey organs flopping forward to stain the ground. The stench of warm blood reached his nostrils, causing an explosion of exhilaration with the success. With no further interest in the dying man, Cappa surveyed the scene before him, seeking a new victim, with wild eyes shining.

Nothing was on offer for the moment, so he stopped for a moment to oversee the skirmish. To his left two barbarians continued to fight, but they now faced six of his men who seemed more intent on capturing them for information. On the right sat Porta, applying a bandage to a deep cut on someone's thigh that had exposed the bone. The face was obscured, but a brief glance assured him that the injured man was a new assignment, not one of the long-term companions. Another quick glance indicated that nobody had been killed, other than the sons-of-whores that had fought against him, while two others had minor head cuts.

He considered how odd that he was able to switch off his emotions so cleanly in battle, refusing to acknowledge an individual's personality, his life. He could act to save a man's life, or kill with a cold efficiency that was admired even by his enemies. Had a friend been lain out on the grass, with a leg almost severed, even that would not have stirred any other reaction than a professional assessment as to whether he posed a hindrance, or could be saved. He would have simply carried on and mourned the loss later. Practical, yes, but still somehow this felt immoral, and it was a loss of humanity that something told him he would never regain.

With a sigh of relief, he turned back to the two remaining Helvetii who had backed away from the others, only to find that a long slope and a crest of trees prevented any further withdrawal. They now stood facing him, faces contorted in hatred, but the fear of their imminent demise was easily seen in their eyes. Fear was the hardest emotion to disguise.

"Kill them quickly, or get them to surrender," Cappa shouted mercilessly. "The few that escaped will be back with more and we do not have time to delay."

Porta saluted, having resumed his position in the line. He had assumed unofficial command of the small group even in Cappa's presence, but with no further ado he raised a barbarian hammer recently retrieved from a nearby corpse. The intended target moved to avoid a lunge by one man and even as the hammer fell it was clear that no amount of speed would avoid this blow. With a sickening crunch the light helmet vanished in a fountain of blood, brains and bone that showered the second barbarian, who immediately dropped his sword and shield to sit on the floor. It seemed his only option for survival, but there was no room for such chivalry now and the hammer fell once more to shatter blood and brains. When he turned to face Cappa again his face was a red mask, and the look of enjoyment made several of the others step away from Porta.

They were not squeamish, but the subsequent blows that had disintegrated the whole head had left them feeling that the excess had been unnecessary. Porta enjoyed killing just that little bit too much. It left them feeling that he could not be trusted. It encouraged them to keep their distance and perhaps this was the very reason for his excessive expression of enjoyment.

"Porta...Porta!" Cappa shouted, shunting the man with his shield to break the battle fever.

"Yes...Yes, what?"

"Move off now and take Constantine with you. Find Scipio's main column and inform him what has taken place here. Tell him that we feel that an immediate attack on the fort will take place soon. We will do our best to delay the enemy here. Off you go."

Cappa watched the youngster follow Porta until he was out of sight, then turned to the remainder and flashed a look of disgust.

"Some legionaries are born to die young and the display I have just witnessed belies the skill of a whore's son at the arena! Now bring that wounded man, and shall we now try and resolve this issue with a little pride in the Legion! Now move!"

Suitably motivated the survivors moved like the wind. Picking up the wounded man, they moved quickly to join Julius, who had already begun to place tree trunks and branches across the far end of the ravine to form a rudimentary barricade. Cappa nodded his approval and set the others to assist. The ambush had lasted barely two minutes from start to finish and only two barbarians had escaped, with at least seventeen killed, although their had been no time to count. All for just one badly wounded and two more with light wounds. Not bad for the moment, but he knew, as they all did, that these had been only the lead elements of a much larger formation.

As he stood and supervised the barricade preparations, he found himself wondering why Porta enjoyed killing so much, and where his hatred truly existed. He knew that all men in battle wear a face of absolute terror. It was in truth the only way to deal with your own fear, by transferring that terror to your enemy. They were all demons in this sort of confrontation, where the slightest hesitation meant certain death. They had ripped the advance party to shreds and the warning would be well received by his opposite number. The next stage would be better planned and executed. They would be lucky to live through the next hour, never mind reach the column. It seemed that Scipio's plan to be rid of them was about to reach fruition.

Shaking his head he smiled, life had a habit of kicking you just that little bit harder when matters were at their worst.

"Are you injured, Cappa?"

He turned to see Julius indicating his right arm. Glancing down his face contorted in confusion and then relaxed as the realisation struck that it was not his blood. The blood on his face was also not his, and on looking at Julius a little closer he could see that the youth was also covered in blood.

"No. No, I am not hurt, Julius. How is the injured man?"

"He will live. The wound was deep, but has only cut the muscle and not the tendons. He will have a long rest for a few weeks and then rejoin us, if he is unlucky."

"Yes, I guess he would have to be to be reassigned to us, eh!" Cappa grinned. "How are the others?"

"Fine. We all seem in good health for the moment."

"Good. Have Marcellus tidy up the minor injuries and make sure everyone has some dried meat. I have a feeling that this day is not over just yet."

Julius touched his left breast and moved back towards the wounded man. So far so good, Cappa thought, but if they were overrun here he would have to leave that man where he was and hope that he would have a short death. The alternative would be to kill him now, as he could not afford to lose any men from the fight to come to take him back to the main column. That was the card fate had dealt him.

Slowly he turned to move back to where Julius had placed all of the pilum available, along with the spare shields and daggers. Now all they could do was wait.

Prince Daxus frowned, turned to look at the men crossing the river with the water line reaching the underside of their chins, and then turned back to face his companions.

Standing at almost six foot five, arms the size of tree trunks, it was unwise to test his prowess in single combat, unless a sudden urgency for suicide had taken control of your senses. The personality matched the physical attributes to create a personage that few dared to approach, let alone confront. To many, in secret, this new escapade was fraught with errors and many feared yet another reversal of fortunes for the combined tribes, but would any dare to inform the Prince? Hardly anyone, save perhaps his father and the spouse, and on this matter he had not permitted any interference and had persuaded the elders single-handedly. To him Roma was far from invincible. Even more so now that her main northern forces were engaged in bitter fighting in Illyricum and along the Danubian river. He knew he would be King, so did they, but some began to concern themselves with just how many would be left to rule.

It was not cowardice. More an innate desire for peace after so many decades of war against the Germanic terror that had finally begun to achieve an ascendancy they could no longer resist. Roma was not an ally, but was perhaps a potential friend. To Daxus this was not an acceptable relationship, as his dreams of conquests and glory clouded any realistic judgement. Devastation and low crop yields had led his people to continually seek aid from Gallia, and on occasion they had even managed peaceful treaties with the Germanic tribes, but that was once upon a time. Now, however, their population was too large for even these measures to assist. The future looked bleak at best and, as for Julius Caesar, war suited his purposes better than any peace agreements.

It was time to move or die, and it was with this sentiment that the elders were finally persuaded by the hot-blooded to act, while the enemy were ill prepared to resist their march to the coastal regions and their subsequent conquest. Power was his ambition and to this *soon-to-be-king* Roma was nothing more than an irritation that he would sweep aside as he built the Helvetii Empire. He would prove this by first destroying the forces moving to secure the Rhodanus Bridge.

Failure was not an option, he told himself regularly, but in truth the Prince had only one real enemy. One true man who could defeat him…Only one…Himself! For the Prince raised many good plans and schemes to win glory for the united tribes, but planning was only the first stage, and invariably the latter stages always led to self-doubt and a lack of any determination to continue, no matter what the consequences entailed. He had the pride of the Verbigini, yet somehow this was never enough. There was something missing, as indeed there was from the plan devised for the fall of the southern fort, which was if anything too elaborate for such a tiny objective. A colleague, Uxudulum, would charge the bridge itself, while the very men now being observed would use the recent landfall and rocky islands to cross the river at the one place the Romans simply did not watch or fortify.

Victory here would force the elders to release the northern coalition into his command, which would mean twenty thousand or more warriors. After his initial success, this multitude would march immediately south, to free all other crossing places on the Rhodanus.

But what if he failed? What would the elders say then? What would his people say?

With eyes as dark as the night and a look of utter disappointment, Daxus looked once more at the low hills facing him, behind the two men kneeling at his feet. They had completed the scouting task requested, but had allowed themselves not only to be seen, but also to be ambushed and defeated. Not a good sign, he thought. The Romans had after all sent a patrol into the woods ahead, and it had seemingly not been a pleasant experience for these two wretches.

However, of what strength was the force they encountered, other than the obvious fact that they were Romans? To which legion or legions did they owe their allegiance? To the fort, or to the forces marching north to aid the fort? The Tenth was known to be along the river crossings, but were there more legions behind waiting to spring a trap and ambush them? The recent advances by the Romans to seal all crossing points had left their elders no other choice but to agree to alter their designs from peace to war.

To him this had been a fact two years before, when they had decided that they would need agricultural lands to endure, and in particular lands in the more fertile lowland of the Roman northern peninsular, if they intended to survive. Now, finally, after he had badgered the elders into action, they had sanctioned a major assault to rid them of the irksome presence of the fort opposite the bridge. Offered command of the flanking move across the ford, he now stood poised to strike the very blow for freedom. And now this! A failure!

Facing only four hundred or so light auxiliaries and slaves in the fort, he had brought with him the entire manhood of his own cantonment, which numbered well over two thousand men. He had also been assigned a contingent of the Boii to assist in his plan to capture the Roman fort and the bridge. Not that he intended for them to rob him of his glory. Their immediate objective was secrecy, their second would be the death of every man in the fort! They would need time to bring the army over and to determine where to strike next, and any survivors could not be tolerated. Secrecy, by the Gods, was the most important part of his plan.

Shaking his head, Daxus realised this first objective might well have already been lost. Not definitively, as it could be redeemed if the enemy decided to make a stand, which was the normal Roman way. If in doubt build a fort and fight to the last man. This thought brought forth a smile.

"If the Romans are in this wood in strength then we need to secure the ford at all costs, as we are not over in full strength," he said aloud, wondering again just how many there actually were. Would he just be moving into a bigger ambush, as this advance party had done? "Issus, take two hundred men and secure the wood. Then scout down the tributary to confirm if any larger forces oppose us."

"It will be a pleasure," replied Issus Cellugda, who had reason enough to be enthusiastic about killing Romans.

Daxus recalled the burning fury on this man's face when informed of his brother's death, at the very same encounter that had sealed the fate of Cappa and friends. The Gods certainly retained their sense of humour.

"Should we seek a prisoner, my Prince?" Issus continued, after a brief pause.

"No. We are in no need of any information. Kill them all."

The smile in response to the command was cold as ice, and within minutes Issus had organised his men into groups of twenty-five. At intervals of a hundred paces he sent them forward to seek out the enemy.

This day he had determined to avenge his brother, or die in the attempt.

⁌⁍

Porta shifted uneasily under the direct gaze of the Tribune, preferring as great a distance as possible. Five paces would be close enough for Scipio to remember his face, so he kept his distance! His hatred for the illustrious leader was almost palpable to those who stood nearby, and yet with an air of arrogance Scipio did not notice, or chose to ignore, Porta's insolence.

Having completed the report on where exactly Cappa was in the foothills of the woods ahead, he now anticipated a swift dismissal and the comfort of rejoining the anonymity of the ranks. His thoughts momentarily dallied on the others still there, but in truth it was not his problem. He finished by stating that Cappa had requested the support of the auxillia, but no one could see any change in Scipio's expression. No reinforcements would be sent to assist Cappa, and Porta again noted that he himself was alive and no longer in the proximity of any barbarians.

He enjoyed killing more than he was willing to admit, but suicide in that wood by trying to stop an army from passing through was not his idea of a good day out. With a lazy salute he turned away from the Tribune, now astride a brown stallion, and walked back toward the endless lines of legionaries to his left. Then he watched as a nearby officer approached astride a white stallion. Valenus!

To one and all this was a man that the Tribune also found impossible to warm to, even in the lowest form of endearment or professional courtesy. That was as obvious as Porta's hatred for Scipio. So why keep him? Porta was lost for words, unable to fathom why the army needed such loathsome people. He knew better than to express such a thought, so he allowed it to drift away. As always it was not his problem. Respect and honour were emotions that were simply not associated with Titanus Scipio, who had great dreams of power yet no methods of obtaining such prowess, except with the blood of his own men. Porta was determined that the blood would not be his!

"It seems we have a problem at the tributary, Centurion," he heard the Tribune greet the pompous Valenus, with gestures of impatience. "Go forward and inform the cavalry decurion to reform the tauma and ride to establish the truth of this report, but to keep a distance away from any conflict. I will bring forward the remainder of the cohort when the situation has been stabilised."

"As you desire, Tribune," replied Valenus, who saluted and spurred the stallion into a gallop.

With a feeling of nausea, Porta watched the stallion pound down the track and grind to a dust flying stop in the dust beside another mounted officer with red plumes in his helmet. If Valenus was to be Cappa's saviour, then he was now doubly sure that to remain right here was the best option all round. With a curt nod he linked onto the end of the first century and smiled as he recognised a few faces.

"Enjoy the break, you louses," he shouted moodily. "I have a feeling this is going to be an eventful day and no mistake. While you lot have enjoyed a nice little walk, I have been parting the hair of a few heathens."

He received a few grumbles in reply, but the majority continued to look straight ahead as they noted the dry blood on his tunic and face. Now was not the time to succour doubts. Now was the time to believe in the might of Roma and the friendship of the man who stood next to you in the battle line. As per usual, many found the fool's words to be inappropriate. Some expressed this opinion vocally to the amusement of the few then, as if by magic, they all lapsed into silence, waiting for the next stage in events to transpire.

As he galloped ahead, these thoughts, surprisingly, also occupied Valenus' mind. Pondering what Scipio had stated after the legionary's report, he found his attitude towards the men had begun to suffer several crucial changes. His loyalty was at breaking point as the recent nightmares had sobered his thoughts about the legionaries. He thought more and more about their families, and the fact that these men might have been their sole provider. His doubts, with nothing to stop them, had grown to the point that he felt lost. Perhaps even betrayed.

The old attitude of absolute loyalty had been severely shaken when Cappa had held a sword to his throat. Before then, the thought of death had never entered his mind and it seemed odd that, in this profession, such a reality had remained so distant. They saw death practically every day and yet it had never occurred to him how mortal they all were and how easily they could perish. With the point of the blade pressing against the carotid artery, that distance had suddenly vanished, and for the last few days Valenus had lain awake, troubled. His dreams had never before been troubled, and with the sudden realisation that he was very unlikely to ever go beyond his current position in life, he found satisfaction in emulating Atronius. If he could not repay the lost lives, then he would make sure that such a foolish event never took place again.

He knew that the Pilum would never forgive, it was simply too soon for such hopes. However, should Atronius ever become Tribune then his efforts would surely be rewarded.

It was an odd thing to happen, but he now found his thoughts drifting back to his father. For years now he had controlled every step of his life and falsely manufactured promotion to Centurion through bribery and the intervention of the tribune, also bribed with a chest of golden plates. He knew that this had developed through connections in Roma of both his father and Scipio's brother, and at first the notoriety had been overwhelming. The thrill of command led him to acknowledge that his real forte was to lead men in battle and victory, and this had sent his confidence on the short trip to the stars. For a few short months he had felt like a God!

When Cappa had led the rebellion after the ambush in the woods, the only thought on Valenus' mind had been revenge. Then the second revolt at the camp and his brush with near death had brought fear into the equation, and the thought of power had diminished equally. Why should these men follow his command, if they believed that only death would result from the stupidity of the orders he had given in those woods? Until that point everything had developed and been perfect. Just as his father had said it would be...

Now, his heart pounding with regret, he knew that so many mistakes had led to over forty men losing their lives.

The face of Porta flashed before his eyes, as recognition flooded across the face. The look of hatred in Porta's eyes served to increase the frustration. He would never forgive.

For a few minutes more, he allowed his mind to hang in the air, not sure how he should proceed. To a stranger the face would have betrayed no real change, but to an acquaintance the new look of stern determination seemed somehow out of place. It had progressed to the point that the whole of the First Century, or rather the survivors, rather than just Cappa's group, had also received the label of the *Damnati!* Now this cruel dishonour was to affect all of them, and his own ambitions!

Of course the centenate had not become privy to such rumours, as they invariably socialised in the higher circle when promoted. However, a man such as Atronius did not maintain his prominent position without keeping a very close eye on the loyalty of the cohort and maintaining a feeling for the entire legion's fealty. He was also the only man that Valenus feared, more so than he feared Tribune Scipio!

Atronius was a perfect example of the efficient officer who had risen through the ranks, a true man of honour, whom most of the men followed without question. To emulate this man would clearly have been the centurion's ambition, had the link to Scipio not been so final and irreversible. The hatred between those two was apparent, even to Valenus, who made every effort to avoid the Tribune's regular wine tasting sessions, but how to bring Atronius onto his side and still retain some immunity to Scipio's scorn?

Pulling back gently on the reins, Valenus waited patiently as the stallion skidded to a halt. Identifying the decurion amongst a small band of cavalry ahead, he approached easily and imparted the Tribune's orders. Without a word these men rode away at speed, leaving him once more with a feeling of no direction in his future. He could not describe the feeling exactly, only that he could not see where his future lay, and when he was alone with his thoughts this feeling permeated his every waking moment.

Sensing the rider's uneasiness, the stallion suddenly neighed and reared onto its hind legs. Gripping tightly, Valenus rose with the change of height, then settled down to regain control of the horse. With no reason to return to the column, the Centurion dismounted and led the horse to the side of the dirt track. The track would soon be replaced with the more permanent roadwork so familiar to a soldier of Roma, but here and now only the mud on his sandals held his attention.

It had been a long time since he had spent a moment alone with his thoughts. Now, as he sat quietly upon a fallen log, those same thoughts reached forward a hand of guilt. Why had he not issued orders for at least some of the cavalry to accompany them on their march to find the enemy horsemen? Why had Scipio ordered heavy infantry to locate the enemy, instead of sending word to Lentulus, whose cavalry was better trained for the task? Even at this point, why had he himself refused the advice of an experienced man such as Cappa? Why had he not taken the full complement of men available or brought along another century, which would have effectively reduced the horsemen's threat?

Questioning every aspect of that day, he realised one main reason for that catalogue of omissions. In short, pride had overcome all sense of duty, along with his additional error of allowing the power of Roma, and the confidence of Scipio in his ability, to cloud his judgement and block the advice of those more experienced. Now he saw this as clearly as the bright sun in the sky. For the first time in his life, Valenus doubted the purposes of his father and saw a future that *he* wished to create, rather than following the whim of others.

As the vanguard approached, he remounted and rode back towards the main column, still troubled by the rebellion experience, and the bombardment of emotions rocked his head until he ached.

As the lead formation came into view and the clink of weapons reached the ears, Valenus solemnly swore to himself that the future would change. The opportunities stood before him, as they did for every man who now marched with Caesar. In this pro-consul, Valenus especially detected a man different from those he had previously met and socialised with, in previous visits home at the family villa.

With a grimace he pulled the horse to one side and allowed the command staff to ride past along with the Tribune. Once past he pulled in beside the first formation, which represented his personal command.

Resigned at this juncture to the hatred of these men, he began to formulate a method to win back their pride and respect. There was a fight up ahead and he had every intention of proving them all wrong in their assessment of his ability. Now the only way out would be to show an exceptional level of personal bravery, and from this day forward he would seek this opportunity.

If Jupiter and Mars would allow a second chance!

At that very second Zeus looked down, mildly distracted just as Valenus made his somewhat foolhardy request. An interesting choice, he mused quietly, and perhaps one he could grant.

We shall see, he promised to himself, perhaps I can find more than one hero in the struggle ahead.

We shall see, if I am not too bored too soon!

Cappilius Paelignus watched as the barbarians identified and marked, with ease, the pits dug by his men over the last week to disrupt any initial charges at the fort. Disappointed that his efforts had clearly been observed, he turned to look at his command, if that was the right word for it.

A professional soldier since the age of seventeen, Cappilius stood six feet, with the normal physique of a man accustomed to physical exertions, and so far had never tasted defeat. With the traditional curly, light brown hair, pointed nose and a powerful jaw, he received remarks that he resembled a hawk, which always made him grimace. Such comments were always made beyond his ears, to avoid a stern reaction, but he would not have been much of a commander if he had not known his men's opinion of him. It was of course a topic of little importance, as the comparison was one of respect and not of derision. His silent acceptance of this slight to his personal appearance was hardly a burning topic when faced with imminent destruction, and his men understood the strength of his character.

Strong in personal valour, he had during several skirmishes risked his own life to save a member of his command, and he was highly respected by those who served with him in the auxiliary regiment and by his commanding officer, Legate Labienus. Now thirty-one, he had served on just about every border known to the Republic, with experience similar to Cappa's.

In a particularly bitter confrontation with a tribe on the Danubian border, he had received his promotion to Centurion, and thus his command within the Tenth Legion, just two years ago. Since then he had used his skills and knowledge to merge and build these men into an efficient light formation capable of fast manoeuvres, and able to react quickly to changing circumstances on any battlefield. Their response had been spectacular on many occasions, but for some this had become a double-edged sword.

When Tribune Actium had been ordered to assume control of another fort to build additional fortifications, he had felt so sure of Cappilius' abilities that he had left him with only his auxiliary troops to hold the fort, which was originally built to house one thousand men. They had initially welcomed the extra room as the camps were normally cramped. A luxury to some, but in others it created concern. It was not good to be so isolated when the border was hardly peaceful. Both received the answer within just a few days when a rider from the legion ordered them to adopt a position of war. The elation had turned rapidly into a feeling of extreme exposure.

Looking about him, Cappilius saw his brother, Aurelias, nodding and smiling with a colleague, no doubt discussing the recent skirmish with the advance guard of the Helvetii. He was quite literally his opposite, and being small in stature he used agility rather than strength in battle and invariably managed to survive. *How* was often the subject of discussion amongst the other men. Many of them held him in awe for his swift thinking, and Cappilius was not a man to ignore a talent for command, even when it was found in his younger brother. It was of some annoyance that at every occasion he took the opportunity to remind him of the time that he had saved his life from roving barbarian horsemen, barely a month ago today. However, this was a small price to pay for the loyalty of an excellent junior officer.

Next to them, and to either side, he looked quietly from man to man, recalling a few names as his eyes recognised particular features. The nonchalant nod or grin from those who had caught his eye served to raise his own spirits. To even the most inexperienced, of which there were many within this fort, the situation looked extremely bad. They could not man the entire perimeter, and it would be only a matter of time before the palisades were breached, thus rendering remaining there impractical.

Turning back, to face the main approach from the bridge that stood directly north of them, he watched the barbarians advance, crouched beneath crude shields of leaves and branches. The cold air froze his face and for a moment he looked over his shoulder, as he thought he could hear the clash of swords in the woods across the tributary. Turning back once more, he noted that the enemy now stood fifty yards beyond the fossa, and whether aid was about to reach them or not was beyond his control. His battle was here and now!

"Stand by to launch pilums!" he shouted, the right arm slowly rising.

Behind him, on the gentle slope leading up to the palisades on either side of the northern gate entrance, the allotted men moved back, stooping to collect two pilums each. At least they had retained the supplies left behind by Actium and they would not go short of projectiles.

"Now!" Cappilius yelled.

In one burst the thirty men ran up to the palisade at a blistering pace to launch the weapons high, stopping just short of the wall itself. With one almighty yell the spears flew true in their arc and descended amongst the crude protection hastily erected by the Helvetii. The result was limited with only a few pilums finding a target. This was not really the effect that Cappilius sought anyway, as the shafts of the pilum were made of soft metal to allow them to bend. His purpose was to delay and confuse the enemy, but, more important, he needed to make them believe that twice as many men as actually were there were defending the fort. Again he raised his right arm.

"Second wave...Now!"

Thirty more pilums landed amongst the approaching men, this time causing several to bolt for the rear.

"Third wave...Now!"

This time the enemy broke and fled leaving only a few men behind. However, a great cheer rose along the palisade as they witnessed this minor victory. The exultation was good for morale and he was not about to stop anything that assisted this predicament. Presently, however, the tentative approach was soon replaced with a more direct line of attack.

"Over there, on the right!" came the warning.

With a calmness that infuriated many of his companions, Cappilius walked over to where his brother now stood counting heads.

"This is not good," he muttered, under his breath so that only the two of them heard.

"Do you think they will charge the wall?" Aurelias asked.

"If they know how many of us there are in here, they will not have to, Aurelias. We cannot defend the whole perimeter. Delaying us here in force and then scaling the fossa and wall at another point unopposed would be the obvious tactic. It will depend on the intelligence of the barbarian leader."

"If that is all we need to worry about then we are saved. We have fought these men on several occasions, but there is one thing we can agree on...their leadership is extremely poor. I mean, we have been here for over a year with barely ten thousand men on this border, and they remained idle until the raids began six weeks ago. If I commanded seventy thousand men, I would have swept us aside last year when we did not have any other legions within ten days support. This attack is pointless, now that we are alerted and reinforcements have almost certainly been sent."

"That may be so, brother, but will they reach us in time? Today we must concentrate on survival. Their strategy may be poor, but they will still seek our destruction, and whether it be a small or large victory will not matter to our bones."

Aurelias smiled, clapped his brother on his shoulder and drew his short sword enthusiastically.

"Then let us make sure they never pass our gates!" he said with conviction. "I propose that I form a separate centubernia to plug any gaps that develop in our ranks. We can also move to cover the other walls and warn of any movement there as well."

"Agreed," Cappilius said, drawing his own sword. "Today we fight for ourselves, Aurelias, and we must fight to live. Roma must glorify itself in our victory, but today we stand alone."

Together they stood, helmets reflecting the sun and the glint of its rays striking both short swords. Resplendent in their uniforms, they moved back towards their respective positions for the combat to be decided on this day. The rain began to subside and the sudden darkness as dark clouds settled overhead led several men to panic.

"It is a sign from the Gods...They do not favour our victory!"

The panic ended as swiftly as it began, as those who had participated noticed Cappilius' unyielding expression. It had not taken even a single word from him to redeem order and discipline, such was the respect that these men had for him. The incident did, however, leave behind a high level of doubt in everyone, and slowly it became clear to both brothers that they would not be able to hold the outer wall, although try they must.

"Centurion!" a voice hailed him to the left.

Cappilius turned and saw the large body of men moving around the side of the camp, well out of range of their pilums. Nodding thanks to the man who had alerted him to the danger, he turned once more to his brother.

"Increase your command to thirty and move off to the left wall. Add those men on station there to yours and defend that side as best you can. If they do not attack, take a few chosen men and picket the right wall as well. Inform the men at the southern gate to be prepared to delay an attack, and I will create a new separate centubernia here. Move!"

Without even a sign of acknowledgement, Aurelias swiftly departed to comply with the instructions and moved not a second too soon. He had barely reached the west wall when the high pitched battle cry reached his ears for the second time that morning.

Pausing only to grab two shaken men by the arms, and to throw them back towards the wall, he waved his sword above his head and then pointed decisively to either side. With no further command necessary, the thirty or so men with him quickly fanned out to either flank and prepared to receive the enemy. What awaited their eyes as they looked over the palisade froze even the most hardened man's heart to the core. A horde of unknown numbers had already reached the fossa and many had begun to scale the steep slope up to the palisade, before they had even drawn their swords.

"Use your pilums to force them back!" commanded Aurelias, but before the first man had been speared, he knew that the wall could not be held.

Grabbing the nearest man, he spun him around to look directly into his face.

"Go back to the Centurion and inform him that this wall is about to be breached. Tell him to withdraw to the inner fort and we will try to hold these barbarians as long as possible."

Glad to be free of the duty to remain, the man sprinted back towards the northern gate, his fear lending him wings.

Cappilius listened to the message and acted in accordance with his brother's assessment. Ordering a few men to remain for five minutes until the whole command had withdrawn, he sent the bulk of the men to the small fort to which his men now gratefully withdrew. Many could remember their curses for a commander who believed in keeping his men active and not allowing any idleness. Now they could understand the wisdom of the man and gleefully headed towards this inner sanctum.

Cappilius meanwhile collected ten men and moved off to assist the west wall. Detaching two men, one to the southern gate to order a retreat, one to the eastern wall to also retire, he reached the west wall just as the first barbarians managed to climb over the palisade. Sword in hand, he charged towards a man caught midway through climbing down onto the Roman side of the palisade. Without stopping he ran headlong into the man, catapulting him high into the air. With a crash, the man landed on the men behind and caused a rolling effect that threw a large group into the fossa.

Cursing and swearing due to the cuts from the brambles, it would take these men a few minutes to recover. Cappilius picked up a discarded pilum and launched this into the group, where it imbedded itself in the back of a man between the shoulder blades. The task done, he looked to either side and moved to assist a man bent over double against a barbarian intent on smashing the embossed shield held over his head.

With these men wearing no armour, it was an easy task to drive the short sword into this man's kidneys, and then push upwards and then forwards. Ripping the blade backwards and forwards to secure a release, the barbarian arched his back in agony and dropped to his knees. Such was the shock of this attack that he had not even shouted, but only managed to exhale gruffly before falling on his front. Dead!

Once more the Centurion had moved unselfishly to assist one of his men instead of seeking the shelter of the inner fort.

"Thank you, Centurion," the soldier said, bleeding from several wounds to his head.

"Move back to the inner fort," Cappilius ordered. "We cannot hold here. Take as many men with you as possible."

The man tried to smile encouragingly then stood slowly. Collecting his pilum, which now had a broken shaft, he moved slowly to the rear, tapping two men to follow. These initially looked to the Centurion for confirmation and with a nod from him they moved off in the general direction ordered.

A few yards off to Cappilius' left stood his brother, who by now had already caked his uniform in blood and lost his cloak to the downward swipe of a broad sword. Sword in hand he had discarded his shield, and now fought with a pilum in his left hand, sword in the right. Stabbing, poking and digging at any target that presented itself, he constantly charged towards the palisade only to be driven back by the weight of numbers.

Ducking beneath a particularly vicious sword swing, he thrust the pilum upward into the man's stomach, whereupon he found that he could not withdraw the weapon. Leaning forward, he forcefully thrust the point right through the torso, no longer interested in its retrieval.

With a gurgling sound the man staggered, raised his sword again and mouthed a few words that none would ever hear. The broad sword dropped from lifeless hands. Aurelias took a step forward and looked the man in the eyes as he thrust his blade deep into the man's throat. Satisfied, he then pushed him down the inner slope, death already this barbarian's destiny.

Moving once more towards the palisade, a few men gathered and tried to assist him in his intentions. However, the enemy had already breached the wall in several places by standing on each other's backs, while also being raised on shields, and literally sending men over the top one at a time. Even then the defenders stood little chance: well over two hundred barbarians were involved in this particular attack, while there had never been more than forty Romans to defend. The situation was hopeless.

Turning to the man with the cornicen, he said:

"Sound the recall. Keep on sounding it until we withdraw to the inner fort!"

"As you command, Centurion."

The cornicen notes blasted above the din of battle. At first the barbarians hesitated and refused to advance beyond the slope. Consolidating their gains so far, they anticipated another trick and stood warily watching the Romans form ranks just a hundred paces from their front. It was not until Uxudulum in person scaled the wall and could see no reason for hesitation that they advanced once more. He also ordered several men to move to the gates to open them immediately and allow the others to enter.

The scent of victory was indeed strong in his nostrils.

Back at the tributary it began to rain again, and Cappa wished that he could take his survivors as far from this place as possible. Of the twenty-four men he had taken into the wood six had been killed and four incapacitated, but of the original twelve companions only Talba had been injured beyond the point of remaining with them.

His wound had reopened as they dashed across the open terrain and Massila had tried to stem the bleeding, but he had passed out during treatment. It was a foreboding thought, but it looked as if he might lose the use of his leg due to blood deprivation, and damage to the nerves. It was a shame, but also a fact of war.

"Are you alright, Cappa? You seem distracted," Porta asked, lounging on the grass.

"I'm fine. Just a little shook up about how many of us failed to come back."

"It's a miracle any of us did!" Constantine added.

"I guess someone on their side must be pretty good at reading the situation. If Marcellus had not seen those men moving north around your flank you would have been surrounded," Porta remarked.

"Yes, that particular barbarian seemed to be acting out of character. But then so is this whole situation."

"How do you mean?" Julius asked, rolling over to face them both, having now been disturbed from a fitful sleep.

"Well, we encountered the scouts…" Cappa began.

"True," agreed Porta. "But you reported that they hardly numbered more than two hundred, perhaps three. I doubt they will pose a problem when we move on to the fort further north?"

"That may be true, if those are all that are hiding in the wood. I would say nearer four hundred anyway," added Marcellus. "Don't forget that you spotted a sizeable formation of scouts in that wood next to the fort, but on the far side of the tributary, Porta."

Porta nodded. "All this means nothing. We did our job, just as the Tribune commanded and we located the enemy, and no doubt he will be calling upon you, Cappa, to report what we found. What he then does is his problem, not ours!"

"It will become ours if my fears are realised, Porta," Cappa admonished. "In my opinion it seems foolish to have so many men across the river if they do not have an escape route. More important, why are they there in the first place, if not to secure the crossing for a larger army? That dip in the far bank must be the location of their ford. One that we are unaware of on our maps."

Olivius bristled with annoyance. Scowling, he raised himself up on one elbow and spat at a white flower in the grass.

"As I've said before, and I'll say it again. I participated in the patrol that charted these waters last year to update the maps. The river up here is too deep and too fast to ford. Furthermore, these heathens are incapable of building a bridge for themselves and to our knowledge they do not have any boats. The idea is ludicrous!"

For a few minutes silence reigned. Then with the clarity of bells ringing in their ears the cornicen trumpeter began sounding the alarm.

As a single motion they jumped to their feet, reaching for their scutums and pilums. Instinctively they began to move closer to the nearest Roman formation, which belonged to Atronius.

For a few minutes confusion reigned. The column had halted at the tributary as per Scipio's orders, and had started to build the traditional camp, when the alarm had been raised. The decision to stop here had raised many doubts in the other officers as the fort to be relieved, and indeed the bridge itself, was only about five or six leagues further north. Cappa had not so far been summoned by Scipio to report, but Atronius had made it obvious to everyone that if the Helvetii had occupied those woods, then it was highly probable that the fort was already under attack.

Scipio ignored the warnings and believed that the barbarians would not dare to attack the fort, and therefore saw no need to march through the afternoon. The Roman tradition was to march approximately ten to fifteen leagues during the morning and then build a stable camp. While the main command would adopt protective positions around the camp, the remainder rotated the chores of collecting the raw materials and erecting the palisades, or the less fortunate might be ordered to dig the fossa, a deep ditch that would surround the defences. Each legionary carried within his own impedimenta a small portion of the fort's construction materials.

However, in the strict rules of command, it was not normal procedure to complete a full palisade within the boundaries of a province considered occupied. The threat was genuine and yet many still doubted the validity of enclosing their troops within another defensive fort. It was a seemingly obvious lesson, to be learnt by way of the difficulties being experienced at the river, that perhaps Scipio should have been satisfied with only a bracken wall and extra torches. In this way some protection was lost, but at least they kept their flexibility to react to whatever the night might throw at them.

Having chosen the very stream that Prince Daxus had viewed from the woods as the site for this camp, the Third Century had been posted to the far side to protect the builders. It was from here that Crassus had raised the warning. He was a capable officer, not prone to panic, although for the first time in his life he had almost given way to his emotions; but everyone could at least rely on him to allow them time to prepare for the expected enemy onslaught.

For a split second he lost control of his white stallion and felt that pang of panic grip his throat. Everywhere he looked there seemed to be barbarians. Regaining control, he watched as the Helvetii horde suddenly descended from the woods in two linear formations, one approximately fifty paces behind the leading line. To his left, Crassus noted the disorganised mounted men also making an appearance around the southern edge of the trees, most probably the same group that Cappa had tangled with a few days before.

With a quick glance at his own men, he noted that, apart from a few anxious looks in his direction, the legionaries all stood their ground. Holding the formation of three deep and forty men long, they banded together behind their cylindrical shields. Trust in their leadership and in the strength of their companion's sword arm was now the only hope left.

"Raise pilums!" Crassus shouted, pulling back once again on the horse's reins. "We will withdraw in formation towards the stream. We will not run! We are soldiers of Roma and we are not accustomed to showing fear to an enemy. Withdraw!"

Yard by yard they began to move, while behind them the pandemonium began to show some order and precision. As Crassus wisely withdrew in the face of a far superior number, he began to try to count heads.

He wiped his brow as, for the first time in his career, he was sweating profusely.

"By Jupiter, I count two thousand in the first line!"

That thought had crossed Cappa's mind as well, just as Atronius rode up to him on a mare.

"Cappa!"

"Here, Centurion!"

"Take your men and join Valenus with the auxiliaries on the extreme right. Your task is to secure our flank to the tributary. Good luck, Cappa, and may Mars and Jupiter fight on our side this day!"

"As you command, Pilum."

With no further words necessary, Atronius rode away to march his men to link up with the vanguard commanded by Crassus. As he rode forward, he sighted Scipio's command staff riding swiftly to the right flank. As if by pure thought alone, a rider arrived at that point to emphasise this fact.

"Primus Pilum, I have been asked by the Tribune to request that you attend the command tent to discuss battle plans."

"I will attend immediately," Atronius responded, returning the cavalryman's salute. Then as a second thought he turned back towards Cappa and shouted.

"Cappa, you will join me at the command tent as well. Leave Porta or Olivius in command in your absence. These barbarians have appeared from the very direction you did. Your information may be decisive in the battle, if it is to be fought this day."

Cappa saluted, and turned to Porta to hand over temporary command, much to the annoyance of Olivius. Delaying only long enough to confirm that they had moved in the right direction, he then lowered his shield to make it easier to carry, and dropped in beside Atronius' horse to run at double pace. Within minutes they had joined Scipio on a small mound, well back from the small stream that ran from north to south, directly across their line of defence. From here a good view of the intended battlefield was available, and apart from Crassus, who had naturally remained with his men, they found the staff with Scipio in an unusually agitated mood.

As they both came to a halt, Atronius on the horse and Cappa sweating profusely from the run, neither man hid their discomfort. Cappa tried desperately not to show his dislike at being in the company of so many members of the centenate. Apart from his companion, he was aware of nobody who regarded him or his men as anything other than expendable. Had it not been for their usefulness in the dangerous march north, Cappa believed that the agreement made by Scipio would have been rescinded days ago.

The fact that only thirty cavalry accompanied the cohort to act as messengers had restricted the ability to scout ahead of the column, to avoid an ambush. Something that Scipio had a private terror of, as he had already blundered into ambushes of one sort or another three times in his career. How the normal procedure of dismissal had been avoided in his case was a mystery that more than a few of those gathered around the small table now pondered.

"Ah, Atronius," Scipio hailed them. "I am in need of your advice."

"I am here to serve, noble Tribune," Atronius responded, indicating to Cappa to follow as he approached the table.

"Has Crassus managed to forward to us a figure as to how many of the heathen are across the stream?"

"Not to my knowledge, but the Optio's scouts returned from that very wood, bringing a prisoner with them. Has this man been questioned?"

Scipio grinned coldly, a look of wild disappointment being thrown in the direction of Lepidus, who physically wilted under such a baleful gaze.

"We discussed the situation with the barbarian, but failed to ascertain any real information as regards the size of the force opposing us," Scipio said coldly. "We will have to act on what we see, Centurion."

Atronius bit down hard to hold his temper, but in doing so failed to see the approach of Cappa, who now stepped forward, saluted and hailed Scipio in the most formal fashion he could muster, while averting his eyes to avoid showing his dislike of the tribune.

"If the Centurion would allow, Tribune, I have a man within the newly formed scouts who has performed miracles with those who are reluctant to speak. Perhaps..."

"Perhaps nothing..." interrupted Scipio. "The barbarian took his knowledge to the grave. In the light of your patrol, what can you unravel for us? We are a little pressed for time."

"The scout's report indicates at least two thousand or more men beyond the woods," Cappa stated respectfully, making sure that he again avoided direct eye contact with any of those present.

Scipio grunted in approval of the statement and then turned to Lepidus and Valenus. "Take your posts and retain order. The final battle plan will be relayed to you in a moment. Valenus, you will command the far right, along with the auxiliaries protecting the tributary flank. Atronius, you will command the far left, with command over the archers stationed there to deal with the horsemen facing you. I am certain that these heathens will not attack today but we will remain in battle array until further notice. Dismissed!"

Without a further word Scipio, looking tired and worn out from earlier exertions, retired to the shade of the tent overhang. One by one the officers moved away to rejoin their troops. All except Cappa and Atronius.

Atronius decided to speak first. "Shall we not try to reinforce the fort, noble Tribune. Or at the minimum assist them to withdraw?"

"Let me remind you, Centurion," Scipio said, deliberately ignoring the true rank of primus pilum, "that I am in command on this battlefield."

Nodding assent, Atronius turned and stormed away, his face red and fuming after the deliberate insult to his rank. Cappa glanced at him as he walked down the small incline to where the main defence line was now being formed by Valenus and Crassus, the latter having now withdrawn his men and archers back across the stream. For a brief moment the air froze, and Cappa looked down at the masquerade in the small valley before him, as if he was in a trance. For a moment he wondered just how many times he had seen similar formations being prepared and the subsequent clash of arms in battle.

Cappa glanced back towards Scipio, who now sat gingerly sipping at some wine in a chalice. Frowning, he took another step forward.

"With respect, noble Tribune, I am willing to commit my men to search out the fort and establish its condition as regards holding until relieved. Should you feel that more auxiliaries from the right..."

"Enough!" Scipio rose with a start. "Take your scum to whatever part of this battlefield you intend to occupy and desist from your ramblings, Optio. I will inform you when you are required to forward an opinion that is above your rank. I command here and I tire of this continual necessity of reminding you and the Pilum precisely what that means. Now leave!"

Cappa stared at the man before him. A man of such experience who had not even tried to discuss tactics with his centurions, never mind make any attempt to assess the situation accurately.

"May I respectfully point out, to the Tribune, the consequences of inactivity," Cappa tried again. "Should the fort fall, we will have to fight a second battle to reach the bridge, at which point they may already have sent over more men to secure its capture. A small detachment sent now would be sufficient to..."

"Damn you, Optio, you are impertinent! You will retire now or I will rescind the status of your heathens and place you all on the cross of execution at dawn. You go too far!"

Cappa stepped back, a gust of wind catching hold of Scipio's cloak as he finished the first outburst, curling it majestically in the air. Normally, some might have taken this as a good omen, a Godlike persona, but to Cappa this only enhanced the scene of insanity and he averted his eyes, lest they give away his contempt for this man. The similarities to Valenus were striking. It was now a certainty that this man had no intention of allowing their earlier defiance to go unpunished.

Atronius now reappeared and quickly grasped Cappa by the arm. Saluting to the Tribune he led the obstinate man away as quickly as possible.

"Do you have a suicide pact with the Dis Pater!" he said, coldly. "That man is close to insanity, along with Valenus. I am praying constantly to Mars to keep the cohort and me alive. Your continual antagonism is not assisting anyone, least of all your men!"

Pulling free, Cappa turned on Atronius. "So we should all just obey without question. I am a soldier. So are you. It is ridiculous to leave those men in the fort without even trying to reinforce them. It is just as much an error to assume no fighting will take place today and order a large portion of our line to continue to build our own camp. We should be attacking those barbarians and forcing the issue, but not that fool! He will wait until we are reinforced and stay safely in the camp until every man at the fort has been killed or captured. I am already under threat of execution, as are all my companions. His threat is empty."

Atronius looked past Cappa to watch the First Century, reduced in number due to the earlier disastrous patrol that had led to Cappa's rebellion, form two lines of fifty men apiece. They were in light order, having left their baggage in the camp behind Scipio's tent. They also seemed to be in a demoralised state with several men actually leaning on their pilums or shields.

"Your old formation will need your help to survive, Cappa, as do your scouts," he said. "In the last six months I have noticed a tendency to rebellion within your heart. You know that your attitude will not be ignored forever."

Cappa nodded in agreement, desperate to keep his temper under control. Atronius was, as usual, annoyingly correct, and if any man would or could assist him, it would be him. Scipio had lied as regards their agreement several days ago, during their so-called rebellion under his command.

It was now obvious that he intended to use the situation to force them all to carry out orders that would ordinarily have been ignored. The realisation dawned on him as if a mountain had fallen on his head, and for a while the blood boiled in his veins and his vision became hazy. People in power never failed to disappoint him, no matter how much hope he had that they would have the right reaction and see matters from both sides of the fence, metaphorically. Anyway, what was the right reaction?

He knew that any act of violence against Scipio would be futile, but the feeling of utter uselessness was fast becoming overwhelming. Sooner or later these issues would have to alter if Roma was to retain any loyalty within the legions. For now it was time to rejoin his companions.

With a parting salute Cappa moved away towards Porta, who had now moved south to take up position amongst the scorpion sections. Atronius watched patiently and groaned inwardly. There walked one of the most experienced members of the legion that he had ever met, and he would place his worth above that of the entire centenate. It was known that he had refused the post of Centurion no less than three times, a fact that amazed everyone including Atronius, as a man's single purpose in serving was to increase his wealth. Not so with that man, and it left everyone trying to figure out why he was so different. It was also the fact that he was different that brought down the scorn of the centenate, rather than their support.

Shaking his head, he mounted the dapple-grey horse nearby and rode away to join the men on the cohort's left flank. Cappa would need to adjust his attitude or he would eventually end not only his own life but also that of all the others he was so eager to protect.

⊰┼⊹┼⊹┼⊱

The presence watched in silence as the two forces began minor operations to realign their positions, each seeking some fraction of an advantage that would secure victory. Such small minds, it thought. So little time to really change anything. It looked briefly into the future to see if the guardians would also be present. No, they were not here, so it was indeed up to these creatures to battle freely. Odd, as Fate and Destiny rarely passed on an opportunity to disrupt this world's existence. It had become almost entertainment, but clearly millennia of this had left them somewhat bored.

A sound similar to a sigh escaped pursed lips as the image began to fade. Even with so much power within the Underworld, it was still possible to hold open this window of observation for only a brief moment. Oft as not the entity wondered why its master bothered with such objects that were so frail. If the dominions obtained access to this world, and others like it, there were no longer the creatures, magic or knowledge to oppose them. What was the fun of victory against no opposition?

With a casual reflection it looked at the destinies that would be affected by these events to be completed shortly on...what was this world called...ah, yes, Earth. So many changes would become possible. It was almost as odd to try and understand why Fate and Destiny even bothered, but its Master was infinitely more powerful and yet this world and dimension still held a fascination it could not comprehend.

Puny, weak, easily killed, less than one hundred years of life... What good were they even as slaves?

For a moment it considered asking the question of the Master but quickly put this to one side. The last creature to do so had been sent to the pit for a thousand, or perhaps...No, a thousand years it was? Yes, it was certain, the Earth had primitive methods of relating to the passage of time. Not that it was even accurate! Knowledge would also change in the next hundred years anyway!

The Caesarean calendar!

Even more odd than the interest in this time was the choice of a particular champion in whom the Master had placed so much faith, Julius Caesar! Why him and not another? This Pompeius Magna seemed a better bet. It had also heard mentioned, briefly, another called Cassius Evictus, who had prayed for eternal life, while his heart was as black as death itself.

Both of these men's hearts sought power and riches, so were easily controllable. Caesar's only difference was that he had no wealth and so the mental necessity to control his actions was less potent. Even so the subjugation of the world by that person seemed erroneous at best. However, it was not there to question, but to view and report back.

Whatever the Master intended, it was about to begin soon. To be late was not advisable, not to mention exceedingly painful!

Cassius looked ahead of him and pondered temporarily about what exactly had happened back at Scipio's camp. Now the voice seemed less believable. He had after all been under enormous stress, or had he imagined it? No, his mind was not prone to illusions. He had lived his whole life studying the black arts and had even participated in the oldest rituals. That had at first been for the orgies that invariably followed, but since that first time he knew that his obsession with keys had taken a new turn. Why did keys interest him so much?

With the recent experiences and voices in his head he now wondered if he had gone mad. There were cases of madness in the Brotherhood and even suicidal tendencies, but he did not feel... mad.

The tension began then, first in his legs, but before he could react his whole body seemed to freeze. Madness was now most definitely a possibility. All around him people moved but none seemed to pay him any attention. What was going on now?

Forcing his eyes down, he saw the earth begin to melt. In his mind he screamed in terror, but he knew no sound was heard. All about him the sky began to flash in vivid, blinding colours, then faded away into nothing.

When the light came he raised his hand across his eyes, thankful of the movement again. This was not like before, when everything had stayed the same, but the voice had spoken to him. This time everything had melted into a black nothingness that had no real form and yet he knew it extended beyond his understanding.

Slowly the brightness faded and he took a step forward, trembling, fighting with difficulty to keep under control.

"*Try if you must!*"

The trembling exploded, almost forcing Cassius to his knees, barely remaining upright. This was not in his head but all around him.

"Try? Try what?" he croaked

"*Control, little fool. If you must try to keep control of your puny mind, then you must, but it will avail you nothing.*"

Cassius fell back a pace, cowering, as if he expected to be struck at any moment. The pain was there in a second. He did not really feel it. It just engulfed his mind but not his physical form. The presence was overwhelming. Painful. He felt confused, hesitant, as the voice seemed able to enter his very soul. He raised his hands to ward off further probing, but this failed, no physical reaction would help. So perhaps if he applied his willpower, he could expel whatever was inside his head?

The laughter was cold and cruel.

"*Try again, fool. Try again. I have need of amusement in this foul pit. Indeed I have much use for your soul. Yes, that is good, now more, harder... fight harder. That is so much better. No, no, no, you are allowing your pathetic compassion to stop your absolute conversion to my beliefs, the truth! Fight cold, Cassius Evictus, as cold as your heart, as the Brotherhood have served me well.*"

Now two eyes appeared in the darkness, red and full of fire. Like needles they pricked and probed into his mind and bit by bit he knew something was changing inside him.

What had this all meant? How had the Brotherhood been of use? With a sudden realisation Cassius screamed in panic.

"Enough! I wish to return!"

"*Return?*" came the reply. "*To where?*"

"The legion! I wish to return now!"

"*To you, the legion, as you say, no longer exists. To the legion you no longer exist. In fact you have never existed at all!*"

"What is meant by this? Release me!"

"*Release you? But this is what you prayed for...Ultimate power is what I offer...Immortality is what I offer...Do you no longer desire these things?*"

"Release meeeeeeeee!"

"*I see the training will take much longer than anticipated. As regards this releasing you, the demand is refused. You have yet to fulfil your bargain. To me you are the key and all I need is the lock to the door. Find me the way to use the key and we can again discuss this...release? Now, to whom shall we send you for the beginning of your training? Ah yes, here is a good place to start. She will be only too happy to assist. The goddess of the* damnati *shall be your initial tutor. I hope you enjoy pain, my fragile mortal, for here you will feel nothing else for five hundred years. Enjoy Orbiana's counsel, enjoy!*"

The probing now became unbearable and Cassius felt his legs fold. He knew this was the end, but something inside him suddenly began to grow faster than he could control. If he wanted to survive he knew he would have to grasp this strength and hold on.

Five hundred years! What was that all about?

On and on went the digging as, bit by bit, humanity slowly fell away. As did the flesh, as each black day passed.

Then the concept of time vanished and his fate became sealed. Always he sensed the presence of the first God, she who ripped asunder his soul and exposed his inner mind, but there, behind this power, was another. Silent, but relentless in its probing of his essence, his soul. Somehow this second presence terrified him more than the first, but as time passed he became less capable of distinguishing between the two, it had all become a blur of perpetual agony.

His last human thought echoed into the void, *betrayal*!

"*By whom?*" laughed the first presence. "*By whom?*"

Zeus looked at the chess set and pondered his next move a little. It had been a long time since he had enjoyed such a game. He wondered if he should give it to the Romans on earth as a gift? No, not just yet, perhaps a little later, when he had developed them a little more.

Then the air moved. The drapes cascaded to the floor and the ground trembled. A few of his companions turned to him, but he deliberately ignored their gaze. Clearly his brother Hades was on the rampage again. The ultimate aim of this new disturbance was of course unknown, but it was only a matter of time before he made his customary mistakes, normally through his ridiculous belief that he was more intelligent that everyone else.

He had already delayed Abundantia—or did she still use that old name of Diana?—against his wishes, when she should have returned thousands of years ago. She was a slight nuisance, as he had always found her to be a little too inquisitive about his personal endeavours. He never did like those members of their elite who felt the urge to dabble in his affairs.

His brother had also travelled to numerous other dimensions of lesser importance, spreading disaster. Always thwarted at the last moment or by some betrayal, the inevitable apologies would follow and he would say that he would never attempt it again. Naturally, as this latest disturbance proved, this was always a lie. Even on his favourite world, Terra, or Earth as some preferred, he knew his brother had been responsible for the destruction of the Minoan peoples, even though he tried to blame his other brother Poseidon, God of the sea. He had had such high hopes for that particular civilisation.

What now, he thought, as he moved the bishop a few squares to the right.

"*The void has begun to flux, Zeus,*" someone offered helpfully.

"*Yes, so it has,*" he replied, scratching his nose as he contemplated his next move in the game they played, a habit that was also an early sign of his temper.

"*Should we not at least investigate, my Lord? Just to be on the safe side.*"
"*I will look later. Your advice on this game would be more useful!*"
"*My Lord, if it...*"

Zeus raised his eyes and the air began to burn, literally.

"*Are we now deaf? Have your powers diminished to such a level that obedience has now equally evaporated?*"

There was to be no answer of course. To reply would have been extremely dangerous, as of late Zeus had been somewhat distracted with this new game that he insisted on playing with every one of them, every day. It had become an obsession.

So the game continued as the void began to expand and contract. The tremors slowly became worse, but in truth it was nothing new to them. Zeus' brother was always up to something, somewhere. As always, it would fall to them all to thwart the plans once more, even if finishing the chess had a greater importance at the moment.

For the moment there was enough time. Or so they thought.

PART FOUR

A BRIEF REST

The air was heavy now as the wind picked up, and the lines of Helvetii moved slowly forward to assume their posts this side of the small stream. It posed no real threat to their continued advance and, to be honest, none of them truly considered the Romans any serious threat either. After all, they numbered at least four times more, and more men were crossing the river as they watched the enemy realign their positions. It was a slow process and many began to wonder why they did not strike now while the enemy was disorganised. It seemed like the perfect opportunity, but those who knew Prince Daxus best knew differently. There would be no battle this day, as the Prince was waiting for even greater odds before he contemplated engaging those before him.

The man himself sat astride a dapple-grey mount that shied with every loud noise. He had been warned that the pony was unreliable and had killed its previous owner.

"If I can not master this damn horse," Daxus had reproached those concerned, "then how am I to master these Romans?"

When none replied the Prince had simply ridden down the small slope to speak to the individual lines of his warriors and those of the Boii. If nothing else, he was a master of the art of manipulation. A man's heart was easily swayed with the prospects of bounty, but the prospect of plentiful food for all was more than enough to make these people fight hard. Some had even brought their womenfolk, which was not uncommon. When the fighting began the women would retire beyond the woods, although the bravest would stay within sight of the conflict. Those few were the breeding stock that the Prince now admired as he rode through the parting lines of Boii.

He despised these people for their high attitudes to peace. They claimed to be more educated and yet none of their chiefs stood on the council. They were weak and compliant, perfect slaves, he suddenly thought, waving in reply to an outburst of battle cries. These fools would gladly die for the cause of finding food for their people, while Daxus fully intended that his people would eventually dominate and then rule all the other tribes in the alliance. Food was only the means to the end. He had greater plans that did not involve sharing one iota of power with anyone, including his father!

Digging his heels into the pony's flanks, he fought briefly as the animal almost turned to bite his calf, whinnied and then finally decided to agree to ascend the hill once more. Turning, he watched as the main chiefs joined him at a fast pace, no doubt seeking confirmation as to whether they would fight. As they approached, he looked once more across the stream and viewed the cylindrical formations of the enemy that seemed so thin in comparison to his own force. Pathetic, he mused, but then why hesitate? Why was he so intent on waiting for more? It did not make sense and yet he found that he could not reach a decision. His mind simply refused to function. Was this fear? Did he truly fear failure so much that he would risk all his people's future?

By the Gods, what was wrong with him?

"Great Prince," a voice said, bringing him out of his internal struggle, "the chiefs are now gathered."

"Then un-gather them!" Daxus snapped. "We fight tomorrow. Post the guards and retire the lines to the wood. Let the enemy sweat for a while, and organise raids to keep them awake all night. Are you deaf? Did you not here my command? Move!"

The warrior flinched as if struck and stumbled back down the small slope to speak to the chiefs, all of whom reacted with open shock to the rebuke. A few began to walk up the final level of the slope but the Prince's personal guard soon stepped forward to end their progress.

"We fight tomorrow!" Daxus shouted and with a final glance rode back into the trees.

⁘※⁘※⁘

Across the stream, astride his horse, Atronius had followed the same tour of inspection. The difference was that he referred to each location with a name rather than an eye for the topography of the land. Even so he found their situation rather precarious at best and wiped the sweat away from his forehead. He had never feared death in itself but he feared a useless death more. Duty was his honour and vice versa. To fail is to die, and on this day he saw little opportunity for success, and this added to his fears that the cohort might well be on the verge of rebellion, due to Scipio's outlandish punishments and tactics, Cappa's so-called rebellion being only one of many such incidents.

With a practised eye he again surveyed the area and breathed a little easier and with some satisfaction. At least what they had was placed to the best advantage.

Flatinius Pinasis, a good-tempered junior officer of promise, commanded the archers on the extreme left, their objective to disorganise any major assault while falling back behind the main lines. A few javeliners had been added to this force to increase this effect, if it proved successful in its initial intent. If anyone could cause havoc it was most definitely Flatinius!

To Atronius' right stood the command of Fabius, with the added weight of Crassus' legionaries alongside, in overall command of the centre. This was not a problem area, he confidently asserted, for here stood their only reserve, initially in the form of Crassus, with a further reserve of Lepidus still building the camp. Besides, Crassus would hold here to the last man. It was not there that he felt concern but more in relation to Valenus and the far right.

Here stood the remains of the first century with Cappa immediately behind them and the main body of javeliners further back at the ford. Not only were these men in poor spirits, but Cappa was on the point of rebellion and the javeliners had never been in any combat, small or large, and were likely to make a run for the woods at the first sign of trouble. If he were the enemy leader he would attack frontally to pin them, send the mounted men around their left and attack across the ford to turn their right. In this way, the barbarians could easily encircle them and force them to retire into the camp, and given the numbers involved it seemed unlikely that they would break out again. They would share the same fate as that of the fort they were supposedly meant to be rescuing.

However, perhaps not today. With the light fading Atronius knew that a battle would not take place, and inwardly he thanked the Gods for this indulgence, by kissing his cloak. To him and many others no sacrifice had been made, and it was not good to anger the Gods, as this foul weather testified. As a result many now stood uneasily at their posts. When the word was finally spread that the lack of light was unlikely to presage a battle, the relief could be seen as a wave of emotion washing across the entire column, as if the loss of the sun presaged an evening of sleep. This was something that many of them now required following the ten league march that morning and the subsequent eight hours standing perfectly still within their respective units. It had been a long day.

Glancing behind, Atronius anticipated that Scipio would already be sending out couriers to order the withdrawal to the camp. For a moment this looked to be correct, as two riders suddenly sped off to the south, away from the command tent. However, it was soon quite clear that instructions to retire had not been given, as they both suddenly sped back towards the main woods to the southeast.

When the riders bypassed the archers, he noted with a smile, Flatinius attempted to stop them in their tracks by threatening to bring them down with his arrows, to establish what their errand involved. One stopped while the other sped past without reducing his speed, knocking two men flying in the process. In anger, one man let loose a shot, which thankfully flew wild and missed by a wide margin. It did not however diminish the anger of the remaining rider, who now looked exceptionally ill at ease.

Atronius chuckled. He shook his head and looked towards the glowing stars. He already knew what Scipio intended even as Flatinius let the rider continue on his errand. They were all to keep the men in line until nightfall and even then they might perhaps issue no recall. At first, as any man would do, Atronius reviewed what could be gained by remaining in battle order, as the sun began to blaze in a beautiful panorama, seemingly directed at him alone, across the horizon.

To all intents and purposes the enemy had withdrawn for the night, and soon perhaps a few raids would be organised to keep them awake and perhaps also to tire them for the morrow. To remain would expose them not only to the javelins but also to the elements, as a heavy downpour had now begun. As if they did not have enough to contend with, the cold now began to bite at exposed arms, faces and legs. With this still in mind, he began a slow canter towards Crassus, who now stood next to one of his century signifiers holding their emblem. As he closed the distance the all too familiar wineskin appeared at the lips to be gulped feverishly and with relish.

Atronius stared at Crassus for a full minute before the latter realised the presence of the superior officer. For all his training and expertise, Atronius had tried to dislike this man, as indeed he had also tried with Cappa. If he was to be honest with his feelings, before him now stood the main threat to his position within the legion, a man who could easily be the next primus pilum. With all the concentration that the God Honus could provide as regards military honour and morality, he continued to try and failed miserably.

Wiping his mouth dry, Crassus saluted and then offered the wineskin up for his pleasure.

"This is a nice place to hold a gathering is it not, Primus Pilum?"

"It is indeed, Crassus, although no doubt our favoured leader would dispute your choice to drink on the battlefield in front of your men."

It was Crassus' turn to stare. He watched the figure on the horse for any sign of displeasure, and finding none he smiled.

"They all know me too well, Pilum. I am unaware of a day that I have not had a wineskin within arms reach. It is my way, as you are more than aware."

Atronius chuckled. "Indeed I am. Indeed I am."

"I assume this is not a social call?" Crassus asked mildly, jerking his head towards the stream.

"I truly wish it were but circumstances have conspired against me. You are unhurt from your earlier experience, I hope?"

It was Crassus' turn to chuckle and the sound rebounded across the small ravine. "We did not stay long enough for those heathens to even try, Pilum. No, I am not even scratched."

"Good news indeed. But what of those very heathens? Who? Numbers? Cappa believes that well over four thousand are in those woods? But if that is true why did they hold back? No, they are staying in those woods for one reason or another and they may number as believed, but they are not ready to attack. It is the only reason that makes sense. But why? They are large enough to contend with us, surely?"

"Unless they have others working around our flanks," suggested Crassus, in between swigs of wine. "We will almost certainly be the last to know due to the lack of our mounted presence, and someone is sure to attack us on the right across that ford. Will the javeliners hold?"

Atronius sighed heavily, recalling his own misgivings only a few moments earlier. "Perhaps some wine after all," he said with a flamboyant grasp of the wineskin while balancing from the horse's flank, for they had no saddles in those days. "They are an unknown factor and never tested in battle," he responded when perched once more on the animal's back. "They seem fine, but the first time in battle is always a very serious test. It was for all of us."

"I cannot even remember the first time," Crassus laughed, retaking his wineskin before it was drained, throwing a look of horror at Atronius for almost emptying it. "Not that they are the real problem on the right, mind you. Valenus is there as well and that makes me extremely nervous. We are outnumbered here no matter how you look at this, and for him to start an attack for personal glory will see us all dead."

"Yes, I know. That is why Cappa is right behind him."

"Ah, yes, Cappa. How is that irksome scrotum? Still as irritating as ever? Yes, I'm not surprised, but then I am not surprised that his people rebelled against Valenus either. Then you have our illustrious leader. Why are we still out here, by the way? Should we not retire to the camp to avoid those raiders that will be coming across that stream as soon as the dark hits?"

"You take the very words from my mouth, Centurion," agreed Atronius, still considering his previous encounter with Scipio.

"I hear on the grapevine that our young Cappa has offended the Tribune once again? What was it this time?"

"Nothing, as usual. We seem to be on a knife's edge, Crassus, and the edge is very sharp."

"Well we could improve matters by retiring to the camp."

Atronius nodded but still hesitated, as he knew Scipio was not going to allow the retirement easily. The earlier riders had shown this to be true. He allowed his mind to wander for a brief moment but soon snapped back as Crassus added his opinion to that of Cappa.

"We have on the other side of that stream, Atronius, well over four thousand barbarians, some of which I have identified as the Boii," he said, pleased with Atronius' look of shock. "Yes, Primus, I said the Boii! The other half seem to be Helvetii but I bet the Vertibrogi are not too far away either."

"Are you sure?"

"I am a little older than the average bear but I think I know the Boii when I see them."

"So they have joined the alliance as well. This was not known when we marched north," Atronius thought aloud. "That camp is all the more inviting." He then added, as an afterthought, "The Boii are well known for their night attacks."

"Indeed they are, Pilum. No doubt our illustrious leader would appreciate the warning!"

Atronius clasped forearms in thanks, turned his horse immediately and rode back to the command tent. Here the guards barred his way briefly, but his expression was sufficient to warn them that he intended to speak to only one person, and they feared to oppose the second-in-command. Automatically, they stepped to one side after a few words. They had done their duty to the Tribune and they now settled down to listen to yet another argument. Even they realised that normal practice was to retire. It had been only a matter of time before the Pilum arrived to discuss this very topic. It had the makings of the best show yet.

"Tribune!" Atronius said, crossing the floor of the tent in just two strides.

Scipio, who had been sitting across a low couch, looked up. "Atronius?"

"I have just been informed by Centurion Crassus that the men we are facing have a faction of the Boii with them. If this is correct then the Helvetii have secured the support of the local tribes. We should retire to the camp immediately!"

Scipio looked down at the table before him lazily, almost as though none had spoken, pouring another glass of wine. For a moment he wondered of what real significance this new piece of information would be, then shrugged.

"Tribune!" frowned Atronius in frustration. "Should we not retire to the camp palisades for the moment and then march onto the fort on the morrow? I am sure you are aware that the Boii are well known for their night tactics of ambush. We should move before the light fails completely."

Scipio again refused to reply, reaching for more wine.

"Tribune?"

With a start Scipio raised his eyes and shrugged indifferently, almost irritated at the Pilum's insistence. He was drunk, Atronius fumed. The damn fool was drunk!

"The Boii you say?"

"Yes."

Scipio, feeling the effects of the wine, forced himself to rise. "Have they been reinforced?"

"Not to my knowledge."

"Have they made any preliminary movement to attack or to force us to manoeuvre further?"

"No, they have remained at the edge of wood to hide their numbers, and it is possible that the rear echelon may already have moved to either flank. It is unknown, but to remain out in the open at night is..."

"Yes...Yes! Then you had better bring the men inside the camp, Pilum. I am surprised that you have not done so already. Just do it!"

Atronius sighed, as for once he did not care about the disrespect shown by Scipio. He had a greater purpose.

"As you command, Tribune."

Scipio raised his voice as Atronius reached the exit. "Also send for the priests. If we are to do battle tomorrow, then we will bring Mars with us."

Atronius groaned inwardly and turned to retire. Outside he motioned for one of the guards to send for Scipio's priests. Then with a savage look he descended on each centenate commander to prepare for a backward move to enter the camp. Within a few minutes, Lepidus arrived to confirm that the fossa and palisade were now completed and that his men would cover the withdrawal of the other units.

Well, Atronius thought, at least they would rest easy tonight and be fresh for the battle that would follow tomorrow. He watched with satisfaction as the first legionaries began to file up the slope.

As the file increased, Atronius remembered the days when they had both served together and held the same rank several years before, when Scipio had proved to be an excellent commander. At the small formation level he excelled. At the more advanced necessities of tactical level, he showed outstanding bravery. Unfortunately, at the cohort level, he seemed to be floundering in a vacuum that was beyond his comprehension.

Too many factors could now alter the outcome. When you fought one to one your only concern was survival, while even at the lower levels of rank you were still expected to stand and fight as an individual. When dealing with a larger confrontation you were never really involved with the bloodletting and your mind was given considerable time to wander. Patience was never this man's greatest strength, and as a result he had oft as not dived headfirst into a poor situation without using the necessary tactics to survey the possibilities, hence his numerous errors. At this level he must now act independently. He should interpret every piece of information to build a picture of the true situation and base the next decision on the previous one, while also identifying the reactions caused by the initial decision.

Furthermore, the ability to change one's plans as the situation dictated was a skill singularly missing from Scipio's personality matrix. It is my plan, why is it not working? Such exclamations did not raise people's morale and a stubborn trait had led the Tribune to question the bravery of the men and accuse many of cowardice. As others excelled, and time began to take its jealous toll of his youth, the man had slowly lost all touch with the common soldier and developed a taste for the better qualities of life, until his former self had been reduced to a mere shadow of his earlier glory. A glory that continued to eat away at his soul and served to increase his hatred of anything that others could, and did, admire.

He was, and he knew this too, more than an image of a man living on the memories of achievements that had not been repeated for over ten years. Scipio had become a politically motivated man who lacked the right connections to progress further. He also lacked the finesse of an orator, such as Julius Caesar or even Labienus, and this restricted his ability to draw people to the banner of future success.

To Atronius the life of a soldier was all the motivation required to satisfy his soul. To him politicians should remain in Roma where they could not interfere with the smooth running of the army. Scipio was now a man who should be relieved of his command, but he retained the post through previous exploits and by a reputation for which Legate Titus Labienus had a high level of respect, even though he was considerably younger than the tribune. Pulling the horse's head to one side, the Pilum rode slowly back towards the camp, patiently allowing the projectile troops and their light scorpions to move their wagons through the gate, before riding behind the protective wall of the palisades.

As he passed the scorpions, he recalled the one occasion on which he had seen these weapons of destruction in action. They were like a horizontal archer's bow but ten times or more the thickness. With tight ropes made from horse's hair and a few levers, the simple art of archery had been improved to the point of firing a large arrow tipped with a metal point. On duty he had seen these weapons pass through a large body of men, ripping and gouging large avenues through the ranks. In a densely packed mass, they were deadly and they were also used in great numbers in sieges. A shiver ran down his back and he wondered why their enemies did not copy such things, but perhaps they lacked the knowledge. It mattered little, as the following morning the ten devices that they had brought along would reap a deadly reward, on an enemy that had chosen to defy Roma.

By Jupiter, Mars and Vulcan, he was so hungry...

As the light rain subsided, the temperature began to fall as the night closed in, drowning the countryside in an impenetrable blanket of darkness. All about them the shadows took on a new life, as hidden horrors seemed to move with the shadows. Grown men of course were not afraid of the dark, but all those that had served for any length of time in the legion knew what dangers could lurk within such depths. They all knew how exposed they had now become, as they did after all only number approximately one thousand while the enemy was known to be twenty times that number. If that was not enough to set the imagination running then nothing would...ever!

One by one, within the camp, domestic fires began to appear at regular intervals, while along the palisade torches became commonplace. Not only were they held by the guards themselves, but they were also erected every five paces along the palisade. Nothing would be able to close on the wall or fossa without being seen from at least forty paces. To ensure this, Atronius had ordered the watch doubled but the normal six hours watch would be halved, to keep as many people as possible fresh for the morning.

It was a morning that held little joy for any of them, although those like Porta clearly looked forward to the opportunity to kill again. Men such as him were invaluable now, but they nevertheless left a sour taste in the mouth and made Atronius especially concerned. However, this was no time to worry about the morality of a few, as he finally arranged the correct rotation of the guards. It was time for him to retire out of sight and allow the legionaries time to relax and sift though their own thoughts.

Around the fires the legionaries congregated to discuss the day's events. Old and new friendships became sealed in the unusual warmth of a fire fuelled by a companionship that could only have developed in a predicament such as this.

Throughout the camp the old hands could be seen cleaning their armour or sharpening a gladius short sword, while all about them sat the less experienced, as though just being close to these men gave them some kind of extra courage for the morrow. All of them had had to remain at their post, or build the camp, within their respective centuries, with no fear of the unknown. There had been no time to dawdle or to discuss openly what they might miss should they fall, or where their experiences and dreams might have taken them in the future. They obeyed because it was their duty to do so.

Now, as they gathered in their small groups around the fires, the conversations were muted and reserved. As the darkness finally engulfed them and the fires cast their eerie glow across the camp, their thoughts turned to their loved ones, their friends and forgotten colleagues elsewhere, or perhaps beyond the boundaries of the living. A memory of an old conversation would suddenly reappear. Men would seek out any excuse for not discussing the issue at hand and others chose laughter rather than gloom. Of course none of this had any effect on the reality that sooner or later would assert itself on each and every man's consciousness: there was little chance of victory against such odds.

To many the stress of being denied the future now overwhelmed their hearts and they took to solitude to seek contentment. Others slept as if tomorrow held no concerns for them, and the officers in particular sought each other's company to avoid the attentions of the men, and thus failed to concern themselves with anything other than the glory victory would bring them. The wine brought forth many different but ludicrous plans of what they would implement on the morrow.

In truth most of the centenate, although experienced, had been appointed to their posts just a few weeks before, as several of the previous centurions had accepted retirement or transferred to quieter posts to finish their twenty-five years service. Only Atronius avoided the command tent and the laughter that flowed as freely as the wine supplied by Scipio. Even Crassus had allowed himself the luxury of a good wineskin, which was undoubtedly of a better quality than his own stock. However, there was little that he could now do to restore or enhance the legionaries' morale.

All he intended now was to show the respect that a commander should have for the men who would from dawn stand by his side and obey without question any order given. Atronius was a firm believer in respect, but saw little possibility of improvements with the command structure as it presently stood. As the evening wore on he became more and more fidgety and took to walking the palisades with little or no rest. He had never felt such foreboding and he had never seen a night as black as this. Not a single star could be seen.

With a grunt, he turned his gaze from the sky and decided to move away from the wall. He checked the nearest gate, the southern one, then gratefully accepted a piece of bread from a guard to nibble as he walked along the main throughway in the centre of the camp. As he walked between the fires his mind wandered down the path of memories long forgotten. Like all men, he was not immune to memories, good and bad, and these were the bad ones, perhaps provoked by his ill feeling about what might or might not happen at dawn.

He recalled many things before he settled on his experiences as a young, inexperienced junior centurion, when he had travelled far and wide. Still in service, but in those days there had been more of a wonder about all the new things to see. He was, as anyone would expect, full of youth and vigour and life was a very splendid experience to enjoy. Then, as he knew, out of all those wonderful experiences, his mind would find the one time where his shame had not dwindled, *could* not dwindle. Of all the people within his vast memory only one continually re-emerged to haunt his every waking moment. He smiled to think that it was not even Scipio!

The name was Lucinius Varas. It rang in his head as loudly as the screams of the innocent thundering through his dreams. Never had a friendship been so firm, but his bitterness at it being shattered in the eastern province would never diminish. He considered his friend's fate, which nobody would have wished upon an enemy, never mind a loyal companion. Or rather, someone who had been a loyal companion until the day they had arrived at this city, but eventually the friendship had diminished into something else, tarnished forever.

The year was not too important. Not that he could remember actually. All he had to remember was the situation that had occurred during the great Mithradatic War. Or more accurately, the third in a series of wars that eventually led to the defeat of the great Persian Empire.

It had been a time of great concern, and the very foundations of the Republic had been challenged from several directions. He was serving with the great Marcus Lucinius Crassus, early in his career. Soon to be the destroyer of Spartacus and the pro-consul of Antioch, the commander already had a reputation for uncommon brutality. Spartacus' six thousand survivors, who were crucified, would be recited as the best-known example.

He had been a junior Centurion with Lucinius in the garrison formations then being formed into a new legion. Marcus Lucinius Crassus, who had then held power within all the eastern provinces, had fought many individual conflicts against the Persians, but so far a decisive victory had eluded his efforts. Both he and Lucinius had fought in the Asia Minor campaign, the Cappadocia campaign and eventually the Pontus campaign, which had finally defeated the last of the eastern threats to Roma, if only temporarily.

With victory came the laurels, and for the legionary a series of promotions took place, elevating numerous men to the rank of senior cohort centurions. It was here that both men accepted this rank gladly and prepared to embark on their return journey to Macedonia, and their new posts in another legion. However, a revolt in southern Asia forced their portion of the legion to be redirected to Ephesus. Here a particularly vicious confrontation took place with armed civilians rioting, because of the lack of victuals.

The Roman governor explained that the indigenous people received sufficient supplies to live, but, on completing an investigation, Lucinius reported to the commanding officer, Legate Avici Numerus, that the reality was completely different.

Atronius smiled as he remembered Numerus. A consummate professional, this man was responsible for his training and education on survival within the legion environment. He too was dead now, killed in a pointless raid by Dacians barely a week after arriving in Macedonia. There, as in this city, the local Roman population had taken to depriving the indigenous people of the necessities to survive. He died trying to restore order.

There and then, however, the wealthy members of Ephesus were hoarding the main supplies of grain, thus starving the city inhabitants. On further investigation it became clear that many of these dignitaries had financial holdings in a company, a property developer, which had recently rebuilt the docks after ten years of decay following the city's conquest, and had made absolute fortune in the process through trading cartels.

It was then not hard to understand that the outer limits of the city were being systematically deprived of food to make the inhabitants sell their homes and, where it was unnecessary to use such methods, people had been brutally beaten into submission. This alienation of the new Roman conquerors had caused the scent of rebellion to reach fever pitch, and even the arrival of one thousand legionaries had done little to diminish the local hatred. Matters rapidly became worse when two youths were beaten to death by a band of callous sons of the merchants who had founded the *Arcani* movement, a name of which none knew the meaning, although it had all the markings of a racial anti-social rabble. The word arcani itself translated as *secret*, but the movement, if nothing else, demonstrated blatantly for all to witness on a daily basis, civilian or military.

The time for talk had slowly evaporated. The citizens decided to act in their own interests and began to raid the warehouses in the docks, taking the food they required but also badly beating several honest guards. It was obvious to Atronius that an act of kindness would have dampened the people's ardour for violence, but the rich demanded reprisals and nothing he could say made any difference whatsoever.

To everyone there was a duty to restore order, which many now considered complete, and Lucinius had already ordered the cohort to prepare to withdraw and rejoin the legion, which had by then continued onto the Danube. Orders to the contrary, however, soon arrived, just as the second major uprising erupted in the dockyards.

With a violence that stunned many people into abject ignorance, five hundred poorly dressed and gaunt people charged several merchant ships in the docks that were laden with foodstuffs fit for a king. At the moment of impact, only forty or so legionaries had been detailed to create a backbone to the local auxiliaries currently acting as a security force for the merchants. They were of course little more than paid brigands and the people knew this well. But this was better than Lucinius and Atronius, or even the merchants themselves, leaving a rather deep hole in their intelligence gathering efforts.

Atronius stopped momentarily, as he recalled the exchange of words that took place that night, as the riot continued outside their barracks. Young, and with no immediate superior from whom to seek advice, the senior Centurion was trapped at the merchant's mansions with a small personal guard. Lucinius fell back on the only training he knew and ordered that the lower town region be put to the torch. By rights he held seniority on this day, but this did not stop Atronius from protesting, as these people only wished to have food. Food that, incidentally, was rightfully owned by them and had been denied not only to them, but also to their children , creating widespread panic.

Lucinius had listened patiently and then, with people starving, had recommended that the governor be removed from office, but he had then received and accepted the advice of the less knowledgeable centenate. Namely, that executions, brute force and the willpower to subjugate a nation and restore order could alone resolve a rebellion.

In the first incident there had only been a few bruises. Then a massacre took place that Atronius, by virtue of his friend's superiority in rank, had no choice but to inflict. That night Atronius' heart finally opened to the true virtues of the Roman elite. For the first time he saw political power being subverted and military power being applied in a fashion in which he saw no real purpose. These people did not deserve this treatment and yet he too had been indoctrinated in unquestioning obedience.

He acted like a man without conscience and little realised what had been ordered or, indeed, what transpired. He simply switched off his mind to all that was taking place around him. He reacted to the ever-shifting situation with increasing ferocity. He blinded his heart to his actions with the lie that he did this as an act of duty. He had been ordered to restore order! His heart now knew this fallacy, but it was too late to change what had happened so many years ago.

That night a friendship died. That night Lucinius vanished. By morning three hundred people, who had asked only for a loaf of bread from the hand of plenty, now lay dead or mutilated. Another thousand had been made homeless and Lucinius' body was found hacked to pieces along with ten other legionaries, in an alley where numerous assailants had waylaid them.

Atronius began to walk again, carefully moving around the individual campfires, then paused a moment to look towards the stars. Earlier it had been a bright sky with little cloud yet now the sky was as black as black could be. For the moment he could not even see the moon, and he sighed. For a moment the memory vanished. Yet, even as he walked, he knew it would return as it always did before any major confrontation. If they had fought yesterday there would have been no time for thought, except for the purpose of life and death. On refusing to fight, the opportunity for all of them to open their thoughts would be a heavy burden that most men would prefer to avoid.

With a resolution that belied his true feelings, he reached the western ramparts and, after saluting the guard, searched the darkness where he knew the enemy would now be resting. What was to occur tomorrow was in the hands of fate. Not even the great Jupiter could avoid the hands of that particular destiny. Lightened by the thought that he was not alone, Atronius mouthed silently a prayer to Jupiter and called upon the powers of the great Mars, the God of war, to fight with them on the morrow.

"Let the fate of the Gods be done," he finished, touching his breast and kissing his cloak, knowing that this was the proper behaviour in his family, but nevertheless still only a ritual.

"Primus?" someone asked, confused.

"Nothing, legionary," he said aloud. "Have there been any disturbances so far on this watch?" he then asked, to avoid further scrutiny.

"None, Primus," the man replied and, seeing no real intention to talk, turned back towards the palisade to continue his vigil.

Atronius breathed deeply, turned away and began to walk back towards his tent. Lepidus was the official senior Centurion on duty for this watch, and he now decided to perhaps seek some kind of rest, be it fitful or disturbed.

Even so the sound remained in his mind, for even now it was the children that he could not forget. It was always the children.

⁕

They rested in a small huddle around the fire that, according to regulations, would support the men of the First Century, who numbered over one hundred. Of those some had drawn the first watch, others had retired, and by this time, with the moon in its full arc, although no one could see a damn thing beyond the cone of light shed by the fire, the night was relatively warm. Only ten men remained around the warmth of the flames, each opening the straps on their armour and placing it to one side. They all knew it would have to be cleaned before retiring, but for the moment that could wait.

Cappa watched as Atronius passed and noted his heavy expression. For a moment he wondered why that man should particularly care about his future. Their agreement with Scipio would not deter any of them from being executed should the Tribune choose to use them as an example of discipline. It was true that he mistrusted and despised most officers within the centenate, but for some reason his judgement refused to solidify against this man.

Always withdrawn and careful to whom he spoke, the Pilum was not a man to make friends easily, and yet the loyalty of the cohort was his to command. He was as experienced as Cappa in battle. Yet, there was something deep within his heart that festered and sought his destruction. What indeed was the reason for such an expression of gloom, he wondered? Then looking once more at the dancing flames he again, for the umpteenth time, tried to discern his own reasons for such a feeling of dread. Something was not right. Something was unnatural and these damn clouds were the first things on his list. This was by no means a normal degree of darkness.

For a moment longer he pondered these thoughts. Then with a shrug he pulled his attention back to the conversation at hand. It could wait, he thought. Everything could wait until tomorrow.

"My apologies, Constantine. You said?"

"I just wondered, Optio..."

"Yes?"

"Well, when we confront the barbarians across that stream on the morrow, will the Gods really be on our side?"

The group smiled almost simultaneously as one by one they nudged each other knowingly. The youth sat solemnly in deep thought after a brief conversation with the "Teacher," Marcellus, who had now retired for reasons that he would not discuss. A woman, no doubt? Not that there was a good selection in the washerwomen, but each to their own.

They all consistently found Marcellus to be extremely educated, for a man who had chosen this profession. In just a few sentences he had literally confused the young Constantine with the philosophies of history and the probability of whether the Gods themselves existed. Then, with a grin as wide as the Adriatic, he had retired to ponder other more personal and relevant thoughts in relation to their present predicament, leaving Constantine well and truly shipwrecked.

"That, my friend," Cappa said, warmly, "is a question more intelligent people have discussed for many centuries."

Constantine blinked, noticed the kind smiles surrounding him and began to timidly look back towards the tents.

"It was just a thought. I mean the officers will be doing the sacrifice and yet we are all still sitting here. You know, I kind of joined the legion because…well…do you ever really discuss the Gods? I mean, who are they? What are they? I try to keep my mind from wandering, but the local village teachers would not allow me to interpret anything my own way. Is it so wrong for me to want to think freely?"

From across the fire, someone called a hail of recognition and momentarily they became distracted. Turning their gaze once more towards the flames, they were happy to ignore the youth. His question was to go unanswered.

Finally Porta said, "I'm not the religious type, but for me there must surely be someone looking after my backside! I mean, how else could I have survived this long?"

A ripple of laughter proceeded around the fire until they all bellowed with merriment.

"The only…God…who would help you…Porta…is the God of the underworld!" laughed Julius, tears freely running down his cheeks.

"You are mistaken, my noble senator's nephew, for my personal body guard is none other than the beautiful Goddess Diana. With her horn of plenty and her heart full of good fortune for my appetites, how can I possibly go wrong!"

The laughter became a roar, attracting more attention. As it began to ebb someone at the next fire shouted. "I doubt that even she would help a heathen such as you, Porta! Besides you eat enough to feed the entire legion as it is, I doubt if even the Goddess could supply enough to keep you satisfied!"

There were nods of agreement. Some clapped enthusiastically and for a brief moment the fire's warmth dispelled their fears.

"Well, who knows anything about the underworld? Who is this unknown guardian of mine?" Porta asked, eager to keep the conversation in motion, happy to be the centre of attention.

"I know of whom you speak, and if you also knew you would choose your words more carefully. There are many who are less inclined to bring down the wrath of the Gods, just for your merriment."

One by one they all turned to look in the direction of the voice. Cappa and Porta both exchanged a glance as they recognised the owner. Marcellus the *Teacher*, having finished his business, had decided to rejoin the group.

With a face that had the weary look of a hardened legionary, which was deceptive, he rarely voiced an opinion on any topic. On more than one occasion Cappa had actually forgotten to establish whether this man was still alive. Always sitting reading something was his image of Marcellus, not the jovial kind of person.

Once, he even forgot his name!

In particular, he now recalled the brief march back into the camp. If anything, this man's knowledge made others extremely nervous, as several people had walked away from him to deliberately avoid a conversation. Then, as he had been earlier, the man could be as crude and direct as the best of them.

"So, Marcellus?" Porta mocked, winking at Constantine, who now floundered in yet another conversation beyond his understanding. "To whom do I owe my good fortune?"

Marcellus cast him a look of anger, a look to freeze stone. Then smiled and winked at Constantine too.

"You mock a subject that you know nothing about, fool! The underworld, or Tatamus, as it is known to many, although I am unsure of the correct written form, is the land of the dead. I for one find your ignorance revealing, Porta. I have often thought that your stench reminded me of the inhabitants of Hades' pit! I look forward to the day when you are sent home, heathen!"

In a flash Porta rose and stepped briskly around the edge of the fire.

"Hades and this pit you mention, Teacher, are Greek Gods and not Roman. I would watch whom you mock on such things. Jupiter and Vulcan would better suit your comments."

Marcellus nodded, looked across to where he had laid his armour almost an hour ago and slowly rose. Then like a lion he sprang around the fire to look Porta directly in the eye.

"I doubt your knowledge would extend far enough to even bother a child, Porta, never mind my intellect. So why don't you sit down and impress Constantine with other matters. Something you know something about!"

With as much agility, if not more, Cappa also rose and, snatching a wineskin as he moved, swung it skilfully to land solidly against Porta's abdomen. His intent was made clear by a look that advised Porta not to respond with his time-honoured fist. Their eyes met, as if a competition in supremacy was in progress, and the struggle mesmerised the group. Then with a wave of the hand Porta smiled.

As the heat of the moment passed the two men grasped each other's forearms and smiled knowingly. One day perhaps Porta and Cappa would not back down, but for now Cappa's strength of will prevailed. Porta raised the wineskin to his lips and drank deeply, then passed the wine to Constantine, who now sat to his left, between the two of them.

"Try some wine, child. It will put hairs on your chest," he said, indifferently, returning to his seat. "So who is Hades? I confess that I have paid priests little attention, Marcellus! Other than the fact that he is a so-called Greek God."

"The matter is not for the light-hearted and I do not wish to bring the displeasure of the Gods on me for a lack of faith. Suffice to say, heathen," Marcellus responded, "you will be well acquainted with Hades and the Underworld when it becomes your turn to leave this plain of existence."

With this parting remark Marcellus walked briskly away from the fire. He retired, while the others shook their heads in wonder. Marcellus was becoming more obscure with each passing day.

"The man speaks in riddles," Julius commented acidly. "I sometimes wonder if he belongs in the legion. Why he is here? I do not know and I am rapidly losing interest."

"His knowledge is of the highest level," Cappa said. "He is very quick to learn and has read more books than I have ever seen, let alone opened. He is somewhat arrogant in his attitude to learning new things, but I think his heart is in the right place. I trust him, which is more than I can say about either of you!"

"Thanks for that, noble Optio," Porta mocked, throwing a look of evil at Cappa. "I think I trust him to fight, that I do not dispute, but there is something about him that is just not right. All this knowledge is not good for a legionary."

Constantine grinned. "Perhaps he has dreams of becoming a legate?"

"No chance of that," said Julius, chuckling. "Much too old already. Hence the question, why is he here at all?"

"To see the world of course," helped Cappa, widening his eyes in mock disbelief. "Are you questioning the great life that we lead, Julius? Join the legion, see the world through the odours of the latrines and from the base of the fossa. An altogether different experience to any other kind of travel."

"I don't think we will be doing much more travelling, Cappa," Constantine said, his eyes solemn and distant.

"Oh, how so?"

"We are hardly in the favour of the Tribune."

"You should not worry too much about that, child," Porta advised. "It is not too good a situation, that is true, but as long as Julius is alive there is hope."

"When we finally rejoin the legion we can put our case to the legate," Julius added confidently. "He will then have Scipio put to death and reinstate our position within the cohort, and then the world will be at our feet, child. Mothers, lock up your daughters!"

"Marcellus will also be of immense help as an orator on our behalf," Cappa said, darting a look at Porta. "We need him on *our* side."

"That is as may be," Porta now said, the anger still bubbling just beneath the surface. "I, for one, will one day be a little tired of being contradicted by the *Teacher*. He is one of us, that we all must agree on, as there will be little chance to change your mind tomorrow, but one of these days I may teach him a few things I learnt in Genoa.

That condescending snake will have lost a fang or two by the time I finish with him!" Porta added, shouting the last sentence so that it carried to Marcellus, who had by then reached the entrance to the tent.

Marcellus turned slowly, but by the firelight Cappa could see that there was no animosity in his eyes. Teacher shrugged, saluted as Primus Pilum passed him and, without looking back, disappeared inside.

After several days of marching, with the ordeal of the ambush and the fight at the barricade, he could see that several of the men had begun to show signs of strain. They needed rest, but before he could confirm this with an order for them all to retire, Marcellus suddenly reappeared. Walking briskly he stopped on the far side of the fire to throw a book towards Porta. Ordinarily Marcellus' education was not an issue, but that night, after all the strain of the past week or so, a pompous, condescending teacher stood too close to Scipio to be acceptable.

Cappa groaned inwardly. If only he had stayed in his tent!

Porta sat and looked intently at the book, but refused to open the cover. "It would break a lifelong habit to open this book and start to read, Teacher. I prefer to stay uneducated," he said, once more the jovial clown.

"Reading a little difficult is it?" Marcellus spat. "You said earlier that you intended to extract a fang or two, how so if you cannot even read a book? Perhaps a book on Socrates or Plato, if that one is not to your liking?"

"*The History of the Gods?*" Porta genuinely smiled. "I suspect that I couldn't name more than five of our bounteous Gods, Marcellus. I leave such things to that oaf Cassius, who seems to be obsessed with such matters. To me the only lesson to be learnt is with the gladius."

"Then it is as well that I am educated and able to help you in your plight. As regards our unfulfilled priest, Cassius, I have only unkind words, which I will not repeat here," retorted Marcellus, smugly.

"Watch your words, Teacher," Cappa warned. "Not all of us choose to read as excessively as you, but many of us are more than capable."

"You need not concern yourself too much, Cappa, but I am sick of being ridiculed for having made something of my life prior to joining the legion. I try to help people if they ask, but beyond that the books are only for my own enjoyment. Why should I have to explain that to you or anyone else?"

"Just remember where you are, that's all. We are all tired, you included, so let us end this night without animosity."

"I agree," Porta added as support. "My words have been, perhaps, too sharp for my own good. Perhaps you could explain a little and my ignorance might dwindle?"

"I doubt that," Constantine jibed. "Take a lifetime to do that, would it not, Teacher?"

Marcellus smiled, resuming his earlier seat by the dwindling fire. "Perhaps my words were also a little barbed. My studies do tend to occupy my head a little too much. I have the tendency to place my head up my rectum..."

"Rectum?" Cappa asked.

"Backside, Optio. My backside!" Marcellus explained bluntly, rolling onto his hip and pointing downwards.

Somewhere a raucous fart echoed, the smell reaching everyone, sparing none.

The laughter began again, each of them relaxing just a little more, understanding that the man opposite was just as tired as their own bags of bones. Now they could once again continue to discuss a serious subject with a little friendly brevity.

"Hades was the son of Saturn in Greece, who, in overall terms, also fathered the great Zeus! However, as their beliefs are recited, Saturn feared the power that his children might inherit from the skies and decided to swallow...yes, swallow, Constantine, all of his children, including Hades. But thanks to the intelligence of their mother, Zeus avoided this fate and on reaching adulthood forced his father to vomit his brothers and sisters back to life. Thus he saved his family, and in the dissection of our existence Hades was given the underworld. That is of course nothing to do with our own, more powerful Gods, Jupiter and Mars being the most commonly known within the legion."

"Even I know of those two," Porta interrupted, nudging Constantine just as he was about to swallow some wine. "Helps if you drink the stuff, not wear it, youngster."

"Why you..."

Constantine and Porta began to wrestle boisterously. Some watched with interest, while others continued to listen to Marcellus. The attention for the latter was, however, diminishing rapidly.

"Romulus and Remus, the founders of our great Republic, are other examples of greatness that we have to draw upon, but we shall be here all night if we continue. Unless of course you all wish for me..."

"No! No!" everyone chorused, and the wrestling expanded into a free for all, and soon devolved into two groups. One led by Porta and the other by Marcellus, forever in competition. Within minutes a crowd had gathered and, in the dim light of the fires, they held their own tiny games. It could not last long for they were all much too tired, but it was long enough for Porta to receive a black eye and a few others a bloody nose. Cappa had declined the invitation to join in, and as he looked at Porta he knew the decision had been the right one.

It must have sounded insane to the barbarians watching their camp. The sounds of merriment hardly fitted in with their understanding. They outnumbered these Romans by seven to one, and by morning they expected this to be even higher. To hear them actually playing arena games in the fort must have raised a few doubts about what exactly the legionary was capable of achieving.

Issus began to wonder what kind of breed of warrior were these Latins? Perhaps that very morning he would find the answers to these concerns, as dawn lay less than five hours away.

The sun brought great relief and warmth to many as they absorbed its life-giving rays. On this particular morning the heat was welcome and well met, as the night had been unusually long and for some time many had contemplated ill omens. It had seemed as though the sun would not rise again. Where such dense clouds could have emanated from none could fathom, and the early morning had certainly been overcast, affecting morale on both sides of the stream.

However, with the sun's warmth, their hopes brightened and one by one, then group by group, and finally by maniples, the camp came to life. To Constantine, it seemed that he alone had sweat pouring down his back. He had seen numerous skirmishes, but he had never before confronted such a large contingent of barbarians. In the wood the day before, he had thought that he would freeze but somehow, by keeping close to one of the more experienced men, oft as not Julius, he had mastered his doubts and kept moving.

He could not completely rid himself of the fear, and the feeling that a terrifying fate would befall him alone this very morning would not be banished, no matter how hard he tried; yet he still felt in high spirits. To Constantine the morning chores of cleaning weaponry and preparing for the struggle ahead had changed irreparably. Before, it had been essential, if only to avoid being on a charge for unclean or damaged equipment, which was deducted from their salary.

If indeed they received any.

It was now a necessary chore. No longer did he look to evade such tasks but gladly took it upon his shoulders to help all those around him that had held his earlier opinion. The petty squabbles between Optio and legionaries had existed forever in the legion, but if it avoided the angry glare of such a disciplinarian, compliance seemed the better option. It also kept them alive longer. The sharper the blade, the easier to kill and to extract the weapon after the dutiful deed. He had never actually believed Cappa when he had first told him that the gladius could become stuck in the torso of a victim due to muscle suction. Having now seen it first hand, he knew the value of a razor sharp implement.

For such a young man, he had learnt swiftly that the only policy was to blend in with the crowd. Volunteers tended to die very quickly and often not necessarily as a result of enemy activities, as the centenate was well known for its brutality. His current predicament after the so-called rebellion under Cappa was more his own choice, as Scipio had offered many men the opportunity to denounce Cappa as the main leader. His honour had prevented any such deed, and so here he sat with a death sentence hanging over his head. If he did not die today it seemed as though Scipio would perform the job in hand at his own leisure.

Constantine shivered involuntarily. He had seen a few men crucified and then returned a week later to find that almost all of them were close to death, but still alive. It was a horrifying death, but one that he deemed necessary if the person deserved such harsh treatment. Of course, he held the high opinion that he and his colleagues did not merit their current dilemma.

If anything, Valenus should have been hacked to pieces for the death of forty good men. Yes, he thought, that is precisely what I would have done. Yet, even as he smiled, he noted how Valenus had seemingly changed over the last couple of days. He seemed almost friendly. He had received nothing but contempt in response but he doggedly kept to the policy of warmth, almost as though he felt guilty. No, he admitted, such men do not fear the death of other men. They expect it to increase their wealth and glory.

The smile drained away and became a distant memory, as the old pain reasserted its dominance. It had been over three years now since the scandal had driven the family away from their village. It all seemed to be so long ago that when he joined the Republican army the thought of going abroad to fight had given him hope. Hope, that is, to return one day and claim Lucilla to be his wife! Of course the others did not know the full story, but he had been refused courtship because of his ludicrous beliefs regarding the gods.

Yes, as always with most of them, a woman was the core of the discontent. Not that it was a cause of her design, but more the result of a forbidden love and the intervention of the local magistrates in the accusations of evil intentions. His open-minded approach to religion had made him numerous enemies in the local community. Nothing could have been further from Constantine's mind, for on the first occasion that they met he and Lucilla had opened their hearts after just one glance. That first exchange of emotions would have melted the sternest of hearts, giving them a true understanding of the real glory of love.

For several weeks the youth refused to allow the natural feelings of desire to dominate, hoping beyond all reason that some miracle would occur to change his circumstances. It never did, for the son of a local teacher had no chance of matrimony with the magister's daughter. So he was left with only his lust and false hopes, and his bitter heart bade him to relinquish this continued agony.

Lucilla seemed to be everywhere, even on a ride far out in the countryside he suddenly found her at his secret meadow. Here he could escape the harshness of life and its boredom. He also knew that people were generally aware of his outlandish attitudes regarding the annual ceremonies for the deities. His proud intentions did not last long and the voluptuous figure of a woman in bloom soon haunted his every dream. Could he somehow achieve an impossible desire?

Could this all be just an illusion, and did Lucilla have nothing but contempt for him? His doubts reigned supreme, but inside there was a nagging hope.

However, no matter how much Lucilla might have desired the same union, the daughter of the magister would not marry him. It was simply unheard of in their backwater area of the Republic. The resultant affair lasted for six months then, on discovery, Constantine had fled the village to avoid the almost certain death penalty that the father would have imposed. Truth or otherwise, he grimaced at the memory of the seven days of them chasing him across the countryside. Those brothers should have learnt when to give up, he smirked, remembering how he had altered his tracks to send them through a swamp.

Constantine shook his head at the thought of Lucilla being close, the softness of her skin, her perfume. How was a man meant to suffer such a loss? How can it be accepted?

If he returned, would it be to discover that the father did not react as anticipated, and instead welcomed him with open arms? Not really, he thought, and continued to clean the blade. Fat chance of that scrotum having a heart. He pushed the memories aside, concentrating on another issue and the conversation last night with Marcellus.

It had always fascinated him how people fussed over the true interpretations of the Gods, and yet Roma had several hundred Gods for every possible aspect of general life. Why? They did not need these deities, or at least not as many as the priests seemed to create out of thin air. For none but the Gods, if they existed, knew the real truth, and as such they could interfere when the desire bade them to do so. If correct, why concern yourself as fate surely had already decided what would befall your very short existence? By the whim of the Gods they all lived, as *they* deemed fit. If that was true, then what was the purpose of life and death and why did so many people fight to retain this one fascinating gift called life?

Here was the other reason for Constantine's extended absence. The local priests were also after his blood for contradicting their Gods and for desecrating the local burial grounds. Of course it had not been him, but suspicion had reared its ugly mantle to destroy and terrorise trust. Emotional deception cut mercilessly through reasonable thought and warped the judgement of even the strongest people. The end result was that he was forced to leave, or face more ridicule than it was possible to tolerate. The magistrate also helped him to come to the decision to leave, and he often wondered to which was attributed the greater reason?

I am not a scholar, he thought, and yet my mind is free of restriction and I intend to keep it that way.

The following two years of wandering also had a lasting effect on him. His faith in people as individuals had disappeared and, although Cappa had restored that faith to some extent, people such as Porta continued to make him feel uneasy. His heart was no longer on his sleeve, but some would have likened this to growing up.

To Constantine, however, the feelings of despair had left him with little hope regarding a fulfilled life of ease. He always expected the worst and oft as not he was correct, but he lacked the confidence to speak his own mind. So instead he kept to himself and allowed the others to do as they wished and to think, as they invariably did, about his real reasons for joining the legion. Experienced legionary, yes, but by no means experienced in blood, but learning with every passing month.

Perhaps these could all be attributed to the hardships of life in general, no one had a bed of roses forever. The loss of trust, however, was a more dangerous trend. Trust was a thing of the past, friendships were unlikely and love impossible, while even acquaintances became strained very quickly. Such was the price of keeping oneself away from the group. In battle, however, trust might be the only thing keeping you alive, as Cappa had shown during the original ambush by the mounted barbarians. If he had not trusted the Optio, he would have run as so many others did, and like them he would have been trampled down by the horses and speared to death.

Only his love for Lucilla had refused to diminish, yet it was also rapidly developing into a distant memory. It had once been all consuming, and the mere sight of her beauty had melted his heart. Almost every night, his head swam with memories of her soft touch, at least initially. Now, once more removed from the group, Constantine again opened his mind's eye to look upon her beauty and felt that all too familiar arousal.

This time though, unlike before, the sensation was fleeting and rapidly diminished, leaving behind yet more frustration to fuel a determination to one day return home and reclaim his love. His heart pounded in his chest to think that only a week or so ago they had met once more, fleetingly, like a couple of ships in the night. He grimaced to think what Porta would have said about such a childish thought, but it felt the same nevertheless.

Would he see her again? She had said that she would come looking for him when news of his legion's return reached her, but that was perhaps too much to ask. Even Cappa had tried to smile supportively, failing to hide his own feelings as to whether she would return. It had of course been Porta who had found out that she was betrothed, albeit against her will. Not that this would stop her father. It all seemed so stupid to be this close and yet so far from any chance of happiness.

"Constantine!" a voice shouted from across the dream, shattering the illusion.

"What?"

"Are you joining us today? Or are you going to wear down that blade with your cloth? We have need of your youthful shoulders to carry our javelins," mocked Porta, grinning.

Constantine stood slowly and sheathed the gladius with a flourish. As he walked back towards the column of men, which now began to gather into the familiar ranks of the maniple, the memory of the evening confrontation between Cappa and Porta reappeared to compound his perplexity. For an instant Constantine could see why many people disliked this rogue, and yet there was something different about that expression of Porta. It terrified him and yet others saw no harm.

What could have happened to make a person barely his senior in age so ruthless? It was always easier to hate than to accommodate new changes.

Porta was of the new breed of men that refused everything other than the spoils that they considered rightfully theirs after every conflict. So this was no time for hesitation, now was the time for him to believe in his companions and trust his Optio, who would directly aid his survival.

"I guess I will join you today, *my lord,* I can spare a few hours."

A few people grinned, while others noted that at long last the youth was becoming a member of the maniple and it was a change for the better, one that perhaps encouraged others to do the same.

PART FIVE

TRIBUTARY SKIRMISH

Silence descended across the valley like a shroud. Nothing moved. Not a sound. None spoke or caused a twig to snap underfoot. Those who listened could feel a light breeze brushing their cheek or lifting their fringe, causing an absent hand to raise and brush back and forwards across the brow. The odd bird, determined to ignore the panoramic scene before it, filled its lungs energetically to thrust its high notes across the valley, its efforts falling on unappreciative ears. On both sides the silence was overpowering. Emotions ran high as neither side deigned to take the first step. All stood firm. All would fight this day, they knew, but who indeed would prevail? More important, who would live?

Standing side by side, the individuals drew support from their companions in the hope of lessening their fears. If fear was the true word to describe the internal mixture of feelings, as each warrior or legionary knew his own worth and had trained scrupulously for events such as this. Apprehension perhaps would be more accurate. None could foresee the future, so their imminent survival or death was an issue designed for ominous contemplation. Many had done so the night before, but in the barbarian camp they had talked only of the victory to win, come the next dawn.

Now that dawn had come and gone, they still stood straining at their invisible ropes, to be permitted to strike terror into their enemies. It was true that all the participants were willing and trained to succeed to the best of their abilities, but this could not diminish the question of whether they would survive this day. This fear was somehow devoid of emotion and secreted in the deepest recess of each man's heart, each willing to strike down the courage of the bravest of the brave. It lay dormant for the moment, but never strayed too far. Each now stared glassy-eyed across the valley at those others, wondering.

They all just waited. The stream was the only obstacle between them. Hesitant to cross, both sides maintained an air of vigilance, bordering on profound paranoia, as if there was something they had missed. Each new sound seemed to rebound across the valley for all to hear. One man dropped his shield, another drew his sword and the distinct sound was carried on the breeze, along with the distant bird song. The notes rang high and low in a beautiful tune that somehow seemed out of place in such a dismal location of imminent destruction.

Emblems gleamed at the tops of poles and the rising sun glinted on spear points, shields and helmets. With a dazzling brilliance the light danced across the scene and for a brief moment hearts pounded. With such a beautiful view several men on both sides became aware of odd comparisons, wondering how such a situation could have developed. The reflection on the water of trees and bushes reversed, the fog covering the stream was awe inspiring and left many of them breathless in the shadow of the bounteous beauty of nature. Mortality was an odd sensation and served to heighten what might or might not be lost, war was almost always received with mixed foreboding and emotional instability.

Anger, hatred, the loss of a loved one, the possibility of a loss, or the protection of a way of life enhanced these emotions. Soon even nature held no power over the determination to rid themselves of the enemy before them.

Even so, a man smiled briefly before the might of Prince Daxus, as he felt the dew on the grass seep through his sandals. The man leaned on his spear and breathed heavily as he watched the air freeze in the morning frost. The bite of the cold sent a shiver down his spine, and he rose slowly to look along the cylindrical formation in which he stood, on the extreme right corner of the barbarian horde. He had never before seen so many men arrayed for battle and another contrast struck a chord with his gentle personality.

While terrifying in the simplicity of battle, the scene was also beautiful and full of wonder. His own compatriots were aligned in four enormous formations, his being to the front of the Prince's guard, which stood apart at the base of a small mound, directly behind them. Each formation numbered well over one thousand and faced the stream, with the Boii to the fore and the Verbigoni to the rear. The latter was his tribe.

The man also knew that more men hid in the woods behind the left side of the mound, and that there was a large group of horsemen out on the far right, but of these he could see nothing. They were there of course, and even if a man knew nothing of tactics, he knew that over two thousand had been brought over the ford during the night, if not more.

Relieved—no, overjoyed—in this knowledge, he had also heard that a large Roman formation was moving northwards to join those across the stream from him. The advantage was here and now, but as the morning continued they stood inactive. Yesterday he had imagined that several reasons had prevented an attack, not really caring, but in his heart he knew beyond any doubt that today many a good man would die, determined to fight for their freedom and the right to move to more fruitful lands in Narbonensis.

For a few seconds more he considered the possibility of his own death and smiled. One person did not really matter, nor did even these six or seven thousand, for behind them were camped four hundred thousand starving people. For them alone, their sacrifice today would define their future and from that he drew comfort.

The Prince and the Gods would decide his fate and, with a resolution that defied the situation, he rose to his full height. Yet another smile crossed his lips as he looked at the smaller Roman formations that followed the curve of the stream. The average height of the enemy would hardly reach his shoulders and yet, in terms of those who stood to either side of him, the man was considered extremely small. Perhaps even tiny, by the Prince's guard!

"This will be easy," he murmured and leaned once more on the spear. "This will be so very easy."

A few glanced at him, momentarily shaken out of their own thoughts, but none replied or even considered a conversation on this morning. Overconfident, perhaps? Thoughts of victory were paramount amongst the barbarians, but so was lack of respect for the Roman commanders and their legions. Recent successes had shown the small number of men available to Roma, and today they once more outnumbered the mighty Roma by seven to one. It was assumed that the morale of the men across the stream must be very low after so many defeats, and for this purpose the Prince had ordered that they remain on show, to increase this disaffection.

It was a fool's policy. Had they understood a fraction of the legionary training regime they would have known that they relied more on the solidarity of their companions, and the potential for spoils, than on any view of the greater picture. Although the legate or centurions might well be aware of the situation as a whole, it was not shared willingly with anyone. Even so, morale in the Roman camp on the topic of battle could not have been higher. It was not morale that concerned them, but more the lack of confidence expressed by the cohort in its leadership. Mid morning came and went and still they remained as if transfixed.

To the Romans, the silence was as much a weapon to cause confusion to the enemy as was, to the barbarians, the great cacophony of sounds that they would make prior to any charge. The former never expressed their tactical intentions until necessary, while the latter used sheer brute force to sway many an engagement, but the stream was more of a hindrance to the larger of the two formations.

Either way, the barbarian Prince had failed utterly to understand the very basic concept of Roma tacticians, and the skills of her generals. To them a life of discipline had inbred an air of indifference to numbers that continued to mystify one and all. They were quite literally immune to such bravado. A Roman legionary was trained to retain the disciplined silence required even when they could easily see that their numbers had been diminished through enemy activity. It was of course not unknown for a Roman army to collapse in defeat, but in the last two hundred years, since the Marius reforms, it had become less and less probable.

Not understanding your enemy was a very serious flaw in any man, be they warrior or politician. Roman arms had not suffered a major defeat for over fifty years and even this engagement would hardly classify as a large battle, more a skirmish, as barely ten thousand were on the battlefield.

Add this lack of understanding to the Prince's growing number of errors, and the reasons for the continued hesitation becomes apparent, perhaps even obvious. Once he had unleashed his people, as Prince Daxus knew, they would be beyond his control and this worried him immensely. The barbarian army was maintained through the experience of the older warriors and by the loyalty of the individual tribes. Individual courage was valued far in excess of any intellectual approach to killing Romans.

No formal training was encouraged and so they fought as an unruly mass. To date they had during their skirmishes only engaged small, detached troops of men that had numbered no more than one hundred. Valenus' ambush and Cappa's plight had been the last major confrontation, about six days before, and on this premise they had now committed themselves to battle. As always, Daxus had nothing based in fact and it was now that he showed his true failing, the lack of the courage to take a chance. He had to act, but found his mind frozen more by his own inactivity than that of the enemy. It was as though he had defeated himself before the first blow had been struck, and Atronius was not the first to mention this to Scipio that morning.

On the far side of the stream stood over one thousand Romans, of which at least three-quarters belonged to the legion. With eyes as cold as ice, and trained to identify even the slightest weakness in an enemy, they found the silence almost welcome. For over two hours, from the crack of dawn, the centenate had yelled and forced the pace to prepare for any eventuality. Now the air was full of nothing but the birds, and way up high many spied a hawk circling to await its own opportunity. To Daxus the songs were not soothing, warm or kind to the senses. To the hawk they signalled the location of a meal and so nature turned once more on its ceaseless journey.

Another aspect of Daxus' folly was to underestimate the centenate, the backbone of any legion. True, the older men had accepted retirement or transferred in the last month or so. However, those who had replaced them, although there were several exceptions such as Valenus, had served for over ten years to achieve the promotion. Of the barbarian leaders, very few had fought against the Romans and even less had any direct experience of full-scale battle, least of all the Prince! He commanded from a distance and rarely saw his enemy face to face. He ordered and his warriors followed, the report was then received, either positive or negative, victory or defeat, as he promptly confirmed to the elders.

A defeat was always miraculously forgotten, as the people only needed to know of the great victories! However, even these had been against very small detachments and never more than a century of eighty to one hundred Romans.

The decision to try and cause disruption in the Roman morale by using a show of force was tantamount to dereliction of duty. With the numbers so much in their favour an immediate attack, as yesterday, was called for and yet hesitation and doubt once again clouded his judgement. He almost believed that the Romans would be terrified, sue for peace and walk away at the mere sight of his army. A foolish thought even in children, but in a leader this was a mistake to be feared.

The unknown warrior who had smiled at the prospect of death was but one small example of the entire barbarian fallacy. Although outnumbered, this small enemy would not be cowed by extended chests and bleating. The man was to be proven correct in his assessment in blood, but not in the overall outcome, Roman discipline being the decisive factor in their downfall. Had he known that for a certainty perhaps he would not have been so eager to fight.

Doubts, of course, were everywhere. Any mortal with a heart felt the same mixture of emotions, but the training enabled the legionaries to retain control better, their camaraderie considerably more potent.

Standing on the mound across the stream, where the command tent had been pitched, both Atronius and Scipio knew this for a fact. The deities had given them a positive sacrifice that morning and the Gods of war had consented to join them to fight this day. This alone raised morale far higher than any speech a man could make, and even Scipio declined the opportunity to preach to the men. The faces had shown a distinct reluctance to hear yet more personal propaganda. Many also had doubts about the overall outcome of the war, but not one doubted their ability to win this fight.

Having supervised their disposition and given the initial orders for the day, both men had removed themselves to the tent to await the inevitable events. At dawn they had held the council of war, and initial opinions had favoured a small assault to relieve the encircled fort with the main command remaining in the fortified camp until reinforcements arrived.

However, even as they discussed this development a messenger arrived from Titus Labienus, stating that two full cohorts of men and Lentulus' cavalry, numbering almost two thousand in total, would be arriving later that day. The messenger then stated that it would not be until early evening, although Julius Caesar had already ridden ahead with the cavalry to assist as much as possible.

They had then all watched Scipio's eyes burn with anticipated laurels. Here was a golden opportunity to shine in the eyes of the newly appointed consular representative of the Senate. How could he allow this to pass him by? The plans were changed immediately and rank combined with duty ended all opposition. They would stand and fight. To cower in the fort was no longer acceptable.

It was the turn of the Romans to be in error. The fort would have been a far more sensible tactic.

However this news prompted Scipio into immediate action and he decided they would array for battle, then remain on the defensive to force the enemy to attack across the stream. This was, in contrast, a sound tactical decision given the numbers involved, but Atronius in particular stated that to fight now would be a waste of lives. It would be more logical to wait for Labienus and then attack with three cohorts. He believed profoundly that the barbarians would not dare to fight such a battle, and the bridge could be secured with as little loss of life as possible.

For the first time since obtaining the tribunal post, Scipio seemed to hesitate, and deliberated over the suggestion. To him this was good advice, but pride and greed began to dominate, forcing a decision based on the benefits of success and not the mortality of the men. He had already taken the first step, why stop now? Perhaps Senator Flavius would not be needed and he could even reap his vengeance on that fool Cappa and his rabble? Especially Julius, who still retained the sword sent to him from Roma by a powerful friend. Indeed the very friend who would be soon approaching Flavius regarding the life of his nephew.

Atronius was ignored and the men marched out at daylight to take up the positions designated by Scipio. At least in this respect the drunkard had not lost all his former proficiency. Placing the archers to the fore with their small cavalry contingent in reserve, Scipio acknowledged that the weakest position stood on the exposed right, near the tributary ford to the north. If the barbarians managed to force their way through at this point then the fort would be completely cut off from aid of any kind.

It was also here that Valenus commanded, and Scipio was wise enough to recognise the same faults in his leadership that Atronius had freely noted. Nevertheless there was little that could be done now. The auxillia javeliners would need to hold the ford itself and Valenus would have to stand and fight, as there was no one to spare. Every other century faced the main enemy body across the stream and would have enough to do just to hold a cohesive line.

They next discussed the far left, where not only could the larger enemy also turn this flank, but had also deployed a large body of horsemen opposite the small incline leading around them towards the camp behind them all. This provided the opportunity to place a force between them, Caesar and any possible reinforcements. This new development was hardly helping their situation. Should any collapse occur, it was assumed that these horsemen would sweep forward into the rear echelons and seek to kill and maim Scipio. As often as not the barbarian philosophy believed that if you cut off the head of the serpent then the body would die. Yet another case of poor judgement on Daxus' list, forever growing as the morning advantage seeped away!

Scipio had no intention of being on the casualty list this day or any other. To try and compensate for the lack of cavalry, he ordered that forty legionaries be mounted on the mules used to pull the wagons, an expedient he recalled that Atronius had used to save Cappa. Many questioned this decision, but in truth it could serve them all well before the end of the day. For once Atronius was strongly in favour of one decision made by Scipio that day!

An additional change to the original plan was to raise a small detachment to protect the camp, as well as the command tent and Scipio. With their resources already stretched to breaking point this seemed extravagant, but nothing unusual, so no protests were made and they satisfied themselves with glances of derision out of Scipio's line of sight. Again it took a brief discussion with Atronius, thankfully one of necessity and calmly delivered, to point out the lack of resources for a large bodyguard. It was therefore decided that Cappa would fall back further to cover the command tent, while twenty chosen legionaries would protect Scipio's person. The camp at that time was irrelevant, as their positions were literally half a league in front of it. If they failed, then the camp would be their first destination.

However, this changed again when Scipio raised the obvious question of the barbarian horse riders who could circumvent their left flank and take the camp in their rear, thus ending any possibilities of refuge, and now even the Pilum nodded assent. Their lack of mobility would be a crippling factor in this engagement.

The result was to place a further fifty legionaries in secondary reserve, within the camp itself. Under the direct orders of Lepidus, who commanded the central reserve, they would not be committed unless absolutely necessary. It was hardly acceptable, but then if this show of strength were to have any chance, then the cooperation of every man was essential. Already other considerations had begun to reveal the numerous flaws in the plan to stand and fight.

Further dispositions left dangerously exposed the right flank reserve of auxiliary javeliners covering the tributary ford. If attacked in force from the north, they would not be of sufficient numbers to hold out for long. To add the final nail in the coffin, Atronius had also discovered that, in their haste to prepare that morning, the javeliners had been told to bring only their projectile weapons, leaving behind their daggers and swords for the sake of manoeuvrability.

Who the hell would make such an order? Surely only a fool would take any men into battle with only a spear! It was in truth beyond belief, but confirmed nonetheless. When he heard of such a foolish order, Atronius immediately told a faction to retrieve the additional weapons and distribute them before it was too late, thus removing another thirty men from the front line.

That left just one further problem, which was slightly offset by the advantage of the marshes, where the stream joined the tributary and stood a little ahead of the ford mentioned already. Here stood Valenus with the remains of his command, and Cappa to hold this position. The latter had been moved to a new position, leaving about one hundred men protecting their hinge with the tributary. Lose this and the ford would follow, and any hope of reaching the isolated fort, and ultimately the bridge, would be extinguished. An attack across the marsh was not expected, but questions were still raised as to whether, with Valenus in command, these men would stand. With no alternative men to bolster this position, however, the situation could not be altered. Events would have to take their course and they would all know sooner rather than later if their fears had been justified.

Meanwhile Fabius and Domitius, the latter placed in temporary charge of Atronius' own command, held the centre, while Atronius would assume control of the left with Crassus to assist.

So arrayed stood both factions, and for another hour they remained in silence watching and waiting, looking for a sign of activity to denote the opening of hostilities. Nothing. The tension began to rise. Instincts began to sing and hairs rose on the back of the neck. It would not be long now.

Then, suddenly, a deafening note sounded high into the air!

Gazes turned towards the sound, as the eerie silence was finally broken. In response a roar erupted amongst the barbarians that shattered the following notes blown on the cornicen. The high-pitched Boii battle cry followed along with the crashing of sword and spear on shields. Seeking to intimidate the Romans further, Daxus ordered that the noise be increased and watched in satisfaction as several legionaries broke for the rear.

Had he watched more closely he would also have noted Atronius riding amongst these men, who had temporarily panicked. Within seconds discipline was restored and the men returned to their comrades. If anything these men, now ashamed of their initial reaction, would fight more fiercely to wipe out the loss of honour. Fear of Atronius was clearly greater than their fear of Daxus!

In reply to the noise the Romans replied with stony discipline, as had been the policy with the silence. For them nothing had changed.

Sitting astride his horse behind and to the left, having left Scipio at the mound, Atronius turned to nod at the nearest cornicen.

"Sound the note! Send forward the archers!" he ordered, raising his voice above the din of the barbarians.

A new note sounded, clear and high. Without a word the archers moved ahead of the nearest century and then vanished into several smaller groups within the fog shrouding the only obstacle before them. Then, one by one, they ascended the small slope towards the stream and vanished.

Atronius watched the far side of the fog, his mouth dry and the palms of his hands moist. They all began to count. Ten, twenty, thirty seconds! It would not be long now and indeed the archers had already reached the far side. Their purpose was to goad and annoy the enemy and to break up any advance. They had to cause as much hesitation and confusion as possible. With this in mind they would draw a bead on any man that looked to be in authority and aim to strike this target.

Kill the leaders and the enemy becomes a useless mass of individuals. Kill the men to make the others fear the dangers of advancing further, lest they become the next corpses.

From a distance Atronius watched as one by one men began to drop with little shafts of wood protruding from the chest. At first, the barbarians raised their shields to protect themselves, but the target then became the leg, and the formation was so dense that they could not miss.

More and more men began to fall and the Boii could do nothing to combat the threat, as they did not employ the bow and arrow, a weapon they saw as useless. Now yet another error became apparent as another barrage of arrows dropped several more men. The lesson would be a bitter one!

The Prince watched in silence.

Then, like the snap of a twig underfoot, the Prince's patience broke: the archers had succeeded. For the first time, the real situation began to loom, its ugly head devouring what courage now remained. Daxus then compensated, allowing his heart to take courage from the sheer size of the host he commanded, but he seemed unable to think straight. Should he stand and wait or should he attack? He decided on neither.

With an air of frustration, he turned to a messenger and sent word to the Boii to advance a skirmish line to deal with the archers skulking in the ravine. Here again the Prince knew only too well the temperament of his own men, the Verbigoni, but failed to make use of the known tendency of the Boii to charge as a single mass. These men had already seen sixty or more of their people fall with no means of striking back.

Receiving the invitation to deal with the archers, the local leaders sought to send only a few men. When these men advanced they were neatly ambushed by the archers and forced to retire. Then, without as much as a shout of warning the left formation, tired of the torment, suddenly surged forward towards the fog. Now the fog almost transparent, Atronius saw with delight the body of men charging, and licked his lips in satisfaction.

Following numerous other foolish enemy decisions, Atronius spurred his horse forward to take advantage of yet another. Reaching Crassus within seconds, he pulled the animal to a stop.

"They are on their way, Crassus," he said from behind. "You must hold in order for Fabius to strike the flank. Understood?"

Crassus grunted, and turned to face Atronius.

"They will not pass this point, Primus. I will reassemble the archers and see to it personally that none go beyond this line," he said, pointing assertively at the forward line of legionaries. "We will advance to contact beyond that point, as soon a Fabius is in action."

Atronius waved a hand in appreciation of Crasus' forethought and knew that his friend would fulfil the required expectations. Taking one last glance across the stream, he noted that the second forward formation of the barbarians had not moved to support the first, thus creating a gap which could be exploited by Fabius. The archers had worked perfectly.

Now all he had to do was explain the plan to Fabius, who was not exactly known for his speed of thought!

❖❖❖

All eyes watched as the archers slowly gave ground while continuing their mission to infuriate the enemy. Some did not move quickly enough and became smothered by the mass of bodies surging across the stream. To every man the sight of the fog seemed ominous and yet in truth they were glad that it hid the real view. Just to hear the barbarians was enough.

Amongst the many stood Julius. Proud and strong, as well as extremely stubborn, he now remained next to Cappa in an effort to maintain a calm outlook. Nothing could have prepared him for the experience to follow in the wake of the rebellion and the ambush. For a moment or two his thoughts jumped back to his family, who now sat eating their morning meal less than twenty-four hours journey away to the east! With a smile, he thought how odd life seemed to be of late. One minute they were all fighting for their lives in the wood, then laughing and joking around the fire last night, and just now this all seemed a little too much to comprehend.

Julius had become a legionary in every sense of the word during those hectic experiences, aided by all his earlier ones. The last few days had provided the lessons, whereas previously, for him, the alternative had been to accept ignorance amongst the crowd, and this had always been unacceptable.

Everything before this day had been a monotony of duties, with the odd skirmish or situation to resolve. Other than that life was relatively easy, or so it seemed to the nephew of a senator of Roma. He was here, you see, to prove a point that men of title were not just given wealth, honour and the positions of power because of their birth. He was here to prove to his friends and family that this was their birthright, and that it was the destiny of the Gods that made certain families great and others puny, thus creating the correct ruling senatorial house. Of course the passions and opinions of a youth were resoundingly ignored, until he stepped forward to volunteer for the legion.

Now he had not only gained the experience required to retain the name of a legionary, but he had also been involved in a rebellion, albeit a very tiny one, and had fought in more conflicts than he even knew had existed back in the luxury of the family villas. He often wondered why he did not just simply up and walk away, for his uncle could certainly resolve any opposition to his retirement, but inside he had changed, and not only from being the rich nephew. He had found a camaraderie here that he had never enjoyed in Roma. He was in no hurry to return to the backbiting life of the capital.

The cacophony of battle cries brought his thoughts crashing back to the present, and his smile vanished as the first Boii crashed into Crassus' front ranks. The pilums had not even slowed their pace and the subsequent charge by the legionaries was comparable to a tortoise trying to stop the ocean.

The noise was horrific. The clash of weapons and the crunch of shields intermingled with the cries of the injured and dying. Somehow Crassus held firm, but after a few minutes it became clear that both flanks of the smaller formation were beginning to be turned, threatening encirclement.

From where they stood, Julius and Cappa watched as if they had already been defeated before they had even had the chance to try. They watched Atronius ride from one point to another shouting encouragement to those who faltered, then using the side of the sword to encourage one or two with slightly less warmth. Nevertheless, not a man passed that dapple-grey horse unless they had received a visible injury.

With their hearts in their mouths they watched as the Primus Pilum charged forward against a small band of Boii that had decided to penetrate to the rear.

"That man has a real problem with living," remarked Porta, standing on the opposite side of Cappa to Julius. "Just look at the way he keeps charging into those heathens. Not a care in the world, that man. Stupid as well, if you ask me."

"No one did," Cappa remarked, acidly.

Porta turned as though to reply, but thought better as Valenus sounded the alarm.

"Our time to dance," he finally said, pointing at the far side of the stream.

"Helmet," Cappa said, quietly, but with as much hidden menace as he could manage.

"Are you kidding? I left it where we stood up. Besides I can fight better without it..."

"Did I ask you for an opinion? Yes? No? Well, by the Gods, Porta, we actually agree on something. Now if you do not wish to visit your new friend, Hades, you will search out your helmet and return before those barbarians reach us. *Clear?*"

Porta flinched, and looked on the brink of again furiously opposing Cappa, but quickly thought better of yet another confrontation. With a look of pure anger he turned and quickly made his way back to their earlier resting-place on the grass before the command tent. You know, sometimes it is extremely hard to like that man, he thought. One day I may just teach him some manners with the point of my gladius!

Further to one side Marcellus grinned as he watched the normal exchange between the two companions. To either side of him in the small line of legionaries, others smiled, joined in and relaxed a little as the more experienced saw no reason to panic, so why should they. Well, if relaxation is the right word for five hundred or more men having been chosen to descend on you and your comrades, who number less than one fifth that number? Perhaps *relax* is the wrong word after all.

Towards the stream the sun caught hold of the fog and scattered the last remnants that had prevented a view of the Boii. Allowing his mind to wander, Marcellus watched the wind bend the treetops and marvelled at the beauty, using this to ignore the imminent danger. The branches bending gracefully, refusing to break, reminded him of Cappa, and he smiled at his own inventiveness. The refreshing wind brought the scent of the spring flowers hurtling towards his sense of smell, causing yet another euphoric loss of concentration.

Then, just as suddenly, a different kind of wind reached his nostrils. The nose wrinkled and the odour was far from pleasant. Taking a glance to either side, the sight of Constantine laughing under his breath created a pause.

"Sorry, my friend, too much wine last night and that meat this morning made me feel ill," he offered as an excuse, but did not halt the laughter.

Marcellus grinned again and wondered if the others in the cohort felt as he did. To him the protection of friends had become paramount in his thoughts. Even with that odour that would kill an elephant, the youth was still the most loyal and kind person he had so far encountered in this lifetime. A youth somehow out of place in the legion. He shuddered involuntarily. Hardly an unknown quantity, he noted, I am hardly the most typical of legionaries.

With a deep sigh he readied his mind and body for the struggle ahead.

"May Jupiter protect me," he whispered, not knowing that Atronius had also offered such a prayer the night before. Perhaps they all had at one time or another.

Constantine now took his turn to daydream as the conflict escalated. It was like a dream come true just a week or so ago. Was it really only that long ago? Surely it was longer? No, he remembered the day distinctly. For over forty years there had not been anything other than skirmishes on this border and Lucilla had been able to visit when leave was distributed. It had been heavenly to see her again but it had only confused the issue. Nothing for so long, then a visit, right out of the blue.

Then this war had exploded from nowhere, he had become involved in two mutinous acts and now faced the greatest threat to life, murderous barbarians. What in Hades name was going on? Nothing made any sense!

As the barbarians reached Valenus' line of legionaries, directly in front of them, he could feel the dread overwhelm his heart. The pulse in his temple suddenly increased. His eyes began to widen and the sight hazed over. The chest tightened, the concentration wandered away to happier memories. Trust suddenly became an issue. Not in the love and loyalty of his spouse, but in the whim of the Gods.

What if he never met his beloved again? To look on her beauty would fill the heart with rapture, and the pain in Constantine's chest increased.

With eyes wide with terror he began to look to either side. Did any of them feel this way? Why did only he acknowledge that death that was approaching? Did mortality terrify them as much as it did him?

The grip was as if a vice had been closed about the biceps muscles in the arm, easing the shudder that ran down the youth's back. Constantine felt the irregular beat of his heart singing the rhythm of his single craving, to be as far away from here as possible. His discomfort reached breaking point and he absently wiped a tear from his eye. Even now he could not bear to think that any of them had seen his emotions.

"Are you alright, youngster?" came a voice over his shoulder. Cappa's!

"I'm *concerned*, Optio. I've done my best, but my Lucilla needs me. I do not wish to die. Why are we fighting against such odds?"

Cappa squeezed the young man's arm tighter.

"You could run, Constantine, but where would you go? Believe me, I have thought about that more times than I can recall. But we are here today and we are under sentence of execution for the camp escapade. We are here because we must defend the province. If you run and these heathens defeat us they will march to Segusio and beyond. Where would your Lucilla be then?"

Cappa removed the hand and allowed the words to sink in as the youngster continued to fidget, drawing and then replacing his sword. To stay or to go would be of little help anyway, he thought. If they were defeated here on this day then the whole northern province would be devastated.

With satisfaction Cappa watched Constantine slowly calm down, but also acknowledged that it had been close. Like a few others, the youngster would need to be watched, as the love of a woman could cause many a foolish decision.

As Cappa turned his attention back to the other men the light suddenly dimmed perceptibly. Almost instinctively the entire formation dropped to their knees, as the sky darkened and lightning suddenly appeared, as if by the whim of the Gods themselves. The flashes terrified them, while all around people froze in mid flow, their weapons held in suspension as their eyes looked to the sky.

"The Gods are angry!" shouted someone, above the din of the thunder.

"We are doomed to servitude in the fires of Hades!" came another cry, and several men suddenly broke for the rear.

Then, almost without warning, Cappa thought he saw several men collapse. Looking through the darkening shadows ahead he strained to confirm this, but the dark wall seemed impenetrable. Irritated he looked for a torch but, on finding none, quickly turned to Marcellus.

"This is not right," he said calmly, almost too calmly, and this unnerved Marcellus considerably, as his face contorted to express *"Really!"*

"Why would the Gods interfere in our affairs? What in Jupiter's name is going on?"

"I do not have any answers, my friend," Marcellus eventually managed, holding his sword with whitened knuckles. "All I know is that I have for the first time in my life a very strong urge to run."

Cappa nodded, turned to look to the left, but the sky was so overcast that Valenus and the remainder of the cohort could not be seen.

Then the phenomena reached them and in the blink of an eye everything went blank. A brief disorientation rendered them all unconscious and for now no further answers would be given, or questions asked. The storm had been one of unusual proportions and after the initial silence of the morning and the brief conflict there was nothing to compare. None remained standing...

Except for one man.

Only one person remained awake. He held the title of betrayer aloft with pride, although to his heart he had only done what his God's desire had bid him. This was his destiny, returned once more to view his work, his betrayal.

"You have done well, Cassius. I have brought you here to see the extent of your betrayal. You have nowhere to run to anymore, they will never accept you back. You are mine now," boomed a voice, seemingly from the cloud itself.

"Thank you, my Lord," Cassius replied, from a prone position, not really knowing in which direction to face. "May I now respectfully request the rewards promised for my devoted service? I fear there may be another issue to discuss, if you will permit me? If I succeed in your demands will I be released?"

A laugh as cold as ice froze the air, sweeping across the valley. For a few moments, which seemed to last forever, the lone figure stood before the ever-darkening cloud, still lost and now perhaps a little frightened by his deeds. Was this his true God and if so why should he not ask for his reward? Cassius became afraid. Perhaps it was not *he* who held the true title of betrayer.

"You will receive what all my servants receive, you puny worm. Nothing more and nothing less, but perhaps my benevolence may change if you serve me better in the future? We have much to do you and I, my little worm. Yes, indeed, we have much to do. I shall enjoy teaching you the true meaning behind the myth of the Tatamus' fire that you were so happy to quote to your companions.

"We shall see firsthand how you will learn the meaning of true pain. We have only just begun, but we take the first of many steps. You are afraid? You need not fear me, betrayer, I have many plans for that black soul of yours. It is refreshing to know such hatred still exists on this pathetic rock!"

Cassius, finally realising that perhaps he had made an error, moved backwards, as the voice began to drive fear into his heart. This was not as before, at the camp he had been taken out of it the same time as all of the others, but he had also retained the ability to stay and watch what happened. Had this not happened before? He could not make his mind work, had his memory now been altered?

A fear that began to envelop his mind soon began to freeze his legs to the ground. He could not move! Sweat poured down his forehead and drenched his back. His neck became sore to the point of bleeding from his struggle to continue to move, but it was all to no avail. All about him darkness engulfed his vision. Panic made him turn to try and run, but as before the legs refused, then his lungs froze. He could not breathe.

"I serve to obey, my Lord," he gasped desperately, "but am I just to be a normal servant? Have I not assisted you beyond the skills of even your most loyal followers? Why do you seek to punish me? How have I offended?"

The laugh again came coldly with brutality, striking a shard of emptiness through the heart. Cassius felt his knees buckle and tried desperately to soften the landing, but there was to be no landing.

"No, my Lord!" he screamed, hysterically. "I do not understand how I have *offended?*"

"*Offended?*" replied the voice, momentarily confused. "*You have not offended me, you fool! You simply show promise, but your heart is not black enough to be trusted, my faithful servant, not yet. I will teach you personally and supervise your training along with Orbiana, who is eager to begin again. I have use of such single-minded lust for power and I hope you enjoy pain my little worm...pain for five...hundred...years! Such is the reward you sought. Such is immortality! So shall it be!*"

Cassius began to struggle fiercely, in a last attempt to break free of the blackness. First his legs, then his knees began to vanish despite his entreaties for clemency. He raised both hands before his face, only to watch his fingers slowly disappear before his eyes.

Then it began in earnest, his struggle renewed. It did not last long as the sensation of falling now began, swamping his tiny mind. He flailed his arms out as a final refusal but he could not escape, he could not compete against such power, so he relaxed his struggle and succumbed to the fall. Forever spinning, his soul was soon confused. In time this left the empty shell once referred to as Cassius Evictus and the blackness claimed another victim, not that he knew of this change. Perhaps he was a willing victim. A *pure* victim, with a heart as black as the night! He was the first mortalkind in aeons to be taken to the underworld...alive!

The laughter above, meanwhile, continued unabated and shook the Earth to its very core. Even the fellow Gods became afraid and turned away from the tasks at hand, for this was the breaking of the dimensions and until that day it had been considered that none could achieve this, no one had that much power. Now a warning had been given and time was running out. The gauntlet had been laid before them and all they needed to know was where the battle would be fought.

Where indeed?

Gaius Julius Caesar looked down on the tributary and felt that his eyes would pull out from his skull, terror gripped his throat, freezing his words. All about the small stream he could see nothing except the bones of the dead, but this was not unusual, as he had expected to see the results of a battle fought by the first cohort, commanded by Tribune Scipio. Here and now, as he looked at the bodily remains, it was as if the flesh had been torn from the limbs, leaving nothing but rags and the odd piece of flesh. None of the eyes remained in the skulls and for a second he felt a powerful cramping sensation grip his throat.

At the back of his mind he fought desperately to hold back a growing urge to fold over, as a cramping sensation gripped his stomach with a power he had never felt before in his entire life. He had seen this kind of ailment in many others, but never had he experienced this stiffening of the spine and the compulsion to cry out. Knowing of nowhere close, where he could hide whatever ailed him, he kicked the horse viciously and headed for the woods on the far side of the stream. Here the ghastly remains were piled higher than anywhere else, the stench was overpowering. The battle had been fought only the day before, so how could their flesh have been torn from their bones?

He reached the cover of the trees with only seconds to spare as the spasm pulled him off the horse's back, his spine going into voilent spasms. He did not consciously reach for the branch, but sank his teeth deep into the bark to prevent any noise. He dare not allow others to see his weakened state. For a moment his mind wandered then, just as swiftly, his body relaxed and he lay sweating on the ground.

How long had he lain on the ground?

Something inside his head told him to rise and as he did so one of the young tribunes, Marcus Antoninus thank the Gods, entered the woods. He composed his stature as best he could.

"What has happened here, Caesar?" Marcus Antoninus asked, his eyes wide with a fear he had rarely felt in all his battle experiences. "Their flesh has been torn from their limbs. Could wolves have done this?"

Caesar nodded coldly. He would grasp any excuse.

"That is so. I have seen this before in Hispania," he lied. "It is a brutal way for the dead to be treated. Have the bodies buried and choose the men carefully. I do not want any ridiculous rumours being spread as regards this situation, *or* these corpses."

"No, Consul, I understand. I will use Aulinius' men, their loyalty is absolute."

"Good, then do not delay any further. The Helvetii have withdrawn back across the river and must now move south, or starve in the mountains. Either choice will make no difference, but we have no time to try and find out what has transpired here."

"I will have this matter resolved shortly."

Caesar gave one nod of approval and remounted as Marcus Antoninus rode away. He was a trusted officer and he saw a good future for him, perhaps even friendship. Whatever the future held, his eyes could not lie, his heart had been wrenched by this sight.

What had happened here?

It was nothing he had ever seen before and he firmly believed that no one else had witnessed the end product of such a slaughter! How could all their flesh have just...dissolved? More important, who had done this deed?

He dallied for a little while longer, but word soon arrived that Lentulus' scouts had found a large band of warriors to their immediate south. With a will of steel, he blocked off the memory and never spoke of the Rhodanus tributary again to another living soul, but this choice was to be haunted by continued seizures and spinal spasms. The fits remained, he was cursed by an illness that no herbalist was able to understand or cure, with the memory slowly burning away until there was nothing left of his soul, his humanity or his faith in the Republic.

Caesar did not know it, but he had been touched by the hand of Hades and had been found wanting. His reward would be the affliction later known as epilepsy, but known to his people only as the *fits*. His punishment would be the eventual fall of all that Roma stood for and the creation of an Empire that Hades was to subvert into hatred and destruction. Although Hades' influence would eventually be diluted, that would avail Caesar naught. Springtime, the month of March particularly, from this day forward held a special meaning for the new pro-consul, but the Gods, let alone a mortal, could not have anticipated such a fateful day.

Unknown to Caesar would be the undercurrent of brutality that the legionaries began to feel while under his command. Brutality was to become the normal way to exact acts of fealty from the local tribes in Gallia, which with each enactment the stronger Hades' hold became over their souls. In time the Aedui, Sequani and Arverni tribes would seek his aid against the Germanic tribe led by Ariovistus.

After numerous debates and manoeuvring of the respective armies, Caesar would learn through a spy that Ariovistus was waiting for the new moon, according to his soothsayers, before he undertook a decisive battle with the Romans. Before this time Caesar, during two years of campaigning in Gallia, had acted with caution, due mainly to his lack of experience in moving such large numbers around a battlefield. With this new information this all changed and Caesar burst forth to force battle upon the shaken Ariovistus who clearly had not expected an attack.

Caesar resoundingly defeated Ariovistus and from this day forward the Germanic tribes would loyally serve him as the mounted arm of all his armies. This alone was notable, but more potent was the persecution of Ariovistus' people who were summarily put to the sword.

Other campaigns would follow, culminating in the defeat of the combined Gallic horde of almost two hundred thousand at Alesia, facing his paltry force of sixty thousand. Caesar may have made a pact with his Gods for victory, but it would seem the rest of the world had not!

Caesar had without knowing it chosen his destiny, but in another dimension the *arrivals* had yet to begin!

PART SIX—

COUNCIL OF LORD AARUN

There came the hunger initially with an insatiable thirst. The disorientation, inability to speak and the general vomiting did little to help any of the survivors of the awakening either, and were classified as the second stage. The experience never altered in this respect, but amongst them several personal afflictions became dominant, always differing slightly for each person. Nevertheless, stage two was seen as a good sign.

Some experienced temporary blindness, and the inability to walk was also experienced, but the most common reaction was the overpowering sense of total loss, primarily of loved ones, young or old. At first, in their haste, the elves had tried to arouse many of the initial cases by way of the lesser magic. This was referred to as the *healing touch,* as it barely touched on any real incantations and most of the maidens knew of such things in the daily healing routines. It should have worked, but somehow the *arrivals* did not follow the normal paths of existence as themselves. The efforts were eventually abandoned when Lord Aarun had arrived and restricted access to only those elves known to *have* the healing touch, incantations being forbidden. The natural approach took over, and the politicians and religious representatives were politely, but firmly, shown the door.

The phenomenon was, to say the least, staggering for them as a species to accept, and several simply could not take on board the magnitude of the situation, resorting to barbarity to hide their fears. The new *arrivals'* minds also struggled and would slip back into blissful sleep and ignorance, refusing to accept the new reality. Was it just a dream? It had to be, for where else would creatures with pointed ears reside? Or was it? They could not tell and for some time many did not wish to, but nature has a way of forcing the mind to face reality sooner or later. The unwilling could not resist the impulse to wake after five hundred years of sleep.

As their experience with coping with such a revelation progressed, the recovery rate increased and the news spread through the region like fire. Lord Aarun had a tough time convincing many of the less intelligent people, while more zealous in enforcing religious stupidity, not to harm the arrivals.

"Zeus protect them!" he was constantly heard to shout at anyone nearby.

Most listened, but a small faction of zealots began to cause riots in the main cities and brought together many of the elven and dwarven factions, who opposed their respective governments. Meanwhile the recovery continued and Aarun was eventually forced to admit that the army would be needed to quell further disturbances. The dwarves had no such forces available, but the local militia had already stamped their authority on the situation, making his life even more potentially explosive. He needed time to organise his defence of the *mortalkind*, but time was not the only element in short supply.

It was, for the Dwarves, a much more difficult time. Within their culture the myth of the mortalkind related to the end of all free civilisation. It was believed, incorrectly, that man had been a descendant of the Elves, and in their texts the species had the title of "Lesser-Elves." When these horrific people offended the Gods, the myth indicated they were cast out of the world, never to return, except to seek revenge on the true followers of Zeus.

This was of course nonsense, and any elf that knew even the basics of their history would know that no mortalkind had ever been in this world. The advantage of a longer life span allowed many elves to question this source but, as was the way of the dwarf, they preferred stubborn resistance to new ideas, rather than a philosophical debate. To many Zeus was the power that decided all, while to others this was a religion of the decadent. It was not an environment that was suited to a political resolution. Hence the deployment of an elven guard archer regiment of the Gallician court as a protection force for all future arrivals.

For the elves the concept of any dimension was an issue of serious debate, even amongst the commoners. A debate that had lasted over a thousand years, and would probably continue for another thousand years, if not more. It had no foreseeable solution, with or without Lord Aarun's help. With neither elf nor dwarf willing to discuss or even compare the ancient scrolls, the dilemma of knowing the real truth had devolved into myth. For the mainstream dwarves, such knowledge was to some extent left to the intellectual faction of their society normally to be found in Hiltar, the southern half of their kingdom. Here in the northwest such non-believers received little warmth and they could not remember the last Hiltar dignitary to visit this precinct of the kingdom. The political hotbed was again ready to catch fire and the elves for once recognised the need for an exceptional arbitrator.

So it was at this point that Lord Aarun of the Gallicia Crown Court was appointed to be that very arbitrator. His task was to complete the revival of the Romans and Helvetii and to secure their safety, as the main appearances had been noted within the Ortovia Forest, which was at this time a political hotbed of religious zealots and anti-government separatists. This placed Lord Aarun squarely in the middle of the most dangerous event to have happened in the last three hundred years. His activities at that point had never gone beyond that of advisor to the great and glorious. Now he set about breaking a few egos, making even more enemies along the way. He could no longer hide behind those who held automatic immunity. They had their own problems in Moravia, where their Queen had opened discussions for peace with the sunorcs. Now it was he and he alone who would stand in the light of the fire and either burn or reduce the flames of duplicity.

Time and topography were his first headaches, his main concern being the dense collection of trees and soggy undergrowth, which would not leave many with the opportunity to survive, should they appear on the surface of the Ortovia marshes. Perhaps some had already done so? He shuddered to imagine such a death: a fate perhaps worse than death, and one he intended them to avoid.

With this in mind, search parties were drafted from the elite archers. It was indeed Aarun's privilege to be their commander, unofficially, while officially their presence on dwarven soil was to assist their neighbours, the dwarves, at this time of crisis. Events soon began to crystallise and the hotheads were quickly rounded up and kept out of the general public's eye for the time being. Not arrested, he reminded them, but detained for the length of this current predicament. It served the dwarves just as well and so little resistance occurred when the archers entered the forest. This policy helped everyone and in time the detainees would be released without charges. Well, most of them anyway! So went the first careful steps.

With the task set and the recovery organised, Aarun next proceeded to deal with the true problem at hand, primarily the Westonian officials! Politicians one and all had now been quietly told to shut up. It was not possible to do this with the Westonian military, even if they did only command militia.

    Over the centuries this faction of the dwarven kingdom had become the most interactive amongst their people. In fact continual couplings with elven maidens had developed these particular dwarves to a considerable height above the normal size, and successive generations had developed a higher level of understanding of politics and financial matters. Militarily they contributed to the defence of the realm, but very few Westonians would serve outside of their borders, and therefore they generally assisted only in the defence of the peninsular itself. Born with an insatiable desire to retire rich, most of the families in this bountiful region had created enormous trade conglomerates designed to control every possible type of business, by fair or foul means. It was not unusual for trade disputes to end in serious injury, and on occasion perhaps a fatality.

    With this in mind, Aarun met with the dwarven Lord Kollis who, as the regional military and political personage, controlled almost every aspect of the Westonian lifestyle, directly representing the trade officials. The meeting was hardly productive, as the Ortovia Forest was a disputed area of land that had for the past fifty years declared itself to be neutral, with no affiliation to either power. It was populated by the most superstitious people in the whole world, and the cry for independence had caused the dwarves to build a border fort, with several hundred warriors to retain order. The Elves reciprocated and tension had once more developed in relation to the sovereignty of the region. Now the added religious implications had not made their lives any easier.

    He had only one thing in his favour, or perhaps two. First, Kollis was already rich beyond even Aarun's imagination, so wealth would not be the deciding factor with this particular person. Second, he was without doubt an intelligent dwarf, but he failed utterly to understand the military factors in the situation. While the militia alone outnumbered the elves by at least ten to one, the latter were spread right across the entire region, while the concentrated archers made an impressive sight marching into Kollis' front yard. Aarun made a gamble and waited for the outcome.

With the locals refusing to hand over any bodies found, and with regional militia commanders opposing all attempts to send in the archers to search the forest, Aarun effectively had as difficult a problem as could be expected. With particular aplomb, the elf Lord approached the problem with skill and ability. Understanding the arrogant stance of the Westonians, he approached with an air of stupidity and gave them the impression of uselessness. This worked well with the lower echelons, but ordering the archers to concentrate at Kollis' mansion was a masterstroke of ingenuity.

With customary aggressiveness, Kollis jumped at the opportunity to retain control, but with very little military presence he knew he could not deal with the whole situation and the troublesome locals. The result was for the elven troops to be applied directly, as originally intended, but under dwarven command! Aarun had already briefed his junior officers to bite their tongues for the moment, and with pride he watched them do so with an enormous effort.

"A small victory," Aarun stated calmly, a verbal congratulation of his own efforts to bite his tongue. Kollis was not an easy dwarf with whom to negotiate a deal involving other people's lives.

To his right Marshal Elvandar, the official archer commander, grunted in agreement as they strode across the main courtyard in Kollis' villa in the city of Lo. Politics were beyond him, he admitted silently, but in recent years he had grown to trust his Lord's judgement on such matters. Now was no different to any other time.

"It seems that the prophecies are coming true, my Lord," he then said, after a pause. "Are your interpretations to be accepted in full? Many of my junior officers are finding all this upheaval disturbing."

"It is unfortunate that so many of our people are as dim-witted as these dwarves, but that is indeed the issue, my friend," Aarun confided. "For the moment we need to concentrate on completing the collection of the new arrivals. The paranoia of these dwarves and the Ortovians will need to be looked at later, there is simply no time now. The situation in Thoria, as far as we can ascertain, has required a substantial proportion of their resources to hold back the goblins. The arrival of the *arrivals* at this juncture is not a coincidence. It is the work of Zeus."

"Or someone else?"

For a few moments more they continued to walk in silence and passed under a high archway leading into an enormous compound.

All about them the trees were full of the spring bloom and the smell of the flowers was almost overpowering. Here a personal guard stood waiting patiently, and on their appearance the guard immediately began to turn towards the main exit leading out towards the west of the city.

"How long do you think it will take to collect the *arrivals*, Elvandar?" Aarun asked, as he mounted a horse provided by a dwarven servant.

"Approximately one week, my Lord."

"You seem uncertain."

"No, not really. Just concerned as regards these swamps. My people do not know them very well, neither do the dwarves."

"Ortovians?"

"Refused to act as guides," Elvandar admitted, still confused, as religion was another issue he had never taken the time to study in depth, other than where it directly related to magic incantations and its historical scrolls.

"Then we must move quickly before they revive in the middle of a forest and are caught by the Ortovians. It would be foolish for any fatalities to occur because of superstition. Speak to the local commanders, I am sure they will know of someone to act as guides. If not, as a last resort mind you, take some Ortovians by force. This is bigger than any local disturbance, my friend. This could signal the beginning of the end or the beginning of the truth. I intend it to be the latter."

"I will organise the search immediately and send the archers forward to complete the task. Do we utilise the dwarven warriors at the border fort?"

"Yes, for the moment, but try and keep them to security duties on the Ortovians. You know that they must feel that they are in charge, my friend?"

"They will never know any different, my Lord."

Aarun smiled. "That is good. We must at all costs avoid this Kollis seeing gold bars for an exchange of the *arrivals*. These Westonians prefer gold over everything, but for now at least some level of morality is keeping his greed in check!"

Elvandar grimaced to think of such single-mindedness but knew little about such matters. His expression became pained as he realised he did not really understand much of anything other than being a soldier, but then sixty years of service tended to do that to the dedicated.

"We can only try," he eventually added.

They rode hard that day and confirmed before nightfall that the entire archer regiment had entered the forest with a local cavalry troop in close support, a fact that was carefully kept from Kollis' attention. It would take time to retrieve everyone, as the sightings seemed to be of only one or two people at a time. All of them were found lying prone on the ground, and to the uninitiated they would have had the appearance of being dead. Time was of the utmost importance. As they moved with consummate skill and Aarun learned of their tireless efforts, he added a constant reminder of their true enemy. Time.

After a few days, Aarun remained at their camp to act as the central controlling point and, although Kollis believed that his staff was processing everything, the local dwarven officers had clearly begun to understand the truth of the situation and started to cooperate openly. The concentrated presence of the archer regiment was the main reason for them offering this help, but to some it was a common courtesy, willingly or otherwise was not the deciding factor.

"This will be a long night," Aarun commented to one dwarven officer at midnight.

"Aye, it will, my Lord. A night of terror for my people."

"How so?"

"The myths, my Lord, are you not aware of them?"

Aarun sighed, then raised his hand to wag a figure. "There are many beliefs in this world that are incorrect, young sir. Should we not keep our minds open to deduce the truth, which is more important than the lie? Is this not so?"

The young officer blanched at such a direct question, but stoically stood firm. "Our beliefs are as strong as yours, perhaps stronger. I do not know what this portends but I do know that because of it our world will never be the same."

"That is undoubted," Aarun agreed. "Undoubted indeed."

With a less than polite grunt the young dwarven officer had then left the room leaving an air of frustration. It was always difficult to deal with superstition, but where possible the truth will always find a way. He did of course have to believe that or face utter madness. Not even he could stop the spread of the news of the *arrivals*. The myths from the depths of the dwarven despair and the end of the world were a hard act to follow. The mortalkind's fame had already been sealed, fair or foul, for good or bad. Only time would tell which it would be. Meanwhile time seemed to be enjoying the endless delays of rain, mud, swamps and local resistance from zealots walking around in blue hoods and chanting ancient poems to ward off evil spirits.

Aarun smiled, it had been many years since he had last been referred to as a spirit. As they worked Aarun also began to question those that had recovered sufficiently, and learnt that these people called themselves Roman, Helvetii, Boii or Verbigoni. This naturally meant nothing to him, but it was a start.

On and on they worked. None slept for forty-eight hours and yet there seemed no end to the demands on those present. Reports came in of another region that had now reported new arrivals. This time, however, the appearances had occurred within the Gallicia Kingdom and there were no political interpretations to adhere to in attending to any medical needs.

It was indeed going to be a long task. If anything, it was going to be a very long week.

⁂

The room began to spin uncontrollably, first in one direction then another.

If this is the result of that wine I consumed at the campfire, he silently fumed, I am going to have Porta's guts on a platter! It was bad enough that he had stolen it from the third century, never mind that his head felt as though someone had boiled it in oil. At any attempt at movement, the feeling of bile certainly burnt his throat. Lying back for the millionth time, he determined to try again soon, but for the moment the thought of vomiting put a stop to any such noble endeavours.

He looked to the top of the tent in which he now lay, apparently as a casualty. Naturally a guess, and how would he know where he was after all that wine, but it seemed to make sense for the moment.

The memories in his head blurred as if his mind was trying in vain to identify an object, any object, but was simply unable to put a name to anything he viewed. The blur increased with the concentration, and after a few more attempts Cappa closed his eyes and let his head sink into the soft pillows. For the moment all that he could manage was the occasional look to either side, to reveal the presence of several beds supporting the inactive forms of more legionaries. Nothing unusual in that, other than that there were no bandages, injuries or orderlies. He quickly ran his fingers over every part of his anatomy he could touch without rising...No, not a single bandage, or even a drop of dried blood, what in Jupiter's name was going on? So why was he here? If not a casualty, then perhaps a sickness? Yes, that would make sense, he could remember the rank before him dropping over as a single mass. But what sickness could have had such a widespread and instantaneous effect?

For the moment recognition was impossible. As he tried in vain to look at the maiden nearby, his eyes continued to refuse to focus, but the image was slowly improving as the subconscious mind continued to force the false reality aside. Of course whatever that reality was mattered little to Cappa, as he noted a blurred figure sitting at the end of his cot.

"Where is this place, Porta?" he said, not recognising the legionary, but knowing it had to be him. No one else would be so profane as to use his illness as an excuse to avoid the daily training all legionaries completed every morning.

"Hey, that's great news. You're feeling better then?"

"Of course I bloody am, why else would I be asking stupid questions!" Cappa tried again. "Where is this place?"

"You should rest, my friend," a voice advised softly off to his left. A hand gently stroked his forehead and he felt sleep begin to switch off his senses. "It will be a few hours before you can stand. Is there anyone I can send for to ease your adjustment?"

"Atronius," Cappa advised, his throat as dry as sand. "This oaf here couldn't help someone out of a wineskin!"

"I have heard of this one," the voice comforted Porta, as though the harsh words were a novelty: clearly a maiden with a heavy accent, Cappa acknowledged. "I will send word for this person to attend to your needs. Please rest in my absence, my friend. Your colleague has been most gracious to sit by your side for many hours this day. A kind word..."

"A kind word be damned," Cappa barked irritably, pushing the hand away from his forehead. "Porta, order the legionaries to prepare for inspection. I will rise soon and they had better not have allowed their weapons to rust or I'll have their hides for a blanket!"

"I see the rest has done nothing to improve your mood!" Porta stated flatly. "I think you are in for a few shocks, so I would rest while you can."

"Are you refusing to obey an order? You loathsome wretch! Where is your helmet, you piece of dirt? Where in the name of Jupiter am I? I recall no injury! Answer me!"

With his voice diminishing Cappa again closed his eyes, trying desperately to dispel the haze. The sound of a tent flap being raised and mumbled voices brought his eyes open again, and with a sigh the vision was considerably better. Porta still remained but had now been joined by Atronius.

"How long...have I...been asleep?" he gasped.

"At this particular point I've been sitting here for about three hours, ever since they advised me that you'd begun to recover," Porta answered, his tones more considerate, for the Pilum's benefit rather than Cappa's. "But the whole situation is beyond my understanding."

"It is for the moment beyond all our understanding," Atronius added after a short silence.

"You are well?" he asked Cappa. "No broken bones?" He then asked the maiden, who shook her head in answer.

"I am fine, as far as I can see," Cappa replied, again performing a brief inspection to count two arms and legs and...yes, that is still intact as well. "I feel as weak as a child, but uninjured. The legion?"

"Gone," Porta answered.

"Gone?"

"Yes. I believe that is what I said, not deaf are we?" Porta snapped, suddenly recalling the harsh words earlier.

"Porta!" Atronius remonstrated. "Keep your tongue silent if you wish for it to remain in your mouth!"

Porta bowed an apology and took a step backwards. After all his patience it seemed as though no gratitude would be forthcoming, so why continue? Let the damn oaf recover without his aid, see if he would care, other matters took prominence now. By the Gods he was in for a serious shock when he stepped outside, he smiled. Nothing was the same any more and he had nothing like the influence he had had before, although he had heard that the officers had voted to determine who should jointly command the legion survivors alongside the Pilum. He began to wonder just who they might have chosen and felt a sudden pang of anger.

Why had the Pilum attended this man's bedside? He had not attended any other. Surely the other legionaries and officers have not voted for this fool? He began to seethe but for the moment held his tongue. It was enough that the Pilum was here. Further proof was not needed.

"You have a great deal of catching up to do," Atronius was saying. "But I'll leave that to the Elves and Lord Aarun."

"Lord Aarun?"

"You will meet him later. You are in for the biggest shock of your entire life, Optio, this title being the first to go I think. I'm still trying to understand it myself, but so far only Marcellus has even begun to fathom what these people have told us. And the people! It is beyond my skills. For now try to rest. I need you fit and ready to command as soon as possible. How long do you require?"

"The way I feel perhaps another day, possibly two. I am uncertain. As I stated, I am not injured, so I cannot determine how long it will be before I recover. I thought it was the wine from last night."

Atronius laughed and the sound made the situation that much easier.

"By the Gods, Optio, some of the maidens here are beautiful beyond belief, and your first thought is to garrotte the wine seller!" mocked Porta, throwing his hands wide in amazement. "There are also many other matters to discuss of more importance, if only..."

"I am not interested...in the quality of...the women!" interrupted Cappa, forcing his body to rise on one elbow in order to look more closely at the source of irritation. Ah, it was Porta just beyond his hazy vision talking to one of the maidens. Why was he not surprised? So he had not left as the Primus had commanded but only made his presence less noticeable.

"What of the legion?"

With a grin Porta turned and once more threw his loose toga over one shoulder and leaned towards Cappa.

"I have already said earlier, the legion is gone. As for the women, you will be interested when you see them, Optio," Porta said, nodding at the Pilum who stood admiring the maiden Ioeta, with whom he had conversed, but she had then politely withdrawn with a smile.

"But you are correct in that such things are not really significant at this point. Are you thirsty, that is the normal reaction?" said a second maiden.

Cappa nodded and a skin full of fresh water was swiftly handed over by the second maiden. Cappa froze!

"Ah, let me introduce you," Porta laughed. "Cappa, it is an honour to introduce to you Eiluna, your personal maiden, assigned by none other than Lord Aarun."

"It is a great honour to have been chosen for such a task, my lord," Eiluna said softly, fluttering her eyes and shyly turning to attend to a bowl of fruit.

Cappa continued to stare, unable to speak for several moments. The comment about the beautiful maidens had been no exaggeration, but it was not that that truly held his gaze. It was the shade of her skin and the extended ears, which rose to create two perfect pinnacles on either side of her head.

"What in the name of *Jupiter*!" he began.

"I'm not even going to try and explain, but here's as much as I have been able to absorb," Porta interrupted, raising both hands defensively, to avoid Eiluna being offended by Cappa's standard profanity. "According to these people, we are no longer on the world we knew or understood to be centred around our glorious Roma. In truth they have indicated that for five hundred years we have been somewhere else, which is not exactly here or on the world we should call home. With me so far?"

Cappa shook his head.

"No, I thought so. That blank look of yours is a dead giveaway, you know. I'll go and collect Marcellus and I guess he'll be able to assist better. Meanwhile I'll concentrate on Eiluna..."

"Find Marcellus first," Cappa barked. "Then find the Pilum again, with his permission, this lord you spoke of, a meeting perhaps?"

"Of course, Optio, but you will see that so much has changed. Nothing is the way that it was before. We..."

"I gave an order! Obey or leave me in peace!"

Porta rose sharply, the command causing an instinctive reaction, saluted and promptly moved to obey, although his look of bewilderment was hidden from Cappa. Atronius Sulla lowered his eyes to look at the trampled ground and quietly withdrew, having remained at the exit momentarily to see how Cappa's recovery progressed.

He knew how tiresome the next few days would be for him, and there was little point trying to improvise respect in a man that had the level of character shown by Cappa. Now outside the tent he was concerned and confided to Valenus these doubts, whether Cappa would support the legion decision after all his previous refusals of promotion. Refusal now was literally not an option. Atronius would command by default but he needed the authenticity that Cappa would give to his position of overall command, although the legion had continued with the reference of Primus to indicate his new rank. In truth they needed each other to some extent, even if his purpose was just that little bit more self-centred.

Back inside, Cappa once more watched Eiluna and for the first time really looked beyond the pointed ears.

With wide brown eyes, a wry smile and sparkling expression she returned his curiosity while retaining a discreet distance. Long brown hair cascaded down her back and the small nose and shapely mouth gave an impression of beauty, but also retained perhaps hidden truths. This maiden had seen the world and Cappa knew this more from the eyes than the youthful face. Smiling, Eiluna returned with some fruit and assisted Cappa in his efforts to eat, for with both hands seemingly unable to grip properly this was not as easy as it sounds. Once satisfied, she then brought some soup that reminded the Optio of tomatoes but clearly the blue colour indicated another substance.

"Brachis," Eiluna offered, with yet another beautiful smile. "It is a fruit we grow in the earth. Very useful for the mass production of food."

Cappa nodded. "Thank you, but I am not used to such... weakness."

"It is common at this time. In a few days your strength will return and I will not be required, but for the moment let me help."

Again Cappa nodded, took the next mouthful and swallowed the smooth-textured liquid, glad of its warmth in his stomach. When his stomach finally rang full his curiosity was again aroused and a glance to either side did little to improve his mood.

Noticing his look, Eiluna sat on the edge of the cot and waited.

"How...How did this...?"

"How did what happen? Your movement here, to our homeland?"

"Yes. I remember nothing. Except perhaps when people began to seemingly fall over."

"Your memory will return with time, but as far as we can tell the great powers that exist beyond our understanding have fought over your existence for five hundred years..."

"Five hundred years!" Cappa gasped, trying to rise, and spitting Brachis in a wide arc.

"Rest...You must rest. Now lie back, that's it, just for a while longer. Yes, for five hundred years you and your people have been suspended in the void between the dimensions that have separated our worlds and kept the universe whole. You are familiar with our God Zeus?"

"Yes, of course, but in my home we referred to our Gods as Jupiter and Mars."

"I see, then this may not be so hard to understand..."

"I am not religious..."

"No matter," Eiluna grinned impishly. "I am a good teacher..."

They talked for hours that day and the next, and slowly a friendship developed that enabled Cappa to extend his understanding of the elves and dwarves and all the other creatures that he now had to learn about. Beautiful as ever, Eiluna also proved true to her word. She was indeed an excellent tutor.

The night before the agreed general meeting, set for the next morning, Lord Aarun arrived at the medical tent and bade the maidens leave. Behind him came Atronius and another enormous elf, which Cappa could only assume to be some kind of bodyguard, as he immediately took up a defensive posture at the exit.

They moved to a side table, on which Aarun placed numerous maps and books, then gestured for Atronius to join him. He kept a few scrolls in his hands and then turned towards Cappa. Before even a word of introduction could be spoken, however, an immense commotion began outside the tent. The larger elf, with a nod from Aarun, moved to investigate.

"It is that oaf Daxus," he eventually called, over his shoulder. "A few of the archers are trying to stop him from entering this tent. Shall I add my weight or allow him to pass?"

Aarun nodded again and Cappa noted how the other elf moved swiftly outside.

"Daxus?" Cappa asked, propped up on his elbows.

"The barbarian leader," Atronius advised with disdain.

"Barbarian!" Cappa shouted, coldly staring at Aarun. "What is the meaning of this?"

Cappa tried to rise, but as soon as his feet touched the floor Atronius was at his side with a look that would have stopped a rampaging bull.

"Rest, Optio, there is much to discuss and you being ill is of no value to your companions. Daxus is not concerned with us or even the elves. He is concerned only with increasing his power base. Here there is no elder council to stand in his way. Here there are those that will follow him blindly."

Cappa glanced at Aarun. "He allows the barbarian to speak at his councils?" he whispered.

"It is so, but against my advice."

"Are we brought so low, so *easily*?"

"There is much for you to learn, Cappa. Roma does not exist here and we are but one thousand strong. We must have allies and at the moment even *Daxus* would be welcome."

"What of the fort? If we are here, are they here as well? Surely they numbered over five hundred?" Cappa asked.

"They are here, commanded by Centurion Cappilius Paelignus, an honourable and capable officer, but numbering less than three hundred. I have spoken with him in great detail and I am certain his loyalty remains with Roma, but here nothing is to be taken for granted. We must play the game of politics, Cappa, then pray that our enemies do not ally against us."

Cappa was about to ask more questions when the larger elf, whom he later learned was called Elvandar, returned with Prince Daxus, his hand wiping away blood from a swollen lip.

"There is to be a great meeting tomorrow," he immediately began, spitting blood onto the floor. "Why? And, more important, *why* have my people been excluded? I demand an *answer*!"

"You demand nothing here, barbarian," barked Elvandar. "Unless you wish the guards to add another bruise to that fat lip you already carry?"

Daxus' eyes were piercing in their malevolence towards the elf, but no move was made to counter the threat.

"I will remind you of this at a more convenient time, elf."

Elvandar snorted, turned back to his post at the exit and proceeded to glare at Daxus, returning the malevolence with glee.

"You wish to know why the meeting has been called tomorrow?" Aarun began, hoping to reduce the air of animosity with his congeniality. "That is simple enough. We need to clarify to everyone what we are going to do. You may or may not have noticed, my friend, but your arrival has caused an immense disturbance to our whole way of living. Until two months ago, we had no proof that mortalkind, Roman or barbarian, had ever existed! There is much to change, if you are to survive."

Daxus reproached himself strongly, nodding his agreement, suddenly realising that prudence would be a better tool if he wanted to establish the truth concerning a secret alliance between the elves and the Romans.

"Perhaps I spoke hastily, my Lord," he apologised, with a slight lowering of the head, as a bow. "But you can hardly deny that these Romans are trying to exclude us from these talks. What good is there in talking, if they intend to continue the war they caused?"

Atronius had only just resumed his seat when the barbed comment was made, intended to cause a reaction. He obliged and rose again from his seat. "We oppose nothing, barbarian. Our purpose is to achieve unity and nothing else."

"The very expression proves I am right. Why are we excluded? Our faction is greater than you are and yet *you,* as always, assume sovereignty." He spat, his right hand resting on the hilt of his gladius.

Aarun rose now and explained to Daxus that the messengers had been sent but, due to lack of cooperation by the tribesmen, they had not been able to find him or Uxudulum, to advise them of the meeting. He also confirmed that Issus had been told, but clearly he had not informed the others.

"I am not surprised," Atronius said. "That fool does not have the brains to think of the bigger picture."

"What, you mean like the glorious Roma!" Daxus provoked again, not waiting for any reply.

Turning to go, he suddenly stopped at the exit and looked directly at Cappa, his look one of pure contempt. "I have heard you are the saviour of the legion. I will remember this meeting: you on your medical bed, sick and feeble, and me in my prime rising to power. I think that one day we will have a reckoning worthy of a story or two."

Without waiting for a reply, as was his normal approach when hurling insults, Daxus then left after a final glare at Elvandar.

"This will not work!" Atronius exploded. "That *fool* is seeking to continue the conflict that was about to begin between Roma and the Helvetii peoples. If he is not willing to seek peace then we cannot unite!"

"If this was going to be easy," Aarun smiled, "then I doubt whether the Gods would have fought so bitterly for so long over your arrival. We must find a way."

"Lord Aarun," said Cappa," we need to find his weakness and exploit it. Perhaps his pride at being the greater faction would be of use. If you can make him feel more directly involved, he might relinquish his position and allow concessions?"

"It is a possibility. However, your exploits and training will be of much greater value than those of the barbarians and, at this time in our struggle, we need people who fight well."

"I do not think you need worry about their fighting ability, my Lord. That is not in question. Their discipline is what you must improve. Our own people will not fight unless they feel they are fighting to achieve a common aim."

Elvandar stirred at the exit. "If by that you are referring to the spoils of war, mortalkind, you had better think again! Our people and the dwarves..."

"Elvandar, enough," Aarun interrupted coldly. "I think this night has seen enough tempers."

"I meant no offence, but the legionaries are professional men who fight for their future. Offer them land for their retirement and payment in gold or something of similar value and they will fight."

Atronius nodded. "That is true enough, but how do we get them to cooperate with their sworn enemy?"

"That I will leave to you, Primus," Cappa said, reaching for the bowl of water nearby.

They stayed for a few good hours that evening, until Cappa fully understood their predicament. They had in the last few weeks progressed immensely but lacked enough respected legionaries to maintain discipline. It was now that Cappa learnt of his promotion to Centurion, whether he liked it or not.

"I will try to honour your decision and serve Jupiter and Mars well," he said in thanks.

"See that you do. Your first task will be to attend the meeting tomorrow. The people of new Roma have demanded your presence," Atronius added, his obvious pride at the choice of creating a new Republic having seemingly received a high level of support.

Cappa could only smile. New Roma, he thought with apprehension. According to his maiden teacher they had been in the void for five hundred years, and yet nothing seemed to have changed. Roma had not come to the legions, so the legion must go to Roma. Or better still, why not just start all over again?

⁂

Later that evening Daxus stood in his own tent. Before him lay a large map that a local had drawn to show this world of Tannis that they now occupied. His mind was in a state of panic. His people demanded action. They demanded to know why their Gods had sent them here and they did not like to be kept waiting. In all his studies of the Gods and the soothsayers, he had never known of such an event and he had no idea of how to proceed. All he knew was that he could not allow his people to become slaves to that pig of a Roman Atronius Sulla.

Who does that upstart think he is? I am a Prince and he is nothing but a commoner! Well, we shall attend the meeting and then we will see. Then, no matter what happened, he would continue to seek other allies, and if that meant the enemy that these arrogant elves and knee-high dwarves were fighting, then so be it!

"Uxudulum!" he bellowed.

A tall man entered the tent and bowed low. "Prince."

"Send out scouts. Find me this enemy the elves speak of. Send them a message that I wish to speak with them."

"Would this be wise?"

"Do I now need to confer with you regarding my right to lead my people?" Daxus' voice rose to a high pitch, eyes bulging.

For a moment Uxudulum's pride flared and his hand twitched in anticipation of grasping his weapon, but something in Daxus' eyes stayed his hand. He had no wish to stand with the Romans any more than his people did, but the alternative was the leadership of this oaf. Making his mind up Uxudulum simply turned, walked outside and beckoned for the nearest warrior to join him.

As the messenger ran off to fulfil the Prince's orders he turned to another messenger and smiled.

"Inform our people that when the time is right we will have a new Prince."

The second messenger nodded, turned quickly and vanished into the darkness. It seemed as though Atronius' assessment of the barbarians was about to be proven correct.

The walking cane was an embarrassment and yet, as the light seeped through the tent entrance, it became clear that not only would the vision be impaired by this so-called "transformation," but also that walking on uneven ground caused no end of trouble. Squinting and crouched over with a wobble that caused many legionaries to turn away and smirk was the plight Cappa found himself in, as he responded to the written request to attend the meeting Aarun had advised him about only yesterday. What to do next!

Who would attend this meeting or, indeed, who had now ascended to power over the last week or so, had evaded his enquiries after Atronius and Aarun had left. He had managed to determine that the legion had voted for Atronius to represent them, taking the title as Primus, to which the elves and dwarves now attributed privileges equal to those of one of their senior military officials.

All the conversations that he overheard within the camp concerned the actions of Atronius in securing solid relations with their erstwhile allies the barbarians. A concession here would then be balanced by way of a refusal elsewhere. Ground to build a home had been a burning issue but most of the legionaries were used to travelling, and so the Pilum had extended the argument deliberately in order to increase the impact of his capitulation later. The barbarians got their plot of land near the river. The Romans received the lowlands further north. The two plots differed little, other than in proximity to the elven kingdom, a people Prince Daxus had so far openly opposed.

However, if last night was an example of progress, he wondered just what else was left to discuss? Aarun had seemingly taken his advice on the land issue, as that had only changed that very morning, as reported by Marcellus.

Atronius was not only the politician, but had also developed into the statesman and the instigator of the new Roma objective. He was also of course the military man. Trained in all aspects over the years, there did not seem to be many issues that he could not resolve... except perhaps one! Who held the dominant position within the mortalkind faction?

Even here a united front could not be accomplished, as the old hatreds had not diminished during their time in the void. Even as he walked he could see the distinct groups of barbarians and Romans. Within the barbarian ranks, the Latabrogi and Boii did not even stand together. He had thought on the matter all night and had discovered a little information from Eiluna, but as far as he was concerned it was still a mystery why these great strategists needed him at the meeting.

Cappa walked, thinking all the time, why? Some, the so-called commoners, all good legionaries of poor education, he knew, had asked that he attend, as the most respected amongst them. He recalled how his mother had pestered him to take more notice of his schooling, but even at a very young age he had known the military life was the only way for him. The plan had always been to remain unknown, but circumstances had played a different game and he now found himself walking toward notoriety.

Atronius would, of course, have been the first to accept his advice. Not that he would necessarily have followed that advice, but he would have at least bothered to listen. Now, in such an arena, Cappa was also the first to admit his failings. His mind worked problems out very quickly and succinctly. That was why he was a good legionary, and his experience made him an exceptional junior officer, but he admitted that he did not have the same abilities as Atronius, or even Valenus.

Others disagreed. He did not! Thinking for too long could be fatal. He acted on a gut reaction, not necessarily what was right or wrong from a purely tactical assessment of any given situation. He was direct to the point of suicide and he admired the fact that he had avoided crucifixion for almost twenty years, almost as much as he admired his levels of knowledge in dealing with new recruits.

To command was another issue altogether!

He smiled as he remembered his tutor. He had tried to teach him how best to kill a man and Cappa had promptly, at a very young age, proceeded to advise his tutor of thirty different strokes that could end a man's life. He then added for effect that he preferred five specific approaches: the stomach, throat, upper femoral artery, the groin and the armpit thrust.

All were lethal if applied with sufficient skill. That was what he knew. Not how to talk down a political argument. It was not that he failed to relate to this New World of Tannis, in which he understood that they occupied only the Northern Hemisphere.

He simply knew very little about the dwarven culture and even less about the barbarian religious rituals. He now knew more about the elven struggle, but he had had put this to one side for fear of being prejudiced. Eiluna had not even attempted to hide her mistrust of the dwarves. No matter how he looked at this situation, he saw nothing but disaster looming towards all of them. They had to find common ground or they would fail even before they began.

The scene that greeted the confused and newly appointed Centurion was not an easy situation to absorb. Once outside, a tall elf had bowed low and, after a brief introduction, had indicated the path to the grove accepted as a local meeting place.

Of course this was of little significance to him, but the land itself, at the extremity of the camp, looked plush and green with an enormous amount of undergrowth. Could this have been a palisade?

He noted a few large trees to the south that stood far above everything else, and the elf politely informed him that they were called Ortovian trees, this being the name the local population had adopted many centuries ago.

They were rare now in this region due to the expansion of the swamps, but in the eastern provinces of Dwarmania, at a place called Thoria, they grew in greater abundance. Cappa nodded his thanks, a habit that had seeped into his daily routine, as the names and places prompted no memories. The land felt normal and yet his heart knew it was not home. The air smelt differently. Everything had changed!

They walked through a city of tents with colours and patterns in smooth materials of an unknown quality, created to fit every possible variation. A sight that was not uncommon in his experience, but the fact that no palisades had been constructed, and no guards were on patrol, indicated that they must surely be in friendly territory. But whose friendly territory, he wondered? The obvious mistrust between the elves and dwarves was an additional burden, and due to the attendance of both, the intended meeting might prove explosive. He had met many people in his life and yet he could not recall two races that were so completely different. Day and night had more in common.

Even so, there could be perceived a grudging sort of respect as they stood against a common enemy, an enemy that the Romans had as yet to meet or recognise as such. Cappa had heard many such stories during his recovery but had not so far voiced his opinion. He could not judge what he had not seen, but he did not deny that the truth had also been spoken.

As they walked, or hobbled, as the case might be, the interest in them was almost uncanny. Cappa would glance at someone pleasingly and perhaps even smile, an event that many saw as awkward. Legionaries were too used to his frowning for him to develop a pleasant personality now!

Maids would stop and stare as word began to spread that Cappa was passing. Within a few minutes, a crowd had begun to follow the two people, and for a moment Cappa found himself embarrassed by this level of attention. In his enforced absence he had become something of a mystery to these gentle people, and to any legionary the first rule was to accept praise when victory laurels were there for the asking; but in his present circumstances most men would seek a hiding place amongst the cohort. Oft as not someone somewhere would be looking for a reason to issue disciplinary actions, and in general the veterans became adept at seeming inconspicuous in the crowd. Now, as yet more people joined the throng, he did not seem to have much choice. His notoriety preceded him.

The entourage stopped by a small guard at an entrance to an enclave surrounded by high oak trees. The two of them entered a circular arena decorated with logs used as seats. On these sat numerous people, several of whom wore clothes that signified a high rank. Slowly Cappa approached and watched as Porta rose from nearby, indicating that he should sit. Cappa assumed that he had been keeping the seat on the stump of a tree for his arrival. Grateful for the courtesy, he smiled and sat down, but still felt exhausted after the ten-minute stroll. The discussion seemed to have halted as they entered, but the issue was by no means resolved.

"Are you well, Cappa?" Atronius said bluntly, his temper obviously at breaking point, similar to the night before.

"I am fine, Primus, my thanks for your concern," Cappa responded, taking a deep breath. "I am, however, extremely confused as to why such a lowly officer as myself has been summoned to such a meeting as this."

A few murmurs followed, and a glare from a proud man on the far side of the circle indicated that at least a few people here agreed with his sentiment. Why, indeed, was this lowly person here?

"You have asked a very interesting question, centurion," Daxus began. "Why are you here?"

"You are perfectly aware why he is here!" blurted Atronius, his face now red with frustration.

"Ah yes, this concept of your legionaries voting for a representative, as you are now elevated above the station of a centurion, are you not?"

"Your point has been made, Prince," spoke a man sitting near him. "Perhaps we should now return to the debate?"

"When I need your advice, Issus, as I advised Uxudulum last night, I will ask for it! Know your place and keep your opinions to yourself. What is to be decided here is the future of our people, and only I can decide that!"

"Wrong!" Issus snapped in reply, twitching the hilt of his sword. Cappa noted that most people seemed to engage in this habit in the company of the Prince.

"Wrong? How dare you? I represent..."

"Your people only. The Boii are represented by me," corrected Uxudulum.

"May we proceed?" encouraged Aarun.

Nobody spoke for a minute or so. Then, changing the topic back to Cappa, the Primus sought to raise his spirits. He was painfully aware of his colleague's inexperience in politics and indeed in senior command. Had it not been for Aarun's insistence, vote or no vote, the Primus would have made excuses and ordered Cappa to remain as far away from this clearing as possible.

"You underestimate your importance to the cohort," Atronius said, earning a glare from the Prince. Unperturbed, he continued, "It is I who should be honoured by your presence, as voted by the legion."

"I am humbled once more, Primus, but still no closer to an answer to my question."

Atronius sighed despondently and leaned heavily forward with both hands resting on either knee. "Such self-pity is no longer an option. Cappa, we do not have time for self-reproach and the denial of greater responsibilities. We held a vote, as is our way, for better or for worse, and we have both received the positions of trust within the legion. Scipio is no longer here to interfere. Whereas Valenus, to everyone's surprise, has been invaluable these past few weeks, with a fire for discipline and learning that surpassed, at times, even Marcellus. We must all work together or perish...a fact that I am trying to get across to this buffoon!"

Cappa looked in the direction of the outstretched finger and watched as the Prince's face reddened, rage almost forcing steam to escape through the ears. However, before he could reply, Lord Aarun intervened aptly.

"We thank you for your clarity, Primus," he said, bowing in his direction, then repeated the same to Daxus. "And we are of course honoured more so by the presence of Daxus..."

"*Prince* Daxus!"

"Yes, of course, Prince Daxus," he bowed once more, and turned to Cappa. "We have a difficult situation in view of the overall problems involved, as regards your own people and those of your fellow Romans. Is that the correct pronunciation? Yes, thank you, that is good, some of these words are somewhat difficult on the tongue. Now where...ah yes, cooperation, it seems will be extremely awkward unless we can resolve this stubborn pride of your species. We have called this meeting to determine how best to proceed. It is my right and my duty to achieve this aim and, with the kind permission of Lord Kollis," a dwarf to Aarun's right nodded in acknowledgement, "we will hopefully achieve this today. We had been talking for many days, and we then took a break as advised by you, Primus. Now it is time for us to make decisions. We have no more time to waste."

Nobody spoke for a while as the weight of Aarun's words lay heavily on all of their consciences, so Cappa took the opportunity to view those who sat on this council. The visual shock of the elves, the abruptness of the dwarves and the seemingly fathomless hatred of Daxus made him wish for a return to his sickbed and the illusion that this was all just a bad dream. He had never seen such a collection of conflicting views, all presented by equally resolute leaders trained in the ways of the statesman. One would accept a specific point, but only in the belief that a second faction would almost certainly refuse to. The task seemed hopeless and yet the elven Lord showed no such misgivings. To all and sundry his face expressed nothing but a warm smile. A smile that made anyone who saw it reciprocate the warmth. Despite all that, Cappa could see no avenue for reconciliation. His all too familiar frown returned to supplant the smile lavishly bestowed on the elven lord.

To the left, moving around the circumference in order of rank, sat the Primus Pilum, Atronius Sulla—which raised the issue of why Tribune Scipio was not in attendance—with the centurions Decimus Crassus and Atia Valenus next in line, and a guard of ten legionaries standing behind them, alert and fully armed.

Directly opposite them sat numerous Dwarves, their existence having been explained to him barely ten minutes earlier, by his guide. Small and squat, they did not seem to pose a threat and yet their skin was weatherworn and the hands callused. These were, if nothing else, a hardy people and the axes held by the honour guard left little doubt as to their prowess in battle. The clothes were heavy and well made with a few wearing the heavier chain mail, in a design that he could not identify. His armour was nowhere to be seen and any enquiry had achieved nothing more than raised eyebrows. Porta had told him, however, that the blacksmiths were already working every waking hour to rectify their lack of body armour and weapons.

Of these people, he decided that the one in the middle with the arched back, and the locked arms gripping both knees resolutely with each hand, was the main dwarven influence. Here sat a person of power, and an ambience that literally flowed from his gaze flooded the circle. It was almost palpable. No one felt the urge to look directly at such a stern countenance.

Next to them, and opposite Cappa, sat the lightly dressed barbarians. The aggressive posture, a hand on the hilt of their weapons, and the bitterness in the eyes left him in no doubt. All held this posture except one. Sitting slightly behind the others, perhaps denoting a lower rank, was a man that he partially recognised. He could not explain this, but when their eyes met it was clear that the other man knew him, perhaps more so, for he leaned behind and spoke softly to another colleague. Issus clearly remembered Cappa!

But who was he and why was he so familiar, went the thought in Cappa's head. It was of course unimportant at that time, but he somehow knew that this man had a greater part to play in these proceedings than his rank indicated. Then again, he thought, so perhaps have I?

Following the circle around further, he ended up once more with the smiling elven Lord Aarun. He too maintained a discreet honour guard but, more strikingly, had an enormous elf standing to one side. Clearly this was Elvandar once again acting as a personal bodyguard or, at a minimum, a senior member of the elven military. Several other elven dignitaries also sat in a small group slightly removed from the circle, while another group of dwarves sat at a similar distance next to them. Perhaps their purpose would be to pass word of what transpired at the meeting to the people throughout the land? It seemed plausible.

"I see that perhaps introductions would be judicious," Lord Aarun finally suggested, noting Cappa's inquisitive inspection of his surroundings. "I am sure that you are familiar with your own colleagues, so I will proceed with those that sit before you."

Cappa nodded and glanced towards the Dwarves once again, allowing Aarun the opportunity to collect his thoughts and begin the introductions. No matter how hard he tried, he could not stop himself beginning to grin insanely. It seemed odd to be treated so grandly. So...unnatural, and out of place for him. But then again there had been little else to feel good about, so why not live the life of a politician for a while, there being no knowing how long this privilege was going to last.

"Immediately on my right sits the great Lord Kollis of Westonia," Aarun began warmly, raising a palm to indicate the personage named. "He has graciously organised the recovery of your people and that of the Helvetii, who are represented by Prince Daxus, Uxudulum and the auspicious Issus. Issus has for several days placed the skills of his men at our disposal in the work of locating any new arrivals, and has earned worthy praise amongst my people. As for me, my name is Lord Aarun of Gallicia, representative of the elven people in this matter. Behind me is the commander of my escort, Marshal Elvandar. I am sure you will acquaint yourself further as the opportunity arises, but we are pressed for time gentlemen and decisions need to be made. Perhaps your assessment would be appreciated, Cappa, as your own people have informed us that you are held in high regard by your legionaries."

"We waste time," cried Daxus. "What his fellow slave drivers feel towards this man is of no importance at all! It is clear that the Romans only wish to create a new state within your lands and begin to fashion another power base to expand their influence and disrupt your kingdoms. If this is allowed they will enslave this world. If you think the hell's spawn you speak of is to be feared, wait until your children are slaves of these Romans, then, when your children's futures are stolen, you will know what fear is!"

"We did what we had to do," defended Atronius. "Just as you would have done. If we had allowed you into Narbonensis our own people would have perished. You demanded the very food that would have left our citizens starving or dead. What you asked for was impossible!"

"What we asked for was land to cultivate for ourselves," Daxus continued, ignoring Atronius as if he had not spoken. "We are not here to create a new empire, but if you listen to the forked tongue of these Romans, that is what you will become part of, or you will be his slaves. We have witnessed their slavery policies in action at first hand! They come bearing gifts and then they enslave your people with technology, science and black magic. They are as evil as the orcs and goblins you speak of so bitterly."

"There is still much more to Roma that you know nothing of, Barbarian! We lived in peace until the Samnites and Etruscans gave us no choice but to fight. Your people began the war between our peoples with your continual raids. We have the right to defend ourselves. It is you that desire an empire, as you did when you isolated the Germanic people and the Rauraci. We are here now and there is no going back. We must stand together or fall individually. Roma has much to offer these people."

"I do not wish to know! I have enough knowledge of your trade policies to realise that slavery is all that Roma brings anywhere!"

"Why do you waste our time with posturing?" snapped Kollis irritably. "Why not at least listen to the Roman for a while and learn if he speaks the truth? Your right to live has not been disputed, although many of my people, the Ortovians especially, would have put you to death if I had not intervened. Many of your people were indeed lost, my people being influenced by religious zealots and a myth that you represented the end of our world! I think you each have complaints against one another, as indeed do we against the elves, but we must now stand together as the Roman has declared. Or fall one by one. You are here now, not in your lands, Daxus, or in your Republic, Primus! It is time to discuss what we will do!"

"Wise words," agreed Aarun.

"We demand lands," Daxus continued once more, ever the protagonist. "We will walk out of these talks right now unless this is confirmed on your honour Lord Aarun!"

"I have put forward your proposals to both governments and they agree in principle, as you are not too numerous, but nothing is guaranteed. You have done nothing to endear the dwarven or elven governments to grant your...demands. They desire to see how you will serve before they are willing to discard centuries of belief that, as mentioned by Kollis, you are indeed not the end of our known world."

Still leaning forward on the walking stick, Cappa took a deep breath and sighed. He had been here barely more than a few minutes, and yet he knew that in his absence Atronius had magnified his personal importance far beyond his own understanding. What he must have said to these important people he had no way of knowing, but inside his heart began to pound ferociously. Here finally was an opportunity to speak for the common soldiers, to stand for their interests, instead of those of the politicians or legates, but he also began to feel like a fish out of water.

As for being highly respected amongst the cohort, he seriously doubted that there was much of an alternative, as many of the men would only be interested in survival, there being precious few officers capable of any guarantees. It was the time-honoured process of voting for your superiors in times of crisis, and it was clear that although Atronius had accepted the vote of confidence in Cappa, others had remained aloof. The issue of authority was the real discussion here, and without unity they had nothing.

Almost without conscious thought, he raised his head and said in a clear voice,

"We should create a unified army or legion. In this way we stand together."

A second's peace followed before everyone began to bellow at once. A few minutes passed, then a new voice boomed out above the conversations continually overlapping each other.

"A capital idea," jumped in Aarun, before the crestfallen Atronius could recover his wits and reopen the discussion yet again. "An army of Alliance. Good, now we have progress at last!"

"Do you agree to this concession, Primus?" Kollis asked acidly, noting Atronius' expression and fearing a severe rebuke or yet another tirade about the failings of the Helvetii.

"I agree. But only if legionaries retain officer rank and the training begins immediately."

"Legionary training!" scoffed Daxus. "Our people have ransacked your capital numerous times in the last one hundred years, due to your expansionistic policies. Why would my people benefit from your training when we are not defeated? Answer me that!"

"If you felt this way, in truth," Cappa spoke again, tentatively, "then you would have attacked us on that first day at the tributary on the Rhodanus River. You did not because you knew that it would take a high level of casualties to defeat one thousand legionaries. Our training is superior, this you *must* concede?"

"We do," said Issus rising to his feet before Daxus could put forward a further rebuke. "Perhaps an exchange of tactics would serve us all well?"

"That it would. More progress. I am beginning to feel hope that this new alliance will serve all our peoples well," prompted Aarun, who as usual beamed a great smile at each of them, one after the other.

Cappa smiled in return, but inside he knew that promises, such as they were, would hold the loyalty of the legionaries as long as they trusted the Primus, hence his promotion to give Atronius authenticity. Their present officers had failed them, and to compensate for this Atronius had so far been very clever and introduced a new point for them all to concentrate on, when the issue of sovereignty was the natural progression.

Now he acted again, as there was only one issue that he would not concede. Romans would lead the army and they would lead the legion, and Atronius Sulla intended to be their Imperator and nothing less was acceptable. Cappa tried to explain why this would be an acceptable demand given Atronius' experience, but he could not sway people such as the Prince or Uxudulum. How to use this to his advantage? He had to think, he needed time to understand where a solution could be found. He changed the subject.

"Perhaps now would be the time to discuss where to settle the few womenfolk who have come with us. I believe even children are here as well," Cappa offered up for discussion, as he continued looking for a way to manipulate the group into accepting Atronius. "I feel that many others here today are fit to make these decisions," he said, digging deeply for as much respect as he could muster. "As far as I am aware, every racial group present in this region has been subject to the interference of the Gods, and moved into this di... dim...diem..."

"Dimension," Lord Aarun assisted.

"Yes, dim-en-sion. Thank you again, my Lord. But the time scale is the most frightening aspect in all this business, more so than the explanations, or even the word itself. Five hundred years! Is it really true? How is it even possible?"

Lord Aarun nodded in response, and waved anxiously for him to proceed, implying that the answers to those questions would have to wait.

"Such time is irreplaceable and I assume that we cannot go back?" he asked.

"There is no going back for any of us," volunteered Atronius, seemingly more calm due to the distraction of the womenfolk. Taking the hint, Cappa turned and bowed succinctly to all three centurions.

"What has transpired so far, Primus? Can you briefly outline the situation? Perhaps if someone could explain my presence here, where such important people are making decisions. I have no knowledge to assist. I feel as a fish out of water."

The curt nod gave the affirmative and Atronius closed both eyes, set his facial muscles in a determined expression and reopened his eyes slowly. So far this morning he had already argued the issue ten times over, and all to no avail. With a resigned expression, he clenched both jaws together and looked directly at Cappa as he retold what had so far transpired at the council, deliberately avoiding Lord Kollis' intent gaze and not looking once in the direction of the Prince.

"The discussions began early this morning and have for most of the time concentrated on the issues of unity. The barbarians..." — Cappa noted Daxus' expression of anger — "believe that if their Gods have deserted them, then they have offended their rituals and deserve nothing other than death. They are still arguing that their primary function must be to save the Helvetii people and all their allies. The fact that they are now all dust, as is the Republic, does not seem to deter them from refusing to aid any of the others. These dwarves have for the last two weeks fed and clothed every new arrival and for this I will be forever grateful..."

Atronius bowed slightly to Kollis, who ignored the sign of respect. "But their issue seems to relate to the actual ownership of us all. So far I have seen only Lord Aarun put forward any sense, and his only wish is to aid our integration into this new world as much as possible. But it seems that there is a war that is drawing to a climax, and it will determine whether any free lands remain for all time. So in my opinion we have only two choices. We either fight to defend any lands given or earned by us all, or we sit here and wait for Hades' spawn to find us individually. Even the barbarians admit that our numbers are too small to stand alone!"

"A resounding speech, Primus," spat Daxus, rising to his feet. "But why not tell your warrior chief what you have suggested to the great Helvetii peoples. The people whom the glorious Republic left to starve in the mountains! To be your workhorses!"

Atronius slowly stood and began to reach for his sword, realising en route that only the guards carried weapons.

"I am tired of your presence where it is not desired or requested. Such filth as yourself should remain where it belongs, under the boot of *Roma*!"

Daxus smiled and then suddenly burst into open laughter. With adept anticipation a legionary suddenly appeared to either side of Atronius and gently, but firmly, held him in check.

"My friends! *My friends*!" shouted Lord Aarun, over the commotion. "This overriding need to express loyalty is heart-warming, I assure you, but you are both ignoring the plain truth of our predicament.

The enemy is destroying Dwarmania as we speak and the people there are desperate for men, dwarves or elves that will stand and defend these lands. There is little time to discuss Kollis' greed, Roman pride or Helvetii arrogance. Our pasts are gone and will never be retrieved, which is the destiny of us all. Should we also help those very same enemies by fighting amongst ourselves? I propose a halfway point that may help all sides…"

"The legionaries should form a full formation now, and leave men to train the Dwarves, Elves and Helvetii to use different tactics," interrupted Cappa, acknowledging the obvious. "The immediate task now is to decide where we will make the most difference."

Aarun's mouth remained open, offset by the sudden sound of support.

"Agreed," he finally managed to say.

"Then, my Lord Aarun, we will need a true picture of the war and the positions of the dwarven warriors who are now defending this land."

All eyes turned to Lord Kollis, who seemed for an instant to wilt under the pressure of so much attention. Primarily a businessman, he had naturally raised large troop formations for the war because it was profitable, but he had no true understanding of tactics and hesitated to respond. Powerful statesman, yes he was, but a tactician most definitely not.

"A true understanding of your people's plight would indeed help matters, my Lord. We have very little understanding of your people or their customs," encouraged Atronius, now seated after receiving some friendly advice from Porta. Why him though? He seemed the most unlikely member to wish to be part of these proceedings. Porta seemed to be wherever a decision was to be made, yet in truth he had no business being there in the first place. This was a puzzle, again, but a puzzle that could wait as Kollis rose slowly and nodded, while placing a hand on the hilt of the broadsword strapped to his waist. Cappa noted with amusement that the dwarf had come to this meeting armed, while everyone else had abided by the terms to make these talks a peaceful process. It was his land after all, but still a rather glaring sign of disrespect.

"The situation is not a simple one, as I am sure you will have accepted. However, my people have for the past twenty years borne the brunt of the enemy's activities, and many of our great people have perished. To the north are the mountain dwarves, who have for the past five hundred years furnished the members of the Priesthood Guards at the caves of Azar-Kad, although numerous Ortovians have also joined them in recent years. The caves occupy the eastern provinces that border the Noborian River where the Thorians take over as nomads, with very few settlements that remain for more than six months: great isolationists with poor manners, if you don't mind me saying so.

"The goblin raids make this an absolute necessity, but manners cost nothing. I find them totally..."

"Can we move on, my Lord?" prompted Aarun.

"Yes, yes, of course. If we move westwards towards us here, we then cross the territory of the Eastonian dwarves, all of whom are skilled at building small coastal quiremes. They are described as a separate part of the kingdom, but really they are Cenitarns who like the water, but refer to themselves as *Boaters*. Ridiculous name! They are simple folk and most of their cities were built next to or on the rivers in the northern regions of the kingdom, but they could not match the northerners for stupidity! Even we, the Westonians, have failed to explain to these people the necessity of wealth and community. They have refused all access to their lands and have on occasion executed dwarves for breaking their laws. Ludicrous..."

"Shall we concentrate on the issue at hand...Please?" prompted Lord Aarun once more, as politely as possible, throwing in the political smile for good measure.

"My apologies, of course. Now where was I? Ah yes, the thieving Northerners..." Aarun frowned and Marshal Elvandar took a pace forward as his patience began to stretch. Kollis hastily returned to the question in hand, throwing a look of irritation at the Elves, who as far as he was concerned never had any patience, except for their own kind.

"Well, as I stated, we failed miserably and the northern mountains have been listed as impassable for the last ten years, due to these brigands. But even so our numbers in the northern peninsular have always been less than in the central regions and in the lower southern peninsular. Here are the Cenitarn and the Hiltar, one supplying the bulk of the army's officers and men, while the other concentrated on education and has developed the best rock engineers in the world. That only leaves the Gretans, in whom few have much faith, as they have on numerous occasions refused to aid our troops in battle, and it is widely believed that they collaborate with the Goblins from Gobli. That is of course unsubstantiated gossip, but nevertheless it is an issue that has led to nobody ever trusting a Gretan dwarf."

"What of the military situation, to the best of your knowledge, my Lord?" asked Cappa, feeling a little more awake as the day ebbed away.

"To my knowledge, the enemy has deployed an enormous army of goblins, hobgoblins and gnomes in the forest, where they have for several months raided throughout Thoria and Gretania. At the moment this is the only activity known, but the last report sent to me by my son indicated that over fifty thousand of the enemy are believed to be in the forest.

"The Gretans normally field about twenty thousand, while the Thorian Army numbers approximately thirty-five thousand. This threat is more than enough to deal with but, in addition, to our northeast the Orcs have also allied with the Goblins. To relieve this pressure Prince Kallum, who commands the northern armies, decided to march to Thoria, taking all but a few of the eighteen thousand that he commanded here in Westonia. I have to date no news of any major battle, but I can only assume that the enemy will amass considerably more than fifty thousand behind the forest for the onslaught that everyone expects."

"Have the Thorians moved to assist the Gretans, and therefore left open the northern approaches to this peninsular?" Cappa asked, having scraped a rough map in the mud with his cane.

"To my knowledge, the central forces are meant to be sending large formations to resolve this, but in one week we have seen no reinforcements and the Prince has not returned. If I am not mistaken, only the Noborian fort posts and the Priesthood Guards have remained to hold the river against the Orcs. I do not believe there is any real danger. The Orcassians suffered a major defeat against General Kol only three months ago, and as yet they do not seem organised to return. I do not believe they will."

"Then you are a fool," snapped Issus, suddenly rising to his feet. "I do not know about my colleagues, but to me it seems obvious that these enemies of Dwarmania are the enemies of all the peoples who wish to live free of tyranny. If I can receive a promise that, should we decide to stand, my people will receive lands and food to survive, then I will pledge my loyalty to any man who accepts these same terms. But to you, my Lord Kollis, I say that you should not rely on your son's reports, as they will be based on the emotions on the front where he serves. It seems to me that your whole northern defences have been manoeuvred for a flanking attack by the very Orcs that you believe to be defeated. In fact, it is because of this defeat that they will have been chosen!"

Issus resumed his seat and for a few seconds they all remained silent, until Aarun suddenly recognised the true worth of this outburst. This intelligent man had given him the key to obtaining this group's cooperation, if only in a temporary arrangement. It was all he had so he decided to gamble.

"You have your promise, my friend," he said, now rising in his turn. "Your pledge will be honoured and I will add to your fine words, by pledging my own personal guard and Marshal Elvandar to protect the northern peninsular. Will the Roma that you have always spoken so highly of and the Helvetii peoples, not to mention our friendly Dwarves, allow such pledges to go forward with no allies!"

Now Cappa suddenly recognised what was afoot. "I agree, my Lord, that we should not allow our honour to be thwarted by the enemies, as they are even though we have not yet met them, who would still seek our destruction. I also pledge to defend this peninsular, if only with my troop of legionaries."

Behind Atronius a cheer rose and on this wave of testosterone, wildly led by Porta, again raising another burning question as to why, the cry of support ran through the entire crowd. With their pride stung deeply, further pledges immediately followed from Uxudulum, Daxus and Atronius, and for a while the crescendo was allowed to follow its natural course, much to the confusion of everyone outside. After a few minutes, the chants slowly ebbed away into an excited silence that deeply moved everyone present.

With all now seated, nobody could find the words to start the discussion again. Taking a chance, Aarun suggested that Atronius had the most extensive level of experience and therefore should be made the commander in chief of the new *Army of Allegiance*. The idea was met with a brief and stony silence, until both Cappa and Issus seconded both Daxus and Kollis as joint commanders, who in turn decided that Uxudulum should also be honoured in this fashion. Atronius would lead, while the others would command individual factions, as they were made available. It seemed to work and everyone visibly relaxed, a few smiles replacing forlorn expressions. Another hurdle had finally been overcome.

The crisis over, Aarun turned to Elvandar and ordered that food and wine be brought in, before further talks continued and they began their recruitment in the local towns and villages. The army itself consisted of only a small force of elven archers, five hundred inexperienced dwarven warriors and an unknown number of men who might or might not be fit to fight by the time they marched. Indeed they had still to discuss where in fact they should take this newly created army.

However, before any maids arrived with the plates of food organised the night before, a commotion began on the extremity of the grove.

Elvandar reacted like a wolf. Drawing the long blade favoured by the elves, he snapped his fingers and watched as seven archers suddenly appeared from the trees to move swiftly behind the Marshal. Cappa noted the elven Lord's obvious anger at the secrecy of this added protection, despite his express wishes, but Elvandar simply shrugged off the shouted rebuke and stalked towards the commotion, where two dwarves had broken through the outer perimeter.

"Hold those two!" Elvandar ordered stoutly, striding forward with the elite archers close behind, quills to their bows. "What is the meaning of this intrusion? Even you are aware of the protocols of a restricted meeting, Khazumar!"

"I am the Lord High Priest Commander of the Priesthood Guards, and I require no formal introductions in order to speak to the regional dignitary of Westonia," retorted the dwarf addressed, standing firmly with both feet planted to either side, fists clenched at the hip.

"The laws of the land are there for all to obey, even me. I..."

"...Am in the way, Elvandar!" interrupted the Dwarf. "I am on important business and I have left my post in an urgent search for the central forces that should have replaced the Prince's soldiers that marched to Thoria, against my wishes I might add! You forget that you are in Dwarmania, elf, and therefore your laws are irrelevant. Now step aside, before I am forced to remove your ugly features from my vision."

With a face of thunder the Marshal began again to close on the dwarf, who now swiftly lifted up a great battle-axe for imminent use.

"That is quite enough," interrupted Aarun, suddenly appearing to one side of Elvandar. "I seriously wish that the pair of you would forget the past. From the two most highly regarded military commanders on either side of the mountains, this childish feud is painful to witness. Rejoin the circle, Elvandar. *Now!*"

Slowly the Marshal backed down and waved irritably towards the archers to lower their bows and return to their posts outside the grove. Having dealt with the explosive temper of the elf, Aarun turned to the dwarf. It looked as though this warrior would also receive the full anger of the elven lord, but just as swiftly as his anger had arisen, a broad smile of recognition replaced the drawn features.

Aarun stepped forward and took one of the dwarf's hands warmly.

"It is good to see you again, Khazumar. It must have been at least ten years ago that your guards company came to our rescue, after the diplomatic journey into Orcassia?"

"Twelve," grunted Khazumar, reluctantly allowing the familiarity of the forearm grip, a custom of the elves that he had never really accepted.

"I see you have not changed, my friend. But you should not hold the Marshal responsible for the loss of your son. We are all soldiers or diplomats serving our peoples. Your son fell bravely defending that ravine, as did many elves."

Khazumar grunted again and pulled the hand free.

"You decided upon the diplomatic journey to organise a treaty with those scum, and it cost my company their lives," Khazumar spat bitterly. "I recall that barely five of your people died that day, and that Orcish commander Igluk was set free by your Marshal to further aide your mission. What you decided was for the best for your people, not for ours. My son died for nothing because Igluk organised the ambush that would have been avoided, had we executed that foul creature there and then. I suggest you seek forgiveness elsewhere and refrain from referring to me as a friend. I am not! Now stand aside. I require to speak to Kollis."

Without further ado the dwarf roughly pushed past Aarun, to gasps and whispers of anger. On recognising Kollis, he quickly closed on his colleague, who for a moment seemed completely terrified. Cappa pondered this momentarily and wondered just who this new dwarf really was. To command the Priesthood Guards was clearly a high position within their society. However, in his discipline, deserting your command was punishable by death. So why had he taken it upon himself to travel, instead of sending a messenger? This would indeed be an interesting discussion.

Without waiting on protocol, Khazumar began to speak to Kollis, in their rough language, as an equal. Behind the Roman faction Marcellus, who had for the last few weeks tried to learn as much of the language as possible, translated the words that could be understood.

It was only at this point that Cappa suddenly realised that every group here spoke a different language, and yet they had all been able to speak to one another without any translators. Full of wonder he glanced at Aarun, who seemingly understood his searching gaze and smiled. Well, however it was done, it was almost certainly his doing that they all now discussed freely and understood each other. But the next question was: Why was Khazumar different?

Of course the question soon evaporated, as the discussion between the two Lords became heated to the point that Khazumar struck violently towards Kollis' head, knocking him to the floor. They both now had the full attention of the entire camp. Anger flourished as several dwarven warriors stepped forward, but Kollis ordered them back.

Standing, this politically powerful, yet physically weak, politician staggered away while Khazumar glared at the departure with open hatred. Turning on his heels, Khazumar now moved to leave but found Aarun directly in his path.

"Move or be moved!" demanded the Dwarf.

Cappa flinched as the words suddenly made sense again. How? Oh, never mind, he thought slowly. What in fire's name was going on?

"I have a proposition for you, Khazumar."

"I am not interested in your heathens. I have heard of the rumours and it is blasphemy against our Gods. They are of no use to me."

"You have already stated that the Caves of Azar-Kad are in danger, and yet you refuse an offer of help. The reinforcements are not here, my friend…"

"I told you not to use that ref..."

"Yes, yes, I heard you the first time. But there is a force here that can move now to your assistance. We have two hundred warriors ready to go to the caves from here, if only you choose to ask. In a few more days a much larger force can follow. I will organise my personal guards along with any other dwarven factions that we find, and march them to the caves as well. With the Prince in Thoria I assume you have news of an impending attack?"

Khazumar nodded.

"Well?" Cappa asked irritably.

"The Orcassians have amassed an army of unknown numbers along the Noborian river forts and, even though my scouts confirmed this, the Prince has ignored all my warnings. Now two of the forts are opposed and under threat of a siege, and for the last seven days nobody has been able to ascertain what is going on. It is obvious that raiding parties must be across the river."

"Then take our aid, Lord Khazumar," offered Atronius. "As commander of the Army of Allegiance, I will place Cappa in command of the contingent that Lord Aarun spoke of and send those men back with you immediately. And I pledge on my word of honour that we will follow with a larger force seven days hence."

"I have no need of your men, but should they wish to accompany my troops then I cannot stop you, as you have the freedom of the northern peninsular, as commanded by Kollis. But do not expect any of my warriors to assist you. We will rest now and march at dawn."

With these last words Khazumar again stormed away, but found a brief moment to throw a glance of hatred towards the Marshal. It was returned with an equally venomous glare. There did not seem to be much room for forgiveness in either of them, and Aarun sighed resignedly.

"I wish things could have been different, but our destinies are already written," he said, glancing after the departing dwarf.

"Such is the wont of the Gods, my Lord," comforted Cappa.

"The Gods? No, my friend. A greater power than the Gods has caused our fates to be encased in reality. Once, long ago, that was not the case. No, on this occasion the Gods are blameless, but not so for many other things. But we shall discuss this another time. Your Primus has given you a task. Can you fulfil it? Khazumar will do nothing to assist you."

"I can and so can the men assigned. It will be good to be active again. I already feel as if this cane is unnecessary," Cappa responded indignantly, his pride stung by the hint of doubt in Aarun's voice.

"Belief me," said Aarun, with a twinkle in his eyes, "by tomorrow it will be."

⸻

Igluk rose with a start, pushing aside the wench and rising in one swift movement. All the hair on his head stood on end, creating an unnatural aura that made all those nearby move away. The wench was perhaps that little bit slower, due to her lethargy. The dream had been as real to him as only reality itself could be, and the blade arched across the hut in wild, slashing cuts. Someone cried in agony, briefly, but he did not notice. He was on automatic. He was back in battle!

The memory of the ambush, so long ago, slowly faded and his vision returned to the present. All around him those that had shared this hut gathered at the far end, and a look of fear and hatred stared back at him defiantly. At his feet lay a prone corpse minus a head, which had inadvertently rolled across the room to lie at the others' feet. It was the wench that he had only moments earlier rutted with, and had now cast aside in as permanent a way possible. He felt nothing. It was good to kill. It always had been.

The old scrolls told of magic beginnings, in which his people had been created by the black arts, but he no more believed this than he understood that an orc loves to sunbathe! Besides, rutting had its advantages.

For a moment he engaged the looks of horror and dared anyone to challenge. When he was certain none would do so, he returned to his straw and began to ponder the dream. It was as if he had been taken back to the valley where he had been killing the dwarves that had captured him so long ago. He recalled one in particular that had fought so valiantly. He had at first considered letting the warrior live, but in a flash he had changed his mind and ordered his archers to shoot, having lost five orcs already. So vivid, so real, that he could smell the blood lust that had set off his reaction earlier. But why would it return now?

He had never felt remorse for anything, and as with most orcs he had only a short-term memory, which lasted barely a month. Unless a specific event occurred that burned a certain memory into his head, there was little chance he would remember the death of one pathetic dwarf over so many others.

Now, after his acquaintance with the Mage, their new *ally*, he had experienced more and more memories of long past deeds. He felt no emotional reaction, but feared that perhaps he was going insane. No, somehow he knew that he would know if his head had fallen, or his brain roasted. No, it had something to do with what the Mage had done to him a week ago. Yes, most definitely, then he had been only a clan chieftain, while now he commanded an entire army. How could such a change occur so swiftly? It had to be the Mage, but how?

So many questions ran around in his head where they had no right to be, but no answers accompanied them. Who could give him answers? At the moment nobody, but perhaps one day he would visit the great goblin-chief at the goblin lairs in Gobli. He would give him answers, for a price of course. For a price.

Igluk dropped back to sleep, but instead of a wench he now held his broadsword across his chest. It was always a good thing to be careful when within the horde. If they did not try to kill you to take your place, then they were just as likely to kill you to take your straw. It was every orc for himself and he had no intention of joining the wench just yet.

Thankfully no more memories came to haunt his sleep.

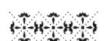

PART SEVEN

AZAR-KAD

Within an hour of the order to break camp the lower chieftains had aroused the masses. One by one the tents and temporary accommodations were torn down, some for future use, but most were burnt to deny the enemy their use. Not that any dwarf or elf would have even entered an orc hut, mind you, let alone reside there, but this was unusually efficient for the orcs.

This enemy now stood only a stone's throw away, across the Noborian River. One by one the masses began to organise themselves into small factions, which then in turn merged to create regiments. Never before had such a large body of orcs moved with such precision and purpose. No longer were they a simple horde hell-bent on death and destruction, for these creatures now understood many concepts that had previously been beyond their comprehension. Brotherhood, loyalty, bravery for honour, personified by Igluk's own rise to command within this very army.

Everything was slowly changing, but changing nevertheless. They could almost sense the air of desperate fear sweeping across the despised dwarven kingdom. The goblin successes in Thoria, the absence of the Gretans and the sudden alliances threatening the lower elven kingdoms were not mere coincidences. Even to orcs it was obvious that something more powerful than they could imagine was brooding over each tiny step, and moving with an insight and patience that had forced it to wait a millennium for the right opportunity. A few more years were of no significance.

To them it was a power to be feared, but also to be embraced as an ally. If they obeyed, then they had nothing to concern themselves with, other than the death of Dwarmania and the killing of elves. After all it was they, the elves and not the orcs, that had stolen the breeding grounds. They, the dwarves and not their brethren, had stolen the goblin's homeland. Why should they talk of peace!

However, the hatred and malevolence emanating from the power was also felt by all of them. They knew without asking that the power would just as happily consume them, as it intended to consume the dwarves and elves in the fires of Tatamus. War was their real God, but in reality who was moving the pieces in this puzzle, and to what purpose? To the average orc, this was of little importance, but to those elevated above, to Igluk, this issue was fast becoming far more important.

As they passed, the marching regiments dared not look upon Igluk directly, fearing reprisals, so they glanced slyly towards the command tent, perhaps seeking a glimpse of this new kind of orc: a leader who could take them to victory, rather than celebrating while thousands of the horde lay slain in a field no one cared to name.

The power of life and death resided with him directly, but the Mage's power itself was there forever, standing in his shadow, never allowing the leash to stretch too far. At first, they questioned why he in particular had been chosen from out of the thousands that now strove to reach the river before the forts could be reinforced. Then, after a spate of strange disappearances, the inquisitive amongst them had wisely chosen to look elsewhere for their answers. It had certainly helped to extend their lives.

Amongst them also marched the hated goblins and gnomes, yet to date their natural mistrust had not fuelled too much conflict. So how did such loyalty emanate from such enemies? Even Igluk had wondered about this phenomenon at first, but there was little purpose in dwelling on an issue that to him now seemed inevitable. He was after all born to lead. So why, or more to the point, how, did he ascertain the best way to retain the cohesion of such a vast number of his brethren, as well as the vainglorious goblins and the thieving gnomes?

Simple really, the promise of future glory kept the goblins happy, and the opportunity to pillage, kill and maim somehow overruled any common sense the gnomes might have, and thus they saw little else worthwhile in their miserable existence other than to obey the goblin king. His brethren only needed to be told of an impending death march for the elves and they would flock to the strongest chief, i.e., him! They needed little encouragement, but the recent defeat in Thoria had left his people more fractious than normal. Only the desire to do what an orc did best kept them together: a mutual desire to see the world of the elves and dwarves fall into ruin. They had destroyed the orc world, and now it was the orcs' turn to destroy what the elves and dwarves loved most, their freedom!

Only a few days ago, Igluk had decapitated a lower-chieftain's offspring after rutting. Many thought Igluk had gone too far, but no orc or goblin challenged his status and even the act of execution, with no fear of retribution, now seemed to be within his powers. His people had no freedom to speak of, so why should any elf? They did not deserve happiness, as they only abused it. No, better for them to serve Orcassia as slaves, then my people will have their revenge.

They all wondered how such a lowly chieftain as Igluk had risen to such prominence. He had shown no great ability, was hated rather than feared by the masses, and his only claim to greatness was the destruction of the elven embassy many years earlier, which in truth most of those now present had no true recollection of. So what favours had been offered in exchange for this power? More important, to whom had the favours been offered?

All of this and more the orcs pondered as they passed that creature on the hill. Did their demise encompass any such promise? It was hard for them to determine anything and yet ponder they did, until the captains noted the glances and reset their priorities with a vicious sword swipe, killing one or two as examples.

On the hill Igluk watched with a deep pride, or as close as an orc could reach to such high emotions, as the enormous orka regiments strode past with their shields and armour gleaming brightly, each company in perfect unison and in the necessary position to assist immediate deployment. Swords crashed against the large shields in salute as they passed and a loud chant boomed across the valley. Magnificent, he thought.

Magnificent!

How could he possibly fail with over one thousand such warriors to whom the enemy had nothing to compare? For him, the rumours of the *new arrivals* would be found to be a fabrication designed by the Dwarves to cause delays and hesitation. Even though he had received direct orders from the Mage only last evening, to execute all mortalkind that he found, Igluk secretly ignored the rumours, which had now seemingly become delirious ramblings, of a higher hierarchy.

Romans indeed, ridiculous!

With a deep, ominous growl he acknowledged the next in line to leave, the feared Regiments of Doom, goblins. These were the largest in this vast army and they terrified Igluk's own personal guard. To them pride was as much an issue as it was for Igluk, but they had been trained for many years before they even marched to any frontier to fight. Now this transfer to a backwater front had tarnished their reputation, as many in their ranks believed that this move was due to some failure that none could remember.

Igluk knew this to be a lie but used it to advantage, by fuelling it in the hope that they would fight more vehemently. A good intuitive plan, he thought, until it had backfired only yesterday, when an unfortunate comment by an orc had led to a brief skirmish that left fifty orcs slain.

When counted, only three goblins had suffered the same fate and, as a consequence, the Doom marched a good league away from the nearest orc column to avoid any repetition.

They were hardly as unified as at first believed, but this was nevertheless the first time that such columns had openly cooperated. It was a concern, but Igluk had deliberately placed the orka in between them and the orcs, with orders to destroy any participants in any future confrontation. So far, so good.

As the Doom goblins moved ahead into the middle distance, he watched with some confusion, trying to understand the goblin race. The Doom was not of the norm! He knew that the Mage, a soothsayer known to have the ear of the *Master*, had said that they were from the same stock and had, millennia ago, actually shared the same homeland, orcs above ground, goblins beneath. He spat, as the thought of such a heritage sickened him. It was almost as good to kill a goblin as it was to kill a dwarf or even an elf, the latter being preferred.

He knew them to be afraid of the light, although they could bear a few hours under extreme circumstances, but generally they preferred tunnels under the mountains and forests. He wondered just how much these goblins owed their abilities to that of the Mage who, as always, appeared and disappeared with such ease that it always left Igluk feeling exposed and vulnerable, which was, no doubt, the reaction intended.

Those within the Doom Regiments, however, walked free in the sunlight and wore black armour as their emblem, and had a reputation for barbaric mutilation of their enemy, of which the unfortunate orcs the day before were proof. Here no sunshades were needed and in the light of the sun these creatures made him feel sick. His own people did not favour river washing but these scum barely even understood the concept of a wash, even before rutting! They were foul, but perhaps if Igluk could have seen his own people, the light of cleanliness would hardly have shone brightly. They were an army of beasts, more concerned with the sharpness of their blades than with their cleanliness. They came to fight and fight they would, with or without Igluk's permission. Now his job was just to point them in the right direction and let their instinct for killing take over. Victory was assured, the glory was already his, and nothing could stop them...Not even the mortalkind!

As the last of the Doom marched past, their banner was held low. He knew that act symbolised the shame of the goblins, and the Doom commander's wrath that they had not killed more orcs in the argument the day before. It was a calculated insult and a bitter sign of disrespect, and was well noted by Igluk. However, the Doom leader was just an individual, who at most was needed for the moment but could be dealt with later. Now the greater task had to take priority.

It was indeed difficult at times to understand on which side these heathens stood.

The *Great One*, or *Master* as the Mage often referred to *him*, must also question their loyalties, and this made him feel all the more adamant that he would act when the time was right. For now he would obey and follow the rules set by the Mage, but sooner or later his opportunity would rise and he would not hesitate to bring his people out of the mire to the power they richly deserved. He would also have the Doom commander's head mounted on a pole.

"Prepare my baggage," Igluk snapped, as the first Orcassian regiments passed below the hill, their garments shabby at best. "Has Bohemoth arrived?"

"Yes, Master," replied the guard, who then motioned to one side at a tall goblin wearing the standard black uniform of an officer of Doom Fortress.

"You are aware of your task?" Igluk said, raising his voice.

Bohemoth turned slowly and nodded, scant acknowledgement in the expression, never mind respect.

"Good. I want the caves of Azar-Kad destroyed beyond recognition. I want every martyr, every statue, and every example of high blood that these dwarves have ever created and honoured destroyed. I want the blood of their culture stained for all time. Failure is not an option. I assume you understand?"

"Yes, the objective is well noted. What troops will be assigned to my command, great leader?" Bohemoth asked, mockingly bowing low and grimacing as he recalled the warning given to him by a colleague.

What threat was this fool to him, Bohemoth of Doom Fortress!

Of course Igluk was swift to acknowledge the insult, and even before anyone could react he had closed both hands around the goblin's throat.

"SSSsssss...Mock me, will you, you filth of Hades' hole. I have been given the seal of Hades..." Igluk noted the look of horror on the goblin's face at the mention of the seal, relishing the power that it gave him, and then, satisfied that the effect had regained obedience, slowly released his grip. "I am the supreme commander of this army and you will be respectful or die! Choose!"

The goblin backed away a few paces and instinctively motioned for his personal guard to close ranks around his personage. They did so but knew from experience that anyone with the seal would also know magic of one sort or another. Bohemoth was their respected leader but he was not worth dying for needlessly, especially when the opportunity to step into his shoes might present itself.

"I naturally choose to live, honoured holder of the seal," he eventually said, his backing down well noted by all the lower chieftains present. "But I ask to see this for...myself."

With a flashy motion of the wrist Igluk produced the seal, which only he knew to be a fake. All about them the revered seal of approval and the sign of absolute power brought most of the guards to their knees. Soon only the two antagonists remained standing. Meanwhile far away the Mage smiled at such theatrics, for he knew the seal to be true and perhaps Igluk doubted its authenticity more than Bohemoth. This amused the great manipulator. It amused the Master.

"I am yours to command," Bohemoth stated obediently, as he finally dropped to one knee. Even he would not dare oppose a holder of the seal.

"That was never in doubt, you fool. Now, to answer your impudent question, which you would be wise to rephrase in future: You will take your own regiment, plus two more of your standard goblins. Three more Orcassian regiments will also be assigned to you, including an entire group of archers. For mobility and scouts I have assigned a regiment of gnomes riding our wolves. They will move ahead of your column and the main army to bring news of reinforcements that will no doubt be sent sooner or later, from further inside the enemy empire. Finally, half a regiment of orka will be assigned to you, but they will act independently of you as they have their own orders from another source."

"When do I leave?" Bohemoth asked, now eager to proceed without delay, as his shame at having kneeled now brought forward further dangerous impulses to strike this impudent orc down. He fought hard to control the urge then..."I foresee only one problem. My commander, Bollak, will stop the splitting of the Regiments of Doom. He will execute me for desertion. How do I deal with that?"

"Kill him and assume overall command," Igluk snapped, with a relish that almost caused a smile, if smile was the right word. "In fact kill him anyway and assume overall command, I require your standard to be raised once more. I have no time for further delays. When we cross the Noborian River only half of the army will be placed in full view of the enemy. This way they will never suspect a full invasion, but prefer to look upon us as only a large raiding party. I will lay siege to the two designated forts for three days, thus drawing all their reserves towards me and leaving your route to those caves open. On the fourth day, I will leave a force to continue the sieges, but with the remainder I will proceed into their nearest province and begin to destroy everything in my path. If the mortalkind exist, they will be forced to stand against this campaign. Is this understood?"

"It is, great leader."

"Then you need not remain here any longer, slug. Be gone before I choose another fool to lead the raid!"

Wincing once again, Bohemoth moved swiftly down the hill and launched himself in the air to land on the back of an unfortunate pony.

From the hilltop, Igluk again turned back to watch the procession roll across the valley before his eyes. He felt again that surge of pride, and the desire for power was almost overwhelming.

"So far so good," he said, rubbing his hands together. "So far so good."

"Uh, sorry, master?" a nearby guard replied, not fully hearing his words.

"What!"

"Uh, I didn't quite catch what you said then. Do you require…"

"Shut up!"

"Y Y Yo…" The guard began, while taking a discreet step backwards as he remembered the earlier punch on the nose.

"You are learning," Igluk declared, incredulously, laughter in his eyes. "I have witnessed yet another…*miracle*."

The last word was spat out with a vengeance and with the purpose of spraying spittle over the guard. On this success, Igluk turned and walked back towards the table where several maps now lay under heavy bowls of fruit. Engrossed in whatever had now become essential, Igluk failed to see the look of glee on the guard's face. Spittle was a lot better than a broken nose!

⁂

They left the city of Lo at dawn, as stated by Lord Khazumar after a very brief conference to re-affirm who would march at the head of the column. Naturally his people demanded this honour. As anticipated, the pace was furious and Khazumar kept his word of offering no help.

As on the previous evening, the dwarf's manners were short and brief. Then, with no further ado, he mounted the nearest pony, a dapple-grey, brought forward by one his four companions, and the march began. All morning they advanced step by painful step. At noon Cappa ordered a halt and the dwarves reluctantly agreed but refused to remain at the camp. Instead they roamed the hills and valleys and recruited anyone left behind who cared to defend their most sacred of places at the caves. They returned with fifty or more warriors of varying age but they asked no questions and took all. None were deferred due to their age or health. All were needed, none spared. Cappa had started to prepare a fossa and palisade. Issus had then laughed and pointed in all directions. This was supposedly friendly land, and the Roman consternation made the barbarians laugh harder.

At first it stung their pride and pulled at their nerves, and Cappa had to fight to maintain order, but Khazumar just frowned and continued without stopping to concern himself with the bitterness of the Romans.

Eventually Khazumar, no longer able to hold his temper, demanded to know why such lack of discipline existed in the Roman ranks. He received in reply a stony wall of silence, but no further fossa would be dug and many exhaled a great sigh of relief. It would be hard enough keeping up with the dwarves, never mind digging fortifications every time they stopped!

As they marched, Cappa spoke with Marcellus and began to learn a little more about the world they had seemingly adopted. Marcellus could throw no real facts into the talk about why they were here, but the teacher's incisive mind did give Cappa's a little peace. Marcellus advised that, even before his own recovery, the blacksmiths had adapted some of the dwarven tools to enable them to build shields, swords and spears.

Helmets and armour had proven a little more difficult, but only that morning those already produced had been freely handed out to the men supporting Lord Khazumar. It was a true mark of how efficient the legion, or even a cohort, was regarding the impedimenta of war. Even when transported to a new, unknown world, the professionals still found ways to replicate the tools of their trade. Every single hour more and more equipment was being produced in the foundries, and within a very short space of time the entire cohort was similarly armed with scutum, pilum, gladius and cuirass. This example of Roman efficiency was not ignored and talk began of arming dwarves and elves in the Roman fashion. It would take some time to create a new legion, but at this juncture Atronius saw this as a chance to keep his men's minds occupied, and so he agreed.

For Cappa's column, the pace of the march had ended further talk, as exhaustion began to take its toll and they concentrated on keeping everyone together. This was going to be a harsh lesson in speed marching.

It was also a march of nightmares and few would forget the ever-forceful will of Khazumar that drove them forward, relentlessly. None had recovered fully but the choices were simple, recover now or fall by the wayside and be left behind. Many stumbled, some fell, but always they picked themselves up and found more energy from a depth inside that Cappa considered mystifying. To him the task was one of pride and to not let the legion down by falling to one side, but in truth these men marched to save but one person's pride, and that was Cappa's. Of course Khazumar was quick to identify this loyalty and noted how, whenever he closed with this captain, the nearest men quickly rose and formed a protective semi-circle within striking range of the dwarf. Such devotion was rare, even amongst his people, and the first step towards mutual respect developed.

Minute by minute Khazumar's own energy began to fail, but still he pushed on regardless and not once did a word of defiance or anger at his merciless orders pass anyone's lips. Hour by hour Khazumar began to forget his differences with these so-called mortalkind. He found it an unusual reference anyway as he himself was mortal, or so he considered, so the name in itself was confusing. The threat to his beliefs, real or imagined, as regards the Romans diminished with every league, but he could not ignore the obvious assumption that everything they knew would change forever.

An event such as this magical appearance of several thousand persons hardly left them with room to fathom whether the arrival would alter their way of life: it was as obvious as the dawn. What worried him was the price of their continued cooperation. Why would they be here and who brought them? These matters he would discuss later, but for now his exhaustion eventually broke down the final barriers, and by dusk Cappa, Issus and Khazumar all moved together, the latter having given up the luxury of the pony and taken to walking. The scouts quickly took his pony for their own as they continued to roam far and wide.

As they marched, Khazumar chanced to remark on the efficiency of the Romans, who rarely broke formation even in the rough terrain. On seeing Cappa's blatant surprise and pleasure at such a comment, he also mentioned that this was the lowland of the Azar-Kad mountain range!

Of course they were not the kind to cower from any adversity, but the outcrop of the lower ridges that they followed the next morning was to test their resolve to breaking point. Accustomed to the mountain ranges, most of the dwarves did not find it difficult, and even the old and infirm seemed to cope. This alone was sufficient to drive the men harder, not that they needed any real incentive as Marcellus pointed North to a blizzard forming at the higher peaks.

At a minimum, they would suffer hail and rain and a bitter wind to freeze their bones. To avoid this, the legionaries actually overtook the dwarves on several occasions, much to Khazumar's surprise.

As Marcellus passed Cappa on one such occasion, they both paused for a brief rest and looked once more towards the gathering storm.

"Do you see what I see?" Marcellus asked.

"I am not sure."

"The clouds, they seem to be following us and the colour, Centurion...they are a deep blue?"

Cappa raised a hand to Marcellus' shoulder. "If anyone is able to answer why the clouds are more blue than the sky, I assume it is you, friend. For now, however, this climb will be the death of me unless I use all my bones to reach these caves."

Marcellus grinned. "I guess that little issue could wait for later. However, I do wish Crassus was here."

"Crassus...Why?"

"I could do with stealing his wine."

Cappa laughed. "I somehow do not think he would willingly give it to the likes of us, but the thought is well received. Perhaps at the caves?"

"Yes, to the caves it is, in the hope that they have at least something for us to drink."

Cappa could only laugh again as Marcellus walked ahead of the column, singing an old tavern drinking song. It was quickly taken up by most of the men, and Khazumar was again mystified as to how these Romans once more overtook him. Cappa simply beamed with pride as he marched past the stupefied dwarf.

On and upwards became the familiar cry, and they did just that as they passed a height that only Marcellus could judge. For many leagues, they could see the lights of fires within small villages, while in the distance a city of unknown proportions stood out on the bank of a major river, running horizontal to their view of the south. It was a magnificent diversion and for a few hours more they trudged ever upwards to the summit of the current ridge, for a brief rest. The beauty of this land became their constant companion.

Here a few broken conversations from dawn were renewed, as the sight before them created an air of nostalgia. The mountain of Azad brought to the fore memories of their own hills of Roma, the seven mounds that had created the very essence of the city. Many had never actually been there, but the phenomenon was well known and respected. Now, before them, stood what Khazumar called the "Toes of Azad," where lay the entrance to the western side of the caves.

On the far side, at the "Toes of Kad," on a series of five mounds, stood their main defences, where it was feared an attack would occur at any moment. They were given barely an hour's rest. Cappa tried in vain to force a further delay to allow energy levels to rise, but the dwarf was formidable and once more turned bitterly to the boasts made by Lord Aarun.

"Bah! March to our assistance, he said. March at dawn, he said," Khazumar raged, once more astride the pony. "You cannot even reach the foot of the western entrance, when there are still another ten leagues to go under the mountain itself. What good will you be on the eastern side if you cannot stand now! By then you will be *useless!*"

So ended the tirade of abuse. So ended Cappa's patience, and he turned to Marcellus and Porta with an evil squint.

"Any man who slows down now I will personally throw over the cliff edge," he said coldly. "We march and we march to beat these irritable sons of Hades and show just how much we can march and fight. To your posts, we do not stop until we reach the western gates."

And so it was that, much to Khazumar's amazement, his dwarves were left behind in the continued march to the western gates. Once more he fell into a confused silence, unable to fathom just who these people really were, or indeed what they meant to his people. He confessed in private that he would use them to save the caves, but beyond that he saw no purpose to their deaths other than that they would mean that less of his people would die. A pang of guilt riddled his mind and he hesitated once more. Had he degenerated so far as to now feel the same coldness as an orc? Would he kill a child orc without mercy? Had this war changed him so much?

He knew these questions must wait, as always, but for a few moments he relaxed his vigil and allowed his anger to dissipate. It had been a long time since he had been able to refer to any person as a friend. Now one person, Marcellus, had made such inroads regarding their language that he no longer had to revert back to the commoner tongue to communicate. It was of course a side effect of Aarun's language incantations, but it was no less impressive to see his rate of learning and his understanding of what he was being taught. Indeed it was impressive in all of these people, whether he believed in their origins or not.

Pushing his thoughts to one side, he now considered the real situation, as the last messenger had advised him of it only an hour earlier. The bedraggled warrior had already ridden three such trips in just one day and his torn red overalls and cloak indicated the hardship of each successive journey. He smiled to note that such devotion to duty would see a rapid rise through the ranks for this youth if he managed to survive, but the smile ebbed slowly as the message once again proved more important than the messenger.

A vast horde had already been sighted, to the south, besieging the Noborian river forts. Reports indicated that the local militia commander had already taken five thousand dwarves to try and relieve these posts, only to be in turn incarcerated within their walls, minus a bitter toll of lives. Other reports had suggested, but not confirmed, that another force had, as feared, been dispatched to destroy the caves and the Kings' Tombs within. Numbers could not be known until confirmed, but the priesthood there numbered only approximately five hundred. Hardly an army!

Khazumar called another brief stop to collect his thoughts. The air had turned bitter and cold, but the refreshing bite did indeed empty his mind. The concentration needed to ignore the bite was soon redirected to seeing into the eyes of an enemy, a skill that he had learnt well many years earlier. There was nothing really to evaluate. The enemy would almost certainly have dispatched someone to the caves. The question was how many, and of what quality were they in comparison to his people?

As his head raced another thought suddenly emerged to add more doubt. For the first time ever a force was comprised of both orcs and goblins, while a third unknown race, believed to be trolls, also ran with this horde. The hobgoblins, or gnomes as the orcs called them, were also present and, unlike on all previous occasions, they cooperated under one leader, rather than by mutual agreement to be at the said battlefield on the right day. This changed everything, and he wondered if any of his people at the caves had acknowledged this previously unknown aspect of this renewed attack? He would have to find his answers later, but to see these hated enemies standing together made his heart sink.

Waving nonchalantly at a colleague to indicate that the rest was over, he rose once more to continue the journey. They began once more to move, but the pace was barely short of a run. Soon the hills bottomed out into a broad valley at least a league wide, where small groups of dwarves could be seen marching with a purpose towards the very gates that marked the first stage of their own journey. Without a word they recognised Khazumar and fell in behind the legionaries, easily falling into step, and even somewhat annoyed at the slower pace. On they marched until their legs burned and the bones ached to a point beyond belief. Some allowed tears of agony to roll down their faces to seek a release, but most soaked up the pain and channelled it into their anger at an enemy they had yet to meet.

Then they reached the gates. Oh joys of joy, their muscles screamed for a rest, but even here there was to be no relief.

The sounds of battle rebounded from the cavern, causing several men to cover their ears. The sensation was temporary and illusionary, as the echoes emanated from beneath the mountain. The distraction of a pause followed, fleetingly, then once more the all-consuming pace of the march. They had travelled at a speed completely unfamiliar to the legionaries, who were no strangers to the long march, but after two days of solid marching even Khazumar looked drawn and exhausted, but there was no time to rest just yet.

Not a single member of any of the factions involved in this column had collapsed on the road to the Western Gate, but, even so, every member of it, including Cappa, was on the brink of physical exhaustion. Nevertheless, on they must go, for now they were close enough to hear the echoes of battle. Rising before them stood the darkness of the tunnels, broken by the torches of the guides and those on the walls.

With a face like thunder, Cappa pushed them on through the gates, then noted their growing number. Two hundred legionaries, one hundred of Issus' warriors and the dwarven factor had brought their total to well over six hundred. All and more would be sorely needed at the Eastern Gate, if they arrived in time. The last effort under the mountain was to prove the hardest portion of a journey that would remain in their memories for the remainder of their lives.

With an angry gesture, Cappa motioned for Porta to raise a small band that had, for the first time, been slow to respond to his urgent calls to move on. Grumbles came thick and fast, but still they moved, still they entered the gate. Without a word, everyone formed ranks as a single mass and began to trudge forward. With a nod from Cappa, Issus immediately took his scouts forward at a trot and within a few minutes they had vanished into the darkness with torches and a few guides. They all needed rest, but the task ahead required an immediate march and Cappa had swiftly realised that to allow these men time to think would result in their refusal to proceed. So far there had been no desertions, but they had as yet to meet the creatures described by Aarun as *Orcs*. There was no reliable way of telling just how they would react when confronted with a mythical creature that even the most devoutly religious did not believe existed. *Could* not exist!

That was yet another obstacle to look forward to with relish!

Now they had passed through the cavern opening, with the guards, standing ten feet high on the palisades, watching in fascination. Occasionally the word *mortalkind* drifted over to them but this they mainly ignored, as the column proceeded into the tunnel by torchlight.

"*Double pace!*" Cappa ordered, once more looking to Porta and Marcellus, who both immediately fell back along the column and prodded a few of the lazy.

As the pace increased, Cappa could not hide a smile as Porta's jokes and jibes floated back and forth, while several replies were beyond repeating, but it kept them all moving. Marcellus had his own way of pushing the men on but, even at this extreme, he began to repeat dwarven words of encouragement, and the warriors to the rear began to chant an unknown melody of war.

The procession slowed only for a moment as they entered the main cavern and for a few seconds the guides became disorientated, which was not surprising as, even with torches, the roof of the cavern was lost in the darkness. Shields, spears and swords jostled together in a rhythmic tune recognised by the legionaries, whilst Issus had returned with a little information on the path ahead, and now moved in almost abject silence. Khazumar's own guides had merged with several other individuals of all sizes, leaving most of them with a few questions as regards their lineage.

At first glance, the dwarves seemed small in stature, yet several of the new arrivals were of a similar height. It was known that the Westonians had bred with local elves, but these always had the distinctive ears of the half-breed, and these dwarves did not. That would be an issue for later, one that Cappa stored in his memory as he returned to the task in hand, wiping sweat from his eyes.

At such a pace, they missed the grandeur and majesty of the cave of tombs, which had been subdued in the flickering shadows for hundreds of years. Some would be permitted no second opportunity, while others would accept none, but either way the stamp of marching feet offered a show of their respect for these great martyrs. They would all fight for their preservation in a war in which Cappa did not understand their role or purpose. He would nevertheless fight, as this was his only way of dealing with the entire predicament. Too often he had lain awake at night to ponder why he was here and not anywhere else. Why him and why his comrades? Why only this little representation of his world and not the remainder of humanity?

The dilemma created an endless list of questions! However, in the usual way of the world, there would be no more time, which had become a luxury none of them could any longer afford. No more time for doubts or hesitation. To survive they must act now, but he had no intention of giving up until he knew the answers to his questions. Sooner or later he would *know*!

The final leagues took the last of their energy and, with heads bowed, they emerged into the light once more, at the Eastern Gate. Their time had come at last. Here Khazumar moved among them and shouted, for all to hear, to let them know what stood before them, and the strengths and weaknesses of all the creatures they would face. He did this for his own people's benefit, as many were farmers who had never been in full battle, while he had permitted the infirm to choose to stand elsewhere at a certain point during the battle to follow. The Romans also watched this dispersal, but it was not for them to question, only to obey. They would stand because Cappa had said so.

The speech ended and Khazumar vanished into the light and took his dwarves with him.

Cappa prepared for the emotional terror to come when they met these orcs, and then ordered his men forward. His own emotions were surprisingly absent, while his thoughts raged: what exactly were they about to face? He thought back to his mother and sought comfort in remembering her untold hundreds of stories about evil creatures that would claim his heart if he was unkind. But this served only to recall memories of long nights beneath the blanket, terrified of the shadows.

He glanced to either side and saw the stony resolve of the nearest men waver occasionally, and as one man faltered a colleague would push from behind, leaving the front rank little choice but to continue. He knew their fears as well as his own, but he also knew how rigid their training had been and that, if nothing else, loyalty to him and to the legion, and the added discipline, would keep them together. It had been ingrained into their minds that together they could survive while, on the battlefield, the individual perished very swiftly. Quite a few had already seen this and while the legionary was an effective weapon on an individual basis, it was the constant cooperation that made them truly deadly.

Cappa quietly looked for the original members who had stood on the hill above the fort. One or two he recognised, but of all the main people only Porta, Marcellus and Julius could be seen, the latter standing content in the front rank. Other names sprang forward but he could not match faces to names, although the exercise served to distract him further as they moved down a slope towards a high palisade that stretched as far as the eye could see, on both flanks. Then he looked beyond the palisade.

At first the creatures could be seen only from a distance, but as they came closer several more men began to backtrack, shaking their heads in disbelief. Terror in a form not previously experienced coursed through their veins and made even the most powerful doubt his vigour. Several barbarians bolted back to the caves and only the stern leadership of Issus made them return. Even then, with courage partially restored, they refused to go beyond the cavern entrance. Cappa set them to work digging ditches and hacking as many spikes as possible from the dead wood lying on the ground. Their last stand would be here, should the palisade fall. Issus meanwhile took charge of those that had remained firm and led them to the left side of their own cylindrical formation, which stood now at closed ranks in the hope of stopping any further desertions.

A great cry of shock and disbelief amongst them almost ended further efforts, and the cohesion in the formation almost evaporated.

It was now the turn of Khazumar's people to be temporarily distracted, while both Cappa and Porta openly began to strike several men who had again tried to break ranks and flee. It was a dangerous moment, to say the least, and, as ever, Cappa rose to the situation to bellow above the din all around them, pointing towards the palisades ahead. If he could not lead them through loyalty, then he would use his last throw of the dice. He would shame them into following him down the slope.

"Who will follow me? Who amongst so many well-armed legionaries has the heart of a true Roman citizen? Who will come with me and return to our arms the glory that Roma demands? I will not stand with any who are weak of heart!" he roared, his face flushed with anger. "Who will follow *me*?" he repeated, drawing his sword.

For a second or two, which felt like an eternity, nobody replied to his hail. The noise momentarily died away into the background and one or two more men took to their heels, but Cappa ignored them. He took a deep breath and was about to try again when finally a voice was heard.

"I *will*!" shouted Porta, who then stepped forward, letting go of a man he had been holding in place, stopping his desertion. "I am not afraid. I believe in our Gods and I will not dishonour the legion! In my honour and in my life I pledge loyalty to the legion and to Centurion *Cappa*!"

"Who *else*?"

Tension shot through the wavering ranks of legionaries. They had been trained to fight the enemies of Roma and now they faced the hell's-spawn that their parents had terrified them with at bedtime when they were children. A few ignored the outburst and continued to bolt, but one by one several groups began to file forward. Some rejoined them, the tactic of shame having had a positive effect.

"These creatures before us are still the enemies of Roma, my friends," Cappa continued, desperately seeking a way to maintain the momentum. "Our brethren, the dwarves, have assigned us a vital mission, to save their holy lands from being despoiled. If this were Roma our wrath would be terrifying to behold. Will you stand with me, or will you allow we few to stand for the honour of Roma?" Several chants began, driving them into frenzy. "Think not of what they look like, my countrymen, but consider whether they would allow us to pass without harm. They are our enemies and our duty on this day is to destroy them. Form ranks!"

"*Form ranks!*" repeated Porta, at the top of his voice.

"*Form ranks!*" bellowed Marcellus, at the other end.

Issus nodded his assent to Cappa and again joined the far left-hand side to bolster their numbers, now with perhaps seventy of his people, more having joined him after Cappa's call for support.

It is hard to know why or how these men suddenly adjusted to their new predicament, but they did so, in a way that left no room for doubt. Never had he felt such a bond between men expressed so openly. They had been snatched away from their loved ones, their homes and their futures and had accepted this as best they could, but now their anger and frustration had found an outlet with the orcs and goblins.

The legion had gone to war once more, not against the expected Helvetii, but against an enemy they knew nothing about. To their anger this was irrelevant, as they would vent their loss on these heathens and hail the Helvetii as brothers in arms. War was their natural business! They renewed their descent down the slope as ordered by Khazumar. Now was their time and not a second too soon!

In the last few days each and every one of them had had to alter his every concept of religion and life in general. It had been far from easy, and along the way several had completely refused to accept this new fate, while one larger group had vanished back into the mountains and refused to ally with anyone, seeking refuge in their own minds but finding only insanity. These factions were now either under heavy guard or watched with some concern in the lowlands further north, and neither had gained the support of the elves or the dwarves. If anything, these people now joined forces with any vagabond that ignored the laws of the land, and in a very short period had organised into roving bands of brigands who preyed on the helpless.

The task of policing the area fell to the elves, but their resources were minimal and the difficulties continued unabated. To the dwarves, they proved beyond doubt that the Romans would bring anarchy to their world. To everyone else, the fact that some could not deal with this world had not been too much of a surprise. However, current circumstances had reduced the importance of that problem.

The fellows now moving with practiced ease had no resemblance to such lowlifes. To them the answer to the question of why they remained loyal lurked in the murky waters of discipline and habit. To most of them their comrades were the only focal point to concentrate on, and to lose them would have been their own doom. So they stayed. They remained also because they *trusted* Cappa. The command structure had changed for the better, and although none of them fully understood what has happened regarding the dimensions, they decided that, for them, the blame rested with these creatures and not their peers. Yes, they would stay and fight and die, so long as they believed in the chances of victory. For the moment this was enough, but even Cappa knew it would not always be the case. Sooner or later further concessions would be needed to retain their loyalty but, as before, other issues now took precedence.

To those present, it felt as though hours had passed and yet in truth only minutes had elapsed. Almost as swiftly as the crisis had developed, the unity of the remainder had returned, and with their pride and honour aroused they marched forward in the standard cylindrical formation, shields touching. When ordered, they expanded out to three paces to either side to allow more freedom for combat, unless a close formation and stabbing approach were desired. The tactics made them all seem larger than perhaps they felt, for as they now crossed the slope towards the Eastern Gate they numbered only three hundred.

Now was a time to stop thinking, and to allow the instincts to resurface. It was time to be once more an integral part of the legion, and to be a legionary. To kill or to die, and perhaps watch a friend die, without breaking formation. Their minds almost achieved a small kind of symbiosis, as they all thought together and acted together as a single unit. Once resigned to their fate, nothing could deter them from their objective...Nothing!

Khazumar watched from the hill immediately to their right and to the south of the Eastern Gate. He and many others saw the advance and wondered just where they intended to go once they had reached the gate. He wondered whether any of them had seen what lay beyond? Khazumar grimaced and wondered if he had after all been correct about the Romans, as he again looked beyond the palisade at the mass of goblins moving forward, and carrying at least six battering rams.

What difference would these Romans make now?

The time for regrets, however, was over and he resigned himself to the last defence that *must* now take place within the caves themselves. One look at the gate indicated its imminent demise, which would allow the swarm behind to trample them all out of the way. No indeed, if they had seen what they were marching towards, he was certain that they would have turned around to hide behind the nearest boulder.

Turning once more to look at the legionaries, he wondered just how he could best use these people. He knew nothing of their fighting prowess and even less about their tactical abilities. His mind raced once more and a brief thought blackened his heart: if these people died fighting, it would mean less for him to deal with in the caves. They wished to make a sacrifice, why should it not be to save some of his people who would otherwise perish defending the broken gate?

"This is going to take some good timing," he said, more to himself than to any companion. "Have the archers converge on the lower slopes of this hill," he added, turning to the nearest messenger. "Then tell Killis to bring over his company to stand before them. They will break the gate with this charge, and we shall see if our ancestors stand with us this day, or perish to preserve what we can. Order all other units to converge on the entrance to the caves, where we will make our final stand."

To either side young messengers, the youths of the guards, swiftly ran off to relay the orders. From the advancing legionaries Cappa watched them go. With a professional eye, like most of the men walking in the same direction, he surveyed the area before them. His eyes beheld a sight that would never dim for the rest of his life, with a clarity that often aroused him from any deep sleep.

Before them stood a mass of creatures that defied description. They could not see them properly due to the distance, but the slope was higher than the palisades, and they could see glimpses beyond the gate.

Cappa noted, as no doubt did the others, that the palisade itself had been drawn too low down the slope and was also compromised by the high hills to the north. It was clearly something that had been created to protect the caves from local vagabonds, not with the presence of mind to defend against a vast army. It made the situation all the more precarious. A few again began to question with their eyes why they were here. A few began to slow their pace, but this time none would be allowed to retire, as Porta and Marcellus, and even Julius, pulled their gladii free of their scabbards. The threat was enough to refocus the men's mind on what lay before them, rather than behind. They perhaps feared their officers more than the enemy, but as long as they fought Cappa did not give a *damn*.

Aarun had been correct in stating that any attempted description would have been pointless, he now realised. They would all need to judge individually of course, but his sword would still be the deciding factor. Once more they faced a decisive and precarious moment as more and more men faltered but, surprisingly, after a little verbal abuse and disagreement, all remained in formation. Stand they would, but would their terror overcome their training? There was only one way to find out, he thought, and it was the best way, the only way.

Cappa allowed one final smile, hidden behind his shield, as he remembered Aarun's reaction when Prince Daxus had accused his people of originating in the fires of hell. The barbarian had then continued to ask why they should not trust those with green skin, when the orcs and goblins were of the same colour? How were they to judge evil from good? That was not too good a start to the relationship between the Helvetii and their benefactors, and the elven Marshall had been close to reacting with violence, while Aarun had simply smiled in his enigmatic disarming way.

He recalled the face of Daxus, who had immediately backed down. Something in the eyes made that elf seem more than his gait implied. This was yet another riddle for him to solve once they survived this day: *if* he survived, of course!

Pulling his thoughts back to the present, his eyes once more roamed the slope, which gently dropped down to the Eastern Gate where it bottomed out to leave the gate high above them. Their pace slackened until a halt was called, now that the far side was no longer in view, and many began to relax. Then, suddenly, everything began to speed up. The first sounds of metal on metal finally reached them through the heavy winds. The bitter screams of the enemy could be heard, if not understood, as the guttural language was unknown.

Then followed the low thump of metal on wood and the gates themselves shuddered and convulsed. One moment, they stood side by side hoping for a brief reprieve, the next they saw the very gates before them split asunder. The time was now upon them and the sight of the denizens of hell did little to increase their resolve, but their resolve they somehow kept. Even if many wished for considerably more numbers they were all used to being outnumbered. Somehow this was different, but there was nobody else.

Here would obviously be the real danger and nobody else was near enough to make a difference. To wait would be suicidal. They must act now and trust in the Gods for guidance and perseverance. They would prevail. They must!

"*Double time!*" came the command. Cappa wiped his short sword on his toga, the habit of a lifetime, and listened with satisfaction as everyone else's blade scraped against their scabbards. This was the sharpest point he had ever managed to place on a blade, and he knew that over the last two days they had all sharpened their edges to the finest cut. Now they would have all the opportunity they required to use that edge. Now they would again kill.

As a single entity, they began to move more swiftly down the slope to the small plain that stood before the damaged doors. As they moved, Cappa glanced to one side where the wall ascended an outcrop of rock covered with light moss and criss-crossed with walkways carved out of the stone. Here he finally sighted Khazumar, at the summit, talking heatedly with another dwarf gowned in a bright red tunic, which clearly signified the guards' uniform. Nothing could be heard of the conversation but clearly the exchange was not between friends. It was of course Killis arguing with Khazumar as to the intended withdrawal.

Cappa glanced away. They could hear quite distinctly the BOOM! BOOM! of the ram and the chanting beyond the gate in a language that somehow sounded familiar, but not too welcoming. At a distance the sound had been unkind to the ears, but this close a rhythmic beat could be discerned.

"Why couldn't they just knock pleasantly?" shouted Marcellus to Cappa.

Cappa grinned. "Manners are short in this dimension as well as in our own, I guess," he replied between breaths. Then, as the gate came within tactical range...

"Halt!"

The word went quickly through the ranks.

"Pilums to the rear!"

Quickly the first two of the four ranks handed back their javelins. Once this was completed, the rear ranks moved back several paces and prepared to launch the projectiles, each having stuck at least eight more into the earth to his right side, for the preferred right arm.

"Porta?" Cappa said, glancing towards the other side of the small plain, where another outcrop of rock protruded from the mountain range that loomed above them all. This was the summit beyond the wall and it stood a good twenty paces higher than the defenders, all of whom had taken to kneeling behind the palisades to avoid almost certain death.

"Take twenty-four men and see if you can find a way to prevent those...creatures from enfilading that wall. If they will follow, take the Dwarves on that side with you and attack the height itself, if you think you can succeed; but do not waste lives. That is the one commodity we need to preserve."

Porta moved with the accustomed speed of one who had finally come home. Cappa could not help but feel a shudder run down his spine, the same feeling he had had at the ambush in the woods. Porta was killing again and somehow that made Cappa uneasy, very uneasy.

They all watched the small detachment march away and for a few moments their progress was of fleeting interest. Then with the sound of splintering wood the door finally gave way, and in a few seconds numerous events took place in swift succession.

First, at the gate the enemy had frozen in blind disbelief at what opposed them on the other side. Expecting Dwarves and an easy finale to their victory, the arrival of the mythical mortalkind had caused them to waver. They had been told they did not exist. Who were they to question their chiefs, but many certainly did so now, but too late to stop, as the great press from behind pushed them forward onto the very swords of the mythical enemy.

Second, to Cappa's right, Khazumar had finally organised the archers and warriors previously collected, and quickly took up station on the small slope at the foot of the outcrop. Here they began to organise themselves, and for the first time they all breathed a sigh of relief. At least that flank was effectively protected. At least these dwarves would stand with them. They were no longer alone!

Then, the third and final event took on the shape of nature renting its fury at the foolish waste of life or, at least, this would have been the romantic's interpretation. To the goblins and orcs at the gate, the thunder and the sudden appearance of black clouds could be interpreted as only one thing, mortalkind magic. To the dwarves, the weather was characteristic of this mountain region, well known for its sudden thunder and lightning storms. The enemy however, whose main ally was superstition, continued to waver in uncertainty, as the dwarves began to crash their shields and raise their battle fury for the struggle ahead, while at the front Cappa remained perfectly calm, along with the legionaries.

At this distance, barely twenty paces, nobody could miss the brutal, ugly facial characteristics of the orc, their tusks rising almost as high as their eyebrows. The size of the goblin was certainly the next item to stand out, and the different shades of green and brown clearly separated the two species, while the howling of wolves outside the gate did little to add to their spirits.

Raising his sword once more, Cappa prepared for the struggle, intending to inflict as much shock on the enemy as possible. If there was one thing he had noticed more than anybody else, it was the shock and horror of the enemy who had initially crossed the threshold. Even with the pressure from behind they still refused to move forward, as the pressure packed them all in tighter than apples in a barrel. They were as unsure of the mortalkind as they were of the orcs and goblins. It was an advantage that must not be wasted.

"Prepare *pilums!*" he shouted, carefully observing the forward elements of goblins that had now regained their courage and taken a few tentative steps forward.

Today they would use the javelins to cause confusion and break up the cohesion of the enemy, and then close to person on person range. Waiting for the right moment to achieve the highest level of effect, Cappa took the opportunity to note the weapons used by the two factions. The orcs seemed to favour the curved sword, some of which looked too long for practical use, a weakness he had exploited effectively against the barbarians at the barricade, because the long blades were not suited to such close proximity. Perhaps the same tactics would also apply here, but only time would tell. The goblins, for the most part, carried axes of enormous size, but as far as he could see very few of either had shields. That would provide yet another advantage, and when he saw the group before him suddenly surge forward, he knew the time had arrived...

Screaming obscenities in a guttural language that nobody else could understand, the goblins sped forwards, looking to smash anything that came within range. Allowing a few seconds for effect, the distance was barely ten paces before the sword was lowered dramatically.

The light became momentarily obscure as the weight of the javelins flew over their heads, over one hundred in all, sailing through the air to search out the sinews and flesh of their targets. As always, the light, sharper projectiles came first, striking the heads and shoulders of the unprotected, while also spreading confusion. With practiced ease, the second wave of heavier pilums landed with a more resounding and sickening thud, as many of the larger goblins began to hack and scream at everything close by, blinded by their agony, with javelins protruding from numerous wounds.

One in particular had a javelin protruding from the throat and yet continued to fight, although in a blinding pain that did not distinguish friend from foe. Yet another tactical note lodged itself in Cappa's little grey cells! Once injured these were as the elephants of Hannibal, a greater danger to themselves than to his own people.

The third and fourth flights had less impact, but on the right Khazumar's archers had begun to fire at point blank range. This had the desired effect and the mass of bodies before them began to waver again, then slowly fall back.

"Now is our time, my friends. Now is our time to take revenge on the scum who caused our loss! Close ranks and advance!"

This was to be Cappa's last direct order for this part of the day, as they moved forward at a slow pace and began their deadly work. As he had anticipated, the orc swords were too large to be used effectively against the closed formation of the legionaries and their heavy cylindrical shields. Hacking and stabbing to wound, Cappa continued to shout *advance*, to allow the men behind to finish off any hostiles that remained alive.

Resistance was at first bitter and full of hatred as the mass of bodies continued to surge forward, but this served only to crush the front ranks into a tiny space and make it easier for the trained professionals to strike with deadly efficiency. In time, Cappa noted that they had almost reached the gate, when suddenly a new threat appeared, as the orcs and goblins split apart, to allow a new formation through the shattered gateway.

For the first time in the history of this world, the *orka* came to battle. They came seeking the blood of their enemies, an enemy they had never met. To them the mortalkind held no secret power, and their black pitiless gaze made even Cappa take a step backwards.

These people had only once before been seen by the dwarves, and very little was known of their origins, other than they had some connection to the orcs of old. They had, however, never been seen in battle. The average orc was between five and seven feet tall, yet none of these creatures was less than eight feet. This in itself was no real problem to the legionaries, except for the fact that this force of approximately three hundred not only outnumbered them, but was also highly trained.

Instinctively, the front ranks retired ten paces and allowed the back two ranks to move forward. Cappa quickly observed how the orka trampled over the living as well as the dead, ignoring all pleas for mercy, eager to come to grips with the mortalkind, to which they chanted death and destruction. Watching the front line, Cappa noted the involuntary backward step taken by a few men who had, he knew, the hearts of lions. He had to admit that the sight of these creatures was far beyond the feelings they normally encountered when facing a larger enemy. With deep foreboding, the newly promoted commander stepped forward and once more took the reins of fate proudly in both hands.

"Shall we dishonour our ancestors by failing now when we have defeated the larger number of our enemies?" he shouted above the din of the chants, knowing that he had barely thirty seconds before the enemy struck. "Stand, fellow Romans, and aid me in my quest to send these spawns of Hades back to the pit where they belong. We are in control of our own destiny. *Prepare to advance!*"

It was a desperate gamble at best and, with or without the speech, several legionaries broke for the rear, but the majority remained and closed the gaps in the line that now seemed so depleted. At this point of crisis, Porta decided to return after sweeping the Toe of Kad of the goblin archers. The return of these men could not have come at a more opportune moment, as the experienced Porta launched his small troop against the flank of the orka formation. Noting this tactic, Khazumar now finally released the dwarven reserve, which in its advance swept up Issus' small command that had earlier reconstituted the final reserve.

They were now committed fully to the defence of the caves, and Cappa could see no real purpose to retaining control of the formation, as the legionaries fought more efficiently on an individual basis.

"*Advance!*" he shouted, but this was not really essential.

Behind him Marcellus had taken the initiative of collecting all possible pilums, and these were launched at point blank range. Seconds later, the forward echelon clashed headlong into the advancing orka that, thanks to Porta's attack, had turned marginally to the right to face this threat. Realising their error, they had then begun to return to their initial line of attack, only to be caught in mid-change by the main Roman faction.

Their training had been considerably greater than that of any orc or goblin, but they could not be expected to stand against such a well-executed assault. Their will broken, several fled almost immediately, while others of stronger character stood their ground. Then, with a weight that belied their size, the dwarves landed on the orka left flank, which had so far remained exposed but unharmed. With cries of delight, the axes completed their downward flight to embed themselves in the throats and skulls of the enemy.

Cappa personally became embroiled in a direct fight with an orka, who wielded the double sword slowly but with great skill. His experience, however, kept the legionary alive. Dodging to one side, Cappa first cut across one knee and then repeated the move on the other. Next he struck the sword arm, ending with a direct stab to the throat.

The gurgling curse became muffled as the orka died, but even to the last the sword was still raised in one last desperate lunge. Uncoordinated and with little strength this of course missed, but it gave Cappa an indication of just what kind of strength of belief they were dealing with in the orka's will to win, as opposed to that of the orc or the goblin. It was a rude awakening.

Taking a step backwards, he now viewed the situation with satisfaction.

Here and there a few of their men had fallen, but the majority of the lifeless forms belonged to the Orka. Step by step, they continued down the small slope and on reaching the shattered gates they began to pile logs across the entrance. The breakthrough had been stopped and it had been a unified effort.

"I am in no hurry to repeat that experience," confided Cappa to Khazumar, who had joined him at the gate. "It was closer than imagined, unless my judgement has begun to fail me."

"It has not," confirmed Khazumar, smiling for the first time since their long march had started several days ago. "We, my King and our people, are in your debt, Roman. I regret my rudeness earlier, but I have had many things to ponder."

Cappa nodded, clapping a hand across the dwarf's shoulder. "My men thrive on this situation, my Lord. They are trained for this and, besides, if they are left to think too much, they will go insane. The busier they are the easier they are to control. It has been a pleasure and an honour."

Cappa finished with a formal bow and Khazumar laughed openly. "I am in need of an aide and perhaps an adviser. Do you have someone who could fill this post?"

Nodding once more, Cappa smiled broadly. "I have the perfect candidate, my Lord." He turned and shouted, "Marcellus!"

"Centurion?"

"I need someone to work with the dwarves as an aide to their command staff. Do you accept?"

"If I am in turn permitted to study their culture, Centurion, then it would be an honour."

"You are permitted to do so," Khazumar said, satisfied to have a mortalkind aide, and perhaps a friend.

"Then that is settled, my Lord. But I have a feeling this day is not quite over."

"My thoughts exactly," echoed the dwarf and together they moved aside to review their forces and defences.

The day had indeed not yet reached a decisive conclusion. Six more attacks took place along the entire perimeter, ranging from projectile attacks to the use of basic ladders. Each in turn was turned back, but not without loss. Hundreds perished, against thousands of the enemy. The Tower of Molarris, on the far side of the ravine that led up to the fortified wall and the entrance to the caves, was lost later that day with the entire post feared dead. The goblins that stormed one wall were the feared Regiments of Doom, identifiable by their black uniforms, if their rags may be so described. These particular creatures were known for their cruelty. They never took prisoners, even when ordered to do so.

Hour by hour they fought on, until the enemy finally retired. They had won a respite and the following dawn they fully expected a renewal of the attack but, eerily, the plain before them had been swept of all enemy as though by magic. This created some satisfaction but also concern as to why the enemy had left in the first place.

They spent the following day burying the dead with full honours. Then they solemnly considered the task of setting off to link up with the main army, now led by Atronius.

They could only pray that they arrived in time... This march would be longer and harder than the previous one, but at least this time they marched as comrades, and the air of suspicion between the dwarven guards and the legion had vanished. Now it all depended on Atronius.

Marcellus sat and stared out across the porch of the small hut at Mount Kad. The whole scene simply could not be related back to the recent bitter fighting at the cave. He sat on the porch barely half a league away, and yet the memory of when he had first seen the orcs, goblins and then the orka lay heavily on his mind.

The tusks and the blind hatred that seemed to have ended all reason.

Then, he had had no time to adjust or to establish any understanding of what had happened to them all. In recent days, here at Lord Khazumar's personal quarters, there had been more than enough time to engage his immense intellect to fathom why, who, and what had occurred.

An educated man, Marcellus spoke Latin and Greek fluently and had quickly grasped the basics of the dwarven language. Therefore the fact of other dimensions, and even that they existed, was not too much of a leap, but to accept that the very Gods his people worshiped actually existed did cause a momentary hesitation on his part. For this, as an intellect, he reproached himself bitterly, as he could not logically unravel this issue without a clear mind.

Religion had its place and he was no different to any other legionary in considering a good omen essential to victory. But this policy tended to dim a little when you have just faced creatures that recently had lived only in your nightmares.

The noise of a hinge creaking made him glance to one side, where Khazumar entered the porch through a small side-door.

"You are well?" he asked, his earlier pig-headed approach having vanished days earlier. "The maids have brought you food, and drink?"

"Yes, my Lord, they have been most kind."

Khazumar nodded, pulled a seat closer to Marcellus' bench and joined him in looking at the vast beauty of Mount Kad.

"I had this place built right here because of this view of Kad," he eventually said, almost in a whisper: a secret revealed. "To me this is what we are fighting for, this beauty, a beauty those people would destroy in a flash. With no remorse."

Another piece of a puzzle had again been put on the table, and Marcellus' perplexed expression became a worry for Khazumar. He was here to learn as much about them as Marcellus wished to learn about him!

"You seem confused?"

"I have managed to come to terms with the theory of what the *arrival* means to your culture and the elves, but this war is beyond me. For what purpose do the enemy fight?"

Khazumar looked back towards the snowy peaks before them. "They fight to destroy. It is their way of life."

"How so? What made them this way? In our lands, before the arrival, a similar situation existed with a race of people called the Helvetii."

"Prince Daxus?"

"Yes. His people were a smaller tribe allied to the main alliance against Roma, but in truth, he and Issus and all their people are Helvetii. They fought for survival because they had no choice but to attack or to die in the mountains."

"I heard this from Issus, yesterday. He stated that many attempts at a peaceful solution were made, but failed. In fact, a man called Gaius Julius Caesar had their diplomats arrested and thrown into slavery. Is this true?"

To avoid a bitter reply, Marcellus clamped his jaws together and bit so hard that he almost drew blood. "Issus has indeed explained their view," he said between closed teeth. Relaxing a little, he continued.

"What he failed to explain is that the Celtic tribes have for the last two hundred years or more raided, killed, pillaged and raped our people in the Republic. There had never been any intention to attack or invade their lands but. when four hundred thousand souls suddenly decided to live in Provence, the mathematics, in terms of victuals alone, made it clear that not everyone could survive in that one area. It was a simple choice. If we allowed them in, then our people would starve. Or, as was decided, we forced them to stay in their own lands. Not an easy choice, but one that had to be made, for our protection."

Khazumar rose slowly and walked to the edge of the porch. At this time of year the grass smelt so fresh. Spring was his favourite season and for a moment he allowed the discussion to abate. Clearly there was more to this division within the mortalkind ranks but, on the other hand, most of them had managed to set aside this hatred to fight side by side.

He allowed his memory to drift back to when his son had died, during the peace negotiation between the three kingdoms. It had failed miserably to end the Orcassian attacks, and yet in truth they had not really even tried to understand why the attacks had happened in the first place. He had never even considered that the orcs might have had a reason other than just the pleasures of pillage!

Not until he had spoken to Issus, of course. The Helvetii had been left with no choice other than to try to live. Even to this day, he was not aware of what had happened to his people, his chief or even his family.

Turning back to Marcellus, he was suddenly struck by the obvious comparison between the two worlds. He had visited the Orcassian plains with Elvandar and Aarun, and yet even then he had not comprehended the desperation of living there. There had been literally no food, no irrigation, no way of creating food for the starving horde. Perhaps there lay the rub? The loss of his son had left him hollow inside and he had switched off all attempts to bring him back to the emotional world. It had been too painful!

Now, as he watched the man before him reach forward and browse through the maps he had brought with him, he knew as with the clarity of a bell that an opportunity to avoid this current war had been there at their feet. If only they had sent a new delegation they might have achieved peace. If they had sent food, cloaks, and garments, and helped with the knowledge to create irrigation and farming then just maybe all this death could have been avoided, just maybe.

"Are there no maps of the whole world?" Marcellus asked as he viewed a small map of northern Thoria.

"No, but I can easily draw an outline, if this is of help?"

"If that is not too much trouble, my Lord. I am just having some difficulty understanding this war. Why has such an army invaded here where, to my mind, the mountains would have prevented any real success?"

Khazumar returned to his seat, called for a maid and asked that paints and papers be brought for him to make the promised drawing. Marcellus watched intently as he sketched the outline of the northern islands of Moravia in the top left-hand corner, and then quickly outlined the main coastline that was Gallicia, Lord Aarun's own land. From here, with a very artistic swish of the wrist, he added the Isle of Sotar and the mainland of Moravia. A minute later and the Dwarmanian peninsular was added and, in smooth circular motions, Orcassia to the east and, further over, the lands of Gobli were painted in what seemed to be record time.

For a moment, Marcellus bit back the urge to ask the flood of questions that began to form, and allowed Khazumar to add the land of Zeutis and the dark lands to their south. Finally he put two large islands in on the top right-hand side, but politely advised that he knew absolutely nothing about either place. In fact he doubted that anyone in Dwarmania or Gallicia did either!

As the dwarf added the mountains, rivers, lakes and main cities, Marcellus could hold back the flood of questions no longer. His brain was almost exploding with curiosity. If he felt that teaching had been a wonderful experience, he now knew that he should never have left the profession. He had enjoyed his stay in the legion but, if he could, he would leave at the first opportunity.

"So this is the Noborian River you spoke of?"

"Yes. Here, here and here are the forts as well. This one and this one were lost, while these two have been encircled. We have had no reports on their condition and we do not have the strength to relieve their struggle. This is the hardest aspect, as we sit here in reasonable comfort while they fight for their lives."

"There are no forces further south? Here...is that Gretan, my Lord?"

"Yes, Gretan. The Prince regent took the main forces in Thoria there, as the goblins had inflicted a severe defeat in the forests. He was then in turn defeated and his army has not been heard of for at least two weeks. How many have survived is unknown."

"Hence the reason for your people staying here, as there may be another attack to destroy the tombs."

"It is a necessary sacrifice. These caves are so important to our people that, were they to be lost, a large part of Thoria would literally up sticks and leave the kingdom. Those who have marched with Cappa will probably not reach the Alliance army in time to help, but I guess they had to try."

Marcellus raised his eyes from the drawing. "The kingdom is so fragile that Thoria would abandon your government?"

"Kingdom!" Khazumar exclaimed. "Some five hundred years ago a group of separate cities decided to call themselves a kingdom. Since then we have been squabbling as much between ourselves as we have with Orcassia and Gobli. Even Zeutis is feared, as the peoples are unknown and wear cloaks to hide their features. Anyone found there is instantly put to death unless they have a permit! No, Marcellus, this world of Tannis is not so bountiful, and the kingdom is more fragile than most of us will admit."

"No doubt your enemies are also aware of this?"

"Of course. So much so that Ortovia, our religious zealots, have demanded their independence more than once. That the Gretans have refused to pay their taxes for fifty years, due to our lack of support to fight the Gobli, is bad enough, but the court officials grow fat on the trade. Even worse, our attack on the goblins, a thousand years ago, to occupy the southern tip of this peninsular is, in my opinion, the real reason for this war. Gobli claim that Sight Fortress is their homeland. Funnily enough, the orcs claim the Lakes of Kor are their breeding grounds."

"Where is that?"

"Here, to the north. About seven hundred years back the elves forced the orcs to leave and built this Iruvian Wall, as they call it, a few hundred years ago. In short, it was a wall to stop the orcs from reaching their breeding grounds. Since then their numbers have dropped significantly. Interesting, don't you think, that the elves practice genocide and yet still stand morally higher than the rest of us? I do not trust any elf, but the orcs detest them with a passion. So why should the goblins be any different towards us?"

Marcellus looked again at the drawing and for the first time could see a slight pattern. He knew that Roma had fought a war against Carthage and that, as a result of that victory, expansionism had taken hold. It had taken seven hundred years for Roma to establish its existence, but then it had taken barely a further one hundred years for Roma to create a significant influence in Athens and to dominate the Hispanic lands of the Celtibernians.

As he looked at the map, it seemed that, from what Khazumar stated, the two kingdoms had followed an expansionistic policy themselves and this was the real cause, or rather perhaps one of the main causes, of this war. For a moment he tried to put aside his natural revulsion for the orc and goblin.

Did their claim to return to their homelands give them the right to fight?

It did if this was the only reason. The expedition to achieve peace, on which Khazumar had lost his own son, had failed because most of the participants were killed. As far as he could ascertain, no attempts at a peaceful solution had been made by the hordes, but was this due to a lack of breeding, or to a greater power that had stopped them?

"It seems this war has many layers, my Lord," he said, after a small delay. "It will take many years to fully understand. I hope you will allow me the opportunity to try?"

"That has already been offered, Marcellus. You will remain my aide until Cappa or someone else assigns you elsewhere. I hope we can both continue to help each other understand this mess better. Perhaps even find a solution?"

Marcellus nodded. "May I keep this drawing?"

"Yes, of course. I must leave you now as there are funerals to attend. Perhaps we can talk again later?"

"It would be an honour."

They rose together and clasped forearms. Khazumar left to fulfil his duties and Marcellus once more sat down and began to study the drawing. He could not understand why, but every few seconds his eyes kept wandering down to the Straits of Jupitannis and the southern tip of the Dwarmanian peninsular. Here he felt a rather strange foreboding.

Sighing, he put the drawing to one side. He was good at education, not strategy, but later he would show the map to Cappa. Perhaps he would know? Picking up a piece of paper, he began to sketch the situation as he remembered it at the tributary. He liked drawing and found it peaceful. By mid-afternoon he had drawn well over thirty!

As he expanded his skill he felt something was knawing at his mind. Something about the map that Khazumar had drawn. It had seemingly resembled the same topography as the Republic and yet differed in many ways, while other aspects of life here also felt familiar. He could not describe the feeling, it was more subdued, but it remained nevertheless.

Not everything here on Tannis was at it seemed at first and for the first time Marcellus began to look at the larger strategy of the Gods. This had not happened for nothing, this arrival and their own personal anguish at being dumped into an unknown world.

Sighing once more he pushed aside his feelings and looked towards the mountain for inspiration. If nothing else there was to be plenty of time for reflecting on why, but for now he began to concentrate on how they will survive. The former would have to wait!

PART EIGHT
BATTLE OF THE RIVER

The two armies stood in silence on either side of the small stream, poised for action, the only obstacle in their path the shallow water, the dividing line. On one side stood the forces of good, on the other the forces of evil. Or so the storyteller would have you believe, but in truth who really fitted the labels best? The orcs and goblins destroyed everything that was not of their making, did not generally build beautiful cities, but had a superior knowledge of survival in harsh environments.

On the opposite side of the coin, the dwarves and elves sought more living room and the recent conflicts had been caused by the expansionism of both kingdoms. To the individual, it was not difficult, if you believed in your superiors, to understand why you stood by your companion's side. However, to you and me the choice was rather more complicated, in terms of the real acclaim for evil. The idealism of goodness somehow becomes a little jaded.

There never could really be a sharp line between evil and good, it was all a matter of perspectives. Living, in itself, was only a series of memories locked away in the brain as an illusion of existence. None, save perhaps the Mages, could foresee the future, and they could not force an act of today to become the reality of the future. No, not even power could change destiny, but their abilities did enable them to retain the advantage by knowing with a fifty-fifty success to failure ratio what might or might not occur.

That was power enough, but to the Mages a greater power existed.

This power bestowed on them dominated more than any other aspect of magic and was the real method by which they maintained control over the lesser peoples they subjugated. The power of the past was far superior to any incantation, for the orc and goblin had no real memory beyond a month, sometimes considerably less. Steal or alter their scrolls, and they would believe whatever replaced the sacred words, no matter how barbaric the transcript. With no way of altering a thousand years of indoctrination, it was therefore impossible for the elves and dwarves to successfully discuss peace.

The orcs especially considered the lakes of Kor as their lost homeland, taken by elves, thus the hatred between them. Meanwhile the goblins considered Sight Mountain, and the fortress that stands on its majestic heights, their birthplace. Both beliefs were clever manipulations by the Mage over many years of influencing the fledgling religions practised by the orcs and goblins, but to any elf or dwarf right of conquest claimed the lands. It was easy to kill a chieftain, but it was almost impossible to kill an ideal, so the hatred continued.

Perception of being right was at best a poor substitute for facts, and the experiences of all the races had little to offer when it came to finding a reason for them *not* to fight. It was almost as if it was too difficult to speak of peace and cooperation. It was also not in the Mage's interests to allow peace.

War was after all what armies were for, was it not? To kill and destroy your enemy.

Here they stood, one defending their homeland, one determined to retake a homeland, while the Mage looked on and laughed. Only he had it all to gain...*Everything*!

A philosopher or a monk would have sent forward negotiators to try again to seek a peaceful solution, but past experience had taught them not to bother. So they now stood and waited for time to have its fun and make them sweat, while fate sat on all their shoulders and decided who would die and who would live. They said that the victor inherits the spoils, but you had to be alive to enjoy them and that was by no means decided as they faced one another across the stream.

The philosophical aspects did not go unnoticed by Atronius, but little other than killing, maiming and mutilation filled the heads of the others. Now was the time for action!

Atronius advised caution, as he had no way of knowing the enemy's strengths or weaknesses, due to the undulations of the ground. During their march across the northern plains, he was also painfully aware that his army was a far from united force. He advocated a defensive policy, as their numbers made it impossible to go on the attack, but the dwarven farmers and labourers had demanded an attack.

In his heart he knew that his advice had fallen on deaf ears, as the barbarians fought as a mass and used their initial charge to break their enemy. The dwarves had a little more discipline with the Westonians, but most of them had either been out of the service for too long, or were simple farmers obeying the call of duty. The few elves with them maintained an air of aloofness, not agreeing or disagreeing with any policy proposed. Then it all started to go wrong as the farmers crossed the stream.

"My Lord." Atronius turned, then lowered his eyes to follow the extended finger.

"By the Gods, what are they doing?" Atronius scowled.

"We have just been advised of another massacre to the south, by the hobgoblins," Lord Kollis put forward as an explanation. "They fear for their children."

Atronius turned to face Kollis. "Even if this information is true, how do they expect to defeat thirty thousand alone? Can none of your officers bring them back?"

"I can try."

"Then do it and do so now! This stupidity has unmasked our left flank on this ridge, Kollis. If they do not return, I fail to see how we can remain here, and if we retire then twenty more villages behind us will perish. I suggest you tell those farmers what they are sacrificing!"

Atronius watched Kollis leave, his face a mask of taut muscles. His fears had been right, and as they all watched it seemed that the farmers now intended to alter his plans and increase their participation, by crossing the stream without prior orders to do so. The defence of this ridge had already failed before they had even begun.

From the crest of the ridge, where he had glued the army created less than ten days ago and given the grandiose name of the *Army of Alliance*, the sight of the dwarves marching forward caused a momentary paralysis. Atronius shook his head, wiped his eyes and then turned to Lepidus who stood beside him, who in turn looked incredulously at Crassus. All eyes now seemed to be following Kollis' progress towards the farmers.

"I have given no such command," Atronius finally blurted out. "We can only pray Kollis can bring them back in time."

"Too late!" snapped Crassus, fairly spitting out the words. "The enemy has already changed their line of placement to encircle those fools. There is nothing we can do for them now!"

Valenus' mouth dropped. "We cannot abandon them. They are the farmers from the villages burned just yesterday by those filthy hobgoblins! We must help them. Many of their children were devoured right before them by that scum over there!"

"If we leave this ridge with this band of misfits," advised Crassus, "we'll be cut to pieces. We are on this ridge, with a stream before us for a reason, you bloody fool! Now those undisciplined fools have ruined everything. Now our left is turned and we have not even killed a single damned enemy!"

"These people have not been trained..." Valenus began.

"That is obvious!" blasted Crassus, turning to Valenus, his hand instinctively reaching for his sword hilt. "Damnable farmers have sealed defeat for us before the enemy has even deployed for battle!"

"Those people..." Valenus defended.

"Enough!" All eyes turned to Atronius, Kollis' progress momentarily forgotten. "We are wasting time. Those fools have ruined this position, so we choose another." He turned again to face Lepidus. "You say you crossed a steep ridge two leagues back, but due to our line of movement most of us marched further south. Do you remember its location? Good, then that is where we move to right now. While they are busy killing those idiots, we will slip away..."

"Retire in the face of an advancing army!" Crassus bellowed. "With a trained legion that would be difficult enough, but half of these fools will run and the army will disintegrate. It cannot be done."

"You have an alternative?"

"No."

"Then we move..."

"Wait."

"In the name of *Jupiter* and *Mars*, if any other fool interrupts me, I will bring back crucifixion!"

"Apologies, Primus," Valenus took a step backwards, offering a low bow as added insurance against the threat of crucifixion, even though he knew their new charter no longer permitted this method of discipline.

"For the love of...Will you speak and get on with it. We have so little time as it is!"

"The enemy, noble Primus, have altered their line of approach as Crassus has advised, but in doing so they have allowed the left column to move across the centre."

"So?" barked Crassus, still a little angered that such a junior officer as Valenus would dare to criticise his comments.

"We are here on this ridge, the stream covering our front, running north to south, along with the numerous traps we created last night. With the left gone already, we must attack, as I believe Crassus is right, this army will disintegrate if we turn and run."

"How does the changed column of movement alter our position, Valenus?" Atronius asked, still seeing red and trying desperately to contain his anger.

"As you advised last night, Primus, this ridge is a perfect defensive location, because the plateau is like a funnel opening out towards this ridge. At the neck the enemy numbers will be restricted and therefore we can fight on an equal parity, but the dwarves may have done us a greater service than they thought possible."

"How so?"

"Look where the dwarves are moving, Primus. They are halfway to the opening of the neck, and this location is vital to the orcs if they are to deploy completely against this ridge. They have occupied a few hills to either side, but from those directions they can only harass us. No, as you intended, this position should force them to attack us head on from a plateau where they can place only half of their army at any given time. We have less than half of the enemy strength, but at least with this plan we had a chance."

"That has now altered, due to the farmers breaking ranks," stated Lepidus, flippantly. "Does this conversation have a point?"

"Can you not see it for yourselves?" Valenus grinned.

"Make your point, Valenus! Time is running out," Atronius snapped.

"On our extreme right is the small gully, there." Valenus pointed enthusiastically off to their right, where the plateau dropped away into a small ravine. "I walked up that stream yesterday, just to make sure there would be no surprises. I found that the ravine follows a small stream, almost to the very base of that hill where we can see the enemy flags. If their left column crosses the centre, then the centre will have to sit behind them until the dwarves have been defeated. Only then would there be room enough for them to continue the advance onto the open plateau. They intend to attack us here, but what if we are not here?"

Atronius now looked at Valenus, and the twinkle in his eye indicated the dawning of a new plan beginning to formulate.

"You are suggesting we move the army into that ravine and attack the southern column while they are busy attacking the dwarves. Their centre will be blocked from intervening, but what of the northern column, the enemy right. That will still leave ten thousand free to move right around the dwarves."

"That is for us to prevent, Primus. They will attack the dwarves with the southern column. Perhaps it contains the expendable soldiers in their army, but the opportunity is now. We must *attack*!"

Atronius filled his lungs with air, breathing hard and contemplating the chances of success if they moved. He also contemplated the most vicious condemnation of a Centurion in the history of this world, but on looking towards the ravine and the obvious fixation the enemy had for the unfortunate farmers, he relented and took to reviewing the maps one last time.

"You say the ravine passes right along the entire plateau, almost to the command tents on that hill."

"Yes, Primus. Approximately half a league short of the lower slopes."

Atronius nodded, by the name of Jupiter the fool was right. The enemy had negated the advantage of numbers by marching their left across their centre, thus blocking the funnel instead of waiting to deploy into the larger space of the plateau. He had never trusted Valenus, and even now did not, since his loyalty had always seemed to be with Scipio, but of late he had become almost irreplaceable.

His work with the men as they travelled across the plains had been exceptional. The endless energy reminded him of Cappa, while the enthusiasm for training reminded him of his belief that a poorly trained legionary was a liability, not an asset. Valenus had definitely changed in the last few weeks and, for now, Atronius left the book of judgements open and kept an open mind. Everything was changing and, although he would prefer another to take Valenus' place, there was simply not enough time to give them the experience of the centurion.

For a brief second his mind wandered away to the caves that Kollis had advised were to their immediate north. How had Cappa and Issus faired in their struggle to save the Dwarvian tombs? Was there another army already marching to cut off his retreat back to the city of Lo, should he be defeated here on this day? As always there seemed to be so many questions and few useful answers. He rubbed his forehead energetically and glared reproachfully down across the plateau. Those damn farmers might already have destroyed any chance of success, so what now?

Enough, his disciplined mind cried out in fury, we have a more pressing issue to hand and no time to dally in pointless remorse over a plan gone astray.

"Has Kollis reached those fools yet?"

"Jumped on his pony and reached them a few moments ago," Valenus said flatly. "It seems he has also ordered forward the Westonian guards, as they are just crossing the stream now, Primus."

"What in all the pits in Tatamus is that dwarf up to now?" Crassus began his tirade again. "There is nobody holding the left flank at all now. We will be *turned*!"

"Only if we are still on this ridge, Crassus." Atronius said.

"What?"

"Bring the army to readiness for a very short march, Valenus, then rejoin your command. If we stay here we lose, so we may as well die taking a chance. War is after all a day of surprises and if we succeed the enemy numbers will not matter. We must make them fear the unknown. Let these orcs and goblins hate us, as long as they also fear our greater skills and courage."

"Do you think we can stop these creatures now?" Crassus asked, as Valenus strode away. "This is madness, Primus. We have known each other for a long time and I tell you this cannot possibly work."

"Perhaps, Crassus, my old friend. I value your opinion as I value the air I breathe, but this day is already lost unless we gamble. Perhaps if we charge forward the farmers will, without trying, have caused the confusion we hoped to achieve with our pits and traps. Whatever the outcome, we must try."

"I hope you are right."

"So do I."

Further along the ridge, Valenus was a blur of activity and did not hear these comments between too old campaigners. If he had, perhaps he would have doubted his own assessment of the predicament. However, the Roman contingent, the most disciplined, had remained in reserve along with Kollis' Westonian Guard Regiment, until Kollis had ordered the latter forward. As Valenus feverishly passed on the necessary orders, as advised by Atronius, he took one last look at the guards striding forward to try and save the farmers.

They numbered less than five hundred and yet walked with an air of thousands. He smiled as he noted their height. They must have taken some kind of growth enhancement, as they all stood at nearly the same height as the legionaries, something Kollis had explained away as a common occurrence amongst Westonians. Valenus suspected some kind of magic but had no real wish to investigate further.

Nevertheless, these warriors had been in reserve along with the legionaries and now the left had been completely abandoned. On the far side, the mass of individual enemy regiments terrified them all, but a calm, professional eye, such as Valenus had shown, had now actually given them a chance perhaps better than before. Atronius had had to abandon a defensive stance now, as they had two choices, run or attack, but realistically the latter was their only option.

Crassus was right, Valenus admitted to himself, damn his soul, half these fools would run if they retreated, especially the barbarians, who would not only run, but also disperse as far and wide as possible. It was in their instincts to avoid capture, Atronius confided silently to himself. He glanced again at the command tent and noted the agitated way in which Valenus was grasping the table, with the hand-drawn map sprawled across for perusal.

He watched the animated way his hands moved across the map, and the fast sharp pointing motion as he named each formation and presumably its role in the coming change of plans. He was too far away to hear, but standing next to Atronius he noticed Crassus return his gaze and raise a hand in salute.

"Are you listening to me?"

Crassus snapped his hand back down to his gladius' hilt. "My apologies, Primus."

Atronius nodded slowly. "Well, if I have your attention, perhaps we may proceed. As I was saying…if we are forced off this ridge, then we will be massacred in detail. The farmers must retire, but we need them to stand and to keep the enemy eyes on them, if nothing else. Crassus, I need you to buy me some time, take Lepidus with you and the two dwarven regiments to your right. I need you to keep that interest alive. Nobody has sanctioned the crossing, but what is done is done. Bring them back across as best you can. I need about three hours to move our forces through the ravine. Can you achieve this, my old friend?"

"I can give you as long as you require. What a ridiculous start but, as you command, Primus, I will move my century forward with Lepidus. What of Fabius though, is he to move forward?"

"Yes, take him as well. I am in your debt, noble Centurion. Do not fail me!"

Crassus nodded his thanks for the compliment and took a brief swallow of the wine attached to the saddle. This reminded him of the tributary skirmish, and again he would be the first in action. Why is that, he pondered? Why always his people first?

With a final nonchalant shrug of the shoulders, he mounted the nearest pony and rode with purpose back to the position where two hundred legionaries stood in four lines of forty, with a fifth line held back slightly behind the front rows. Here he stopped momentarily to survey the scene once more developing before him, initially noticing that Valenus had momentarily vanished from sight.

Looking across the stream, he saw a lone horseman desperately riding from side to side with both arms flapping in the air: Kollis. What a fool! He had no control over those dwarves and he had also compounded the disastrous start by taking the guards with him to help a group of idiots who were already dead.

As far as Crassus could determine, about two thousand dwarves had marched across the river for no reason other than to attack the enemy. The guarantee of defeat precluded any real objective designed by a leader of any kind. Furthermore, leaderless people on a battlefield could easily become more of a hindrance than an aid. They had learnt only yesterday, from the scouts, that several thousand orcs had been sent south to raid the coastal villages, and Crassus assumed this must be where many of those dwarves lived.

Fear for their relatives had diminished their fear of the enemy, who now stood between them and their loved ones. At best it was a forlorn gesture, as the raiders already had a day's head start and would already have wreaked havoc. Now many of these fools would pay dearly for their sense of responsibility, such a waste. On the ridge they would have made a better account of themselves, but now they would be lucky to survive the next ten minutes.

Crassus looked at the group of junior officers who now gathered near him for orders. Even before he spoke one of them announced the preparation to advance. Like a precise machine, the entire formation moved forward, breaking their line only to circumvent the traps built the night before by the small faction of engineers present, another waste of valuable time and effort.

Such was the metal of his people that there was little or no grumbling, and as they again moved forward to fight against unthinkable odds, his heart rose with unabated pride. If he were to die this day it would be amongst these honourable legionaries of Roma, and he could think of nothing better.

As they approached the stream, the far bank, which stood six spans high, briefly obscured the scene ahead. Crassus emerged on the far side to watch the momentary confusion as their formation regrouped in a deep and very muddy ravine. After a few sharp commands by the juniors they emerged on the far side. The dwarves now stood approximately half a league ahead and to their immediate left diagonal, where the funnel that Valenus had described began to open out onto the main plateau.

Behind him both Fabius, to his left, and Lepidus, to his right, had also circumvented the stream and had paused momentarily to straighten their lines. Now moving again, each step brought them closer. As they continued, the dawning of realism amongst these desperate people trying to save their families became apparent, but it was too late. To either side of the valley so many advancing enemy regiments were crammed tightly, thousands beyond count. On the left came the long armed orcs, on the right moved the considerably larger goblins, while the centre, as expected, had come to a halt. All carried weapons of various descriptions. All began to chant in their garish and yet somehow melodic tongues, the translation as always escaping them.

To Kollis, standing behind the farmers' scant line of defence, this sight was the last straw. Damn all farmers to the fires of hell, if they failed to hold this initial charge. To damnation and the pits of Hades, he swore these fools could go to their doom, his place was back on the ridge. He knew he could turn the well-disciplined guards around, but these fools would panic and break and then the wolves would hunt them from behind and seal their doom. But there was nothing more to be done.

Turning his pony's head, he was about to strike its flanks and launch into a gallop when his eyes befell a young dwarf. Something struck him as so familiar that he held his pony in abeyance. The dwarf could barely be old enough to have enlisted, but why did he look so familiar?

"Kozar!"

The dwarf turned. "Uncle Kollis! I can explain...I was at one of the villages attacked..."

"There is no time for such foolishness. We will have little or no opportunity to make a profit for the family, if you are dead *here*. Go back to the ridge immediately and report to the Primus. You are of royal blood and should not be serving in the ranks. Now go!"

"*But?*"

"No argument. Just go, *immediately*!"

The dwarf nodded and began to shuffle back to the ridge. Kollis could hardly stop smiling at the difficulty the fool had in walking in the armour, never mind participating in a battle. Well, he sighed, I guess there is no way that I can leave now that he has confessed, as he watched Crassus emerge from the final slope a quarter of a league behind them. The Romans had clearly decided to stand here and now, and he could hardly abandon his own people.

Dismounting, he noted the sudden arrival of Crassus on his pony and smiled up at the powerful centurion. He had been wrong about the Romans again, which was nothing new, he admonished himself in silence. The three advancing columns would not be long in arriving, so perhaps they could keep some of these fools alive after all. As he glanced behind him, off to his left, he watched his disciplined guard regiment form up on the farmers' extreme left. Even with these experienced warriors finally joining him, he still had only two thousand five hundred to face over ten thousand, bleak at best. Survive they might, but how many?

Behind this unfolding situation, Valenus had also noted with satisfaction the arrival of the dwarven guards. At least Kollis now had a slim chance of holding the bottleneck of the funnel. Turning to an aide, he ordered him to ride to the command for specific directions. The man returned a few minutes later.

"We have been ordered to go and join the elves in the ravine off to our right. It seems we are to attack the flank. The Primus has adopted your suggestion in full, Centurion."

"Will anyone remain to hold the ridge in our absence?" Valenus asked.

"The Primus did not indicate that any force will remain on the ridge, but I can only presume some kind of defence would have to be maintained."

"True. Prepare the men to march immediately. It seems I will be learning more of my trade after all."

"Your pardon, Centurion?"

"Nothing. Just a point raised by Lepidus many moons ago. Now hurry, we do not have much time. The enemy will already be driving against Crassus as we speak."

Never had a statement contained so much truth.

To Crassus, the enemy up close brought home to him the descriptions used by the elven lord and the dwarves, as though someone had struck him across the head. Nothing except seeing for yourself could prepare you for the sight of the rampaging orcs, tusks and all! The stench of the goblins alone was sufficient to make several men wretch, but afterwards they only smiled and stated that they now felt considerably better. Crassus applauded the bravery, but found the response in some a little exaggerated, leading as it did to a spate of men poking fingers down their own throats to somehow lose the stench themselves. One man in particular actually stated that he could not smell anything unusual.

"That's due to your own smell being stronger!" someone shouted.

A ripple of mirth flowed along the line and the bravery of these men created pride and honour in all the officers. It was barely a moment, a window of peace, then there was no more time. Faces became drawn. Their training took over as each man swiftly adjusted his equipment and glanced nervously to either side.

To their left, the orcs clashed heavily with the dwarves and yet somehow failed to break the thinly held line of inexperienced warriors. On the right, Crassus rotated the lines of legionaries and slowly gave ground, covering the vacated space with the injured and dead. Those in the centre waited patiently, knowing only too well that their effort would be called upon soon. Casualties were not heavy, but even at this rate they understood that sheer numbers would claim them all one by one.

Crassus rode over to Kollis and spat in disgust.

"This is ludicrous. You must give ground so that we can retire to the ridge!"

Kollis shook his head, equally adamant. "I understand what you intend, Centurion, but if we retire by even one step they will turn and run. They must stand or run. These are not trained men, not in the sense that your people are trained!"

Crassus fought for a few seconds with the pony as it reared majestically onto its hind legs, threatening to launch him skywards.

Then, after a few deep breaths, he looked around at the *dwarves*. To all intents and purposes they were terrified. None of them could cooperate correctly and in truth Kollis was correct. They would run. The only thing keeping them together was the common desire to live. All thoughts of bravely marching south had vanished as soon as they had reached this flat plateau.

"It will only be a matter of time before they move around our flanks. The only reason they have not done so already is overconfidence. They believe we are all that they face," Crassus stated intensely. "If that is true then we may have a chance, if the Primus times his move just right."

"I do not understand. What do you mean?" Kollis asked, his hands extended in bewilderment.

"Suffice to say, my Lord, we have sufficient troops to deal with one column at a time, but perhaps not all three together."

"I see."

"We must hold for as long as possible."

"As I said earlier, I do not believe we have much choice as regards where we go!"

Crassus nodded. Then without thinking he reached down and took hold of Kollis' raised arm. Grasping the forearm he nodded again.

"Honour and victory, my Lord."

Kollis nodded in return and watched as the mortalkind rode back to his men on the other side of the defence line. The forearm shaking custom was a strange one and yet it had immediately dropped his guard. For that split second, all racial barriers had vanished and Kollis had smiled broadly as the extended hand offered the soldierly hand of friendship, a common bond. The prophecy regarding the arrival of the Romans was correct, but he now doubted the validity of the *bringers* of doom paragraph. They were too eager to help! Just too damned helpful to be considered evil. He sighed heavily, nothing seemed to make any sense any more. Why? Why had his clear mind been so heavily disturbed?

A sudden crash behind him ended all further remonstrances, as yet another orc formation charged.

"Hold them!" he screamed, above the crescendo of clashing steel and the cry of the wounded. *"Hold them, I said!"*

✧·҉·✧·҉·✧

Prince Daxus stood on the crest of the ridge and looked down at the sorry sight of Crassus' advance attempting to save those vermin farmers. With a look of absolute hatred, he glanced towards the table where Atronius still stood discussing heatedly, with messengers, the points to where individual factions of the army had to move to enable him to implement Valenus' plan.

Daxus laughed at this point and glared at a legionary who sought the reason for his merriment. With a grunt the Helvetii Prince walked away. This day was marked with only one thing that had truly annoyed him. His messenger to the enemy camp had not returned. He saw the orcs as a better ally than these high and mighty elves and these dung-smelling dwarves.

"Are our people ready?" he asked, as he turned down a small incline where several warriors waited patiently.

"All is ready, Prince Daxus. A few have refused to leave and Uxudulum has yet to confirm that his people will join us. But our people in the majority will retire when ordered, Prince."

"How many will stay?"

The warriors looked at one another pensively. They had not been entirely truthful.

"Do I need to ask again?" Daxus turned on the nearest warrior. "How many will stay?" he demanded.

"Barely nine hundred have agreed to defect, Prince," another man advised. "Uxudulum believes a further thousand will follow him, but they will not follow you."

Daxus turned to the second warrior and nodded. It was too late to try and add more numbers to his force. The number mentioned would be enough to march to the mountains and set up a new tribal power base. It would seem that the Ortovian people were ripe for the plucking. While these fools died here, he would destroy their pathetic council and usurp power. Then, with this central position and control of what the dwarves called the East Tower, he could effectively cut off Dwarmania from direct assistance from Gallicia. More important, when the final defeat of these fools occurred, he would be seen to have helped the orcs achieve victory and in so doing he would be granted further riches and more power. This was the perfect time to destroy the alliance.

"Send the word," he said. "We move in ten minutes."

By the time Atronius discovered this betrayal by almost one thousand barbarians of the army, they would have placed a good league between them and this ridge, Daxus considered. Atronius would not be able to pursue, as his main forces were committed to his new strategy.

The Prince grimaced bitterly, now it was his turn to take what *he* demanded!

Along the crest of the southern rim of the plateau, a totally different kind of discussion now proceeded within a group whose interests extended far beyond the immediate task of survival.

Igluk swore vehemently as yet another goblin chief began to rant and rave about not having been told that the mortalkind did exist! That their beliefs of old no longer mattered, for the end of the world was at hand, due to the arrival of *them*!

"You sorry bag of bones for a warlord," Igluk screamed at the nearest goblin chieftain, beckoning his bodyguard to move closer. "They are not the threat that you believe! These mortalkind are weak and small, no match for our great warriors or the orka. Our master informed me personally that they are here and yet do you see fear in my eyes? We outnumber them by over three to one and we will prevail, if you stand together with us."

"It is easy for you to speak, Igluk," spat a chieftain who had one eye missing. "But it is not you who must face these devils, it is us!"

"Face them...face them!" Igluk screamed at an even higher pitch, his throat aching from the effort. "There are but five thousand across that stream and you fear such numbers!"

"I fear nothing!" the chieftain replied, in disgust at the mere suggestion that he was afraid.

"Then move to crush those pathetic dwarves and let us today end the occupation of the goblin homelands."

For a moment the group of leaders swayed hesitantly, looking to one another, as if seeking inspiration. Then with as much loathing as possible the one-eyed chief spat in the direction of Igluk, and began to reach for the gigantic sword at his side.

Igluk frowned and slowly licked his tusks, saliva running down his jaw. With no effort, he cast a short incantation that slowed down time just as the Mage had shown him, and stepped forward so that only he and the chief could hear one another. Drawing his own short dagger he proceeded to gut the chief and slit his throat, while enjoying the look of horror on the goblin's face as he felt each sensation. Only Igluk was outside of the normal time frame, and perhaps he was beginning to like this particular skill a little too much.

To everyone else, it seemed as though the one-eyed chief's stomach had simply exploded outwards, while his throat suddenly split asunder and began to gush with a deep green sea of blood. Unable to speak or react, the victim dropped to his knees and began to convulse violently. Still kneeling, his life essence vanished and with total contempt Igluk sent a bone-breaking kick to the chief's chest to send the corpse rolling down the slope. At the bottom the ravenous hobgoblins swiftly devoured the corpse. No need to waste fresh meat, they chanted happily.

"I assume there will be no more disputes," Igluk then said to nobody in particular, tensing for the possibility of speaking the incantation again.

When no words of dissent burst forth, he rounded on the group and began to issue orders, and watched with satisfaction as each chief stepped backwards every time he approached. Power was indeed a unique joy, he thought suddenly. I want more!

With the drama over it was astounding how the individual goblins swiftly forgot all friendship towards a corpse. Within seconds several of the hesitant chiefs had moved off and rejoined their command to support the advance party, which was at this moment fighting the dwarves and mortalkind. The situation was a poor one, but not beyond repair.

On the far side the orcs had engaged without orders, due to their blood lust for combat. Others had begun to move around the dwarves, seeking to surround them. Igluk now intended the same for the mortalkind, but the goblins on the left, in their eagerness to join the fray, had also crossed over the path of the elite forces in the centre, and in doing so the fools had opened a door of opportunity.

As he adjusted his chest armour the sight before him began to take on a more detached sensation. The people moved and yet Igluk somehow felt as though he was not there physically. It was a detached sensation he had felt before during an ambush, which he had organised to assassinate an elven and dwarven delegation travelling to Orcassia to speak of peace, but that thought brought back the same memories as his recent nightmares, so he swiftly changed his thoughts.

Why should this feeling suddenly resurface now? What could possibly be the link between the two events? Who knows, he thought, scratching his backside, I will find out soon enough.

With a grunt he moved back towards the far side of the slope where he could better see the ridge beyond, which was obscured slightly by the rise of the valley entrance ahead. Nothing could be seen of the enemy main force and for a moment this struck him as odd. To his mind it seemed a logical approach to hold the forces on the far side of the ridge to avoid having their numbers counted, but the gnomes riding the wolves had managed to do this. Nevertheless, there was that odd sensation that this information suddenly began to fuel into a fire.

"Where is that half-wit Nittos!" he bellowed, summoning the commander of the riders.

A few moments of disorder saw the small, thin and seemingly weak creature brought before Igluk, where he bowed several times before stopping to keep his eyes on the ground.

Silence reigned for a few moments as they all surveyed this whimsical animal that could barely be called sentient. Indeed their cousins, the goblins, fought almost incessantly with this smaller version of themselves, which resorted to direct murder and stealing just to survive in Gobli. Commoners called them hobgoblins, but this was actually wrong, as time had changed them significantly, but they still retained some obvious traces of their origins, the pointed nose being the most pertinent reminder. One and all despised them and yet they were the only creatures that the wolves would permit to ride on their backs. Nobody had ever been able to ascertain why. It was not really an issue of import and yet Igluk felt the familiar dislike rise in his chest at the grovelling Nittos.

Standing four feet with dark green skin and brown scraggy hair, the hobgoblins detested washing of any sort and used their long pointed noses as homing beacons on food. It was rumoured they could smell an elf or dwarf from a distance of five leagues, but this was more than likely an exaggeration.

"Your stench is commendable, Nittos," Igluk stated flatly, holding his nose.

"I thank you, oh great Lord of the...MASSSTER! How may I best serve your highnesssss?"

"Take your heathens to the north and find a suitable crossing place for the siege train. Your task is to move behind this scum who oppose us and attack their rear. But before you do this I want an up-to-date count of their numbers, within two hours. Do you understand, worm?"

"I do master. I do indeed."

"Then be gone before I have you burnt alive to rid us of your stench!"

They all watched as the hobgoblin slunk away and began chanting in the high-pitched shriek that passed as an attempt at a battle cry.

Within minutes the cry received a reply and within five more an enormous band of wolves began to ride north, each with a screaming hobgoblin astride its back, waving a sword above his head.

The small band that had originally pinned the dwarves also turned tail to join the main band, creating considerable confusion in the orcs' lines, and offering Kollis an opportunity to realign his front, which had been buckling due to the added fear of the wolves. The enemy surged forward to attack the exposed flank of several regiments, forcing them again to retire. The angry response was inevitable, as several hundred had perished in achieving the buckling in the dwarven line, and it had all been for nothing. Several orcs took matters further and physically attacked a small detachment of the hobgoblins.

Igluk also noted that his army was not as unified as it appeared to his enemy. Gnomes, or hobgoblins, or whatever name you chose, did have their uses, but loyalty was not one of them, and the wolves quickly turned on several orcs for killing their rider. Further confusion reigned as a free-for-all conflict suddenly exploded within his ranks. In a flash two hundred riders had been unsaddled and summarily executed and the wolves driven off.

Thankfully Nittos was unaware of this development. Igluk watched as they disappeared to the north, the wind still bringing their stench to burn his nose. Those wolves would soon descend onto the ridge, while here the goblins now began to reorganise the flanking attacks on the enemy to their front. After a while the orcs also reorganised and seemed galvanised to attack again, and with satisfaction Igluk watched as several regiments marched forward to move right behind the dwarves.

Everything was back on schedule, if somewhat delayed by the ludicrous fear they had shown of the mortalkind, who wore small chain mail shirts and carried square shields.

I will succeed, nothing can stop victory being achieved, but that sensation he had felt earlier would not go away. A sense of foreboding was rapidly beginning to develop...

Cappa stood on the ramparts at the shattered gate and, for a brief moment, allowed the wind to massage his face. Breathing deeply he looked first to the left then to the right, satisfied that no enemy had remained, yet secretly glad that the ordeal had ended when it had, for they were all exhausted. For the moment, the air was not dominated by the stench of the dead and carried the light pollen of countless flowers, which caught the Roman off guard and brought forth a series of sneezes, causing the nearby guard to smile. With his eyes red, a nose as runny as a stream and a light heart, Cappa smiled in reply and allowed himself a brief respite, to think of the summer and all things beautiful. It was to be a brief respite, but welcome nonetheless.

It was now two days since the battle and all memories of it had as usual drifted away on the wind. In the end they had lost barely anyone, but nearly a thousand enemy corpses had been burned just the day before, in large bonfires that had left the ground blackened with ash. He wondered whether any grass would ever grow at these spots again. They had saved the caves and the obvious decision had been to rush to Atronius' aid, but this had seemingly not been the case. Throughout the day they had all discussed in detail the battle that had taken place a few days before, and it had been argued that, if they left the caves, then all those who had perished would have done so for no reason. They had fought the enemy to a standstill and denied them access to the sacred caves.

Lord Khazumar had openly thanked the entire group for their help in repelling the orka at the gate. It all seemed to have taken place a lifetime ago but, as the talks continued, this day had yet to be covered by the blanket of darkness. It seemed ridiculous and somehow understandable, and this was the only reason why Cappa had not ignored Khazumar and left anyway. He had taken an oath to serve him until the caves were safe and, in truth, if he was honest, he did not believe they could reach any battlefield in time to make any difference, so it seemed that here they would remain.

Here victory had been assured, but Cappa knew that, if they moved now, it was almost certain that some kind of enemy force would be waiting at the bottom of the valley just to finish the job attempted earlier. If he allowed this, then all the sacrifice would have been for nothing, but surely they could send some of their people, even if only as a pointless gesture?

As the pollen gripped his reflexes again, his thoughts again wandered back to the summer. All about him the mountains had the feel of life, and the red and yellow blossoms lightened his mood. He turned, bowed to the guard respectfully and retired just as the sun began to set. Had Atronius engaged the main enemy forces yet? It was known that they had marched towards the great city of Lo, burning everything they encountered. If so, had they also been victorious?

Many did not ask the question for fear of hearing a negative response. Rolling his shoulders once more to ease away the stiffness caused by excessive use, a sign of old age, Cappa descended the steps off to the left and waved nonchalantly at Porta, who had already started to cook an entire pig for victuals. Greedy bastard!

Choosing not to join them just yet, he continued to walk up the hill to the caves. For a few moments, he stood at the entrance, in awe of the enormity of this enclave carved out of the mountain's base. Such architecture was not too uncommon in Roma, but on this scale he doubted whether even the Republic had any wonders to match the sight.

The Republic!

What did that mean anymore, he thought, casting a sideways glance down the hill, where his men were recovering from their experiences. Did any of them really believe their fate? Had the

Gods truly deserted them? Could he as an individual try and secure whatever future was left for them, to seize and hold on to for dear life? He spat out such questions, but as yet no answers, knowing that if the Gods existed then they were playing a cruel game.

Not here, not now and certainly not until he again had the opportunity to talk to that elven lord…What was his name…? Aarun…Yes, that was his name. He knew far more than he was letting on to anyone, and it was his obligation now, and his duty to the men, and to himself perhaps, to find out precisely what secrets this Aarun was keeping to himself.

Cappa sighed and rubbed both eyes soothingly. Time to sleep, he scolded, and promptly moved back towards the camp. As he reached the edge of the fire's glow, his thoughts returned to the main column and for a split second his pace faltered. Then with a resolution that surprised even him, the Centurion marched through the camp and retired without food.

Tomorrow they would march to find Atronius and Aarun and ask several searching questions! Questions that demanded answers!

<hr/>

Aarun stood red-faced and horrified, sweating from the hard march that they had endured to place them within striking distance of the enemy, only to find that Atronius had developed symptoms of cowardice. Earlier that day, he had taken their only mounted force north to try and defend the fords on the stream before them, and had fought bitterly with the gnomes and wolves. The riders had then turned away after it had become obvious that more than a few of them would perish just to force the crossing. With typical disloyalty they had decided that a village further north would offer easier targets. Now Aarun's blood was up and the lust for revenge for those elves that had died was almost overpowering.

"This is madness!" he shouted, pacing back and forth at the base of the ravine that separated them from the battle in progress, his words scolding Atronius. "They are your people dying out there!"

If the words caused any anger Atronius did not show it, but continued to follow the events with an almost complete lack of emotion. The ranting elven Lord continued, but refused to usurp the fragile authority they had over this odd mixture of peoples who could easily disband at the drop of a hat. He did indeed rant, but he had also made sure that they were not within earshot of the waiting forces behind them in the ravine.

Allowing the words to flow over his head, the Primus stood at the crest of the ravine, which offered a wide view that enabled him to observe in safety the struggle of Crassus, Lepidus and Fabius. He caught only glimpses of the dwarves on the far side, thanks to the undulating plateau floor nearer his hiding place in this ravine, but somehow he knew that Kollis was still fighting.

At the crest of the ravine, several scouts lay waiting, to inform him not only when the enemy moved the regiments just beyond, but also who stood between him and the enemy command tents. Their only chance was to cut the serpent's head off and then concentrate on killing the body later. Earlier, Aarun had told him that he had never before seen any orc and goblin force cooperate so freely, and he had surmised that either the Mage or a lesser-Mage was maintaining this with magic.

If true, then it was quite possible that, if they lost that cohesion, the mass would turn on each other and victory would be secured... perhaps? Meanwhile, not including those currently fighting, he could now deploy five thousand soldiers against the southern column of the enemy, whose losses numbered ten thousand. Now, due to Crassus' expertise, they enemy must have lost at least a quarter of the original numbers sent against him.

A scout to his left signalled with three fingers and pointed. Several more enemy regiments were moving into the fray and weakening the defences of the command tents, and he nodded with satisfaction. Now it needed just a few more to increase the pressure on their colleagues, and expose their chieftains. Atronius cast another worrying look at Fabius' command. This nearest flank was almost at breaking point in the fading light.

The enemy was relentlessly adding new regiments as others became tired, and this was bearing results as both flanks began to fold, threatening to encircle them all. They had no fresh recruits to rotate those fighting in the front line. For the brave there would be no respite, and they had already stood alone for most of the day.

But not yet, he noted, not *quite* yet. Hold. Hold and let the enemy rotate more regiments and deplete their personal protection and morale, as Kollis and Crassus defied the odds. Cut off the serpent's head and the body is defenceless: that was to be the additional policy in Valenus' plan. With this in mind Atronius intended to take the heads of the enemy generals, where he believed the cohesion must lie. If he was wrong, they would all be marching straight into the arms of an army that was known to have numbered well over thirty thousand, while they at dawn had numbered just under nine thousand.

But not yet, he repeated in his head! A little longer...hold them Crassus, my godlike professional executioner. Kill as many, maim as many, and tire as many as you can, trade space for lives.

For a few moments more he watched and waited. With razor-sharp eyes he watched as Fabius was taken down from his mount to face an unknown fate. Even when several groups of Helvetii charged across the stream into the enemy flank, and the Westonian Guard's last company of reserves was committed to defend their Lord Kollis, still he waited. Then came the signal that he had waited for and, with a grin, he ascended the slope to watch gleefully as the four regiments before them began to march to meet the added strength of Uxudulum's Boii. A leaderless rabble, but nevertheless a rabble Crassus was pleased to see.

"Now it is our time," he finally ordered, and patted Aarun solidly on the shoulder. "Take your archers and bombard those four regiments. Disorganise them to enable Crassus to cause as much damage as possible to the barbarians, and then inform Elvandar that he now commands the dwarven contingent. He will march first, and then I will follow with Valenus and the remainder of the legion. The Helvetii with us will be launched on a frenzied attack behind those facing Crassus. Are we ready?"

Aarun nodded silently for the first time in over half an hour. He was by no means inexperienced at fighting, but had never before witnessed such a large gathering of people so intent on destruction. The whole experience was threatening to overwhelm the elven lord. He was fighting to control his emotions, and he had hoped that Elvandar would remain at his side, but clearly that was no longer possible. He would cope alone.

Looking a little concerned, Atronius watched the elf descend the slope and briefly speak with the much larger Elvandar. Within minutes, however, the elven marshal was a blur of activity and quickly asserted total control over the dwarven faction in this flanking movement. Then, with a level of pride that surpassed even his expectations, the dwarves marched forward in good order and ascended the small incline to the crest of the slope.

With a wave of the hand, Valenus acknowledged the order and moved forward in perfect formation to support the dwarves, while the archers launched a mass of arrows into the four regiments that had now moved into a small gully far to the rear of Fabius' flank.

Here the guards came upon the mass of confused goblins, in which all order had melted away. For the slightest instant the guards hesitated, as they reached the lip of the gully and saw the terror in the eyes of the enemy.

Then the memories of suffering came flooding back, and slowly the chant arose as they walked forward mercilessly, hacking and stabbing everything before them. Caught between the archers and the guards, the goblins swiftly broke for the rear, but even there safety was still beyond their reach, as Atronius launched forward five hundred Helvetii, who fell on their flank with terrifying weight. Few, very few, reached the safety of their own line, and the barbarians continued on their way until they reached the rear of the main goblin effort.

At first the shock was palpable, but just as swiftly these goblins recovered and simply turned to face the new threat. They were not the Doom regiments, but they would not break easily, and they continued to fight on two fronts for several minutes before they too began to turn in an attempt to retire in order.

At first only one or two took to flight, but in a short while the entire formation had begun to withdraw, some doing so in good order, thus preventing a full-scale defeat. Crassus quickly regrouped and immediately took back the ground he had so far lost that day. If nothing else, the barbarians had gained them a pause and they now gladly joined him to stand against the renewed goblin attack, which did not keep them waiting long.

Such was the position before Atronius as the dwarves and the legionaries fell upon Igluk on the mound that he had personally chosen to show his faith in the prospects of victory. On the mound itself Igluk's eyes widened in astonishment as his blatant error landed resoundingly, right between his eyes!

There was literally nothing to do, except depart at a very rapid pace leaving behind all paraphernalia. Pandemonium reigned as several chieftains again took to arguing while mounting their steeds to hasten their retirement. Seeking a resolution, Igluk turned first one way, but no, the Regiments of Doom had already been employed against the mortalkind only moments before. Then his eyes looked to the other side of the valley...the Orka!

Keeping pace with the bodyguard, he manoeuvred two orc regiments in front of the advancing enemy and then promptly left them to their own resources, which soon took on the form of following their chieftains! However, the delay was sufficient for the mischievous orc to reach the orka and signal a general advance by the enormous warriors.

"Now we'll see who commands this field!" he gloated, as the cylindrical formations of orka marched forward in perfect cohesion.

The point of no return had now been irrevocably reached.

Even as Atronius reached the mound and they easily sent packing another goblin attack, the orka finally smashed through the dwarves on the far left, while Kollis' survivors ran for the ridge in terror. Turning to their left, the orka next fell heavily on Crassus' survivors, who had amalgamated into one command. Fabius was nowhere to be seen. Not that it mattered, as these tired legionaries were soon swept aside and the Westonian Guards, in their turn, were dispersed with little effort. It was not looking good.

On the ridge, Prince Daxus turned to the nearest chieftain and stated flatly that the battle was lost and, without hesitation, turned his command of a thousand warriors around to march as far away as possible. Obedience being their lifeblood many obeyed without question but a few refused, and then suddenly their numbers increased, stung by pride. However with no leader they might as well have been on the stars, for all the help that they could offer the retiring Crassus.

Now. It must be *now*!

The nod was brief but nonetheless spoke volumes. Before their journey across the dimensions Atronius would not have trusted Valenus with a burial detail, yet now the fate of the entire army was plainly on his shoulders. Committed to stand on the mound with Elvandar, Atronius watched as the small force of perhaps four hundred legionaries, their last hope, descended the slope to cross the small gully, where earlier the guards had devastated the goblins. Before them stood a mass of warriors standing head and shoulders above them, and brandishing hammers and swords that were as wide as their shields.

To their rear rode Valenus and to one side rode Lepidus, who had seemingly been separated from his command, terror controlling his seemingly obvious reluctance to ride further.

Then, as if they had suddenly appeared out of the earth itself, Aarun's archers rose in unison. Catching sight of this activity, the orka hesitated in their pursuit of Crassus, and several formations turned to face the elves as they rained down as many arrows as possible. As Atronius knew, this method of surprise tactics would have some effect, but many of these giants simply stood stock still with ten or more shards protruding from their hides. A few did fall, but looked more like porcupines than hideous Orka!

Then, amazingly, as they crested the gully to march onto the level plateau that Crassus had defended for so long, Valenus rode ahead of the men and signalled for a halt. Ensignia officers passed the orders to the trumpeters and three sharp, short notes flowed effortlessly across the battlefield. The mass came to a halt as if in one motion. Silence engulfed the scene and most of those present found themselves suddenly holding their breadth.

Crassus also stopped and in total wonder watched the pony ride up and down the length of the orka line in open defiance.

Then...

"We, the free people of this world, denounce your existence and call upon our Gods to deliver us from your evils!" shouted Valenus. "I give you the opportunity to surrender now and avoid the prospect of your imminent death! Do you accept your defeat?"

For an instant the demand went unchallenged. Then the ranks separated and Igluk rode forward with a banner carrying the orka emblem, a burning tower. Pulling to a stop before Valenus he grimaced and spat towards a blossoming flower that had somehow avoided being trodden flat in the confusion of the battle.

"Do I not know thee, mortalkind?" he said, squinting.

"I am unaware of any acquaintance with the spawn of all evils, foul heathen," retorted Valenus, drawing his sword in preparation for an attack. "Your people have done enough this day. I am here to end your pillaging!"

"You?" Igluk mocked, raising an accusing finger. "You and your filth will die beneath our boots to be forever forgotten! Your hate-filled dwarves and elves invaded Orcassis and Gobli for your own purposes, killing and maiming thousands of our peoples. It is you who will be stopped!"

For a moment Valenus hesitated as the words, spoken slowly, sunk in, having never contemplated the obvious dilemma of there being two sides to this conflict. These creatures, as foul as they looked, had not openly harmed him. Were they here for the right reasons? Why were they here in the first place? Dimensions and the wrath of Hades were both issues unknown to him, and indeed the only real truth lay in the freedom of no longer being controlled by his father.

He had been wrong before and as he watched Igluk he realised that he was in danger of being wrong again.

"No," he said sternly. "I have been wrong before, but I am not on this day. Stand aside and retire or face my wrath!"

There was no reply as Igluk simply spun the pony around and waved towards the silent ranks of the orka. With a few steps the goblin archers advanced and launched into the air a vast number of arrows. Calmly, in fact more calmly than he could ever recall, the Centurion turned and rode back to the linear formations of legionaries and dismounted.

The arrows had reached the pivot of their arc and now began to descend.

"Tortoise!" Valenus ordered, and stepped forward with a shield to add to the overhead protection, as shields were closed about each group of men.

The arrows landed, but failed to penetrate the cylindrical shields so expertly held together to form a wall of protection around each group of legionaries. Then within seconds of the last arrows landing, they regained their formations and, at the signal from Valenus, began to tramp towards the waiting orka. Now it was his turn. If only Lepidus' intentions had matched those of the men now so valiantly exposed...

It was a few minutes before the cry of treachery was heard. One by one Valenus' command stopped in their tracks, and confusion reigned as they looked behind to see their comrades still at the gully crest. Looking ahead, it was now just as clear that Igluk did not intend to waste this opportunity, and the orka began to move.

Fear afflicted many of those legionaries as they stood in abject terror. In some the numbness of the recent experiences was now beginning to wear off, and one by one several now turned to run from the sight before them. During this crisis Lepidus remained transfixed by the orka and refused to move. He had again usurped control of perhaps one hundred legionaries, leaving Valenus dangerously exposed on the plain.

Atronius had to act!

Kicking hard into the heels of his pony he set off towards Aarun, whose archers had began to withdraw, seeing that half of the legionaries had remained behind. Cloak flapping in the wind and his mind racing, Atronius could not have even anticipated the use of magic, far less acknowledge its use.

For now Igluk drew all of his strength forward and flung the same incantation that he had used on the goblin chief to engulf the hapless Atronius. Time began to slow and then came to a halt. For him the battle was over. For Igluk the concentration was strenuous, but the sight of the orka marching to victory began to increase his durability.

Yet another crisis!

With Atronius imprisoned, Valenus exposed and certain to be destroyed shortly, only Crassus and Elvandar were left to act freely before they too became pinned. With a strength of character so far hidden within the recesses of his heart, Valenus maintained control over the majority and, seizing the moment, stole the nearest mount and rode back to face Lepidus. Meanwhile Crassus' survivors and the Helvetii began to regroup.

"What is the meaning of this!" screamed Valenus, in a voice that resonated high above the din of battle. "You have left my command to die, fool. Move these men forward immediately!"

"You do not command here, you ignoramus!" Lepidus retorted, his face red with outrage. "Primus Pilum commands and I have received orders to remain here!"

"That is a lie."

"You dare to question the word of a senior centurion? You forget your place in this world, Valenus. As do these heathen barbarians. Why should we risk our lives to save them?"

"I doubt not your words, but I implore you to understand that the enemy is well acquainted with black magic," Valenus said, changing tack. "Is it not possible that your thoughts have been manipulated? We must stand together!"

For a moment it seemed as though the words had achieved the desired result, as Lepidus turned to his aide and ordered the men forward. The trumpet sounded in one clear note. But would it be in time? Already Valenus could see the first elements of the orka clashing bitterly with his deserted command. Then a scream that split the air with a heart stopping clarity ripped all their eyes in one direction, towards Lepidus.

They all looked to see where the sound had originated, but that was a fool's game and none of them had the time. All that could be accepted, as fact, was that Lepidus had dropped from his horse and now lay motionless on the ground, both of his eyes seemingly...gone! A rush of panic hit those nearest, but Valenus quickly rose to the occasion and ordered them to retain formation and continue ahead. Pulling off his cloak he quickly dropped it over the prone body of the Centurion and took a deep breath. Whatever had happened to him, it was not a fate Valenus was willing to accept. With a cry he pulled the horse's head around and returned just as the two groups linked together.

"For Roma, the Republic and for the honour of the Legion!" he cried, as his horse plummeted into the nearest rank of the enemy, whose exposed heads he began to attack systematically.

Crassus, as mentioned, acted with equal strength and pleaded with Uxudulum's warriors to rejoin the fray, as the survivors had started back to the small plateau after suffering several setbacks. For a few desperate seconds it seemed as though Crassus had succeeded, but the interference of Uxudulum ended further cooperation and he ordered his tribesmen back to the ridge. A scuffle ensued between the lower-chieftains and Uxudulum, with groups of men taking one side or the other; and, in a flash, before any level headed advice could be given, Uxudulum lay in a pool of his own blood. No one usurped the gap of authority and for a few seconds more the barbarians procrastinated, uncertain as to what to do.

Only one man's voice could be heard over the din of the battle all around these desperate Helvetii.

He said, "We have fought well so far this day, but now we stand idle, while those who have chosen to fight have done so with honour and have died to retain our freedom. *We* are dishonoured, our Gods will have disowned our souls. I for one will not accept further insult. I will fight! *Who will follow?*"

Crassus never knew this man's name, nor could he find him afterwards to offer any thanks, but those words were instrumental in adding another two thousand to those who now turned around and looked to him, for his command as to where they should fight!

Crassus would never forget the words spoken on that day. It was plain to everyone that had that short speech not been made, then all the other soldiers would have returned to the ridge without a second glance, perhaps even joined Daxus' betrayal. In addition, Kollis rallied the dwarves and, placing the guards at their centre, began to push the orcs back, while Elvandar attacked behind the orka to pin the enemy elite, who now moved to join the fight on Valenus' right.

By the time this crisis arrived, the battle had raged for eight hours, and the sun was beginning to set. Then, when it finally did, the day was decided in a very short space of time. Igluk, now intent on his incantation, could not supervise the orka, or indeed the goblins and orcs. This lack of control led the chieftains to bicker, even when the enemy was literally upon them. Individually they fought well but, in brief, both Crassus and Valenus cooperated to fall first on one position of advantage, soak up the weight of the counter attack, and then move onto the next. This meant that the orka were never able to bring their numbers to bear, and within a short period of time barely half their numbers remained standing. All about Igluk the cohesion of the regiments began to falter. One by one the leaders were killed, and their people lost faith and decided that this bottleneck was the last place they wished to be.

By this time, Igluk was aware that he personally was in danger and that the situation was beyond redemption.

In swift succession the orcs broke and fled, the goblins followed and only the Black Regiments of Doom remained, while the orka had now been surrounded and faced extinction.

"I am defeated," Igluk muttered in total disbelief. "How? How has this happened?"

A good question, one that perhaps a few others might wish to ask, he thought. This was a question that also began to haunt the now despondent orc. Indeed his masters would ask the very same question, in tones of less endearment of course, but it was the Mage he feared...it was the *Mage*!

Meanwhile Aarun stood before the orka survivors with fire in his eyes. To others he might have shown mercy, but it was now known that these creatures had already massacred two whole villages on the Noborian River.

Mercy was no longer an option.

"Fire!"

The final act of the day now began, as the elves sent arrows tipped in flame high in the air. Defiance welled up in the orka eyes, but even as death claimed them Aarun could not prevent a tear escaping and running down his cheek. So many of their people had perished, so many.

"This day is over, at last," he said, in a barely audible voice.

"But have we won tomorrow?" added Atronius, now unburdened by Igluk's incantation, but still feeling as if he would vomit each time he spoke.

"I am a new man," contributed Valenus. "Never have I seen such devotion to duty and honour."

"It is indeed a day to remember," agreed Elvandar, clapping Valenus on the shoulder.

"At a price," finalised Crassus, as he drank more wine. "A price that has seen Daxus betray us all. Uxudulum is dead. So are Fabius and Lepidus, Kollis has been wounded. We have won a brief respite, but now we must secure the immediate future. This army is vanquished, but we must still prevent even a single member of it from rejoining the next army they send against us."

"Yes," agreed Atronius. "Crassus, organise a pursuit. We must also care for the wounded and see to the dead. We will pursue these heathens tomorrow with the main force, but for now we must send as many mounted auxiliaries as possible, to keep the pressure on them and prevent them from reorganising."

Exhaustion prevented any serious pressure on the enemy survivors for more than a day, no matter how hard Crassus pushed and pulled his men to follow the enemy. None of them had ever experienced such a bitter confrontation. Indeed, it was not until dawn on the third day that Atronius finally renewed the advance east to the Noborian River, minus a small band detailed to defend the wounded that had to be left behind. However, every day there came a report from the mounted dwarves of how many of the enemy they had hunted down and executed. Surrender was never offered to any of the orcs.

The Alliance numbers had dwindled by almost fifty percent and the odds were now greater than ever. They were far more outnumbered by the enemy than they had been when they started. Yet no enemy would stand before them. The only real victory was the core of experienced warriors that the river battle had produced, and the blooding of the legionaries against the spawn of Hades. They had not faltered, nor had the barbarians who had stood beside them, and all were now more unified than ever. Perhaps unity was the real prize on this day.

They had won, but for how long! If Igluk had only looked about him he could easily have fought a second battle and achieved his desired victory, but it was not his army now running for the river, it was *Igluk* himself!

※ ※ ※

A week later they heard of the barbaric raids carried out by Daxus' rebels on the Ortovians. Lord Kollis, recuperating from his wounds, sent Atronius a report requesting reinforcements, as his militia could not cope with such well-trained warriors.

Of course there was no way Atronius could send anyone, for he had barely five thousand to defeat the encirclement of three Noborian forts but, as a gesture, he ordered Marcellus, Julius and Valenus to take one hundred legionaries to the city of Lo. Here they were to train the dwarves in legion tactics and the best ways of countering the great strength of the Helvetii broadsword. The raids ended and the seeds of a dwarven legion were sown, but Daxus remained in the mountains, unassailable.

All made a note of the intention to return to make Daxus pay for his betrayal, but for now nothing more could be done, except contain his activities. Julius and Valenus returned to the army, while Marcellus continued the training and would rejoin them later.

Daxus' day of reckoning would have to wait, but Kollis especially did not intend to let him wait too long!

※ ※ ※

The pace had been horrendous, but if there was one thing Igluk intended to ensure on this escapade, it was that he himself would avoid capture. The battle had been fought well, and strategically the enemy should have been broken. The combination of archers, orka and Black goblin regiments, added to the sheer brute force of his own orcs, had singularly failed, but why?

Over the last five days he had forced the pace, as his fear of reprisals from the dwarves increased. The reports he received indicated that several villages had been destroyed and, at one place in particular, the wolves had even consumed the children. The logic was infallible. If their existence ended now, then they could not reach adulthood and thus pose a more significant threat to the wolves' own intentions. However, the resultant anger had brought forward thousands of farmers, who would ordinarily have refused to join an advancing horde. Now Igluk found every river barred, and a clear determination to make them pay with their own lives for this campaign of terror, a factor that had not originally even entered Igluk's mind.

The experience of fighting the mortalkind had made clear to Igluk his complete lack of control of at least sixty percent of the army. More than once the goblin archers had retired without orders, while the gnomes had taken it upon themselves to raid a village when their sole purpose should have been to attack the enemy flank.

Arguments between the senior chieftains had also made it difficult to coordinate the orcs and goblins, who invariably descended upon the enemy one after the other, thus losing their greatest advantage, numbers. In truth the enemy had certainly fought with an unusual level of stubbornness. On four occasions he had believed them to be on the brink of victory, when suddenly a new force had appeared, as if by magic. Yes, he suddenly thought, magic, was that how they had defeated me?

"Not a very convincing argument under the circumstances. I would make the standard attempts to blame the chieftains, if I were in your sandals."

Igluk spun on his heels and brought the sword sweeping around at head height. The sound of metal on metal indicated a block and instinctively he sidestepped and brought the blade down with his entire strength, only to suddenly find that he could not move.

"Mage!" he spat, struggling to free his mind from the incantation that had frozen time. "Free me now or face the consequences!"

"Consequences? Why, Igluk, you have indeed improved your vocabulary," the Mage replied. "I am also reliably informed that you have acquired a very strong taste for fruit. Now that is extremely unusual for your species. I am somewhat confused, I have to confess."

Now sweating from his exertions, Igluk tried to look about for the bodyguards who normally accompanied him everywhere. On either side he could see at least five huge orcs who fitted this description, but they remained totally oblivious to what was taking place next to them.

The Mage followed his gaze and chuckled.

"They will not interfere in our little discussion," he said. "They are not in this time frame, but then you would already know that, wouldn't you?"

"Release..."

"Release *me*. Yes, yes, we have covered this issue already," the Mage interrupted irritably, waving his fingers at the prone orc. "We have a rather odd issue of more importance to hand. Where is the mortalkind dead you promised when you were placed in command of the Orcassian army? Why did you retire beyond the Noborian River and allowed three dwarven forts to remain intact? Your command still numbers over fifteen thousand and yet you are moving north. Why? Where are you going, Igluk? Are you so foolish as to believe that I would not seek out the answers to these questions? Or has your little mind been fried in the sun? Do you now aim a little higher than we agreed?"

For a moment the Mage stopped and began to look around him. He had watched in anticipation as the battle had unfurled and still remembered the bitter disappointment of failure. A failure that he had yet to report to *his* master!

The mortalkind contingent had been the deciding factor, and just when Dwarmania was on the brink of collapse the great Zeus had chosen to interfere. Now this simpering fool had been given too much freedom, and in this mistake the Mage could see a lifetime of pain ahead for the person who discussed the subject with the master. It was then that he had a bright idea.

"Yes, it would serve my purposes for you to report to the master, instead of me."

"I command the Orcassian A..."

"You command nothing. It is done!"

The blinding light was all the warning received, and all those too close fled in terror as the heat increased with every passing second. With a final flash the crest of the hill where had stood, only a few seconds before, their leader Igluk, now burned crisply, the grass turning black. Of Igluk there was no sign, and they wisely decided not to hang around and find out precisely what had happened. If magic had claimed him, then they did not want the performance repeated on them. Within minutes the orcs had scattered to the four winds. The goblins maintained more control and began to march southwards, once again under the command of the Black Goblins, of whom there were no surviving officers.

However that did not matter, as they were going home to Gobli and their line of march might well surprise the Gretans, and offer sweet pickings for revenge. They chose new leaders as they marched!

For Igluk the situation was not quite so easy. The second the Mage had completed the incantation, he lost consciousness and was to awake in a cell with no armour and no weapons of any description.

"This is not good," he whispered, fearing that others might be listening. "This is definitely *not* good."

From deep within the fear began to rise, as he tried to consider just exactly where he was in relation to where he had originally stood. At first he could not understand the fear, for it was a long time since he had been alone without a bodyguard, but deep down something was chewing at his mind. Why does this place feel so...familiar?

The answer would not arrive for some time, but when the thought pushed through the fog of fear it replaced everything with a sense of dread.

"*The Haderian Tower*," he whispered, after a few more seconds. "If I am there, then I have much to fear. But all is not lost, the Mage would surely have disposed of me if I was no longer of any use, but to what use will he now seek to jeopardise my life? I need a way out of here. Soon."

The last statement was more a stab at fatalism rather than realism, as he knew, having sent people here for punishment, that nobody ever left the *Tower*. Or rather, if they did they were no longer the being that had initially gone in! This was the centre of their empire!

A shiver ran down his arched spinal cord, causing him to grimace. What were those questions that filth had asked just before they had vanished? Despite all his efforts, he could recall nothing of the discussion. Well, if he could not remember now he was certain that the questions would be asked again. In the meantime he began to search the cell and found that, on its far side, several bunks had collapsed. Here he broke free a metal bar and having obtained at least some kind of weapon, he settled down to sleep.

It was not long before he heard distinct steps outside, and he leapt to his feet, holding the bar. The keys jangled in the lock and he flexed his muscles in anticipation of the struggle to come, but as before there was to be no struggle. Another bright light, although less bright than before, engulfed his vision. When it cleared he was no longer in the cell, but standing beside a gigantic, bottomless pit. Ahead and slightly to one side stood the Mage. With him was another hooded figure, and two others that had lowered their hoods to show mortalkind features.

As they approached, he looked down to see if the bar had also travelled, and found his clenched fist empty.

Igluk swallowed hard and looked feverishly for an exit. This was indeed turning out to be an interesting day...

In the next few days, Igluk occasionally stirred from his hay and meandered aimlessly around his cell. Or rather it felt as though the days had gone by, but there was no real way of knowing. No natural light ever reached as far beneath the tower as this. He knew that after a couple more days of this his mind would be completely disorientated, and he would almost certainly be at his wits' end. Why did that pig of a Mage keep him waiting?

A daring plan had begun to form in his head, but every time he decided on a course of action he would mysteriously lose all context, and he had to start all over again. This had to be some kind of mind control, but dispelling such an enchantment was beyond his knowledge. So he sat down again and looked into the darkness, which was at least something he could do with ease, his eyes being exceptionally good, even for an orc.

He did not really feel the incantation when it finally collected him, but on arrival in a massive chamber he felt the sudden urge to vomit. A transportation incantation, the Mage's little speciality. Shaking his head, Igluk looked around. His brethren by now would have charged madly at the nearest person seeking a weapon of some kind, but for the moment he held his anger in check. In spite of the Mage's obvious haste, he walked slowly towards the large table set about a hundred paces off to his right. His eyes were transfixed momentarily by the cliff edge marking the fall into the bottomless pit, but he realised that this was not helping, and continued at a much faster pace!

He took a few shambling steps towards the wall, but could see no exits, although he did wonder at the ornate decorations. The picture just off to the right, at the edge of his vision, held his gaze. Then he noticed that the gargoyles and the depictions of beheadings, in particular, were marvellous to see. The wooden carvings were exquisite and for a further annoying moment he stopped to admire a picture of a landscape. As he watched it seemed to change. Yes, the picture was constantly moving in and out of focus. He watched as large rectangular formations marched against one another. He guessed they must be an orka legion.

The battle scene began to develop rapidly, as the two armies charged. Death was rampant and the picture changed to show a single man on a horse riding back and forth. He thought it must be the despicable general who had defeated him at the river, but as he watched it was clearly not that one.

"Gaius Julius Caesar," said the Mage.

"Uh!"

"The person in whom you show such an interest. He is a pet of our Master. It is good to watch his history. His life is a good one, but permitted only by the power of the Master."

Igluk thought about replying, even of asking why he was not commanding them instead of this fool, but he thought better of it and held his tongue. He had after all just lost the best part of thirty thousand warriors in one campaign!

There was a long silence as more people entered. A gigantic goblin moved, awkwardly, its blubber rolling along the floor, to a large dais nearby, but then made no move to walk to the table. Probably too much of an effort, Igluk laughed inside, his upper lip rising slightly, the closest an orc came to ever smiling.

A mortalkind entered from behind and brushed past him as though he did not exist, then sat next to the Mage. Moving forward, Igluk felt a sinking feeling in his stomach. The mortalkind had to be the second Mage he had heard of, who was responsible for training the Orka. Meanwhile the fat globular puss-bucket could only be the goblin King from Gashar, the tower of gobli, which his own horde called the *Fortress of Doom!* That place was even worse than here for nobody ever returned! Perhaps there was hope yet?

"You know why you are here?" barked the Mage.

"No."

"No!" scoffed the mortalkind. "Why waste time, just throw him down the pit. The Master will not be pleased if we summon him for such a trivial issue."

The Mage only nodded, but made no move to comply. "You are here because I contend that you were treasonous at the river in Thoria. You are here to plead your cause and to save your hide from a punishment saved for only the very stupid. How do you plead?"

Plead? What an odd word, Igluk thought. What it meant was beyond him, but he was not dead yet, so perhaps he would still be useful after all.

"I led and the army followed," Igluk began, "but you all failed me and those *fighting* for our cause. You were the ones who knew the Romans had arrived, and knew what effect this would have on the army. The treason was yours and not mine!"

For a moment, the Mage considered his testimony and recalled the smashed body of a messenger that had been caught some weeks before by some goblins near the Noborian River. The face had been eaten, and he had not considered the possibility that the *arrival* had begun. He had in truth not contemplated the possibility that his Master could be outwitted.

"What of that corpse brought to you by my garrison?" asked the goblin King. "Is there any truth to this worm's testimony?"

"If the face had not been eaten?"

"Hunger is hunger. We do not banter over fresh meat. You are indeed lucky to have seen anything of it at all!"

There began another brief silence as Igluk looked from one face to another. The mortalkind was in consultation with the Mage, while the goblin King simply watched him coldly.

"I would taste foul," Igluk spat, for he knew he would not die now. His confidence began to return. "Why do we not call upon the Master to further explain this fiasco! I am certain he will be interested to know that the Mage knew of the Romans' arrival and yet did not inform him."

Igluk was beckoned closer to the table. At first he refused but then a compulsion to comply filled his head. Damn that Mage! He sat awkwardly in the chair as it was designed for Romans or goblins, not arched-back orcs. He tried once more to glean something, anything, from the faces of the mortalkind and the Mage, but it was like looking into an empty hole. Both sets of eyes simply held no life. There was nothing to glean from either.

"Call in those spies," the Mage finally spoke.

"Spies?" Igluk demanded. "You had spies watching me!"

"Did you think we would allow such scum as you to lead without being watched?" the Mage laughed bitterly. "I am impressed with your arrogance, Igluk. But do not try my patience, fool." Then, turning to a small band of goblins, he said, "You watched closely?"

"Yes," their chosen speaker advised. "He did what was necessary, but the mortalkind intervention stopped many from fighting well. The plateau was well chosen by the enemy Captain, as it was tight at our end, open at the ridge only. It was the mortalkind who decided the battle."

"And Azar-Kad?" the mortalkind shouted. "My orka were left to fight unaided and died for nothing!"

"They stopped at the gate because of the Romans. They should have been told of the *arrival*. We can only spy on those named, but we cannot interfere in their decisions. That power is not given to us by the Master." The goblin bowed low, and the Mage waved him away.

Once more there was silence. This time however, Igluk noticed that the mortalkind kept watching the goblin. He could not see if it was hatred or perhaps an alliance against the Mage, but it was interesting nonetheless, and information he could perhaps use at a later date.

"The battle was but a diversion anyway," Igluk said, tired of this growing silence, "so why worry about the death of the *horde*. There are many others to take its place. The Master has plans for an invasion, does he not? What part will I play?"

The Mage looked towards the orc with a slow movement of the head. The question had taken him by surprise.

"What part will you play?" he said, while at the back of his mind he could feel the first tingle of a summons from the Master. "You will have none. For the moment, for what reason I do not know, you have received a stay of execution, Igluk. For your sake I hope your performance improves, but in our desperation you might just be useful."

"Alive is all I ask."

The mortalkind grunted. "That will depend on how you fare during my training. You are seconded to me, orc! And I intend to make you pay for the death of my Orka!"

"I protest! I will not serve with this mortalkind. I am a chieftain, I am…"

"Nothing, unless I say otherwise. Now leave me, all of you. The Master is summoning me and I must leave for some time. Prepare for the final struggle. Make plans for the invasion of Dwarmania. We will prevail."

As the trio left, the Mage walked over to the pit and calmly stepped over the edge. The sensation of falling was always a little odd, he knew that here he was in limbo and did nothing, literally. Here he simply did not *exist* and falling was still the first sensation of many that would bombard his senses. Next came the tearing feeling as though his flesh was melting and yet was also dead, so why was this feeling so apparent?

"*You still cling to your humanity, Mage. Pathetic! Report to me on the battle. Leave nothing out. Why was I not informed of the arrival of the mortalkind?*"

The Mage felt a sinking feeling in his soul. The Master had known all along!

So began a long debate between a God and a spirit inhabiting an empty shell. The Mage answered all that was asked of him. Remember, *only* what was asked of him. The defeat at the river became Igluk's cross. The unknown *arrival* the goblin king's. The failure of the *orka* to achieve victory was the mortalkind's. It seemed as though nothing was going right, but as the debate continued so his own discomfort increased.

The God had little use for lies so it took the truth by force and left the Mage in agony, his soul ripped asunder. He would remake the fool soon enough, but for now he left the essence writhing in pain and enjoyed the infliction of unwanted suffering. Would this Mage never learn? He was the God, not him!

PART NINE

A NEW ALLIANCE

The wind blew in gusts, lifting her hair across her forehead to briefly obscure the sight. It was not often she found the time to be alone these days, but for these precious seconds she looked out across the mountains in awe. The season was about to change, she noted, not that it affected these ancient rocks as they always maintained their head of snow. She wondered whether there would ever be time to climb those peaks again. Looking across the small ridge, she spied a small rock protruding from the grass, her usual seat of contemplation. She drew closer, noticing that the rock was still covered in powdery snowflakes, now melting.

Ordinarily this would have been a reason for concern, bringing on the breeze the early indications of summer, preventing her from assuming her normal seat. To Helin, however, on this day alone, it was, as always, the most beautiful feeling to stand on such a high precipice, and revel in the sensations of power that nature constantly performed before her very eyes. The changing seasons, the wildlife and the ever-present feelings so embodied in what the future might hold for them all.

The ridge was her favourite location in the mountain ranges, to the north of the dwarf's northern peninsular. It had for many centuries remained one of the most secret gardens of her people, but day by day the earth dwindled, and the ridge had collapsed to descend the three thousand paces straight down to the valley below. A journey she had felt that, for some strange reason, had a kind of affinity to having never left these high mountains. She again pondered what lay beyond this valley. An eagle appeared through a nearby cloud and Helin smiled to think of its freedom, and how it represented her own desire to go beyond the valley.

To her, the view was forever changing and never a bore. As far as the eye could see, the clouds shifted in their lazy mannerisms that defied any formality. Sometimes, the more she stared, the more she might perhaps see an abstract conformity, but to whose laws she could not even try to understand.

Nature itself was beyond all their understanding, and this was the reasoning behind the warrior's belief that you must seek a oneness with the naturalness of the universe. The individual can only matter if you are absorbed into nature itself. She smiled to recall her father's endless efforts to make her understand this aspect of her training, but she felt it more important to enjoy life: to live the moment, rather than worry about the concept of the moment. Somehow everything became so complicated when you tried to analyse even a single raindrop.

Her eyes drifted over to the valley. On some days it could be seen far below, yet within minutes it could just as easily become hidden, engulfed in the very clouds she admired so much. On other days, the sea on the far side of the peninsular could not be seen, but then the following day it would appear as a thin blue line bordering the horizon. Nothing remained the same from one day to the next, perhaps that was the attraction.

Today the view was clearer than ever before and, along with the breeze, the warmth from the sun beat down on Helin's forehead with a love and affection she had come to cherish. All in all, this place had always reminded her of peace and internal harmony, and it signified the very essence of why this small individual had chosen to become a warrior.

Here on the ledge, as always when she sat on this rock, memories of her training began to return, and of how the instructor had religiously followed her progress. She sometimes wondered if this had been because of her exceptional ability, or because her father was the High Marshal of the Valleys. Either way, it had given her the advantage of almost private tuition on a daily basis, an opportunity that she did not waste. Now, as a fully commissioned officer, her reputation as a direct, clinically precise commander would be more of a modest description rather than the truth.

If any warrior chose to accept in all honesty what Helin stood for, he or she would have to concede that she was highly respected by her regimental staff, but avoided by the other maidens in the command. Perhaps they held her in a slightly healthier respect than her male rivals, who tended to believe that maidens should retain their femininity and stick to childbirth.

Helin grinned wolfishly. If only they could see her now! She gazed in amazement at the very complexity of the Yander flower, with its bright yellow petals. It always amazed her just how gullible the masses really were about people's true worth. Perhaps it was an inherent weakness of her people alone, who seemed to be influenced only by what they could see on the surface, rather than by what could perhaps be perceived underneath. There was a depth to their culture, but perhaps their minds had become as trapped by the warrior ethos as a people trapped in the mountain valleys they also so adored.

The grin slowly vanished as the weight of the dilemma returned with a vengeance. Moving away from her rock, she sat heavily at the base of the largest tree on the ridge, touching her fingers into a steeple, a habit that reminded many of her father, and let her mind again review the issues the high council had discussed earlier that day.

It was always difficult and for a time she tried, truly she tried, but it was no good. A warrior was not a politician!

It was then, after an hour or so, that the hairs on her neck began to rise. Muscles tensed, her hands tightened and increased the pressure to execute a fast movement to one side. Her training was indeed of the highest order.

"When you disappear, I am sincerely grateful that it is not too difficult to find you again, my daughter."

Helin visibly relaxed. "You have grown careless in your old age, my father. I heard you at least ten yards away."

"I saw no purpose in using stealth when approaching my own daughter. Perhaps next time I will not be so lenient. But I did not come here to dispute our individual abilities, that is beyond discussion..."

"Why you pompous, old...!"

"Now, my daughter, keep your dignity intact," Arnim said smoothly, raising both hands defensively. "Has your sense of humour totally deserted you?"

Helin smiled warmly and gazed at her father. "Not quite, although I feel that perhaps our people do not laugh as much as they should, or as they used to."

Arnim nodded as he claimed a seat at the base of the same tree. "Duty has become more important. The generations before us allowed their free spirits to soar, only to find that the outside world was not quite so welcoming. Even those who went in the guise of a northern dwarf found those lands to be barren and lifeless in comparison to our valleys. Somewhere along the way society depicted that open emotions were no longer necessary, and our military background did little to alter this, now or then. But I am weary of debates."

Leaning back on the tree, Helin gazed forward and tried to remember the last time she had heard her father openly laugh. Oh, there had been love, attention and even funny moments, but their social structure had always restricted how, even as a child, the individual responded. It had undeniably made them tougher and stronger but, on the other hand, something else was always missing.

"It is almost time to leave," Arnim said suddenly. "I presume you are prepared?"

"Yes."

"The council have just finished the final forum and it has been decided that we leave today. My objections have been over-ruled."

"If you wanted the army to seize power..."

"As I stated earlier, I did not come here for any debate..."

"But father, our people..."

"Will obey the consensus of the council, as we decided over a century ago, to diminish the control of the military. You were too young then, my daughter, but we came close to civil war. Us! The people of the mountains...the people of *peace*! We trained to preserve all this and yet there remained a faction of my colleagues who desired war, conquest and glory. Our ancestors would have turned in their graves."

Helin watched as the diplomat suddenly appeared, fearsome and erect with a pride that had retained order in the valleys for over fifty years. However, she found some difficulty in agreeing with his statement. To her, the military would be more efficient than the long delays inherent in the council ramblings. It was too slow, and perhaps that was her weakness, no patience?

The messenger appeared as if out of thin air, causing even Helin to jump when the tiny voice spoke almost in Arnim's ear.

"My Lord Marshal, the council awaits the final dispatch of the detachment to the city of Lo."

"Inform the council, Arrim, that I will attend them shortly. It is also good to see that you have retained those special skills of yours, they may be of use."

Arrim bowed deeply and took two steps backwards. "I live to serve, Lord Marshal, as we all do."

Arnim turned and watched the messenger return to the archway that led down to the plateau, where their army was slowly gathering for the descent into the northern passes.

"I do not know why, but that oaf gives me the creeps," Helin said, shaking briefly as if to rid her of the clammy feeling covering her back and forearms.

"I know what you mean, my daughter, but Arrim is a thoroughly accomplished warrior who has led several expeditions into Orcassia."

"Orcassia!" Helin gasped, jaw gaping.

Arnim turned back to face her and smiled warmly. Leaning over to gently brush his lips to her forehead, he said, "Times change. Once upon a time we lived in total seclusion, but even within our valleys bands of goblins suddenly arrived early last summer. Where from or how we do not know, but the religious people tell us of magic that could teleport people across the world. However, they have never seen it used and know nothing of how to prevent it happening again. Luckily the incidents were only minor and the general public was kept from learning of these disturbing incidents."

"Why are they disturbing, father? We have had raids before. By orcs, dwarves and even elves!"

"That is true, but none of them used magic to appear wherever they chose. I believe that someone knows of our existence, and is using these incidents to speed up our involvement in the dwarven war with the orcs. Why else would only small bands be sent to cause as much confusion as possible? Even the general population of the dwarven and elven kingdoms are not aware of our existence."

"Perhaps the powers could not send more than a few?" Helin offered, although the subject of magic was far beyond her understanding.

"Maybe. Perhaps this venture is a blessing in disguise after all."

"How so?"

Arnim sighed. "It is only a matter of time before the military way of life slowly diminishes to the point of being almost unnecessary. Perhaps my time has ended and I should step aside for the new era to begin. We cannot forever remain on the sidelines, while the elves and dwarves fight for their very existence."

Helin shrugged and moved forward to lean against her knees.

"You disagree?" Arnim asked, puzzled.

"I just find it difficult to see how the war could enter the mountains? Surely we are able to defend our valleys?"

"That may be true now, Helin, but in time there will be armies on our doorstep rather than the odd band of twenty raiders. No, even if we remain neutral, do you really think the orcs will be satisfied with just the peninsular? Even if they then fought a war with the elves, how long could they resist on their own? The passes, if need be, can be circumvented, indeed we have done so ourselves. Should we deny our enemies the same abilities after the magical show of strength?"

Helin shook her head in resignation, knowing only too well that this very argument had been regurgitated and debated beyond counting in the last few weeks. She opposed the army leaving the valleys, while her father supported the move, but advocated some delay. To him it was only a matter of time, but for Helin the dream of everything passing them by dominated, even though it was honestly recognised as being impractical.

"We have remained neutral for centuries," Arnim continued. "It is time to join those free-speaking peoples who oppose the orcs. Their own people, because of their close relationship to all of us, hate the northern *dwarves*. They too have now accepted that they can no longer ignore the plight of the entire kingdom, and so shall we support their decision to join the struggle."

"Many of our young people may never return."

"That is the fate of all warriors..."

"But not necessarily the fate of all the peoples in this world and their cultures. Their wars have raged since the beginning of my adulthood and yet there are no signs of the carnage abating. If the dwarves fall, why should we also concern ourselves? We are too small an enterprise to warrant an invasion. If we remain neutral, perhaps our borders will be honoured?"

Arnim turned to face his daughter with a look of anger that normally froze the recipient, but Helin was more than familiar with her father's personality and stubbornly returned the stare.

"You suggest a truce with the *Orcs?*"

"No. Just an acceptance of ignorance will suffice."

"And when they have this *Ignorance* agreed, how long will it be before the armies on our doorstep number in thousands? Ten years, twenty, thirty?"

"It would give us time to devise a more stable way of retaining our freedom. Time is what we require, not a rash descent into the peninsular for us all to perish before we need to. I am all for defending our lands, but I do not share this necessity that the older factions seem to feel, a need to die now. Personally I would gladly accept another thirty years, and then I would happily give my life for my people!"

Helin rose and moved a few paces away, turned sharply and raised an accusing finger towards her father.

"I opposed all intentions of leaving, but your words swayed the council. You then tried to obtain a delay. Why?"

"To bring the next level of trainees into the fold. With them we could take ten thousand and still leave a large force of recruits with experienced warriors to protect the valleys. It was a simple mathematical calculation. Additionally, the elves have not mobilised yet, and although a large army has started to march south they will not arrive for another two or three months. The advance guard at the city of Lo is but ten thousand strong. Is it not strategically sound to join the greatest force so as to enhance our survival prospects?"

Still breathing heavily, Helin nodded and realised that anger had fuelled her harsh outburst. "I am sorry, father. I have always been incapable of understanding the larger picture. You say that only a third of the elves are marching south?"

"Yes, and even they may arrive too late."

"Then why has the council decided to move now, of all times?"

Arnim grimaced and for a moment fell into a deep silence.

"They have received news of a great defeat inflicted on the Orcassian army in the northern peninsular..."

"I remember," interrupted Helin, thoughtfully. "The mortalkind, Romans they call themselves, had arrived as foretold, but the location was rather odd. Nevertheless, they defeated the invasion and forced the enemy back. Why should that be relevant?"

"The situation has been reversed. The dwarves in Thoria have been devastated at the Battle of Thor's Fingers down the Noborian River. Half the Thorian plains and forts have been lost along with at least two thirds of the army. Furthermore, the enemy has landed in the southern peninsular and the end is near for the *dwarves*. The council feels that we should move now and seek to join the forces in the southern peninsular before there is nothing left."

"But if the northern peninsular is lost, we will be trapped."

A nod of the head gave the confirmation she sought. Helin resumed her seat, but this time leant against the raised knees of her father rather than the tree trunk.

"Father..."

"Daughter..."

"Can we prevail?"

"We can but try."

"That does not answer my question."

"Then my answer is no. But we will *still* try. We will always try. We will have to trust in Zeus and pray for guidance that will enable us to make a difference."

"How long will we be away?"

"I do not know."

"Nothing will be the same when we return."

"Everything must change. We are no different."

The wind had died away by the time they both fell silent, lost in their own thoughts. The spring leaves on the ground could no longer be seen to fly in their circular motion across the ridge. The sun began to beat down, and shone through the leaves and branches to further enhance the beauty of the scene. Nature had finally managed to bring the debate to a close. Nature was after all the strongest force known to either person. Or should I say *Hobbit*!

Even as Arnim glanced at the reflection the sun created on Helin's platted brown hair, the combined strength of these small doughty people began to arrange their regimental columns in his mind. They had developed new ways to defend themselves and, over the centuries, few, if any, in the outside world had known of their existence, believing the northern mountains to be impassable except for the dwarven and elven Gate Towers. Both towers protected either the dwarven or elven interest in the passes that circumvented the highest mountain range in the world.

Barely four foot five inches, Arnim was considered a very tall Hobbit. Helin herself was one of the largest their people had ever seen, a fact that many blamed on the new spring waters, as they did not know where they originated. Their contents were suspected of being contaminated, but to date nobody had keeled over and so the young had not only consumed the water, but also bathed in the river on a regular basis.

With curly hair, a round face and strong arms and legs, these people never wore shoes, as their soles naturally grew an inch thick. It was this fact that had led to initial trials with wrestling, and eventually to a system of fighting they referred to as *Hobi*. The system involved using the hands and feet, plus other less obvious parts of the anatomy, to strike an opponent and bring them to the floor.

At first this knowledge was restricted to only the richest families, as a form of sport, but with the crisis three hundred years before the system had been quickly altered. At that time, a band of fifty orcs had raided one valley and set up camp due to their curiosity about the hobbits themselves. This not only helped these people to retain their secrecy, as not a single orc ever left that valley, but the birth of Hobi became essential.

Tomar Bobirus was the name of the founder of the new system!

Refined swords and shields became the first things to change. Then almost naturally the method of unarmed fighting became a subject for the maidens, who were at that time excluded from the armed forces. They approached Bobirus and asked to be taught the basics, to protect themselves and their honour. He showed them the hand chop, the sidekick to the knees and then the grip to freeze the breath. Then came the most important question of all time.

"How do we apply this to a creature twice our size?"

Nobody remembers who asked the question, but the result was that additional application, and the study of all creatures' anatomies, were added to the ever-growing requirements a warrior was asked to learn. Soon a select warrior band was chosen and eventually the academy was created, leading to the creation of an army within fifty years. Under the tree, Arnim watched his daughter rise and felt the joy of pride surge through his veins. Here stood a young officer who had proven that the maidens could stand side by side with the males and defend their homeland.

Arnim's thoughts became disturbed as Helin gently shook his right shoulder.

"Father...are you listening?"

"Oh, my apologies. You were saying...?"

"It is time for us to join the others at the plateau. Are you coming now or will you join us later?"

The older warrior slowly rose to his feet and smiled warmly at the forthright approach of his daughter. He could not help but realise that her lack of patience might prove her doom, as the world was a place where such an approach could save lives, but might also rashly expend them.

"Not at this precise moment, Helin, perhaps in a moment or two," he said, adjusting the curved blade he carried on his left hip. "Prepare your vanguard and proceed to secure the valley floor. I will follow with the first formations in five hours."

Helin bowed formally, stepped forward to kiss her father's cheek lovingly and, with a final knowing look, took off at a brisk pace towards the archway.

"Where to now?" Arnim whispered to himself. "Where to now?"

Less than an hour later, Helin proudly moved across a small ravine that had been circumvented with a rope bridge, and descended to the bottom of the small hill on the far side. Resplendent in her bright red armour, she moved solemnly towards a low-lying ridge and looked beyond. Behind her the commotion of movement was almost inaudible as the entire maiden regiment also moved towards the ridge with their hearts pounding.

Then with a sigh that many overheard, the youngster led the chosen vanguard forward to destiny. Helin's future was for the moment unknown. As indeed was her people's!

They moved though the shadows with an unknown purpose. If it had been for good then the local highway would have sufficed, but for these warriors of the night the empty darkness was their only friend, but a friend nonetheless.

Nobody knew their real purpose in the long run, but many used the name of Black Thorians to describe a minority that stood side by side with the orcs! These were dwarves that had chosen the dark side, the kingdom's inevitable fall having already been accepted. They saw no reason to struggle further, and promises of power, land and wealth kept many of them fighting against their very own people.

In reality, thankfully, their numbers remained small and their actual influence on the global events was very minor. However, as covert spies they had proven their worth to the enemy. Nobody knew where they had originated, but rumour and misunderstandings had led to the common belief that they were descended from dwarves captured in Gobli one hundred years before. It was believed that an entire camp of over two thousand had been taken prisoner, for the very secret purpose of bending their will to that of Hades' disciples. Another well-known myth was that they had orchestrated an assassination attempt on one of the dwarven kings centuries before, but no one knew if this was true, or of any links to the fools who had failed.

Since then disillusioned dwarves, and even elves, had joined this so-called power base that sought the survival of their species after the eventual defeat they expected to transpire. There were barely ten or twenty within the ranks that the great Hades would personally trust with any task of serious importance, and it was these honoured few who entered the camp by the great river or, more accurately, the Kikonos River, to give it its real name.

No, they came from all walks of life, and within their ranks stood any dwarves or elves that had a grudge against their own people. At the top stood an elf and dwarf that none of this group had so far even met, yet it was understood that both had served actively abroad as spies for the Mage. They lived on deceit and even admired a truly evil plan to deceive and destroy an enemy. Alliances were common, and in their own darklands, far to the south, they fought many clan wars for power and riches. There was no limit to their deviousness, and their eagerness for gold was their main reason for being here now.

Freedom and mistrust were hardly the cornerstones of a new age, and yet for this band of ten the current task was as essential as the breath they drew every morning. But why refrain from following the Mage blindly, as indeed the orcs, goblins, gnomes and wolves freely admitted they did?

No, you see, their own arrogance kept them above such fools as the Mage, whom they despised almost as much as the goblins. No amount of depravity could bring them to work with those heathens. Yet they held no special position in the hierarchy of the orcs and, if anything, they were the lowest of the low, and this led to the intense training and their use for espionage, which had high expectations of fatality.

None of the ten anticipated returning home.

Yet here they were walking through an enemy camp with thousands of warriors on all sides. Gold. That was all it was...gold. For any that survived there lay waiting a pot of one thousand pieces that would allow them to live as kings in the south. If they survived.

Home, now there was a contradiction and no mistake. During their training, they lived in the shadow of Mount Doom in Haderia and, due to the intense heat of the upper lands, they dwelt well beneath the surface in elaborate caves. This was nothing unusual for a dwarf, but these caves still retained their previous occupants and only recently a successful conclusion had been achieved in the Caves War, as it had become known.

For ten years they had fought in the tunnels, and cave after cave had fallen under their control after suffering horrifying losses. Eventually the trolls, the original occupants, were forced out into the sun, where they turned to stone. It was of course rumoured that the southern trolls would avenge the extinction of the northern cave trolls, but they were too set in their isolation and would probably have enjoyed killing one another more than seeking retribution.

However, it was also rumoured that several southern trolls travelled with the Mage, and this was the topic of discussion this very morning. Nothing could be substantiated of course, but it did not stop two elves from drawing knives. Such stupidity was short lived. Trolls or not was of no importance to them, as they stood in the middle of the greatest army the enemy had ever assembled, well over five hundred leagues from their own lands. Unity was their greatest strength.

Their number was quickly reduced to eight!

During the cave war the population had suffered, but even as the war continued more and more people joined their ranks, and even a few Romans had in recent months appeared from an unknown direction. Life was hard and the training even more trying, and yet most of them succeeded in joining what they called an "Arcani Group."

Here infiltration and covert operations, such as assassinations, were their trademark, although there had been little opportunity in the last five years for them to make any distinctive contribution to their cause. Then, suddenly, they received orders to organise this operation. This in itself was not a surprise, but the type of mission requested was a shock. Kidnapping was not their normal approach, as it was invariably easier to simply kill the target. However, on pain of death, they had been told to bring the target back alive! They were also threatened with the loss of gold pieces! The latter had more effect!

Within the hour all ten, sorry eight, of their group had been informed of their role in the task ahead. Fires, confusion, shouting and general mayhem were their only allies. In one hand their leader held the orb of transportation, sent by the Mage, and his task was to find their target.

The orb was an incantation that required only that they throw it within five feet of the target, and all would be transported out of the camp and given an initial head start for the coast. Here a vessel would be waiting. It seemed simple, perhaps too simple.

A peculiar addition to the orders was that another spy was actually within the camp of the elven lord Aarun, but his name was not mentioned. However, his participation was expected and was to be accepted if he offered identification, in the form of a seal from the Mage. If the task alone was not enough pressure, they now had an unknown factor that could seal their doom or become their saviour on his or her whim. Thinking absently, their leader guessed that this was the reason he personally did not trust the Mage.

For security purposes, until this very day none of them had even known of the others' allegiance to the orcs. They had all been trained and, from the date of their infiltration, only certain contacts had been maintained, and they had never been in a group of more than four operatives at any given time. In truth, several had been totally lost for words on arriving at the one and only meeting, two hours previously. Three were captains of reasonable distinction who had so far served with honour, but had to date not been forwarded to any front line formation.

The surprise had quickly dissipated with the arrival of the leading member, and they were all quickly brought up to date.

In short, they were all being sacrificed to achieve the kidnap, although in reality a few might survive if they were lucky, but being captured and subsequently interrogated was not an option open to any of them. They had therefore consumed a slow working poison that would give them twenty-four hours in which to drink the antidote, fifteen if there was to be no error in judgement and survival a certainty.

Now, as the training dictated, they moved quickly through the outer camp where only a rudimentary guard was maintained due to the masses on site. However, it was not long before the inner camp border became apparent and the captain-guard stepped across their path and called for a halt.

No word was uttered. Each moved with that practiced skill of any assassin, using friendship and that all too deadly art of familiarity. Those that stood before them were dwarves, after all. However, even the snake in the bosom would wait patiently for the right time to strike. Even so, the guards saw only a group of dwarves wearing the livery of the Westonian Guard Regiment, hardly something to treat with suspicion, so the guard-captain walked forward with arms wide and smiling. As did his executioner. That night it was their only mistake. It was their last mistake.

Swiftly they threw the four bodies, plus one of their own number, inside an empty tent in the knowledge that the change of the guards was due anytime now, perhaps in a few minutes, perhaps a few hours. None of them knew the timetable. With a nod from the leader, the survivors spread out to act in pairs and began to set fire to as much as possible. The nearby stables and hay provided a perfect target and swiftly threw a deep blanket of black smoke across their vision, stinging the eyes.

Shouts could be heard above the din.

"Fire! Fire! Call out the guards, some fool has set fire to the stables!"

At first, there was an orderly response as the inner guards were trained, but quickly the three captains began to assume the authority associated with their rank, and within a few minutes nobody knew whether they were coming or going. Meanwhile the fire caught hold of several tents and the pandemonium increased threefold. With a practiced eye, the leader nodded towards the two captains at his side, and the three made their way back along the central line of tents, seeking the golden flag. It was not long before it came into view.

Behind them someone shouted a challenge, but they ignored this and increased their pace to a slight jog. Everyone else was now moving towards the fire, while they concentrated on moving away at an ever-increasing pace. In fact, they moved so rapidly that the tent guards were set upon and dispatched before they had even drawn their swords or uttered a challenge.

They were now inside and the alarm would almost certainly have been raised. There was little more than ten seconds to find the target.

"Go outside. Delay any one's entry," the leader commanded, condemning them both to almost certain death.

Neither hesitated and with a scream they charged outside and set upon the nearest dwarves with enthusiasm. This new shock caused further delay, and even with a more determined response nobody initially realised the real threat, that someone else was still inside the golden tent. They approached guardedly two captains that had seemingly gone insane.

Then the penny had dropped!

"Black Thorians!" came the cry through the tent to the leader inside. "Death!" became the chant!

Then there was a rustle. A man rose sleepily from a nearby enclave in the tent, still groggy with sleep. One swift movement, and the orb flew across the tent to land next to Atronius, who instantaneously dropped back on to the furs that constituted a bed.

One step brought the leader within the sphere of the teleportation incantation, and together they vanished, just as Cappa and Elvandar entered the tent. Too late! By the Gods only seconds too late, but still in time to see the Black Thorian leader smile coldly in triumph.

"We must find them!" exclaimed Elvandar.

"How? Where? What the hell did they do to leave...magic, I suppose?"

"You suppose correctly. Organise the searches north and south, Cappa. I will see to the other areas. We must act swiftly for the incantation will have moved them only a league or two. We still have a chance of finding him, if we are quick enough."

Neither needed any further encouragement and they set about the task with energy. Frantically Cappa sought those he knew to be efficient organisers. All the while his mind raced. Without Atronius, what would happen to this army of mixed-up peoples that at best had agreed to sit at the same table, never mind fight together.

The enemy had indeed been clever in their choice of target. In the past few months, Atronius had single-handedly moulded the small Army of Allegiance into a formidable army that functioned almost as effectively as the legions. There were of course differences, but somehow their own people had become more at home with their predicament. The uncontrollable outbursts, even racial comments, had diminished, although not entirely.

Even as he searched, he knew that the escape would have been planned meticulously. They must broaden their search area. He sped off in search of Porta, Julius, Marcellus and Valenus.

In the end, twenty bodies were recovered as dawn broke on the horizon, and Aarun knew of only two who could definitely be identified as the Black Thorians. For a few hours, they tried to establish what had taken place, but in the end they gave up and decided that they must try and locate where exactly the incantation had taken Atronius.

Aarun returned to Cappa and Elvandar for reports on their patrols. He knew, as did Elvandar that the incantation could not work for more than a few leagues and so they began more intensive searches. As they were looking towards the coast, they were all surprised when Porta had quickly taken up the challenge and had said that he would cover this region. Before there could be any refusal, he took a band of Helvetii and Romans and marched off in search of blood.

"I find it difficult to understand your friend, Cappa," Aarun stated in bemusement, as they watched the odd band march away. "Only yesterday Porta was caught in a brawl over a maiden elven captain whom he had approached for...how shall we say...unseemly attention. Now Atronius is missing and he has suddenly developed into an avenger. It is a mystery, is it not?"

Cappa nodded. "It is true, however, that the Primus saved Porta's life at one point," he offered, by way of explanation. "But he has, nevertheless, been acting quite strangely the last few days. Almost as though he was seeking trouble, rather than the normal Porta, who usually found it sooner or later anyway."

"I hope he succeeds, for it will make a leader of him and we could use another centurion," Aarun suggested.

"True. We need everyone," Cappa agreed, but in the back of his mind something was beginning to take form. Something was definitely not right, but *what*?

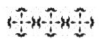

Of course they never found Atronius, for even as Porta marched to the coast he was already concealed on the ship that had begun to sail south under the Mage's protection. It was the beginning of his true nightmare. A nightmare that he could not even envision with all the might of Hades, for he was being taken to the Dark Tower and nobody returned from there...Ever!

The Mage watched the shimmering picture of the ship before him and smiled. Now perhaps the Master would forgive him for trusting that fool Igluk with the northern expedition. This was indeed a coup. The only force now capable of standing against the Master was the Oracle and now, as determined by his spies, he was in their power. Surely he had succeeded, and who better to have as the Oracle than a filthy mortalkind! This also explained why the Romans had been brought to this dimension after all. Their numbers were unimportant, as the only reason was to bring the Oracle here.

No matter, he thought, I shall remain on guard for the entire night, if necessary, and guide the ships to their ports. Nothing must happen to this treasure...*not anything*!

Helin watched from a distance as two of her most able warriors closed on one another. They were in a field south of the city of Lo, and only that morning they had informed the local magistrate that they did indeed exist. She had enjoyed that moment immensely but today she had ordered a day of rest. They would compete with the other regiments, give the locals a demonstration of their prowess and dazzle the males with her maiden warriors. In all her years of dealing with her own people she had learnt one valuable lesson. Nothing could last long in an argument against any leather-clad female. A poor lesson perhaps, but it had won her more arguments against her superiors than her fighting prowess could ever hope to achieve.

Now as Molisis and Armolin closed together, they began to almost play-fight.

The strikes were clean, as their training demanded, but the weight applied was hardly noticeable. Blending each foot movement with a rotational hip adjustment would simply project a clenched fist straight towards the other, arousing several gasps from the gathering crowd. Helin knew better of course, for even before contact was made the head tilted slightly and the palm easily deflected the strike to one side. Within a split second a different approach followed, by which each would lose in turn, hence prolonging the demonstration that was literally a dance, as far as Helin could see. Of course to the uninitiated it was spectacular.

One punch would flow into another and be swiftly followed by a kick, all being blocked, as indeed were the counter measures, which involved a magical spinning kick over one body height in the air. Helin had openly laughed at that spectacle and waved an acknowledgement to the smiling Molisis. Such kicks were always fun, although she had for many years discouraged such ineffectual tactics for any real combat situation, but this was not a fight and so the crowd applauded wildly. Nearby an instructor in unarmed combat clapped his hands, and the two warriors increased their speed and began to incorporate more spinning kicks and jumping kicks, and adapted many moves to finish with throws.

Molisis was the master in everything as her hand reached for Armolin and twisted the wrist, but she resisted, so a leg sweep was applied to encourage her descent. On and on they continued for at least ten minutes before the final explosion left both warriors on the floor. Now they fought for the honour of the teacher's praise, and the techniques were dirty.

A final clap of the hand brought them both to a stop, just before control was lost, but the two gladly smiled and clasped each other's forearms. They trained hard and would play hard, as neither would have stopped due to Helin's presence. You see, both were up for promotion to a captainship next month, and only Helin knew that Molisis would prevail, but it would be good for Armolin to keep trying. Her time would come next year, as nobody thought for a second that either would remain at the lower rank for very long. Helin beckoned for them both to join her at the edge of the field. Molisis as usual arrived first and saluted grandly, but with a smile. They were after all off duty.

"Jumping spinning kicks indeed," mocked Helin, spinning on her heels. "My father should have allowed Armolin to teach you a lesson. What have I told you about...?"

"Yes, okay, my Lady, I get the message," Molisis said, once more bowing in mock subservience. "I will endeavour to avoid such childish tricks in the future."

"I just hope she does not teach her people to do that," chided Armolin, raising an impudent finger to wag in her face.

"No, would I do that?"

"Yes!"

"True, but I have emphasised the difference between that which is practical and that which is not. If you doubt me, my learned colleagues, perhaps a tournament tomorrow, to see who commands the best in the regiment?"

"Yes, why not," agreed Armolin, grinning broadly. "My people have been lazing around all day. It is about time they did some work."

"I doubt they have been lazy on this day," informed Helin, a serious look clouding her expression ominously.

"Why so?" both juniors chorused together.

"My father has ordered extensive patrols to the south to locate the dwarven army. We have heard rumours of a great defeat to the south. It seems we may arrive too late anyway."

"Ha! You jest, surely," roared Molisis, puffing her chest out like a man and stamping her feet. "When we few arrive, defeat or otherwise, we will prevail. I doubt not the success of our endeavours."

It was hard not to laugh, but the news was still enough to dampen their spirits.

"No fight tomorrow then?" Armolin confirmed.

"No, I'm afraid not, we march at dawn and we will be in those mountains to the south within five days. From there we will be on a war status. I have heard that one of our patrols has engaged a small band of orcs not too far south. Grave news, if true."

Molisis nodded, but on glancing across the field found her attention wandering.

"Mmmm. What did you say? Oh, sorry, my Lady, you were saying?"

"I was saying that we march at dawn…but clearly…You…are… Who is she looking at?" Helin eventually whispered to Armolin, while searching the far side of the field.

"Artonin, my Lady, first lieutenant to the tenth regiment. He has asked to court the young Molisis, love at first glance I believe…"

"Love…" snapped Molisis, turning sharply. "By the Gods it is lust, I'll have you know. Have you seen how tall he is? Almost five-five and built like a stone shit…"

"Yes, yes," Helin interrupted mildly. "I think we can pass on the details, but I must confess he is quite delicious. Perhaps I will take him for myself?"

Molisis turned as if she had been struck between the eyes with a blunt instrument, and stared coldly at them both in turn.

"You would not dare, my Lady. Would you?"

Both grinned, but it was not long before their better natures took a firm hold on their conscience, and Helin's smile was seemingly enough reassurance. However, even so small a doubt still lingered, and for the rest of the day Molisis remained a little subdued. In her past she had emotionally betrayed others, and it was difficult to imagine that someone would not do the same to her. Her heart wept at such a prospect. With a grimace she turned abruptly and walked away in silence. Some things were simply not funny, she thought, feeling guilty about her youthful escapades.

"She will be fine, Helin," Armolin confided later that evening, over some hot bread and broth. "She will live, I am sure. It is odd to think that males are the only weakness Molisis seems to have."

Helin grinned in appreciation of Armolin's comment and clapped her roughly on the shoulder. Further words were unnecessary as, later that evening, they again spied Molisis dreamily watching the object of her desires, and completely oblivious to their earlier taunts. For a moment they both laughed, but just as quickly each realised that perhaps their friend had the real key to survival. Fatalism would certainly play into the hands of the enemy, as they would all be fighting for one reason or another, but without really understanding or believing in the reasons.

Maybe they no longer needed to believe, but to look for justification as best they could under the circumstances. Perhaps her blind following of a youthful officer, who clearly had a future, gave their friend an insight into her possible future as well, thus giving her hope. Hope that their task would not be a final journey, but only a beginning. Yes, perhaps, whatever the reason, the main point was to maintain hope. None wished to die and all would desire a reunion with their loved ones, but fate rarely helped anyone. So without certainty, the next best thing was the hope of once more walking the high valleys of their homeland.

Of course it was always possible that she would die, but Helin was too well trained in her belief that all things would happen, regardless of their hopes or dreams, to allow this to cloud her judgement. It was best to simply allow the Gods to have their immortal distractions with their fleeting lives, and make the best out of a bad deal that had singled her out to be unusual...In truth it had not been difficult for her or her people, but that was all about to change. Now they were known, now they were no longer just an unconfirmed myth, now they could no longer hide.

These thoughts and many others became the topic of discussion as they set forth on the march the following dawn. The main issue was whether fate and destiny actually existed, or whether the Gods had created such beliefs to make matters more manageable with the unpredictable elves and dwarves.

Although the discussion was not heated, many of the military intellects stood amongst them and the hours drifted from the positives to the negatives without prejudice. With their minds occupied, their feet walked all the more swiftly and within a few days they had traversed the vast northern peninsular of the Dwarmania, which, suffice to say, did not really turn their heads with its beauty.

Then, one morning, the central mountain range suddenly appeared before them, rising in many places to over ten thousand paces and taking their breath away. For many, the homesickness became unbearable, duty being the only reason that they remained in a country that had nothing for them. Thoughts drifted back to their loved ones, and for the first time Helin realised just where they now stood, far from home. Barely ten days ago they had left their mountain fortress, but now none of them could see what the future held. Could they even make a difference? Why had she allowed her father to convince her to leave their homeland? Doubts and fears welled up in her chest, heartfelt and painful, and all about her the same feelings were literally written on the faces of her warriors.

That night Helin decided to confront her father, but again Arnim refused to be baited into yet another debate. They could hardly go back to hiding in the mountains, he fumed, they would continue *south*. They must, as news had reached them of another defeat in Gretania, smaller than before, but a defeat nonetheless.

"Our numbers are now required more than ever because the Gretan army has been decimated," Arnim had confided, as a final statement. "We no longer have time to debate or dally anywhere. We must march and we must march *now*. We will have an hour's break every ten hours. We march through the night from this time forward. Make it so, Helin!"

With that, Arnim had turned to the problem of victuals for their continued journey and pointedly ignored his daughter. Deflated, Helin had left the tent feeling stupid. She should have known better than to try and take them all back, for even if they did go the dwarves now knew of their existence and almost certainly so did the enemy. Now that their course had been chosen for them, there was no other choice but to stay the course, but for all her loyalty she could not help feel a growing awareness of dread.

Something was wrong or, more to the point, she felt as though a greater force was controlling precisely what happened and where. She could not put her finger on precisely what force, but a dwarf had recently told her that the power of the Oracle was well known for bringing the forces of good together, even across the dimensions void.

"Oracle?" she asked.

"He is our greatest ally, my Lady. The voice of Zeus and a powerful Mage."

"So this Oracle is the opposite of the Mage of Darkness?"

"Yes."

"So who is this Oracle?"

"Nobody knows," the dwarf replied, looking rather sheepish. "It is the most guarded secret in the kingdom."

"So how do you know the Oracle even exists?"

"What?"

"How do you know the Oracle even exists?"

A look of indignation crossed the dwarf's face, as he turned without another word and stormed away in disgust, ending the debate. Religion, she thought, what a load of rubbish to base a society on. Had they all gone senile? If this Oracle was so powerful why did he not simply sweep his enemies before them and save so many lives? It seemed as though the greatest hope for the dwarves was steeped in mythology rather than the bare facts, that they were losing the war and losing it very quickly.

Of course, neither could have known what had happened that very day in the great camp to the south, for Atronius was unknown to any of them, and his kidnapping would have been of little importance.

Perhaps it was this occurrence that filled Helin with so much dread, perhaps?

Well, she sighed resignedly after a brief pause in her walk, once we enter these mountains and reach the great river there would no turning back. Now it was time to do what she was best at...to fight!

"You," she indicated to a nearby guard. "Have the first regiment brought to arms immediately. All scouting sections to move forward at the highest pace to spy the land before us, as the dwarves seem unable to do so. We march ahead of the army to secure safe passage on the roads. Clear?"

"As the blue sky, my Lady."

"Then go. I will be on the ridge to the south. Have the company commanders join me there."

So it was finally to happen. In a way she was glad that she could finally forget all her feelings and concentrate on the task in hand. With a weight lifted from her shoulders, it was not long before the maiden regiment was thoroughly organised and marching into the night, with scouts ahead in the dark, and the smaller columns advancing by torchlight. After sending a messenger to her father at dawn, she had then followed the regiment and soon caught up with the footsore warriors, who had already begun to sing heartily as the sun rose before them.

It was a beautiful spring morning, and it was the day that Helin finally went to war.

Lord Aarun sat comfortably on pillows in the tent kindly supplied by the local inhabitants after his own had mysteriously vanished. With a central pole the facility to light a fire was magnificent and very good at keeping the spring chill from his bones. A fact that he had already noticed was becoming more and more of a problem: the task of remaining warm and achieving any kind of comfort was becoming ever more tricky. For a few moments, he blindly rifled through a few papers and then consumed the last piece of meat on the side table nearby, before finally allowing a slight incline in his posture to enable him to sink more comfortably into the cushions.

For the moment, everything seemed of little importance, for this night was without doubt his greatest moment. His theories had finally been proven to be correct but, by the Gods, he had had no idea that the proof would be so astounding. Hobbits did exist, and his papers on the elusive people had already become highly popular in Gallicia. He was known there as the exclusive expert on the race of people known in the histories as the *forgotten people*.

In the histories of time past, which he now associated with another dimension, as this was the only way it made any sense, a great war had been fought to preserve a world and its people. But little if anything was ever known as fact concerning exactly what had transpired during this conflict. It was known that the elves had forsaken that world forever and had decided that the dominance of the mortalkind had destroyed their dominions, to which they were accustomed. Thus the real magic of life had ended for them.

It was commonly believed that they had then travelled here to Gallicia, and that their old lands had existed on the other side of the circumference of this world. Of course Aarun had learnt quickly that this was not true, and that explorers had found an ancient civilisation on the other side of the world, but it had not matched any elven or dwarven architecture. In fact, it did not even match orcish, goblin, gnome or troll civilisation either.

For centuries that mystery had given rise to speculations, which over time had become almost the law of the land. In truth, however, Aarun had always known that their ancestors had come from another dimension, just as they had too, and his dreams had told him he was correct. In this he knew Zeus spoke to him directly, but many a time the messages had been a little confused, or certain parts had been deliberately left out to avoid further erroneous enquiries. Aarun had spent most of his youth fascinated by the myth of the hobbits. Now he was finally proven to be the real genius at the King's court. Not those overbearing idiots who still believed that the Romans were lesser elves that had been punished for betraying Zeus at the beginning of time.

Aarun chuckled with satisfaction. The fact that Time in itself was an entity true unto itself did not seem to deter his elders from their folly, but that really was a different story and felt like a lifetime ago. Now his mind was completely focused on what this evening would mean to him, for the two hobbit dignitaries were joining him shortly for a brief discussion, General Kol being far too busy to welcome this new reinforcement from the north.

What's that? Aarun forced his eyes to refocus, pushing away the momentary lapse into self-congratulation he had permitted, and looked just in time to see these two very dignitaries enter his tent. He began to sweat and noted almost offhandedly that he had never felt like this, except in the presence of his own king. What should he do now, he suddenly panicked, bow? With a flourish he rose, but for the first time in his life he failed utterly to find the right words, and nothing seemed to help his dilemma.

"We seem to be having this effect on most people these days, my daughter," Marshal Arnim said, with a smile. Then, turning back to Aarun, he continued. "It is an honour to meet you, Lord Aarun of Gallicia. I have heard your name many times in our reports."

"Name...reports...me?" Aarun stammered, much to Elvandar and Cappa's amusement, as they too entered the tent. "What possible use would my name be to you?"

"Shall we sit first and partake of a drink perhaps?" Arnim suggested, having already spotted a very large cushion that looked absolutely irresistible. Without waiting for a reply he quickly took a step and claimed his space before any opposition could be uttered. It was indeed comfortable. Perfect after a ten-league march that had worn him down to his very bones: he wondered if anything was left of his feet.

"This is a great day, Lord...?" Aarun began, still unsure of the correct diplomatic approach, his mind still racing as the two hobbits quickly assumed seats.

"Please, Lord Aarun, call me Arnim, but the official title is that of Marshal. However this is of little help to us and perhaps an informal discussion would suit us better."

"And...?"

"My daughter, Regiment-Captain of the First Regiment, Helin Arnim."

"But...?"

"Ah, yes, here comes that all too familiar *but* again, my daughter," Arnim smiled, with an affectionate pat on Helin's shoulder. "It seems the novelty will be some time in wearing off."

"It seems that the maidens of their culture are useful only for childbirth, father," Helin replied, indicating her displeasure to Aarun, who had now been joined by Cappa and Elvandar. "Perhaps another demonstration is required?"

"Demonstration?" Elvandar smiled, raising his hand to gently close Aarun's mouth.

"At the city of Lo the people did not believe we were of the warrior caste," Helin explained, returning the smile. "I ordered my junior officers to prepare a brief demonstration, and in this way the city supplied us with victuals. It was an entertaining day."

"I bet," laughed Cappa, loudly. "I am having difficulty with this myself. Even I have heard of your people, and all the storytellers agree on one point...that you were a myth. You seem rather alive and well for a myth."

Helin turned to look for the first time at a mortalkind and found the sight not displeasing at all. The rumours that all of them were small, ugly and forceful by nature were clearly not true of this example, and proved just how prejudiced the dwarves had become. If anything the strong eyes and stature denoted a very powerful person, but also one of wisdom. Or was it just his experience?

"You are?" she asked, still smiling a smile that for a moment froze Cappa to the spot.

"Marius Cappa, Centurion of the Tenth Legion of the Army of Alliance. Formerly of the Roman Republic, to which I one day hope to return to fulfil my duty to Caesar."

"A noble name," added Arnim, and glanced at Elvandar.

"Elvandar, my Lord Arnim, of the Empire of Gallicia, and personal bodyguard to Lord Aarun."

"Yet another noble name to add to that of Lord Aarun with whom I am familiar, although we have never met in person. I, nay, *we*, are honoured beyond any expectation."

"So now that we all know each other, where do I begin?" Aarun said, finally regaining his voice and dropping back onto his cushions with a dull thud.

"Perhaps I could answer a few questions, if I explained the reasoning behind our decision to join your struggle?" suggested Arnim.

"Please," Aarun urged. "Please proceed."

"Well, where indeed to begin? A difficult question when we have so little time. I guess the best place to start is to answer the issue of whether we are indeed a myth?" A chuckle lightened the atmosphere further and both Cappa and Elvandar assumed seats, placing their weapons to one side. "A myth we most definitely have never been, but a shy and protective people we most definitely have been for many centuries...too many."

"So why reappear now?" interrupted Elvandar, earning an irritating glare from Aarun.

"If we allow him to proceed uninterrupted perhaps we'll find out."

"It is fine," Arnim consoled. "We have had the same questions for the last fourteen or more days. I can only hope that this will be the last time, as this explanation is a very simple one. In the last five years or so, we have experienced a constant disruption from raids within the high mountain valleys that we had closed off many centuries ago. We saw no reason to bring the ills of the world amongst us and we lived in relative peace. Of course we kept watch on the wars but, in truth, no conflict has reached this level of success before, and it became clear that if the dwarves fell then we must surely be the next targets. So we had a choice, help the dwarves win or wait and fight alone. Our presence here proves how that decision has faired."

"Indeed it has," agreed Aarun. "But how have your lady-folk become warriors? Why did the raids suddenly begin only five years ago? How have you maintained your secrecy for so long? How is your society maintained? As far as my knowledge extends, you were never a warrior race but one of peace, unless provoked. However, nobody could produce an army in just five years!"

Arnim laughed heartily and raised both hands as though to surrender. "Wow, slow down, my Lord. Questions I have had before but never with such vivacity."

"I apologise," Aarun said, this time throwing a grin at Elvandar. "It seems I reprimand my greatest friend and then proceed to do exactly the same as him and interrupt."

"We are very familiar with your work regarding our people, my Lord," advised Helin, tired of being the dutiful daughter and just as eager to learn about the Romans as they were about her people's history. "Your papers have been read by our people for many years with great interest."

"Yes, you indicated this earlier. How could my work interest you? I suspect that most of the assumptions are incorrect."

"To some extent, but not altogether," Arnim added with a slight inclination of the head. "On the contrary, your work has matched a great deal of our own histories, but in this we must confess that we are left with as much myth as yourselves. According to our histories, we arrived in this land at the same time as the elves, but immediately went our own way and chose the mountain valleys, this time a place where we could dig our hobbit holes in freedom, no more flatlands for us. As regards your earlier questions, we have always suffered from raids of one sort or another. In time, we found the northern dwarves to be our only friends, and for this they were ostracised from their own civilisation, and for the first time we felt pangs of guilt for our single-minded pursuit of isolationism. A mistake that perhaps is one of the main reasons we are here.

"As for the lady-folk, they became warriors when the army almost caused a civil war amongst us. The army was born because of the lessons learnt in a previous great war of which we sat ignorant for far too long. Being of a small stature we therefore learnt unarmed combat and developed our curved sword, which helped us to draw larger swords around our smaller waists. Our solid foot soles enabled us to toughen them almost to the same strength as wood, and gave us a very strong kick, similar to that of a mule, but employed with more skill. Our society is based on a council of elders, as are most autocratic systems, but the decision to join this struggle only came when the raids began to increase. We could no longer stand alone."

"If the raids had stopped," Cappa asked, leaning forward, "then you would have remained alone and without any intention of helping anyone but yourselves?"

"Yes."

"That seems impossible to believe," Aarun spoke almost at a whisper. "Your people are remembered for their high level of prowess, kindness and spiritual strength. How could you have remained for so long watching others suffer?"

"You speak of prowess, Aarun," Arnim began, his eyes now lowered. "But to us the word honour would be more accurate. We became trapped by our own efforts for preservation. In time we believed we had all the answers, but in truth we had nothing."

"That is not true!" exclaimed Helin, turning to face her father. "We have accomplished more than our ancestors could possibly have dreamed. We are stronger than before, more focused and have a greater purpose. Never before has our population been so high..."

"This is a personal debate that is not suited to today, Helin, and we ended this argument several days ago. We are here, and to debate the possibility of returning is pointless."

"The enemy will already know of your presence by now, anyway," Cappa stated flatly, his mind not really taking in the topic. He could not take his eyes off the hobbit maiden's eyes. Never before had his eyes encountered such a perfect face, and the leather overalls were just too much of a distraction.

"Quite so," agreed Aarun. "Quite so. It therefore falls to me to advise you of what our commander, General Kol, had advised me just before your arrival."

"Please begin. We were advised that Kol was too busy to speak to us this evening. I find this acceptable under the circumstances, but many of the young...it is difficult sometimes to curb their enthusiasm."

"Yes, I can understand your predicament, but for the moment it seems that we are all taken aback by your arrival. Kol has requested that you perform the duties of his personal guard until the situation is clearer, and your purpose in this struggle can be identified."

"What!" screamed Helin. "We have exposed our entire people to be nursemaids for your great General Kol! This is an *insult*!"

"*Sit down*!" roared Arnim. Clearly all was not well between father and daughter, but in truth they simply had no time for such outbursts, and no time to delve any deeper than the surface irritation that the continual outbursts were creating.

"I must apologise for my daughter," Arnim continued, as soon as he regained his composure. "We will of course do what is required of us. However, the night draws to a close and my weary bones need their rest. With your permission, we shall retire, and perhaps continue this discussion tomorrow?"

"Of course. But tomorrow I am to set off on my own journey," confided Aarun. "Perhaps when I return?"

"Of course. I look forward to our discussion."

"Perhaps we could talk to this oracle instead then?" demanded Helin, again bridling at yet another rebuke from her father. "Perhaps we could better serve him instead of this Kol, who clearly needs a *nursemaid*!"

"Helin!"

"No, no it is okay. The young act in many ways that seem odd to us of greater years, so patience does indeed become a virtue," said Aarun, hoping to avoid another exchange between father and daughter. "Perhaps our journey tomorrow should require participation by your people, Helin? An active part to reduce the dented pride, perhaps?"

"And the oracle?" Helin demanded. "I hear tell he is a great Mage. Perhaps he should sweep our enemies before us, on this journey you so freely mention?"

"That is not possible," Aarun began to explain, but then thought differently about confiding in someone he had met barely an hour earlier. Especially as the Thorian rebel raid was still fresh in his memory, and the abduction of Atronius still caused a pang of guilt. "Perhaps at a later date?"

"Then tomorrow will have to suffice. For now! We will join your journey, and tell our people of the trust you have placed in us all. I am honoured. Perhaps in this way we can all begin to work more closely together, we are after all on the same side."

A series of bows followed that final sentence. Then, just as swiftly as they had arrived, the hobbits left with Elvandar as their guide. For a moment Aarun remained standing and exchanged a few glances with Cappa.

"That could have gone better," Cappa said finally, with a shake of his head.

"Yes."

"Rather odd though that they would request to see the oracle. Do you think they had anything to do with the abduction?"

"No."

"Feeling talkative again, I see?"

"Yes."

PART TEN

A JOURNEY SOUTH

Aarun sat in silence, solemnly embroiled in his own thoughts, noticing only absently, out of the corner of his eye, the entrance of Elvandar. Swathed in shadows, the tent gave the Marshall an air of resolution, an intentness that Aarun had seen during many other confrontations on the battlefield. Taking a deep breath to put steel into his resolve, he waited for the outburst he knew would come. He watched the sway of the matted hair and the long, powerful stride that covered the length of the tent swiftly.

With a smooth movement that betrayed the elf's finesse, Elvandar approached, completed the traditional salute of respect and patiently waited for permission to speak. Amongst the higher echelons of Gallician society, the Marshall was often referred to as an oaf, but here was the diplomatic side of him that few, if any, had ever seen. The silence became monumental.

"How are you this fine evening, Elvandar," said Aarun, with a wry grin. "There is still a sharp bite in the air, do you not agree? You seem angry, I feel perhaps there is something troubling you? Please, sit, tell me if I can assist."

"Do not *friend* me, my Lord," retorted the elf, furiously. "I have just been informed that an expedition to Haderia is to be organised for your personal business. What *personal* business would you have in those lands that excludes me?"

"Is that not my own counsel, Marshall, or should I now consult you on every decision?"

"Then it is true! You have lost your mind! If you..."

"I am *not* aware that I am expected to explain my purposes to *you*!" Aarun stated vigorously, rising threateningly from his seat to point at the map on the table. "You forget yourself, my friend. I, not you, hold the seal of Gallicia and my orders will be obeyed. I have a separate task that must be undertaken before all else fails. The details are not your concern and I will be travelling south without you, do we understand each other? Your destiny is no longer with me, but here with this army."

With a look of horror the elven warrior dropped to one knee. He knew he had gone too far and allowed his friendship to override his customary calmness yet, when Cappa had advised him of this journey, his anguish at such a foolhardy expedition had left him lost for words. Only a few scant hours ago he had met, for the first time, the halflings of lore, and now he had to accept that his liege-lord was about to undertake a suicidal journey into the very nest of the evil that they defied, preferring the protection of this *Helin* over his own. He was now to be left behind, his duty as a bodyguard ignored, and his pride had been stung deeply.

"I beg forgiveness, my Lord. I am concerned only for your safety, nothing more. I will, of course, obey without question. I simply see nothing to be gained by sending a few hundred people to Haderia, not when we need every blade here at the river. I disagree with you as regards my duty: I feel it is by your side as a shield."

Aarun nodded and raised his hand to hide a smile, one of self-congratulation. He had known almost with certainty how the elf would react when someone finally informed him of his intended journey. Furthermore, Elvandar's exclamation was so loud that it could have been heard in Gantran, never mind by the several people near his tent every dawn. Enemy agents were all around them, and he knew that a few were in their camp, and he hoped that his journey would be reported. The raid by the Black Thorians to take Atronius had proved their existence beyond doubt.

It was a cruel way to exploit such a great friend's loyalty, but his only weakness was a blind fury, which on release was nigh on impossible to control. This, coupled with a lack of understanding of the subtleties of espionage, had made Cappa's earlier announcement all the more genuine. Hopefully, this would lead the enemy to their own shores, perhaps in anticipation of a counter-invasion, but their true objective was the retrieval of Atronius.

It was a ruse to buy as much time as possible, a commodity that seemed to be rapidly running out. He did however understand why Elvandar thought this a fool's errand, but since the abduction and the arrival of the hobbits he had had a gut-wrenching foreboding that the next stage would have to involve a showdown with the Mage. He knew nothing of this creature other than the assumption that he too was from the mortalkind brought to this world. Why, who, what powers did he possess, indeed what purpose he had for this world was unknown, but Aarun had to find out!

Resuming his seat, he waved a hand nonchalantly, and speaking gruffly, to imply a deep anger at Elvandar's breach of etiquette, he again pointed at the map before him on the table.

"The enemy have raided our camp on several occasions," he said. "They have successfully kidnapped the one person that we could ill afford to lose, our Oracle. Atronius must be rescued, and it is our belief he has been taken to the Pits of Doom in Pitlas."

"If that is true, then he is already dead," Elvandar commented coldly, rising once more to his feet. "They will torture him until he breaks."

"Cappa has stated that the Pilum has a high pain threshold. He feels the strength of this man will last for several days, perhaps a week, but that we should always remember that magic has never been a part of his beliefs. We must therefore act now, while the winds are favourable for a return journey to Haderia. It is the last thing they will expect. Furthermore, the greater part of their forces will be here, thus giving us at least a chance of saving the Oracle. We must at least try."

"Is he so important? It is only the Ortovians, not our people, who surely believe in these tales of an Oracle who speaks to the gods. Why would our enemy be so concerned over this one person?"

"Him? No. Nobody is too important in the overall scheme of the dimensions, my friend, but the act of kidnapping him has shown they themselves believe in the myths. Do you not see that the longer they pursue this activity, then the longer the Mage remains from the frontline, and the greater our chances of victory become? Kol needs time to mould the army and I must try and give him that time. To achieve this, we must perpetuate the dream they have of breaking Atronius, and thus the Oracle, and learning our most sacred secrets. This illusion will prevent them from throwing their full weight against Kol at the River Bridge, and give us the valuable time we seek to recover from the recent defeats."

Elvandar grunted unsatisfactorily as he stretched his hands high and yawned. Exhaustion was plainly written on his face, and his eyes looked distant, tired and heavy, and the crow's-feet had tripled in depth. "We were not totally defeated in the southern peninsular, my

Lord, it was simply a strategy decided upon by the General, due to the army's lack of experience. He chose to withdraw."

"Yes," agreed Aarun, again all smiles. "But the enemy is not aware of this. Also, the armies sent to outflank Kol would hardly have waited for an opportune moment, no they would have struck immediately. The withdrawal was the right decision. We are not defeated, but we are still in a very precarious situation and the more they believe we are unable to resist, the less detailed their plans will become. You are needed here to mould the recruits into a fighting force for Kol to command. At present we still have the divisions of race and creed. This cannot continue for much longer."

"Why has the council not forwarded the reinforcements promised several months ago?"

It was now Aarun's turn to groan inwardly. His smile drained away and a cloud, which the candlelight could not hide, covered his face.

"That, my friend, is the very reason for our journey. As desperate as it sounds, it may not be so in the light of what I am about to tell you. Our council will be sending no more soldiers…"

Elvandar stopped in mid-yawn and a look of disbelief flashed across his eyes. Momentarily he recomposed his expression but the shock remained in his eyes.

"Yes, it is hard to believe, isn't it?" continued Aarun. "However, the council have received news from Moravia. If we do not send them an army, they will sign a peace treaty with the sunorcs of Innan-Unar, to protect their people from further raids."

"Peace! With the sunorcs, but they are the most vicious of the lot! They never take prisoners of any kind and they use poisoned arrows, unless they wish to each fresh meat!"

"True, but the council has also learnt that the elven confederation in the east has already signed an agreement with the Orcassians. If this battle we intend to fight at this river is not conclusive, we may be ordered to retire from the peninsular entirely. It seems that doubt and suspicion have swayed the council into believing that, if they stand on their own borders, the Haderian army will remain content to stay south of the North Mountains, and will not ascend the mountain crossroads into Hiba."

Elvandar began to pace the floor. "But that is foolhardy, beyond understanding. Who could possibly have convinced them of such a stupid policy? Even the hobbits have determined that to stand without a friend is to die alone. Surely the council are above such a selfish policy?"

"I am not sure which party within the council has advocated such a foolhardy act, but I have made enquiries, the answers to which will not reach us here in time to make a difference."

A heavy silence fell on them both while they listened absently to the wind buffeting the entrance flap, each dwelling briefly on the repercussions of what had been said.

"If they will not reinforce us, then where will the Internal Army be sent?" Elvandar asked, after the pause had become unbearable.

"It will hold a defensive position between both fronts at Fantal. The Moravian Queen will hopefully be reassured by their close proximity, while they will be able to block the mountain passes, should we fall. In other words, they will help no one."

"What do they hope to gain by this betrayal of the trade and alliance agreements with Dwarmania? The dwarves will not tolerate this, nor should they!"

"The army numbers over fifty thousand, Elvandar, so the Moravian Queen will be impressed. Why they are not able to defend their own lands is beyond me. I met her only once and it was enough. She will not send us any aid, but by politically forcing our council to fight for our own kind, she has effectively crippled any effort to stop Haderia in this peninsular. If we win, I hope we can bring about some kind of retribution for that devilish maiden!"

Elvandar closed his eyes. "We have been here for months now, spilling our blood to help the *dwarves*. I am not sure I can accept this betrayal."

"It is but another manifestation of the fear and doubt that the enemy wishes to fester in all of our hearts, Elvandar. They try to turn us against each other and hope that we will fight amongst ourselves, thus diminishing our efforts. In this they were successful with our council, but the hobbits have arrived and from this we must draw faith. Our efforts may prevail, and we must not give up hope."

Aarun gestured towards the wine then thanked Elvandar as the liquid was handed over, with a ceremonial bow, in a silver goblet. "The Moravian Queen has already sent her foreign minister to a meeting with the sunorcs. I have it on good authority that she has no intention of maintaining a state of war against the sunorcs. For us here this is not too serious, as she is no fool, and she will delay the negotiations. What worries me is the elf who will accompany the minister, he is..."

"*Horta!*" Elvandar spat, instinctively reaching for his dagger.

"Yes. Horta."

"But he left the kingdom ten years ago. He went to Orcassia, where he believed the true Gods lived. I am not sure I have ever met a more conniving, devious soul in all my years!"

"That is not in dispute. Horta has had something to do with the change of heart in the Moravian court, and the dwarves also think he is the founder of the Black Thorians. It is rumoured that he has the ear of the queen herself, but even I find that idea too painful to accept. If there was ever a person who fitted the dwarven notion of a *dark-elf*, he surely is the first in line. But whatever the circumstances, we cannot dally on this topic for long. If the enemy learn the truth from Atronius, they will push all the harder. The more they push us, the more likely Moravia will succumb. We *must* throw them off balance before we are smothered and unable to see the good for too much evil."

"But, my Lord, Haderia will still be thick with the enemy. Surely you cannot think that you can reach Pitlas!"

"We must try."

The Marshall rose once more, intent on his pledge to serve Aarun, and if that meant protect him from himself, then so be it. This expedition was utter madness. However, just as he was about to renew the discussion, in marched Cappa and Porta, the latter with that ever-present grin.

At first nobody spoke, while Elvandar's eyes clearly emphasised the unwelcome interruption, and Cappa sensed the heavy atmosphere.

"Have you broken the news yet, my Lord?" Cappa asked, after perching on the table next to Elvandar, and returning his stare with a grin as wide as Porta's.

"I have."

"Then all is well. I have come to confirm that the travel arrangements are complete and that we can leave for the port tomorrow morning, with your consent."

"Consider it given, General Cappa," Aarun responded, formally. "We leave at dawn. Please also inform the admiral that we will be taking Lord Kollis of Westonia with us, as well as a small faction of the hobbits under the command of Helin."

Cappa lowered his eyes, jumped off the table and saluted to his left breast, turned to leave, only to stop at the exit.

"Is there something on your mind, General?" Aarun asked.

"The hobbits are a strange creature and I am a little concerned as regards their battle worthiness. In many cases their stature is even lower than the dwarves'."

"I feel that we will be surprised by their efficiency," replied Elvandar, turning to face Cappa. "My people have believed in their existence for centuries, but to my knowledge only Lord Aarun has ever met one. They are greater than their appearance implies, we should not doubt their heart. In addition, several of my aides have been training with them, and their skills with the curved blades are exceptional. The reach of their arm may be limited, but the reach of those blades most certainly is not."

"Perhaps, but it is my job to be concerned, and I am sure General Kol will also find it difficult to determine a true purpose for them."

Elvandar nodded. "It is perhaps an issue that we should clear up tonight. They have a meal each evening for their officers. If you would care to join me, I have an invitation..."

"It would be the perfect opportunity for you both to become more familiar with our allies," advised Aarun, walking to the exit and clapping Cappa on the shoulder. "The Marshall could do with a little light entertainment, my friend. Perhaps you could see that he finds it?"

With a mild chuckle from Porta the air suddenly lightened and, resigning himself to the task assigned, Elvandar moved to join Cappa and Porta.

"I see that I am being given little choice," he stated, the anger still apparent in his eyes.

"True, my friend. True indeed! The task is set and your destiny is for you to create. You do not need me to assist any longer. Your place is beside Kol, not on the warships going south."

"I am not best pleased either, Marshall," consoled Porta. "Cappa here is leaving me behind as well. He is also not willing to tell me exactly where you are sailing to, only that it is south, hardly a friendly disposition."

"I cannot divulge every order given, Porta."

Aarun smiled once more. "True enough, now off with you all, I need time to complete my own preparations."

All three were bundled unceremoniously outside, much to Cappa's annoyance, but it was not long before they were all quietly walking towards the hobbit camp. It had been a long week, one that had seen the enemy sweep through the southern peninsular after their initial landings. Had so much taken place in barely seven days! To all intents and purposes, Elvandar had been correct in his assessment that the final confrontation on Mount Holvidar had ended in a draw.

However, the sheer number of the enemy had allowed them to place fresh regiments before them on the second day of the battle, while Kol's had remained exhausted. The new formations had required time to assimilate their recent experiences and achieve the transition from raw recruits to experienced soldiers. Difficult manoeuvres in the face of a very active enemy would not have allowed them to do this, so Kol had retired behind this Great River, which he found out later was actually called the Kikonos.

The river was vast with a width of three leagues at its greatest point, while here at the bridge it was barely half a league across. Nearer the west coast the river ran relatively strong, but rarely damaged any of the smaller bridges that had existed before the withdrawal. After the destruction of every bridge other than the Great Bridge that stood before them all, as a lure to the enemy, his advisers told Elvandar that the river to the east was impassable. Almost as wide as a lake, vast cliffs, three hundred paces high, flanked the river. These alone were sufficient to prevent any major attempt to turn this flank, while the other side was too close to the Great Bridge for any success to be possible there. No, it was here that the enemy would have to attack, as this was the only realistic place to cross if they intended to keep their army intact.

Many, especially the Hildar, opposed such a withdrawal, as this would leave the inhabitants to the south exposed to the cruelty of the goblins. A policy of small rearguard actions had allowed most of the civilians to evacuate, but invariably many were still caught by the roving bands of orcs and hobgoblins riding wolves, then handed over to the goblins for a particularly brutal act of revenge.

However, if they had remained it was generally accepted that at least half their current strength would have bolted for home. Eventually even the Hildar accepted this fact, but it did not stop them from continually badgering Kol to open an offensive to recapture the lost territory. The political pressures of the Cenitarn and the Hildar were yet another hurdle to surmount, along with a King who so far had refused to release his capital guards to reinforce those who stood at the river! *Politics!* On the brink of extinction people still tried to vie for power.

Another factor had also decided Kol on his withdrawal policy: the severe losses the cavalry had suffered at the hands of the hobgoblins using wolves instead of horses. The cavalry had always been weak in this arm of the Alliance, but this campaign had reduced it to a shadow of its former strength. They had therefore been almost powerless to stop the hobgoblin raids on the villages.

The main losses had been in animals rather than civilians, but no longer having this arm to protect their supply wagons, after that first day of fighting, simply added weight to the final decision. Many had to be abandoned!

Back in his tent, Aarun launched another log onto the fire and watched the sparks dance. They needed more time and he intended to give Kol just that, even if it did mean their own end. Himself, Cappa, Kollis, Helin and one hundred elite warriors, with the five hundred or so sailors, would leave at dawn and be at Haderia after seven days sailing. It would not take long for them to find Atronius, but it was hoped that the Mage's castle would be lightly held, due to the arrogance of the enemy. It was a slim hope to wish that the entire enemy was now in the peninsular, but it was all they had for the moment.

Kneeling, he began to pray. The next seven days would be much longer than the last seven, and fraught with dangers. He prayed for guidance, but also for any help possible, for he needed all the help he could find.

<hr />

The very next dawn saw a conglomerate of peoples boarding a small fleet destined for a southern shore. Only a few knew of their destination and they most certainly did not include the sailors, who would have refused to obey had they known it was Haderia. The fleet had suffered at the hands of the enemy, but had eventually achieved a status quo. However, it would be, at a minimum, a miracle for such a small number of warships to succeed in reaching the enemy's main shores at this juncture in the hostile invasion of the peninsular. To add to this, the fact that twenty-one maidens had been taken on board one of the warships did little to allay their superstitions!

Unaware of this dilemma, Helin arrived at the crack of dawn with her escort, as ordered, and within the hour they had all set sail. No fanfare, just business as usual, to avoid any unnecessary attention. The others had arrived earlier, so the final preparations had taken little effort.

Aarun, ever aware of the watching eyes, had deliberately left a map depicting their intended journey, although not its purpose, in his tent in the hope of discovery. He had momentarily Porta at his tent and advised him to leave the map for his attendants to put away. He had then asked for certain items to be brought and then, without a second thought, he left the tent after a quick scan to see if anyone was nearby. Apart from his trusted guards, there was nobody, but this did not necessarily mean anything. He would have to trust to the deviousness of the enemy to set in motion the plan that he hoped would lead to the final confrontation.

Trust, and a few more prayers to Zeus!

⟨·⁝·⟩⋇⟨·⁝·⟩⋇⟨·⁝·⟩

As the ships of the small fleet moved further west, the port soon became a distant blur on the horizon. Their course appeared to be towards the lands of the Zeutisii, to confuse any unwanted watchers, but then they would turn south to avoid the southern tip of the Zuetis Isles. The wind this fair morning was strong enough to travel, but many of the sailors pointed out that no great distance could be covered during the first day. When asked why, they had simply frowned and walked away, crossing their chests.

Bloody superstitious sailors, Cappa had roared in their wake, with a scowl that most people took a great deal of pain to avoid. The cook shied away from him as he ordered food to be supplied to his legionaries. This was going to be a long, long journey, rather than the short one predicted by Aarun!

That same morning the threatening clouds to the south became another topic for discussion. The sailors drew on their vast experience and stated airily that it was not a natural storm. Some crossed their chests again and spat over the side. These few had been in a fleet that had been hit by a similar storm off the coast of Haderia. Of the twenty warships, only two ever a safe port, while the fate of the others was never known, although these survivors managed to dramatise it ever more brilliantly.

More bloody bad omens, cursed Cappa, silently. How on earth did these sailors ever manage to get out of their hammocks each day, never mind hold out against the fleets of Haderia? It was one of those days when he could not understand how such a small race of people had survived for so long, under the shadow of Haderia. Irrespective of his opinion, however, the fact remained that they had survived and, more than that, they had thrived and built a vast kingdom.

Now the old hands claimed that, in case of bad weather, they should sail close to the shore, but Aarun had insisted that the last place anyone would expect them would be far out to sea. Even at the best of times, their vessels were not built to survive a heavy storm. The argument had lasted an hour before Aarun's implacable will had restored a modest level of control.

Even so, if any problems arose, they would now require several days sailing to reach the shore, and in that time absolutely anything could happen. Morale in turn suffered to the point that the sailors openly avoided contact with any of their passengers. They had only been out to sea one lousy morning and already the famous sailor-soldier hatred was influencing the probable success or failure of the task. Cappa could not help feeling that they had begun a fool's errand, as Elvandar had advised. It was all quite unique, if you consider that they had been travelling only a short while before the first grumbles began, the southern storm started to follow them to the south and the ill-will between the army and navy exerted itself, ever more potently with each passing hour.

Only Aarun recognised the truth behind this aggravated attitude between the services. Without mercy, the Mage was seeking to force them to fight amongst themselves, thus robbing them of any unified effort or clear, precise strategy. Instead they did little more than argue over trivial matters, which in the greater scheme meant nothing. He had known this beyond question when the sailors complained about sailing out to sea.

A sailor afraid to sail, that was just a little too much to bear!

For now he needed to bide his time, and literally weather the storm, until he could impose a little magic of his own and try to dispel some of the Mage's influence. His personal disadvantage lay in the realm of showing his hand too much. If he reversed the Mage's influence completely, then his attention would be even more concentrated on them than it was already. He could not afford to use too much of his own power just yet, so they would just have to continue their debates, while he concentrated on avoiding any bloodshed. The Mage had to remain focused on Atronius, not him!

Cappa and Helin had also watched the heated debates with apprehension, but due to their lack of knowledge of seafaring they saw no real benefit in any intervention. Indeed they found the debate illuminating. In particular, Helin found the remark regarding sea monsters, which dwelled more than ten leagues from any shore, especially amusing and had to leave the room to avoid offence. Cappa had followed and mimicked a stern father admonishing the daughter for being so rude, which inevitably added to her laughter. In the past two days, their friendship had seemed to blossom and many a rumour had followed, but is it not true that in life kindred spirits will meet, friendship being the cornerstone of any society?

To others who saw this change in Cappa, especially his own men, it was unusual to see him so jovial. Why did this most highly respected, professional officer, recently voted into his present rank, favour someone so small and from a different race? Had his skills in distinguishing a true warrior from these children diminished, due to their being at sea? If so, how could sailing alter a man's character? They all knew of the bewitching ways of the world, but to them the blending of two peoples still held a bitter taste. For the Romans, this was a particularly harsh pill to swallow, as their numbers and the purity of their race had in recent months become a matter of intense debate.

They were all elite, professional soldiers, and yet to see Cappa and Helin being frivolous somehow made both hobbit and legionary concerned for the purity of their futures. As always, they did not truly expect a fully detailed report of the purpose of their journey, but they did expect to have at least sufficient faith in their leadership to stand a chance of returning. Such laughter and light-hearted cheerfulness seemed out of place in the light of the serious task ahead of them. The task ahead was, therefore, put into serious jeopardy by too much open discussion amongst the soldiers, with no direction from the officers, leaving the soldiers to fabricate numerous horrific stories about what lay ahead.

This was a serious breach in both etiquette and command and control, and in it Molisis, Helin's junior in this task, found her first taste of leadership difficulties, having to quench the first sparks of rebellion. This was of course an exaggerated way to describe the grumblings of elite soldiers, but never in her life had Molisis had heard any of her people moan and groan so much while on duty.

It was true that none of the hobbits were very comfortable at sea. They were even less impressed by the lack of honour Helin was showing by expressing her favour for the tall mortalkind, rather than one of their own warriors. For the moment, Molisis applied duty and honour as the controlling elements, but she knew this would not be sufficient for long, so she determined to advise Helin later of her doubts. But what was causing such dissent? Why was Helin being so neglectful of her duties but, more important, how could her own warriors have fallen into rumour and disrespect so quickly? It was baffling, but it all still had to be resolved, so in Helin's place she assumed complete dominance, waiting for her commander to return to normal.

Thus stood the situation when Aarun emerged from the cabin, triumphant for the moment. The main army at the bridge was outnumbered three to one. The sailors on this journey had already shown an intention to mutiny on finishing this duty, although they knew nothing of where they were going. Additionally, the legionary and the hobbit guard had now held secret discussions on what was ahead, particularly relating to their destination, where it was said an entire dwarven fleet had been destroyed by the same storm that seemed to be following them on the southern horizon.

"We continue west for another day and then we will turn south," announced Aarun, eventually. "Set the sails accordingly!"

At these words, the warship captain translated his brief request into an elongated series of commands to the sailors. The grumbling seemed to ebb away momentarily.

It was true that if left idle the mind would create either a world of beauty or wallow in the shadow of darkness, whilst a busy mind had little time for thoughts of good or bad omens. This was true of the sailors but, as Aarun returned below, Cappa for the first time noted the sullen looks on the faces of his men. At least he was beginning to realise he had neglected his duties!

"Inspection, one hour!" he snapped, watching the junior ranks spring into action to motivate the others.

Satisfied, he moved to join Aarun. He had numerous questions that needed answers. A conversation with Porta at the dockside had involved several maps that had been left for all to see back at the tent. He was naturally concerned with this breach of security.

If there was, however, one thing he had learnt about this elf lord, it was that he was never careless unless there was a reason. Clearly he suspected there were more spies in the camp and perhaps the map had been a decoy? Having not seen which map had been left out, Cappa had ordered Porta to remain behind and secure the maps.

"Go back to the tent and put the maps away. I am not sure what Aarun's intentions are but perhaps we should find out," he had said to Porta, at the dockside.

Now he intended to do just that and find out what the elf intended.

As he entered the stairway, he saw the warship captain enter Aarun's quarters. Moving closer, he listened through the open door, as they discussed the further reports that the captain had received just before they had set sail earlier that day: clearly more issues worried the sailor. Having had no time to review them, he was heatedly advocating a return to port.

As he listened, Cappa looked at the exquisite carving on the doorframe and allowed his eyes to wander around the corridor in general. The wood was beautiful beyond words, marble being the only substance he admired more, and yet it was also pure in its beauty as well, easy on the eye. He smiled as he made another mental note that he was becoming more and more appreciative of the lighter things in life: the dusk or the dawn, panoramic views of sunset and sunrise. He also appreciated the way the light cascaded along the corridor, but the décor did not allow it to become blinding at any point.

He became aware of the recent naval battles, and contemplated how such a fight would have been fought, how he would have felt in such a confined environment, knowing instantly that he had no idea whatsoever and no experience. For the moment, he decided to sit on a small bench and take the opportunity to relax, mulling over the grand idea of being an admiral. He listened to the creaking, groaning life of the warship and as the rhythmic sound continued his eyes began to grow heavy.

His questions for Aarun could wait a little longer.

"Now every warship is more than ever crucial to our trade routes and keeping the enemy from any further landings up the coast." The captain was pleading his case. "My squadron is only five warships, but they are experienced sailors and the replacements do not even have the ability to sail to Zuetis and back, never mind fight a battle!"

"That is true, but do you think that I would have contacted your Admiral prior to requesting that this journey be made, if I had felt that it was not absolutely vital?" retorted Aarun. "I understand that you wish to stand with your friends, Captain, but our duty lies elsewhere. I cannot say what our task is, but I do assure you of its vast importance. I do realise, however, that one word from you and your people will turn around with, or without, my permission, so I need to know whether you will remain loyal."

The last sentence aroused Cappa from his slumber, the tone in Aarun's voice being more than enough warning. Rising, he entered the small cabin without knocking and as he stepped through the doorway he nodded in recognition to Aarun. The captain turned, frowned, but also nodded in recognition that perhaps this was a matter he would have to concede on or, quite literally, tell his people to mutiny. The elf had the seal of authority from Admiral Kommodos and this was enough to force his compliance, but something still nagged at the back of his head. His flotilla, these beloved warships, was about to be sacrificed for a reason that this elf would not divulge.

"I see your people are as loyal as mine, Lord Aarun. But you need not concern yourself. My dwarves are exceptional sailors, and they are few and far between, but traitors we are not. We will follow you, but bear in mind that we are superstitious at the best of times, and to have Romans and halflings on the same warships is a recipe for disaster. Mark my words."

"Your advice is duly noted." Aarun smiled, pleased that the topic could now be set aside. "General Cappa, is there something of importance?"

"I see you are busy, my Lord. I can..."

"No. Please come in. If that is all, Captain? Yes, good, then perhaps you could forgive the interruption and see that our course is held true. Thank you."

The captain left, but not before glaring up at Cappa, to emphasise that the legionary's status was not to be taken for granted.

"Now there is a cheerful character," said Cappa, after the door had closed. "Makes me wish for the company of Khazumar no less!"

Aarun felt the chuckle rise in his throat and smiled broadly.

"A little too immersed in wives' tales about monsters, I feel. How may I help you?"

"The people are restless. The storm has made everyone a little jumpy. It's not every day that a storm follows a warship, or at least that is how it feels. The winds are blowing the other way and we are almost standing still at the moment, yet those clouds are still moving against the wind."

"I feel you have come for a more significant reason than that?"

Cappa hesitated, knowing that loyalty had already been discussed with the sailor, but he had to know precisely where they intended to go. *South* was not enough information!

"As regards monsters, I think my people have had a little more to deal with than these sailors. Where are we going, my Lord?"

"Haderia."

"*What?*"

"We have to rescue Atronius."

"If he is the Oracle, as you, the dwarves, the elves and also our enemy believe, then I can only agree, but why so many warships? And why leave the maps, which state exactly where we are going, in your tent?"

"We needed to be noticed somewhat, so we made as much commotion as possible, so that the enemy spies would not miss such an opportunity to report back to the Mage, but not sufficiently to draw an enemy fleet. The maps were just an added bonus, as we most assuredly have more Thorians in our camp, more than we are perhaps prepared to admit. No, I wanted the attention of the Mage to drift from Atronius to our journey, and I feel this is working to some extent. We must save him from further torture."

"Is that the only reason?"

"Meaning!" retorted Aarun, incredulously.

"I have seen your stressed look, my Lord, ever since the abduction. You may be able to fool everyone else, but not me, and certainly not Elvandar. What else is there?"

"For now I must keep my own council."

"That is not good enough…"

Aarun turned sharply, his face a contorted mask of ravines and stress lines, his eyes burning with malice. "It will have to do! Now leave me, I have work to do. Do your duty, is this too much to ask! Leave the greater scheme to those who can make a difference! Now *leave!*"

"Answer my question..."

"Leave! *Now!*"

The hand was on the hilt of his sword before Cappa even knew he had moved, but the look in Aarun's eyes told a different story. This was not the normal elf he had grown to know in the last few months. The emptiness in the eyes reminded him of the stories the dwarves told around the fire, of a great magic that the elven descendants had once wielded, although he doubted the authenticity of it. Of course magic was nothing to him, but the sweaty palms and blurred vision left him in no doubt. Aarun was capable of magic. He had suspected as much at the council meetings, but had said nothing.

Without a word he turned and closed the door with a kick. The corridor no longer held any interest, as he pondered the arrival of the storm and wondered if it was the magic of the enemy that had created such animosity between friends, where before there had existed trust. Had Aarun just applied his own variation, to prevent him from drawing his gladius? Why had he been so quick to temper? There was more being applied here than he could fathom, but he was not the sort of person to step aside simply because he did not understand. No, that made no sense. If Aarun had wanted to stop him, he could just have used a more direct approach, but for now Cappa would have to wait.

The enemy was more than capable of destroying this expedition, so why waste time on manifesting the storm? Why had the storm not smashed them into tiny pieces? The storm defied nature, but it did not close on them, so it must be the elf that was opposing its progress?

As always, Cappa found the topic of magic just a little too much to grasp, and on reaching the deck he walked over to the captain, who stood with a worried gaze directed at the gathering storm to the south.

He had gone below to get answers, but had ended up with only more questions.

They had stood between the enemy armada and the shores of the southern peninsular. They had sailed defiantly, attacking several smaller fleets that had been sent initially to test their resolve but, on finding them determined, the main enemy battle fleet had set sail to put an end to their continued resistance. Only then did they create great carnage amongst the smaller warships of the dwarven fleet.

Many of those who now sailed with Aarun had lost friends and family in those initial battles. Now, as they turned south, they had reached those very same waters that many believed were haunted, where monsters dwelt, waiting to devour them, ship and all! They could not avoid the fact that for the last three days the storm had remained, and yet it had stayed always a league or two to their south. How?

Below decks in his cabin, Aarun recapped the recent events and fought against his own conscience, his own fears. He tried desperately to justify this sacrifice these people were about to make, willingly or unwillingly. His mind was battered with the guilt that many of those with him now would perish. Did he have the right to do this? He must find a way to justify this journey! In the name of all the Gods, Zeus please help me!

He recalled the report received from Admiral Kommodos, according to which the enemy had numbered over a thousand warships of all descriptions. He recalled a brief journey north to the kingdom's courts, where the dwarven King had flatly refused to co-ordinate any of their efforts, declining that which was available, against not only his advice but Kol's as well. Even Admiral Kommodos' experience was ignored. Did the Mage also have power over this king's mind? It was a constant worry.

Split between the southern fleet of two hundred ships, the western fleet, perhaps eighty ships, the eastern fleet, barely one hundred more, and the northern fleet, which was seconded to the support of Moravia, and numbered another sixty ships, their combined force would have stood a chance. Or so they believed at the time. However, the royal advisers had feared invasions everywhere, while the knowledgeable would have advised the king that the one safe location was in the southern region of the peninsular, close to Haderia, where supplies could be brought across the Straits of Jupitannis with ease.

Whatever the decisions, General Kol had under his direct control only the southern fleet to oppose the landings, or rather to delay them to obtain as much warning as possible. These few sailors were now directly commanded by Admiral Kommodos, after Kol had admitted to having little understanding of how to apply such a small resource against such a vast enemy. With consummate skill, Kommodos sailed rings around the orc sailors, who still had a great suspicion of all things watery! Even with the Mage's aide, they could not entirely ignore this inbred fear.

Kommodos eventually bought Kol two invaluable weeks before the enemy finally landed!

So with great bravado, and a healthy appetite for suicide, the two hundred sails engaged the enemy fleets between the Zeutis Isles and the dwarmanian coast. Here, with unfavourable winds, the orcish fleet had floundered, finding itself hemmed in, and with so many sails they had little opportunity to manoeuvre.

Indeed, with so many their numbers now worked against them, and by the time the wind had changed, the dwarven fleet had sunk or captured over one hundred orc warships, while many lay burning, with many more severely damaged. Dwarven losses had amounted to less than thirty, but such a small loss was critical. As always, the preponderance of the enemy allowed them to accept such wastage, but Kommodos and Kol could ill afford the loss of a single warship, let alone so many. It was only a matter of time before Kommodos would have to retire, leaving the sea open to the enemy.

Aarun moved to the poop deck and allowed his thoughts to wander back to that first meeting with Kol and Kommodos.

He recalled Kol's sheer confidence in Kommodos' ability to delay the enemy. Neither, in his opinion, were born leaders, more, he thought, chosen. Yes, Kol had been chosen for his role, while Kommodos was Kol's choice. Indeed, perhaps they were all chosen?

As the deck rolled with the swell of the waves, the first conversation spilled into his memory.

"I cannot order the eastern fleet to join Kommodos, Lord Aarun!" Kol was screaming. "What you are asking me to do is treason. Our King has ordered that those ships protect the eastern shore. What do you suppose I should do, inform his Majesty when the enemy land on that shore? No! We must wait for permission from the King before we change our dispositions."

It was a valid point. Kol had only just been transferred to this part of the kingdom after falling foul of the King's advisers, and he feared a further reversal of his fortunes. The advisers had ordered the Prince to take his forces out of Thoria to support the Noborian River, which had led to the ludicrous defeat of the Prince and Kol in Gretan by the goblins. This in turn had then led to the River Battle and the severe losses encountered in the civilian population. Clearly the high and mighty had then sought a scapegoat, and he was it! They had moved him to this area, rather than berate a prince of the realm, because it was felt that an invasion might occur, but that it was more likely the goblins would attack Thoria first. This position had therefore initially been a secondary one, a safe place to let Kol rot.

Of course the main army was kept in the central region of the kingdom to facilitate a rapid march north or south, but Kol in theory commanded. In reality he had become nothing more than a figurehead, as one dignitary after another had continued to interfere in the running of the army.

When they had been transferred to this region to rest and recuperate, Lord Kollis' Westonian Regiment and Lord Khazumar's Priesthood Guards were a blessing in disguise. Now the three together, Kol, Kommodos and Kollis, began to organise matters to deter an enemy invasion, but the local resistance was if anything more formidable than the orcs.

The Hildar had lived for a thousand years in the southern half of the kingdom, and on more than one occasion had led a semi-autonomous existence. Being the scholars, teachers, scientists and general all-round geniuses, they made horrendous soldiers with their continual habit of suggesting better ways of resolving the issues to hand. They were far from obedient and, as often as not, demanded Hildar officers for Hildar regiments, but none had the experience for such posts. And so the arguments continued.

Into this arena stepped Aarun, bringing a force of fifteen thousand elves from Gallicia with Marshall Elvandar, with the argument that all forces should be used collectively. Gratitude was not forthcoming! In fact, Kol had him arrested and escorted from the camp, with orders not to return for at least a week. Of course he did no such thing, returning the very next day.

Aarun smiled. That was one day where he had seen a powerful dwarf brought low by the weight of administrative matters that were, for once, literally beyond his abilities. The staff was incompetent, apart from Kollis, Elvandar and Khazumar, while Cappa and Aarun helped to some extent, but decisions invariably had to have Kol's seal of approval. Independent thought was not in abundance and, to cap it all, the previous regional commander, Lord Komar, now stood within Sight Fortress and openly ignored every summons to attend Kol's staff meetings to discuss tactics. Anarchy would have been a more pleasant description, as no one seemed eager to stand together and unity had become a foul word. The small Army of Allegiance, then commanded by Atronius, did wonders to reduce Kol's stress, but the simple fact was that six thousand experienced soldiers could not defeat an invasion by fifty times that number. He needed his head free to organise training, not resolve issues of who controlled which aspect of the command staff. To Aarun, however, administration was his life and blood. Raised in the turmoil of the ever-changing political arena of Gallicia, he had always surmounted every problem and obtained a solution. Indeed, had it not been for his immediate transfer to command the elven forces supporting Kol, he was certain that the border dispute that had been his original assignment would have brought about his first personal defeat. Fortune favours the brave, he had always believed, but it did little or nothing for the superstitious border regions and the money-mad Westonians.

Now, with an energy that both shocked and puzzled Kol, due to his earlier rebuke, Aarun set about winning over the support of the Hildar by wooing their vanity and exaggerating their importance in all decision-making processes. Kol was a soldier and used to obedience, while the Hildar did not accept brute force, and it was this strength that Aarun now tapped into with exceptional success.

"It is just a case of knowing the people you are dealing with, General," he confided to Kol smugly. "If you wish, I am happy to assume the role of intermediary."

Kol had simply nodded.

At first the General was present at all the meetings, then at only a few, finally practically none. Left to deal with the army itself, Kol also began to excel and brought a little more cohesion to their varied formations. The incompetents were transferred to the eastern coastal posts, while those of promise suddenly found posts commanding regiments and companies. Much to their surprise, many well-known officers were purged, causing the expected political anger at such effrontery. Of the officers dismissed, over sixty percent had been Cenitarns. However, Kol had no need for politically correct officers, he needed leadership at the regimental level, which was their weakest link within the command structure.

Luckily they were abundantly provided for in the realms of generalship, and when discussing tactics several people came to mind. However, what indeed would be their tactics? Cappa and Crassus were busy training every day, to create two new legions of elves and dwarves, while others also began to learn how to use the elven bow with efficiency. The mortalkind was organised into official cohorts consisting of one hundred and fifty legionaries and fifty or so barbarians. It became the cohort commander's responsibility to train the new recruits, and on paper the legion began to look formidable. A second *Helvetii Legio* was formed to train alongside the elves and dwarves, but their inability to march efficiently and retain discipline made them of little value, in comparison to the legionaries.

Tactically nobody truly knew, however, what would transpire and to this end, as in Thoria, Kol decided to maintain a central position and defend the coast with delaying actions. In this way the majority of his forces could be used to fight a decisive battle at the right moment or, if they failed, a large portion of their troops would escape to the great river to their north across the Hildar plains, thus avoiding any elaborate coastal trap.

He later sent Crassus to the south with an assortment of dwarves, Romans and Helvetii totalling approximately fifteen thousand. They were to take station on the isthmus beyond the Inner Sea, and use the many rivers and valleys to delay any landings along the southern coast. It had been determined that this would not be a large landing site, but their supplies could be threatened by a march along the southern coast to reach the eastern shore and a march to the river. So it was an important role, and Crassus had decided to take his dwarven legion with him.

To the east Kol sent, initially, Admiral Kommodos, with five thousand new recruits and the warships to protect the beaches, and also to rebuild the fleet. This too was not thought likely to be a decisive theatre in the coming struggle, but in time an active fleet raiding supply ships in the Straits of Jupitannis could only help, if they were to have any hope of success.

"No," Aarun remembered Kol stating during one of their many meetings. "No, the south and east will be diversionary attacks. The main assault will be to encircle Sight Fortress and any other forces in that lesser peninsular within those magnificent walls. At first, I also saw the advantages of the fortress and the defensive bonuses, but I have waged too much war in the open where an army can breathe, to shut myself up in that trap. No. Here is where the first battle will be fought. Here, at Mount Holvidar."

It was astonishing to think that any one person could be so adamant that he knew what the enemy thought, and indeed what they intended to do to bring about their destruction. Some called it arrogance, but several had served with Kol before and knew better of their commander in chief, and it was not long before all murmuring had gone and a high level of self-confidence began to exist.

If Kol said so, then so it would be!

This was dangerous, Elvandar had advised, but at that moment news of a great defeat in Thoria had left them no choice but to encourage Kol's approach. Victory for the orcs in Thoria would almost certainly be followed by an invasion here in the south.

Looking back, it all seemed childish, but the troops had needed that blind belief in Kol and, to be honest, so had Aarun! Only a few, scant days later, news reached them of yet another defeat. Prince Kallum had once again been defeated, this time in Gretan, for the second time, leaving them all numb with disbelief.

Without these mountain and forest fighters tying up fifty thousand goblins in Gretania, these would now be free to join any invasion the enemy intended. It had been bitter news and was the low point of the entire war for the free kingdoms.

After discussion of the two defeats, Cappa had told Aarun that he remembered that Kol had sent Elvandar with a further twenty-five thousand to the western shore, taking with him the fifteen thousand elves currently under arms, including those elves trained by Cappa in Roman tactics on the battlefield. When asked about the efficiency of the dwarven and elven legions, Cappa had honestly stated that the latter had shown exceptional prowess during the training. The dwarves had also shown exceptional adaptability, but had less discipline and were prone to want to break formation to use their axes; however, used correctly, both new formations would fight well. It helped, Aarun recalled, as trained warriors were in short supply and time was no longer in abundance.

With the central army numbering approximately sixty thousand and Lord Komar's private army of ten thousand in Sight Fortress, their dispositions numbered one hundred and fifteen thousand.

On paper this looked impressive, considering they had had only a few scant months to prepare this army, but in fact they did not know the real truth of their situation, and perhaps for many this was a good thing. In reality four times their number stood in Haderia alone, waiting to land on their shores. Had the raw recruits known of this they would have fled long before any fighting began.

Those final, hectic few weeks were indeed some of the hardest days that Aarun could remember, but he also felt a burning pride that they had all done as much as possible to oppose the enslavement that would be their fate if they failed.

He turned as a hand was laid gently on his shoulder, to find Cappa looking quizzical.

"I wish to apologise for my interference a few days back," Cappa said. "You seem weighed down by heavy thought, my Lord. A gold coin if you share them?"

Aarun smiled, and nodded for Helin to join them. She perched on the lower rail, carefully avoiding the swell of the vessel and the possibility of falling overboard, by gripping the upper level.

"Not thoughts, my friend," Aarun then said to them both. "Memories."

"Of?"

"The campaign in the southern peninsular and that nagging thought that we should have stayed to fight on that second day."

"Mount Holvidar was the largest conflict that I have ever witnessed," Cappa confided even as the grim memories flooded back. "But I agreed with Kol then and I still do, my Lord. Had Kol remained for one more day, a greater portion of the new recruits would have been lost. In one day we lost ten percent from desertion, plus another ten percent from casualties. The army would have disintegrated."

"We had trained a high proportion of the new levies and many actually took to your methods better than our own. We stood triumphant after numerous defeats and the loss of Sight Fortress. Those people needed a victory."

"Not there and not then."

"Why?"

"In my experience of battle, my Lord, many men develop fast and learn quickly in order to survive, but the dwarves, who made up seventy percent of the army, did not learn quickly. They were brave and fought on many occasions with the hearts of lions. However, had it not been for the arrival of Kommodos and the eastern division, plus our own standing, that of the Priesthood Guards, and the reinforcement of Elvandar, who had marched one hundred leagues around the mountains to assist, we would have failed. That still left Julius to delay the enemy charges north on the other side of the mountains, but that did not influence Holvidar. I felt that Kol would not stand on the first day, never mind the second."

Aarun nodded and, out of concern, Helin placed her hand on his sleeve. Even for her the sudden closeness she had developed for this elf surprised her, normally reserved in all approaches to deep friendships, but this elf was somehow different.

"I know it is hard, my Lord," she said. "But we were not there. My people had not gone south and your task had been to organise the bridge, when the army marched beyond the Great River. Had it not been for you, many more of our people would have perished needlessly. The dwarves needed time to assimilate their experiences and develop their reactions accordingly. Even the Hildar no longer argued, as they could see that so many had perished to defend their lands and as such, many more would die to recapture them."

"It just seems that the river is not the best place for a counter-strike. How can we alter what has taken place?" Aarun asked.

"We cannot!" said Cappa. "That is the choice of the Gods, we are but pawns in their games and our choices help them define theirs. We can only hope that we will prevail. It is not like you, my Lord, to have such doubts."

"Do you think that I have no doubts, Cappa? I am an elf and beset with as many emotions as you. I doubt my actions every day. Every day."

"We will still prevail," Cappa stated defiantly.

"Do you think we will, Helin?" asked Aarun, bluntly.

"I do not know. But I do know that we will proceed and still try because giving up is not an option. We must succeed, whatever your reasons for taking us on this journey. If we keep the Mage occupied, then his powers will not be with the enemy as they were at Holvidar. It was only the sheer size of the battle that prevented him from being in two places at once, may Zeus forbid!"

Aarun chuckled, then repeated, "May *all* the Gods forbid!"

They sat for a few more minutes quietly discussing what might lie ahead. For the moment their fears had been extinguished, but it was perhaps natural to have some doubts, as this was one of the many ways that they identified the good in each other with their levels of doubt, humility, even compassion. Strength was not always the best indicator.

Beyond the Great River another powerful mind also stood in reflection on the southern peninsular campaign, but with a totally different agenda. Even as Aarun and company sailed into the sunset, Titanus Scipio stood on his mound of earth, which rose above the local ravines, and watched the Great Bridge with growing anticipation.

To him the campaign had been glorious!

For the Master, several great battles had been won, while several lesser Mages had proven themselves to be capable, with the exception of Java. Perhaps there remained a semblance of the original mortalkind within his soul, thus causing his lazy march north to outflank Mount Holvidar. Perhaps his sympathies had still gained a momentum, thus holding his hand when a small force of the enemy elite had been cut off and should have been destroyed. Either way the disappointing performance had led to his removal back to Sight Fortress to assist the Mage in interrogating the Oracle of Zeus. Fail there and Scipio would have his head!

What a find, he laughed openly, drawing several strange glances. What fools would keep their greatest asset in an open camp where he could send his minions to kidnap him with little or no difficulty? The taking of the Oracle had virtually destroyed the fool's morale before this final battle had even begun.

Furthermore, who would discuss such issues where people could overhear? Many had at first doubted the information of the Black Thorians, but on reflection there was no reason to doubt the validity of the significance of Atronius Sulla. Yes, Atronius, of all the Romans possible, it had to be him! His soul cried out for revenge for all those memories of that filthy mortalkind continually undermining his authority. Yes, it had to be him all right! No one else would have had the arrogance to accept such a role!

Deprived of this emblem of power, in Hildar the enemy had been easy to outmanoeuvre and defeat. The plan had been simple, perhaps to some too simple, but it never paid to complicate matters when dealing with dullards. Indeed, if the truth be known, goblins were little more than dirt, while the orcs showed some levels of intelligence, with the orka almost matching his own intelligence. The Orka, he pondered...my creation! *My creation!*

Scipio moved back towards his personal tent to look once more at the maps laid out for his perusal, for his gloating. There had been seven landings in all, with each part playing a significant role. Come to think about it, the plan had involved several attempts to delude the defenders into committing themselves early to a decisive battle. In that he admitted to an error.

Sight Fortress was meant to have been a magnet to their pride, but the enemy leader—Kol was his name, he believed—held back his main forces and awaited developments. This was a tactic so reminiscent of Atronius that it was now Scipio's own encouragement that had the Mage working on the torture of the Oracle, rather than being here. The purpose had been to remove the Mage from interfering and in that Scipio had been successful, and now any further glory would be his alone.

Not that the damn Mage was needed, he spat defiantly. The puny forces across the river would not last long. Yesterday they had acted without due care, attacking across the waterfalls with the orcs ill-prepared. Ten thousand perished, but as their long-term planning came of age this loss was rapidly being replaced.

For the delay, and the humiliating defeat, he intended to destroy them all!

When they had landed in the kingdom, just ten days ago, a pincer movement had been planned. To the north Java would land with a staggering eighty thousand, with the task of pushing inland to split his force. Half would then march south to link up with the main landings for a joint advance between the tip of the Holvidar Mountains and the Inner Sea, the key to the whole peninsular. Meanwhile, the other half would immediately drive north, striving to move around the northern end beyond the Holvidar Mountains, to circumvent the Central Mountains and fall on the enemy supply line stretching back to this river.

Not only did the defenders destroy the initial landing force, but Java had also lost one hundred vessels at sea to a raid from the north by a smaller dwarven fleet. He had then decided to add to this failure by not matching his own progress, causing numerous delays elsewhere. The elven defenders had been allowed to choose and defend their own battlefield although the goblin losses were severe, twenty thousand to the estimated enemy loss of three thousand. The elves and their leaders were finally broken, but too late to influence the main effort, led by Scipio's forces at Sight Fortress.

Java had followed close behind the survivors who had marched north to the Kulla river then, as agreed, sent the balance marching south to join Scipio at Sight Fortress.

Here Scipio had personally supervised the main forces, which landed with little or no opposition. North of the fortress the Mage and thirty thousand landed, while to the south three beaches were used for the one hundred thousand commanded by him personally.

"What fools," he growled vehemently, his memory flushing his anger. "We had victory within our grasp and they allowed themselves to be dragged into minor skirmishing for an entire day!"

It was here that Scipio had intended to lock up tightly at least fifty thousand of the enemy who were intending to defend the fortress to the last. The fortress was a formidable sight and commanded the entire toe of the peninsular for twenty leagues or more. However, their progress was slow and it became increasingly obvious that the forces before them were tiny in comparison to the expected resistance. The result was a further three days of intense combat, which saw first the Upper Gatehouses overrun, then the Lower, with the Central Palisade falling on the last day and, even then, only with the Mage's assistance.

It had cost them forty thousand casualties, while less than six thousand dwarves had been mutilated. It was then they discovered the caves burrowed beneath the Central Palisade. Leaving ten thousand goblins to dig out any resistance, Scipio had then ignored this development and had immediately begun his march for the toe of the mountains, only to receive news of three more heavy defeats.

Igluk, that slime of life that should have been exterminated after the northern peninsular fiasco, had failed abysmally.

With a force of thirty thousand under his direct command, he also had the ten thousand Black Thorians in support, landing on the eastern shoreline, but the fool had failed to destroy even those that had opposed him. The Thorians had played little part in the three successive defeats over the same three days as the battle for Sight Fortress. The orcs had maintained their advance, but had suffered almost fifty percent casualties, over twenty thousand, due to ambushes, and had not once accounted for more than a few thousand of the enemy.

They advanced, they all advanced, but the decisive victory was yet to be achieved.

However, it was still within their grasp, as Scipio confirmed that Kol had taken up a position at Mount Holvidar, offering the chance to settle the issue in one major confrontation. The invitation was accepted greedily, but he also identified the typical central, defensive position, so expected of Kol! At this time, all Scipio could think about was the whereabouts of Atronius. So far he had not been seen on any battlefield. What was he up to?

His initial disappointment at not having gained this central position for the Haderian army vanished when news arrived that the second wave of troops had successfully landed at Sight Fortress. Sixty thousand more soldiers had been landed with confirmation of the same number within a week. He knew that barely eighty thousand of Kol's forces remained, and even though the trap at the fortress had failed, while Igluk's defeats and delays and Java's consummate defeat in the north had all served to their enemy's advantage, his forces had remained intact.

There were now four armies converging on Mount Holvidar. Kol stood with a scouting estimate of eighty thousand under arms, while the orka legions numbered twenty thousand, Igluk numbered approximately twenty thousand again, Bata in the north of Holvidar, in the toe of the mountains, stood at a further twenty and his own command already equalled that of Kol's. Defeat was not an issue. Time was the deciding factor and the enemy had none left.

Scipio descended onto the feather pillows and looked up as his memories flooded back on the greatest two days of his existence. He remembered the excitement of battle burning in his veins and the rush of adrenaline pulsing through his brain. The clouds and the rain were being buffeted across the sky, as he ascended the hill now chosen as his command post. From here the whole field could be viewed with godlike freedom.

He now stood on that central hill, which rose off to the left just south of the western spur of Mount Holvidar, which overshadowed the local region with a crest over two thousand paces high. To the left also stood a small plain that separated this spur from the eastern outcrop, barely two leagues distant, but clearly the crest rose to twice the height on the eastern spur. However, on either side of the stream that descended into the valley before him stood the three hills the defenders occupied.

The prize this day was Dwarmania!

Scipio's own positions were cramped within these hills, with a wide expanse of lowlands off to his right, where Igluk could be seen advancing in the distance. Across the river the enemy positions were more spread out. All three occupied hills had several palisades built on them to prevent any easy passage. The intersecting gullies had not received any such attention and it was clear that the intention was for them to attack in the gullies and subsequently be massacred on the far side, where he also knew that a ridge ran the entire length of the hills further east.

Could the enemy be surprised, and thus forced out of one of those hills? On this fine day of rain and cloud it would be a simple matter to order forward twenty regiments of orcs to find out. Proceed, or hold? The entire army was not present and to attack piecemeal might mean a lack of the concentrated effort required to achieve victory. Igluk's error! To wait might enable the enemy to obtain reinforcements of their own, thus further deflating his chances. Oh, that joyous knowledge of absolute power swept across his being, as the words seemed to flow out of his lips once more.

"We will advance across the stream and take that small central hill," he had said with conviction, and did not hear a single word of contradiction. "Ten regiments to either side should be sufficient, but keep five more in readiness for any counter attack."

With a wave of the hand, the orc leaders had quickly left, eager to impress their new Master. For Scipio's own Master had imbued in his people an understanding that, in the absence of the Mage, they would obey without question his commands. It was intoxicating, this power of life and death combined with the knowledge that he himself was immortal. These creatures would die at his bidding and yet he felt nothing for their anguish or pain, if they felt such things of course. Only victory mattered, even at the cost of the entire army!

They would all do his bidding!

Lord Khazumar looked out beyond the hazy horizon on the central hill, created by the mixture of heat and the rain, and grimaced. This rain was impossible, and where did it come from? No rain clouds, no bad weather beforehand, not even a raised level of wind! This had something to do with that Mage, he thought.

"I heard the drums myself, my Lord," his colleague repeated again, still waiting for a reply.

"Keep on the alert, Komad, and report any additional noises that may be carried on the wind. I will report this to Kol. Under cover of this downpour, we may be in for an interesting day after all."

The guard nodded while Khazumar strolled back to the tents on the eastern slope of the hill designated as his responsibility in the coming struggle. A surprise attack to secure this vital hill in the centre would not be beyond the enemy's capabilities, and it was something that he was not willing to take a chance on. Here he had only his personal Priesthood Guards, numbering barely two thousand, although more would be sent forward the next morning, but that was a good twelve hours away. Better to be safe than sorry, he thought, as his mother had repeatedly advised him.

He launched himself over a small wall and nodded to the guard who quickly turned, raising and lowering a spear in recognition. It would take a few minutes to reach the tents and from there perhaps ten minutes for a rider to reach Kol's, which stood well over three leagues away on the ridge now designated as the point of no return. The ridge had been chosen as the line where their final stand would be made, should they face a reversal in tomorrow's expected battle.

Of course they believed in their eventual victory. The news that Crassus had engaged and defeated the enemy before him three times had raised their spirits, but in truth the small force he commanded had been compelled to give ground in order to achieve these victories, small as they might have been. Each successive river line the enemy crossed exposed their left flank and supplies through the Kikonos and Hildar plains. Sometimes even a victory was poor fettle indeed!

Elvandar's own victory on the northern front at the Tulla River had been overshadowed by subsequent defeat trying to hold the Kulla River further north, where the odds had been over three to one. With his army divided during the subsequent retreat, the next stage would be decided here at Holvidar.

Khazumar's eyes became moist as he remembered visiting this region as a youth while in training for his captaincy. He wondered just how many others had felt that way at one point or another during this entire war.

Hopping lightly over a tent wire he nodded again to another guard and turned to hail one of his junior officers.

"Killis, order the two senior companies to form ranks, will you? We may have a problem, but if nothing comes of the report, we will stand them down to rest in two hours."

"As you wish, my Lord."

"Oh, and can you change the schedule to have the next two companies stand the morning watch, and see that the captains are informed?" he then added, as he once more resumed his journey. "On second thoughts, I will speak to them personally."

Then he was gone. Killis watched Khazumar wander off towards the central line of tents, where he knew the command maps could be found. For a moment he hesitated as he pondered what Khazumar had asked him to deliver. Then knowing Khazumar as a stickler for prompt action, the young captain moved swiftly along the tents and, finding the desired officers, informed them to arouse their commands. This did not, thankfully, include his own, but on raising the alarm the two officers asked for him to remain to assist in establishing what was to transpire, and indeed where they were to march.

That was the one thing Khazumar had not mentioned. Where indeed should they go? For what seemed an eternity, Killis feverishly tried to decide on what he should do next. Both the senior dwarves standing before him were ten years his senior in experience, but they had no information to work on and now looked to him for guidance. The responsibility was almost unbearable, as there did not seem to be any solution to the problem. Then with a snap of his fingers Killis turned and suggested that one company rapidly run to one extreme of their palisade and the other to the other extreme, and there await developments.

The suggestion was accepted, albeit with a little scepticism and with the odd expression of disdain thrown in his direction but, nevertheless, whatever happened next would be their problem and not his!

For the third time that day Killis stopped in hesitation. Perhaps Khazumar had said where they were meant to go, but he had not listened sufficiently? With a pace that surprised all and sundry, the young captain set off towards the command tent and on the way told his own company to rise. He had not gone far when the distinctive sound of battle reached his ears. Something had definitely gone wrong!

As in all life, Fate always seemed to play an unending game with the fortunes of the mortal world. Those that could interfere for their own interests tried to do so with great aplomb, but most of them invariably failed and lived the lives designed for them at birth. Of course they never knew this truth, for to the Gods it was an issue that was never discussed with mortals, for in their eyes the truth could well destroy the individual's mind. They were simply not intelligent enough to understand the full picture.

On that day, as the rain pelted down in torrents, nobody could see more than thirty paces in any direction. Fate had, for reasons unknown, permitted a breach in the natural laws, by allowing rain that had no origins, no clouds, only an empty power that moved water from the sea to fall on Holvidar for an unknown purpose.

For the guards this was a nightmare, while for the aggressors it was a double-edged sword. On the one hand, they could approach practically unseen while, on the other, each formation could not see the next and so cohesion was quickly lost in the quagmires of muddy water that flowed freely across the valley.

Fate was indeed busy this day. What it gave with one hand it took away with the other, and smiled at the resulting chaos.

Even as Killis ran to find Khazumar, the two guards companies marched swiftly to either side of their palisade, and they arrived at precisely the same time as the guards raised the alarm. Six regiments of orcs, three to either flank, had struck both flanks of the palisade, causing instantaneous panic. Had Killis not split the two companies it is hard to say what would have happened, but his decision certainly made the orcs halt at least momentarily.

They had expected limited resistance, then a delay after the brief struggle for the central hill, before a counter-attack could be organised. They would have used this delay to extend the palisades as much as possible. Now it was clear that the enemy were not only alert, but also actually prepared to receive their attack. To add to their woes, this rain made firing arrows impractical because the wind just blew them away, and spears were also rendered almost useless. They had no choice but to raise their battle fever to a crescendo and revert back to the old ways, a bitter charge to overawe an enemy and kill everything in sight.

Scipio stood and watched from his hill, the rain no obstacle to his vision, as the orcs clashed heavily with the *dwarves*. Red, he noticed, red uniforms, what does this signify, he began to think, but for the moment the memory eluded him. Where had this uniform been mentioned before to him in a report? It was Igluk! The fool of an orc had sent the Black Regiments of Gobli and one formation of the orka against these warriors and failed miserably.

This hill was indeed the key to their position, and the fact that his people had failed before caused him to become a little anxious. Not for the lives of his orcs, but at the possibility that this skirmish could develop into something bigger when he was not quite ready. Once more he had a simple choice: send more into the fighting now and retain the upper hand, or withdraw now and limit his losses and take the hill the following day.

"Send in the second wave," he decided, not willing to wait any longer. "They cannot hold against such numbers. The rain and wind will smother the sound of battle from the other hills. Strike! Strike now while they are isolated!"

Satisfied to watch the messengers speed away on wolves, Scipio again looked at the red cloaks. They were known as the Priesthood Guards, if he remembered correctly. Pah! Priesthood! None of them were priests and none of them cherished life, as they so happily told his people to do! Scipio laughed heartily as the first clash began on the slope of the hill across the valley, and inch by inch the palisade was being turned. Such stupidity to have not extended the palisades across the entire valley, perhaps they had not had enough time?

Whatever they intended it would not be enough. Already his sunorcs had pushed around the base of the hill, forcing the dwarves back beyond the crest of the hill. Soon they would push inwards behind the palisade to kill all that were trapped there. This was too easy, he laughed to the wind, and I am victorious already!

✦✦✦✦

Khazumar acted with the speed of light. Kilk's decision had saved the day and he clapped him heartily on the shoulder when he met him. After a few kind words of congratulation, he then told him to take command of the support companies in their entirety, plus any others who might join them, and bring them when organised to the crest of the hill.

Meanwhile he sent messengers to the elves and Romans on either side, requesting immediate assistance. At this time in the crisis, two hundred on either side held back three thousand orcs, with barely four hundred more being swift enough to join the front ranks and help repel the first onslaught. He roused the rest of his command, but even then his situation was poor at best.

With a sickening feeling, he acknowledged that they would all rue the day that they had not finished the palisade across the gully floor, as requested by Crassus the day before last, a rare mistake and perhaps one that might also be costly. Now would be a true test of their mettle!

Companies became intermingled and for a few moments they tried desperately to create the correct formations, but Khazumar quickly saw that this would take too long. Ordering the captains to move swiftly with whatever they had to hand, only Killis was told to remain to bring together the stragglers. The regiment would fight piecemeal as the surprise had been total. It would now take desperate action if they were to survive the next ten minutes, but all was not beyond redemption just yet, if they received reinforcements on time.

Khazumar was literally everywhere at one and the same time. One warrior would waver, a small gap in the line appeared, and then with a yell their leader would arrive with the chosen few to block any holes. Bitterly the dwarves fought shield to shield, shoulder to shoulder. Dodging one way to allow a colleague to strike, only to step forward as the same colleague also sidestepped to avoid an enemy's blow, for them to also strike down an orc. It was true that the enemy had probably identified their red uniforms, but as Khazumar returned again and again in his vital role, he noted that they seemed more deep green, from the splashes of orcish blood, than the traditional red.

With his consummate energy, moments of wisdom and exceptional axe arm, he led the guards slowly back to the crest of the hill, but never allowed their line to break. To bend a little was not a problem, but it could not be allowed to break. Killis on several occasions led his own charge to restore the line, but the rain was an uncomfortable hindrance. On the extreme left the rain obscured the right, and vice versa, and the problem persisted. It was only a matter of time before they disintegrated and broke. Already several hundred now lay wounded or dead, while many others lifted them to safety, only to be wounded themselves whilst carrying out this charitable act. Khazumar eventually had to order that all wounded were to fend for themselves. No able-bodied warrior was permitted to leave the line. They were losing, slowly, but nevertheless losing.

Where was their help?

Where indeed! Crassus, Valenus and Marcellus had reacted swiftly to the arrival of the messenger, but they could not hear the sound of battle through the downpour. However, after one brief request for a confirmation, they acted swiftly to raise the alarm.

"Marcellus, march now with the guard and take those dwarven archers with you. Use them at close range, as this wind will simply take the arrows away," barked Crassus. "Julius, raise the legion and prepare to march forward in unison, should it become necessary. I will move forward to bring Cappilius' men to assist our friends on the hill."

With a nod, a brief forearm grip and a knowing smile, the three moved off to complete their tasks, fighting the wind and rain as they moved through the long line of temporary accommodation. Crassus had already faced his baptism of fire, but to date neither Julius nor Marcellus had actually *commanded* men in a battle. Now would be their baptism of leadership and it was never an easy step to take, but they had no time to think and so relied on their experience and training. Unhesitating, quick to act, a commanding voice when giving orders, Crassus knew both of them were going to be fine.

Turning to his own objective, Crassus decided to add Issus' velites to his force. Here was another man who had so far only participated in skirmishes but who, on the word of Cappilius, now commanded a recently formed Helvetii velites regiment. As they moved through the rain, Crassus quickly explained the situation.

"Where do you need me?" Issus asked, gripping the extended forearm awkwardly, but thankful for the gesture of friendship.

"Your men have been in combat for three days without rest, Issus. They should rest."

"We have fought the spawn of this God Hades and lived. Our Gods have favoured us with many victories, Roman. You asked for us to cooperate, we have done so, here and in the northern peninsular. You ask, then speak as though we are but your slaves to do your bidding. This is not what I promised my men."

"You have fought with honour and pride, Helvetii, but this is not the time for politics. I think only of your abilities to stand and at this moment you are yourself exhausted."

"You doubt our conviction due to our refusal to stand on the fourth river chosen by you. There we were tired, Roman. There we needed rest and so we took that rest while on the march here. We were flanked by a large body of lightly armed goblins moving rapidly to encircle our position, the decision to fight was wrong. Had we stayed we would not have joined you here or anywhere else, except perhaps in the afterlife!"

Crassus pulled free of the grip and looked keenly into the barbarian's eyes. Even though he believed completely in his loyalty to their cause, it always seemed difficult to eradicate the suspicions of betrayal. However, if he was honest to his own heart, what would he gain, other than eternal damnation, if he condemned these men?

"You have your wish, Issus," he said after a brief hesitation. "Take half of your men to join Marcellus. There, he will command, but the remainder must stay here to support the legion. Understood?"

"It shall be as you command, Centurion."

The matter decided, Crassus resumed his march and began to breathe heavily with the tiring effort. Where in the name of Zeus was Elvandar! Khazumar would have sent for his assistance from his flank as well and, even at a minimum, Cappilius' light troops should have joined him almost immediately. Now he would have to go and find them personally. More delays!

Moving swiftly through the gully, between the two rearward hills, the path wound round in ever increasing circular rotations. There was simply not enough time to run to either wide ravine that enabled passage through the pits dug within the gullies, which were now filled with hot pitch and oil, ready to be set alight. Any spark, any mistake, and they would all roast.

"Who are you?" a voice then shouted, out of the gloom.

"It is Crassus. Centurion of the army of Alliance and I must speak to Elvandar urgently."

"Approach and be identified!"

"Cappilius!" Crassus admonished, when he closed on the person that had issued the challenge. "This is no time for damned joviality!"

"I am sorry, friend, but that mud puddle you stopped in was just too much for me."

"*Enough*, where is Elvandar?"

"At the command tent. Why?"

Crassus frowned. "Has a messenger arrived from Khazumar yet?"

"Yes," Cappilius confirmed, still a little taken aback by the blunt interrogation. "He spoke of some kind of attack on the central hill."

"And?"

"Elvandar told him that to attack in this weather was a ludicrous suggestion, and the messenger should go and return with more conclusive information. We can hear nothing from here."

"Elvandar said this?"

"Of course. Khazumar commands the centre, you the left, Kol and Cappa with the main line, and Kommodos with the reserve. What is this all about?"

"Cappilius," Crassus began, trying desperately to control his rising anger. "Khazumar has now been in mortal battle with five times his number for the last hour, while Elvandar has remained inactive and you are playing practical jokes. Marcellus and Issus are on their way to assist, but we will need you and some elven archers to move with us in support."

"By the Gods," Cappilius exclaimed. "Had I known for certain, I would..."

"Yes. Yes, I am sure. But we must find Elvandar."

"Follow me."

They crossed the outer lines and walked around the southern extremity of the palisade on the northern hill, to find Elvandar ensconced within the comfort of the tents supplied by the *dwarves*. On this occasion, Crassus did not wait on ceremony and stormed right through the entrance to find an elven woman combing the Marshall's dreadlocks.

"What is the meaning of this!" bellowed Elvandar, rising swiftly and reaching for the nearby sword.

"Meaning?" countered Crassus, incredulously. "The meaning, oh great and merciful elven lord, is why in Zeus' name are you not marching to Khazumar's support? You have commanded an entire army and you know of the central hill's importance to our defences, and yet you remain inactive. Explain!"

"I do not have to answer to you, Roman. General Kol commands here, not *Khazumar*. I have been told to hold this hill and the outcrop of the eastern extremities of Holvidar. I do not go running to assist beggars."

"What?" retorted Crassus, stepping further inside and momentarily sensing Cappilius' presence to his left. "They are our friends. Khazumar has fought in many battles and never once allowed any elf to be sacrificed needlessly. To these dwarves the guards are the elite and if they lose them, then we may lose half of their number by tomorrow. A messenger was sent and was received by you. Why have you ignored this call for assistance? I have never seen you so dilatory."

Elvandar towered over Crassus, his expression betraying the desire to strike down this impertinent man. As in many such instances, however, friendship finally dominated the urge and the sword was smoothly resheathed and the maiden dismissed, while a heavy atmosphere lay on them all. Cappilius was openly breathing heavily, knowing only too well, after serving with the elf, just how powerfully his temper could be expressed.

"What is it between you two that compels you to ignore a plea for help and risk failure for all of us, Elvandar?" demanded Crassus, stepping closer to the elf.

"It is a long story. Perhaps..."

"There are no more *Perhaps* left in my patience, Marshall. This will continue to delay your reactions and I must know the reasons for your actions. It might may decide all our fates, should it recur at the wrong time."

"You mean Kol may determine to remove me from command instead of that vermin *Khazumar*!"

"If that would serve our purposes better than an internal feud, which has to date not been explained, then I would support that very decision. Unless I knew why such bitterness existed."

"Then I will explain. Ten years ago I was a young, enthusiastic captain. I had for the first time achieved a task of insurmountable prowess. Gallicia and Dwarmania had decided to send an ambassador to the Orcassians to try and begin peace talks. I commanded the elven guard, Khazumar the dwarves."

"We have heard this before, Elvandar," Crassus stated irritably. "We are somewhat short of time for the long version of this tale."

A hand moved to wipe the brow and a sigh escaped the lips as the truth finally dawned on the Marshall.

"Perhaps in some ways Khazumar's hatred of me is justified, but I was young and full of my own pride and stature, in terms of beating anyone who dared to stand before us. We numbered barely two hundred and the first attack was easily repelled, due to considerable confusion on the orcs' part. They attacked in small groups, trying to wear us down, but we retained a deep formation and used the bows to cut them down before they even reached our positions. It was a massacre and the ease of the victory made me overconfident. We charged, defeated the main body and captured their leader and several others."

"Victory is hardly a reason to hate!"

"No, but due to our peaceful intentions, I convinced the ambassador to let the prisoners go, as a goodwill gesture. Me, not the ambassador, or the dwarves, only I wanted them released. I expected them to be grateful. To run to their people and to show them all how we believed in mercy and sympathy."

"They took it as a sign of weakness," Crassus said, already knowing that he was correct.

"Yes. Igluk was the name of their leader. That foul beast now commands the force that faces our left and that orc remains in my nightmares for my stupidity. He returned to his people and used the fact that he had survived to overthrow the ruling chieftain and usurp power. Now he has returned, but with the entire tribe rather than the small faction that supported his earlier ranting. Killing was all he was good at, and nothing would stop his plans to gain power within that horde. I had it in my power the ability to slay that foul creature before the main Dwarmanian conflict began, but I chose to let mercy rule my council."

"It was a childish decision, one born of hope for peace, but with a lack of experience. As you stated, you were young. I am still at a loss as to why such a hatred exists."

"The orcs returned, Crassus, only this time in thousands. We were fighting for our lives from the very next day and for three whole days we retreated towards the Noborian River in the hope of finding some assistance."

"How many made it?" Cappilius asked, the story completely holding his attention now, the battle momentarily forgotten.

"Ten."

"Ten!"

"Yes, ten from two hundred. The ambassador was injured and Khazumar's only son was slain and his body openly cut to pieces by Igluk personally. I obtained my rank only through the intervention of my good friend Aarun. Had it not been for his patience I am sure that I would have been banished."

"Banished?"

"The ambassador had been the first son of the King. But when we entered Orcassia we did not wish for it to look like an invasion, so we took only a minimal escort. It was a mistake and we all paid dearly for this misguided attempt to find peace."

For a moment none of them spoke, as the weight of this news began to sink in, neither having known of the reasons behind the continued feud, which had left them both somewhat numb as to why such a great leader would refuse to support a colleague.

Crassus turned back towards the exit then, looking again at Elvandar, he knelt and spoke solemnly.

"I, Crassus, of the Roma Legion do solemnly swear allegiance to Marshall Elvandar of Gallicia, to whom I attribute the highest level of honour and pride. From this moment forward I swear to obey and follow the directions so chosen and beg for him to now obey the call of assistance from the priesthood guards."

Cappilius then knelt, repeating the oath. "It is time to redeem your honour, Elvandar," said Crassus, rising. "You could not save the son, but perhaps you can save the father and all of his new sons that make up the Priesthood Guards. We should not delay any longer!"

Without waiting for a reply, they left the tent and began moving back towards the main position where a new formation, created from the auxiliary survivors and appropriate Helvetii warriors, stood to arms awaiting their commander's return. This wild mixture had been training with Cappilius every day and had so far in training proved more than capable. Behind them, without looking, they could hear the distinct horn blows of the elven horns sounding the call to arms. Within minutes all three began a march onto the sunorcs' left flank at the head of six thousand, and their presence had an immediate effect.

So it was not long before Elvandar did indeed save Khazumar in more than just an act of fealty. In the heat of battle, he sought out the dwarf and for a moment the two faced each other, not truly knowing whether to attack each other or the advancing orcs. Then, taking Crassus' example, Elvandar knelt before Khazumar and formally apologised for the loss of the dwarf's son, then swore an oath to repay the loss, binding his life to Khazumar's family. The oath was well received, even though the look of shock took several weeks to vanish. The two turned to face their enemy together, finally putting to rest the spectre that had haunted their companionship for years.

Friends they would never be but, from that moment forward, they never spoke of the issue again and the two became inseparable on the battlefield. Finally they had come of age! Finally, two of the greatest tacticians in the army willingly fought side by side, and adversity was creating a formidable weapon.

So ended Scipio's surprise assault. One by one his regiments were forced to retire and the reserve came under heavy projectile fire when the wind finally subsided, forcing even them to retire beyond the danger zone. The assault had served to galvanise Kol to act without caution but, had it not been for their superior leadership, greater damage would almost certainly have been inflicted. The crisis abated and Kol relaxed, for now it would be decided at dawn.

Killis received the highest praise for his insight in splitting the two companies roused after the initial alarm, and was promoted to Senior-Captain and placed in command of his own regiment. Unfortunately, he was not to survive beyond the next day to enjoy this accolade as

Fate once more took a hand in his destiny, but for those few hours this young warrior was the talk of the entire kingdom.

Khazumar would never forget that brief discussion with a young officer that he had until then known only by name. It was odd how even the efforts of the small personalities made the difference when the whole was later reviewed. It was never the mass that decided any given issue, but the sacrifice of the individuals that collectively created the end result.

For Scipio the disappointment was temporary, as the two flanking formations and the orka began to arrive later that day, for the next act in this play. Meanwhile, Fate began to consider how it could once more turn the fortunes of each side. It had no real understanding of good or evil, the concepts being unknown to it, but it still interfered far more than the cosmic order usually permitted.

It was now that Zeus decided that this minor irritation was easily dealt with, and cast Fate into another dimension. He also included Time and Destiny, which feverishly tried to stop any mortal creature from understanding the concept of the passage of the days, in order to slow down any culture's natural development.

It was obvious to all three that the mortalkind especially had a vast skill in learning new sciences at a rapid pace, which in turn made them look over their shoulder apprehensively. It was ludicrous really, the mortalkind had a further billion years' wait before they would even understand or see Fate, Destiny and Time with their own poor, inadequate vision. The retina and optic nerve were such poor tools for seeing the universe in its true format, quite clumsy really. To feel it necessary to continually interfere was odd, while his activities... Well, it was just fun, nothing more.

Besides, it would only take them about a thousand years or so to find a way to return but, for now, they could only watch earlier interference reaching fruition, but no longer intercede directly. In this way, Zeus allowed the mortals to fight on an even plain. Neither he, nor his brother, could assist. It was now their time to step forward and claim a destiny for themselves.

PART ELEVEN

HOLVIDAR

From the central hill Kol watched in silence, his heart a mass of conflicting emotions that he barely managed to keep under control. Yesterday the enemy had almost undone his entire strategy by capturing the central hill. Even now, in the light of day, he still could not shake an unerring feeling of foreboding. This was not the right place to make a stand, but to leave now would be just as disastrous.

He did not doubt their willingness to fight, but a vast number of his people lacked experience. He had that very morning sent word to Aarun, to begin constructing palisades along the Great River and to have all other bridges destroyed, save the main central one that led to the capital. Here the ground would favour the defenders, and the wooded terrain might afford the opportunity of a flanking attack. In case of defeat his mind was already formulating alternatives.

Before him the two armies, massed on either side of the valley, began to deploy. From here he could easily see the preponderance of formations facing his centre and left. Clearly the enemy intended to try for their centre, having failed in their night attack. This suited his own plans perfectly, but even before the real struggle began he was aware of their singular disadvantage in numbers. Could they hold? Could they even withdraw in good order, to fight another day? Only time would tell.

At the centre the enemy would again face Khazumar, reinforced by several dwarven regiments, while on the southern hill there now stood Crassus and Marcellus with a mixture of troops. The issue would be decided in the central zone, he knew, and he thus placed a large portion of the reserve there, with Cappa, to counter this conclusion. The one true ace that Kol recognised that he had was the good road that ran the length of the ridge behind him, and allowed his reserves to travel almost anywhere along his lines with relative ease. The enemy had to traverse rough terrain and so major delay would be unavoidable, time he could hopefully put to good use.

In addition, news had arrived that Kommodos had temporarily abandoned the fleet and had arrived with ten thousand sailors to assist, thus doubling the numbers originally placed beyond the rearward ridge, where the entire reserve now stood. They had arrived late yesterday evening, tired beyond description. Many had simply slept where they halted. Others sought out accommodation but, on finding nothing except a few old tents, began to create their own little camps, while a few were simply too tired to sleep.

Kol had inspected them that night. They had marched a staggering distance, even greater than Elvandar's march, but their subsequent exhausted condition did not increase the army's effective strength. They would be too tired to fight this day. However, circumstances might make it necessary to commit them anyway. They were more than welcome, and words could not describe his pleasure in seeing his people make such a selfless effort, but even so he needed more trained warriors, not sailors full of heart to fight to the death. No matter how romantic the gesture sounded, it was still suicidal.

The sun shone brightly through the cloudy sky onto spears, shields and drawn swords, even onto the upturned faces of the legionaries, dwarves and elves. The wind had abated somewhat, leaving the archers free to continue their deadly work, but the overcast clouds threatened another downpour across the valley.

At first everyone simply sat and waited. The orcs, sunorcs, goblins, hobgoblins and a few trolls began their normal chanting, but the distance dispelled most of this noise. The air seemed heavier than normal, with the sky becoming ever darker and cloudier. It was a fitting setting for this day's work. Every now and again the sun would break through the clouds, almost in a fit of defiance.

Then it began, just as in a nightmare.

What followed was pretty much a blur. As with Khazumar at the hill the previous day, Kol seemed to be everywhere at the same time, offering support and encouragement to any that needed it, and often to those who did not. Crassus and Elvandar also cooperated well and maintained absolute control of the centre, while Valenus moved to stand with Marcellus to watch the extreme left, where a dust cloud had now been identified as the orc chieftain Igluk's army.

In the mountains, Issus and Cappilius, both sent there by Elvandar that very morning, found their true forte, as they fought many bitter skirmishes along the many tracks that criss-crossed the eastern spur. Their day had begun at dawn and the struggle involved more desperation than tactics, as their numbers were less than those of the orcs, who were seeking the passes that would enable them to move behind Kol's ridge. Despite this, their continued cooperation ensured that the enemy's attempts across their right failed.

It was of course a distraction to try and draw Elvandar and Crassus up into the mountains, but their most efficient application of their training was in this valley and, in truth, the enemy had not committed too much to this enterprise. Scipio clearly expected Atronius to ignore any distraction.

He had no way of knowing that Atronius was not commanding and had, for the past three weeks, tried in vain to make the dwarven King release his capital guards, which numbered almost thirty thousand. In this he had failed, but this in turn meant he would miss this battle.

On the other side of the valley, Scipio did not rest either and never permitted any attack to proceed without his express attendance. This was indeed the one weakness that enabled Kol to hang on. Both Igluk and Baka, a relatively new commander from Gobli, had little or no esteem for their overall commander and they actively sought to delay the assaults, in order to throw doubts on his leadership. In these circumstances it was by pure willpower that anything took place at all, but the summary execution of Baka stopped any further tricks by the now subdued Igluk, who sullenly rejoined his people on the far right, where he received the instruction to attack behind the southern hill.

Of course Igluk knew that the *power* retained Scipio's control, and that all the delays in the world would not transfer command of the army to him. However, the day had been boring so far and he saw no other way of antagonising the hated Scipio. In his own way he continued to delay and hesitate, but never when Scipio was sufficiently close at hand to strike him directly.

The disjointed attacks confused Kol, but they enabled each spear point to be blunted by the efforts of the reserve and by Kol's quick thinking as to where the next blow would land. The pits in the valley filled with burning oils worked exceptionally well, and when they were lit several Sunorc regiments perished in a blaze that turned the remainder away in terror. The effect was staggering, but only fleeting as order was quickly restored and the pressure resumed. After five assaults on the centre and two across the spur, the casualties, strain and overall pressure began to tell, as the Orcassians and the wolf-riders finally secured the central hill, so valiantly defended by Khazumar the night before.

Noting this development, Elvandar organised a counter attack, and here that young Kilk's sorrowful destiny took a turn for the worse. He perished, sword in hand, trying desperately to drive his companions to the hill's summit, but the enemy isolated his people and easily drove Elvandar back, leaving Kilk's small band of one hundred encircled. He and his entire company failed to return.

Others had watched this, and some had moved to try and assist their withdrawal, but the arrival of Kol in person halted a very unwise surge forward of the remaining troops in line. Now it was time to withdraw and hold their position on the ridge, where there remained only the exhausted recruits and sailors of Kommodos' column, with Cappa in attendance.

This crisis had barely receded when news arrived that the southern hill was now dangerously exposed. For a few moments it became clear to any fool that the day was lost. An immediate assault by the orcs over the central hill, to support the goblin attack on the southern hill, would have sounded the death bell, forcing an immediate retreat.

However, the General was astonished to see the advancing columns suddenly turn southwards and head straight for Marcellus and Valenus.

"Are they blind?" he asked incredulously, dancing around madly waving both arms. "We are beaten and they decide to turn southwards? By the Gods, we will make them pay for this error! Tell Elvandar to bring everything to the central plain. Hurry, before they realise their mistake."

Messengers ran like the wind, jumping and running over and around the bodies of the dead and the dying to bring Kol's verbal orders.

Along the entire centre, Kol now provided Elvandar with a second force of relatively fresh formations, and threw them wholeheartedly into the flank of the exposed columns. Valenus waited patiently with their own southern reserve, while Marcellus bitterly contested the rear slopes of the southern hill. Then, with consummate professionalism, the cylindrical formations of the Legion, with additional dwarven and two elven formations trained to cooperate, smashed into the left flank of the advancing orcassians.

Behind these very same orcs, Elvandar struck first while Crassus drove several regiments further west to try once again to retake the central hill. However, the arrival of Scipio soon ended this attempt, as he marched at the head of the orka legions. The enemy elite!

Crassus stopped, raised both hands and bellowed as loudly as he could to ensure that every warrior heard his words.

"I stand before the evils of this world and defy them to advance. I, like many of you, have stood this ground before and I call upon you all to strike again for the freedom of our peoples. *Shall we stand?*"

The words swelled their chests like an electrical current, running through their hearts and swelling their pride, leaving them no other choice...They would stand! Once more, as Cappa had done at the caves, Crassus defied the horrors that stood before him and felt his heart beat all the faster as the possibility of death became ever more apparent. Was this his day? Would they stand? Could they stand!

To Scipio the defiance was pathetic. No more than five thousand opposed the whole orka legion of twice that number, while the forces attacking the orcassians were also only half their number. It was true that they were trapped and were fighting on three sides, but so far they had shown no signs of panic and, for once, he praised the scumbag Igluk for the discipline of his regiments.

He had recognised the moment of truth and thus moved forward with the elite, expecting to see the orcassians advancing against the ridge. The fact that they had turned south had surprised him, but the fact that the elite had only half their number to oppose them destroyed any doubts that might have arisen.

This would be the final decision.

"Here we stand, my proud creation, on the verge of absolute domination," Scipio began, gesticulating wildly. "We cannot fail. These fools are committed against our brethren, the orcs. Look, and look hard, my Legion, for we stand on the brink of victory. March! March forward and bring back the glory our true Master deserves! Find the maidens, despoil their purity and cut out their hearts to feast on their flesh! March!"

Step by step the orka moved closer and closer to Crassus' thin line of defenders. Then, with a blaring trumpet, another formation suddenly appeared off to the far right, where it was hidden by the local terrain. Who were they? Many would never know the answer, and Crassus's heavy heart suddenly beat all the faster when he was brought news that another formation was advancing from the northern hill, thus rendering their current position untenable.

"Do we know who they are?" he asked with a frown, spitting in frustration.

"They are covered too much by that long grass and they have just entered the northern gully," replied the messenger. "As far as we can tell they are carrying black flags, which suggests they are goblins. Perhaps the eastern spur has been overrun?"

"Find out. Take whoever you require, but..." began Crassus, but then a new trumpet call caught his ears.

With a swift look at the orka's progress—yes, they would be at least another five minutes advancing along the central gully—he quickly turned and ran through the line of men and dwarves that represented their last reserves, apart from Kommodos' recruits of course.

"That call sign," he chanted excitedly. "Where in Zeus' memory have I heard it before?"

The call came again just as the unknown formation began to ascend the lower rise off to their right, and the said warriors quickly formed into four cylindrical formations. The transformation took barely a minute and then the advance proceeded once more, accompanied for the third time by the call.

Black flags? By the Gods, black flags they did indeed have but, more to the point, it was not goblins, but dwarves that carried them.

"Kollis!" shouted Crassus, jubilantly. "It is the Westonians."

"It cannot be," someone challenged. "They are holding the eastern spur with the mountain dwarves, Cappilius and Issus. How could they be here?"

"I do not know. All I know is that before me is the mass of Kollis' regiment and they do not seem to have lost many of their number. Order the command to form five cohorts. We are no longer on the defensive. Order a small retreat to link up with these warriors. Tell the archers to advance and skirmish with the orka to slow them down. Understood?"

"Understood."

For a few seconds Scipio had watched the arrival of black flags, recognising them as those of the Doom regiments. He was too far away to identify them correctly, and for a few precious minutes he allowed a foolish belief dominate his strategy. They had to be the goblins, who else could be marching from the eastern spur carrying black flags?

However, on realising his mistake he sent for his own reserve of two more orka legions to join him now. They would be at least an hour behind the current force, but he still seemed to see no reason to doubt the outcome previously predicted. It simply meant that two thousand more would perish along with those already numbered!

Thus did the ever-changing arena alter the plans of both sides.

Scipio was now well beyond the lowest point of the central gully and beginning the ascent to the ridge summit. Crassus had withdrawn towards the palisades on the ridge, and deliberately allowed them all to be limited in their manoeuvrability. They were going to be the bait as the Westonians advanced on his far right, perpendicular to the Orka. Several of their formations slowed their pace and then stopped altogether, to face this new threat. However, by doing so they exposed their own flanks to an attack from Crassus, who waited patiently at the top of the ridge.

Kol also watched, while Valenus and Cappa had managed to disengage a large portion of the Roman legion on the southern hill, reform the line and march to strike the orka's' right. Here again they stopped to turn and face the new threat, creating further opportunities for Crassus to attack the weak points.

"Triangle!" came the single word, and with practiced ease Crassus' command formed two enormous triangles, with spears protruding from every space.

Crassus had remembered that this tactic had been used by the Persian King Mithradates who had, in turn, learnt it from the great tactics of Alexander the Great. It was clearly one that the enemy had never seen, and as far as they could tell no Roman formation used this as a standard battle tactic. For Crassus the gamble was about to secure an advantage, but even so it was odd how the enemy had trained themselves to fight in Roman formations! He had felt this at the caves when Cappa had informed him of the details, but there the realisation had not fully taken hold. Now, as he watched the reactions of the orka, it was as plain as night and day that they were fighting with traditional Roman tactics.

Here, on the ridge, the triangles meant nothing other than a defensive position to stand and die. The sudden charge down the slope achieved absolute surprise and swiftly cut two great holes in the orka lines, but it was still not going to be easy to destroy them. Scipio had no doubts, for his orka were well trained and their sheer size would be enough to trample through this resistance.

On Scipio's left the Westonians charged with a bitterness that saw even the orka hesitate. On his right Valenus landed with a smaller force, but attacked with such ferocity that even the size of the orka saw them begin to give ground.

"The wolf-riders. Give me the wolf-riders!" shouted Scipio. "Where is the second orka legion?"

No one could answer his question, for the wolf-riders had long since charged off to assail the southern hill, on orders from Igluk. Finding their losses mounting, they had then decided to attack several nearby villages instead. As at the River Battle, the wolf-riders once more showed their complete lack of cooperation and deprived their allies of the mounted assault when it was most dearly needed. The wolves were the strong point of any such charge! Of the second orka legion, nothing could be confirmed as the heavy downpour had sent them off in the wrong direction. They now faced the southern hill, but nowhere near the centre, where their presence would have ended the alliance's efforts once and for all.

The final stage was far from over, but even Scipio could see that to remain would be foolish. Assailed on three sides, with the Orcassians having already bolted, the remaining orka would not arrive in time if he sent relocation orders.

Scipio left first, fearing for his own safety, leaving the orka to find their own way back. Many did not! From a distance Crassus observed the riders withdraw and for a few seconds the entire line of orka began to take several backward steps, unsure as to why their leadership had now fled. For a brief moment his sympathy went out to them, as any soldier was fully aware of his profession's dangers. It was something else when the inspirational leaders suddenly took to their heels. The feeling swiftly vanished as his eye caught some unusual movement off to the left. With Scipio no longer maintaining their discipline, several orka had broken ranks and were proceeding to hack to pieces the prone bodies of their fallen colleagues.

The sight was enough to galvanise several others into breaking out to charge these heathens and repay them for the dishonour bestowed on the dead. Crassus then realised that one of the impaled heads was that of a messenger. That was always the hardest aspect of a battle. Someone, somewhere eventually forced you to put a face and a name to the decimated torso. The sight was sickening and the wish for an end to all this slaughter overwhelmed the young man, who barely six months before had been but a junior officer in the first cohort of the tenth legion of Roma.

Roma, he reminisced, momentarily lost in his own thoughts. What had happened in their absence? Had the new consul achieved the results that so many had believed in? Had Roma even managed to continue to exist to this present time? A wave of nostalgia now followed the bitter memory of the five hundred years within the void. Everything…everything was no more! Not a single thing would remain and they could never go back. Why them? *Why me!*

Lord Kollis had watched from a short distance as Crassus raised a hand to his forehead. When he withdrew it the distinctive red stain of blood had caused the centurion to stagger for a moment, and with deliberate steps the dwarf stood ready to support a person for whom he had developed a deep respect. Ever since the council of Aarun, this man's character had made possible the integration of all their peoples and enabled them to fight side by side.

In the months following the initial awakening, Kollis had played little part but, at the King's request, he had proudly accepted the commission to command the Westonian Guards Regiment, a reward for his part at the River Battle. It all seemed so long ago. He had not been home in six months and had never once obtained any information as to whether his nephew was still alive. For now such thoughts would have to be subdued as Crassus faltered, now was the time to prove their friendship.

As he staggered a second time, the dwarf placed a hand on his arm to help stabilise his balance, and the contact pulled Crassus out of his reverie.

"Are you well?" asked Kollis, indicating the blood.

"I am fine, my Lord. The blood is not entirely mine."

Kollis jerked his head towards the sad scene of revenge currently being enacted off to the left.

"We should push forward again. It seems they are attempting to retire."

"Yes. Yes, we should. How are you bearing up, my Lord? Your people took heavy losses."

"No more than anyone else, Crassus."

Crassus nodded, wiped a drop of blood from his eyebrow and turned to survey the scene ahead. The Orka Legion, still keeping a reasonably steady line, continued to retire in good order, but now numbered no more than half their original total. Off to the right, at a slight angle, Kollis' warriors had quickly moved and now awaited the return of their commander, which Crassus did not delay for much longer, thanking the dwarf with the time-honoured forearm grip of friendship. Kollis rejoined his battered regiment.

In another glance off to the far left, he saw Marcellus, Valenus and Cappa, the latter organising everything they had into similar triangular formations. But now they actually stood southwest of the retreating enemy, and a thought entered his head. There was no time to find Kol, so he immediately grabbed a nearby legionary and sent him on his way. Could they drive north and cut off the enemy?

"You," Crassus commanded. "Run, fly or jump over there, I do not care, but tell Cappa to throw everything in a northern direction to cut off these scum. Understood?"

"Yes, Centurion."

"Then off you go," he said, then shouted to Kollis. "It is our task to slow down their retreat and the only way to do that is to feign another rout. I will pass the word along that we will charge, fight a little and then turn as if in panic. If they break to follow I want you to fall immediately on their left and keep pushing. Has Elvandar contacted you at all?"

"No. The last I heard of him was during your assault on the Orcassian advance south. If anything he is either with Cappa, or with Kol."

"Are there any other formations on the northern hill that we could throw in here?"

"Only two regiments of Hildar, but they refused to accept my orders when I tried to add them to the regiment's initial arrival."

"Try again. It is..."

"Look! Look they are bolting!" shouted someone.

They both looked back to see the meagre cavalry force that they commanded storm across the southern hill and drive through the lower echelons of the Orka. With this defeat the remainder simply turned and ran.

The fighting on this day was finally over.

"I guess we will be holding on that plan for now," Crassus shouted, then lowered his voice when he realised that Kollis had rejoined him. "Time for us to await the next onslaught."

"Should we not see if we can retake the central hill?" Kollis suggested, full of enthusiasm after the recent successes on the eastern spur.

Even before Crassus could reply, the ill-conceived cavalry charge was now sent packing in its turn, by the long overdue appearance of the wolf-riders. Casualties were few, but the effect on the ponies was instantaneous, and many actually threw their riders. The following scene need not be described, but that day's conflict ended with the few riders in the alliance decimated.

The enemy still held the central hill as ten thousand more orka finally moved to secure its status. The fading light only served to add to the scenes of horror spread across the once serene and beautiful valley. It seemed as though the entire countryside, for leagues around, was covered by the dead and dying. Horses, ponies, wolves and all sorts of wagons added to the assortment of views, but as they retired to the prepared positions on the ridge, Crassus thought back to the burned corpses of the sunorcs that had attacked the gullies in that first assault in the morning. Their screams still seemed to echo in the air, and their scorched corpses created yet another feeling of pity.

The exhaustion felt was genuine. Only Kommodos' recruits had not been committed. Even the sailors had been thrown onto the eastern spur, when the mountain dwarves had reported that without the Westonians they would be forced out of the hills.

That night they all counted their losses and the final tally brought a tear to many a noble eye. Of the original eighty thousand, it was known that between twenty and twenty-five thousand now lay incapacitated or dead. This figure did not include the additional tally of twenty thousand of more that had received light wounds, such as the glancing blow that had split open Crassus' scalp, even though he was wearing his helmet.

The numbers were almost beyond belief, but Kol was quick to assert that if their loss was this great, then that of the enemy must have been far greater. It was poor comfort for those who remained. With no additional reinforcements, Kol made it clear that they *must* retire that night, taking their wounded with them. The first stop was to be a small range of hills about thirty leagues away, but Scipio gave them no rest. Only four days later did they arrive at the Great Bridge, exhausted, bedraggled and deeply thankful for the palisades built by Aarun.

Had they won a decisive victory? To them the enemy numbers had not diminished, and so it was widely felt that the forces of evil could not have suffered as greatly as their own leaders claimed. They were of course not privy to the fact that Scipio had received enormous reinforcements, almost two days after the battle, and these made his losses almost irrelevant. However, his army had set out with over one hundred and twenty thousand, and the following day barely half that number gave pursuit.

Holvidar had been a decisive victory marred only by the need to retire. This did not alter the fact that by this very day, a few days before it was decided that Aarun should sail westward, one third of the Dwarmanian peninsular now lay in the hands of the enemy. Morale was at an all-time low, desertions were rising and defeat seemed imminent.

In addition, there was the final insult: the Black Thorians had stolen their greatest symbol, the man they now called the Oracle, Atronius, a few days after the army had returned to the Bridge. It was only by dint of Herculean efforts that Kol had managed to keep the army from disintegrating there and then.

Never before had the future looked so dim and cast in shadow. Never before had Kol wept for the lives lost in the southern peninsular campaign, which had seen the enemy suffer three times more, and yet still they continued to advance.

Kol had never felt so alone.

⁛※⁛※⁛

In the relentless glare of the early morning the open sea shone like the cold edge of a sword. The eyes had to be shaded against the glare of its brilliance. We now jump back to the present, where Aarun's efforts and the sailing south had reached their seventh day. Many had served at Holvidar, but for now this was a distant memory as they watched the southern storm continue to block their journey south.

As in so many other seas, there was nothing to distinguish this part of the coast from any other, except for the looming clouds that still sat ominously to the south. To the east, the sun still shone brightly and caused many a lookout to cup his or her hands over their eyes. To port and starboard, sailed the other warships in their tiny fleet, while a further two had drifted slightly astern and could only just be seen by their topmasts on the horizon. It was always a worrying sign when any fleet found itself separated at dawn, but during the pitch darkness they had sailed through last night there had been no effective method of keeping them together. This invariably made them feel more vulnerable.

Behind Cappa, the captain of their warship loftily called "Full sails!" with such a bellow that even Helin jumped involuntarily.

Within a few breaths the warship seemed to rear into the air as the wind caught the sails in full extension. Ropes were pulled, tied and then altered as the strain of the wind began to take effect on the rigging, which incessantly creaked under their relentless master, the wind. Spray splashed across the entire warship and for a few moments they stood in awe of the power of nature, and smiled at the wet look that Cappa now seemed to have adopted. He, as always, replied with a deep frown while his stern hand wiped the water from his forehead.

A little later Aarun climbed the steps to the deck and sought an audience with the captain. The storm ahead was causing some concerns and they seemed to be heading into the storm, a course he felt they should avoid. Even as Kol and Scipio sat submerged in their memories, watching one another across the river, he now faced yet another dilemma.

"No choice, my Lord," the Captain responded to the enquiry. "We will never go around that width in time, so we may as well go straight through. If you still intend going south, mind you."

"I do."

"Then into the storm we go. However..."

"It would have been more logical to remained nearer the land, where we could have sat out this storm in relative safety," Aarun finished.

"Yes, my Lord. I mean no offence, but you were told that right at the beginning. Now we are thirty leagues or more from the shore and if we do hit hard times the probability of survivors will not be high."

"Have your men been complaining again, Captain?"

"Them? They always complain. Don't you worry about them, they will do what I command. But it would help if you gave *them* a little breathing space now and again. You see, they *are* the sailors."

Aarun turned at the obvious effrontery, but simply acknowledged his lecture with his resigned gaze. He had after all been wrong and now they had to sail right into the storm, with no landfall possible. For the past few days he had fought desperately to keep the storm from reaching them, but the Mage's power was far superior to his. If he applied his full power, then the Mage's attention would move to him, and Atronius' sacrifice would have been for nothing. No, the storm would now have to be defeated, and for that he would have to rely on the sailors. They would all have to rely on them.

When he returned to the cabin, Cappa tossed over a small wineskin and smiled, having had enough of being drenched.

"Had your ears cuffed, my Lord?" he grinned.

"You could say that."

"Is the storm a problem?" asked Helin, in between gulps of wine, well aware of Aarun's strained condition over the last few days. "I must admit we only have lakes in the mountains, but the storms we have there are quite rough, and many inexperienced sailors have perished."

"From what the captain said, it is unlikely that we can keep the fleet together. As it is, two vessels somehow became separated last night."

"I heard one sailor saying that they had never seen a darker night," Cappa stated, reaching again for the wineskin, which Aarun had absentmindedly dropped onto a table. "None of the lookouts could see even their hands in front of their faces, and it was most definitely not natural. When they called to keep in touch with their colleagues in the other warships they heard not a single sound in reply. There was no wind, yet their voices just died in the air. I have a feeling the storm ahead is also of an unusual variety."

Aarun walked back outside, feeling the deck dance under every stride. They were following a southeasterly course, which ought to bring them back to their own mainland, but not before the storm managed to catch them. He felt the spray hit his face and momentarily forgot their predicament. The air felt so clean, and the smell was far from the aroma of war. For a few brief days, it had almost been like a pleasure cruise.

Only yesterday, Helin and her people had begun to teach Cappa's legionaries a few tricks of the trade in unarmed fighting. Some had shown an enormous aptitude for the training and Cappa, especially, was soon learning several forms designed for individual practice. There seemed to be a most unusual link between Helin and Cappa, but the verdict on this relationship, whether for good or for bad, was as yet reserved.

The warmth of the last few days had helped them all. Yet their very predicament was rapidly seeking them out in the one hideaway that Aarun thought the enemy had not covered. It seems that he had been wrong about that as well. The enemy's eyes saw the sea as well as the land.

With a friendly slap on the shoulder, Cappa rejoined the elven lord who, in his opinion, took too seriously his responsibility for the task ahead. In truth Atronius, to whom he still had difficulty attributing the status of the Oracle, had agreed to be the bait for the enemy, while the true identity had remained a secret. Guilt perhaps made it all the harder, for the Mage would at this very moment be using everything possible to make him talk.

How long could he last?

It had already been over seven days since his abduction. Had the Mage already broken Atronius' spirit and revealed the ruse, and was this the reason for the storm? Did the Mage have the ability to descend into the very soul of any living thing, as was rumoured? If so, then the pain that Atronius would suffer would be terrifying to comprehend.

It seemed also that Aarun considered it his fault! Realistically, Aarun was to some extent responsible, but it was more the thought of someone suffering in his place that was so daunting, and on many occasions Aarun stopped and wondered what this journey was actually expected to achieve. They numbered but a few and yet they hoped that the whole of the enemy's attention would remain on the southern peninsular, while they sneaked in to raid the Haderian Fortress itself, and rescue Atronius. Suicide? Perhaps, but then what was not suicidal in this age, where all things good seemed to be on the brink of destruction.

For the sake of argument, were the other societies really evil or simply the exact opposite of the free kingdoms? In their own arrogance had they just given them the label of evil, as those orcs he had spoken to had not under any circumstances considered themselves evil-minded. No, such doubts were only their doubts. Somehow it seemed unlikely that an orc would have any such hesitation, but the fact that another controlled their hearts and souls made them so dangerous. However, if that force could be removed, what then would be the reaction of the orcs and goblins? Would they then exist in peace?

It was difficult to see it from the other side, and the Gods on both sides failed to see anything other than the continuation of the hostilities. Did the Gods ever talk amongst themselves? He knew that once, long ago, they had dwelt together, but had become separated after many bitter struggles. Why was not important. Aarun consistently felt the lack of any reason why their lives should be dominated by the whims of the Gods, for good or evil?

They never really benefited from their presence, and indeed very few were known to have a direct method of communication. It was believed that, in the scrolls before time, it was ordained that only six from each level of existence would gain the gift of being an oracle. The orcs and goblins called them Mages, while they retained the reference Oracle, of which there seemed to be only one amongst the peoples fighting in Dwarmania. Of the Mages it was known that at least four existed, possibly five. How then could the balance be justified, the hand being stacked before they even began their struggle for the right to exist in peace?

Aarun looked sheepishly out to sea and for a moment watched the swell of the waves, occasionally wiping the spray from his face. The storm ahead was not natural, as even he could see, and the mood of evil foreboding was difficult to ignore. Everywhere you turned the sailors continued to cross their chests and pray to Zeus or Thor for guidance. Even as this thought touched his subconscious, up ahead lightning began to strike ominously close to the surface. Was the thought connected to this reaction?

"What the hell is that?" exclaimed someone, rushing ahead to the bow.

"A whirlpool? Here, in the middle of the sea?" Someone else replied, "Ridiculous!"

Aarun arrived at the same time as the captain, who had moved with expert agility through the rigging to reach the bow of the warship in seconds.

"Whirlpool?" asked Aarun, unsure of what exactly this meant.

"It is the point where two tidal currents converge and both refuse to give way. The end result is that the water swirls around at vast speeds and creates a kind of suction in the central area. I do not know the teacher's description, but I know enough to say that they are common close to the shore, mainly within certain bays along the western coast."

"But not out to sea?"

"No. Not to my knowledge."

"Then how?"

"I guess this comes from the same place as this storm," the Captain suggested, turning to another dwarf, whom Aarun recognised as the second in command. "Get everybody in the rigging. Raise the central sail and tighten it down for speed. If we gain enough, we can simply sail along the horizon and reach the coast. Difficult, but possible."

"We should have stayed close to the coast!"

"Yes, yes. No time now, matey, get those sails adjusted..."

"One of the other warships has gone in!" another sailor interrupted, grabbing the captain roughly. "By the Gods, the main masts are snapping like twigs!"

All eyes looked ahead as one of the previously trailing warships, which had somehow managed to catch them up, rolled over onto its side. A tearing explosion reached out to them, then a great snapping sound followed.

"The hull," someone whispered in terror. "The hull just snapped in two."

"What do we do?"

"We pray and we work, or we'll go the same way!"

"Jump overboard, we are close enough to swim to the shore!" someone shouted in terror. Panic had set in and the sight of the shore, so tantalisingly close on the horizon, made several sailors attempt this ludicrous solution.

"Stop that! Get those bloody idiots out of the water. If we keep our heads we will not even go close. Those fools ahead have paid for their racing. Now, do as I ordered, and we will survive. *Go!*"

The warship became a bedlam of activity and both Cappa and Helin ordered their soldiers to assist wherever possible. The task ahead looked impossible, as the warship had already begun to turn into the whirlpool's current.

It would be a miracle, but sometimes miracles occur when they are least expected. Perhaps this would be one such occasion.

⁂

Sweat, like a waterfall, blended together, just as the flow bundled over the eyebrows to make a torrent that stung Aarun's eyes. A hand moved irritably to sweep away the slight stinging from the salt in the sweat, but only served to make it worse, reminding him of ground onions and how they irritated his eyes when peeled. Rising slowly, he stopped short and found that he could not straighten his spinal cord. Initially perplexed, he finally shrugged and decided to remain doubled over, knowing that he was perhaps still dreaming or, worse still, he was in the land between wakefulness and a deep sleep. He stumbled over a folded rug, and swore vehemently as his question was unceremoniously answered.

Throughout his life he had been able to accept the dangers that he had invariably had to face. They came with a choice, and with that came the possibility of success, or even failure, but it was still by his conscious decision and by no one else's. Now, as his mind reeled in the attempt to re-establish at least a resemblance of reality, he knew without even thinking that he would fail, as he no longer had any control. Perhaps it was this fact alone that always produced such potent emotions of anger whenever Zeus chose to appear in his dreams. Maybe it was also resentment that he could be so easily overpowered. Nobody could really say except perhaps Zeus, but nonetheless the feelings existed.

You would think that being blessed by a God was a wondrous event but all he could remember, after thirty or more years, was the feeling of being used for a greater purpose, as yet unknown to him. Being used was never really a gift no matter how hard you tried to delude your pride. He again tried to see through the mist that always surrounded the shady image of Zeus as he spoke, to understand his feeling better and, by doing so, understand how he might resist, but this simply drove him to his knees as the torch spun uncontrollably before his eyes. He tried to stand again, but fell back, remembering that this routine occurred at every visitation.

It was a strange sensation. He knew he could stand, he knew that his body had not ceased to function and that his mind still worked, if a little fuzzily, but his vision was, as always, blurred almost to blindness. He remembered his dreams, as a child, of being blinded in an accident, and just how terrible such a fate would be. Other events, such as the loss of his mother while he was still a child, smothered his will to continue to resist, the emotions overpowering, the tears warm as they rolled down his cheek.

Such love, such motherly adoration, such a bond had never existed with any other person, but his embarrassment that these feelings always appeared whenever Zeus walked into his dreams never entirely vanished. Why should such a blessing bring forth such emotions? It never seemed to make sense. Then there was the dream or, more accurately, the memory, of his discussion with Elvandar about this journey south, and the futility of such a gesture as the attempt to save Atronius.

Again the powerful emotions that existed between two friends surged to the forefront of his mind, a bond that had stood before death and survived so many times. They had forgotten the last incident where they had each done so alone.

For a moment Aarun remained prone, but with an effort that defied logic he was soon to resist again the creeping drowsiness. I will stand, he demanded of himself, I will not be controlled like some useless toy of the gods. Damn them. Damn them all!

The effort was pointless, as stand he could not, so the feeling of defeat flooded his heart. To raise his spirits he began to sing an old lullaby his mother had taught him just before her passing.

"Hulinas are red, our life is fine
The flowers to bloom, colours sublime
Nature is within us all
Through me, you, bread and wine
Here can we dream, all for you

A dream to choose, red or blue
Ours to keep
Where we both belong
Me and you
Me and you..."

He felt his throat slowly constrict and his voice became gravely, it was too painful to continue the nursery song. It brought forth so many memories that he momentarily forgot his current predicament. But in only a moment or two Zeus once more focused his attention. Such a power to dominate and to control his very being, and yet this power was not used against their enemies. He ground his teeth in frustration and suddenly found he was on his feet, staggering maybe, but upright nonetheless.

Damn this method of communication for making him so puny, so powerless to control his own destiny.

"*Elves,*" a voice then reverberated inside his head. "*Such stubbornness, never willing to leave things as they are. Always seeking to meddle or change the truth behind any existence, theirs or the rest of the worlds. Then you wonder why your mirror souls seek your destruction?*"

"Zeus, my God, I seek only the real truth and to stand before those who judge me and my people," Aarun responded, again dropping to his knees, exhausted by this effort. But inside there was a need to keep resisting which he could not describe, an itch to defy. "If we do not seek such things as the truth, do we not defeat ourselves."

"*More questions, more stupidity. Even if I explained to you in the simplest format, you could not possibly understand the very fabric of time and space. By what right do you make a claim for such knowledge, elf?*"

"I claim this in the name of all mortals who wish to be freed from the tyranny of the Gods that seek to enslave us. Is it not better to speak of the truth, than to base an existence on lies?"

"*A lie can be as much the truth as the teller wishes it to be, while a God can alter the existence to match the lie. If such power exists, then where lies your truth, elf?*"

"I am honest in my endeavours, my Zeus, I have no need to visit people in their sleep and prove my worth by dominating a puny being such as I. I have nothing to prove to anything, or anyone!" retorted Aarun, suddenly furious at being made to look like a newborn baby, fresh from the womb, unable to stand free of assistance. "I seek the truth behind all things, the knowledge that you Gods are forever keeping from us!"

"*Truth again?*" said the voice with a little more potency. "*What do you know of the truth, elf? I bring what help I can, but the void and the dimensions, put there for your protection, prevent my direct intervention and the existence of life is beyond even my knowledge to explain, for it began aeons before my existence. You speak of matters of which you have no knowledge...*"

"If that is so, then my ignorance is at your bidding, my Lord. I..." Aarun began to respond, once again trying to stand, and failing miserably.

"*Will you not sit down, you fool! The incantation is for your dreams and yet you defy the very fabric of time by trying to bend it to your will.*"

With relief Aarun finally obeyed and rolled back onto his bedding. So time was the way in which Zeus created these visitations, he thought. He must stop time in itself and thus freeze the dimensions temporarily, to allow his spirit to traverse the distance between them. How far did he travel? How was this done? Once he knew, he could then prevent this, and perhaps regain control of his soul!

"*That is far enough elf. Again you are looking for answers to matters you cannot possibly understand,*" came the reply to the unspoken questions. "*Also, for now, your understanding of this debate is sufficient, but not exactly correct. I cannot freeze time, but I can slow it down to the point that time is unaware of my presence, but there are only a few minutes before the ruse is discovered. So I have little patience, elf, if you catch my meaning, for philosophical debates. Speak less and listen more, we have a need to discuss the current events.*"

All Aarun could manage by then was a nod, now that the drowsiness had increased. "Will I, as always, remember nothing of this conversation, my Lord?" he eventually asked. "If we are to speak, can we not speak plainly instead of the standard riddles and innuendoes?"

For a moment it seemed as though he had gone too far and allowed his anger to control his motives. He was after all addressing these questions to a God, yet he did not seem to fear any reprisal. Had he become so arrogant, due to this gift, that he would dare to defy a God? For a moment he felt a searing pain deep within his mind and tried desperately to retain consciousness, but just as his senses seemed to be on the brink of closing the pain vanished.

"*I often wonder why I test my patience with you mortals,*" the voice began, but this time Aarun detected a certain level of amusement in the deep voice. "*Perhaps it is this infernal self-importance that keeps me so interested. However, do not try my patience too hard, elf, and no, this time you will remember everything. Time is running out for our cause and the enemy is close to understanding how they can achieve victory. You must know some of the reasons for what has transpired. You wished for the truth. Now we shall see how your mind copes with your wish when granted.*"

"I live to obey, great Zeus, I live only to obey."

"*I know of your true value, elf, but perhaps you do not. I have brought the memory of Elvandar back to you, to remind you of your purpose in this journey south. You must not falter. You must continue, no matter what happens. Your life and mine are at stake. You must succeed!*"

"But the storm has already claimed a warship! Will any of us survive? If we cannot reach the land of the Sunorcs, how will we save Atronius?" Aarun blathered, again trying to rise.

A sound similar to a grunt rebounded through his head and for a full minute he could hear nothing, nor move. Never before had he felt such an anxious desire fill his heart. Would he be given an answer to issues that had troubled him from his birth? How could he just abandon his friends? Would...

"*Stop your blathering, you fool, you are distorting the link. I will answer your ridiculous questions when your destiny is fulfilled. That alone should keep your arrogance at bay. Elves! If I could but have created such a link with a dwarf, it would have been so much easier.*

"*Those fools still think Thor exists, if only they could comprehend a change of clothing and the collection of a hammer! Now shut up and listen, the storm is as you have suspected and is not of a natural origin, but it will not destroy you all, and you must continue south. Sight Fortress is now your target, elf, Atronius Sulla is there, not at Pitlas. This Mage of Hades is shrewd indeed. Here he can keep watch on the battles and interrogate the mortal at the same time. Most logical indeed, but you must prepare yourself for further sacrifices, others are of no significance. You must prepare for a final confrontation, for it is near, very near.*"

"When...where?"

"*You will know, elf. You will know very soon.*"

With that the sensation began to fade, but he had so many questions, so much to learn. Nooooo...why should the Gods play such heartless games with their lives? Others did matter, they were his friends, his colleagues! Why did his God, in whom he believed absolutely, refuse him the answers? There was more to this than he was being told, but he had to find out. For now there was nothing to do but sleep. Yes, sleep now and try to find a way to help them all survive. He must find a way...there must be a way.

Aarun slept away the rest of the day. Deep in his subconscious, Zeus surreptitiously submerged the door needed for him to partake in the final conflict. He needed to be there, for the elf had no real concept of his true worth. He did not know that Zeus could indeed control him, that his essence had been drawn from the very fabric of time itself.

To him a freak of nature, to Hades an opportunity, to Aarun a gift of such power that he had even yet to fathom its worth, and Zeus was happy for it to remain so. Zeus could control, but he did not have the power to destroy Aarun even if he had desired to do so, and neither did Hades. Banish perhaps, but not destroy.

Mmmmm...Aarun was indeed unique for the power had yet to corrupt him, and Zeus had never seen a mortal retain his morals for very long when he discovered immortality. However, time was running out and this meant that desperate measures were now unavoidable.

There was less time than he was willing to admit, even though he had temporarily banished Fate, Destiny and Time. In fact there was nothing else left for him but to force the confrontation mentioned and so...it was his storm and not one of Hades', or the Mage's.

It was his storm.

Hades needed Aarun alive, not that any storm or even the sea would have killed him, as he could jump overboard and sink to the ocean floor, if he so desired, and breath as naturally as in the fresh air.

However, there was no safe way for Aarun to persuade any of the sailors to land at Sight Fortress, so he had taken it upon himself to steer them, as best he could, to the final act of this game. Hopefully, this would be without the Mage realising Zeus' involvement in their sudden appearance, thus the necessary sacrifices. The Mage must believe that their shipwrecked survival at the fortress was a freak of nature, and not of his doing. This whole charade had now lasted for two thousand years. It was becoming a little tedious.

Aarun was the more important aspect. Zeus considered the other mortals inconsequential, except perhaps this Cappa who, for some reason, remained in his thoughts whenever he spoke to this Aarun.

He must do what he could to stop Hades, his brother, before the very fabric of the dimensions disintegrated. The effect of such a calamity was too dire to contemplate, and he must succeed, and at any cost. Any cost!

⊹·⊹·⊹·⊹·⊹

It was not at all clear what had started the argument, or why the two formations had determined on such a confrontation and ignored their officers, and offered them no explanation. It was, in brief, a simple soldierly disagreement that had been allowed to get out of control. It was at this very juncture that Porta and Elvandar passed the end tent in a long line of the same deep green colours. The hobbit colours!

On one side stood a full patrol of thirty legionaries, while the opposition was a group of twenty or so hobbits. The legionaries stood in full body armour, while the hobbits wore only strong leather, as a form of light armour. Either way, words had seemingly become exhausted, a parley no longer practicable. The Latin, of the sort nobody cared to repeat, blended together as the crescendo increased. Then, without warning, one legionary suddenly drew his short sword and stepped forward to end the discussion.

It was a sight that froze Porta, who stopped in mid-stride, in disbelief.

No legionary drew a sword unless he intended to use it to deadly purpose, and this man was well known to all. Hadrian's skill had been fashioned in the bitter campaigns of home, where many shared memories of those lost forever, but his heart was lost in an unknown existence and fretted to find its true worth.

The release of a gasp was not singular. If anything, one and all watched in amazement as the sword was thrust forward, towards the hobbit's chest. Surely nobody could avoid such a thrust, yet the defender had not even tried to draw a weapon, or parry the blow with a shield. Instead, in a blur, the hobbit stepped outside the thrust, gripped the legionary's wrist, rotated the blade inwards, toward the legionary's throat, forcing him to lurch backwards to avoid his own cutting edge.

Then, with one agile step back in the original direction, the hobbit again rotated the wrist and arm to propel the soldier cleanly and effortlessly to the ground. The shield, meanwhile, went flying through the air to land harmlessly at Porta's feet.

Nobody moved for an instant. Nobody dared. Then what had actually happened sunk in, and before Crassus could react the result was a free-for-all, incorporating a series of repeats of the aforementioned incident. He had at first expected a totally different climax, but this sight was astounding. He knew better than most that any legionary preferred a gladius to fighting unarmed, but even so they were all highly trained in wrestling. Indeed any one of them could easily crush the life from any other, never mind from a hobbit that barely reached their shoulders. That is, of course, had they been able to lay their hands on them!

One after another the legionaries coordinated their efforts, but while the initial confrontation had involved a raised sword, the followers had the sense to resort to physical intimidation only. It would perhaps have served them better to learn from the first example given, but such is the stubbornness of men. All three men, Crassus, Elvandar and Porta, grimaced as they saw one man lunge towards a hobbit that seemingly had no cause for alarm.

With a snap of the leg, the hobbit's shin rose smoothly to crush the legionary's testicles between his legs, the extended foot being the reason for their grimace. As was to be expected, this particular man failed to rejoin the scuffle. Next to this scene, several hobbits seemed to have inherited springs in their feet, as they continued to bounce in the air, repeatedly kicking while in mid-air. The result was many a sore nose, with a sprinkling of black eyes.

A little further on, one man lunged forward, only to find that his prey had stepped to one side, extended a leg and turned in a full circle to press his hip into the pit of his stomach. Then, with a wail, the man suddenly cartwheeled over the hobbit's hip to land unceremoniously in a heap on the floor. It had taken literally ten seconds for the remainder to realise that their health was more important than their pride.

For a few heavy breaths longer, an irritable tension between the two groups could be felt, as Crassus pushed forward to intervene. With a nod from Porta, he quickly began to reassert his authority, even though he outranked Porta and on occasion was known to express annoyance. The predicament had stung his pride deeply. Such a show of wanton aggression to an ally was normally the Roman way, and yet even the legionaries had begun to see the folly of their ways. The night patrol had been a long one.

A semblance of control of the hobbits was reasserted only on the arrival of a maiden wearing a light blue toga, adorned in bright jewellery that none of them recognised, initially. Perhaps it was the evening attire for these people, Porta thought, but it reminded him so much of his mother's. It was the first time he had allowed any thought of what he had lost, and he suddenly felt the pain that this day had involved for the others, which so far he had chosen to ignore. It was strange that this young maiden should arouse such feelings, he mused in his head, and winced again as Elvandar slapped him on the stomach and winked.

"Not bad for a Hobbit, even if I say so myself," he said, grinning so broadly that the moon was almost eclipsed, and returning the Marshall's familiarity. Wine was always the best equaliser at any social status.

"Shut up, Porta," Crassus barked from his horse, finding the grin for the first time extremely irritating. Odd that after so many years, such small expressions could provoke his anger, and yet somehow it seemed as though it always did since they had arrived in this world.

Cappa too had mentioned the apparent increase in Porta's arrogance in recent months. What could have changed to bring about such a wanton disregard for authority? More important, given the patrol's actions, did this mean that discipline in general was failing? With a shake of his head, he put these feelings down to a brief irritation regarding the new arrival. But was it just that? He simply could not tell.

"Have you naught to keep you occupied?" he finally said, coldly.

"Oh, yes," confided Porta. "I have a meeting with the very same elf-maiden who acquainted herself with Cappa, General. But I guess he just didn't notice..."

"But you did?" helped Elvandar.

With a slight nod Porta turned and marched away along another line of tents that led to the elven side of the camps, leaving both Elvandar and Crassus to ponder what the word "acquainted" might hold in store for their companion's ambitions. The sound of raised voices brought their attention back to the scene of the recent, friendly disagreement.

From the stance it took, from which even the larger soldiers now recoiled, it was apparent that no ordinary hobbit now stood with its back to them. It was also clear that such a lack of discipline could not be tolerated.

"You," the hobbit shouted. "What is the meaning of this disturbance?"

"I..." began the flustered warrior.

"Are you without wits? Are you all so eager to achieve injuries? There are over one hundred thousand demons across that river, yet you decide to pick a fight with our allies. I desire to know the reason and we will remain here until I hear it!"

A warrior at one end of the line stepped forward, saluted briskly and proceeded to offer a reply.

"The Romans stated that we were too small to be of any use, and that it was no wonder they had to do all the patrols, while we remained in the camps, Captain Armolin. Their insolence was intolerable. Their attitude required retraining."

Crassus watched the newcomer bear down on the forthright orator, who seemed to wilt under the direct stare that was no doubt aimed squarely between his eyes.

"We have had to suffer jibes and childish comments against our people for decades, and never before has such a display occurred. Why now, Sullas? In the absence of Lady Helin, do you propose to stand before me and fight our allies?"

"We are a long way from home, Captain. We have seen things that our elders have only talked about," someone offered from the back.

"Perhaps we needed something to do," offered another, smiling. "We have, after all, not been given even a position in the battle line, which will be fought here soon. From the day we arrived, we have been insulted."

"We came here to fight, not to guard their tents," chorused the remainder.

"Your requirements are what I tell you they are!" bellowed Armolin. "In the absence of Lady Helin, I command the First Regiment of the Honour Guards. Such childish attitudes we left in the mountains, and I will not tolerate such behaviour. You, Sullas, will report to Marshall Arnim and inform him that you will be returned to the general population, demoted by two levels in rank. You, Under-Captain, will join the reserve training companies and remain there until I inform you that your honour has been redeemed. For the remainder, I will determine a relevant punishment tomorrow. For now, get out of my sight!"

With a look of horror, a look that Elvandar recognised after his recent exchange with his own Lord, the column of hobbits moved away. Amongst them not a head was raised and clearly, although it was in the end a mild rebuke, the significance to these people of the under-captain's demotion was profound.

Still angered, Armolin now turned on them, her eyes burning with indignation. "What part do you play in this fiasco, gentlefolk? Or must I also play a game of words with you to determine the truth?"

"We arrived on the scene late, Captain," confided Elvandar, slipping easily into the formal politician, a role he normally assumed only in Aarun's company. "I assume it was nothing more than a friendly disagreement that went one step too far. We have not met previously."

"No, we have not. I am Captain Armolin. As I said earlier, in the absence of Lady Helin, I command the regiment. I find it necessary to apologise for my manners, but such a lack of discipline is unacceptable."

"I concur," added Crassus, smiling, a fact that did not escape the elf's attention. A rarity indeed! "I am sure I can find a suitable way of punishing our people as well. It is a shame that we cannot order a decimation, but these days we are in need of every sword."

"Decimation?" Elvandar asked.

"Every one in ten, within a maniple, is beaten to death by his companions to avoid further loss of discipline!" Crassus explained.

"That is only to be expected, but perhaps too harsh on this day?" said Armolin, more to herself than them, as she watched Sullas march away. Her demotion would hurt her pride immensely, but with the battle coming she knew that such officers would not be replaced. It was a foregone conclusion that Marshall Arnim would reverse her decision, but that was of little importance at this time. "This continued inactivity is driving us all insane."

"I agree," Elvandar concurred. "I do not know why we are waiting for the enemy to grow stronger, but we have been here for seven days without even raiding the enemy camp."

"The tactics of Kol are not privy to just anyone," confided Crassus. "I suspect it has something to do with the journey Cappa and Aarun have taken. But who knows for sure?"

"The war will not end here," Armolin offered. "Also the enemy will devise a way to go around this river, unless we attack them and sting their pride into making them fight us here."

"A sound policy," both of them chorused. "Perhaps all three of us should visit Kol and put this to him," added Crassus.

"We could take your men and ours as the strike force, Captain," Elvandar suggested, smiling ever more broadly, his mind warped by the wine he had consumed this fine evening. Only two hours earlier Kol had advised that him he must not be disturbed until the morning.

"*Men?*" Armolin remarked, her face awash with amusement. "Is this a term for males?"

"Yes," they replied. "Why?"

"Sullas is female, as are her warriors."

"Not gentlehobbits then, Captain," Elvandar offered, helpfully.

"Gentlehobbits? Do you seek to insult Sullas further?"

Crassus looked oddly at Elvandar, who returned the gaze with a shake of the head.

"Then...?" they chorused together.

"They are the First Regiment of the Honour Guards. The first maiden Guards. They are the personal bodyguard of Lady Helin and of Marshall Arnim, who commands our entire army here, although he also has a small male bodyguard."

"Females?" they both chorused, again.

"Yes. Is this so unusual?"

"No!" stated Elvandar, warmly.

"Yes!" added Crassus. At which point they both began to laugh profusely.

"Are you going to tell your good friend Cappa of this night?" asked Elvandar, between bouts of laughter. "Or shall I?"

"Oh, I think I will save that precious moment for myself, Elvandar."

"Elvandar?" Armolin jumped at the mention of this name. "The great elven Marshall, who held up the enemy during the entire withdrawal to this river?"

"The same," Crassus confirmed.

"While here stands the great Crassus, one of the Generals of the Romans, until the return of Atronius. We are all three unique, are we not? We were a little remiss in the introductions earlier."

Now it was the turn of all three to laugh and, still full of jovial spirit, they retired to Armolin's tent to take some victuals and so never reached the planned evening officers' meal, for which Armolin had seemingly dressed. Elvandar paid for this on the following morning, with a sharp rebuke from Kol for not arriving at the general meeting until mid-morning.

Before long the elf and the hobbit had developed a strong bond with each other, and became inseparable except when duty prevented their being in each other's company. To anyone's knowledge this was the first joining of hobbit and elf, but such times did little to help any of the budding relationships. Later that day Armolin was called for, and advised that her suggestion to raid the far bank of the Great River had been accepted.

The only change was that she would not be going over the bridge.

⟨·⊺·⟩⋈⟨·⊺·⟩⋈⟨·⊺·⟩

Cappa flinched, sat upright and swore vehemently, something he had not done for quite some time. His eyes bulged as he tried to focus, then a low whimper to one side made him turn. A dream, it was a dream, but one that had been so real that he wondered if he had actually been there a second time? Was that even possible? Shaking his head, he lay back down and snuggled in closer to Helin, who automatically wriggled to find as comfortable a position as possible without waking. They had been fighting the storm for two days now, and there was little hope of survival. They had finished a ten-hour shift and now rested, but soon they would be back on deck, fighting the winds and the whirlpools.

Closing his eyes he began to relax, but not to sleep. Never before had a dream been so clear in his memory. He now knew for certain that they would not reach the land of the sunorcs. They were going to a fortress of some kind, but the only one near them was Sight Fortress, but if their journey had gone as planned, it should still be one hundred leagues further south. They had avoided the whirlpool, although another warship had not, but such a long journey south was simply not possible in just ten days!

He closed his eyes and felt the soft brush of Helin's breath on his neck. They had not shared a bed yet, but they were now so close to one another as to make this a foregone conclusion, although something in his heart told him not to allow too much of an attachment while the war was still inconclusive. So he kept avoiding the issue of love making, using the lack of privacy as an excuse, not that this would have really bothered him.

Someone was pulling strings and the longer he was on this journey, the more he felt that foreboding of disaster reach out and pull down his inner strength.

A massive creaking sound made him turn his head, and then a wrenching snapping of wood from above ended any further pretence. He rose slowly to allow Helin to continue to rest and made for the doorway. Whatever that noise represented, it was definitely not good at all!

❖❖❖❖

Kol stood on the stone palisade of the watchtower and looked beyond the rising river: a recent downpour had added to their defences by making the current thrice as potent as normal. The small rise of ground he knew to be deceptive, as nothing could prepare you for the undulating pathways hidden behind the initial promontory. In these mysterious ravines an entire regiment could hide with immunity. This gave the terrain an air of mystery and danger, and allowed an enemy to move regiments around the battlefield without his knowledge.

As his gaze settled on the small hill immediately across the water, he saw an unexpected, sudden movement in the woods beyond. Here heavy mist rolled between the foliage and the tree trunks, while in some places a whole tree was smothered beneath a dark foreboding light, which did little to set his mind at rest. The unnatural clouds, the heavy rain, the lack of sunshine and this damnable fog were all attempts by the Mage to lower their will to resist. This he knew, but even the knowing did little to dilute the effect on morale. Although the poor weather was not especially harsh, it was consistently and permanently wet or damp.

It was now, as always when he faced a trial, that an unexpected old memory or part of a dream would resurface, drawing forth a single, small tear. Normally it involved a moral that his conscious mind refused to learn, and so his subconscious brought forth these memories to emphasise the point, leaving him no choice.

Today it was simply a fond memory, one that had now altered forever, of a moment in his past, when the free spirit of a youth had decided to take a chance and ask a young maiden to join him for a walk. It was in these very woods that Kol had plucked up the courage to also seek his first kiss. The maiden's name had for some reason slipped his memory, as for the past thirty years he had remained happy in matrimony with a wife of singular quality, and such thoughts had long since departed. Even so, the tear traced a fine line down his cheek and the stern chin, then fell harmlessly over the side of the stone palisade.

"One more tear for my memories," he said solemnly, wiping a hand across his cheek.

"Your pardon, my Lord, I could not hear."

"It is nothing, Karr. Only a fond memory from a long time ago, a lifetime ago, which refuses to be buried. Inappropriate for these times, I think."

"If I can assist, my Lord?"

"No, but your offer is well received, friend. I am fine."

"Then with your permission, my Lord, I will seek victuals for the guard and organise your bed for the night, but perhaps we must all hold onto our memories? Everything has changed."

Kol nodded, knowing that no acknowledgement would have been necessary, as Karr never left his side for anything other than food, drink or to locate the bedding, but the melancholy was unusual. In recent months it had been nigh on impossible to attend to Karr's needs, yet not a single word of complaint had been heard to pass his lips. Such was the level of his devotion and trust. Kol quietly vowed to himself that, in the fullness of time, such devotion would not go unrewarded.

Time, he groaned inwardly, how much longer did they have left? According to the clerks there was little or nothing left of the victuals. Their supplies had all but run out, because their main granaries lay south of the Great River. In the last two weeks, the bitter struggle to hold the lower half of the kingdom had failed after several major engagements that had left thousands of dwarves killed or wounded.

His only reward was the knowledge that a considerable number of the dwarven regiments had now been blooded and had fought with distinction, while the Priesthood Guards had taken on almost mythical proportions after holding the central hill at Holvidar. Another aspect from which he drew a little comfort was the performance of the new elven and dwarven legions. The elite element of the army was no longer restricted to the Roman formations, and this also enabled him to rest a little easier at night.

Apart from this, however, their losses had been appalling and the enemy had thrown away their lives with abandon. With such reckless hatred, how could they win? He needed the Dwalini city guard, but Atronius had failed to induce the king to release these for immediate service, because he preferred to keep them to defend the capital. With such leadership, did they deserve to triumph?

It now all seemed to have been for nothing. The hobbits were a welcome addition to his forces and the elves were stout warriors, but too few in numbers to make any real difference. His hopes rested with the poorly trained dwarves and the elitist Romans, who would put some backbone into the less experienced.

Indeed on several occasions the superior Roman training had saved the day when the will to fight on had been broken, with many bolting for the rear. This was the real problem. They had enormous numbers at this location facing the Great Bridge, but barely forty percent of this multitude had any significant combat experience. Matters were improving with every day that these formations remained in training with Crassus, Julius, Marcellus and Valenus, but if they were to prevent the enemy capturing the whole peninsular, they needed a miracle.

Where that would come from remained a mystery, so they continued to hope for something that might perhaps never happen. Kol prayed that Aarun's folly would be the miracle he sought while, across the river, Scipio's prayers were directed towards breaking Atronius.

Kol glanced back across the river, then chose to look towards the waterfall off to his left, where a blanket of steam arose from the cascading water. More memories flooded back, as swiftly as the water descended the ledge of stone to fall over the Kicos Island rapids. Memories of boat races and swimming competitions years ago produced a heavy heart, as reports had indicated that the enemy had now almost sealed off the entire island and the garrison was locked up in the small fort, built barely a week ago in preparation for a final stand at this very location.

For a few minutes more the general stood transfixed by the mist rising up above the waterfall, and sought to control the urge to leave this place of desolation, where so many friends and colleagues would soon lose their most precious gift. The gift of life! Conflicting emotions surfaced in quick succession. Why were they here? To what purpose was all this suffering, and who truly benefited? Why had the arrival happened in the first place?

If the enemy had remained within their borders and they had remained within theirs, there would not now be two vast armies facing one another across a river that had, to date, been viewed as the life-blood of Dwarmania. Who had instigated these wars that had, for the past hundred years, given successive generations nothing but suffering and deprivation?

It all seemed pointless and yet he knew without a doubt that, should they decide to leave and subsequently refused to fight, the alternative fate would be to live as Haderian slaves. No, they had to fight on, if only to stop the enemy from overrunning everything they held precious. With a surge of pride, Kol expanded his chest with a mighty intake of air and exhaled, with a purposeful stare towards the waterfall.

"They will never stop our people!" he said, through clenched teeth. "Even if we fail here, we will fall back and fight on. We must! If not for ourselves, then we must accept this sacrifice for the next generation and defend their future peace. *We must not fail!*"

The last words, spoken in the full bloom of his fitness, were carried on the wind throughout the tower. The heavy sound of footsteps on the stairs on either side indicated that the general's guard was far from drowsy after a night's duty. As they appeared on either side on the palisade walkway, their expressions of bewilderment caused Kol to smile. Not knowing what evil they were to encounter, several of the warriors had drawn their weapons and now retired almost in disappointment, having hoped to cleave a few orc heads.

Fortunately, or unfortunately, Kol's own council had not been intended for anyone's ears but his own. With an apologetic wave of the hand he dismissed the guards. Satisfied, the majority obeyed, but a few remained on the stairs in full view of their beloved general. For them, none save those most trusted would be allowed to ascend those steps and, with this security, Kol again relaxed and pondered what might happen over the next few days.

Once more the silence was broken only by the light wind, and the mist that seemed to slowly roll forward, continually decreasing the distance to the far side of the Great Bridge altered his mood. The sound of laughter encouraged Kol to turn, but he resisted the temptation, realising that his thoughts had been disturbed enough this morning. The laughter increased and was now accompanied by the jangle of cutlery. With a face like thunder, the general finally succumbed, turned toward the noise and ventured forward to vent his displeasure in full on the culprit responsible for this cacophony of noise.

However, after only a few steps, and long before he reached the descending doorway to the stairway, there appeared an apparition that made him rub both eyes in disbelief. The annoyance subsided and then vanished altogether, as Karr suddenly appeared on the walkway balancing a tray so full of food that it was a miracle he still stood, while between his teeth he stoutly held a large wineskin of wine.

"What in Zeus' name are you doing?" asked Kol incredulously, feeling the first burst of merriment flooding though his chest.

"Ummnph...Food...My Lord," Karr struggled to reply, tripping dangerously on the last step.

Laughing now in a full, deep boom, the guards on either side joined in, at the sight of the general's personal aide weighed down with a tray that held an entire roasted chicken and an enormous volume of fruit.

Catching hold of the tray, Kol turned and placed the food to one side, then offered a hand to his friend, who had by this time dropped to one knee.

"A proposal, my friend, surely we have not known each other long enough..."

"You are not funny, my Lord," Karr chastised, yanking his hand free and glaring at Kol. "That tray was heavier than an ox!"

"An ox you say," chided Kol, warmly. "Perhaps I should pass on your sentiment to my father, along with your dowry. A chicken and a flagon of wine hardly constitute a worthy price for my hand, my friend."

Slowly Karr rose and glanced toward the general, throwing daggers with both eyes.

"You jest, my Lord. Besides I am more than happy with my own wife. I am in no need of another wench. Especially one as short as you, my Lord."

"Well played, my friend, well played indeed!"

The laughter increased and for many, as so often in the environment of war, the sound had the power to release their concerns for a brief moment. Others, such as Crassus and Marcellus, could not see or understand the cause of this merriment, and failed wholeheartedly to participate. However, Crassus was not so foolish as to intervene and restore discipline, as he had grown to understand people need to relax before any conflict.

Glancing up towards the palisade, the Centurion shaded the view from the sun's glare, watched for a split second, then quietly pushed past the merriment to join Valenus outside the tower by the main gates facing west. For this man there was a more pressing issue to resolve.

"Has everything been prepared, Valenus?" he asked, conspiratorially.

"I have organised a special group of our best men, Crassus. We will leave in the next few minutes."

Crassus grimaced, placing a hand on his colleague's shoulder. "You know what to do?"

"Yes. We need to know who has trained the orka to fight in the formations that mimic our own tactics. Are you sure that there is a traitor?"

"It is the only possible explanation of this situation. Kol is blinded by loyalty but, in short, every move we planned has been countered by one of us, a traitor who sits close to the army staff. It is impossible to believe that these heathens, the orcs, are capable of countering our tactics. Either way, we need to confirm this before we are all destroyed."

Valenus grimaced. "I will try, Centurion. I will seek out the information required, but I truly wish that we had Cappa here for this task. He would have been the obvious choice."

"That is not an issue to discuss. His fate is on another path. Yours is the destiny of this task. I have total faith in your ability to succeed."

"Thank you, noble Centurion, but if it is all the same to you I prefer to retain my doubts."

"Why?"

"They keep me from becoming careless."

He clasped Crassus' forearm and the two men looked into each other's eyes, as if to try and see what the future held for them both. It was then that Valenus suddenly thought that he would never see this man again. It was beyond his ability to understand why this revelation had appeared and, without another thought, he turned and signalled to a small column of men fully armed in the traditional Roman weaponry, but with less heavy armour.

Will I ever see any of them again, he wondered, as they descended towards the nearest side entrance to the bridge, where Marcellus was ready to pass them through Khazumar's defences. Pushing the melancholy to one side, Valenus raised a hand to wave to Marcellus then, ignoring everything but the wood ahead, took the twenty men in his command into the fog at a great pace. Within an hour of leaving the bridge they had entered the expanding mist, just as hidden from the orcs as from their own people. Then, just as swiftly, the small band vanished into the triangular wood to the right of the bridge.

On the tower's palisade, Kol and Karr remained in high spirits, knowing nothing of the secret mission assigned to Valenus. They too would soon have enough to occupy their minds, and their merriment slowly subsided as they considered Armolin's suggestion of further raids across the river, even though the last two had achieved very little. Crassus had in the meantime decided to keep his own counsel, ignoring Kol, and for Valenus it was a decision well made, as he continued to seek the respect of the legionaries!

In the valley before the southern entrance to the bridge, the first column of the enemy suddenly appeared, then another and another. Each column converged on Khazumar's barricades. His small detachment, left on the far side of the river to delay the enemy crossing as long as possible, to avoid any surprise assaults, began to look inadequate. At the base of the tower, Crassus once again grimaced and understood that his colleague had left just in time, and felt a pang of guilt at having sent twenty men to almost certain death, but he had had no choice.

"So it begins again," he said. "So it will end...at this bridge rather than the one on the Rhodanus."

"I should return to my command, Centurion," said Marcellus, having returned up the hill to advise Crassus of Valenus' safe departure. "The enemy seems to feel a little more active this morning."

"Go with good fortune, Marcellus Sabinus. May the Gods fight for us on this day, and find Cappa and Aarun in high spirits."

"The same to you, Decimus Crassus. Today may be our end, but what a glorious end we will make it!"

Crassus had no response to that statement but, as he watched Marcellus descend the hill, he could not help but think that there was far more yet to be discovered in that man's destiny. Of all the people seemingly brought here by the Gods, Marcellus was the only one who seemed to have utterly accepted his fate, almost as though the Gods had confided in him their true destiny.

Marcellus' friendship with Khazumar and Kollis, his ability to advise Kol without hesitation and his capacity to learn so quickly, had pushed him forward so much so that when the bridge command came up, Crassus had not hesitated in appointing the former teacher.

Turning, he watched Karr walking back to the kitchen with the empty tray. How many of these people would be here tomorrow, he wondered. Would he be here?

By Jupiter, I need a new wineskin!

On the far side of the river, three more pairs of eyes watched the columns, now increased to ten, slowly and purposefully advance towards the thin wall of defence placed to create a semi-circular formation around the entrance. All three knew they were the baited hooks in the first stage of this battle. A great responsibility had been laid upon their shoulders. Today they had one purpose, to fight fiercely, but always remaining aware that they must retire in stages, but not at a pace that would lead the enemy to believe they were doing so deliberately.

It would not be difficult to fool the local leaders but, in truth, the group of riders that now appeared on the lower slope of the hill rising up towards the barricade would be more wary. Watching intently, the three not only stood resolutely, but also represented the conglomerate of the forces that defended the bridge and ultimately Dwarmania. Dwarves, elves and men stood together in a tight circular wall designed for defence and to maximise the destruction of the enemy.

To this end, the riders they could see watched their columns converge, then with loud trumpet calls the advance ended as abruptly as it began. With practiced skill, the columns now quickly organised their structures to allow long cylindrical formations to stand side by side and, with another call, the first three began to march forward. These were Orcs, but not all of those opposing them were so!

With a calm that surprised most of the people who knew him, Khazumar ordered the forward echelon of dwarven warriors to stand ready. Turning slightly to look at Abraxis, the commander of the elven archers, he received a nod of acknowledgement, then the commander left to rejoin his comrades. To one side Marcellus looked on with a grim determination, his forehead damp with sweat from his brisk walk from the watchtower. His task was to act as a minor representative of the alliance. It was felt that some men should stand with this contingent to demonstrate unity of purpose. It surprised many that Crassus had chosen to elevate Marcellus to command, but in the absence of Cappa this was not a surprise to everyone.

It was not widely known that Khazumar, not Crassus, had really made the choice. The friendship that had started at the caves of Azar-Kad had been further enhanced by yet another close encounter with death.

"This will need perfect timing," Khazumar said in Dwarvish.

"It will indeed, my Lord," Marcellus replied, in a heavily accented response. "Where do you require my men to stand?"

"Where they are at the bridge will allow us to have a final standpoint. That will serve our purposes better than any foolish repositioning of our forces."

"Then I will bid you farewell, my lord, and pray that we shall fare the better on this day."

Khazumar glanced towards Marcellus, who now turned and walked back towards the bridge. It had now been several months since the *arrivals* had changed not only the social structure of the kingdom but had also, unwittingly, forced the dwarven people to see the bigger picture, not just their own.

At the Azar-Kad caves, the Romans had saved their religious and monarchical symbols, earning the respect of the nobility and, should they prevail in this struggle, several land concessions. Then, in the southern peninsular campaign, further concessions followed the training and the exchange of knowledge that the Roman engineers gave the dwarven engineers, for example, the scorpions. They were now an integral part of the army. Where it would all end was beyond his understanding, but today was its greatest test.

This very morning the enemy that marched towards their defensive ring of the Priesthood Guards, increased in strength on the King's orders, would have to be held temporarily, then fooled into a rash charge across the bridge.

The plan was, to many, at best risky, because, if the enemy managed to organise their defence promptly on the far bank, they would be able to maintain a bridgehead. If that happened, then it would only be a matter of time before their whole position was compromised and they were forced to retreat again. However, should the bridge be destroyed as planned, by the heavy oils and the so-called Fire Company, trained specifically for this one task of burning the bridge, success would be assured. If they succeeded, they firmly believed that several thousand orcs would be trapped on the far side, ready for Crassus to massacre, hopefully damaging enemy morale and gaining a few more days respite.

None of them laboured under the false illusion that victory was a real possibility, as even the common warrior was aware that they were outnumbered at least three to one. No, he thought, this battle would be a question of buying time for the real task that both Lord Aarun and Cappa had undertaken over a week ago. For a few moments the commander's thoughts wandered, as he tried to establish just where that secret party had gone. Where were they? Had they succeeded? Only they knew the full truth about their mission. With this train of thought, he also began to wonder why a small band of Romans had suddenly appeared on this side of the bridge, less than two hours ago.

Nothing but questions, again!

Orcs! Yes, foul creatures indeed, but they were fearless in battle and as determined as his own people to prevail, whatever their racial objectives. Khazumar took a deep breath and clapped both hands together to throw a swift prayer to the gods. He did not really care which one heard this time, as long as they answered. Then with a resolved expression he marched towards the small mound that now served as the command focal point. Dressed in the bright reds of the

Priesthood Guards, he summarily dismissed his personal guard and sent them all to the front line.

"Pass the word to prepare!" he bellowed, listening to the repeated order follow the circumference via each company commander.

There was of course nothing more to prepare, so they all waited.

It was the chant that reached them first, followed closely by the clashing of shields in rhythm with the chant. The guttural language was full of basic words, but few dwarves understood Orcish. Maim. Kill. Enemies. Destroy. Destruction. Death. These were the few words that Khazumar recognised, but as the enemy drew nearer the translation became lost in the melodic chant.

"Arrows!" he bellowed, above the din, and watched as the highly trained elves moved forward to take position behind the dwarves.

Then, just as he intended to give the order to fire, the columns suddenly stopped in their tracks and fell into a surprising silence on the far side of the small ravine, immediately in front of them. Puzzled, Khazumar moved forward a few steps to try to discern why they had stopped. The tiny ravine was barely ten paces across and no obstacle to this mass, and yet the eerie silence sent a chill down everyone's spine. Why? *Why?*

Gritting his teeth, the dwarf turned and waved a hand towards Marcellus. At a fast pace the man reached the perplexed commander, who was pacing from side to side on the little mound, agitated.

"Why?" he stated bluntly. "I do not understand! Anywhere else they would have broken ranks by now and surged forwards to destroy us in detail. What can they gain by standing still?"

"Our attention, Khazumar," offered Marcellus, still lightly panting after the brief run. "Perhaps their full force has not yet arrived and they are reluctant to engage us until additional forces arrive?"

"Orka Legion?"

"Perhaps."

Khazumar slowly came to a halt and tried desperately to see through the mist over the far hill, in the hope of identifying the enemy's intentions.

"If they are waiting for the orka we had better try and precipitate an attack. Where did they develop this level of discipline? It is so out of character."

Marcellus' lips tightened as he placed a hand on his friend's shoulder. "I have no idea, but even at the caves and in the peninsular only the orka showed this level of tactical understanding. The masses generally kept to the normal chants and then the madness of a charge."

"Something has changed and I have a feeling that we are not going to appreciate this at all," Khazumar remarked glumly. "Return to your men, Marcellus, we will undoubtedly do our utmost to dispel these orcs." As Marcellus moved to obey the command, several warriors arrived on foot, panting heavily.

"Well?"

"The enemy are moving several formations to the river on either flank, my Lord," one of them stated, between gasps.

"It seems they have no intention of attacking us here, but will try and capture the far side without coming to grips with us directly," added a second.

Khazumar nodded, and dismissed the messengers to return to their respective captains. Orcs detested water and feared small boats, or at least this was his understanding. Yet another personality trait had somehow changed over the last few days. How could this be? What evil could achieve sufficient control over their minds to make them believe something against their very nature?

It was then that the realisation of their real peril struck home, like a thunderclap. Sweeping away everything, Khazumar knew that he now finally understood just what kind of evil they now opposed.

"One or more of *The Six* are here," he said quietly, seeking his own council. "If this is true, then the only person to counter this magic is the Oracle and he has been captured by the enemy. This day will be the end of Dwarmania. It is the end of the world. Well, so be it. I will take as many of these foul creatures with me as I can."

However, as the words passed his lips a further realisation forced itself to the forefront of the warrior's thoughts.

How? If the enemy could traverse this position without even using the bridge, then this stance was useless. Despair began to slowly engulf his mind and, as if in a dream, Khazumar found himself to be trembling. With an enormous effort he regained his thoughts, and fought desperately to regain control of his senses. What in Zeus' name was wrong with him?

"Khazumar! Khazumar!"

It was Marcellus, shouting hoarsely for the commander to join him at the bridge. With heavy feet the warrior moved and found that each step became harder and that, rather than moving closer to the bridge, it seemed to grow further away, while his senses again began to throb in the effort just to see the bridge.

From the bridge itself Marcellus watched in horror as the orcs broke through the thinly held perimeter and headed straight for Khazumar's mound. For a few seconds he expected the commander to burst into action and send messengers all over the ground in the normal response, as they had agreed they should retreat across the bridge. Only then had the cloud surrounded the mound and the small warrior became lost to sight.

He sent several men to investigate but they too vanished. It was more of that Underworld magic!

That was the only answer. Throughout their experiences, he had not really believed in Mages and the like, but this now dispelled all doubts.

Moving to the nearest soldier, he rapped him on the helmet. "Lucius..."

"Centurion."

"Retain command here and keep this bridge open for as long as possible. If I am not back in time withdraw, as I discussed with you earlier."

"As you command, Centurion."

Moving quickly Marcellus ran across the small slope to the mound and reached forward to drag the dwarf out of the cloud. Just as he was on the brink of success, lightning came out of nowhere and struck Marcellus a glancing blow across the eyes. His scream of pain was lost in the whirlwind of activity, as the orcs that had broken through reached the far side of the mound.

Blinded, Marcellus tried desperately to return to the bridge, but he knew this was hopeless when a peal of laughter sounded behind them. Khazumar was almost unconscious, but making a slight recovery. Throughout the entire battle the commander had remained on the mound, motionless. Now they were about to die, as the entire dwarven line collapsed inwards.

Lucius took one look and moved a small group towards the struggling officers. With their lives they protected their withdrawal and Lucius was amongst the fallen, to be mourned later. Marcellus never knew of this sacrifice.

The battle raged for several more moments before the entire command broke and fled, due to no overall command structure. Initially this was deemed a great victory by the orcs and, as expected, the discipline shown previously disintegrated. As a mass they began to cross the bridge and on the far side Crassus watched anxiously. Previously he had observed the sudden cloud that had emerged around Khazumar and had associated this too with magic. Expecting the same outcome for himself, he therefore gave the word for the individual junior officers to attend a brief council.

Meanwhile Marcellus and a few of the bridge guard continued along the far side of the river, seeking any shelter that the topography of the ground might offer.

The battle for the survival of Dwarmania had started, but not in the way intended, and without the control expected.

Marcellus knew that some kind of Mage had prevented Khazumar from commanding correctly and that the individual captains had fought with bravery but, in the absence of firm leadership, all cohesion had been lost.

So far he had not even considered his loss of vision. So far no one else had either!

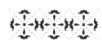

PART TWELVE

VALENUS

The light was still murky, almost as if the leaves and trees had decided to be reluctant about throwing off the veil of darkness surrounding them. However, inch by inch the majestic determination of the sun rose slowly against the darkness, and at first small areas began to show signs of life and vitality, pinioned in a column of bright warmth. The light became a beacon for the animals, which had for days been deprived of this comfort and denied any warmth. No birds had flown freely through the trees for fear of whatever evil now stalked them.

The small band of legionaries felt their hearts become oddly calm for a few seconds, but a single moment was as long as it lasted, a single breath, no more! Within seconds there emerged a cloud so dense that it made each man's resolve falter, and soon it was impossible for the sun to offer its warmth. This reminded Valenus of a dog with its tail between its legs, and he gritted his teeth in determination as the warmth vanished.

The heavens had tried to achieve a degree of resistance and failed miserably, echoing his feelings as the light faded once more. The darkness had come with the enemy, a power far beyond their understanding, and the resistance of nature held sway within the confines of this wood and the surrounding valleys. Under normal circumstances life for many of them was hard enough, but now even the creatures that would kill for sport now roamed these very woods, and life had become exceedingly fragile.

Any warmth, any light was something to reach out for, but it was almost as though someone watched that same hope and felt it increase, only then to snatch it away in the knowledge that despair would supplant it. It was not always so, as the darkness was a blanket from the bright sun for the goblins and the Orcassian orcs, who despised direct sunlight for extended periods. Amongst the enemy only the hobgoblins, wolves and especially the sunorcs, were able to stand in bright sunlight for an entire day, the latter living in lands, far away in the south, that were practically a desert. If it were possible to use magic to rid them of this protection then the advantage would most definitely stand with the alliance.

This thought occupied Valenus' mind as he tried to utilise the momentary warmth from the sun to finally throw off the experiences of the night before. With the warmth gone, he put aside this somewhat childish effort, turning slowly to look all around and establish whether it was safe to move back through the foliage.

He could not help but feel that the enemy had actually destroyed the sun, as so many others had begun to believe. A stupid thought, he knew, but as he strove to put his mind to work, with exhaustion not far off, he could not remember the last day of bright sunlight. There had been the odd glimpse, but nothing more. He frowned, then thought of Cappa, which made him smile, then picked up his gladius and began to crawl towards the nearest bush of brambles. Cappa would hardly have allowed a little cloudy sky and some rain to thwart his efforts!

It was of course magic that kept the sun's glare from reaching these trees. His imagination created a picture of the upper branches actually stretching forth like fingers, as though seeking to break through the dense clouds far above. It was of course an illusion, but a pleasant one nonetheless. As with the light, however, this feeling too often evaporated as swiftly as it had appeared.

Reaching the brambles, he cursed mildly under his breath as he suffered about the hundredth deep scratch from the thick thorns. Never before had he seen such sharp edges on a plant. It was a ludicrously small thorn, but the points sank so far into the skin that it became almost impossible to remove them without wrenching the skin. Looking tentatively at his hands, he noted at least five more cuts on each.

Was his weakness from the probable loss of blood or from exhaustion? Or was his mind playing tricks on him? Either way the thorns were beginning to test his nerves. He smiled again, loss of blood from a few scratches...what on earth was he thinking?

All night his small band of legionaries had moved from one muddy hole to the next, avoiding the searching claws of the enemy. Wet one moment, caked in leaves and mud the next. Finally, hiding in a very small cave they had found only a few hours ago in the midst of a night-time skirmish, they had managed to kill all the enemy scouts before another group could arrive, but the night had taken its toll. The stress had been enormous and, though the others were just as adept as he was at hiding the truth, they had all been shaken by how close they had come to detection and death.

So close, and yet so far, he mocked, looking once more for signs ahead of any orcs. The cave had been a godsend and had saved their lives, of that he was sure, but uncertainty came with the how and why? Fate, he thought to himself, must have had a very important part in what had occurred the night before.

Had Tatrius not fallen down a small ravine, they would not have followed the stream. Had Hadrian not twisted his ankle on a tree root, he would not have fallen through the bush that had probably hidden the cave for centuries, and then capture or death would have been a certainty. Valenus could only guess, but at least five hundred orcs had entered the wood at dusk yesterday, or as close to dusk as he could determine in this eternal darkness.

Why was always a guess, but perhaps it was not so difficult to formulate the truth. An important dignitary must have arrived at the enemy camp, and the very reason Crassus had sent him here was to find out exactly who this person was. If there was a high-level spy in their camp, then it would he here that he would find him, or *her*! The sunorcs were also investigating the sudden loss of several patrols in these woods and a slight fear of the trees had helped them immensely, but he was just as positive that the enemy did not know of *his* presence.

He knew that he would have to find the spy by dusk, as this was the fourth day since crossing the great bridge. Daily the searches had intensified and, although none of them had been seen by any enemy who remained alive, he knew that someone in the enemy camp understood that something was not right in this wood...they simply did not know what. To an orc there were as many good powers that would devour them, as evil powers would be happy to devour Valenus, both ancient and long forgotten by the peoples of Tannis.

Magic, he grunted, only a Mage could sense beyond the natural boundaries. Even the foul orcs could not change their natural abilities, but could easily smell another creature at a hundred paces. Sweat and bathing oils were the most common error applied by people using stealth. What fools, when a little mud and dirt can go a long way to securing a little protection. Their heavy armour had been put to one side in the cave. They needed to move fast and light and the advice of Issus prior to crossing the river had been invaluable.

It had worked so far, but for how much longer? No, they had to finish their task today and retire from this wood as best they could. They would not survive another night as, whoever the enemy was, their hiding place would sooner or later be discovered. As long as they had a small advantage of surprise, then they still had a chance.

Accepting this decision, Valenus rose to a crouched posture and looked intently in a full circle before daring to move a second time. A bramble thorn caught his eyebrow and a droplet of blood ran down his cheek from another cut, but the sensation went unnoticed. Nothing moved as he again surveyed the area, not even the leaves in the wind. No sound either, so it's now or never.

Within minutes he had reached the stream and acknowledged Hadrian who sat on watch at the mouth of the cave, his entire body submerged within the nearby bushes. It was only because Valenus knew he was there that he could perceive anything, and he was again amazed at how well Hadrian and the others had taken to this secret form of soldiering.

Roma no longer existed for them and this was a bitter and constant memory. For all of them, there was no going back, and the bitterness was more profound. They had little chance of survival, as they had been told when they volunteered, but the temptation of victory, spoils and glory always managed to bring forth someone for these missions. Greed, women and gold were the main recruitment tools and even here such practices still worked wonders.

As he entered the cave, he tried to recall the last number identified by their numerous scouting activities, and he recalled that they had finally agreed on a figure of over one hundred thousand. Even then it was mere speculation, as the formations had almost certainly been double-counted at one point or another, and from this wood they could not see the entire enemy army. Even so…seventy-five did not sound too much of an exaggeration and, from the size of this battlefield, they could easily double that number and probably still fall short of the true number employed by the enemy in this campaign.

"Ave Centurion, any change in the approaches to the hill?" greeted Tatrius, reaching to clasp forearms, and pulling Valenus' mind back to the present.

Once inside, the cave was large enough to stand in and, before answering, Valenus nodded his thanks to Bruti, on receiving a small mug of the warm liquid the dwarves called kintas, which was special because the liquid used spices which kept the drink hot with no fire required. He breathed deeply on the heavily spiced liquid and sat on a nearby rock.

"No change, Tatrius. The approaches are still guarded beyond our strength to alter."

"Do you think the spy theory is true, then?"

"Why? That the hill is defended so well is not new to you or me. Hardly proof, Tatrius, we need more information about this spy to be certain, but there is no easy way of obtaining any in the time we have left."

"And the lights we saw last night..."

"*You* saw last night, Tatrius," someone at the back interrupted crudely.

"Shove your face into a lion's mouth, Bruti! I know what I saw. I may be unable to understand what has happened to us and why we are here, but I have seen enough magic to recognise it when I see it."

Valenus closed his eyes in frustration, but he had to agree. Most of these men were stout of heart, but lacking in brains. Tatrius, however, simply loved to fight and found waiting behind in reserve an impossible strain on his carnal desire to rip, smash and destroy anything. His mind worked towards one goal in life and that was to achieve the coveted rank of centurion. He was also the best legionary here, hence the guarded comment from the back of the cave, to avoid retribution, for many would call him the equal to Cappa. He suddenly wondered what their family names were, but why that was important was illusory. He let the thought go, gulped down some more kintas and nodded to Tatrius.

"I have no doubt magic was used last night, Tatrius," he agreed. "But we are in need of proof, and then we have the small task of bringing this news to Crassus and the alliance generals."

"Shall we deal with one issue at a time?" scoffed Tatrius, in his airy way, which annoyed most people, but Valenus had learnt from Cappa to listen to his juniors. He opened a hand inquisitively, his sanction affirmed, as Tatrius crouched on his heels. "What we are in need of is a very large distraction. We draw the guards in one direction, and then you can get in close this very dawn and find the proof. Then you send the messenger back and, if we are lucky and the Gods are with us, then in all the confusion the identity will reach Crassus. Beyond that it is in the hands of the Gods."

"What kind of distraction?" Bruti asked, his interest peaked by the opportunity to burn something. Many believed he had a rather odd issue with fires.

Tatrius groaned noisily. "The military sort...you know, when we employ our skills as trained legionaries. Too many of you fools have become soft and use our predicament as an excuse to avoid the practice training ordered by Crassus."

A murmur ran through the group, a legionary rose threateningly to his feet, and the name Volas leapt into Valenus' head. "Some of us did not leave their wives behind, so I would choose your words more carefully, toad."

"And if I do not? You will do *what* exactly..." Tatrius allowed his sentence to hang in the air, and for a moment Volas looked ready to strike, his right hand reaching for his gladius. Then, just as quickly, he glanced at Valenus and withdrew.

"Just as I thought...no backbone," jeered Tatrius, grinning broadly. "Next time I'll gut you like a fish, if you dare to oppose me while standing before the centurion. Let this be a warning..."

"Enough." Valenus rose to his feet irritably and gestured towards Bruti for some more kintas. "This is getting us nowhere. A diversion has been decided upon," he affirmed, glaring at Tatrius to end any further delays. "It is almost dawn and I am certain that few of us will see the next sunrise. Make your prayers to the Gods and prepare for the final fight. I intend to find a glorious death that will be worthy of a song. See that you all set your minds to achieve the same, and do not dishonour your families. Their memories are still with us and we owe them this honour. Tatrius, you and Jarvi will come with me, as the latter is our fastest runner and our youngest blood. May the Gods bless the wind to carry his footsteps. Volas, you will command the diversion with Hadrian. Everything else we will leave to the Gods. Now make ready."

The sound of a few hands striking a few breasts could be heard as Valenus moved back outside, to find on guard a legionary whose name momentarily escaped him.

"Jarvi, Centurion. I joined the Tenth one week before the storm."

They had obviously changed the sentry, and it irked him that he had not noticed, but he also thought *you poor bastard*. What did you do to annoy the Gods? Just one more week and you would still have been in Italia, free and able to live a normal life. In fact what had any of them done to deserve this wrenching separation from their entire existence?

Valenus felt his lips flatten as he tried to smile, but he knew even before he began that he had failed abysmally. That was one aspect he still had to work on, encouraging others when he did not feel very enthusiastic.

"You will fight with me and Tatrius this day. Go and find some peace of mind and finish your prayers to the Gods. I will keep watch for the next hour or so."

"Thank you, Centurion."

Valenus turned to look back at the entrance to the cave and settled down for the vigil, Jarvi willingly withdrew to rest. As his eyes scanned the ravine, searching every bush meticulously, his mind worked feverishly to justify his own prayers. He had never had any problems before, but now such things seemed rather foolish. The Gods here were not the same, except for the name of Zeus of course, which was not Roman anyway. Greek or Roman, what difference did it make to them?

Everything was different and he found himself wondering how he would face his end, if his original beliefs no longer counted. Even now he had an almost impossible compulsion to find a deer or rabbit to slaughter as a sacrifice to Mars especially, chanting for victory. Anything would have served this purpose, but such a commotion would have brought the orcs running. There would be time enough to stand eye to eye with the enemy and declare their intentions as true Romans invariably did, but for the moment stealth was their greater ally.

A noise off to his right made him turn. A branch from a dead tree crashed through the bushes. It was nothing to him, but anything nearby would almost certainly investigate. He waited patiently and sure enough the bushes immediately to his left shuddered as an orc crashed through, scimitar drawn, ready for use. The face was hideous and the stench repugnant, but Valenus forced himself to remain perfectly still. He waited, knowing from experience that, before they appeared, others would be waiting to see if this one died. Ugly they were, but not necessarily always stupid.

A guttural cry screeched from the orc's mouth, and answering cries followed, but still nobody else entered the ravine. Valenus imagined the silent preparations inside the cave as they waited patiently for him to act, but noted for reference that he had heard not a single sound. Of course the orc's hearing was significantly better than his, but it still made no obvious move towards the cave. They were safe for the moment.

Another cry ripped through the wood and was promptly followed by the appearance of five more orcs, all wearing dark red cloaks. Valenus racked his brains for what Crassus had tried to teach him. The easiest way to identify your enemy was to look at the skins. The goblins had a slightly green tint to their skin, orcs had a bluish-brown tint, but generally were smaller than goblins, while hobgoblins were barely the size of a boy of ten and had very pointed features, such as the nose and chin. Orcs as a rule had protruding tusks and goblins normally had rounded mandible bones. So these were not orcs or goblins, but sunorcs or possibly hobgoblins!

They most definitely did not belong to the mainstream orcs that had searched for them all night. These were different and their obvious tracking skills indicated that they were scouts. How good their skills were was about to be tested. The answer came as swiftly as the thought. The leading creature began to sniff intently and at first its eyes only gleamed across the foliage, but slowly it became obvious that it had heard nothing, but smelt everything.

"*Kinkasssss!*" It spat coldly, its eyes now staring right at Valenus' hiding place. Had it smelt his breath?

"*Siryu bukbukis arundish!*"

Two more creatures began to circle to either side of the leader.

"*Imka hahatnash ni su killo!*"

The scimitar was raised and, with a sweeping thrash to emphasise the intent, was now pointing directly at the cave.

"*Cavunis!*"

Valenus felt a chill go down his spine. If there was ever a word that held such menace yet was not understood, that was definitely the one. Even the sound implied the meaning of a cave.

They could hide no longer as two creatures moved towards the cave, eyes searching the ground frantically for trodden grass or broken leaves. One looked up and he swore that their eyes met, but no attack followed. The scout did not see what his own eyes did, and he remembered that he was caked in mud from head to toe. They were hunting by smell, not sight! He had never before been so glad of a mud bath and, surprisingly, he wondered what his mother would have thought, since he had, after all, not played in a mud pile since the age of ten.

Such an odd thought.

His right hand glided effortlessly across his abdomen and smoothly drew his gladius. Then in one step he emerged as if from the ground itself and thrust the tip deep into the scout's throat, just above where he assumed the clavicle bone would be. There was no resistance from armour and the extraction was easily achieved.

With a gasp the first dropped to its knees and died. With practiced ease Valenus stepped to one side and thrust the gladius again. This time he aimed for the lower side of the body, easily avoiding a desperate swing of the scimitar. Feeling resistance, he lunged forward and pushed hard, while looking straight into the eyes of the creature. Green fluid bubbled up through its mouth and for a second it seemed to falter then, realising its own life was over, it fiercely pushed Valenus away and sought to take him as well.

The attempt was perfect and would have succeeded but for Bruti, whose arrow lodged itself into the creature's throat. It staggered and fell to one side, and in one step Valenus moved on, picking up the fallen scimitar, as his gladius was still within the enemy's torso.

"To one knee," Valenus heard behind him, and dutifully dropped.

Three arrows sang past his ears as he bent down to watch as three of the remaining four were dropped, but what of the last one?

"One has escaped," Tatrius stated blandly, relishing the sucking and bone-breaking efforts to retrieve Valenus' gladius.

"Then we have no more time left," concluded Valenus. "We act now, or not at all."

A resounding series of nods gave consent just as a third piercing screech cut across all of their thoughts. It would not be long before they had more company. It was time to meet their fate.

"What were they?" asked Jarvi.

"I am not sure," Valenus replied. "Issus and Crassus explained that the enemy generally use sunorcs or hobgoblins for scouting, but from the look of the features of these scum, I think they are sunorcs."

"They were good," Volas added. "I think they found you by smell alone, Centurion."

Valenus shuddered. "When that creature looked directly at the cave and then at me, I confess my heart stopped beating. It was a moment not to forget for a while, but we must move now before it is too late. Volas, take your legionaries south. Make as much noise as possible and draw the enemy to you. Find honour in your deeds today. Now go. Tatrius and Jarvi, you are with me. What is the delay...*move*...all of you. Jarvi, pick up that bow, we may have a use for it, and you will have a particular task ahead of you. Are you up to this task?"

Jarvi nodded mutely, giving rise to a little doubt. A few murmured, considering in their vanity that all they desired was not to be forgotten. That this sacrifice had not been pointless, but had in fact been an absolute necessity that brought nothing but honour to their memory. Sensing this sudden change from the normal boisterous arrogance towards enemy weakness, Valenus stepped forward and clasped the youngster's forearm. He was trained and he had the ability, that much they both knew and understood, but the void had changed all of them. They had been forced to adapt their values, morals, understanding and learning skills, or they would have been driven individually insane.

Doubts were commonplace, perhaps expected, but the difference was that, as a leader, he could not express them, no matter how much he considered the advantages for his own sanity in admitting his own doubts. He was after all the same, but for them he had to be different. He had to be strong where they felt weak. His confidence in his own skills must remain superior, or they would ask why he commanded in the first place.

"I do not doubt your ability, Jarvi, and neither should these fools. I have seen your skills at remaining unseen and the speed of your run. It is those skills that will keep you alive."

"I will not fail you or any of the others, Centurion."

Valenus glanced at his men one last time and, after a second of silence, Volas began banging his shield viciously. "Legionaries to me, form line. One cohort to the right, one to the left, reserves to attack west!" He began to chant, much to the amusement of the others. They numbered only sixteen, but they would fight and die as if they were a thousand.

"Burn them back to Hades' pit," shouted Tatrius, in approval. "Make them fear the name of the *legion*!"

"We will, Tatrius," retorted his colleagues from the dense undergrowth. "We will take them all to the pit with us."

Then they were gone and the undergrowth swallowed them. They would perhaps never meet again in this time, thought Tatrius, suddenly. He knew without a shadow of a doubt that these few were his only true friends. It grieved him that they would all perish, but then he too might well meet his end today.

"So be it," he said following closely on Valenus' heels.

"What?" Valenus gasped, momentarily stopping.

"Nothing, Centurion."

"Then shut up and move. We must reach the base of the stream, if we are to have any hope."

Then they too were gone and only the bodies of the sunorcs remained to rot. Nobody mourned these creatures' passing.

The stream left the undergrowth a few paces ahead and wound its peaceful way around the base of the higher ground that rose before them. Apart from some high grass for a few paces at the base, there did not seem much hope of approaching the summit without being seen. To charge straight up the hill would have been just as ridiculous as, even from their poor position, they could see several enormous creatures on guard. Valenus assumed these were trolls, but had no way of knowing for certain, as nobody had ever seen one before.

They had scouted north and south to see if there was any other approach, but nothing gave them any hope. To reach the tent would be impossible without the planned distraction being considerably more disruptive.

"Is there nothing we can do?" asked Jarvi, despondent at their sudden lack of progress.

Only moments earlier he had avoided an orc patrol by literally lying on the ground, barely a pace to one side of the path. One stagger, one misplaced step, and for him all would have ended. Valenus noted how the youth's voice seemed to quiver slightly. The experience had unnerved him and he found it impossible not to sympathise. His own nerves seemed more taut than usual.

He looked again at the stream, trying to fathom what he should do. The second they walked into the open, the nearest group of orcs would fall upon them without mercy. If they remained here, then assuredly the sacrifice of Volas would have been for nothing, and he did not intend for his ancestors to be so dishonoured. He had skulked around in the mud for long enough, perhaps it was time to stop hiding.

In the last few months, especially at Mount Holvidar, where he personally had saved Tatrius' life, he had won the loyalty of a few legionaries, and this meant more to him than he could possibly express. Now, as he watched a troop of orcs march past, he counted at least five hundred in this group alone, and he wondered just what else he could do, if anything.

"We need the distraction to cause more mayhem, they are not moving the forces in front of the hill to the far side," Valenus finally answered.

"I may be able to..." Tatrius began.

"No, I will need you to take Jarvi back to Crassus. That will be your task. I have a sinking feeling in my stomach that I cannot seem to lose, but somehow I must see the identity of this spy."

"A foreboding, Centurion. About what?" asked Jarvi, concerned that if Valenus was as terrified as he was, then perhaps they should all go back to Crassus now. He began to question the decision to volunteer for this task, but everyone was forever telling him that promotion was awarded only to the brave. Now he was here and decidedly unhappy.

"The spy," was all that Valenus whispered in reply. "I think there is only one person it can be. It is impossible to think that it could be anyone else, but Cappa had his suspicions, as did Crassus, but it just seems impossible to believe."

"Who?" snapped Tatrius, irritably. I wish these officers would say what they mean the first time around. "If you know...why are we here at all?"

"To confirm a fear. A doubt that has grown in the heart of Crassus, ever since the enemy knew our dispositions at Holvidar. It had been festering, until it became unbearable. Ever since Cappa left, we have known we had to find a way to prove our fears right or wrong."

Tatrius shook his head violently. "And you intend to achieve this by doing what exactly? I count at least two thousand within visual range of this hill alone...never mind whatever is on the other side!"

"Keep your voice down, you fool." Valenus turned and drew his gladius, threateningly. "You will obey instructions. Only I will approach the hill. When I know who it is, I will shout the name and you will both run like the wind to report to Crassus, and then we can finally fight without a viper in our midst."

"As you command, Centurion," mocked Tatrius, knowing, as he always did, that once more he had pushed that little bit too far.

In his mind, however, he saw this as the sure way of achieving his objective of becoming a centurion. In the legion strength was rewarded, not dithering ineptitude. He began to recall why they had hated this idiot before but, even as these thoughts resurfaced, he recalled the many battles in which Valenus had shown a different side. He had even saved Tatrius' life by slaying an orc that had forced a way behind him. He was grateful for this act, but in truth any legionary would have done the same for any other under the same circumstances, so he owed no one any exceptional loyalty.

Fine, for the moment he would remain dutiful, but when he reached Crassus he would be the only person claiming the laurels, as was his right, of course.

Valenus sheathed his sword and looked at the hill again. "It is no good. The only way is for me to walk up that hill."

"Are you mad?" grimaced Tatrius, managing to keep his voice down this time.

"No, I do not think so. It will be the last thing they expect. It may work and I may get close enough to do some damage. Look there, those lights have begun again. The spy has returned just before dawn, as always."

"Centurion, look there," added Jarvi. "They begin to move their cohorts."

"Some luck at last. Volas has finally started to do the task correctly," jeered Tatrius.

Sure enough, several formations had suddenly swung around and vanished across the crest of the hill, working their way towards the southern edge of the wood. Within minutes, barely an orc was left within half a league of the northern slope of the hill. Volas' efforts had achieved the desired result. All their eyes must be turned to the west and he must act now, before it was realised how small the distraction was.

"Keep your very special ears tuned for the name, Jarvi," advised Valenus. "I may be able to say it only once. I bid you both glory, and pray Jupiter and Mars will favour success in your task. I will see you on the other side, where we will again exchange stories of times gone by."

With a final clasping of the forearms, both Tatrius and Jarvi watched the man walk forward into the open air and proudly ascend the slope. Neither knew what he intended, but if a name was called out that they recognised, then they would take it back to Crassus as ordered. Either way, as they both agreed in the single glance they exchanged, they were glad that Valenus had not ordered them to also climb the slope.

✧·𐤟·✧·𐤟·✧

Volas felt his teeth grinding together as he plucked the arrow shaft out of his arm. The pain was piercing, but in that instant he knew there was no going back. Not for him and perhaps not for any of the others.

"I think this small rise will be enough for our needs," he shouted between blooded teeth. "Shall we end our service here, Hadrian? Shall we cut down the enemy before us as they charge? Destroy these scum that dare to stand before us!"

A resounding chorus of shouted replies echoed across the small glade, where they could see the southern plains stretching out of sight. Some of the legionaries banged their shields, while Hadrian began a filthy dirge about a prostitute in Roma. Some smiled at the sound of the familiar song, but for a few memories of the past stung them yet again, causing pangs of regret. That infernal question... again and again...why us?

Volas allowed Hadrian to finish the song in full, even though the last verse was almost lost in the high-pitched yells of the orcs ahead of them. The sound travelled and it became clear there were just as many behind them and on either side. All of them remained out of sight for the moment, having learnt unpleasant lessons about hasty attacks. Volas looked to either flank in satisfaction to think that so far only three of their number had fallen, although at least fifty of the enemy would no longer trouble anyone.

"Do you think Bruti will make it?" Volas turned to see Hadrian standing beside him. "Well?"

"It is hard to say," replied Volas, solemnly. "These orcs rip everything to pieces, you have seen it enough times already. Playing dead may have become a reality."

"Not to him it won't," grinned Hadrian. "That idiot has the luck of the Gods. He has won my wages ten times over with the dice."

"Then at least our act today will be remembered," sighed Volas. "That is good. I have been honoured to serve with you, Hadrian. We have seen many wonderful places…"

"And many wonderful whores as well…"

"Yes, that too, but today it is our turn to join the Gods and, if we die well, then our honour will be our banner to take us forward."

"I am looking forward to the rest," joked Hadrian, then gripped Volas' forearm with a strength that had always surprised the older man.

"To your post."

Hadrian pulled upright and moved his scutum to sit comfortably on his left shoulder. "We use the tortoise, I suppose?"

"Yes," commanded Volas, drawing his gladius.

"Prepare to form the tortoise!" bellowed Hadrian, high above the screams of the enemy. "We will march in a southwesterly direction to draw the enemy away with us," he continued, in a lower tone to avoid any prying ears.

The tortoise was a rectangular formation with interlocking shields, which gave them complete protection from arrows. Volas knew it was the wrong formation for this terrain, but they were in such small numbers that he knew the arrows would pick them off within seconds if they did not protect themselves. It was their only hope.

The legionaries now acted as a single unit, one thought giving rise to only one purpose: to sell each and every life at as dear a price as possible, and perhaps find a chest of gold along the way. Volas grinned as he wondered why he had thought these foul creatures actually had any gold, but it had seemed like a good idea at the time, and he could no longer tolerate sitting around thinking about his wife.

The pain and loneliness had become too great for even him to bear. Now, as they completed the change in formation, arrows began to rain down on them, but the tortoise was initially too good to penetrate. The orcs watched in wonder, for this was something they had not seen before, and once again they began to hesitate.

Those in front continued to lead the way as the tortoise moved forward down through the glade. To either side, jeering screams could be heard, but they ignored them and marched on. Ahead, a small band of orcs suddenly rushed them, but in an instant the back of the formation opened up and launched several pilums at the charging mass. The group attacking hesitated just a fraction too long, and the front row of legionaries now broke formation and began to hack and thrust indiscriminately at everything within reach.

Blood flowed and the frustration began to grow, as the enemy made attack after attack but failed to break the formation, mainly because of the dense trees so close on either side. A few orcs actually jumped onto the roof of the shields to hack downwards, but they were quickly allowed to fall inside, where each one shared, in reverse, the fate they had intended for the Romans.

Volas took one final glance back the way they had come and wondered if their diversion had helped Valenus. There was no way of knowing, of course, and there was nothing he could do for him, so he turned back to the task assigned. He felt the shield above him vibrating with the impact of arrows. He heard one of the men curse: with an arrow protruding from his throat he collapsed, the curses fading away. The formation seemed to stumble over the prostrate form on the ground and, without warning, a wave of orcs struck at this very juncture, sending many of them sprawling. Sensing victory, the mass charged and the end was near.

Volas' arm became numb with thrusting and hacking, but one by one they began to fall and soon it would he his turn.

Soon, *he knew*, it would be his turn.

The gentle wind felt fresher than ever as Valenus reached the summit of the slope. The aroma in the air filled his nostrils and he breathed deeply, and for a brief moment he allowed faded memories to reappear. The breeze pulled gently at his hair so as he again pulled his gladius free his vision was partially obscured, although he heard the guttural outcry of the alarm being raised.

Once more he was on centre stage and this aspect of his personality had never altered, no matter how hard he tried. Vainglorious he was and vainglorious he would remain and, to be fair, in this particular instance it would be this obstinate, blind obsession with his own importance that would convince his enemies of his genuine intentions to betray the alliance.

As he crossed over a ditch another voice, more powerful and holding the hint of magic, cut across his thoughts. A Mage almost certainly stood before him now, and his thoughts drifted back to Tatrius and Jarvi. If only his damnable hair would remove itself. He began to regret allowing it to grow so long. The breeze was suddenly becoming an irritant.

"By the Gods," a voice then mocked him off to his right. "An assassin no less."

"The commotion in the woods is now clear, My Lord," mocked a second voice, a voice that chilled his spine.

"We should cower in fear. We should run to the hills and seek a hole to hide in!" continued the first voice.

"That we should, My Lord. The master would approve our actions, when faced with such a formidable enemy!"

The words froze Valenus' blood.

At first Valenus accepted this abuse and indeed remained silent to further his own purposes. Assassination was the obvious reaction, as was mockery, but his true intention had to be implied as a desire to betray Kol and Crassus. Or rather he needed them to believe this was the case. He had no wish to die on this day and, as he walked up the slope, he had determined that his best strategy now was to join the enemy. Damn all those that had led him to this day. He filled his head with red rage and allowed his remembered hatred for Cappa to burn through his mind, seeking to block the search that the Mage would obviously implement.

He stopped and finally the breeze removed his hair from his vision. The second voice had seemed so familiar. It was not so much that he recognised the voice, but that he could not shake the chilling experience of hearing it. He physically detested the owner, he knew, almost as much as Cappa in the old days, and the next logical assumption was that to his left stood the spy. To the right would be the Mage, but as the name crossed his lips, nothing could have prepared him for the revelation destined for his eyes on that windy morning.

"Porta!" exclaimed Valenus, his breath catching in his throat. Now he no longer needed to force his hatred, for in his heart this was true enough beyond any form of measurement known to man. Crassus and Cappa had both been right!

To find that Porta was the spy simply broke something inside. Had it all been for nothing? Had he just been a pawn in the plans of his enemies? He had suspected, but now, with the proof before him, he felt such a fool.

Laughter was the only reply he received.

"You have yet to perceive my name, Centurion. Are you as shocked to see me stand before you, as you are this whelp?"

Valenus slowly turned and gasped. "Scipio?" he said, incredulously. "How can this be?"

For a moment Valenus was crestfallen. Suddenly the new enemy tactics on the battlefield all made sense. Scipio's knowledge alone would have been sufficient for this purpose, but it also explained why the implementation of these said plans had failed to totally defeat them...as yet. Scipio's record as a Tribune of Roma was being extended into the service of darkness, but clearly not all was as it had been.

Porta's betrayal reminded him of the light-hearted discussions between the two after many a junior officers' meeting, where the council of the alliance passed on the commands of the generals, but here was a personal edge to the knife he felt twisting in his stomach.

For a second his legs stumbled, his coordination diminished and he knew both betrayers had seen his lack of faith. His breathing became irregular, and the gladius in his right hand unexpectedly weighed as much as a mountain, but even now, at this low point, an inner strength began to surge through his veins.

He assumed that Tatrius and Jarvi were already on their way back to Crassus, and they had in fact left a considerable time before, but for Valenus time had stopped. It was this hope, above all others, that raised his spirits. Now it was his task to keep the darkness focused on him for as long as possible, to allow those two to escape. To also give Volas or any survivors of his group the chance to escape.

"I should not have been so surprised to see you both here," he began, searching desperately for the right words to hook the bait. "It will make my purpose all the more...suitable."

"Suitable?" quizzed Porta, as his eyes narrowed and he took a pace towards the centurion. "I suggest we do not trust this fool, my Lord. At Holvidar he fought with distinction and it is unlikely that he wishes to aid our cause..."

"Lord!" scoffed Valenus. "You call Scipio...*Lord*! I find that insulting, you heathen piece of shit! I sought his favour long before he even knew of your pathetic existence. I am here to offer your master the very plans of the Alliance. What do you bring, but the pathetic ramblings of a junior officer!"

"The information has served us well so far!" retorted Porta, stepping closer. "If you felt the way you say, why then did you not make this known to me?"

"I am not in the habit of dealing with lowlife. I gave you what you wanted to hear and then I waited for the right moment. We all suspected you anyway, after your pathetic efforts to track down the culprits who kidnapped Atronius. Hardly inspiring."

Porta opened his mouth to pronounce a long list of profanities, but then his throat began to burn. He wondered, briefly, if he had some ailment, but as the heat increased he realised what was about to happen.

"Perhaps your services are no longer required," spat Scipio, his eyes having turned as black as death. "Perhaps Valenus, as he says, could be of more service? Perhaps, but either way, end this pathetic banter. I have more important issues to hand."

Porta gasped as the incantation was released and dropped to his knees, gripping his throat. His expression was one of desperation, but his eyes never left Valenus. He would wait for now, but if any lie was told he would not hesitate to reveal it, thus securing his own status again. He also planned revenge on Scipio...nobody treated him like an underling...he would talk to the Mage and see just how much he valued his efforts. Yes, the dark Mage would help him get rid of the fat Scipio.

"You say you bring the enemy plans with you," continued Scipio, as though the pain he had inflicted on his *master-spy* was insignificant. "Furthermore, who ordered this raid and to what end?"

Valenus breathed easier now and dropped his scutum, and placing his gladius on one side, but making a note of its whereabouts. A glance to either side indicated how useless both would have been, as all about them the mass of orcs had returned. Volas' last stand had evidently ended. On either side a large troll looked hungrily at his miniature form. This would have to be a performance to match the greatest orators he had ever known, if he were to live beyond a minute more...

"The alliance is seeking to move around your right flank, where you have rebuilt the old cart-bridge. Already Kol has dispatched ten thousand dwarves with the elite elves and velites to cross, and when they succeed a further ten will be sent to break your centre."

"Lies...nothing but lies!" screamed Porta, exultantly. "I know for a fact that a bridge of boats is planned to our left, beyond these very woods. You have been sent to scout the woods. Do not take us for fools."

"Scout? No we were not sent to do any scouting. That information I kept from you, and I told the legionaries only when we were in the wood. As I said, we already suspected you..."

"*A lie*!" hollered Porta, spittle spraying from his mouth. "I heard Crassus in person discussing the plan with that filthy dwarf Kollis. Do you deny that fact?"

"No, but Crassus did not have his normal bodyguard with him, and he did look directly at you, which startled you. It was intended to, and you did not even know of your error," said Valenus, gambling on Crassus' habit of always looking at all those who stood close enough to stick a sword in his gullet. He had a careful nature, nurtured in the halls of deceit in Roma.

"Yes...I remember...he..."

"...Saw you for what you were and let you have the information needed to fool you further," finished Scipio, raising a hand to prevent any further rebuttal. "A veritable victory, Valenus. You are to be commended, but I wish to know the reasons for the raid and how many came with you. All this seems rather elaborate, just for you to take the plunge into betrayal. I am sure at many times I have witnessed you fighting as never before, yet now you ask me to believe that you wish to betray your so-called friends. It is...somehow...too much to ask. Would you not agree?"

Valenus watched as the words rolled from Scipio's tongue and for a second he felt unusually warm. Even though he had never felt magic, he knew instantaneously that the words themselves were an incantation and that if he lingered too long his bluff would fail, but how to bring Scipio closer? Could he convince this parody of evil to drop his guard for just one moment?

"Your incantations will only tell you what I want you to be told. Countermeasures and training have enabled us to block…" Valenus felt his knees buckle…"You will not learn…" Now he dropped onto his palms before everything began to go black.

The hand movement had seemingly come from nowhere, as far as Porta could discern, but in that split second both Scipio and Valenus vanished into a darkened hemisphere. He watched with glee as he recalled his own journey into such a bubble of despair, where Scipio plied his trade. Valenus' mind would be torn apart and probed beyond the understanding of anyone other than a Mage, but the more he thought about it, the more he relished the idea of Valenus in agony.

His villa had been attacked during a slave rebellion. His father had known nothing and neither had his father's brothers. They were nonetheless sentenced to crucifixion, and in his heart a seed of revenge had grown. He, his mother and his sister had been spared because they were slaves of value to work in the fields, but very shortly afterwards another revolt had started, following the rape locally of several maiden slaves.

To the Romans it was their right, to the slaves it was yet another reason to believe in freedom, only to find, sadly, that it existed only for Roman citizens. The bloodbath lasted a week and had given him the opportunity to thrust a dagger into the heart of his own master, but could not find the ultimate culprit, a senator, that had ordered the death of his father. He found this senator much later, but the memory of his mother and sister began to resurface and his heart would not permit these experiences to return. There was too much pain and hatred, more than even he could control!

From that moment on there was no going back, and to surrender would have meant a terrible death on the cross. So with nothing to lose he had brusquely walked into the recruiting station in the nearest large town and, given his young age, signed on as a stable lad, seemingly hoping to join the legion when he was older. The similarity to Cappa was astounding.

To his amazement it had worked and he had avoided retribution, but his very nature had always made him rebel against authority, which had eventually transferred him to the Tenth and eventually to Valenus' century. As he watched the darkness begin to fade, he pondered on just how oddly it had all linked together, as though he was meant to be there, and each series of events had been preordained.

He closed his memories, as Scipio once more appeared while Valenus could be seen sprawled on the ground.

"His mind is indeed strong," said Scipio absently, his face strained after the exertions of breaking down this man's natural mental barriers. "However, I must know of their plans and that is paramount. You will return to their camp," he then said, turning and pointing at Porta. "Find out from this Crassus…"

"If I return I will be arrested…you heard what that fool said. I am suspected."

Scipio turned towards the table behind. "I care little about your welfare, spy. You made your alliance with the Master and you will obey…"

"I serve the Master, as you say, not *you*…"

The argument was soon in full flow. To both of them the heated exchange was of the highest importance, but Valenus heard the words as though spoken from a distant hill, faint and muffled. His hand reached across slowly, all the guards' eyes fixed on the argument. He did not think of striking down Scipio, only that the gladius felt cold to the touch, comforting; it was just an instinctive action. He would rather die fighting than on his knees a broken man. He did not consider, as he rose, that he would succeed.

The gladius slipped smoothly into the back of Scipio, passing through where the third and fourth rib should have been, on the right-hand side. Or rather where it would have been, if the body Scipio occupied had been alive, because inside only the remains of his soul existed within a husk. The sensation did not hurt in any real sense, as there was nothing to kill or damage, but the husk had been broken and he had for only a second dropped his guard, to concentrate on the transportation incantation for Porta.

As they argued, they had forgotten about Valenus, accepting that he was a broken man. Scipio gasped as the power keeping him on this plain of existence evaporated. The heat burned all around him and a faint scream reached his ears, but there was no time to consider what this meant. He fought desperately to reseal the power, but it was already too late. This husk was dead and he must return to Pitlas and the Underworld to retrieve another.

"Fight on..." he stammered to Porta. "Hold the left and keep attacking the centre, they will break eventually...You must..."

Time ran out, Scipio was removed to Pitlas, and out of his tent stepped Igluk.

Valenus dropped to the ground, his face a mess of open burns. For a few seconds he just lay there awaiting the final thrust that would end his life. He knew nothing of what had happened in the darkness, but sensed that a great struggle had drained part of his mind. His face stung and his right arm hung limp at his side, but the final strike never came. All about him he could hear screams of panic. Could he have done so much? The dagger had struck home, that much he knew, but ordinarily such a blow need not have been fatal.

Scipio had vanished, as far as he could see, and Porta had run off somewhere. Now only a large orc stood at the tent entrance and, although the creature had looked at him directly, there had been a look of approval in its eyes. Valenus was of no importance to this creature. Valenus was already dead.

He was not sure why or from where, but that look of absolute certainty goaded Valenus into action. A spark of survival made its appearance felt and, even if the final blow were to fall, he would meet it as any true Roman would, head on and with pride. In this madness, would anyone see him crawl down the slope? Only a few yards away stood the ravine, but to his tortured mind it looked a league or more.

But he would try. Damn this world and everything in it...he would try!

Using his one good arm he began to drag his body towards the slope. Each movement was an agony and his vision became blurred. More than once he fought back a sensation from within, which he knew and understood to be unconsciousness. On reaching the edge of the slope, he looked down feverishly at the angle and at the welcoming undergrowth at its base. If he could just reach the wood... closing his eyes he dropped his body forward into a roll, and felt the acceleration pound his shoulders mercilessly. If only he could reach the brushwood was his last thought, as the darkness finally took him once more.

At the top of the slope, Igluk watched in fascination, yet he did not feel compelled to order the nearest troll to follow and smash the prone body to pieces. He was probably dead or dying anyway, and what could one fool do against his new power? Let him have his five minutes of glory at surviving against such odds, he thought absently, it would mean all the more satisfaction when they found him in the wood later and brought his head to Igluk's tent as a trophy.

Yes...he would look forward to that later, but for now he had more important issues to resolve.

Scipio's husk had been destroyed and his essence would be forced to travel back to the Master to find a new one. In the meantime this left Igluk in charge. Now it was time to finally win this war!

⁂

Tatrius moved like a man possessed. The wood was almost empty, and any orcs they met he easily dispatched due to the element of surprise. Mostly they melted back into the trees, fearing another example of the ferocious warriors they had met earlier that morning, but it was only a matter of time before they came across more serious opposition.

The first he knew of this was when an arrow took his breath away and sent him sprawling. A second hit his shield with a thud, while a third glanced off his helmet. Tatrius' breastplate saved his life, no doubt there, but the arrow had still penetrated at least an inch beyond the punctured metal. How, he had no idea, but he was well acquainted with this kind of injury and his instincts told him to leave the shaft exactly where it protruded from his chest. Snapping it a hands' breadth from the feathers, he was back on his feet within seconds, ignoring the nausea and pain.

Jarvi stopped dead in his tracks, turned and looked to find his companion, but the orcish battle cry was already all about them.

"Go you fool, what are you waiting for!" shouted Tatrius irritably, throwing a stone at the still motionless Jarvi, still moving but too slowly to avoid the impending charge.

"I will not leave you," retorted Jarvi, stubbornly.

Tatrius threw another stone. "You idiot...the information you have is far more important than me...do your duty, legionary. You must live to let Crassus know the truth. Now go!"

Jarvi listened of course, hesitating as his conscience fought for the right decision, but his young heart would not abandon a companion in such a way, no matter what the reason. His eyes quickly spied a deep hollow in the bracken, and as Tatrius bitterly swore at his wilful defiance, he lunged at him and flung them both into the hollow.

They descended fast and landed even harder with a crash, cut from head to toe by brambles. As Jarvi had suspected, the roots were relatively clear of the sharp barbs and when they could breathe again, they righted themselves. Jarvi took one look at the protruding shaft and sighed with relief. No puss was visible, so there was no poison.

Up above them the frantic activity of the orcs searching for them began with the bushes and undergrowth being set alight and pierced through with spears of vengeance. In the hollow, both men slowly slid further and further along the gully, until they could see open ground ahead. They watched for a little while, contemplating what they must do next, but the open ground looked as though it would take a miracle to cover without being seen. A fully fit man would take at least an hour to cross that distance, but Tatrius was wounded and bleeding, even though he was also stronger than most.

Now there was no choice and Jarvi would have to leave, but this time he grasped the extended forearm with equality. He could look Tatrius in the eye and know he had given him a chance to survive, however small. He was leaving his companion with hope.

"I will draw them away from you, so stay here at first. Here, you may as well take the last of my food. I will not need it. My only chance is the river and even then it might carry me as far as the bridge. If that happens, then I will have to dodge ten thousand and not just the dozen or so who are pursuing us here," Jarvi summed up, with a grin.

"Head north west then, Jarvi," gasped Tatrius, realising that his lung had been punctured. "I think Centurion Galienus will have began crossing the river by now, or at least created the boat bridge to the west. You may run into his outposts."

"That is Julius, is it not?"

"Yes. If I remember Valenus correctly, we are using both flanks as diversions, but we were not told where the main blow would fall, in case any of us were captured."

"Then northwest it is. I will keep the food warm for your return, Tatrius."

"Bugger off now, before I decide to come with you and make you carry me all the way. Go now, Jarvi, before it is too late!"

Jarvi smiled in gratitude and after one more glance at the wound was up and away. Tatrius watched for a moment and wondered if the enemy had any cavalry. He could not recall seeing any, but if they did Jarvi would not reach the top of the hill. He coughed into his hand and watched the blood flow over his fingers ominously. Either way any part he had to play in this great adventure was probably over, he thought, looking mournfully at his poor food.

"Ah well, I may as well have a final meal," he said softly, and promptly finished the food in a few mouthfuls.

He would never make centurion now, but he would surely make them pay dearly for his life, he fumed, as he rose to his feet and bit back the searing pain that forced a small groan to escape his lips. Almost immediately, as in reply to the groan, he heard a faint sniffing sound off to his right and, without hesitation, swiftly plunged his gladius into the bush to feel the satisfactory squelch of the edge entering flesh. A strangled yelp ended another orc's life, and he counted that as the one hundred and fiftieth since the beginning of this strange fate that had befallen them all.

Stepping to one side, he slashed at another bush and felt rather than saw the orc's head, severed from his shoulders, drop to the ground. This time there was no outcry.

It was going to be a glorious ending. Tatrius grimaced in pain and glanced upwards, half-hoping to catch a glimpse of the sun. A glorious end to a glorious day!

※

Igluk looked out beyond the mound and saw before him the mass of the army of Haderia. The sight filled his chest with a powerful pride and his eyes gleamed with anticipation. Could he rebel against the *Master* with this army and destroy all those who opposed the rise of the orc *Empire*? Could he just fall upon these fools at the bridge and push on through to Gallicia? He could retake the Lakes of Kol and re-establish their rutting grounds, and be overlord of the whole *world!*

Maybe, he stared angrily at the dark clouds above. Maybe, but not just yet, as there would be those who would doubt his intentions. Defeat the elves in Gallicia and nobody would dare stand against him and this army. Not the Mage, nor the goblin king, nor the sunorcs or orka, not even the *Master*! All would flock to his banners. All who desired power would kneel at his feet!

He pondered the issues to hand. The enemy plans to attack his right and thus weaken their centre had been confirmed, and even though that foul spy had run away, the Roman betrayal had been true. He would strengthen his central attack this day and sweep them off the ridge on the far side of the river. He would also simultaneously attack across the wooden bridges to the east, where the wolf-riders were waiting to cross and sweep north to the Dwarmanian capital in Kol's rear, to spread panic and fear.

Victory would be his and the Master would praise him and nobody else. The second Mage, Scipio, had failed. The others who always wore the heavy cowl were nowhere to be seen. As before, he was at the right place at the right time. The enemy would fall beneath his army's feet and they would set Dwarmania alight. Then it would be him that stood next to the Master, not that scum in the cowl. Rebellion could wait for later.

Bruti lay in the bushes and held his breath. The idea of having a few of them lie prone as corpses in order to have at least a mild chance of survival was one of Hadrian's better suggestions. Currently he was, however, wishing they had chosen someone else to do it. For several hours now he lay on the ground with the smell of foul orcs all around, choking his breath. This was a new kind of warfare and the new terror that came with it was breaking his nerves.

He knew he had volunteered because at the final end the main group would not be able to try, as the orcs would shred their corpses to confirm their death, but then they had all known at dawn that few would be returning.

As he lay he wondered if that was why they had all agreed in the first place. He knew that personally he found no particular difficulty in accepting that the Gods had taken it upon themselves to move him from one existence to another. He had had little to lose in the other life, but he did pine for the warmth of a good maiden. There had been a small faction of maidens with the cohort to clean clothes and cook, but in recent months Atronius had set them to one side to avoid any loss of discipline. Even now, in this predicament, he contemplated how he could get a little closer.

Never mind, he sighed, opened one eye, spied an orc nearby, swung his gladius to hack both legs asunder, rolled over to thrust the blade into the throat quickly to stop any scream, and pulled himself up onto his haunches. In less than a second he was up and running. Off to his left ran another legionary. Was it Hadrian? No, he was with the others making a last stand, a diversion for Valenus. It was Sullai.

Bruti watched as six orcs quickly closed off Sullai's escape route and set upon him with relish. He thought momentarily of going to help, but knew that if he did he would only add his death to Sullai's. He fought well and three orcs were easily dispatched, but in the end a scimitar cut off his right arm, and Bruti swore he would remember the name of Sullai Viscanis.

Just before he reached the far side of the wood he was forced to ambush two more orcs. On looking around he spied the body of Tatrius lying prone and unmoving. He wondered if Jarvi had managed to reach the river. All about the body lay more than ten orc corpses. He had given his life for a belief that in truth had no real bearing on any of them. What would they gain from the victory the elves and dwarves sought? Land, food, freedom to live and to build as well! Was this enough?

Bruti began to run into the open ground and noted with satisfaction that there were flags flying on the high ground to the west. The Alliance had indeed crossed the river that morning, but not in strength.

He wondered if any of the others would reach the river. Where was Jarvi at this very moment? Would any of the others ever be made aware of his success in reaching their lines, and had Valenus succeeded in his own task?

There was of course no way for him to know one way or another. So for now he ignored this and concentrated on reaching the crest of the hill and safety. There he would begin to write the story of the final stand of Valenus' volunteers. It would be a long and glorious one!

PART THIRTEEN

REUNIONS

The hatred permeated the air like a living essence, devouring all that could be consumed, good or evil; it had no real preference. Morality was for the weak and unsure. It had no such vices, it considered the world its due inheritance. Indeed it felt that it had been robbed—no, duped would be better—of its rightful place in the universe.

Atronius stirred. His arms and legs ached incessantly, but the sleep he desired had been tormented by dreams of torture and destruction, and of the enemy's final victory. He felt just as tired as before the rest. The plan had been a desperate one, but both he and Aarun had thought that, if he took the role, which has now led to his abduction, it might enable them to gain a little time. If he had known this deception involved this abduction, he most definitely would have had second thoughts.

Atronius knew that he was suspended in the air, an instinct more than anything told him so, but he could not see any bonds. It struck him as rather interesting that he was now held in the same position as one being crucified. Yet he could see neither cross nor nails, although he felt the pain intensely. It also made him think about where such knowledge of crucifixion might have been learnt.

Pain. Yes, this pain, never ending, had initially been almost unbearable as the mental torture progressed. Several goblins had taken it in turns to batter his head physically, while the Mage had continued to batter the inside of his head relentlessly with endless questions. Eventually though, for Atronius, the constant pain had become almost old pain, as his muscles and bones could not truly register any more, the nerve ends having been nullified.

Most of the time there was little point to the question or answer and so he gave them the truth willingly, yet even then it was never believed, nor were his lies. However, twenty years of serving in the legion had prepared the body for such an ordeal and the pain had slowly become easier. There was after all only so much they could do before he passed out or died. Yes, there was only so much, but deep inside he knew he was close to his breaking point, but would the Mage be able to find this out?

I will not cry out again, though, he admonished himself, as the Mage re-entered the circle of light. He could discern no walls, chairs, tables or even the floor, for all he could see was the bright circle of light that surrounded him. He clenched his fists, knowing that the first action would try to wrench his mind apart. He prepared. Felt the first probing thoughts. Then he screamed. He screamed until his lungs burned, until his jaw ached with the effort, but still the pain increased.

It seemed like an eternity, although barely a few seconds had passed, then he slumped down to hang by his wrists. This was a different kind of pain, he noted. This had not been to obtain information. This had been for the Mage's pleasure alone.

So he was frustrating this foul creature. He was still serving a purpose. A ray of hope returned and he looked up at the Mage. He tried to smile but he was clearly beyond this tiny act of defiance, although his eyes said enough to make the Mage once more raise his hands.

Atronius held on for a few seconds. I will not cry out, his mind yelled, insistent that his pride held strong. Then he screamed and screamed and screamed, all the harder for his resistance.

As always it ended rather abruptly and he was somewhat surprised to find his lungs still functioning properly. Why did they delay killing him, he wondered? What was so important that it made them go only so far, then fear his death? There must be a very simple answer to this riddle and yet his mind could not work correctly, or else refused to do so, and this line of reasoning had eluded him for the moment. He took comfort that the pain had ended, knowing it would start again soon.

With a sigh he tried to fathom just how much his body had been beaten, his mind distorted. Could he even function properly any more? By the Gods, how he longed to feel the grip of the gladius again and to die a true Roman, but he knew this was not in the plan, as his mind again considered the puzzle of why he was still alive.

The respite lasted a few minutes then the mind games began. At first they were rather childish, but in time their complexity began to strain his nerves. Always the fear of a double-edged sword, always the fear that the answer might be of more significance than his tired mind could comprehend. He was fighting to understand every structured sentence and to make sure that his pain did not guide his answers.

First there came the reports that the Alliance had been destroyed and that Dwarmania had surrendered. If true, then he ought to disclose his secrets, as such a continued sacrifice was no longer required. If untrue, at which Atronius laughed, why was the Mage still here, trying to obtain such secrets as remained to be told? That was the small defiance that had earned him the current escapade, with both arms now feeling as though they would break free of their sockets. No matter what the pain, he had to continue to defy this Mage. If only for a day, for he knew this would aide Aarun in whatever task he had undertaken for the common good.

A long time ago, Atronius had once seen such a thing done during a skirmish, where a brute of a Boii warrior had literally torn a man's arms out of their sockets. It had been garish to watch, and it had taken ten men five minutes to send the barbarian to his maker, with two more men injured in the process. No, stupid mind games were of no use against him and the Mage knew this, so why try? He already considered his life over, but to delay meant gaining time and if that was the only service he could now offer his friends, then that was precisely what he would try to give them, *time*!

"Time is a funny concept, Atronius Sulla, is it not?"

The voice as usual came from the darkness and did not seem to travel to his ears, but rather appeared within his head. He squinted to try and see his persecutor, but the light was too dim and his eyes had already begun to hurt just from this tiny effort. The Mage had seemingly retired back into the darkness. Perhaps he needed to recuperate after using the power? Perhaps this was a weakness he could use?

"I can take away that pain, if you wish," the voice began again. "If you cooperate."

"I have answered your questions, Mage," he replied, breathing deeply after almost every word, which was rasping and painful to the throat. "I do not know what else you require."

"Well, now, what do I require indeed, Roman? I could take your soul, but the secrets I require may be so deeply embedded that even you do not know they exist. You see, one of you must be the Oracle of Zeus. The gateway that enabled him to free you from the void, the void that my Master cast you all into in the early stages of this war."

"Zeus is not my God. Certainly not Roman either, as only the people in this world accept him as a predominant God. Only the dwarves and elves accept his existence. My people do not."

"Oh, come now. Are we really going to have a conversation about the Gods? Are you truly so stupid as to not know anything of the real truth?" The Mage now stepped into the light again. He had underestimated this man and his Master was becoming impatient. "What do you know of your Gods?"

"I followed the faiths that existed. I know of their names and purpose. That is all I have ever needed. I am a legionary. Not a priest!"

"Pah, you are a fool to not have recognised the real truth. Why have you been brought to this world, Atronius? Why would Gods of any description bring you here? You, the elves, the dwarves and all of us! Why is it so important that you are here?"

Atronius forced his puffy eyes to open, while his mind raced. He had tried desperately to understand that very issue and had sought answers from Aarun, their acknowledged expert. So far he had been given only small pieces of information, but had Aarun lied to him? Was the truth too damning for their Gods, as well as for this Mage's?

"I see you have no knowledge other than that which I offered you on your arrival," began the Mage, his voice now silky with satisfaction at insinuating the first doubts into Atronius' mind. Now to work a little more!

"Jupiter, he was the master of the Gods and the main deity of you Romans, was he not?"

"Yes."

"Jupiter is your supreme God, sometimes referred to as the shining father, as many of you mortalkind often referred to this useless waste of power. So touching, emotional, *pathetic*! He is supposedly the God of your light and blue sky, protector of the senatorial state and its defunct laws. You worshipped him especially as Jupiter Optimus Maximus...*all good and all powerful*. This refers not only to his domination over the universe, but also to his purpose of controlling the realm of the Gods and making his will, and no other, known through his *oracles*! A God to be feared and honoured with war, no less! A God who has left you in the greatest peril, Oracle, and yet you still remain loyal. Why?"

Atronius fought desperately to keep his mind focused. What was the point of this conversation? It wasted time, so perhaps he should indulge this Mage's ego, but why bother with this information? He was not a priest!

"Mars was the God of war, not Jupiter!" offered Atronius. Let's just keep him talking and waste more time.

"Ah, yes, thank you for the correction. It all seems so difficult. Mars is indeed the *Roman* God of war, and therefore one of the most important and widely worshipped deities. According to your pathetic histories, he is also the father of *Romulus* and *Remus* by the virgin Ilia. You will forgive me if I laugh at this point…virgin indeed? Do you still see your destiny as a son of Mars…even now? You do not look like one to me."

"What is your point?"

"My point? That is as clear as the light in this circle, Atronius Sulla. What are the attributes of Zeus? Who is Hades, or Vulcan or Poseidon? Do you not see what is so obvious?"

"I do not understand…"

"Think! Atronius, just think! I can erase your pain, if you will *just* see the truth!"

Atronius closed his eyes. *See the truth*, what was this Mage aiming for now? What is the point of discussing Greek Gods or Roman Gods? He just could not…what is the connection…could they all be the same one…then it was all so simple.

The connection was so flimsy that even a fool such as he could see it! Why had Aarun not mentioned this before? Even Marcellus would have known about this, and the obvious assumption that they might all be the same Gods was unavoidable, but how could this be? They existed in two different worlds, different civilisations. Two different dimensions! Mars had set the beginnings of the Republic in motion!

"If they are the same Gods," Atronius began, his mind still reeling, "you will have to offer a little more proof than a list of names!"

The Mage laughed silently. The only indication of his amusement was the slight rustling of his cowl.

"More proof, the Centurion has asked for. More proof. Juno, she was the wife of Jupiter, the Goddess of all maidens and fertility. Her symbols were a pomegranate and a peacock, probably Zeus' Venus, now she was the Goddess of love and beauty and used her skills to seduce all those she chose to use. While Minerva was meant to be the Goddess of wisdom, learning, art crafts and industry. Her symbol was the owl, but to my eyes only the owl benefited.

"Neptune, now here was the all-powerful God of the sea, Poseidon being his true name, but he rarely took it upon his honour to explain this to the deeper creatures of the ocean that none have seen for centuries. There you will find a new deception, an evil far greater than the one being experienced in this world. His symbol was the trident: you Romans used his ideas in your gladiator games, while he used it to execute those who opposed his power.

"Ceres, mind you, was the Goddess of the harvest, always depicted carrying a bundle of grain, pathetic really, when poison would have served her much better in her quest to see Zeus fall! All had both Greek and Roman names, yet no connection has ever been made. Is this arrogance or stupidity, Atronius? Is this enough proof of your Gods' duplicity? No, then perhaps we should look again at the name of Vulcan, the blacksmith to the Gods! He is also a God of the Underworld, but we should really use his correct and preferred names of Hades or, as you Romans prefer, *Pluto*! I mean, in your dimension Hades is now revered and linked to all death, not just yours, and yet you stand here and ask for proof! There are now those who believe he is the God of good fortune and luck!

"If my Master stoked his furnace too hard volcanoes would erupt. He was the God of all the blacksmiths and manipulator of all the volcanoes! Creator of life in unknown designs, all here to stand, all here to fall. Your people have no true Gods. When Zeus saw his pet civilisation falter, after that fool Alexander took to bedding boys, he had him poisoned and set in motion his next task: to manipulate the Romans! To dominate his pet world!"

"This is all fabrication!"

"Fabrication! Can you not use your own mind? You are a pawn in a family squabble that has lasted aeons!"

"The future of man in this world, or any other, is not determined by any Gods. They guide…"

"Guide! *Guide!*" screamed the Mage. "If it had not been for Zeus' infidelity in the first place there would have been no Roma. It began with the seduction of Diana, the hunter and keeper of the silent moons of the universe, by the despicable manifestation called Bacchus, a name used by Zeus when he felt like seducing a maiden, God-kind, mortalkind. He was interested in anything that moved outside the existence of his sisters and brothers! In this guise he was the God of wine and partying. Naturally, he was one of Roma's most popular Gods, at first. You all took him to your hearts completely, if I recall correctly, but not everyone in the family was amused by the spreading of the seeds of the Gods to lesser creatures!

"Mercury, forever the messenger of the Gods, with his wings on his helmet and sandals, grew more and more despondent. He began to travel wherever a God might choose to send him, even through the void, temporarily. Many referred to him as the God of travellers or tradesmen, there never having been a surer way of influencing the hearts of men than by gold. But when he discovered Jupiter's profanity at siring his bastard children with mortalkind, he informed Hades and a great roar filled the universe. My Master had always and forever been told never to interfere with creation, although the power rested with only a few of the Gods. Now the great lawmaker himself had broken his own rules. For his loyalty to my Master, Zeus took Mercury's wings away and then cast him out of the higher dominions, and in time the voids were strengthened to stop them both returning."

"And?"

"We intend to return and cast down those who stood in judgement of us. It was not we who created a universe so diverse as to be completely uncontrollable. It was not we who created the void!"

"So why not take what you want from me and leave me be!"

Atronius expected a sudden explosion of pain, but when it did not appear he opened his eyes again and looked directly at the Mage. No reply came. The Mage had finished his tirade and, interesting as this information was, Atronius now saw no real depth to its reasoning. He could not alter what had happened aeons ago and at this moment his only thought rested with Aarun. This strategy helped Atronius, not the Mage, so why continue?

Atronius waited. Still no reply came, just a continuing wave of conceit and hatred, a feeling that there was more to this line of questioning than was obvious to the naked eye. Why was he still alive?

"That's it, isn't it?" said Atronius, seeing perhaps another ray of hope. "You need me to give you the secrets willingly? A safety valve for Zeus, or bloody Jupiter, whichever name befits him. A God to be reckoned with and one the dwarven faith has ratified, as he obviously seems to have the intelligence to outwit you. I see he is as strong as the dwarves tell me..."

"*Silence!*" screamed the Mage.

"A little touchy, are we?" Atronius continued, raising his head. "I'm not surprised, really, your *Mmmmaaaaster* must be furious with you. I've been here almost seven days, I think, and all your tricks have done nothing, other than batter my body and damage my soul; but you cannot kill me for fear of the secrets dying with me. A little sad, don't you think? How do you expect to prevail when you cannot even break me, a mere mortalkind?"

The Mage listened in silence, but something in the air bade farewell to any further attempts to fool Atronius. His Master was indeed furious but, willingly or otherwise, this broken mortalkind would reveal the secrets given to him by Zeus, or face an eternity of hell for his puny resistance. There were far worse existences in this universe than life or death. They were just two examples.

Furious or not, his Master would demand some kind of progress, so with a renewed bitterness the Mage closed in to look the Roman directly in the face. If he had any ability to feel he would have felt Atronius' breath on his face, but there was nothing for the air to touch.

From within the cowl two deep holes seemed to exist. Red they seemed at first, but as the Mage grew closer he knew them to be a multitude of colours, as though they were on fire. Bright oranges and yellows danced amongst the majority of reds, but always in the background there skulked the deeper black of the underworld.

"You seem to enjoy pushing your luck to the limit, Atronius. This is something we have all come to expect," said the Mage, eventually. "There is of course so much more for you to know. You see the *Republic*," — the word fairly spat out of the Mage's mouth — "was founded *by* Jupiter. Do you know of the historical theories of this birth?"

Atronius shook his head meekly.

"It all began with the creation *by* Jupiter of the Etruscan City State and the revolt against their King Tarquin. It was before your time of course, but for five centuries Roma witnessed a revolt against the rule of these Etruscans. The popular story, handed down from father to son and passed through the ages, was that Sextus, the son of King Tarquinius Superbus, raped the wife of a nobleman, Tarquinius Collatinus. The people's rage was unquenchable. Etruscan rule was already deeply unpopular and this rape was too great an offence to be tolerated by the Roman nobles..."

"What has this to do with your task, Mage? You dither and waste time, for you know what your punishment will be if you fail again!"

"You will see, Atronius, you will see how this is relevant. You see the void was not quite as strong then as it is now. It had been allowed to decay and my Master fuelled Roma's hatred and sent the soul of Mercury through the void, to supplant that of Iunius Brutus. The Romans rose in revolt against the Etruscans and Sextus fled, but Mercury soon found him and had him executed. Would you like to know why?"

"You are telling this history, not me, Mage!"

"Of course, so you would like to know why. You see Sextus was *Jupiter* in disguise, off on one of his numerous seductions. So you see, your little Republic was founded on a lie created by Jupiter and he has been doing the same in this dimension, as he has done for aeons long forgotten!"

Atronius closed his eyes. If he remembered his history correctly the Etruscan King with his two brothers escaped to Caere. Then, aided by the city, they returned and fought a battle against his rebellious subjects, but failed to win back his city. So he called upon the help of his fellow Etruscan king Lars Porsenna, who promptly besieged Roma.

However, when Porsenna finally captured Roma he did not restore Tarquinius to the throne, and to Atronius' mind this indicated that he planned on ruling the city in person. If that was true, and if Mercury was there as Iunius Brutus, then Porsenna could easily also have been Jupiter. Did this mean that we have all been manipulated, right from the beginning? But Roma, though occupied, must have remained defiant? The cities in Latium revolted against Etruscan domination and clearly this again defeated Zeus' designs, but what kind of game used lives as such unimportant pieces?

"It did not end there, mighty Atronius. The struggle continued with the void being slowly strengthened. More significantly however, your history has been nothing but the influence of my master foiling your Gods' petty interference in the lives of the Romans."

"You have no proof," Atronius began, his voice barely a whisper. "We Romans carved our name across the lands and there is much that we would...*did* achieve."

"No, Atronius. You achieved what the Gods desired and nothing more. Your existence was a mistake and a profanity to the Gods themselves. So my Master set about Roma with a vengeance, to bring the Romans to their knees once and for all. War with Etruria, the Volscians and Aequians helped Roma rid itself of its Etruscan enemies, but enemies still loomed all around, and the Etruscans remained a potent force in the Sabellian and Oscan hills. Roma was therefore always at war, attacked by or attacking her Etruscan neighbours the Veii, or the Volscians or the Aequians, or an occasional Latin city, murdering all. Each death delighted my Master every day, as the mortalkind numbers began to fall rapidly. He sent Mercury once more with the plague to aid their final destruction, and to end Zeus' continual interference. Roma would be my Master's tool to destroy the very civilisation that your God created, and you are part of that success..."

"No. None of us would have had this knowledge!"

"Do you think the millions who died have any interest in your guilt? Roma next fought and exterminated the Hernicans, a tribe wedged between the Aequians and the Volscians, after the Aequians initially, then the Volscians soon after, agreed an alliance with Roma. It was a typical example of the ingenious Roman tactics of dividing and conquering, so easy and yet so difficult to prevent when near completion. That particular escapade kept my Master enthralled for many years!"

Atronius was now so very tired and confused. He knew that there was magic in the Mage's voice, but inch by inch Atronius began to feel his mind unveil itself. The more he heard this new truth, the more he began to doubt the word of Aarun. This doubt then created a lack of faith, why had Aarun kept this from him?

"Stop. That is enough! Our history was fraught with dangers. We had to fight to defend ourselves. The Etruscans were not good people at all!"

"Really, that is a rather odd assumption, seeing that you now employ them extensively in your Republic. You see, even Romans could now see an opportunity and, for the first time, my Master began to see the extent of the mortalkind weakness for power and riches. I recall one very notable incident in the Aequian wars, when a Roman army was sent to attack an enemy garrison on Mount Algidus.

"It was a trap, of course, and they needed urgent help if any were to survive. A relief force was quickly put together for Lucius Quinctius Cincinnatus to command, and he was offered the powers of dictatorship. Cincinnatus ran to take up the shield, having been called from his fields to fill this power vacuum, then led his forces against the Aesquians and managed to free the trapped army. He then returned, relinquished his power and returned home to tend his farm.

"At that very point, every soul of the Roman Republic was handed to my Master and a door was created through the void. To freely give up so much power, when no one in their right mind would have done so, leaving it in the hands of Mercury, no less. He made sure that by the end of that century Roma had become the mistress of Latium. Your fate was sealed, so why not give me the secrets I require, and I can then release you from this pain? Is it really worth the friendship of that pathetic elf Aarun to continue this suffering!"

"I am not sure...what to think!"

The Mage slowly turned away and, imperceptibly, waved a hand and loosened the bonds that held Atronius up high. The pain eased slightly. Without turning the Mage continued his tirade.

"Of course it did not end even there. Jupiter was stung with jealousy and began to send enemy after enemy against my Master. The Gallic tribes were the first, but we also turned this to our advantage. You see, we managed to infiltrate their camps with spies and sent them first through Etruria, then had the entire Senate meet for the last time, as Jupiter sent Brennus to massacre them all! The attack sacked our power base, but from the ashes rose an even greater Roma and one that quickly conquered the devastated Etruria." The Mage turned back to face Atronius.

"I must remember to thank Jupiter for his help in bringing the greater power to our *feet*."

Atronius reeled under a coughing fit and then spat blood onto the floor. Could all this be true?

"If such power was at your feet, why did your Master not appear in person to end all further resistance?"

"That is obvious!"

"The *void*."

"Of course, the void, you fool! Neither God could appear in person, but they could use a suitable soul when one became available."

"Is that what you were once? A suitable soul!"

"Perhaps, but we are again drifting off the very topic we are here to resolve. What do you think came next, Atronius? Did you ever make use of that *Teacher* Marcellus Sabinus?"

"I spoke many times with him, as did many others. If you are now going to tell me that the Samnites and the Spartans were Jupiter's pawns, you will have to forgive my *laughter*!"

"The first war was very brief," offered the Mage, solemnly.

"Yes. Barely two years, if my memory serves me right."

"It does. It does indeed. The Samnites were not the pawns of Jupiter. That was the pleasure of the Latin league of cities, which betrayed Roma and forced us to betray the Campanians. But the Spartans, now they were a different breed altogether. Their society was even more perverse than your own and their understanding of sexual deviancy set even my Master's teeth on edge, if you will forgive the pun?

"In the second war of course, we had more influence. This was set to rights, as the Bruttia also now stood against us. The weakened Greeks then screamed for help from Sparta, and how we laughed at such a choice by Jupiter. Nevertheless they sent King Archidamus, but his army failed too! When Alexander the *so-called* Great was starting on that pathetic attempt to conquer the world with Jupiter's banners, after he had had the temerity to refuse my Master's offering of power and riches, Jupiter sent his uncle Alexander *Mossian* from Epirus to further forestall our task. His success was initially rapid, but after a night of passion with two maidens his efforts were cut short by the dagger of an assassin..."

"Mercury no less."

"Now you seem to be getting the right idea."

"I think you are getting ahead of yourself, Mage. I recall that the second war was a defeat at Caudine Faroks."

"You are mistaken."

"I think not. Marcellus did a better job than you think." Another ray of hope. "What did Jupiter try next?"

"He tried King Phyrrus and the Carthaginians. You recall Hannibal, no doubt?"

"Of course!"

"Did you not think it odd that for fifteen years he eluded your armies, even when you sent eighty thousand against his thirty thousand at Cannae? Surely it was odd that the skills of a barbarian were able to massacre eighty thousand!"

"Is that all? Have you nothing else to advise? Nothing else to coax me into supporting your claims that your *Master* is what made Roma great?"

"Only one. In your history do you recall the great slave rebellion of Sicilia?"

"Yes, I recall Fulvius Flacchus was called to deal with a terrifying rebellion of the slave population in Sicilia. The revolt was accompanied by savage atrocities by the slaves against their masters. Its suppression was marked by wholesale atrocities on the part of Flacchus. At one place he crucified twenty thousand slaves. What of it?"

"Slave rebellions are much closer to home than you think, Atronius, but my point is that they also represented Jupiter, and your people are doing the same now."

"Your point is well made. But my will, albeit tested, for which I thank you for all your efforts, cannot bend to your demands. I will not release what you desire."

The Mage's eyes flared with uncontrollable anger.

"I grow weary of this ordeal. I have given you the proof of your folly and, no, I cannot permit your death, no matter how much it might be *desired*. However, perhaps I am no longer interested in your mind and will seek my goal another way?"

A feeling of dread filled Atronius' heart, as several people were slowly forced into the circle to stand beside their tormentor.

"What is this?" he asked, struggling defiantly against the power that held him suspended. "They are not even in uniform. What do they have to do with this? Let them go! This..."

The sentence trailed away into obscurity as the screams filled the room, wrenching all ears and causing them all to wince, all except the Mage, who smiled.

One of the prisoners dropped to the floor, with an enormous hole where his chest had been. The exit point of his heart could be clearly seen, while the Mage now held the heart firmly in his left hand.

"Such fragility," he mocked. "Now, how should we proceed? Ah, yes, I have not done this to someone for quite some time. Now let me see, how did that incantation begin..."

"Stop!"

"Yes, that is just how it begins, but whom shall we practice on? Mmmmmmm... *You!*"

Slowly the writhing body began to levitate...

"This is madness!" shouted Atronius, in vain.

The arms and legs became extended...

"You must stop this!"

This time there was no scream. Only a kind of soft grunt, a sound of total surprise rather than pain as, one by one, each leg and arm was dislocated and separated from the torso. Then the pain and realisation sank in, but the screams rapidly became a sob as the Mage allowed the torso to drop with a sickening crunch that ended all sound.

"Are we now more willing to cooperate, or shall we move onto the next one?"

"If you think that this will make me give you the secrets, you are mistaken," Atronius responded with tears of frustration glistening in his eyes. "I will never give in. I am used to death, as are all legionaries, but we are averse to the useless waste of life. However, if you wish to kill your new subjects, then go ahead. I think you will find that, when the dwarves return, you will need to beg hard and long for their forgiveness. Even then it will serve only to achieve your swift death."

"Oh, please," mocked the Mage, pointing towards the remaining prisoners. "These heathens are of no importance to me. What I want is back in the world that we left behind..."

"We?"

"Yes, *we*, you fool! Do you think that all the Romans went to serve that oaf Zeus? What I want is the total domination of all Romans, under *my* domain. It has already been promised, and all you are achieving here is a minor delay."

"You may do with me as you wish, Mage, but I will not fold. Not now that your folly has turned into blind hatred. You know this better than me. Try again. Look deeply into my mind, what do you see? No, really, what do you truly see? Yes, that is right, friend, oh greatest power that has ever lived, my *master*. I am incapable of surrender. Surely your powers, immense and terrible, can confirm this fact for you? If I was the sort to give up because of some level of discomfort, I would have joined Scipio's band of useless parasites, but instead I continued to fight against all the odds. Against everyone and everything, as though pain were my middle name, Mage, and I have all the time in the world. How much time do you have?"

The Mage nodded, taking Atronius by surprise with such benevolence, but then slowly raised his eyes to look directly into his.

"Do you not recognise me, Primus?" he said softly, stepping closer and closer, the hatred now literally crawling down Atronius' spine. This time the cowl was not steeped in shadows, but illuminated.

"Yes...Yes...I know who you are. Cappa referred to you as *Black* Cassius because you believed in the dark magic, the powers of the underworld. You are Cassius Evictus, which hardly changes matters now, does it? I am still here crucified and you are still incompetent, a fool in a fool's cloak! A seething piece of *scum* that the Gods decided to spit out...!" The final word hung in the air as the breath caught in Atronius' throat, and the pain seared through his windpipe. Hot fire descended, burning the soft tissue and scorching his tongue, bringing forth his breath in short, painful gasps.

"I may not be able to bring your existence to an end," the Mage swore, through clenched teeth. "But I sure as hell can make every breath so painful that you will *beg* me to end the pain."

"Pain is pointless," Atronius gasped, still defiant, even as the pain truly reached his breaking point. The air had become so hot that even the thought of breathing caused severe pain. Everything burned and the searing crispness of the throat brought forward tears of shame. Shame that he had finally reached the point of no return. It was becoming too much.

The Mage moved closer, sensing the change, rather than seeing it, as the mortalkind's face remained screwed up in agony, making his expression unreadable. Yes, now to increase the pain further. Yes, more, much more! His eyes narrowed in anticipation. This was it, this was the final glory. The doorway to the void and the entrance into a world that knew nothing of true power, or rather had allowed the truth to fall away into myths. Not any more! He would return triumphant and ally himself with the most perverse power available. Then, with its help, he would destroy and kill as many people as possible, before showing the full extent of the magic, thus making the final conquest so much the easier.

"*Stop!*" screamed a voice, seemingly from behind the Mage, who immediately spun around to seek its origin in the very darkness that had earlier allowed his own obscurity. "*Stop!*"

"Who speaks?" demanded the Mage, while in his mind the fire incantation began to take life in his left hand.

"Someone who dares to stand before you and your Master in defiance," came the reply. "Someone who brings your doom."

"Doom," laughed the Mage. "Doom? I am the bringer of doom, not you! Show yourself, so that I may laugh a little louder. Ah, an elf, I should have guessed. So why should I quake with fear, my young elf? I am the Mage of the Pit of Doom, Deathslayer to the orcs and goblins. I am death itself, for death fears *me*! Whom do I address?"

"I am Aarun, Lord of Gallicia, my friend, and it is I whom you seek and not Atronius."

"What?"

"You heard."

"Then you are..."

"By the Gods...are all you Mages so slow to keep pace. I think this will indeed be much easier than anticipated."

"You are the *Oracle*? But if you...then who is this?" screamed the Mage, furious once more, but equally dumbstruck by the magnitude of the error, and by the nerve of this fool in defying the Master.

"That, my friend, is a fine fellow who agreed to become the decoy for your fascinations. We knew you had several spies in the camp and so we let them hear precisely what you wanted to hear, although I was definitely surprised by the kidnapping. It is safe to say that surprised everyone."

The Mage's mouth opened and shut several times and the fire incantation was quite forgotten. Then, finding his voice...

"You have made a grave error, Oracle. This is now my domain and you have crossed over the threshold. Your powers will be non-existent here."

"Oh I think I will be able to match a fool such as you," Aarun responded, deliberately moving in a wide circle, hoping to free the

Roman with a swift teleportation incantation. It would leave him exposed for a few seconds, but Atronius looked in a bad way and the blood rolling down the chest from his mouth was not a good sign.

"You circle like a maiden, elf," mocked the Mage, remembering once more the fire incantation. "If this fool allowed such torture, then he is worthless, even less as regards my purposes."

"His life is more precious than my own," Aarun said, finishing the incantation. Then with a snap of his fingers the Roman slowly dissolved and then vanished, with a small *pop*. "He has not gone far and I will rejoin him later. For now I believe we have some unfinished business."

"That we do, elf, and I am looking forward to my *Master* finally putting your God to rest for his continual interference."

"We shall see, we shall see."

"Something is wrong," Cappa whispered, clenching his gladius all the more tighter. "This does not feel right."

"Explain," said Helin. "How exactly?"

"I don't know, I kind of just feel that something is not right."

Constantine stirred to one side and scratched his head irritably. "Come on, Cappa, we will need more than just a feeling. The scouts are up ahead and we need to move now, or not at all, if we are to find that elven lord."

They were crouched at the base of a hill that had, for the entire journey, been completely covered in darkness by the vastness of Sight Fortress. The storm had eventually won the contest and smashed their warship against the rocks on the coast.

Even the moon could not compete with the shadows that engulfed them, giving a sense of protection. All around the survivors the shrubbery had remained unoccupied, and yet they had all moved with so much stealth that a distance of just one league had taken them well over three hours. Then suddenly Cappa had stopped, frozen in his tracks.

"This has all been too easy," he said, searching for the right words. "Our intelligence reported that well over ten thousand goblins had remained to occupy the fortress and rebuild its walls. If that is true, where are they?"

Helin looked bewildered, but refrained from allowing her impatience to get the better of a judgement that had so far kept her alive.

"You think we are walking into a trap?"

"No, not exactly."

"Then what?" snapped Constantine, a little fraught to say the least, as the small force still with them consisted of only a few legionaries, but they were *his* legionaries. As Cappa had anticipated, the youth was indeed blossoming into a very solid and reliable commander. Quick to support, he had also reprimanded a much older man for not properly cleaning his blade, risking rust. They had few supplies, but what there was had to be cared for correctly.

The older man had taken the reprimand in good grace and a growing confidence emanated from Constantine, and it was beginning to be infectious.

"We've come this far, surely we cannot be considering pulling back?" the youth asked, in earnest. "Perhaps a small band such as ours has slipped through the patrols? Either way, after the shipwreck, where else could the elves have gone?"

"Perhaps. Then again, perhaps not. Where are the scouts?"

"Ahead. Far ahead by now, possibly even at the base of the road that leads to the central palisade."

"Are we certain that Aarun entered this way?" Cappa asked again, turning to look at the elves off to his right, although he managed only to recognise a shadow nearby, which feverishly moved its head in approval. "But the scouts have not returned?"

"No."

"I do not like this. How could this place be so large, and yet I can see no fires, no torches and, even more to the point, *no* guards. Why not?"

To one and all the question was unanswerable, for the simple fact was that the dwarves had stated that, if there was any light within the fortress, then little, if any, of it would show outside. All the guardrooms were cleverly concealed within certain folds in the rock wall as it ascended towards the central gates, which stood well over two thousand paces above them.

Once there they would then need to enter the main tunnel leading to the inner gate, which was again protected by ravelins and high walls. The tunnel had apparently been collapsed on the enemy during the three-day battle to hold the gate, killing hundreds, and the only way in was to climb over the debris, unless the goblins had become tidy in their absence. Those few dwarves who had consented to follow Cappa, Kollis having vanished with most of the dwarven warriors who had survived the storm, knew this was the wrong place to enter the fortress, if stealth was the object of your approach.

So why had Aarun marched straight up this road and through the gate with no challenge?

Where were the guards? Why had they not been challenged so far? Was the dark power in use and, if so, from where, and could any of them counteract its effects? For the millionth time Cappa found his judgement muddled, as he fought to understand how the powers affected all their lives now. He knew that he had difficulty with theories on the dimensions but, as Aarun had already stated, this was an issue best left to the Gods, and to those with the knowledge to make heads or tails of the complex subject. He knew that any commander who showed hesitation might irreparably damage any loyalty his people felt and possibly even induce a rebellion, but on this one issue he was completely at a loss. Now he felt torn, as he recalled the earlier disagreements at the beach.

After many discussions, it had been established that both Lord Kollis and Lord Aarun were missing. Helin had immediately assumed the worst and accused the elven Lord of treachery, as she still could not understand how Atronius had been kidnapped in the first place. She cited the elf's sudden disappearance and his aloofness since the landing, which had been so unceremonious, so close to Sight Fortress, as proof. That this was hardly compelling evidence was the obvious rebuttal, but Cappa had been surprised by the strength of her opinions.

In truth nobody agreed with her, as she had known him for only a very short period. Eventually, Cappa could not either, for he simply had too many memories of the northern peninsular to believe that Aarun was a traitor. That made no sense to him, but it did make sense when Constantine had suggested that he no longer had control of his actions. Perhaps he had been taken over by the Mage and this was how the enemy had known of their plan to sail south, thus the storm, which had practically shadowed their fleet for so many days. Five vessels had started out, two had been sunk, one had vanished without trace and the last two had been grounded on the rocks.

It had then been decided to rescue Aarun, but only after five hours of argument. Helin, who still believed the elf was the spy, simply refused to accept that he had had good intentions in disappearing, and she believed that he had rejoined his allies. Cappa had confronted her at this point, to prevent any further objections fuelled by the loss of ten hobbits in the shipwreck. The loss she felt for her people was admirable, but they were not the only ones who had perished. Thankfully her vocal disapproval slowly diminished with the added persuasion of Molisis.

The other elves had been confused by their Lord's actions, but refused to believe in any kind of betrayal and maintained an air of superiority: Lord Aarun was incapable of being a traitor. Their absolute faith set them off on another round of arguments. Eventually Helin had not entirely dissuaded them of the possibility, but a decision to act was finally reached.

Only Constantine's feelings on the issue caused some concern, as his inexperience led to a few choice comments, which did not sit too well with the surviving elves. Numerous outbursts of anger, more from frustration and fear in their new predicament than from concern about Aarun's guilt (or otherwise), had almost set the dwarves and elves at each other's throats. It may have been this final bout of disagreements that led Kollis to decide to leave, taking most of his people with him. Where he had gone was a further mystery, but his greater knowledge of the terrain did give him a slight advantage over the rest of them. Cappa was the first to point out that even the elves did not know exactly which part of the coast they occupied.

In all honesty, whether Aarun was a spy or not was secondary, as they literally had nowhere else to go. To try and march north along the coast, as some of the sailors had decided to do, would have been suicidal, as the coast would be permanently watched by the large fleets employed daily. How their shipwreck had gone unreported was yet another question with no apparent answer.

To go anywhere else was pointless, and so, to give them all hope, Cappa had decided that they would seek answers from the elven Lord in person, face to face. But it was as if the elf had literally vanished. There were no tracks in the mud, and no broken leaves or twigs on any of the trees or bushes to indicate his passing.

Moving to the fortress was, as far as he could ascertain, the right decision, but what had happened to Aarun? More important, why had he decided to go alone, when it had been his decision to make this journey south in the first place? He had said quite emphatically, however, that their destination had been the Haderian coast. So how could the storm have landed them here? They had to get inside the fortress, and maybe Aarun could answer some of the questions burning inside his head!

"There are definitely no other ways to enter the fortress?" asked Cappa.

"No, General," replied a dwarven voice in the dark. "We received extensive reports from a few farmers. They had sailed north in tiny coastal vessels to escape the enemy, who were seeking slaves to repair the fortress damage, as soon as the Haderia army had marched to Holvidar. Thousands were slain as the farmers refused to comply, while the remainder were taken as slaves. The lucky ones were kept to try and rebuild the damage to the fortress, but the goblins soon gave up and began to fight amongst themselves. This was when a lot of the farmers escaped, but not all of them."

"No hidden doors or passageways?" Constantine asked hopefully, grinning in the dark, knowing that it would be exceptional to seek revenge on the goblins using their own tactics. Sneak in, kill them all, sneak back out without a loss, before they even knew they had arrived.

"No. No passageways are known to any of us. Of course, Lord Komar's own regiments were fiercely loyal and could have been told of, or created, new secret entrances, but they would not serve us here. In addition, several farmers have stated that the fighting is still going on within the fortress walls. They are unsure as to how, but the goblins are continually bringing wounded out of the southern tower."

"That would be impossible. Komar perished with his entire command," said Constantine, feeling that familiar fire in his chest, as he recalled the dwarven lord who had attended Kol's camp only once, to deny Kol's right to command the Alliance army.

"That is another issue to add to all the others, Constantine, but the main point is to find a way in that does not seem so obviously a trap," said Cappa. "Is this not the way by which the goblins entered and were massacred?"

"It is," the dwarf confirmed. "The archway was the weakest wall in the fortress and so to increase its defence the archway was constructed, and designed to collapse on an enemy. However, the fool of a Mage tried to use magic and this just dropped the archway too soon. If only they had had more defenders..."

"Explain."

"It was widely believed by the farmers that Komar had not died, and that the goblins had publicly announced that four thousand dwarves had perished in the fortress, so further resistance was futile."

"But there must have been over ten thousand in Komar's command?"

"Nearer fourteen thousand, when you consider those who stood with the warriors, but belonged to no regiment."

"Why would they play down the number of losses?" Helin asked, intrigued.

"To make the victory final," Cappa announced. "There must have been numerous tunnels and caves dug beneath the mountain where Komar retreated, and these goblins must have had to go in to destroy him in detail. The battle may still be raging even now, but they would not have been able to cope with resistance both outside and inside."

"So they may have few or no guards here," added Constantine. "And the major push at the river would have reduced them even more."

"Yes."

"So what are we waiting for? Let's get up there and find the elf and run as fast as possible back to the river!" Constantine suggested.

"You are forgetting one thing, youngster," said Cappa, frowning. "It has been weeks since we retired north. How do we know that Komar still fights on and that this is not a trap?"

"Life is full of risks. If the elf went in, then surely so can we, but sitting here will not answer our questions. If we stay, it is a certainty we will be discovered sooner or later."

Cappa nodded again, knotted his eyebrows in the heaviest frown of the day, receiving a few knowledgeable smiles in response, and reluctantly waved to either side, for them to proceed to climb the slope ahead. They numbered less than two hundred now, and he had a feeling they would number considerably less by the end of this night.

The small band of mixed warriors, who began to move forward in small groups of ten, acknowledged the wave and proceeded as fast as their legs permitted. None of them had any idea what lay ahead and yet they implicitly trusted Cappa's judgement. None questioned and some would never have dared to do so, yet Cappa held in reserve a hope that perhaps it would help more if someone did challenge his authority every now and again. Not too much mind you, just enough to increase his own natural levels of caution. Now, as he personally broke cover and began the slow ascent up the mountain road, the earlier feelings of dread simply doubled.

Was something wrong? Was there something terrible? But he could not be positive that it was not in their interests. No guards, so no fight. No fight, so no more fatalities, but such a prize as Sight Fortress must be defended, even if only by a token force. It was the guards, the guards. Where were they?

"Are you still worried?" jeered Constantine, childishly, running slightly ahead of him and excited by the prospect of a fight. "We have not seen any trouble so far. Have we?"

"No."

"Then everything will be fine. Maybe the glory of retaking the fortress will be ours? Maybe the Mage has called them to the river up north to reinforce them after a defeat? Perhaps they are, even now, scouring the countryside for further escaped prisoners, and do not even suspect we are here?"

"Constantine."

"Yes, Cappa."

"Do me a favour?"

"You have only to ask, Cappa."

"Shut up."

"Shut up?"

"Yes, shut up. I am not aware your ears are afflicted?"

"No...No...My..." Cappa frowned deeply as the youth turned to confirm the command, somewhat confused by the request. On viewing his expression, however, he took solace in the fact that they had marched halfway up the approaches and had still not been challenged, thus proving his assessment correct after all.

He also shut up.

Only a few wore leather armour, most having had to throw it away to swim to the shore, and so they moved in almost total silence, each lost in his own thoughts. Cappa could not help but think back to what Atronius had told him about the massacre that a friend had ordered many years ago, while returning from the Mithradatic war. The screams of the children dying and afterwards, when the survivors had tried to revive their mothers by pressing on their blood soaked chests, had stained his memory for life. Cappa knew that life was cheap and that to remain in existence you joined Roma or perished.

Now, with no such barriers, they had all been forced to change their interpretations of life. The most obvious change was that their original enemy, the Helvetii, which had defied Roma, were now an ally and an integral part of the legion. This was still not accepted by all, but they had no other choice but to work with them.

Atronius had told him about the raising of the swords and the plunging spear points that had ended so many lives, although these people had requested only food from a fattened senator and his cronies. With the death of the senior centurion, Atronius had ordered that the food be immediately distributed, defying the senator's orders. Since that day he had suffered from nightmares, and he considered this act of kindness the reason why he had never been promoted to Legate and given the command of his own legion. Ever since their arrival in these lands, however, the nightmares had ended and the Primus had never been so contented, and the earlier bonds of admiration and respect had blossomed into friendship. His kidnapping had been a heavy blow to them all.

Now, as Cappa reached the foot of the massive boulders, which heralded the beginning of the collapsed tunnel, that friendship reached its greatest moment. He stopped, causing everyone else to also pause, muscles taut in anticipation.

Aarun had wished to land in the enemy's territory and seek out Atronius Sulla, as they had all desired, but Aarun had left them at the beach before most of them had even organised themselves. Why? Cappa groaned and nodded to Constantine knowingly, causing the youngster to look back, perplexed. He ignored the look of confusion and looked up ahead, where against the skyline he could see the shadow of the few elves that now acted as their scouts. Then, as certain as he was of the sky, Cappa knew that Atronius was here and not at Pitlas, as the dwarves coldly loved to quote.

Up ahead was a man he could not be sure was still alive. All these thoughts circled inside his head, and he felt his pause begin to feel like hesitation, robbing him of his normal alertness, until of course the running horde were almost literally upon them.

"By the Gods," shouted Constantine, looking to Cappa for guidance. "A trap! A trap!"

The goblins seemed to be coming from everywhere at once, screaming obscenities in their guttural language that, as usual, nobody tried to translate but easily understood. They came swinging clubs and brandishing swords, and many already had horrific battle wounds, the green blood staining their garments. The number was unknown and to count them would have wasted valuable seconds. Cappa had already lost time by being taken by surprise once, and twice was not an option.

"Everyone to me!" Cappa ordered, pushing and shoving those nearest to him to form some kind of order. "Move it, you fool! Do you want to sell your soul so cheaply?"

All about them the enemy charged, with the all too familiar battle cry. Cappa felt the normal gut-wrenching imbalance as his battle-fury rose swiftly, his grip on the gladius' hilt tightening. His breath came in short, sharp wheezes, forced through clenched teeth, but rather than associate this with fear, he liked this feeling of uncertainty. For the first time in his life, he admitted wholeheartedly that he enjoyed the freedom of battle. No more morals, no more restrictions or forlorn debates, just kill, kill, kill and kill some more! The rage surged through his veins and all semblance of control vanished, as his survival instincts took over. They did not have to count, for they all knew it was time to die. Nobody would be walking back down the mountain.

The surprise was too great to allow them to work together on the broken ground, but small groups did manage to link together to fight for their own survival, although most of them quickly became separated. Cappa found himself alone, after a few brief encounters with five goblins bearing down on him with a vengeance. He looked, but there was nobody near enough to him to assist. This would be his greatest challenge yet.

He screamed defiance and allowed his anger to swell to gigantic proportions, at which nobody could have retained control. The first assailant was a blur of green blood flowing into the air and the absent memory of metal grinding on bone. The second was more deliberate, as with a side step and downward strike he separated an arm from the shoulder, while the backward, slashing motion decapitated the screaming goblin, ending its futile anger.

The third began to strike viciously and Cappa parried with skill, but could see no direct opening, as the last two closed in on either side to join in at the finish. Then the attacking goblin tripped on the rolling head of the earlier fatality and stumbled, whereupon Cappa pounced to drive the short sword deep into the throat and with both hands thrust downwards into the torso. Blood gushed everywhere, making the hilt too slippery for him to retrieve. Cappa panicked and took several steps backwards, as the two remaining goblins moved closer, knocking aside their dying comrade.

"*Ishtka I'asaissinai bo nu genikeral*," one growled deeply, seemingly grinning in anticipation of the kill.

"*Ishtka*," repeated the second and lunged forward clumsily.

Cappa sidestepped and, as Helin had taught him, drove his knee high to strike the torso. The sound of breaking bone was satisfying, but the goblin had stopped only momentarily before again turning to face him. Looking to either side, he saw nothing but gigantic boulders, no clear way of escape. If he turned his back then death would be the only escape and he was not quite ready to give up. Not just yet!

A second lunge and a new sidestep brought a hand down on the wrist, releasing the curved blade favoured by the goblin. A heavy kick to the face sent the goblin sprawling and his failure to retrieve it left Cappa with the weapon, but the first swipe was too high and the goblin withdrew easily, to pick up another discarded blade. It was now the turn of the last goblin to move forward with rotational cuts that indicated a much higher skill level, thus a more difficult opponent. Cappa's new sword was unwieldy and considerably heavier than a normal blade, and he needed all of his skill just to parry the blows. A few wild, circular swings at least made his opponents advance cautiously, but he was running out of space as the boulders closed in on all sides.

Bracketed and with no shield or body armour, Cappa was in a desperate situation. The battle madness had not dissipated, but it was obvious that a chance had to be taken. Steeling himself for the effort he ducked beneath a new onslaught and rolled forward. Thankfully, the creature remained stationary for a split second, having lost sight of the intended target, and unsure of the next move.

It was to be a fatal pause. With surprising strength, Cappa sent the curved blade singing through the air at a low level to make contact with both ankles, smoothly severing both feet.

He did not even notice the scream as the goblin dropped to both knees, for he was concentrating on rising. Once up he swung the blade again in a full circle to increase the rotational speed and impact, where the edge made contact with the back of the neck. With a look of insanity Cappa laughed belatedly, as the second head rolled away, while the final goblin stood to one side screaming defiance.

With one step and a practiced swing, a third head rolled and Cappa had survived another impossible situation, but it was not over yet. More and more goblins came over the crest of the hill, intent on killing them all, or so it seemed at first. Cappa rejoined a small group nearby, intending to continue the fight, which had literally devolved into a series of individual battles between a few antagonists on either side. No mercy was given or asked, as the blood toll rose. From that moment onwards Cappa remembered little, as the killing went on and on. Some of their own fell as did a few of the enemy, but it soon became apparent that the main objective of the goblins was apparently to bypass them and escape down the valley.

The bitterness of this skirmish however had left no quarter, and it was not long before his sword arm ached beyond description and the very act of lifting the blade was extremely painful. He remembered desparately looking for Helin, but he could not see even one hobbit, let alone his beloved, and, fearing the worst, his anger exploded once more.

Bodies lay everywhere and the dead and dying had taken every pose possible. Some lay sprawled across a stone or the bottom of some flatland. Others sat looking in shock at a dismembered part of their anatomy, as their lifeblood ebbed away in the dirt. Some tried to bandage a colleague's injury, but then became victims themselves, as a goblin swung a passing cut to strike them down.

Nearby two brothers lay side by side with at least twenty corpses around them, their lives having taken a toll the enemy could ill afford. Another group sat in total exhaustion nearby with the same number of slain around them, but were just as incapable of rejoining the fight as he now felt. They could not go on, as Cappa knew, for he himself could no longer raise the adopted goblin blade to defend his head.

"It is over," he confessed, to nobody in particular, dropping to his knees and looking to the skies. "*Over!*"

To those present it did indeed seem so but, as was the way of any skirmish, the enemy vanished as quickly as they had appeared, leaving the survivors shocked and disorientated.

"Perhaps a little hasty." Oh, God, Cappa thought, that sweet voice, that sweet, beautiful voice. "It seems we are saved after all. It looks as though Kollis is standing above us, and I presume an apology of some sort will be demanded?"

Cappa nodded, it was all he could manage, just a nod.

"How?" he asked, as Kollis joined them.

"It is a total secret," Kollis explained, "but amongst many of our people such things never remain so for long, and it was well documented that Komar had begun excavations underneath the fortress."

"I guess that is where you went from the beach?" suggested Helin.

"I considered it the best chance we had of survival. On board the ship, the sailors advised me that the farmers had counted only four thousand corpses reported by the goblins. It was obvious they were hiding something. It was a guess but, as you can see, my Lord Komar is most certainly alive and has actually now retaken the fortress."

Kollis indicated a muddy figure above on a tall rock, who was seemingly trying to organize the survivors to be taken inside the fortress. He did not look especially significant, but it was obvious that this dwarf was yet another who believed in leading people by example. Anything his warriors did he would willingly do too.

"How many...?" began Cappa, but stopped when it seemed to his eyes that few of the people who had begun the ascent were still alive. "Any wounded?" he asked instead.

"No. None. Only slight wounds where the injured person was able to continue to fight," confirmed Helin, solemnly. "We should bandage that leg while we wait, Cappa, or we will be adding you to the list of the fallen."

For the first time, Cappa looked down and noticed the dark red stain of dried blood covering one leg. The wound was not deep, but for all his willpower he could not remember when the injury had occurred.

"I do not even..." he began then, realising that he had lost sight of the youngster, asked, "Constantine?"

"He is fine. A few have gone ahead to help find any stragglers that may still be in the fortress," Kollis replied, helping Cappa to stand.

"Stragglers?"

"Komar has been fighting these heathens since the time they occupied the three tower fortifications, which make up the fortress. They tried to dig down to him and tried to overrun their caves, but each successive ambush became more and more expensive. Eventually the loss ratio left Komar with the advantage, and this very night he counterattacked and retook the fortress. It is an amazing achievement!"

Cappa smiled, then laughed with the joy of having survived once again. He was glad Kollis was still alive, Helin too, but there was still one issue left to resolve.

"Have you seen Aarun?" he asked firmly, his face screwed up in anger.

"No, not personally, but there are reports that flashes of magic have been seen in the upper palisades. Constantine and a few others have gone to investigate."

"You sent Constantine?" asked Cappa, incredulously.

"He insisted," Kollis confessed. "Something about being under your shadow for long enough, and he had to prove his own worth."

Cappa grunted, then grimaced as the pain in the leg broke through the battle weariness, and the residue of adrenaline from the near death experiences faded.

"I think he will be fine," Helin said. "He has had a good instructor."

"We all must stand alone sooner or later," added Kollis. "Look at me when I commanded the Westonians at Holvidar. I too have learnt a great deal."

"True, but I would still like to follow just in case that fool of a youngster decides to take on the whole goblin army single-handedly."

Kollis grinned. "That I can truly understand. I will supply a guide, but in truth the way is simple enough."

"Thank you, my Lord, you saved our lives."

"I saved what I could, just as you would have done, General, nothing more. I only regret my dismissal of your people all those months ago, when my pride dictated my actions. I should have been more understanding, but this is the greatest lesson I have learnt."

"On this day, my Lord, you have repaid that insult many times over."

They separated then and moved off in three different directions. Kollis rejoined Komar, who waved briefly before turning to deal with a new threat in the lower palisades. Apparently five hundred or more goblins had been trapped in the central hall, and any offer of peace would not be accepted.

Everything seemed to be on the up from there, and even Helin kissed Cappa longingly on the lips before she moved away with the six hobbits that still survived of her original twenty, Molisis in close support with a deep head wound; the others he did not know by name. They began to tend for the dwarven wounded, many of who had not seen the sky for the past few weeks. These people had achieved an amazing success, and Helin was proud to be part of the recovery, and worked all the harder to make the injured comfortable.

Cappa meanwhile set off after Constantine with Kole, an old but well-respected dwarf of no rank. They went after the youngster, a slight limp betraying his wound. It was only then, as they began to climb a nearby set of stone steps, that the familiar feeling of dread returned to Cappa, implying that whatever it foretold had yet to pass.

Cappa began to feel nervous again. If what he had experienced earlier was not enough to rid him of this feeling, then whatever was up ahead should be left well alone, he suddenly thought. Then again, he could not just abandon the youngster. Right, bring that fool Constantine back and then go for a very long rest. God, this leg was beginning to ache.

How many more of these steps are there anyhow!

Even as Cappa ascended those very steps, a meeting between friends had just begun hundreds of leagues away to the north. Just as he had no idea of their intentions, this small group dwelled heavily on the ships missing from the small fleet, which had supposedly sailed south several weeks earlier. One ship had returned with its main masts ripped asunder and half the crew missing, presumed drowned. Of the other four, nothing was known and nobody had any intention of sailing south to establish the truth, as local fisherman confirmed that the storm described had begun to travel along the coast, destroying everything in its path that was not tied down.

Nobody could remember a storm of such ferocity before, and the winds had been known to lift people into the air and throw them down leagues away inland. It was this very storm that had required this meeting, along with the fighting that day at the river.

Decisions had to be made and Kol was the person to make them.

He sat now in a comfortable armchair, smoking a pipe and wearing a long overcoat of bright red facings, the colour of the Priesthood Guards. The tight trousers and boots lent him an almost comical look, but to date nobody had challenged the commander-in-chief. The fact that he had not so far left the tower during all the fighting left none of them in any doubt about his sincerity when he claimed he would not retire another step. He would rather perish in this tower than run to the mountains and hide. The officers had not missed the sentiment, neither had the rank and file, both earning more and more laurels with their bravery.

With a practiced eye Kol looked around the table and nodded in recognition to each in turn. He had personally sent word for each to attend this evening and noted with pride that none had taken the time to wash or refresh, having remained with their respective commands, and attending only at the first signs of any drop in the enemy activity. Those who had begun this campaign as inexperienced commanders were now fully-fledged generals, and highly respected by the troops. He could not have wished for a better command staff. He had to be proud, for it had cost them the southern peninsular to mould this army and it was increasing in efficiency with every day.

Elvandar was to his immediate right and looked exhausted, more so than the others, and seemed somewhat agitated, as he constantly looked to either side. Kol signalled with a hand and, as if by magic, a tall chair arrived and the elven marshal smiled in gratitude. Just a few weeks ago, the elf's face had shown great strain as Aarun had left to sail south. Now, with the news that the fleet was lost and the Lord with it, the stress had increased enormously. His hair, normally tied back, now fell loose across his eyes in an attempt to hide his grief, but those who stood close enough knew better.

Next in line around the table was Khazumar, with a white bandage wrapped around his forehead, a small red patch indicating an injury of some sort. The dwarf had taken numerous steps to enhance the efficiency of the dwarven regiments, and it was universally agreed that without his presence half the army would have bolted weeks ago. He was now a force to be reckoned with, and could easily usurp the power to command from Kol with little resistance; but this outspoken, loud dwarf had never shown the slightest level of disloyalty to Kol. If anything, he had shown undying loyalty, something that was as priceless as a further fifty thousand warriors, indeed irreplaceable.

Of all the people present, the only real unknown quantity was Arnim, who commanded the hobbit forces, which numbered about five thousand, of which it was known that perhaps five hundred were maidens. The story of Crassus' encounter with a small group of these maidens was well known to them all but, for political reasons, Kol had asked that the hobbits be kept in reserve, to avoid any arguments from the Hildar, who refused to fight besides maidens. It was just not done and it offended their high sensibilities. Old fashioned perhaps, but Kol could not help but feel that on this subject they were correct.

To avoid offence, he had asked them to become his personal escort and the local regimental commander, in the absence of Helin, Arnim's daughter, had readily accepted the honour. He believed her name was Armolin and she stood at the back in silence. It was odd to be surrounded by such beautiful creatures all day, and it often served to distract the general from his tasks, but they were if nothing else highly motivated and, even this evening, they had searched all of the generals, including Arnim, before allowing them to enter this room.

They were of course not as delicious as the dwarven maidens or his spouse, as they did not have a beard, although the current dwarven fashion was to shave the beard off completely, something he had found rather disturbing at first. Thankfully his own wife had resisted this new fashion and retained a good head of hair, which made the cold nights ever more comfortable.

After passing more time with the hobbits, however, he found their company quite soothing, if not a luxury, in this camp. Kol smiled as he recalled Crassus' indignation at having been searched and having his ever-present short sword removed and placed to one side, to await his return. That one was a strange beast and no mistake. Creative, powerful in stature and yet never seen without some kind of wine within arms reach. How he managed to consume such quantities of wine and still remain standing was the subject of an ongoing debate amongst the others. However, their initial worries regarding his efficiency had been dispelled at Holvidar, where Crassus had fought off the final assault in the centre and simultaneously defended the ridge, as the rearguard fought to delay the enemy's pursuit.

That had taken a cool head, not a drunkard, and since then their faith had never faltered. Kol wondered why he drank so much, but never pressed the topic. Each person had their own problems, and each had suffered a personal loss since their association had started many months before. Was that really only six months ago? No, it must surely be more?

Kol refilled his pipe and pointed towards the last of the group, the youngster Julius Galienus, who smiled in reply as he leaned on the table to move a few markers as he brought to them the latest news from the waterfall. The youth reminded Kol of his own son, who had forever a smile and never seemed to lose any enthusiasm for anything. Always active, the youth seemed to be everywhere at one and the same time, and it was for this ceaseless activity that, after the River Battle, Crassus had joined with him to hunt down Igluk's survivors.

It had been an efficient partnership and, combined with Julius' skilful withdrawal along the western coast—now referred to as the Seven Day Battle—it had earned him the respect of young and old warriors alike. Sometimes perhaps he lacked that aloofness a decisive commander required, and perhaps he was liked a little too much, but he was now a trusted member of this staff.

Besides Crassus was never too far away from him. Julius was given a lead, but not allowed to stray too far. However, the partnership's recent efforts, to create a bridgehead across the bridge of warships to the south, had borne less fruit than their previous tasks. This was the total of those at the table, which was slightly to his right and a little distance away to allow a small table to sit at his feet. If someone had stated that in six months he would be commanding an army of dwarves, elves and two mythical creatures, the Romans and hobbits, he would have laughed until his sides ached. Even Karr would have laughed. He was a strong warrior and full of loyalty beyond restraint, and yet his faith had been shattered when they first sighted the Romans. Now they had reached the final decisions and they could not ignore an almost blatant fatality about the meeting, possibly also a little defeatism.

"Aarun is lost," Elvandar stated gloomily, starting the more serious discussion. "There can be no profit in awaiting the results of their journey."

"Which was?" Khazumar asked, raising an eyebrow quizzically. "Some of us were not exactly too clear what the intention was anyway."

"Was it a rescue attempt?" Julius guessed. "Probably seeking Atronius."

With one movement all heads turned towards Kol, who shifted uneasily in his comfortable chair, the smoke thick around his head and the smell, to some, most unpleasant. He nodded in agreement with Julius, but refrained from joining in just yet. Sometimes a free rein provoked a few little truths that made possible a more educated assessment of what his staff really thought.

"Atronius?" scoffed Khazumar. "A mere mortalkind, and we have lost the very person to keep the elves in line..."

"And what have I been doing today, my good Khazumar, twiddling my thumbs?" Elvandar retorted, reaching for a blade that was no longer within the scabbard.

"I only meant that those remaining have shown a lack of discipline, nothing more."

"They will stand," said Crassus, coldly. "Or I am a fool."

"Such comments should not be made lightly, Centurion, for they have a habit of coming true," Khazumar barked. "And while we are on the topic, what was that raid by twenty or so legionaries into those woods to the south of the great bridge all about?"

"It was to find proof of a spy here in our camp," defended Crassus.

"If you wanted proof of this you had only to ask, as we are aware of at least thirty," said Elvandar, closing his eyes. "When we need every warrior possible, I think we should avoid further personal joyrides into the woods."

"You should have a care, Elvandar," retorted Julius. "The spy Crassus sought was very close to us all in this camp, and has been since we arrived in this God-forsaken world!"

"If it is so distasteful, leave now!"

Julius made to walk around the table, but stopped when his eyes met Kol's.

"Did you establish the identity of the spy?" Kol asked, lighting his pipe for the third time that evening.

"It was Cornelius Porta."

"Porta?" repeated Kol, incredulously. "That is an ill wind indeed. Have we apprehended him?"

"No, he vanished," offered Julius, by way of an explanation, walking back to his original place at the table.

"That is very true, Julius, but now we can plan without him revealing our intentions..." Crassus began to add.

Julius smiled again and the mood lightened a little. "Not another one that is wine induced, I hope."

"No, indeed, noble youngster, a much more daring plan than before."

"Which is?" asked Khazumar, again raising an eyebrow, an expression that he most assuredly had picked up from Marcellus, who they all knew to be recovering from his wounds.

"You know, every time I see you, my Lord, you look all the more like my good friend Marcellus. Those eyebrows, Julius, it is the eyebrows don't you think?"

"Most definitely," Julius said conspiratorially, throwing a knowing smile to Kol.

"The plan," Khazumar continued, ignoring the attempted joke.

"Plan?"

"You spoke of a plan, Crassus, or are we again just wasting time?"

"Well it involves us all stripping naked, carrying off all the maidens orcs, leaving of course the ugly ones for Julius..."

"What?"

"And then keeping all the males from cavorting with our chosen mates, at which point the enemy will be joined to us and..."

"Is this serious?" Khazumar asked, looking towards Kol, but receiving only a smile for the effort. "Do we have *time* for this?"

"We should make time." Arnim spoke for the first time. "It is good that we are able to lighten the mood before we begin the more serious debate."

"Which is?" Elvandar snapped.

"That is obvious. After today's fighting it must be clear to everyone that we can no longer hold this river line."

"Why not?" snapped Elvandar once more, looking down at the hobbit marshal from on high.

"The enemy has rebuilt the central bridge…"

"And we destroyed it again…"

"Three times, Marshall. Three times! How long can we sustain the same level of losses inflicted upon us today? It is not only the bridge either. The Lower Island and fort have been lost along with some of Julius' finest people, and your people, Khazumar, suffered horrifying losses to stop them crossing the crest of the waterfall. I tell you, we cannot continue here."

"What do you suggest then? A retreat north, where we can protect your mountain valleys, no doubt?" Elvandar mocked, crossing his arms and looking to Kol for support.

"We could do much worse," Arnim argued, pointing at the map stretched across the table. "If we pulled back and incorporated all the troops to the north, we could amass over two hundred thousand and fight them in the open at the base of the northern mountains. I can guarantee a further five thousand, and the army on the Gallician border could easily give support and still remain close to Moravia. It is the most logical thing to do."

"Is it?" pondered Crassus, aloud. "If we pull back from here the whole of the Dwarmanian peninsular and their capital will be left open to the ravages of the enemy. Where will the people go, Arnim? We rely on them for sustenance and yet they are hardly likely to support us if we turn and run. No, we must stand and fall right here."

"I agree," Julius added, after a brief pause. "But if we are to fall, I would rather we did it going forward rather than standing here waiting for them to kill us all one by one."

"What do you have in mind?" Kol asked, noting everyone's expressions of surprise as he listened to the youth's opinion. "Please, continue. If I did not value your opinion, I would not have sent you the invitation to this meeting."

Julius smiled and visibly relaxed a little more. Looking first at Crassus, who grinned, and then at Elvandar, who nodded, he turned to the map and began in earnest.

"The enemy have forced two bridgeheads across the river at the upper Cart Bridge, which they repaired while we fought elsewhere, and at the waterfall. We could debate all night, but we do not have the time or the energy, so we must decide now and quickly. We know the enemy has sent a large force to our left flank, where Issus' scouts have also reported a major bridge in the making. He does not have the strength to attack the forces there, but has delegated the task of delaying them to his barbarians alone, and we can ill afford to reinforce him yet..."

"My own people could perform that task," suggested Arnim, painfully aware that his people had not taken part in any of the fighting so far. "With your consent, General Kol?"

"Issue the orders when you leave, Arnim," confirmed Kol. "But please leave your maidens with me, I've a feeling they have a special part to play by my side."

"Of course, they will deem it an honour to remain as your bodyguard."

"Good." Kol looked back towards Julius and pointed at the map with his pipe. "Please continue, Julius."

"Well, in truth we need either to pin the enemy or drive them back..."

"Yes, yes," snapped Khazumar, impatiently. "We all know this, but what is your suggestion?"

"That we do exactly the opposite."

"What?" shouted Elvandar. "If we are to hold here, youngster, we must throw them back into the river..."

"And as soon as we do that they will attack across the Great Bridge, divide again and rebuild over and over...again. Every time we move our reserves to plug a break, they attack at the bridge again. We send our best to hold the bridge, and they attack elsewhere and create a new breach. They only stopped because of the night, but they continued to raid our lines in earnest."

"How does this help us?" Crassus asked, now intrigued, as he did not doubt the youth's tactics, and was perhaps now beginning to see the advantage of doing exactly the opposite of what the enemy expected. If anything, in Cappa's absence he had taught him well, and Julius had been a swift learner.

"Let them cross. Let them build their bridging points. Pull our main forces back beyond the ridge, allow some to run..."

"Make them think we are bolting!" Arnim stated with enthusiasm.

"Exactly! Bring them forward, on and on."

"Then?" asked Kol flatly, catching Julius' eyes in a death-like glare. "What do you want us to do in the meantime?"

"We will cross back over the river using a bridge made of warships. The mouth of the river is wide enough and all we need is six warships to link together with those that carried our recce force across yesterday, and we can be over within a few hours."

"That is where you rescued the messenger sent by Valenus?" Kol now asked, his tone showing a doubt for the first time.

"It was, but the enemy simply ignored our presence, and there is literally nothing to the west of the triangular wood to stop us crossing."

"I still do not see how that will help us," said Crassus, his eyes scouring the maps. "Surely a better place to cross would be to the east, where we can utilise this bridge they are building."

"Our weakness is in numbers, is it not? Yes...agreed? Good. Well, if we allow two thirds to cross the river we can use the advantage of numbers to deal with those left on the far side. Here we stand and pray, across the river we fight to kill the Mage. On the far side, surprise will be our greatest weapon and at least give us equal numbers on one part of this battlefield. They have already sent a third of their forces to turn our left. If Issus and Arnim could hold them for just one day, even if they only make them hesitate to join the bridgeheads, we will have victory and will be able to crush their centre and left from both sides of the river."

Crassus' mouth opened and closed, searching to find the right words. Elvandar just stared into space and refused to even consider the idea, while Khazumar instantaneously whooped for joy.

"By the Gods, lad, but that is an ingenious and foolhardy plan, but I feel that it may be beyond our forces to perform."

"Why?" chorused Kol, Julius and Arnim.

"Well, for one there are a high number of inexperienced warriors within our ranks. Each has been blooded in turn, as the saying goes, and many have faltered, some have stood strong and others have excelled. Overall, however, we are still a young army with little or no manoeuvring experience. Second, still keeping the first point in mind, if we strip the best troops from the initial lines of defence, how will the remainder stand without the true backbone of the army?"

"A point well made," Kol said, finally rising to join them at the table, discreetly placing the pipe to one side. "How can we circumvent this difficulty?"

"You are not seriously considering this plan?" jeered Elvandar, shuffling from one foot to another.

"Nervous, Marshall?" asked Kol.

"Nervous?"

"Yes, I believe the choice of word is correct. Earlier it was suggested that your elves are showing signs of poor discipline. You are not thinking of retiring without us, are you?"

Kol's challenge fell like a heavy weight through a window, shattering any pretence of a friendly joke between companions. The face reddened, the eyes bulged in fury and the hand again reached for the missing weapon. It was painfully obvious that Aarun was not only this elf's lord and friend, but that he had also been the pressure valve to keep this great elf's temper in check. It was to be a painful lesson for Kol to learn.

"You dare to question our loyalty after so many of us have fallen? Who was it that argued against a withdrawal? Me, that's who. Me! For your insult I should lead my people away, or perhaps we should join the enemy instead!"

"I merely suggested that your people were tired, and not up to this task," placated Kol, still keeping his tone flat, as Aarun had suggested, in allowing the great elf to draw his own conclusions.

"Place us anywhere and we will do our duty five-fold. I pledge my honour and the honour of Gallicia on this oath."

Kol nodded solemnly and looked to the others. "Thank you, Marshall, I am sure I will have need of your bravery. And I am sure that no further sitting on the fence will occur. We must decide what to do. Just as Julius has so aptly stated, we have little time in which to set things in motion. I need a true assessment of our status."

"I think we are tired, but not yet beaten," stated Crassus proudly, speaking for them all. "I am sure we can hold the bridgeheads for tomorrow with a reasonable force, if we build palisades and place as many obstacles as possible on the hill where we stand now. However, we would be forgetting our duty if we did not consider an alternative."

"Which is?"

"The possibility that we could march the entire army and strike the forces on our left. With our entire force we could smash through, over the very bridge the enemy has so kindly built for us."

A grunt sounded to Kol's left. "You disagree, Julius?"

"Yes, so much for experience and an open mind, Noble Centurion."

Crassus' laughter again broke the tense atmosphere, as they all chuckled to hear the youth's minor insult. "You will have to do better than that if you wish to insult my thick skin, youngster, but I am not too old to accept good advice. Why would it be wrong to concentrate on the left?"

"I offer my..."

"There is no time for that, Julius," reprimanded Kol. "We need to move on. Explain your comment."

Julius smarted under the stern gaze of Kol and hesitated. He was always amazed how his nerve never failed him when facing the enemy, but here, in this small room, Kol's personality was overpowering. Cappa had always made him feel the same when in his company, but with him there had at least been professional companionship. With Kol, except for a few very close attendants, most had little opportunity to break down the barriers and become firm friends, for he was always at a distance. Cappa was, if anything, the exact opposite. When he lowered his guard, it was more an issue of catching him in the right mood.

Julius allowed his thoughts to wander a little, where were Cappa and Aarun now, and what of the lost fleet? No matter how hard he tried, it was just impossible to think of them as dead, and, if they were, he was certain that he would somehow feel differently. However, for some reason he knew Cappa was alive, but he was not so sure about Aarun.

"Julius...*Julius!*"

"Yes...I'm sorry, I suddenly just remembered Cappa...I just..."

"The left," prompted Crassus. "My lesson in tactics? I am still waiting."

"I feel the same as you, lad," soothed Khazumar, thrusting an elbow into Crassus' ribs. "Somehow, I too just feel that he is not dead. I do not know why, but..."

The sentence drifted into silence as they all bowed their heads, each remembering someone who had sailed with Aarun.

"My thoughts were just that, if we moved to the left, it would not alter our situation," Julius began, reaching for the wineskin offered by Crassus as an apology. "You see we will still be fighting over a bridge, with our flank turned by a bridgehead, except that this time it would be to our right. According to Issus' report, there are no strong ridges to aid our defence, and dense woodlands break up the area. Excellent for delaying tactics, but an army would find it difficult to move and attack other than in small numbers. The enemy would always fight on a one-to-one basis, even though we could outnumber them briefly in the initial confrontation."

Crassus raised his hands in mock defeat. "I bow to the better plan. I believe we should go with the youngster's plan, Kol. It is bold and definitely the last thing they will expect. We could roll up their entire army."

Kol closed his eyes, then relit his pipe. "Is everyone in agreement?" One by one they nodded assent, although the elf did so with obvious reluctance, while Arnim again stubbornly suggested the option of withdrawing north. "No, I think we have a good chance of success if we remain here. What we now need to decide is who goes and who stays."

"Well, now there's a problem and no mistake," laughed Crassus, as he retrieved the wineskin from Julius, his fourth since entering the small room two hours ago. "Shall we organize some food first? I am ravenous."

"It is organised. We eat when we have concluded the plans. Shall we begin..."

It took them two more hours to mull over who was best placed and qualified to turn west and head for the makeshift bridge. Kol had already sent word for the bridge to be built and estimated it would be ready by dawn, with several Roman engineers supervising. The final decision was for Julius and Khazumar to command the forces selected to cross. Arnim would take command of the far left and, along with his own people, take two thousand dwarves to delay the enemy at their new bridge.

Elvandar would command at the Great Bridge and the Waterfall, effectively the army's centre, while Crassus would organise the dwarven and elven legions to launch a surprise attack on the lower island fort, to delay and occupy the enemy. Kol would command from the tower, but if necessary he would cross and join Khazumar in a drive into the enemy flank. For this purpose, they would send most of the experienced dwarven regiments, some new ones and most of the Hildar, in the belief that the task of retrieving their homeland would make them fight all the harder.

Most of the legionaries also went with Julius, and Cappilius gladly accepted his seniority, even though he was the more experienced. In total, forty thousand would cross and for a few seconds Kol remembered Cappa describing the youth as a senator's nephew, and how their Tribune had tried to use his presence to influence their government to obtain greater status.

In Julius, he recognised a great tactician and one who would continue to develop, and would always leave his enemy guessing about his next move. He was the perfect choice for the tactical envelopment of the Haderian left, by using the woods and undulating ground to mask the movement.

With consummate skill Julius quickly named Cappilius as the velites commander he would need, none disagreed. With Issus already away on their left flank fighting the goblins there was no one else. They considered whether to summon him to this meeting to offer his views on capturing the West Hill above the warship bridge, but these issues could easily be resolved with Crassus, so he was allowed a few more hours of sleep.

Now they needed a tactic designed to fool the enemy into utilising the advantage of attacking the Alliance's left flank, using the fixation of crossing the Great River in force, and of course a little luck. Just the mention of this word made Julius glance at Crassus who had also noticed the word. For months now they had all taken to avoiding the word, as within their culture Hades was believed to be the God of good fortune and luck. However, this had thankfully been a new concept and had not been taken too seriously by any of the legionaries, but the belief was still known to many of them.

Crassus smiled at Julius and nodded once more at the maps. Neither of them had any real understanding of religion, so for the moment they put aside this somewhat abstract concern. There were more important matters to occupy their minds, such as how they would move a third of their army across a river of enormous tidal fluctuations, without the enemy realising what they were about.

They moved and planned all night, managing a few hours sleep just before dawn. Then everything was ready. They would begin their greatest gamble, and possibly their last, to defeat an enemy that still outnumbered them at least two to one. Perhaps now would be a good time for the miracle so desired by Kol to make an appearance, or perhaps they would create their own miracle.

PART FOURTEEN

DIVINE INTERVENTION

The air had become heavy, making the ascent more difficult. The sight on leaving the central tower of the fortress had been daunting, to say the least. At a brief glance, Cappa had counted ten flights of almost vertical stairs stretching out before them, and his eyes strained to see the summit, so very far above them. He could of course see the upper palisades of the third tower, over one thousand paces above. Even in this dim light it was hard to miss. It was up there, in the high tower, that Komar had heard the rumour of flashing lights, and the severe nausea experienced by anyone who watched them for even a few seconds.

Mind you, not being of the pro-magic fraternity, Komar had blatantly neglected to investigate the cause. Cappa's arrival barely a few hours ago had invariably given rise to the assumption that Aarun might be found in the high tower. Komar was quick to recommend a well-known guide called Kola.

Now all he had to do was walk up a mountainside, using these damnable steps.

They began at a jaunty pace, much to Cappa's hurt pride, as the old dwarf did not seem daunted by the climb ahead. At first neither old age or Cappa's injury seemed to slow them down. It was not to last, of course. As they reached the third set of steps, where several had been smashed asunder for one reason or another, the pain felt as though it had sneaked up on his senses and laid a perfect ambush. A shooting pain in the groin was his first recollection, a cry of agony his second.

Noting Kola's look of anguish only fuelled Cappa's pride, and he forced the pace again. He ignored the pain. Then the pain ignored him, as his leg began to go numb then, without warning, it simply collapsed under him and he rolled unceremoniously back down several stone steps, to land in a muddy puddle on one of the many landings they had traversed. His language followed swiftly and even the dwarf tried to close off his ears to such profanity, but Cappa had only one way to reach the top of these infernal steps and that was through sheer anger.

So on he pushed, grunting and groaning and wishing all the destruction his mind could fathom on Aarun, the Mage and all of the Gods. He then extended this to include everyone in existence, except for the dwarf who faithfully helped him to walk, as his leg was soaked in blood again and the pain excruciating. They reached the ninth level and sat down for a rest. They sat in silence, watching one another.

As always, Cappa immediately wondered why him and why here! Why did he have to find the youth? He was bloody injured! Meanwhile the dwarf simply sat and wondered how such responsibility had been handed to such an uncouth man as this. Well, that really was all he could say. This was a perfect specimen of a man and their manners obviously lacked a great deal.

Cappa rose awkwardly, gesturing for aid. Kola grunted under his weight and also rose. How could an old dwarf and an injured mortalkind be the deciding factor in all their futures, thought the dwarf, ironically. Nothing made sense any more. Nothing!

Dutifully Cappa again struggled to put on a brave face, as they set off once more for the summit, which now, thankfully, was much closer. Each step required more effort, his thighs burning as though someone had set him on fire. Each movement of his legs was slower than the last. To make it even harder, the steps had not been designed to accommodate the height of anyone other than a dwarf. This meant that he had to take irritatingly small steps, or two at a time, either choice aggravating his injury.

Kola was now actively encouraging him a little too much, thus earning himself a bitter tirade of unknown words. Unperturbed, he advised that the lower gates to the third tower were just up ahead. They should not despair! Then, low and behold, if they did not see them as they rounded one of the annoying turns in the ascent. They now stood between the main steps and the last hundred or so that led to the tower's main southern entrance. Made of iron, but topped with silver and gold claps of thunder, signifying the deity of Zeus, they were a welcome sight.

Kola now happily began to talk of better times, when he had enjoyed many a wonderful party up here on the promenade, with so many friends who were no longer with them. Cappa tried to listen, but soon the words began to fade and he knew the blood loss was beginning to have a severe affect on his senses. He had to reach the summit or die an ignominious death on some stone floor with an old dwarf, who knew these mountains like the back of his hand, but had failed to bring a change for his bandages. Come to that, so had he!

By the time they reached the lower gate entrance his patience had, nonetheless, all but evaporated and his tongue had become as sharp as his sword. He staggered and looked across the path, nodding with thanks at his guide, but there was now nothing more he could do to help.

The air here had changed. It was heavier somehow, harder to breathe, and his panting was a sure sign that the heat up here was also unnatural. He hated the heat. Cappa swore and spat over the wall he now leaned on and watched the spittle drop away to the depths below. Up ahead he could see the bright flashes of light that he knew to be nothing other than billowing magic, which probably explained the change in the air.

Having a few more years under his belt, Kola was openly fearful of magic and was not afraid to show his uncertainty. Cappa smiled understanding the dwarf's apprehension and nodded his thanks. He sympathised with the old dwarf, aware of his own lack of understanding, but also knowing with equal certainty that he would continue from here on his own.

The air itself literally smelt of burning oxygen and his nostrils flared apprehensively. Neither could ignore the electrical tension all around, and any contact with the metal gates caused a momentary shock, not painful, but one that could all too easily be read as a warning to turn back there and then!

Of course Kola had no reason to proceed and, without a word, gave a brief wave of farewell, pointed to the gate and, with walking fingers, indicated where to go, then promptly turned around. For a moment Cappa watched him descend the steps in long, bounding jumps, with never a rearward look, and felt a brief envy that he was unable to follow. Up ahead there would be nothing but pain and perhaps even death, as he began to remember his overbearing feeling of dread and now solemnly wished that he had insisted on others accompanying him. But somehow in his heart he knew this was a journey only he could take.

Even so, as he turned back to enter the tunnel leading to the upper gate, a small hope still flourished. All about them, even with the fortress back in their hands, the goblin hordes walked freely throughout the southern half of the dwarven peninsular with a preponderance of numbers that defied a mathematical solution, but somewhere, deep inside, Cappa refused to give up.

He would never give up!

None of them would, and perhaps this simple stubbornness was the source of their real strength. Within the horde the individuals generally acted as a mass, with little or no personality or freedom. They did not act out of any higher purpose of preserving their way of life, or so he believed, but rather to dominate others, or so it seemed to Cappa as he stood at this gate and watched the flashing shadows on the wall. It was hard to see that this would have been their choice, and he suddenly saw the parallels with Julius Caesar.

It was a lifetime ago and yet the comparison seemed so obvious. The Helvetii tribes in truth had asked for and then demanded only a simple right to exist. To farm and grow food in fertile ground within the coastal areas, perhaps a province was their only wish and maybe land could have been found. In time perhaps they might have become more allied to Roma, to a greater extent than any military solution could have produced. The policy of Roma he now saw in all its barbarity. Food for Romans, but the other populations could starve and would do so at the bidding of senatorial edicts.

This then invariably led to more and more trade influence outside of their borders. In truth it had only been a matter of time before Julius Caesar saw his opportunity and closed the borders to the Helvetii, and by doing so forced them to take desperate measures. Perhaps, in one way or another, Caesar was also responsible for them being here?

He began to think about his mother and her terror, due to their ancestor's exploits against the Senate of Roma and the Roman people. He had hated them then and despised those who had sought him out to load his life with such trauma from a very early age. He had not committed the betrayal, so why should he suffer, for he was a loyal Roman citizen.

Some had been justified, and he knew better than anyone how cantankerous and stubborn he could be, but only when absolutely necessary. Even the revolt with Valenus had somehow turned out for the better. Scipio was no more, or so he thought, and neither was the legion. The men now had a much more open path to seek a true happiness, but for many the loss of their family would eventually be too much. For them he felt a great sorrow but, with no return journey, they must all cope as best they could and hope to triumph.

Cappa entered the tunnel beyond the tower gates and found his mind wandering back to Valenus, who had created a hatred amongst the men that had, at one point, surpassed even their loathing of Scipio. Yet now, in this new existence, Valenus had, with Crassus' aid, developed, during the southern campaign, into an invaluable officer and although the men did not yet trust him completely, they obeyed willingly. Authority was useful here, but was not really the deciding factor. They had all needed to learn new ways to lead the men and integrate them into the other social policies, while keeping at least a semblance of their own identities. It had not been easy.

Cappa had not fought directly at Holvidar, but had served more as an aide to Kol. It had been a bitter struggle, and several times he had found himself demanding permission to lead his legionaries in battle but, rightly or not, Kol had ordered him to remain, where in truth his own insight had enabled Crassus to defeat Scipio's final charge in the centre.

Cappa smiled as he recalled his first meeting with Helin's personal guard. It was surprising how much Cappa, Crassus, Julius, Valenus and Elvandar could laugh when the moment caught them. It had been the first time they had met warrior-maidens and for a moment he stopped, trying to calculate on his fingers just exactly how many weeks before this had happened. No matter how much he tried, he could not discern how much time had elapsed.

Well, it did not really matter. Helin was safe with Kollis and all he now had to do was find Atronius, if alive, and Aarun, if he was in this tower. On entering a lighted dome, he looked up to see the tower rise to touch the clouds through an open aperture in the roof. He rubbed his eyes, momentarily disconcerted, as the tower seemed to almost wink in and out of focus.

Why, he thought? Yet another problem to fathom, but the whole area seemed to be here and yet...not here? By Jupiter, this way of thinking seriously gave him a headache. Let's move on, he encouraged, and picked up pace to reach another opening that looked much like a welcoming foyer.

Moving on through, Cappa reached the top of another small flight of stairs and faced yet another landing. A sigh of relief escaped through his teeth, as he spied no more steps on either side. He noted how this one differed slightly from any of the others he had found since leaving his guide, as before him now stood doorways. All three seemed to be ascending and there was a natural pause, as he pondered exactly which way to go.

Where was the guide when you really needed one?

All three were decorated with doors hanging from their hinges, but the entrance was not barred, and there was just enough room to squeeze past. The next question was, which one to take? If only the guide could have told him about this room, Cappa fumed silently. A mistake now could send him to the wrong part of the tower and steal vital minutes, minutes that might decide the success or failure of this attempt to find Aarun.

⊹−∗−⊹−∗−⊹

"He is coming!" the Mage stated, acidly.

"*He cannot change anything. He has no power*," Hades replied absently, almost mocking the Mage's lack of faith.

"You do not know this man, he must be stopped."

"*We cannot divert any power for such a trivial end. Do not be a fool!*"

"Then he must be delayed! You must delay...delay...*delay!*"

⊹−∗−⊹−∗−⊹

Cappa hesitated, wondering whether he should go back and find the guide? Yes, perhaps that would not take too long...Of course, he realised almost immediately it would have taken forever in terms of any rescue attempt. It would in fact have been an admission of failure to turn back now and, as always, he knew it was beyond his conscience to do so, but how in all the God's names was he to choose?

The groan came from the right. He thought the sound was familiar, but could he be sure? Even if the sound was mortalkind, who could possibly be up here now? Constantine was here somewhere, but the guide had indicated that his followers had traversed the base of the tower. It was not known whether they had entered the tower. The groan reached his ears again and, with the foreboding of a trap, he knew his decision had been made for him. The right door it was then, he thought resignedly. For a moment his thigh began to burn. Taking a deep breath he forced the pain out of his mind.

Now was not the time to give into any easy road of despair either. Going back or using his injury as an excuse seemed no different. Both could be seen only as an admission of failure. So, with the injury forgotten, he dropped low and drew the short sword once again, with practised ease. A few paces brought him to the door, and a swift glance inside revealed only a wide room in which a body lay prone on the floor. A second glance indicated that the room was extremely large, but there was no way to see if there was anyone else there, other than by going inside.

With a deep breath and a heart racing at an unnatural pace, Cappa dived through the gap, side-stepped twice and made wild sweeping slashes with his blade to either flank, where someone might have been waiting to attack. Relief spread across his face when it became clear that nobody was about to charge and that the prone body was the only mystery. He wiped the sweat from his brow and wondered if that had been caused by the exertion, the heat or his leg? Taking yet another quick look to either side, he finally knelt beside the body and pulled gently on the shoulder, rolling the body onto its back.

"Atronius," he gasped, glad to see him alive, but also well aware he needed medical attention, and soon. "By Jupiter, what have they done to you?"

Atronius opened his eyes, blinked as if to focus and smiled weakly. "It is good...to see you...my friend."

"Are you hurt? I cannot find any wounds? No blood?"

"They are wounds...of the mind, Marius. Of the mind...and the blood has dried."

"I don't understand."

"It is quite simple, you oaf," spoke a familiar voice from behind. "The Mage has broken his mind."

A voice as familiar to Cappa, as breathing was to any other.

Cappa froze for an instant, for the voice was like a blow to the depths of his very soul. He could not speak as the realisation of who was behind him overwhelmed his training. He had been strange, yes, but this? No it was not possible, not even he would stoop to this level of betrayal!

Cappa moved then, but it was too late. The blade bit deeply into his back, forcing him to gasp and stumble sideways. The stumble had saved his life, but as he glanced towards his assailant it was clear that his demise would not be long delayed.

"He is like you, Marius Capparticus, descendant of the Brundisium betrayer. Long overdue my personal attention."

The blade dug deeper the second time and the pain shot through Cappa's shoulder, causing him to arch and lose control momentarily. He knew that such wounds were not to kill, they were to cripple and humiliate an enemy. This oaf was toying with him, and he reached out and flailed desperately to retain that thought. Then, from within, came that familiar anger. Here was not my time, his head screamed and his body responded...he rolled away from his assailant.

"That is hardly going to help. However, I may as well finish off this fool now, seeing as you will not be going anywhere."

Cappa fought desperately to break the haze that masked his vision with pain. The backs of both legs felt sticky with blood, the wounds were deep and began to raise a small doubt, just a small one, but it would be enough to make him collapse. No, his mind screamed again, if that happened it would be over and, as before, as always, he was not ready for defeat just yet. He allowed a momentary pause in a kneeling position and looked up for the first time.

"Porta?" he said, the voice rising an octave, the eyes widening in disbelief.

"Surprised?" smiled Porta, taking a step towards him and viciously swinging a blade he carried in the right hand, then sidestepped to try and dig once more with the dagger in the left.

Cappa again rolled, but as soon as his back touched the floor both legs collapsed and his vision blurred. The next few moves were instinctive, as a lifetime of training took over and he rolled twice to the left and was again on his knees, prone for the next move. I cannot see, the pain is winning. Must...keep him occupied...I must talk...

"Why?"

"Why what, you fool?"

"Why this betrayal? We were like a family, all of us. We never wanted this to happen, but we are here now and nobody had a choice, but to survive as best we could. No one has betrayed you!"

"Very sweet, Cappa, very sweet indeed. It is also a whole load of shit! Shit designed by your heathen leaders and given freely by your Gods, to keep you happily sacrificing your puny existence for their pleasure!" raged Porta, spittle rolling off his chin, while all Cappa could do was wait for his vision to return. "I tried to forget, but you all made it impossible. Valenus, Scipio, *you*! Nothing could wipe away the memory...nothing!"

Cappa rose to stand, quickly spotting Porta on the far side of Atronius, with roughly ten paces between them. "Memory?" he asked, trying again to delay any further heavy movements, as his free hand checked the wounds more closely. "Explain."

"Explain?" Porta began.

The insanity in his voice finally brought home to Cappa what the feeling of dread had been trying to tell him. Here was the spy, not Aarun. Porta! That laugh, this was why it had irritated him so much recently. All those tiny innuendoes, odd expressions and barbed comments now began to fit into place.

"I'll explain alright," Porta continued, swaying from side to side, almost babbling the words out in a mad rush to vindicate his actions. "The rape and murder of my mother and sister by a Roman senator, Flavius. Senator Flavius no less, Julius' uncle, do you think I joined the legion by accident! Yes, you can sneer, Cappa, but I am a runaway slave, but not just anyone, for I have the blood of a senator on my hands and the memory brings me immense pleasure."

Porta laughed like a lunatic, while the swaying almost toppled him over. Cappa took a few steps forward, but the eyes soon opened again and the hatred was terrifying.

"Going somewhere, my *General*," Porta mocked, again crouching into a guarded position, moving closer to the prone Atronius. "I think not. This is somewhat boring, so why not come over here and I will put you out of your misery."

"Misery, Porta. What would you know of misery? A slave! So what!" Cappa shouted, knowing the only way to remain conscious now was to become angry and stay mad. Not really too difficult under the circumstances.

They began to circle slowly, each more than aware that any misjudgement or slip would now decide this uneven contest. It was obvious that Porta had only to wait and allow the inflicted injuries to weaken Cappa, who already showed the white pallor of someone seriously ill from blood loss.

Porta had started to listen to Cappa's heated response, but after the first sentence or so it had all seemed irrelevant. All he could think about was his hatred of what this man stood for and fought to defend. What all of those fools fought to defend. He knew better, though, as the Mage had explained everything quite clearly and had promised revenge on all those who had brought such terror to a happy family from Macedonia. Or rather that was where his mother had originated, while the father had defied Roma and the descendants had been sold into slavery, pain and eventual rape and death. His father and his brothers were the first to die under the injustice of Roman law.

He recalled the rain as he ran back to the villa, having barely turned sixteen, to find that the senator and his guests had decided that a little fun was called for, and had proceeded to rape his mother and sister after some recent slave rebellion had been defeated. His sister had only just turned eighteen. Such barbarity, such evil, could not have gone unpunished and they had plotted to poison the senator and then run to the mountains and freedom.

A stupid plan really, with little or no hope of success, and his sister had already decided otherwise: she committed suicide. It had been the last straw, *the last insult*. A few months later a second slave rebellion had exploded across the region and Porta used this distraction to avoid the guards, who naturally stood at the villa's defences rather than search a child.

The poison had worked well on the senator and his aide and, deciding escape was impossible, Porta's mother had told him to leave and gain a head start. There was after all no point in both of them dying for this crime, as the local citizens would almost certainly demand retribution. He had refused at first, torn between his loyalty and the desire to flee. He had tried to convince her that they could escape together, but she was fifty now and the mountain life would have killed her anyway. No, he must leave now.

He had gone no further than the courtyard before returning to the main living quarters, where, miraculously, no other servants had appeared to discover the dying senator. He had one last thing to do...

"He screamed like a stuffed pig!" Porta stated aloud, shocked to hear his own voice, but continued anyway, not caring about whatever Cappa had said. "A *pig*, by Hades, a compliment to such a *fat* buffoon."

"The senator? You mean the senator?" asked Cappa, noticing that Porta had slowly closed the circle without noticing where Atronius lay. A few hand signals had enabled the two to agree that, should he pass close enough, Atronius would grab at the legs and Cappa would make his one and only strike for survival. Looking back at Porta, he smiled and lowered his sword marginally. "The one you killed?"

"Yes. Yes, I stuck my dagger deep into the throat and twisted it down and down. I did it slowly so that he could feel each tiny movement and I watched the horror creep up into his eyes. Then he started to kick and fight, but the poison was designed to shrink the throat to prevent the victim from calling for help. So he struggled and I think it is that part I remember most. Just as I did with that brat of his..."

"Brat?" Cappa's eyes widened, suddenly realising why the name Flavius had rung so many bells. It was Julius' uncle! Why had this admission refused to register in his head?

"Yes, that scum Julius!"

"He is here?"

"Yes, and I stuck my dagger in his throat and watched with pleasure as the blood flowed onto the cobbled floor. It was odd, he took a long time to die that one, almost made me sorry to have to slit his throat."

Cappa stopped circling suddenly, the anger had reached breaking point, and the blood loss was reaching the point of no return. Julius, the youngster, here and now...*dead*, but that was impossible, he was at the river! *Constantine?*

"You back-stabbing, treacherous heathen!" he screamed, and lunged with such speed that the sword bit deeply into Porta's sword arm. A scream and the sound of the metal clanging on the stone signified the release of the weapon, but his blind fury just kept his own blade swinging hard for Porta's head.

"Die, you heathen!" he screamed again and again, and struck numerous times, but never with a killing weight and his energy began to fade, the vision blurred. "Damn you to hell for all eternity, Porta," he cursed. "We have all had a hard life, but we have not taken it upon ourselves to walk the path you have chosen. Damn you to hell! Julius is at the river you fool. *Constantine* is here with us. Julius was not the person you killed."

"No? Well, no matter. I will skewer that scum at a later date. Your friends are failing at the river and soon the whole world will be at our disposal. Shall I let you live, Marius? Should I let you have a life...as my slave? No, I could never trust you. So death it is!"

Porta retrieved his sword easily, and the sweeping strike struck Cappa's good leg causing him to drop to his knees, unable to lift his own sword in defence. His lack of energy and loss of blood had ended further resistance.

"I will go where I please, Cappa. If anything, my Master has a very long list of plans for your soul. It is not me who will be going to hell. It is *you*!"

Cappa watched the blade rise slowly and sat back on his haunches. The feeling of gloom had dissipated and vanished now and the vision finally darkened to blot out the inevitable blow that would end his life. Perhaps it was now finally over? Perhaps now he would be allowed to sleep in peace?

Issus crouched on the crest of the hill and slowly moved forward to peer through the long grass. What awaited him belied any possible description. He was a simple man who believed in defending his own people, but the recent events had robbed them all of this basic purpose to their fighting. Now, for the first time, he suddenly realised that, although he had previously supported peace with Roma, the flush of excitement when war had been declared had been greater. Now, as then, his people did not seem to have much of a choice in this world either. Fight or die. Perhaps that was nature's way? Only the strong survive to perpetuate the species, and yet the suffering involved must surely make Mother Nature evil and cold-hearted.

Issus chuckled softly as he watched a long, winding column of goblins cross the very crude bridge, built at the narrowest part of this Great River. It would not have taken much to set it on fire with a few barges soaked in oils, but the plans had now altered. Now the forces across the river were to be allowed to cross and those with him would seek to delay their advance as much as possible. Twenty-four hours they had demanded. They would be lucky to get ten!

Behind him the grass rustled lightly, as another person assumed a prone position next to him.

"Any estimate as to how many are now over, Issus?" Arnim asked politely, having already accepted that Issus would command, due to his skirmishing experience.

"No, my Lord," Issus began, still watching the bridge. "A force of wolves and those tiny creatures crossed and rode north, but we have nobody to counter their speed and we are better off with them not here. At a guess I would say about ten thousand or so have so far crossed, but..."

"But?" echoed Arnim.

"A little earlier the forces on the far side suddenly took up the march, but went back the way they had come. Then several formations crossed again and others began to build a camp, as though they did not intend to move or to attack our left. It was bizarre, but I am not complaining."

Arnim's face was full of anxiety, as two more large formations of orcs began to sing as they tramped back across the bridge, which swayed and jolted with the river's flow.

"Do you think they know of our plan?" he asked, not taking his eyes from the bridge.

"How? You said yourself that only five of you attended the meeting. Now I am added to that list."

"Yes, but perhaps they are recalling them for their own purposes. Perhaps a change in command has made them alter their own plans? It is not unheard of for a new commander to choose other options to achieve better results."

Issus nodded, pondering a little the real purpose of his task, to tie up as many of the enemy as possible on a flank that would be unimportant this day, then he slowly crawled back to the far side of the hill to sit in more comfort. Arnim followed.

"How many did you bring with you, my Lord?"

"Four thousand of my own warriors, two thousand dwarves, two hundred elven archers."

"While I have eight hundred of my people here, giving us a total of around seven thousand."

Arnim expression became resigned to his duty, he then waved for a small group of officers to join them. Issus turned to look at the hobbit. They were odd, small, hairy and yet extremely strong and hardy. They had taken his people by surprise simply by their size, but they wielded their weapons with skill and fought unarmed in a way that mesmerised most of them. Proud and yet humble, this hobbit had the authority to seize command, but had without hesitation accepted that Issus should initially remain in charge, as he knew the ground and the most effective way to delay a larger enemy. Now, it seemed, this was about to change…

"We should attack them at the bridge," Issus suggested, already knowing the answer.

"Yes." There was nothing else to say.

"Then you should command, not me. My experience is better used harassing the enemy and striking in small groups."

"Yes."

"How do we proceed?"

Arnim reached over and lightly gripped Issus' shoulder to acknowledge the weight of the admission.

"We strike fast and hard. No formations and no formalities, then with the dwarves and elves we demonstrate in the woods to make as much noise as possible. It is essential that we pin down here as many of them here as possible."

Issus rose as Arnim's officers joined them, it would be a short discussion.

"I will leave the details to you, my lord," he said, with a slight bow of the head. "Meanwhile I will take my people and rearrange a few heads in preparation."

Arnim smiled as Issus moved away to gather together the chosen few to join him in the initial foray. This task would be their day and no mistake. Today they would write a history worthy of his decision to leave the mountain fortress of the hobbits and join the struggle for freedom. He regretted only that his daughter might already have joined the Gods, but something told him she was not dead. He could not put a finger on why, it was almost a premonition, a superstition perhaps.

If she was dead, he would somehow know and that feeling had yet to smother his last hope of seeing Helin again. He had to keep on hoping, no matter what transpired here as the goblins reacted to Issus' disruptive raid.

This would be a long day.

A few leagues to the west, General Kol stood atop the tower and looked out at the array of enemy regiments poised to strike across the Great River.

Against the lower island stood Elvandar with the remaining elves and a sprinkling of dwarven regiments. Facing the waterfall stood Crassus with the Roman contingent that had not gone with Julius, the dwarven legion and the elven legion, plus all the archers that could be gathered and another sprinkling of dwarven regiments, serving to bolster the central defence.

At long last the catapult and scorpion projectile weapons had arrived from the capital, where a contractor had spent months building them. These weapons had been placed halfway down the hill to fire directly at the bridge or the waterfall, whichever was required. Crassus had sworn by their efficiency to destroy enemy charges, but Kol was sceptical of anything that pinned him to an unmoveable defence. However, he knew they had little choice other than to use them, so he had ordered Crassus to place them at the most advantageous location possible. It would then be the dictates of the final battle to come that would vindicate Crassus' faith.

At the Great Bridge, or rather its remains, where four out of six large pillars still stood, the enemy preparations for the crossing could be openly observed. Here stood the few dwarven regiments known to be of stout heart and ability, following the Roman training, which had benefited even the most experienced warriors. It was here that the greatest fear rested and yet at the upper bridge, the Cart Bridge, the enemy had already established a small bridgehead and fully intended to expand this captured ground, this very morning.

It was here that Arnim rode out to join Issus. If they failed, then their left flank would be overwhelmed and they would have no choice except retreat. So much depended on them, but the plans of last night could not be undone now.

With the dispositions agreed, they now stood outnumbered almost four to one at the broken bridge, yet they had to fight with utter determination and give ground, to draw at least half the enemy across the river. It would then be a simple matter of killing, and who could do it faster. If he planned the commitment of his reserve of twenty regiments correctly, then they could push the enemy into a tight semicircle with their backs to the river. If they were then so tightly packed that they could not fight effectively, his troops on the circumference would face no restrictions.

It would be difficult, and it would be a matter of killing and nothing else. Just killing.

Kol turned to see a dwarf watching him sternly, and for a few seconds could not place the face...

"Khazumar?"

"It is just a flying visit, General," Khazumar stammered, exhaustion written across his face; or could it be consternation? "I must return, but we did not wish to send this by messenger."

"Continue."

"We have sighted a vast force of the enemy returning to their central position from the enemy's far right at the Cart Bridge. It seems they are not going to attack Arnim after all. Should we proceed? We still have time to retire, should you desire us to do so."

Retire? Now! No, they had to go on. To retreat now was unthinkable!

"No, it is too late. The enemy are preparing to strike across the bridge. We cannot retire in broad daylight in the face of an attacking enemy. No, we are committed with no return, Khazumar. Your warriors will not arrive back here in time to help any decision at this point, or on the left. No, continue on, and if the Gods are with us we will prevail."

Khazumar smiled, and Kol wondered when he had last seen the dwarf do so, but before he could remember the dwarven lord was gone. He had turned abruptly and vanished down the stairs, the very stairs that Karr had ascended with the tray of chicken and wine hanging from his mouth just yesterday, or was it the day before? The days had blended together to fade his timeline.

Now it was Kol's turn to smile as the memory flooded back. He had remembered the last smile, it had been during a drinking contest many moons ago. The memory was a welcome distraction.

It was going to be a long day.

⟨⇵⟩⋇⟨⇵⟩⋇⟨⇵⟩

Igluk spat in contempt towards the nearest chieftain and kicked another.

"Filth, scum, vagabonds of shit!" he screamed, kicking a third chief. "You dare to disobey!"

The fingers rose, the magic flashed and one chief, Igluk did not even notice which, screamed in a high-pitched voice before the very flesh on his torso began to melt. The screams continued while the others backed away, watching his internal organs fall to the floor, sizzling, as the chief tried desperately to put them back in, but failing.

"Who is next?" Igluk ranted, his eyes glowing with hatred and, as if the dying chief had not existed, he stepped over the corpse towards one of the more vocal opponents of his plans. "*Well*! No one left with any guts? Now isn't this so sweet to smell, your *fear*! Return to those filthy cretins you call your tribes and prepare for the morning's work. Where that Scipio mortalkind filth failed, we will succeed, and the *Master* will reward us all."

"We should wait for the flanking forces to return..."

The fingers flashed again, and this time the head exploded majestically, spraying all but Igluk with the brains of the speaker.

"Still *here*?"

In brief, no they were not, as they had all, including the black-goblin and orka leaders, moved rapidly to rejoin their peoples. The further away they remained from this uncontrollable fool the safer they felt.

This was the final day, as Igluk knew in his bones. The alliance had been bled for over two weeks now and must be at the end of its endurance. Yes, now was the time to strike. He would attack all three crossing points together and, in case of disaster, use the flank forces as a reserve. He would not be caught again as he had the last time. No, he would keep a reserve to add weight to the final victory.

It was going to be a short day, because by dawn tomorrow he would be at that tower, and he would personally take Kol's head.

Yessss...*Personally*!

<hr />

There it was again. A voice faint, but distinctly familiar, which seemed to float on the very air. Then a word, but what was the word? Distant, as though it was in your mind and not spoken, quietly spoken as if not to disturb, yet so familiar. So familiar...

Did it matter? Did you really want to know? Yes, but why? The word was too far away and would take a great effort to find. Could you really be bothered, as here and now was so peaceful, almost pure blissfulness? No hatred, no treachery, just a peaceful calm that soaked through every negative thought to replace it with a warmth of such depth that even a sceptic, such as he was, could not resist.

But the voice was so familiar...

Familiar...

Who? Who was calling me? Yes, that was it! The word was my name, of course, but the voice...who did the voice belong to? Was it the Gods speaking to him? No, somehow they would make themselves known and yet, as the thought developed, it vanished to be replaced with a light, then another light. Two small pinpricks in the sky tempted his further investigation, but were somehow far beyond his reach. Was it the sky?

Then the voice again...

Helin wiped away the tears, grinning insanely, as Cappa opened one eye and then the other, blinked a few times and weakly returned her smile.

The voice had indeed been very familiar. Just as familiar as the sun that slowly rose in the sky every morning. While Igluk dreamed of victory and glory, Kol of survival, Julius and Khazumar of keeping the surprise element, Issus and Arnim of selling their lives dearly, Cappa had already fought his own battle and had won a brief reprieve. He would see another dawn.

While the Mage, in the tower where Cappa lay, had only just begun!

It was already a long day!

Zeus sat beside a large pool and silently fumed. His brother's skill at manipulating the acts of mortalkind had almost brought about the destruction of the one creature that might possibly save the day. In all his years he had never really cared much about the mortalkind. The procreation was illuminating, but their incessant demands to improve their status had always been an irritant.

Ever since Hades had interfered in his creation of the Republic, sending numerous enemy armies under the command of that oaf Mercury, this whole situation had become more and more annoying.

He would rather have just let his brother believe he had won, so as to have at least some idea of where the next scheme would originate. How was he to know that a soul as black as Cassius Evictus would be born in the time of the Romans? It was almost five thousand years since any mortalkind had had a direct link with any of the higher beings in this universe, and even then it had only been one or two who had deigned to visit them and begin the interference.

Why did some deities always have to interfere?

Hades had chosen his domain. Why should it be any of his business, if he chose to seduce the odd mortal for his own interests? So what if the Romans called him Jupiter? He had loads of different names. In fact he could not recall what his original one had been! Did they even have names at the beginning? He simply could not recall.

Anyway, if that brother wanted to argue, *he* had refused to use his real name and was known to the mortals as Vulcan or Pluto! So why were his interests so constantly ridiculed? Had he defeated his father to have them regurgitated, for them to continually ridicule him? No, so why could he not simply live within his own domain?

Hades' constant interference was due to boredom. Zeus had known this before he had thought of such childish questions. They had distributed the domains evenly between them after his father had been deposed, and it was his brother's overpowering jealousy that continually drove him to such useless wastes of energy. There was after all an entire galaxy to be explored, but no, it always had to be on this earth, where the void had existed for an eternity, that his interference took form. Zeus could not resist a small chuckle, and yet peace had never been theirs to keep even by mortalkind's hands, never mind the constant bickering of the Gods.

He turned as another deity, a shimmering cloud of bright colours, joined him, but refused to change into the familiar form of a mortalkind. It was so demeaning, she thought.

"*No!*" said Zeus, irritably.

"*I wish you wouldn't do that!*" Venus replied, just as irritably.

"*If my brother wants her to attend him any longer, then he is to stop this infernal interference with the void and the dimensions. Otherwise...she stays here with me!*" Zeus said, looking away in disgust.

"*You are both acting like spoilt children. Why can't either of you leave those poor creatures alone? Are you truly disputing who may go though the void and who must remain?*" Venus laughed, still unable to fathom how such an argument had lasted so long.

"*It is far more than that and you of all our kind should recognise the fact that Hades is untrustworthy! If he breaks the void, then we will all have to live with those vermin he has created, using skills that were not his to use. Are you happy to live with that lot? Well? No, I did not think so. Now leave! I have things to consider and this matter is becoming extremely tedious and boring. Go and fill someone's stockings or something!*"

"*You must discuss this with your brother, my Lord.*"

"*Why?*"

"*This cannot only be because of the kidnapping of Persephone. Is it possible there may be another reason that Hades and his minions are trying to leave…?*"

"*Did I not tell you to leave me in peace?*"

"*We must…*"

"*Leave!*"

Zeus never noticed her leave, yet the feelings of guilt still reappeared to further irritate his stretched nerves. Why did she always make him feel guilty? Why did she always attach herself to the forlorn, the needy and the unhappy? Why did she always arrive just at the very peak of his emotional disarray, then abruptly throw all possible blackmail at him? Of course he knew precisely why, her powers related mainly to procreation, a basic instinct, then giving it to any creature in overwhelming quantity.

If she liked the creature she would control the inundation, but to those she disliked she would give without stopping. Even to Zeus, the complete arrival of everything ever desired at the very same time would be enough to send him insane, never mind to the minds of lesser creatures.

It was her great skill.

Too much of a good thing always invariably became an emotional strain. Domination therefore was gained, not only by the promise of more of the same, but also by the promise to take it away. Quite ingenious, he thought. Less fun though, as he personally preferred to vaporise those who had decided that disrespect was in their best interests.

Well not this time! I have enough to cope with and I think it is time I made a personal appearance, he decided.

It is time this ended once and for all!

It had started as a long day, but he was about to make it considerably shorter for someone!

✧✦✧✦✧

The air was dense, hard to breathe, and even the attempt sent shearing pain through his chest. His lungs moved, but even the slightest expansion brought tears of pain to Cappa's eyes. The room was full of hobbits and dwarves while, on the far side, Atronius Sulla was receiving the attention he so desperately needed but, even through the mists of pain, he knew there was something missing.

"Where is Porta?" he demanded, rising to one elbow and biting back the searing pain that ran across his back. "He…"

"I know," Helin soothed, wiping the sweat from his brow and encouraging the injured man to lie back and relax, with little success it must be said. "From what we can see it is clear he was the spy and not Aarun, as you suspected. I was wrong to blame Aarun for the death of my warrior-maidens. Porta's treachery here proves this beyond doubt. I am still finding it difficult to believe…poor Aarun, we have greatly misjudged him…"

"Yes, but I think it was mainly you, Helin," interrupted Cappa, refusing the kind hand urging him to lay back. "But where is he?"

"He?"

"Porta? His body…where is it? It may give us some idea as to where Aarun is."

"You should rest…"

"There is no time, Helin. Just tell me! He was here for a reason. How else could he have travelled here, if it was not by the hand of that Mage, who must also be in this tower. What happened? Why did he not finish me off?"

It was obvious in that dust-ridden room that Cappa was not so injured as to allow such pain to prevent his force of will dominating the situation. Many now saw, for the first time, his depth of character, a character held deep within, rather than expressed outwardly. They began to doubt their Lord Komar's rash decision not to support this mortalkind many weeks ago, as he now seemed to show true strength and leadership quality, a fact that did not escape Komar's attention either. He felt his earlier guilt resurface.

"I can answer that in part," Komar said, walking over and kneeling. "Helin became concerned when you did not return, but Kola and the lights above us gave me some doubts as to your decision to even go in the first place. So we came to look for you and to determine what was happening in the upper chambers. Before we got here, however, we came across by pure chance your Porta, about to strike you down. A minute later and he would have finished the deed, as you clearly expected."

"So what happened to make him change his mind?"

"Helin did that all by herself. She moved in and with a speed I cannot begin to describe, she brought her foot up to strike the dropping arm holding the sword. A few inches more and the blade would have bitten too deep for any medicine to help. You would have died, friend, and no mistake."

Cappa nodded his head in recognition of thanks for the deed and forced himself to rise further. He permitted a brief smile to Helin and for a moment he found the world to be a better place. His eyes floundered in hers and the urge to just let go and surrender to whatever fate had decided made him dizzy. Then, with the familiar sharpness, his training took over again and the moment was gone, leaving Helin's heart beating all the faster for the loss.

"You should rest..." protested Helin again, in vain, but she allowed the full weight of the words to drift away as Cappa offered her the cold stare of disobedience. His was not the will to allow a maiden to issue orders, but he was of course very grateful for the helping hand as he tried to stand.

"I have already told you that there is no time, Helin. Porta was brought here for a reason. He was here either to kill Atronius, or to counter something else, but what? Until we know this reason none of us can rest..."

Komar held Cappa tightly as he staggered for the umpteenth time, and watched with fascination as the man bit his own lip to make it bleed profusely, to prevent any outcry. With a gentle push Komar helped him stand again and their eyes met briefly, and the strength of character suddenly made everything clear, so much so that Komar laughed, as the obvious was no longer hidden in the clouds of doubt and superstition. Porta was the counterbalance to this man. A mortalkind for a mortalkind, it was so obvious as to have been oblivious in their search for the superstitious reasons.

"It is you, General," he said, deliberately using the correct rank, finally accepting that matters were far beyond his control. "He was here to stop you from doing something that perhaps you are fated to complete. Perhaps you are the missing variable that the enemy fears? Perhaps you are their real enemy."

"I am not that important. It must be something else, surely?"

"No!" shouted Atronius, as forcefully as possible, causing everyone to turn momentarily. "During the interrogation, Cappa, you were the second topic they demanded to discuss." A series of gasps made Atronius smile inwardly, as he almost began to enjoy the pain. Had he changed so much? They must have fooled just about everyone with his deception, where he pretended to be the oracle instead of the elf, which made it all the more satisfying.

"Yes, my friends, I am not the Oracle as your own people openly stated, just an ordinary legionary. Of course they did not know this, and we bought time for everyone to fight on and to allow the true Oracle to achieve his destiny. While they tortured me, Aarun had time to evaluate the enemy's true purpose and thus give us all at least a chance of victory."

"Surely not me!" Cappa exclaimed, pulling a face of utter disbelief.

"No, no of course not. It is *Aarun*! Why on earth did you think we discussed the deception? Komar is right about the equilibrium of good and evil, the Mage admitted this to me. You are the opposite to Porta..."

Cappa brushed aside Komar's helping arm and moved back towards the original entrance. It all made sense now. At the time he had assumed the deception was completely true and the arrival of his people had foretold the equally majestic arrival of the *Oracle of Zeus*.

He had once more not paid enough attention, but when people had discussed mystical issues he had for some reason been completely baffled and bored. Now that lack of patience and understanding had led him to this place, without ever truly understanding the faith and trust given to him by Aarun six months ago, in that tiny garden. By the Gods, he could be so ignorant sometimes!

"Do we know where Aarun is now?" he asked, without looking round. "Has anyone made a search?"

"I think it is pretty obvious, he is in the upper chambers," Atronius stated, clearly struggling to remain conscious, and now speaking with both eyes closed.

Cappa grimaced as a familiar feeling of dread, more profound than ever, flooded back into his mind. What in all the Gods' names was *he* doing here? Why now? Aarun was the oracle in the tapestries...Great! So why did he not simply destroy their enemies and finish this war and save so many lives? Which was the evil side? Was it them, for wanting to enslave and destroy and return to the true homelands? Or us, for allowing this slaughter to continue? Would it have been so difficult to achieve peace? How many more fatherless families must there be before someone or something stepped in to end this perpetual strife!

Cappa frowned and sighed heavily, a fact that brought many a smile to those still in the room. He was slowly becoming the Cappa recognised and respected by all. The pain had indeed subsided, but he knew the injuries had been severe. His pain was but a fraction of that which so many others had experienced, and it galled him to think that others would lose their loved ones by the end of this day. He could do nothing to prevent this. Or could he?

"Nobody has confirmed what happened to Porta?" he eventually asked, turning to face Helin. "Well?"

"I cut him to pieces," Helin responded with pride, and a smile that belied the real danger she had actually faced.

Porta had not, by any stretch of the imagination, been easy to finish off. It had taken six of them, three of whom were injured in the struggle, before they had cornered the fiend whose eyes had begun to burn red. Not wishing to allow anyone else the honour, Helin had then thrown down her weapons and advanced on the prone creature that only resembled Porta, and proceeded to systematically break bones.

When Porta began a circular lunge with his remaining dagger, she simply ducked and trapped the arm between her two hands, which were moving in opposite directions, and the first break made them all cringe. The scream had been satisfying, but not as much as the sight of the white bone on the black leather armour. The arm had snapped at the elbow like a twig. With nowhere to go the struggle of course continued with Porta standing tall over the hobbit, and yet he too remembered the favourite story of the encounter of the legionary and the hobbit. It was about to be repeated, but something in Porta's expression had changed. There was no longer a look of certainty, as he began to hesitate.

Helin's extended foot easily blocked a wild kick from Porta and the snap of his shin was audible to everyone. The pain, however, did not seem to matter to Porta, who continued to shuffle on his broken limbs, as if nothing had happened. His good left arm had reached for her throat and for a few seconds the grip astonished her with its ferocity, and panic momentarily froze her reaction, as her breath became shorter and shorter. Had he been using two hands she would almost certainly have had her throat crushed, but with only one hand it was easy to dislodge the fingers and break the grip. Then, with an almost nonchalant sidestep, she twisted the arm in a full circle. This arm did not break, but the tendons and muscles tore apart with a tearing wrench that brought the creature to its knees.

"For my love and for all those betrayed," Helin had then said vehemently, as she spun in a complete circle to drive her heel into the man's throat to snap the neck, as cleanly as if she had decapitated him with a sword.

"He is dead, but his body crumpled to dust before our very eyes," added Komar, eventually, bringing Helin back from those very fresh memories.

"Then we need to find Aarun and we need to do so soon."

Within a minute Cappa was moving towards the upper chamber. Behind him Helin was astonished by the speed at which he moved, while Komar reached forward and gripped her arm.

"He is on a different journey, young one. He must make this one alone."

At first Helin struggled, but not too hard. What Komar had said was somehow true and she knew that, if anyone followed, they would only be in the way. Nonetheless this did not diminish the desire to go and her heart weighed heavily, as the sound of his footsteps dwindled in the corridor.

Outside Cappa moved swiftly along the corridor against a heavy wind that bit through his garments and caused him to shiver. How he managed to remain standing was a miracle in itself, as was the clarity of his mind. The thought that his actions were no longer his own ebbed and flowed in his subconscious, causing him to stop at corners and again try to reason out what his real purpose was, beyond the task of finding Aarun. If he did find him, for example, what chance would he have against the Mage? He slowly felt the familiar anger rising yet again, just as it had at the fortress gate.

That experience had been only a few hours ago and yet he now stood, after a near-death experience, gazing suspiciously at the high steps before him. His wounds had been fatal, he knew that from inflicting so many on so many other people that he had lost count. Yet, here he stood, proof that someone had intervened. His memory gave Helin's voice as the cause for his return, but that did not explain the sudden loss of pain due to the wounds. Even at a minimum he ought to convalesce for at least a month with the two cuts Porta had inflicted. More to the point, how much blood does the mortalkind body hold? He must have lost at least half, so how was he still standing?

He knew he had someone to thank, but it would have to wait.

Where the hell was this corridor going anyway, he cursed, and began to move a little slower. Up ahead he saw a prone shape and looked behind. No, nothing following, but up ahead someone was definitely leaning against the wall. Where is that...good...at least I had the brains to retrieve my gladius!

Cappa knelt as low as possible and inched forward in order to keep the sound of his steps to a minimum. On the smooth floor and wall at this pace it was not too difficult, but it was always best to be a little cautious. The form looked mortalkind...yes, definitely mortalkind. Who?

Then it came to Cappa like a thunderbolt.

"Constantine!" he said almost without thinking, then crouched a little lower in case the person ahead was not a friend after all.

However, there was no reaction, nothing. Rising a little, but keeping a good prone posture, Cappa moved forward a little more and noted that several other bodies were blocking the corridor. The curved nature of the passageway had hidden this from him, but as he took a few more steps it was obvious that none of them were alive.

He now saw the blood running along the floor, and noted the mixture of green and red, which merged to develop a tinted bluish purple.

As he took a few more tentative steps, a shudder ran down his back, and as he gazed at the first body he felt his stomach churn. Porta had been wrong, as he had tried to tell him. As he had suspected, Porta had not killed Julius, but Constantine and the other survivors from the gate. For a moment Cappa stood transfixed by the large blood clots on the youth's throat, where the trachea had been ripped open by a short blade. Death would have been slow if the aggressor had chosen, but on this occasion the strike had been deep and only the youngster's will to live had made the ordeal last longer.

The whole of the torso was covered in a deep red coverlet, where the lifeblood had found a ready exit. Of the others there was little to say, except that Cappa identified a few of the legionaries. They lay with their faces up, while a few lay faced down on the floor. An enormous axe was buried deep in the back of one, exposing the man's spinal cord. Another axe protruded from the ribs, from behind, of another.

A large group of goblins had clearly ambushed them at the clearing on the far side, where the tunnel ended, and had cut them all down. By the layout, it seemed probable that the youngster had spotted a band of goblins and eagerly chased after them, only to be waylaid later by a force ten times his number, led by Porta. They had fought and died well, if that was any consolation, killing well over thirty of their assailants. It had eventually come down to numbers and in this respect Constantine was deficient and therefore lost.

Cappa stopped at the far side after hopping through the cavalcade of corpses and took one last look at Constantine. What a waste! Why had the stupid fool run off like that after the skirmish at the middle-gate? Just a little patience and he could have gone with them, but he had been too occupied with finding Helin. Now the youth would see no more sunsets and somehow Cappa felt it was his fault. He had let Constantine down, who had never wanted much other than to remain in Cappa's good favour, and to retain his rank, no matter how lowly. Now it did not matter.

The melancholy might have continued for quite some time, as Cappa remembered the youth at the ambush in the woods, just south of the tributary bridge across the Rhodanus. He had been so eager to please and had never flinched when the death sentence was held over them for their alleged rebellion.

But Cappa was not allowed to wallow in self-pity for long. Other schedules began to pull on his sense of duty once again, as the floor began to vibrate. Slowly at first, and barely noticeable initially, but the jarring effect soon began to increase. Then, with sudden violence, the entire wall cracked and the floor began to rise and split asunder. The sound of thunder rolled along the corridor, forcing Cappa to cover his ears. Then, just as swiftly, a heavy silence filled the air punctuated by the fall of loose debris, but not before Cappa had been catapulted forwards, landing near a second wide opening in this maze of corridors.

Now there was no time to think, only time to act.

Up ahead was obviously where Aarun and the Mage had decided to resolve their differences, and perhaps decide the fate of the entire world. The air was dancing with small rivulets of lights, and although his breathing had been heavy before, Cappa now began to feel a constant pressure on his shoulders, almost buckling his legs. The pain returned to his back and thigh, while his head throbbed with a pain that was fast becoming unbearable. Magic had somehow been his protection, by Aarun no doubt, but this had now been withdrawn, leaving him a heap on the floor.

When the screech reached his ears it was a terrifying sound that reverberated through his head and brought instantaneous paralysis. Cappa could not move, dared not move, as the shadow fell across the broken corridor. With an effort he managed to stand, but he could not avoid taking several rearward paces, as a second screech filled the air. For the first time in his life Cappa felt *real* fear. Felt the icy breath of death on his face, and veered away from looking directly at the abomination that stood between him and Aarun.

"By the Gods, what are you?" he said, not really expecting an answer.

"*I am you, but from the other side. I am my enemy,*" the creature hissed. "*I am your hatred, your love of killing, your prejudices and your vices rolled into one entity. Manifested in one force, a force that protects this gateway to my Master's domain. Here you traverse the real world to the world of magic, mortalkind, how does it feel?*"

"I am but a mortal!" Cappa began, taking a deep breath and venturing forward a few steps. "Surely I am not worthy of your attention?"

"*Attention? No, you are not worthy of a long delay, but I find your attempts to delay your death amusing, mortal. Try again!*"

The wings now began to beat rapidly and Cappa quickly retreated along the corridor. This time it was not fear that carried him, but the fact that, further back the way he had come, the corridor was not so tall and considerably narrower. There the creature's wings would be neutralised and he could perhaps strike back as it pursued. Not much of a plan, but it might give him a chance. His only chance. As always the policy was never to give up, but for once the task seemed beyond his ability.

He reached the corridor only to find that the creature was now ahead of him and no longer following. By the Gods, how did that happen?

"Stupid mortalkind. Did you not listen? I am you, fool. I am you!"

It is me? What is that supposed to mean? If this thing is a part of me, on the dark side, then if I kill it, then do I kill myself on this side as well? How could it be me? What the hell do I do now?

"It is not you, Cappa! It is but fooling you because you know nothing of how the power affects your brain patterns, my friend. It is not in the corridor. It is only in your mind. It cannot harm you. Only you can harm yourself by allowing your mind to be broken. My enemy seeks to delay you. Look deeply within your heart Cappa, seek those arrogant ideals, and ignore the real world. Ignore the magic and seek your true destiny here with me. Help me fight this evil!"

"Aarun! Aarun! Where the hell are you?" shouted Cappa, shocked by the sudden voice echoing in his head.

"Do not despair, my friend, I am here and I am not. I have transported my thoughts, while I am in the next chamber, where I need you to distract our enemy. I need but a few seconds to allow our Lord Zeus to arrive, but the dark power is creating a permanent barrier. You...must...hurry, I...am...weakening."

It was, it has to be said, good to hear a friendly voice. To be honest, it had come at just the right moment, but even as Cappa searched his heart his feet still refused to move.

"What do you mean, this creature cannot harm me?"

"It is you. It...is...you. Hurry my friend. We must end this now. I feel that *HE* is coming. We must stop *HIM*. I cannot defeat *HIM*."

"Who?" Cappa yelled into thin air, unable even to notice the creature ahead of him, which began to advance on his prone position by the fallen rocks.

"To Hell with you and all that you represent!" Cappa spat as the creature neared, his fears now dominated by his friend's troubles. He had lost enough friends. "You do not exist!"

The image wavered, faded, returned, then finally vanished. A damnable game! That Mage was playing with his mind. Well, Aarun needs a distraction. Let's see if we can oblige.

Cappa was finally about to lose his temper!

⁃※⁃※⁃※⁃

"There it is," Issus gestured, with his outstretched hand. "We can hardly capture it, but maybe we can burn it a little!"

Arnim looked. Below them stretched a wide belt of tall lativicus trees, tall and conical shaped with deep green leaves. Beneath them heavy undergrowth was strangling the trunks. Looking a little further, he could see the open ground beyond undulating downwards in diminishing prominence towards a bridge, which was somehow rather disturbing.

On either side more trees rose just as high, but the open ground in between enabled a clear view of the bridge, which held their gaze. Constructed of numerous small boats, which seemed to struggle against the tidal current of the river, it seemed to sway and to give the impression of imminent collapse but, as each passing moment proved, it not only stayed afloat, but also resisted the powerful river. Here, at the one place where the cliffs of the lower river were surmountable, the great boulders further up river reduced the current sufficiently to protect the construction.

They had now been bitterly contesting the open ground north of the Orc Bridge for several hours. Little by little their numbers had dwindled and, as Arnim glanced to either side, he could not see a single warrior who did not have an injury of one kind or another.

"If we burn it," Arnim called back, "they will have to send others to repair it. A final effort is all we need."

Issus could only sigh in reply. He was as fit as ever and yet the bitterness of the fighting so far this day had diminished his reserves. He had fought the orcs and goblins several times and yet these seemed to have developed a greater level of cooperation. They fought better individually and, in short, their training must have been extensive. Either that or a great deal of magic was being used to make them so.

"We send most of our people back to the woods," Arnim continued. "There is little point in all of us perishing. We need only a few hundred for this final task. Issus, you will organise the people to return to the Great Bridge..."

"My Lord, I am better suited..."

"Do not argue. Look, they are already reorganising their ranks. It will not be long before they charge again. Take your people and the dwarves and leave immediately. The two southern companies I have already sent back to the bridge. The remainder of my people will take the honour of this final sacrifice."

"Surely there must be another way. If we retire to the woods we can delay them further..."

"And what will make them follow, Issus? No, if we charge they will see our desperation. They may assume we are defeated and charge forward once more into the woods. Then your people can add the final ambush before retiring."

"What of the elven archers?"

"Have many survived?"

Issus looked broken-hearted for a moment, as he recalled when the archers had been overrun by goblins, one hour earlier. In a flash they seemed to vanish from sight, as the bodies piled high and the screams of the goblins were horrifying. Not many of the elves returned from the melee, and the usual elven veneer of those that did had been shaken to its very core. Some even had tears on their cheeks. The well-known strength of the elf had broken but, just as quickly as it had happened, the survivors had banded together and immediately struck back by killing the goblin leader with a well aimed arrow.

"Not many," was all he could manage for a reply.

"Then take them with you as well."

Issus sighed once more, grasped the hobbit's forearm, which was tiny in comparison to his, but the grip was like iron.

"You know if you charge into the gap we created they will simply surround you at the bridge."

Arnim's eyes betrayed his understanding and seeking to hide this from Issus withdrew his forearm and reached down to his left side. With a swiftness that made even Issus step back he drew the curved blade from its sheath. Holding it high he noted how the sun glinted off of the edged weapon and felt his pride rise immeasurably. He had

had a good life and he could always see Helin in the next one. That was his only sadness, as he began to walk forward. Behind him he heard the singular scrape of the blades being drawn and the chosen five hundred kept pace with him as they approached the bridge.

Issus watched for a few seconds and then turned to the officers behind him.

"Pull our people back to the woods. We can do nothing more than delay these heathens now."

As they moved, they looked behind them hoping to catch a glimpse of the hobbits, but the sheer size of the goblins prevented this. What they did see was the flying arms and heads separated from the bodies of the unfortunate. That was enough to signal that Arnim had not been lost just yet but, as predicted, the enemy quickly surrounded them at the bridge. Issus ran to the top of the nearest rise. He had known the hobbit barely a day, and yet his friendship for this person had become immense.

Straining his eyes he searched the battlefield, but all he could see was the smoke from the burning bridge. When a great chorus of cheers went up in the enemy ranks he knew it was over. One by one the enemy turned back towards him, the sacrifice had worked.

"Tell the archers to try and slow down those orcs as much as possible," he commanded, to nobody in particular. Someone simply took up the responsibility and bolted off to forward the request. "Everyone else back to the woods. Now!" he added, as he caught up with some hobbits that refused to retire any further.

"There is nothing more to be done here."

He began to slap the tiny warriors wildly. Pushing a few towards the river. A few of the hobbit officers also began to do the same, but these hardy people simply ignored all further commands.

"What is wrong with you!" snapped Issus. "We all cared for Arnim, he was a great warrior. His last order was for you to retire to the wood. He has gone now. There is nothing you can do here except obey his last request!"

"His body must be retrieved," a warrior stated, flatly. "We are honour-bound to do so. Some of us cannot leave."

"That is sheer suicide! What would be the point of dying here? You must fight on in the trees and bring more honour to his name. To die a worthless death is an insult to his memory!"

Like a flash, ten or more swords were drawn, two expertly raised to Issus' throat.

"You would be wise to choose your words more carefully," a voice said over his shoulder. "These are Arnim's personal bodyguards."

Issus closed his eyes. "The more we argue here the closer the enemy steps and the less time we will have to set the ambush. Order these fools to lower their weapons!"

For a few seconds the sword's edge ran lightly against Issus' throat and he could feel the sticky flow of blood seeping down to his collar.

"Lower your weapons," said the voice.

Issus opened his eyes, turned to look at an older warrior. The eyes made him blink, as the stare returned was so potent he could not hold the gaze.

"You are?"

"Arrim."

"Well, Arrim, you would serve these people best if you could make them retire to the wood, where we will again stand and fight."

"They will not go," Arrim advised quietly, stepping closer to the warriors who had drawn their swords. "To us honour and duty mean everything. Ippanos!"

"Captain."

"You are correct in that you have not recovered Marshall Arnim's body. You are dishonoured, as indeed is the entire guard. Retrieve the corpse or die trying, if you wish to regain your honour! The remainder will move to the woods."

"As you command, Captain."

Issus watched as the small band of warriors quickly organised the surviving hobbits into four new companies. Then Ippanos swiftly organised captains for each group and one by one ordered them to the woods. Within a few minutes he returned, and with a small band of perhaps fifty hobbits Ippanos started to walk back the way they had all retired, back towards the bridge.

"What is the point of this?"

"They will die to regain the honour of the guard. They failed in their duty to keep him alive. Now they must join him or bring back his corpse. It is the code of the warrior."

Issus screamed. "Get back to the woods! This lunacy has gone on for long enough!"

Arrim bowed low and slowly walked back towards the last hobbit company, but it was already too late. Ippanos joined Arnim and for all its intent the sacrifice only added to the list of the dead.

It had been a pointless gesture, but one that perhaps made the other hobbits continue to fight. Issus was simply unable to understand.

Cappilius looked beyond the small hill and gazed at the triangular wood standing directly across their path. Here the ground was good for a flanking assault with not too many undulations in it to break up the formations. However, to the south and beyond the wood, he could clearly see a larger hill that fell away to break into several ridges interspersed with broken ground similar to where he now stood. Any fighting there would be bitter and free with little or no formation, while in the woods the tree-hugging conflict would be terrible. The day was already looking to be a long one. The crossing had been achieved, but there was so much they now had to accomplish.

He did not doubt that they would succeed, but in the back of his mind there lingered a single thought: just who exactly was destined to survive. Others claimed they never felt this foreboding before any conflict. If you were there you just had to get on with it and leave the results to the Gods, but this somehow seemed so lame. Did someone actually sit and point the finger...yes...you...it is your time. Cappilius smirked at the thought and wondered if that someone looked anything like Cappa? Must be, he added, just must be, otherwise there would no sense to this world.

For a moment his thoughts went back to the Rhodanus fort, where the Helvetii Uxudulum had killed his brother. Why he had not put that foul heathen to death at first sight was beyond him to understand, but for peace and unity he had agreed to stay his hand of vengeance. Later his own people had murdered him, but he still wished that duty had fallen to his hand. If the arrival had been just one hour earlier, his brother would have been alive and this fate would have been a little more bearable, but when did the Gods ever listen to a mortalkind's wishes?

To each side of him, and as far as the eye could see, a mass of men, dwarves and elves marched to try and envelope the enemy left, as agreed, and drive forward as quickly as possible. He noted how slow their progress was, for their training had been rudimentary at best. Some of the dwarven regiments struggled to keep in formation, never mind moving swiftly into the bargain. Not that it mattered as long as they fought, but at least a third of those present were of dubious quality in that respect too. Julius had described this as a gamble and the more he looked at the bedraggled formations out of line he wondered just how much of a gamble, and how many would actually stand?

The most dubious were the Cenitarn Regiments, which had originally stated that they served to protect the king and that fighting south of the river was not their duty. If not, then who else was to accept this duty? Indeed, would they stand? If they ran they would take a third of the total strength. He noted that a few cylindrical lines had reached his positions and identified the very Cenitarn he considered the weakest part of their line. Thanks for sending them to me, Julius!

He noted the Hildar following. Someone had seen sense and sent them ahead of everyone else giving them no choice as they stood to the forefront. Stand and fight, or run straight into the avenging arms of their brethren, who followed next. Mercy was not a trend that was well known to the Hildar, and one equalled only by their superiority and arrogance.

"This is going to be a really long day," Cappilius mumbled, and began to walk a little further along the hill to where his velites were resting from the night's exertions.

"What?" Julius enquired, turning in the saddle of the dapple-grey.

"Nothing, Julius, nothing at all. I just realised this was going to be a long day."

"True, noble friend, very true," Julius agreed. Then, after glancing off to his right, he asked, expectantly, "That broken ground to the south is going to cause us problems isn't it?"

"I'm afraid so. As soon as any formations reach that area they will break like waves on a beach. Then it will be up to the individual. The only real line of advance is along the riverbank or through that central wood before us."

"Well, I guess I can now tell you where your velites will stand, Cappilius."

"Sorry?"

"I want your people to lead the advance in that part of the field to the south, but do not expose your men too much. I have a feeling we will need all the experience we have later this day. I need someone there I can trust."

Cappilius nodded and felt as though fate herself had decided that his gaze would fall on the ravines, thus influencing Julius' decision. This caused a momentarily pang of annoyance regarding this youth. It did not last long, for his professional bearing soon reasserted itself. However, the lesser doubts stayed for much longer.

Had they chosen the right person for this responsibility? Julius was indeed unique and matched all the seniors in the ability to command, but he still lacked that emotional stability. Would the stress of so much responsibility weigh too heavily? Would he break? Would they all break, due to a lack of belief in his ability?

It was time for them all to find out!

"A delaying action to tie them up in the broken ground, no less," he eventually confirmed, making sure his gaze never faced the youth.

"I'm afraid so," said Julius , as he turned his horse's head to face his standing colleague. "I am also giving you the Cenitarns, my friend."

"Cenitarns!"

"Yes. There is nobody else who can possibly control the main dissenters. Khazumar cannot afford any confusion at the river. Here we will have the decisive battle. That leaves only the extreme right. So to you they must go."

"You really are trying to cheer me up this morning, General," mocked Cappilius, while Julius smiled broadly. "Do tell if there are any others that are less likely to stand in a fight and send them along too, quick as you like."

Now Julius laughed, causing a few people to turn in surprise. It also brought Khazumar to their discussion.

"I see humour is still with us," he said, struggling with his pony.

"It is," Julius hailed. "Did you speak to Kol?"

"Yes. We are to proceed regardless of the changing forces on the enemy right. It is too late for us to change. Kol is right, by the time we had turned around and returned, everyone else would already have decided our fate. So we must determine our own on this flank."

"Then we should delay no longer," agreed Julius, then turned to look back at Cappilius. "I am always glad to see that you retain your sense of humour, Cappilius, but the task set for you is nevertheless vital. You are able to accomplish this duty?"

Cappilius nodded his assent, knowing full well that the broken ground would be the best-defended part of the field, and also the most likely place for the enemy to counterattack. It offered considerable cover from the majority of the area through which Julius and Khazumar had chosen to advance. Already numerous skirmishes had occurred in the course of the evening, but no significant effort had developed while they had been moving the large force across their ramshackle bridge built by the warships roped together.

That had been their most vulnerable moment, when Cappilius had only his three hundred velites to defend the far bank of the river. A concentrated effort would have thrown them back, and perhaps even allowed the enemy to capture a fully functioning bridge to turn against them. However, no such effort had been made and, after the first few encounters, the local patrols seemed more eager to avoid them than openly oppose them.

Then the game of waiting began, with both sides vying to establish the best view of the opposing side. A small troop of smaller orcs wearing bright red jackets, which he now knew were the dyed skins of numerous creatures that the individual had killed, had especially peaked his irritation in the last three hours. If he was assigned to the broken ground, it was almost a certainty that he would face this same enemy.

Yes, it would be the same ones, as they had shown an enormous degree of cunning in their tactics. When one band showed stupidity in making a stand, these would retire and then suddenly launch an ambush, not to kill, but to continually delay. Issus used the very same tactics, he suddenly thought, as Khazumar reigned into one side of him.

"Are you ready for the struggle ahead, Cappilius?" he asked, and on receiving a curt nod in the affirmative, continued. "We are sorry to give you the Cenitarns, but we have no choice. The main blow will fall through the woods and along the riverbank to retake this side of their crossings, and trap them on the far side. They will fight, I am sure, but I also advise you not to rely too heavily upon them for long!"

"I will keep my eyes open, but before I take my people to that area I have one request."

"Name it," prompted Julius, slightly distracted by the arrival of the legion, or rather what was left of the battered few, now numbering less than eight hundred. With Crassus' contingent they had barely six hundred here, and that would have to be enough.

"Let me take the maiden hobbits with me," grinned Cappilius, bowing low. "We will be nice to them and I am sure their skills will be well rewarded."

Both Julius and Khazumar looked at each other and shrugged. They had been expressly forbidden to place these warriors in the front line, as they had only been released after Kol had realised that there was literally nobody else to give them for the flank attack.

"We are ordered by Kol, as you well know, to hold them in reserve and only commit them if absolutely necessary" responded Khazumar, still looking at Julius. "But there was nothing said about sending them on scouting missions."

"Scouting in force, you mean?" added Julius, with a smirk.

"They are after all warriors and well trained at that," agreed Cappilius, his hopes rising with every second.

"Kol has retained one hundred as his personal guard, thus releasing the normal regiment for service and we can ill afford to have four hundred efficient warriors watching our baggage," stated Khazumar, more seriously. "That flank will probably not be used for the full counterstroke, if they have time to organize it, as we will keep them busy at the river. But later in the day they will be sorely tested. Cappilius will need their help."

"Some good fortune at last!" exclaimed Cappilius, waving a fist in triumph and remembering Captain Armolin, so beautiful. Looking up, both Khazumar and Julius frowned in tandem. "I'm sorry, General, Lord Khazumar, but the moment took a hold of me. It will not happen again."

"Let's hope not," admonished Khazumar, with a nod, while the familiar grin replaced Julius' frown. He was so much like Cappa sometimes.

"I wonder what happened to Porta?" asked Cappilius, finally, as the legion clashed their shields to their shoulders in salute to Julius. None of the three responded, they did not have to!

"I do not know," said Julius, as he remembered the ridiculous conversation with Elvandar just before their meeting with Kol last night. "Elvandar stated that they had sent messengers all through the camp, but nobody had any news of him since dusk yesterday. It is odd that he vanished just when Valenus finally confirmed him as the spy."

"Is there any news of Valenus?" Cappilius asked.

"No, not yet. If he is alive he will be in that wood, but there is no way of knowing yet."

"Porta the spy. I still find it hard to believe," Cappilius admitted.

"I know what you mean," Khazumar added, putting his hand to his heart to ward off evil spirits. "I spoke with him just a few days ago and he seemed to totally ignore me, as if he was in a trance. I sent for the medics, but by the time they arrived he had gone. Definitely an air of magic that was, mark my words. Definitely magic!"

"What, Porta?" scoffed Cappilius, flatly. "Never in a million years, Khazumar. He would not even know where to begin!"

"In my experience of magic, Cappilius, you will not often use the magic, but it is always there if you look hard enough."

"Still, it does sound odd that Porta was the spy and used magic to leave the camp. I just hope it is not the portent of more ill news."

For a moment the three sat or stood in silence. They contemplated what had been suggested. Magic meant the enemy. Magic associated him with the spy that nobody had found, even after his discovery. The nursemaids had been questioned! Paranoia had reigned in the camp for weeks. Then there was the abduction of Atronius, where Porta had immediately assumed command of the search party sent to the coast, where it was firmly believed the escape warship had been harboured. The participants said that they had marched at a lazy pace and never once broke into a sweat. This had raised questions, but aimed more at Porta's competency than his loyalty.

"It hurts too much to contemplate such things," said Julius finally, to change the subject. "How is Marcellus?"

Khazumar immediately brightened, as he had Marcellus before returning from his early morning discussion with Kol.

"He is recovering well," he reported enthusiastically. "The wounds are healing and he says he can see, but only in shadows. He does not see any features, only people's shadows, which are different shapes in various degrees of grey. It is certain that his eyesight will not return fully, but it is good news nonetheless."

They all gave their approval fervently, for the *Teacher* was well liked amongst all the people for his swift wit, deep knowledge and understanding of everything.

"How are your new recruits doing?" Julius then asked, throwing a look of despair at the realisation that not only dwarves and elves had joined his velites, but that several of the barbarians had also chosen to do so. Cappilius' personal command had only seventy-five Romans out of three hundred or more men.

"We are fine, Julius," Cappilius replied, with an anger that both riders knew to be an act. "We thank you for your concern and we eagerly await the arrival of the maiden regiment. It will certainly make this an interesting day."

Julius and Khazumar nodded once in unison and then looked in a full circle, to see that their hill was completely surrounded by their own formations. It was time to go back to business.

"Cappilius."

"My Lord."

"Take your people and keep that broken ground clear of any heathens and protect our flank. You have your three hundred, the four hundred hobbits and...How many Cenitarns do we have with us? Really? Fine, well, you will also have those three thousand under your direct command. I hope that will be sufficient, but I have held two more Hildar off to the far right just in case. Do not wait for me to release them, they have instructions to obey you directly or me by messenger. Take them if needed, but make sure I know you have done so."

"I will not let you down, Youngster," Cappilius said, and with a brief wave trotted lightly down the slope to rouse his own command to begin the short change in positions.

"Do you think they will try our flank?" Khazumar asked, as soon as he could not be heard.

"I do not know, in truth. It is certain they will try to take the ground just to force us to defend the far side, if their leaders have any sense, and they have shown plenty of that recently. We can only wait. Our task is here, at the riverside and the wood. Which do you prefer?"

"I like to have room to swing my axe, Julius. I will stay at the riverside as agreed," Khazumar decided sternly, as he began to set his mind to the task ahead.

"We go at midday," Julius reminded.

"Midday it is then, and I wish you all the luck of the Gods...May I use...?"

"Please do," Julius smiled. "I sometimes forget that I have yet to reach thirty. I guess to most people I am the youngster, although Crassus must be as old as the Gods!"

Khazumar's booming laugh turned heads just as easily as Julius' had earlier. Then, with no further words required, the two clasped forearms and looked deeply into each other's faces. Then, as an afterthought, Khazumar's face became more stern than normal.

"No fear, Youngster. We must have no fear."

"No fear, my Lord Khazumar. We will never fear."

With that the industrious dwarf rode off to the left and wound his way around the numerous formations. Now the waiting was finally about to draw to a close.

Igluk looked at the map and glanced suspiciously over the top of the woods obscuring his left flank. The trees bordered his East Hill, as it had now become known in its capacity as the command centre, and they gave rise to a nagging doubt.

He pondered slowly and deliberately. Why would any force try to capture the wood? If successful they would be stopped by this very hill and the rising slopes to the north. An attack along the river could threaten his contact with those on the northern bank of the Great River, but, even with his limited knowledge of tactics, it seemed ridiculous for the enemy to split their forces in such a desperate tactic. It did not make sense, especially when his orcs had just smashed through their centre and were very close to capturing Kol's tower.

Again he looked at the map. The recent reports of a dawn attack on the right flank, where the goblin king had control, had not really altered his plans. He had discussed them briefly with the chieftains earlier and killed two of them just to prove a point. They would do as they were told, or simply die. His discussion had taken the form of a severe rebuke for the continual defeats at the waterfall, where piles of his orcs' corpses ten paces high could now be found. The river had not turned red, but it had definitely taken on a deeper shade of green.

Not that this especially bothered him, and they would continue to do his bidding. If the goblins on his right folded, he would just send the orka legion to restore order and then return to the centre, but not just yet. With ten thousand already across the river, ten thousand on the southern bank waiting to cross and the other twenty thousand standing on the extreme right-reserve region, that flank was in little danger of collapsing. He did of course keep the right-reserve ready for commitment into the central battle or, if required, they could help the goblins, but for now they would remain where they stood, even if he had ordered them to close the distance to march to the centre.

If anything, the goblin king, with well over thirty thousand at his disposal, should be able to attack the enemy left, thus forcing Kol to send reinforcements, which in turn would weaken the central defences. Only a few moments ago he had sent word for ten thousand to return, to add to the currently depleted right flank's reserve. On their arrival there, he could then deplete this force by the same number a second time to create a central reserve here, at his command tent, but they would not arrive until late in the afternoon.

To this reserve he had already added the five elite *Black Regiments of Gobli* and the two newly created legions of orka, numbering a further ten thousand. The force requested to return consisted of the other orka legions, which Scipio had sent off to support the goblin king. As far as Igluk was concerned, these elite soldiers should be as close to him as possible, not sitting on the flank fighting a skirmish of little consequence. Even if the goblins continued to call for reinforcements and send bitter claims about being abandoned, which did not seem justified, he wanted all twenty thousand orka right here at his feet.

No, the right was safe. It might be battered, but it was unlikely to be defeated. It was the left, only the left. Why had they crossed with such force? Indeed how many had crossed? The sunorcs had for once failed to ascertain the enemy strength, but for the woods alone this still seemed strategically foolish. Surely not so with this dwarf Kol, but perhaps they intended to cause a distraction, pull his reserves left and right and deny him the strength to finish them off on either flank or at the centre?

Yes, that seemed logical, he determined. Absently he walked to the edge of the slope that Valenus had rolled over and looked down, as if he expected to see the corpse of the Roman at the foot of the slope. Disappointed, he turned to reach for a large mug of wine and some fruit to parch his thirst and hunger. Fruit, why fruit? Bloody fruit!

Igluk increasingly gazed towards the west, where the West Hill was crawling with a force that the *Reds*, a large formation consisting of sunorcs trained for scouting purposes and experienced fighters from Moravia, had estimated at ten thousand. However, that had been during the night. Early this morning they had been driven from the hill and their attempts to return had been foiled, so he now had no real estimate of the enemy strength beyond the wood.

So it was safe to assume that perhaps a small reserve sat behind the hill. So...fifteen thousand stood on his left flank and he had his main forces poised to strike across the Great River, but why had they decided to split their forces?

The thought would not go away!

Igluk was stuck, and for the first time he realised just how important Scipio had been. Scipio had known the tactics and the minds of the enemy, as he most definitely did not, and he needed this knowledge more than ever, now that this flanking attack was developing. As far as he was aware, the Mage had recalled the spy and time was running out, if he was to seize this opportunity for power. Scipio would only be gone for a day or two and he must attack today, but something was making him hesitate. His left flank made him hesitate, but perhaps this was its sole purpose, to buy time. Of course...time!

They were expecting reinforcements! If the dwarven king had suddenly had a change of heart and had sent the thirty thousand or more that he knew were held at the capital to assist, then they would be able to release a flanking force. Had they arrived? There was no way of knowing but, if so, then surely they would have attacked by now?

Igluk began to pace and found it impossible to make a decision. With each passing minute Issus and Arrim pushed his right flank harder only to withdraw, to ambush any pursuit.

On the West Hill, Julius and Khazumar watched in vain as Igluk sent no reinforcements to the northern bank, and they wondered whether the enemy had decided to turn on them instead.

Kol, at the centre, stood with Crassus and watched as his troops feverishly tried to build a rampart from the wood and other materials nearby, to help their defence.

All had nothing to do except wait.

Then, without warning, one regiment of dwarves at the Great Bridge began to move backwards. Had Kol given the order, Julius wondered? If so it was early, considering no attack had begun! Then, inexplicably, a second regiment began to retire, as the first literally fell into a breakneck sprint over Tower Hill. Nothing could stop them, not even Kol. Within minutes five more Cenitarn regiments, the last of those still with Kol, had turned and fled. It was indeed the wrong time in their plans, but across the river Igluk looked on in surprise.

"The reinforcements are expected, but they have not arrived," he said to himself, and grimaced evilly. "Tell the front formations to get across that bridge. We have wasted enough time with these fools to our left. Send the orka to destroy them quickly and deploy the Black Regiments into the wood for the moment. Take the messages *now!*"

As though struck, the nearest messenger withdrew and sprinted for the nearest batch of hobgoblins, which acted as fast riders on their wolves and would verbally pass on the messages to the regiment chiefs. The retreat had not been planned, but now served Kol more than if Igluk had decided to attack at dawn, as expected. It was now mid-morning, and the enemy had freely given them the vital time to finish their deployments.

Igluk had not ignored the left, but had merely decided to delay any decision, and he would use his orka to gain the time to make it the right decision. Then the orka would redeploy and form the core of the final attack on Tower Hill. Once past that position, there would be nothing to stop him marching on the capital. Victory would be his and *his* alone. His crackling roar of triumph was by now familiar in the tent, but outside the guards watched each other in silence. They did not share Igluk's optimism. No indeed, they definitely did not! It was going to be a long day, no matter what their new chief said. A very long day!

⸻ ⁕ ⸻ ⁕ ⸻

As fate watched her cards fall from a distance and draw together the individual factions for the final dance, a lone man stood leaning on his spear and once more contemplated the similarities to today's coming experience. Before he had stood as a proud man in Prince Daxus' army facing the Romans at the Rhodanus tributary, where they had all anticipated an easy victory. Here he stood with a different spear of better quality, but with a new allegiance forged in friendship and an open heart.

He had never hated Roma or its people, but he had felt sorry for their confined lives and the lack of true natural beauty in the mountains. Starvation had forced their hand and, trained as they were to protect their village, it seemed only correct for them to stand beside their elders and accept the council's decision to fight, should Roma oppose their descent to the coast.

It had been foolish really, he thought, looking back, to think they would not be opposed. Four hundred thousand tribesmen descending on any province would have caused any local statesman to cry for help, and the only source available was the military. This proved to be their downfall and eventually the reason for their current predicament.

Things had obviously changed so much that he found it difficult to even hate the enemy here, just as he had respected the right of Roma to defend itself, and why were the orcs' and goblins' situations any different to his own people's previous plight? He would of course have killed the Roman legionary then and the orcs now, but somehow this fight did not seem so clear-cut. It involved some very odd issues that he found difficult to comprehend. He was not stupid, nor a genius, but from recent conversations he had gleamed enough to know that he was not alone.

The question was simple, why did they fight at all?

Before they had had the obvious reason of survival, or starvation in the mountains. Here, however, was it not the enemy who now claimed this right to live in freedom and to defend their borders from the expanding Dwarmanian Kingdom? Did they not have a society, although one clearly less efficient than the Helvetii or even the Romans', but it nevertheless existed and required space to cultivate. Even within this kingdom numerous divisions existed, especially between the Hildar and Cenitarn dwarves.

The former considered they had a rightful position of dominance over all the other factions of the kingdom, while the latter claimed sovereignty over people who did not want their leadership. The Westonians were little more than one step up from pirates in their desire for gold, while the Northerners were a people that had previously dealt with orcs peacefully and a few served in the armed forces. If this was not enough, the Gretans openly rebelled at every opportunity and the Thorians accepted only their own military leadership and were fiercely loyal to their generals, while openly defiant of their king.

Meanwhile, to add to the pot, the mortalkind then came along to dispel all previously known lore and prove that those Romans, or lesser elves as many now called them, did indeed exist. Within their own group, three major factions had quickly asserted authority over those present, in the form of Atronius for the Romans, Daxus for the Helvetii and Issus for the Latabrogi and Boii, lesser tribes within the larger body of barbarians. Then came the elves.

Here the man sighed and rose to stand well above his colleagues on either side. He had to admit that he had found the elves very difficult to understand and, no matter how hard he tried, he could not bring himself to trust them. There was something in their lofty attitude that always left him feeling they had not told them the whole truth.

He fought now to defend his own honour, in that his Prince had accepted a truce until the end of this conflict, and although Daxus had then abandoned the Alliance, right at the beginning, he himself would not. With the Prince gone, Uxudulum murdered and Issus assigned elsewhere, many had not known what to do and in desperation had approached Cappa, previously a junior officer, and had spoken quite freely. Where could they fulfil their oath?

It was then that this amalgamated formation was designed with the intention of using the larger men to reinforce the legionaries. Over the last six months they had all shown enormous improvements. Their greatest accolade came at Holvidar, where they had acted and looked like a combined legion, not two different peoples fighting side by side. Yes, he remembered, that final advance over the charred remains of the orcs had left a lasting impression on him. They had died in pain and in that case they surely deserved to find peace, and perhaps they fought only for that divine right to exist.

If we stopped, perhaps they would too?

Somehow he knew it to be a vain hope and that a greater evil existed to control those poor creatures. If he did not honour his new companions, he could at least set free the orcs from their tyrannical leaders. It was perhaps the real reason he stayed. It justified the killing by giving it a moral reasoning. They were a people enslaved and he fought for their freedom as well as his own. It sounded arrogant, much like his thoughts of an easy victory at the tributary, but he had been much younger then. Five hundred years younger to be precise!

As always the sound of laughter turned heads. All about the man people began to stir. It was midday now and the real issue was about to begin, and the laughter died in his throat as the orka came into view. They matched his height and yet he felt no fear.

Life was but an endless series of memories, he suddenly thought, his mind going into overdrive. Memories that always seemed to be in the past tense. If that was true, then why worry about the future, as he would not know about it until it had occurred and by then, if death was to be the end of this day's journey, he would be the last to know. Or was that the first to know? Only time left now to kill and die. Fate was indeed busy this day and not only at this location either.

Up ahead the elven archers had already launched their first offerings of the day and the man watched fascinated as the arrows, specially weighted for a heavier impact, crashed into the orka formations moving towards their hill from the south of the wood ahead. Blood splashed into the air and a cheer wrenched the silence apart, as it was now clear that the training and the experiments would indeed bear fruit. At long last the firing would be slower, but the results would aid them considerably more.

The orka were suddenly not quite so intimidating…

PART FIFTEEN

RETURN OF THE GODS

Cappilius watched in awe as the four gigantic cylindrical formations traversed the eastern slope of the West Hill. Moving through the small gap between the wood and the broken ground he now occupied on the Alliance's extreme right flank, they smoothly constricted their cohorts to avoid any confusion in the ranks, and the enclosed space did not even hinder them for more than a blink of the eye.

From a small rise, above a deep mud pit on its front, he observed the way the orka broke each flanking cohort momentarily to offer cover in the rough terrain, avoiding an ambush, then beyond the break they swiftly closed ranks to reform.

It was a sight to cause admiration and a little despair. He also developed a keen interest in breaking up those formations or, at a minimum, disorganising the advance up the slope to allow Julius time to organise his response.

The sooner the better!

They would all stand a much better chance of surviving if the enemy was much more disgruntled, and perhaps a little hesitant about their continued success. Of one thing he was sure, only those who had gone with Cappa to the caves of Azar-Kad had ever seen the orka in such numbers before, or tested their prowess against them for any length of time. The caves and the River Battle had only involved five hundred orka altogether. As the chanting boom of these enormous masses slowly progressed, Cappilius began to doubt if they could stop an enemy so disciplined.

In his experience fighting in the legions, he had witnessed, during several engagements, how the discipline of the legion had time and time again smashed through an enemy three or four times their strength, by the elitist training regime imposed on all legionaries. It looked as though someone had now taught these valuable lessons to the enemy. Perhaps it was Porta, the spy, who was responsible, but somehow he did not seem likely to have had so much knowledge.

Looking to either side Cappilius nodded twice, the signal for those armed with bows to move forward and add their weight to the elven archers, who were beginning to inflict casualties. The orka marched with shields at least a third larger than a legionary's scutum and wielded swords that looked impossibly heavy, yet for them they were not. Almost with an air of childish play they rotated these blades high above their heads.

This alone was not too hard to accept from a professional point of view, comparing the scene with his experiences of fighting the Helvetii and Germanic tribes who had wielded swords of almost equal length. No, it was the way the sword's cutting edge swished through the air with so little effort. Even the hardest of hearts missed a beat, as these elite soldiers, bred to believe in their own invincibility, walked without faltering towards an enemy they considered already defeated.

The armour worn was leather with strips of metal at vital points, although one cohort did wear a complete cuirass of a sort, while the helmet was the only dense protection, apart from their weapons. It made Cappilius recall the legions' early days and the hurried armament program that had not catered for the numbers involved.

It also reminded him of the orka's one single weakness. Their sheer size in comparison to all the others made the combination of sword and shield almost impossible. Like small dogs the dwarves and legionary whipped around their legs, hacking and tearing apart the shins and tendons. When crippled and on their knees, they would then resort to their natural thrusting strikes to the chest, throat and face.

Cappilius smiled as he thought of his brother and the habitual lesson he had continually quoted...

"Wound them all and then move on," he had usually stated, matter-of-factly. "Leave the finishing off for the men behind!"

It was of course the standard procedure, but it seemed damn odd to be using it against a combatant's knees!

He could hear the drums more clearly now and searched ever harder over each flank of the enemy for the red-jacketed scouts they had encountered during their crossing last night. A minimum of ten thousand orka walked in perfect unison, while the red scouts were by far the most effective soldiers the enemy employed. In his opinion of course, for his own expertise was in the scouting role and the disruption of the enemy as a skirmish line. He could match this skill with his own people and fully intended to do so today.

Even so, as he watched the orka advance, leaving the odd prone corpse behind, it did not seem to make absolute sense. Why commit the elite to secure this flank? Perhaps the spy had learnt of their plans after all, and they now stood in peril of being decimated? Or could they have failed to understand precisely how many had come across the river with Julius and Khazumar? If the latter, then it followed that the enemy scouts had failed to obtain any new information since the night skirmishes, which had ended with them withdrawing.

They had for most of the morning kept the larger formations behind the West Hill, out of sight of the red scouts. Even with this in mind, it was still impossible to think that these orka expected to meet only a few thousand, an easy fight and a swift return to the centre. Just a brief look across the West Hill would have shown the extent of the forces deployed to attack, irrespective of those kept beyond the summit.

If the enemy leader considered this move nothing other than a delaying tactic, then it would make sense to deal a heavy blow here, to free the orka for the decisive blow in the centre. Even so, clad as heavy soldiers it was foolish to think they could fight a decisive flanking action and also partake in the central conflict, all within a few hours, so he began to search for the support columns. His next thought was to perhaps win the conflict with the orka and then leave the other orcs to finish the task, but he could see no supporting archers, velites or auxiliaries.

With the recent clear-cut copying of the cylindrical formations and the use of legion tactics, it seemed impossible that there were no auxiliaries before the orka line, and no archers and javeliners moving from behind to support the attack. His own people functioned in this capacity for their own army, and their absence left the orka extremely exposed from all sides.

"Where are the auxiliaries?" he asked nobody in particular.

"More importantly, Centurion," a voice replied from behind, "why are they here at all? They normally send the orcs or goblins to soften us up first before they commit their best. Not very bright, if you ask me?"

Cappilius turned and grinned conspiratorially. "I agree. Send someone behind that formation and confirm if they are closely supported. You, yes *you*, move now and report to Julius that, in my humble opinion, we should retire behind the hill and allow these fools to the summit, before we close in on all sides. This could be just the start we needed."

Within seconds two experienced men ran to complete the tasks assigned, and a few watched them circumvent some of the rough terrain, but their interest was quickly diverted back to the orka. The ten cylindrical formations consisted of ten thousand orka in total. All about them milled the archers who fought in small groups, and the bodies left behind confirmed that the heavily weighted arrows had not only been irritating, as the lighter shafts had proven. The additional weights on the arrowheads were proving most effective.

Cappilius watched several orka fall dead, while the remainder simply trampled the corpses into the mud. One gripped its throat, where a green waterfall marked the point of penetration of the arrow point through his neck. The other had simply dropped down to pull an arrow from an eye and seemed at first eager to stand and then rejoin the formation, but then he suddenly keeled over onto the trampled grass.

In its back could be seen four great shafts, as the parent formation had moved far enough ahead for the individually wounded to be targeted by the elven archers. All of the wounded were systematically hunted down, as no supporting formations or light troops kept them from doing so. The enemy losses began to rise.

On and on they came, seemingly unconcerned by how many of their companions dropped, but the front line always remained mysteriously complete. He knew, however, that from behind there would be rents in the back areas, where losses had slowly mounted. They had been told only light resistance opposed them, and yet this did not seem light to them. Nevertheless, on they marched, as the training dictated! They were invincible, all resistance would melt away before them. None would dare stand and fight!

Cappilius watched the forward line of four cylindrical formations slow their pace, to realign and allow the two following in close support to close a gap that had unwisely been created by the line of movement. The rearward formations, also numbering four, also slowed, but did not stop, knowing only too well that they must all keep moving or perish.

He could imagine the feelings in those lumbering masses, as they suddenly began to realise that no supporting auxiliaries marched with them, and nobody covered their flanks. A few glanced to either side, but none broke out in panic, their discipline was simply too great for that, but many more did begin to show signs of reluctance to proceed up the hill.

Meanwhile the archers continued to kill indiscriminately.

As they passed, the orka left behind prone corpses or struggling wounded, which were quickly finished off by the elves. The grass was stained by the deep green blood, which ran like a river down the slope to coagulate into a pool at the base, where it met the broken ground to the south. Still they moved forward, step by step.

They were now less than five thousand paces from the summit of the hill when Julius, as instructed by Cappilius, ordered the forward dwarven regiments to retire behind the summit, out of sight of the advancing horde. Here a long line of new archers, adding to those already deployed, swiftly replaced them and the solemn ranks of the dwarven legion quietly moved in behind.

It would take the best to break the orka, with or without support! The Roman legion was also on standby, Julius having made it quite clear that they might also be needed to survive this crisis.

Just as Cappilius ordered his own auxiliaries to add their javelins to the party, Julius waved frantically for the archers to begin their deadly work. Then off to the enemy's right Julius gazed at the advancing legion. Crassus should have commanded them, but his duty lay elsewhere and on this day Arrecinus Neros had been promoted to command in Julius' absence. Only time would applaud or condemn this decision, and that time was fast approaching.

The entire enemy now walked up the hill with Cappilius on their left, Julius to their front and the legion survivors on the right along with the elven legion, with archers along the entire circumference. They were, in short, surrounded, but without even a sign of hesitation, the summit now within sight, the orka quickened the pace. Those who now opposed them were everything the enemy could send, as they had been informed only ten thousand stood on the West Hill. Unknown to them, Julius now commanded over forty thousand.

Of these, Julius had not even committed all of the archers at his disposal. Any leader of any skill would have seen this for himself, and decided that a retreat back to the woods was the best option, then perhaps a return with a more organised force might prevail. At this time, however, the orka leaders had no idea of the true situation, which was about to be made painfully clear to them all!

"Now," screamed Julius, as loud as he could above the loud thump of the orka drums. "Now, archers, now is your time. Fly high! Fly high!"

Like a wave over a stone, the elven archers previously held in reserve advanced over the hill summit and for a few seconds they stopped to gaze in awe, as Cappilius had done, at the orka, who now approached at less than five hundred paces. A few well-chosen commands from their officers, however, broke the reverie and the fact of the very real danger they faced suddenly came home.

The people before them had hardly come this far to sit and parley, but the normal air of calm around most elves was soon re-established. They had come to kill the enemy and to preserve their own lives. To do this they must now kill with the utmost efficiency allowed by the elves' superb skills with the bow. Where a legionary could withstand the charge of an elephant if called upon to do so, an elf could shoot the elephant in the eye with an arrow.

It would take courage to aim under such pressure, but these were elves from strong stock and within a few seconds they had quickly formed two long ranks of raised bows.

Behind them Julius waited a few more moments, as the orka crossed the one hundred pace marker, put there at his request, then took a deep breath to yell one last word.

"*Fire!*"

With a sound like a high-pitched whistle the arrows flew directly into the air, where at their pinnacle of flight the weights on the shafts turned them over to point earthwards. Then, with a different sound, they descended to crash into the forward echelons of the nearest cylindrical formation. For the first time the screams of the enemy were heard, as shoulders were smashed and arms left useless, heads were cleaved open by the arrow points and the blood literally splashed into the air, as every tip found a target, such was the preponderance of orka to arrows.

On either side dwarven archers added their weight to the attack by extending across most of the hill, where Julius now rode frantically back and forth.

"Load," he shouted with eyes wide with the surge of imminent battle, his inexperience forgotten. "Front rank fire low this time. Rear rank fire high. Ready, *fire!*"

The arrows once more sang into the air and were joined by Cappilius' spears and javelins, while the hobbits fired their lighter arrows to add just a little more misery. On the far side Neros, for the first time, using his own judgement, ordered both the elven and Roman legions under his command to launch their pilum, which proceeded to decimate the far right of the orka, whose numbers had been cruelly diminished.

It was now the turn of the second wave to strike home and the front ranks of the orka seemed to stop in their tracks, as one arrow after another smashed through their shields to splinter forearms and strike torsos. On either side, the enemy dropped in increasing ratios to the continually increasing forces opposing them, but still they trusted their leadership, even though almost a third of their number now lay dead or dying.

On they came, forever looking for that glorious moment when they could break formation and close with those puny animals before them that dared to stand and fight. They would seek revenge with such hatred that they would never dare face their wrath again, and they would march onto the Dwarmanian capital and ultimate victory.

All along the lines, the command to halt and redress the lines could be heard, and the deep boom, boom of the chant itself soon answered the call of the battle chant. Meanwhile the drums beat faster as the four frontal formations moved together to create one long line of terror.

"Ready," Julius continued, unaffected by the sight ahead, barely out of pilum range. "*Fire!*"

This time they all fired low. The effect was staggering, as the whole front line was thrown backwards with three or four shafts protruding from the enemy armour. Shields shattered into useless scrap and the screams now began to affect the enemy.

It was not really something anyone noticed specifically, but at fifty paces the enemy had most definitely slowed. Individuals now began to shout and beat their own people fiercely, one actually killing the only orka known to have retreated willingly. The others took note and resumed the ascent, only to be met by an even greater forest of arrows and spears, as the dwarven legion made itself known with the odd flying axe.

The orka paused, redressed the line for the millionth time and with an air of calm, which was somewhat disturbing, prepared to apply their pilums. The command to prepare was heard clearly by Julius, who momentarily pulled his horse to a halt. Had he not done so it was a foregone conclusion that he would have died during the orka's first charge. To his right, on his intended path, no less than six enormous spears flashed past his head to bury themselves into the hill a few paces to the rear, some also finding victims.

All about him, the archers were hit hard by the javelins, and the front two ranks of the orka charged fiercely to cause further disruption, but the pressure was insufficient to perturb the elves. With an equal level of calm their arrows were again aimed low and the charge dissipated in one cavalcade of blood. Few orka achieved the pleasure of personally striking down an elf and within a few heartbeats order had been restored. Not a single orka had lived through the charge.

From where Cappilius stood it looked as though the enemy still advanced, as the six formations behind the front line continued on regardless, and it was then that he knew the situation was about to be decided. Without thinking he turned to the nearest people and began to collect them together to facilitate loose fighting.

"Come on," he shouted. "If we hold some of these heathen up down here, then the front rank may break. Let's not let them reinforce the front line!"

With a cheer that carried to the top of the hill they charged up the slope and began to attack the nearest enemy, never staying long enough to be drawn into a direct conflict, but moving swiftly onto the next and the next. By the time the enemy had reacted and turned to face the new threat, they had vanished into the undergrowth to charge the next formation. On the far side Neros watched in fascination, but soon realised why Cappilius was risking so much. The time for delay was over. Julius had not given the command to attack, but he knew that he should not allow the rear formations to reinforce the front line.

"Legion," he shouted above the din of battle. "We will advance in formation for the glory of the Alliance. Trumpeters! Ready! *Advance!*"

As though each man had been joined at the hip, they moved forward to strike at the enemy, which, as they stepped forward, looked for the first time to be taking a few steps back down the slope. Had they retired a few steps? No surely not! Yes, there, a few more have bolted! There are some more, they are breaking, *they are breaking!*

May the Gods be praised, the orka have been broken!

Julius watched as the rear lines of the front linear formation suddenly broke for the rear. They had never done so before and had always preferred death to defeat, but on this day, with no support, no archers to deal with the elves and completely surrounded, they had suddenly done the most unexpected thing. He wiped his eyes several times in case he was seeing things, but the view did not alter even after several attempts, and he could not now remember when such joy had filled his heart.

It was not over, but the panicking few took others with them and the rear formations became disorganised, although they would only be so for a very short period. Turning around in the saddle, he searched for Kubios, the dwarven legion commander, and spotted him on the far side congratulating his warriors. He was a vain dwarf and not the one that he would have chosen to train people as legionaries, but so far he had proven to be a good officer. So far!

"Kubios!" he yelled, ignoring all formalities. "Take your people down this hill and send those scum back to where they belong!"

Kubios bowed low and smiled. Then without a word he began to march down the hill. Julius watched as his own people simply followed in group order and the line slowly moved down the hill obliquely, driving the enemy towards Neros who, he noted, had also begun to advance to cut off the retreat, rather than move back to the woods and safety.

It was hardly necessary, as the orka suddenly turned into a mass of fugitives that almost literally headed directly for the very woods mentioned. Nothing could have stopped them, but as they passed the archers continued to snipe and caught a few hundred more. On the hill the wounded were hunted down and executed without hesitation. None of them would be allowed to live out this day.

Julius watched the enemy reach the woods and then looked down the hill. He tried to count the enemy dead, but there were thousands, and it seemed as though at least two legions had marched against them. That must mean at least ten thousand. He looked hard and tried to find pride in the work, but found his heart heavy with the loss of life before him. Perhaps the futility of this carnage had created his melancholy.

He tried to keep his mind on the fact that these were creatures from the underworld, creatures of foul existence, and yet nobody could ignore the bravery of such a charge. Nobody could ignore the strength of character and conviction that had brought these people forward, and the futility of committing them with no archers or support whatsoever was criminal.

He tried to count once more and noted that others were doing the same for one reason or another. Their own losses had been relatively light.

"Six thousand is the count so far," panted Cappilius, having sprinted up the hill. "Six thousand!" he repeated, shocked by the very extent of this success. "What are our losses, do you think?"

"A few hundred, if that," Julius responded, his attention attracted by the sudden movement again on the eastern hill.

"Do you know why they never sent support with them?" asked Cappilius, still excited at the success, still trying to fathom the stupidity of their opposite numbers.

"No. I guess that will have to wait, though."

"What?"

"On the far side, Cappilius. I think those dwarves that you left in your place are about to have a very warm welcome."

"I guess I had better return then, before those damnable Cenitarns decide to take to their heels."

Julius gesticulated wildly and Cappilius again ran down the hill, but this time had to move around the large clumps of corpses that had only minutes ago been the most terrifying sight he had ever seen. Yet, even now, he knew there would be more killing before this day ended.

So much more!

⁙⁙⁙

It took him almost twenty minutes to rejoin his comrades, and the stench of orka blood had done little to improve his temperament. It had been glorious to watch such bravery, but now the whole area was as slippery as the Underworld and the smell was offensive to even the most unclean amongst them. It was a longer journey for the stomach than the body.

Nevertheless he arrived just as the feared red-coated sunorcs began to make a new appearance at the eastern end of the broken ground. Moving in light order, they began to creep forward and apply their light arrows to the dwarves, using the same tactics the elves had used on the orka. The effect was minimal and more of a strain on the nerves of these inexperienced regiments. A few warriors dropped with injuries, but most of the arrows just hit the shields, some of which were pierced by numerous shafts.

"How many?" Cappilius asked indiscriminately, not caring who answered.

"About a thousand so far," someone behind him answered. "But we are certain another large group is trying to work behind us. Perhaps it also numbers a thousand? That is uncertain."

"Thank you, my friend," Cappilius nodded, turned and began to view the entire horizon from their slightly elevated hillock.

Indeed off to the right the dry dust had the telltale signs of large bodies of people moving, but only to the trained eye. Indeed the dwarven regimental captains had looked incessantly and refused to move, as long as they could see no such proof of a flanking force. Now it was obvious that the advantage had been lost and the only way to restore the equilibrium would be the hard way, the very painful way.

"You will keep your regiments here and hold this line at all costs," he said, indicating the three dwarven captains, then turned once more towards his own people. "Meanwhile we will drop back and take the hobbit regiment with us and deal with those heathens.

"You, yes *you* again, stop looking at those maidens, from experience I can assure you they are not to be taken lightly. I like to send those that I can trust and for now that means you. Remove yourself off back to Julius and inform him of exactly what is happening, and say that it may be prudent to have someone ready to reinforce those already behind us. Is that clear? Yes? Good, well be off with you. Now let's move before we take root."

They moved in the very same angled formation taught to them by Issus, which allowed them to move fast, but also to cover a very large area. Behind them Cappilius waved and the maiden hobbit regiment broke formation, to form small bands of twenty to reinforce their positions, as and when it became necessary. They crossed one small ravine swiftly and began to cover the next, and then, on the crest, they saw several figures clearly retreating before them.

"Extend outwards," Cappilius shouted. "Hobbits to the rear, help when called for, but not at any other time." He turned to emphasise the point to the hobbits and, when satisfied that Armolin had accepted his command, he continued. "We hold them and if necessary give ground rather than suffer losses. Understood?"

Nobody replied and he took this as a positive response, and with a smooth action drew his short sword and adjusted the position of the circular shield in his left hand. Now they would see the true bitterness between the antagonists, leaving nobody with the comfort of mercy.

Even more so, they knew it would be kill or be killed.

At one point the orka had had a choice, but their subsequent actions at the river had ended any acts of mercy. They had fought earlier, but had had little conviction to enter the true conflict. At this point it was definitely their turn, on the Alliance's far right flank, to fight. This was where the turning would occur, this was the end of the line. There was nobody else beyond this point, only them.

They moved across the next small ravine where the grass had grown wild. They moved swiftly and their eyes kept looking from side to side. The situation and the sun made them all sweat but, as with all things, the only concern was where and when the enemy would strike.

A bird suddenly broke free from the grass and in an instant they crouched to a low stance, keeping the lower knee just above the ground. Another broke free, but was swiftly followed by a shrill call that carried clear to Julius, never mind those in the small ravine.

Cappilius waved for the flanks to close in, and they soon stood along an open flatland perhaps three hundred paces in length and one hundred in width, dominated by the small incline to the bottom of the ravine, which was covered by the grass. The call had come from directly ahead, but nobody could be seen and the sudden feeling of being watched made each person nervous. By Jupiter, why did something not happen?

The second call, obviously some method of contact, came from the left and the third from the right. Then nothing and the air seemed heavy with anticipation, raising the anxiety with each passing minute. These facts Cappilius acknowledged when he saw a young man slowly begin to edge back up the rear slope. These sunorcs were good, damn good.

Cappilius looked along the far side to the rise beyond the grass and began to wave a few people forward, as he deemed this to be delaying tactics and nothing more.

Even as the very thought entered his head the enemy suddenly struck, standing from prone positions in the grass. The first reaction was shock, the second for many was the terrifying realisation that an arrow now protruded from their chest. The lucky few died instantly, the unlucky choked on their own blood as they tried to retire to a safe area, not knowing that the poison would work much too quickly for any to reach the top of the rear slope.

There would be no medical help when dealing with sunorcs!

Cappilius felt the feathers of one such arrow brush his throat, as the wind must surely have altered its flight by a fraction of a degree, saving his life. That was enough to confirm that his position was untenable and he quickly ordered a fast retreat. They did not need telling twice.

With a speed that defied logic Cappilius began to scramble back up the slope into the other ravine. His legs seemed to drag with each step, and his breath came in short bursts and at any moment he expected an arrow point to pierce his spine. All his velites wore the heavy leather chest protection, but nothing else, and although he liked the helmet many had discarded it as useless, preferring to fight with wide open movements and smaller shields.

What a time to start comparing different methods of fighting, he thought, and why the hell was the top of this hill so far away!

With a little anxiety he risked a look over his shoulder, where he saw the orcs in pursuit, but a clear fifty paces behind. A dwarf was hit nearby and spun in tight circles, as three separate arrows struck home. A spray of blood was almost suspended in the air as he dropped, descending a split second later.

Then, thankfully, Cappilius was up and over the crest, where he saw the orderly formation of the hobbits rapidly reforming to offer protection. Catching a deep breath, he paused to turn and look behind again. All of his people, apart from the ten or so dead, had managed to retire. A sudden yell to the left made him duck instinctively, allowing a curved blade to swish through thin air. Another step found his own blade plunging deeply into the exposed torso and a solid shoulder push sent the aggressor rolling back down the hill to sweep away a following group's legs.

"Hobbits!" he yelled, as loudly as possible. "Hobbits advance to open order. Move to the oblique right." Cappilius had noted that more of the sunorcs had congregated on the right side of the ravine. "*Move it!*"

At first the hobbits looked to Armolin who had originally ordered the regiment to reform. It was all they knew. This kind of fighting was normally left to the other regiments, and for a heart-wrenching moment they stood still and hesitated. In truth they had never been in open battle before and had only fought a few skirmishes at the river, and these had hardly been against an organised enemy. Initially they sought clarification, but the age-old training that Helin had given Armolin identified Cappilius as their lawful commander and they quickly moved to obey, but it was now too late. The hesitation had been just a few seconds too long!

Far to their right, the sunorcs suddenly reached the crest of the hill and sent a shower of arrows into their blocked formation. What had happened to the orka, now happened to the hobbits, but on a far smaller scale. This time, however, the tips were covered in a poison that made even a scratch potentially lethal.

Cappilius ran madly towards them and began to beat, kick and push to open up their formation. Again a second arrow came close and struck his sword, which had only momentarily been raised. Had it missed, the arrow would have struck his throat without a doubt. Another passed harmlessly overhead, but a muffled cry made him turn, where a young maiden hobbit tried desperately to pull the barb free of her stomach. It snapped and she looked up with a hazed expression, as her knees gave way and without a sound her body fell forward, dead before hitting the ground. So beautiful, so young, so final an ending.

"Forward," someone was shouting, ahead. "Forward! Why die here if we can kill a few of them as well!"

Cappilius snapped out of his trance and knew, without even looking, that their only chance was indeed to go forward. He smiled warmly to Armolin, out of place in such circumstances, but she was the voice of reason they had all heard so clearly above the din of battle. Here they would all be killed, as this ravine was even broader than the place of the ambush. It had perhaps been planned so as to leave the sunorcs an open killing field.

Either way they had to move and why not go forward, he thought. Yes, why not show these heathen how we stand and fight? As Cappa always said, the angrier you are, the better you fight.

"She is right," he concurred, moving to the front, where he could see for the first time that at least a third of the regiment had been killed by the arrows. "Wait for them to fire the next lot of arrows, and while they reload run like demons to catch them in mid pull and put them to the sword. Think of your friends and family who have all lost someone this day. It is time for revenge, just as we repaid the orka!"

A solemn silence followed, but from their eyes he knew they had all agreed. At the top of the slope the sunorcs once more prepared a flurry of arrows, anticipating an easy kill.

They were in for a surprise!

The air was heavy to breathe and hot, so hot that the top of his mouth had been burnt. The eyes had become little more than waterfalls and even with a squint the vision was blurred. All this was nothing more than a minor inconvenience in comparison to the pain that pulsed behind both eyes.

A searing pain, which had no starting place or end and caused him to stumble blindly, as he struggled to move down the corridor to the great chamber he knew to stand less than fifty paces away. Yet, even now, as he struggled once more to his feet, it might as well have been fifty leagues.

All about him flashes of red, blue, green and a blinding bright white had added to his discomfort. He had long ago forgotten, or rather, chosen to ignore, all thoughts of revenge for the earlier embarrassment of being fooled by the Mage's tricks. Now all he wanted was to run, as the fear now engulfing him was fast becoming unbearable, a fact that terrified him more than death itself. He thought he had known fear earlier, but now he was truly afraid!

Not of dying, not of pain or torture, but of losing his pride, which seemed brittle and pointless. He recalled the emaciated form of Atronius and thought hard about how much pain he must have endured, and yet he had survived, but he was not Cappa. They were not the same. Atronius had embraced this New World with open arms and, although he had bitterly contested the barbarian involvement at first, he was also the main force behind the amalgamated legion that incorporated those erstwhile enemies.

Cappa had taken time to discuss magic with everyone possible and had tried to understand its tactical uses, and indeed what and who knew which incantations. He had struggled in the very first discussion with Aarun and from that moment had almost willingly ignored its existence, much to Aarun's amusement.

He was a simple man and had very simple needs and he knew all there was to know about fighting an enemy made up of flesh and blood. Tactics had been the main reason why, at the original council, the men had chosen him to be their representative. They knew he would fight for the individual and not for what Roma, Atronius, the elves or dwarves thought, and especially not what the barbarians thought, good enough for them.

Magic had never once even entered his mind.

Oh, yes, he knew about the dimensions and the void and that they had been held in suspension for five hundred years; that was not too difficult as long as you remained away from the finer points. However, here and now, in this corridor there was no escaping those details, as they were bursting his eardrums.

Cappa screamed, as he dropped onto both knees and clapped a hand to either ear. Nobody heard the scream, he did not even hear it himself, but it had felt good to release the ever-increasing frustration, so he carried on screaming until his lungs ached with the effort.

Stay angry, he screamed in his head, *stay angry and alive*, but it was no good. Nothing took away the pain and his whole body felt as though it was being torn to pieces, bit by bit. He felt helpless and fear made a new appearance, tugging at his survival instincts.

Run, run now and live forever! Stay and you will die! There is nothing you can do to help Aarun, he is as good as dead! You have done all you can, why should you die as well?

No! No! I will not run! I am an officer of the Alliance Army and I fight for the freedom of my people!

This is not your fight, fool, from the beginning. You are here by fluke, nobody wished for you to be here. Go! Go now and live. Stay and you will die!

If I leave then Aarun will fail!

He has failed already!

No!

Yes! Yes! Yes! You pitiful fool, go now and leave. This is a fight for the Gods and you are nothing but a puny mortalkind. Who are you to pretend that you are needed here? Who are you?

The tears of unbearable pain came then and he knew, just as Atronius had known, that he was beaten. He knew he was broken and the will to go on was evaporating. He fought on and felt the pain simply increase. Five paces, then ten, now he was at the entrance, but the pain blacked out all that could be seen and he dropped to the floor unconscious.

How long he lay there he did not know, but the cacophony of noise had not abated, indeed if anything it had increased, yet somehow the pain had subsided. It had not gone completely, as the numbness now covered his entire body and both arms felt heavy, while his legs simply did not respond. Had he been struck? Cappa panicked and began to struggle, feeling something heavy on his back. Fearing the worst he pulled and twisted and felt relieved when the weight suddenly shifted to the left and rolled away.

Rocks, he looked, a *bloody rock* had landed square on his head and had enabled him to recuperate. He smiled as he tried to rise onto his haunches and looked around a little more. In front of him the whole area was illuminated from one side of the hall to the other by a red flame, which seemed to be trying to encompass a small white circle. Within this circle could be seen a small figure, both hands extended to the ceiling. Something told Cappa this was Aarun, who looked to be losing, if not at the brink of total defeat.

Earlier Aarun had said that all he needed was a distraction to do something that could win this fight, to open a back door for Zeus to utilise. However, he knew no magic and the gladius had been lost back in the corridor, where he now realised the Mage had concentrated a portion of his powers on destroying him. Maybe that was the key. He did not have to have a weapon, the Mage would allow the distraction because of some kind of link. Even Komar had seen a destiny in this fortress that nobody else had even contemplated.

Fate, as far as Cappa was concerned, was just more gibberish, but if the enemy believed he had some kind of power, then perhaps he *could* help. Perhaps it was because he knew nothing and understood nothing of magic that he was able to survive. Perhaps if you believed in the power the effects were greater? Only the Gods could answer that question and there did not seem to be any about at the moment, so he would have to guess.

"Is this the great Mage that I have been told about?" he scoffed, rising to his feet.

It was the end, as he knew beyond any doubt. It would end here, in this chamber, so there was nothing left to fear. Only to die this day Roman and avoid any dishonour which might befall his mother's memory.

"If you are so great why has it taken you so long to dispose of the elf? More to the point, how could a mere mortalkind fool you into believing Atronius Sulla was the *Oracle*? You are the fool, not *them!*"

Cappa spat out the last word and waited.

For a long time there did not seem to be any reaction, but then the red light suddenly stopped and the Mage turned towards him, the face grotesquely distorted. He knew his presence alone was about to have a profound effect on this contest.

"*No!*" A voice echoed across the chamber. "*You fool...leave the mortalkind! He is no threat. Finish the oracle and victory is ours. Do as I demand, kill the Oracle!*"

"No," replied the Mage, staggering as if some unknown power was trying to drag him sideways to force him to obey. "No. I do not need you any longer! I will be *Master* now. I will command, you will obey and for starters I will shred this scum inside out!"

"*No you fool. The Oracle! Destroy the Oracle! We are so close and so many. Destroy the Oracle and open the door for my minions, then we can destroy all together! Ignore this puny wretch, he cannot harm us now!*"

The Mage began to swear profusely and Cappa took this opportunity to try and reach Aarun, but long before he reached his friend the Mage's attention turned on him once more, with a vengeance.

"Now, how shall we apply your death, Marius? How indeed?"

Cappa froze and turned. "You know me?"

"Do I know you?" The Mage laughed heartily. "My dear Cappa... You made me! Did Atronius not inform you as to who I am?"

"What? How? I have no powers! How could I have made you? Did Atronius even know who you are?"

The Mage's hand rose and from the fingertips a cloud appeared, and from within Cappa watched as Hades made his first appearance as Cassius Evictus, coldly known as *Black Cassius* amongst their own century, presumed dead prior to the *arrival*. It all felt such a long time ago, a lifetime ago. He watched as the body was stripped of flesh and grimaced at the pain that wrenched the bones from the soul, leaving nothing but a small circle of light that rapidly turned grey and then vanished altogether.

A few moments later a new body appeared, and for the next few seconds Cappa watched as the vile creature that now stood before him was trained and created, but always with one purpose in mind... the destruction of Cappa's soul!

"You gave me my purpose throughout all of the agony. You gave me the reason to allow the Gods to enter my soul, for I possessed the key and this elf is the doorway. Without your cruelty do you think I would have gone? *Do you!* For five hundred years I have dreamed of your death. Now it is here I am at a loss as to which method befits your crimes."

"You never offered any friendship to anyone." Cappa began to play for time, as Aarun was now back on his feet and the white light was steadily growing. "How could we have known?"

"You did not want to know!" The Mage screamed hysterically. "None of you did, so I took the power offered and now I will seek your soul, as I intended all those years before."

"*The Oracle you fool! Why do you disobey? Together we can rule the cosmos, if you obey me now!*"

"Who is that?" Cappa asked, still walking towards the elf. "Is he your God? Why is he not commanding here?"

The Mage again staggered, his face contorting horribly as the unknown forces within his mind vied for ascendancy.

"Oh he wants to, yes indeed, but I am in charge now. I have the power to allow him through or to hold him back. I am, after all, the key."

"And if you die?"

"Then the key is either taken or destroyed, but that will not happen, fool, I am beyond your comprehension. I am a *GOD!*"

The last word hung in the air and for a moment Cappa felt the urge to run, but before he could move the whole chamber became a blinding light and nothing could be seen.

He knelt and pushed both hands forwards, while closing his eyes. So this was what it was like to die, he thought, but it was not death that answered, but a new voice. A voice as powerful as Cassius' Master.

"Not quite yet a God and I have had just about enough of my brother's interference to last a millennium! It is time this was brought to a conclusion! And that time is now!"

Of all the different stages of the past two hours, none was remotely capable of preparing Cappa for what he now saw. Before him the entire chamber wall seemed to waver and then began to fade. Pieces began to shimmer and the Mage's face twisted to show an agony beyond description. Blood flowed freely from his eyes and mouth and his ears had almost melted into his skull, making him shudder as he remembered the blood that had covered his own hands only moments before.

Pain was no longer the issue, as he literally bathed in the light and felt it heal the open wounds. He thought of Helin and smiled as Aarun joined him near the entrance to the chamber.

"What is happening?" he asked, his own voice sounding distant and cold in this light.

"You have achieved your destiny, my friend, but I must now seek mine."

"Destiny? What exactly have I done? Other than annoy that fool, who could easily have destroyed me. Is there more to be done?"

"No," Aarun laughed, raising a finger to point at the Mage. "This is over. The Mage had me at his mercy and for the sake of vengeance, he moved away from me, to strike at you. When he did so Zeus was able to use our doorway. For as long as my whole being was fighting the Mage, I could not allow his entry into the struggle.

"I had lost, but you gave me that diversion and Zeus was able to use my body in order to join this world and apply his powers directly. The Mage, as you heard, decided that he no longer needed his Master and that, as he was the key, he could lock out his ally. His vanity was his downfall. Had he not done so, we would not be here and the world would have been lost forever."

"It was that close?"

"Yes, it most certainly was, but we need not concern ourselves with this now. I must speak to you as a friend, Cappa, as you will be the last to whom I will speak in this dimension."

"This dimension?" Cappa asked, feeling that all too familiar confusion rising to smother his brains.

"Yes, my friend, I am no longer able to return with you and although the enemy will has been broken, so has my mortal coil linking me to this world; but there is still so much more work to be done."

"Such as? Have the orcs not been defeated at the river? Did Kol lose that fight?"

"No he has been victorious, but at such a high price. With that I am not concerned. Only the future concerns me now."

"If the fighting is over, how can the future be under threat?"

Aarun closed on Cappa and laid a hand across his shoulder. "Now that I have ascended, the Gods have permitted me to see certain truths, Cappa. You are not the first *arrivals*."

"What!"

"I cannot divulge any details, my friend, but you must find the ancient scrolls that were written before the lesser scrolls. There is much more for you to learn, Cappa, but you will know when it is time to seek out the priests."

"Priests? Now look here, Aarun, this is fine, but how am I to influence the minds of a kingdom or even Roma? You must tell me who the other arrivals were and when they occurred!"

"I am not permitted, but ahead of you is a long journey and I will help when I can, but you are more entwined within the fabric of the future than you know, my friend. Find the other arrivals and find the ancient scrolls, but first secure peace with Haderia."

"Peace with Haderia! After what they have done!"

"You must find a way to unite all of the peoples, Cappa, only you can achieve this! Beware of the spy, he has not perished despite Helin's efforts, and Hades is only banished, he may find another way to return. Avoid Time, Destiny and Fate, they are forever vigilant in seeking your destruction."

"Do you mean Porta? I can handle his interference, but what of these others you have mentioned? To me they are nothing more than phrases the priests use to make us fight all the more harder."

"Yes, this is true, I mean Porta, but not as you know him. His appearance may have changed. As regards the others, they hold ancient names that even the Gods refuse to repeat, and at the beginning of all existence they thrived on the souls of the living, but here in this universe there was no living entity, as we would use such a description. So they changed what already existed to match everything they desired. They existed within all living creatures and they created the first souls, the Gods, to help them feed."

Cappa took a step backwards, his mind again reeling. "So there are other creatures we must fear other than the Gods?"

Aarun sighed, had Zeus chosen the right person?

"In the beginning, Cappa, only light and dark existed in this universe and throughout all of its dimensions. They coexisted in pure harmony, so enthralled in their existence that the arrival of these three entities from another place, which is unknown, was ignored for millennia, until it was too late. The ancients called them Fatalis, Aetas and Fatum."

"Fate, Time and Destiny," Cappa chorused.

"Yes, just so, Cappa. With the Gods created, they could feed on their souls, until one day they grew too powerful for light and darkness, whose ancient names are also unknown, if any names ever existed. As time moved on, the Gods created the worlds and finally tricked Fatalis, Aetas and Fatum into leaving their souls alone and feeding on those created by them. Soon the Gods grew stronger than them and they were thrown out of the dimensions, never to physically return, but now the Gods are few and their power is waning."

"They are seeking to return?"

"No, not them, they are now too weak to defy Zeus, but another power has been awakened in the Underworld, more greater and more terrifying than Hades. Did you not wonder why he wished to escape his kingdom in the first place?"

"No, I guess that is something I did not think about. More interested in how to defeat an enemy, not to understand them."

"This must change, Cappa. Beware of the goblins and sunorcs, but befriend Igluk, he is a future ally."

"*Igluk*! The one that killed Khazumar's son?"

"Befriend him, Cappa. You *must* unite the peoples or all this suffering will have been for nothing, this is but the next stage of a war that has been waged for many centuries. I wish you luck, my friend, but I am being summoned, so I must leave. I have convinced my Lord that you should be given a second chance..."

"Second chance? What, you mean I am actually dead?"

"Your body has been rebuilt, my friend, without the injuries...in fact without any imperfections and with an extended life span. Zeus has decided that you will be his champion in my absence and will combine the forces of freedom, but he has also warned me that you must be wary of our people becoming the evil faction in their zest to correct Hades' work. In this, Hades has laid a very powerful enchantment that will devour those of lesser minds. The enemy is free of Hades' willpower, but they will turn to their own Lesser-Mages for guidance, if the dwarves, especially, revert to their expansionistic policies. Defeat the last few remnants of Hades' willpower, and peace may be there for everyone to enjoy."

Cappa nodded and, with a look of utter despair, he turned to Aarun and clasped his arm. "Then this is goodbye."

"No, it is just a small interlude, my friend, we will meet again. It is apparently written in both of our destinies."

"And Cassius?"

"He decided his own fate many centuries ago and even now still struggles to hold onto the power. I hear him scream for his master to help, but as with Hades and all his minions, he will never openly defy his brother, so he has abandoned the Mage."

"*Brother?*"

"It is another aspect of our story, but yes, both Zeus and Hades share the same father."

"Then the gibberish Atronius called out before Porta attacked me is true?"

"Tell me what he said and if I am permitted, I will answer?"

"He simply said that Zeus had many names, the most common being Jupiter. That in reality there is no Greek Gods and Roman Gods, as they are all the same deities. We have not been supported by a separate group of Gods, but that the same Gods who created Roma, also created Greece."

Aarun hesitated, knowing that to answer would violate the trust given to him by Zeus, but this time he did not care. So many people had died in this ridiculous war and, if he could, he would see it ended.

"What was all this sacrifice about, Aarun?" Cappa forcefully prompted when no reply was forthcoming.

"This war has had many different causes and reasons why the individuals have accepted the ultimate sacrifice of losing their lives. To me there is only one real force that has remained above all others. It is our religious intolerance, where we as elves, were full of scorn for the religion of those who believed in Hades. Hades beliefs were hostile and had only one purpose, to close people's minds to the truth, oppress the minds of orcs, goblins, trolls and even man with the concept of eternal damnation in the pit of hell. To an orc for example just the proof of Hades' existence was, at best, childish and their religion had been generally based on nonsense, manifested and enforced by the Mage, Scipio, Porta and the goblin king, as only these few had actually seen him in person.

"Ancient rituals built around the empty ramblings of using evolution to rebut the notion that without Hades there can be no strength, no power of unity or a safe haven for the raising of their young. This created the hatred we all associate to the orc or goblin; but how strong is our own mistrust of our religious leadership? Did our own hatred fuel this war as much as the orc's? Zeus insists that religion is a conflict-ridden and tyrannical force when linked to his brother and yet I see no real freedom within his realm either, which God is telling the truth?

"Did we really need the Kor lakes? Did we really need to throw out the orc and if we had tried to live in unison, would it have created peace, instead of everlasting war? We all give our sympathies and emotions a realistic value, but in our misguided pride and arrogance are we to blame for all this sacrifice? I can not see a more devastating attack on our moralistic high ground than our efforts to force the orc into extinction, to corrupt his very religion and the fabric of their culture.

"Regardless if you agree or do not agree, Cappa, we must all accept a little portion of the blame for all this suffering. It is time we found a way to believe in one religion or a way to become more tolerant and supportive of those cultures we find offensive to look upon. One God or another has influenced us all in one way or another, but it is now more than ever a time for someone like you, Cappa, to step forward and prevent this from happening again. Ahead of us there waits a greater struggle, but it is faith in the false Gods that will be the greatest enemy, for this will destroy us from within."

"Are you saying that religion does more harm than good? If so, how am I to alter the way any of us deal with our own mortality. To die, in battle or otherwise and then ascend to the higher status of standing with the Gods is the foundation of most religions. How can I change this belief in one life-time?"

"You will find a way, Cappa," Aarun said with a smile. "There is more to your future than you realise, but I must solve a few of my own riddles before we discuss your destiny further. There are fewer Gods than you suspect, Cappa. There are fewer than twenty. They are not immortal, but live beyond our understanding; however, they have never been numerous."

"So we have all been manipulated for their amusement?"

"Perhaps we will have time for such debates later, if matters become less pressing. For now what I have told you must suffice. You will need to leave, as this entire tower is not exactly in the same time or place as you or I, and is held together only by my will. You must escape and bring the peoples back to the ways of peace, Cappa. It is not too late for any of you."

Cappa frowned. "I was kind of hoping I could have rested here for a bit. The harmony in this white light is something I have never felt before."

"It is not your time, my friend. Not yet, seek out Helin, never let her go and be happy, my friend, but also be forever vigilant. You will know when it is time to act. Unite the peoples, Cappa, or this has all been for nothing, remember!"

Cappa felt his heart ache and was about to expand on his feelings for Helin, when the entire room began to shake violently. The roof began to collapse, so he moved rapidly for the exit. Somehow he knew Aarun could not be harmed by anything as small as a piece of masonry. However, Cappa's head was not quite so hard!

He barely escaped the tower before the whole building suddenly folded inwardly. Not odd in itself, except that he observed that not a single rock fell outside of the circle of its original design. Not a single person was injured as a mountain of rock cascaded down. It was awesome to watch and also terrifying. In fact, if he really thought about it, the tower did not really collapse, but almost vanished into itself, but saying it had seemed the easier explanation.

He wondered more and more about Helin as he ran down the stone steps. He could not prevent his unease increasing, as they had all been in the tower in the lower chambers. Had they escaped as well?

"*No, my friend, they are not injured,*" the voice echoed between his ears, making him ponder whether he had anything in between them. He smiled at his own self-criticism, Helin was fine and that was all that mattered to him now. "*I have managed to move them without too much disruption. They await you at the lower palisades by the main gate. Take care, my friend, we shall talk again soon. Soon...*"

Cappa shook his head defiantly, as the voice began to fade and then, suddenly, smiled.

"Not too soon, I hope. Not too bloody soon!"

"By all that is sacred. Will you look at that?" a young elven warrior stated flatly.

"Look at what?" asked his companion incredulously, not certain where he was meant to be looking.

"Them!" A raised finger pointed accusingly.

"Are we all now incapable of seeing *them*?"

"No."

"Then please be quiet. We have enough on our minds, without having to listen to you. We can see for ourselves where the orcs are charging" stated the elf, airily.

"Only trying to lighten the burden..."

"Lighten the burden? How exactly?"

"That is just your problem, friend, a right misery guts with little chance of enlightenment. If I am to end my days here, then I will do so at my bidding, not at an orc's. I'm at a loss as to why I bother to help you."

"Me too! So will you for the love of Gantran and Imtal...*please* be quiet! An elf needs moments like this to contemplate and think of happier times, before those heathens reach us."

"Oh, yeah, you mean that bounteous maiden that was tending to Arfleus no doubt."

"I am not aware of what you mean," his colleague replied, embarrassed.

"Are we now to believe you, but not me, I think not? Besides you think too much for your own good. Now if I had a chance with the same maiden, I would not have any regrets now."

"Silence in the ranks," barked an officer, further along the line.

The voice belonged to Elvandar who had listened while astride his great mare, which had so far that morning carried him dutifully up and down the line from the waterfalls to the area beyond the island in the river captured by the orcs.

The two warriors he listened to had bandaged foreheads, injuries from several engagements this morning to repel the enemy, and their helmets had dents where the blows had fallen, yet their spirits had not been affected. It was truly amazing how these raw recruits had changed before his eyes during the southern campaign.

The regiments had been large in comparison to their dwarven compatriots, and this had led Kol to split many of them in two, to enable a greater level of flexibility. Even so, the remainder had now shrunk to barely sixty percent of the original number and all of those remaining had been injured somewhere or other on their anatomy.

Here stood the last reserve, now comprised of all the walking wounded, while before them they could see the bitter struggle to hold onto this side of the river above the waterfall. The orcs had brought wooden ramps, which had been quickly roped together to form a very crude bridge. It had not been too hard to destroy those rickety constructions, but as soon as one was cast down two more suddenly appeared, with different boulders as the central pillars.

Each rock was capable of holding over fifty orcs apiece. On several of these many of the enemy had been abandoned, as their walkways had been burned or simply smashed apart by the defenders. Even as they watched, a group of twenty elves dashed forward to thwart the attempts of more orcs to cross the river, where they outnumbered the defenders at least five to one. Before their mad charge had reached the bridge, five had fallen to arrows and for the umpteenth time the orcs surged ashore and swept the brave survivors aside.

This time, however, Elvandar did not react but remained bolt upright on the mare's back. He noted the two warriors looking at him, as if to implore him to give the order to advance. He could see in their eyes the bitter anger of having to watch their fellow elves being butchered, while they stood on the hill in relative safety. It was of course part of the plan, a plan not known by the river defenders. It was now essential to give ground and to entice the enemy over the river. To feign defeat and then unleash the next stage of the battle.

"Hold your line!" Elvandar bellowed, as several warriors began to move down the hill. "If you are required to advance, I will command you to do so! Now get back in formation, before I decide to offer punishments long before those orcs attack!"

The elves moved reluctantly back, but only because of his status. In their eyes there remained an open wound to their honour, resentment at having orders issued that effectively abandoned those still fighting at the waterfall to almost certain death. He felt an overpowering urge to explain, to lighten *his* burden. Aarun was dead, or so they believed, for he found it difficult to accept anything else. Nobody had returned from the lost warships and nobody had reported survivors being captured or escaping back north. Even so, he was going to the enemy lord's tower anyway, from where nobody came back...Nobody...*Ever*!

"We should advance, my Lord," offered a warrior with a heavily bandaged arm.

"It is not our policy," Elvandar offered, as an explanation. "It is not our time to advance just yet. Stay strong and obey the orders. This will be a hard won day and we will need your trust, my friend."

"You have our trust and our honour, my Lord, and we will stand or run, where you command us to do so. All we ask is that the sacrifice now is justifiable."

"It is a sacrifice we will remember for all time."

"Then we will stand."

The warrior looked to left and right and with a small chant began to sing an old child's song. It sounded ridiculous to hear a child's fable in the midst of such devastation, but one by one the next company, then the adjoining regiments, began to join in, the sound becoming almost audible over the din of the orcs. For one tiny instant the orcs stopped, fearing some kind of trick. Many of them looked off to either side, but could see no other major formations at the crest of the hill, so these fools were not about to charge. So why sing?

"*Noei Ish'Airyack!*" chanted a larger member of the throng. "*Noei Ish'Airyack!*" came the chant again and slowly the boom of their reply echoed across the valley. Ten thousand orcs sang in their deep voices and clashed their shields, as they started to advance. This was of course no orka formation and the bitter waterfall fighting had destroyed all semblance of order, as the great mass closed on the slender line of elves.

The leaders had mostly been felled so now they continued to fight for the loss of their own people and to satisfy their own hatred of the elves. To an orc they were the real reason for the dwarven expansion through Orcassia, and the real reason for revenge.

All about them the elven survivors of the river line stampeded back, and others pulled them into new lines. They talked, they pleaded, they badgered and if that did not work they bullied them back into the new line. They were tired and the sight of their own people standing by while they bled and died had been enough for them to break, their faith broken.

To end this, Crassus crowded them together, stopping the rout, and decided to tell them the entire battle plan. He explained that in the bushes behind stood forty or more arrow-launching scorpion weapons, each capable of killing ten or more of the enemy. Ten catapults lined the far valley and, even as they spoke, were now being armed with scolding stones covered in inflammable liquids to burn the Great Bridge. He knew his job well and few of the survivors passed him, but pass him they did and Kol from the Tower noted the loss.

"This is the test," he said through clenched teeth. "This is the final test."

Beside him Karr nodded, but said nothing. Here they would only be spectators of the final clash. Crassus would lead the final reserve forward after the scorpions had done their deadly work. It was an odd feeling to finally lose all his doubts, as the final decision did not seem to be theirs to make. Others had made it for them.

With a calm that surprised him, Karr looked far across the river and watched the first of Julius' and Khazumar's forces move towards the triangulated wood, leaving no room to either side to allow any distractions. They too had reached the same impasse and the final decision would soon be known. Whether they took the wood or were forced back would not truly aid them on this side of the river, unless Khazumar was able to drive forward and cut off the enemy's line of retreat back across the bridge.

As Karr watched the action unfold, he spied a large group of the enemy frantically increasing the ramshackle repairs to the Great Bridge. Once they were completed, a vast number of the enemy would be able to surge across seeking their blood. To him the facts were plain. In all their wars, the enemy losses had always been five times greater than their own. This did not diminish the pain felt by the families who suffered such losses, as the sacrifice on many occasions had been great, perhaps sometimes too great. Only this day they believed that their own losses had been equal to the enemy and, should they fail, there would be nothing to stand between them and the Dwarmanian capital.

It did not seem to matter, but the orcs had indeed suffered most grievously, yet they recovered and came back for more bloodshed and devastation. It was after all a simple case of numbers. In the last five years of this conflict, their borders had slowly been driven inwards, and the field army they had previously commanded had numbered well over two hundred thousand. Now they fielded a force of barely eighty thousand. It was only a matter of time before the elves and dwarves, and now the men as well, could no longer replace those lost, and then they would fail.

Karr reached down and clasped a wineskin. For a moment he allowed the glint of the afternoon sun on the golden texture to distract him, admiring the bright colours of the reflection, which reminded him of a rainbow. He finished the drink in two large gulps and then looked for Kol, who now stood at the far end, the better to observe Elvandar and Crassus.

For a moment he hesitated, feeling despondent. Why was he here? What possible good was he standing next to Kol, when others stood side by side and made the ultimate sacrifice? Even before his pride could answer, he knew he was destined to serve Kol and no other. He would have served no real purpose given his damaged leg, and would only have added to the corpses littering the river's edge. He turned to look once more at the wood and wondered just what was going through their minds right now.

Here the blades had been temporarily sheathed, but in that wood the sound of fighting travelled easily on the light wind.

Only time would tell...

⋄⋅⋈⋅⋄⋅⋈⋅⋄

Julius watched the new developments and felt his stomach begin to churn. The bile rose in his throat. The stench was something nobody could describe, and it caused a reaction you felt rather than acknowledged. If you thought about it even for a second, as many indeed did, the stomach did not hold out very long, and the morning meal made its second appearance. At first this brought some mild relief, but after a few hundred people had reacted in the same way their combined bile simply added to the stench. For some this meant a third or even a fourth appearance!

The horse seemed to sense his irritation and struggled to leave this foul area, where the disgusting odour was stifling its nostrils. Its eyes were wide and Julius could not blame the beast, which to date had never even seen a battlefield, never mind experienced one. Like the rider, the horse was learning first-hand what it was like to sit and watch.

"What is he doing?" barked Julius, startling the nearby aides by the ferocity of the exclamation, and making them shuffle about aimlessly looking at each other for support.

"How can he retain the linear formation when the wood is in flames?" Julius shouted, somehow unable to fathom what Neros was attempting.

The legion marched in mutually supporting cylindrical formations towards the triangular wood, which had been deliberately set alight by Neros who had, you may recall, been made temporary commander of the legion in Crassus' absence. There was not a complete wall of fire, and at certain intervals the wood still remained intact, but it was only a matter of time before the spreading flames consumed everything.

Julius spurred his horse forwards, gesticulating bitterly towards where Neros stood. The latter was too far away to even notice the approach of his commander. They had indeed chosen the wrong man, as Julius desperately admitted. He had acted with bravery against the orka, but his inexperience had now led him to believe that he could defeat the enemy single-handedly, and the whole of the legion was about to be taken into the wood, to its certain destruction.

That was, of course, unless he could reach there in time to stop the advance, the benefits of which had been nullified by the very fire they marched towards. Neros was about to repeat what the enemy commander had done earlier with the orka, thus giving the enemy the equilibrium instead of using their own advantage correctly.

By the Gods, they had just devastated a large portion of the enemy army, and now a fool was about to inflict the same torture on their own people. Let them all burn, he spat, as he rode down the slope, why take our people into the wood as well? Let all the heathens in the wood burn. They did not need to enter, as they could go around the southern edge. This was ridiculous!

As he rode the mare at the gallop, it became plain that nothing would arrive in time to stop the doomed advance. Time had finally run out and Neros was about to find a very furious Julius landing very heavily on his shoulders...

※ ※ ※

They moved like a wave rolling up the beach, only this time there were no cliffs to stem the advance. They waited and watched, as the stench of the orcs moved closer and closer, causing many a stout heart to drift into despair. They manned their new machines of war, but none of them had had more than a few hours tuition in their practical use. Nobody doubted that the devastation the scorpion wrought would be anything less than spectacular, but before the elven line charged a mass of pure hatred. Perhaps more than a few extra large arrows would be required to prevent the fall of Kol's tower?

Sweat beaded on their foreheads, as they crouched beside the large wooden arrows, tipped with sharpened points created only this morning by the hardiest of dwarven blacksmiths. They were sharpened beyond normal levels, and five blacksmiths had been injured just lifting the damn things, with cuts to the forearms and legs, never mind what would be unleashed onto the orcs.

The tension was extreme as they watched the enemy come closer and closer.

How were they supposed to survive, if the generals had miscalculated? Each weapon would take at least thirty counts to reload. In that time even the oldest dwarf could cover at least eighty paces, never mind battle hardened veterans such as these orcs.

This was suicide, they decided, almost simultaneously, and a few rose slightly to use the light-footed approach. The thought existed of course, what person in such close proximity to death did not feel some level of fear? They had their loved ones, their partners and friends, some of whom shared their ordeal, and they naturally questioned the validity of the sacrifice required of them this day.

This was true, but no matter how tempting the thought, not a single warrior left his post, as the horde reached the small incline twenty paces below them on the slope. The crest of the hill was just a few paces behind them, where safety could be found if they left now.

Some needed a stern look from a friend or senior, but most of them simply sat and waited. A few prayed to Zeus for guidance, but did not truly hold their breath. This was a mortal conflict and they would decide what transpired here, not the Gods.

"Make ready!" someone shouted, so loudly that the nearest orcs stopped suddenly, unsure of what lay in the bushes ahead.

The pause was only momentary, as the great press from behind suddenly forced them to move again and, whether they wished to make a choice or not, the opportunity was snatched away by those following. So on they came after a few nervous looks beyond the undergrowth, where the crest of the hill was clear of all foliage.

The rush of activity that followed the order was of course hidden from the enemy by the very same foliage, but the first shot would almost certainly clear up any misunderstandings, leaving them all exposed to retribution, but there was nothing left to do but continue. Besides, where could they go now? Even if they ran the orcs would probably just catch them on the hill, rather than right here.

"Adjust sights!" Crassus gave the final warning, and according to who had this responsibility, a few scorpions were moved marginally a nudge or two to either side, all the better to kill!

On the hill, Elvandar suddenly rose and looked down at the long mass of black leather that stared back with red, yellow and white eyes of hatred. The chanting became louder than ever for the orcs always enjoyed ripping apart a hero, as they had already done more than a few times that morning. Now, on a stupid animal, sat another fool for the slaughter.

They began to chant and push and bash one another as they marched on once more, and their intent became apparent, to kill the elf on the horse. They would reach the top and rip his body to shreds and roll down to victory on the far side. This was a good day to be part of the horde. Whether you were sunorc, orc or one of the untrustworthy goblins, victory was now only two hundred paces away.

Step by step they neared their goal. Morale was high, despite their horrific casualties. They had no reason to doubt their purpose. On they strode to a victory, which, unknown to them, had already slipped them by.

They would never make those two hundred paces!

"Fire!" screamed Elvandar, using the full force of his lungs, and feeling a new excitement grip him. It was the feeling of a chance being grasped from almost certain defeat. "Fire!" rebounded down the long line of foliage on each side and then the first arrows struck.

Julius had described how the weapon worked, but only Crassus had actually been present at a live performance. His description was not even close!

Elvandar watched as one arrow slashed through the mass of bodies that could not avoid the massive blade, due to their compactness. Great swathes of blood trailed behind, as it struck at perfect head height, decapitating more than one unfortunate. Another struck barely a few paces to the left and skewered three orcs, which were lifted bodily into the air and flung back down the slope to tumble into the crowd, to cut and injure several more.

Off to the left he watched a mass of the enemy, who had just stopped in their tracks, look to one another for explanations as to where their legs or arms had gone. One in particular staggered ahead with both hands flailing blindly, as no face remained on the head. More could be seen off to the right, where a massive hole had suddenly appeared in the mass, but nothing could be seen of their comrades' remains, which had been catapulted far over their heads, some actually landing back in the river itself.

"Reload!" ordered Elvandar frantically, finally snapping out of the shock. It was an unnecessary order, but it was reassuring to know he could still respond to any eventuality of battle.

"Fire!" someone else shouted, and even before an attempt at recovery had been made more carnage rained down on the orcs.

More orcs than before were cut to ribbons and the free flow of blood now caused many others to slip on the steep slope. A lucky soul did just that, and one particular arrowhead passed inches above his head, then decapitated the three officers who had stood directly behind, discussing a change in tactics.

A swift glance told him there would be no further instructions from them and there was literally no way back, as the orcs below were only marginally aware of the danger and continued to push them forwards toward the barbed points of hell.

He looked frantically from one side to the next, seeking a good place to hide until some kind of order was achieved. Then he would rejoin the front rank for the glorious march up the hill, but where exactly? All about him the arrows flailed and cut into the mass, leaving behind more orcs injured than able to continue to advance. He knelt sheepishly next to a wounded comrade who simply swore at him, then shoved so hard that he stumbled on the wet, sticky blood. This was madness!

He rose to turn back, fully prepared to kill anyone who stood in his way.

The point penetrated his torso just below the ribcage and ripped the whole of the left side of his body away in one silent wrench. He gasped once or twice and then tried to move his arm, but found that everything had suddenly begun to fade. His hatred vanished as he remembered his home and wondered whether his mate had remained true or taken another, it had been over three years after all.

Then he died.

All along the small ridge Elvandar watched the carnage grow to the point where nobody could advance to harm the scorpions, due to the natural barricade of dead bodies. Such was the damage that he ordered Crassus to move the counterattack off to the left to circumvent the worst locations, where they would be unable to keep their own formations. Crassus had simply remained silent, had drunk deeply from a wineskin and vanished amidst the numerous regiments poised to make the attack.

It was now only a matter of knowing when to go. Not yet, Elvandar thought, let the catapults destroy their flimsy bridges first, along with the repairs to the Great Bridge. Let us truly trap them, while the scorpions continue to do their deadly work.

He glanced momentarily at the far side of the river and felt his heart rise majestically, as there seemed to be a mass of regiments steadily advancing past the trees towards the far side of the Great Bridge. Even from here he recognised the Red emblems of Khazumar, even though the Priesthood Guards now stood with Crassus. The plan was working...By all the Gods, it was actually working!

Nothing had worked so far and the feeling of imminent destruction could be seen in all of their eyes, yet now suddenly the air seemed fresher and the old indestructibility returned.

"Now is the time, Elvandar, for the Mage is past."

"What? Who? What trick is this?"

A gentle laugh was his only reply. A laugh so familiar that a tear welled up and broke free to run the gauntlet of mud and blood covering his face.

"Aarun?" he shouted, helplessly. "Is that you?"

"Yes and no, my friend, but now is not the time for reunions, Elvandar, you must finish your task. Now is your time to fulfil your destiny...the Mage is dead!"

"You are certain?"

"I destroyed him with the aid of our great Zeus. Strike now, my friend. Strike now!"

"But where are you? I need to know if you still live? What has happened? Where have you been, my Lord, your people need you? Aarun...*Aarun!*"

Elvandar turned the horse's head, as his own whirled at the sudden arrival of the voice. There was nobody near him...*Nothing*! It was impossible...How? He had been told to strike now, but why now? Nothing had changed, they still needed to destroy those before them. It was stress, he admitted, he had finally cracked after the loss of his friend and benefactor. It was his own stupid imagination but, in that case, was that approaching storm also his imagination? The speed of its approach was definitely unnatural. Then it was true: the Gods had finally destroyed the Mage!

"Crassus! Where is Crassus?"

"Here, Elvandar, how may I help?" responded a voice, from amongst the nearest regiment.

"How goes the relocation?" Elvandar asked.

"We have five or so regiments in place, but the bulk are still moving. Why?"

"We strike now!"

"What!"

"We strike now! Now Crassus, do not delay, for the Gods themselves have spoken and the wind yonder brings news of the death of the Mage. We strike now!"

And with that Elvandar charged down the hill and took the Priesthood Guards with him. Vengeance was to be his, one way or another, and whom better to take on this journey than the first warriors to fight in this new conflict at the Azar-Kad caves.

It was early evening.

⸻ ※ ⸻ ※ ⸻

Cappilius sat for a moment as he tried desperately to recover his breath, which burned in his throat. Recent exertions had left them all short of breath and their numbers whittled down to a fraction of their former strength. All around this temporary refuge hundreds of prone bodies lay still in their caricatures of death, while a scattered few continued to move, struggling to keep hold of their lifeline, a struggle he knew would fail.

Any wounded were likely to have poison running in their veins and the mortalkind, dwarf or hobbit heart would not be able to resist for long. That was why none of the survivors had made any attempt to save them or treat their wounds. To begin with they had done so, but after numerous failures the facts had become known and the healers had picked up a sword instead of their herbs.

It had been a heart-rending moment to see a friend injured, apparently only mildly, by a scratch across the neck or arm, and yet know that they would die. Then calmly turning your back on them. The look in a person's eyes when the realisation dawned, as they themselves often never even acknowledged the injury, or did so only when they caught the eye of the very friend who was turning away.

In that moment many decided to die taking a few of the enemy with them, but so many simply sat down and gave up, some lost in their grief. To die was to die, but to do so in such a ridiculous manner left many proud men devastated. It had in a way hardened their resistance and improved their aim, to prevent the orcs from shooting their deadly arrows.

Even so they did not seem to be winning.

Their struggle no longer had anything to do with the greater conflict. They had long ago forgotten the developments elsewhere, as their own struggle to survive had seen almost half their number slain. Here was a conflict of skill rather than hatred and neither side would relinquish the field, thus prolonging an unnecessary confrontation. Or so it would have seemed to a casual observer, but to any still standing it felt as though the war and all the minor confrontations would be decided on this rough terrain, with its undulations and death-trap valley floors.

They had all bled and died to protect the main army's extreme right flank, but in truth the sunorc numbers had been reduced so much that, even if they had won, they would no longer have been able to influence the bigger picture. No, as stated, this was purely an issue of skill and the hatred of the morning had vanished, as soon as emotional energy was needed simply to stand, never mind fight.

Cappilius knew his job had been to pin the enemy here for as long as he could, but in truth there was no front line regiments of the enemy left, other than the opposing light auxiliaries. They now occupied a position on the extreme right of the broken ground and were still looking to go around their flank. For six hours they had fought hand to hand with an enemy that had shown not only cunning, but also a high level of intelligence.

Cappilius began to wonder just how much of the information given to him about the orcs had been falsified, to give him confidence. Perhaps some clever propaganda had been applied, as regards their real purpose? Or perhaps they had used the true nature of the orc as a generalisation? Whatever the reason, it was plain to see that these sunorcs had somewhat disproved the usual claims.

A sudden movement to his left focused his mind, causing a momentary quickening of the heartbeat. Had he been taken by surprise? Had he allowed his eyes to close for just a few seconds? No, it was fine, it was Armolin the hobbit captain standing over him and casting a very welcome shadow on his forehead.

"We cannot continue like this," she panted, her own exhaustion obvious as she crouched, both hands resting heavily on her knees, the breath rasping in her throat. "We are at the point of exhaustion, Cappilius. We must retire before it is too late. Even if they are as tired as us, they still outnumber us three to one."

Cappilius raised his shoulders indifferently, but numbers had never really bothered him before, and was there any reason for them to do so now...? No! Not really, he had already kind of accepted that few of them would celebrate or commiserate that evening anyway, so numbers really did not matter.

"If we fold, then they will sweep into the right flank of the army, Armolin. As beautiful as you are, I am still not willing to face that youth, Julius, with news of a failure. He may be young, but Cappa and Crassus are not and he holds their seal of command. We must stand, there is no other choice."

Frowning, the hobbit crouched beside him and jabbed her finger into his ribs. "Flattery will get you nowhere and Julius is not the issue, Cappilius, a point that I have reminded you of at least five times this day. As handsome as you are and as terrible as your youthful commander may be, I am still not willing to allow my people to be massacred here or anywhere else. My Lady would skin me alive!"

"If you leave it will be your choice. I have none, as I have already explained. I must stay and so will my people."

"What!" said Armolin, shocked to hear such a foolish statement from such an experienced warrior. "You'd number no more than one hundred if we retired, as we must do to avoid certain death. Honour is all well and good, but those sunorcs are not going to be honourable. They will charge very shortly and we will not be able to hold them. Unless we have reinforcements, we will *not* succeed."

Cappilius drew a deep breath, where could they seek reinforcements at this late stage in the battle? He had tried earlier with the Cenitarns, but they had stoutly refused to move any further into the broken terrain, as the orders given to them encompassed offering support to this point only, but no further.

It was the sign of a good officer to recognise when circumstances during battle required a personal interpretation of orders given several hours earlier, but these dwarves were already known to be weak and had been sent only as a gesture. They had stoutly referred to the loss of personal honour, if they moved without fresh orders, but just as stoutly refused to support the right flank in their struggle.

"The Cenitarns will not offer support unless *we* retire, but I am damned if I will do so and expose Julius' rear echelons to harassment! Too many of my comrades have fallen this day to give up now. No, if we are to fail, then why not do so here, where we can honour our glorious dead! We will attack them!"

"Glory? Attack a force superior in numbers, as well as experience?"

"Yes, why not?" said Cappilius, with increased enthusiasm. "What is the last thing those sunorcs will expect at this time?" he continued, seemingly oblivious to Armolin's glare of absolute disbelief. "Well? You do not know, because it is too stupid for even us to try, but it may just be exactly the right thing to do. Don't look at me like that. I am *not* insane. This sun has not quite scrambled my brain yet..."

"Not too far off though, eh?" Armolin laughed, and again jabbed her finger forward, but with a smile of mockery this time rather than irritation. "Come to think about it, I guess I'm just as bad."

"How so?"

"Well, I said that we should leave, but I have yet to do so. Perhaps I know deep down that even if ordered, my people would not leave without you. Only the Gods know why of course!"

"Listen, Armolin, what I said earlier..."

"About what they would expect least?"

"Yes. Do you know what I am thinking?" asked Cappilius, moving a little closer to the hobbit and, with the expression of a child, encouraging her to agree.

"If we attack, where do we do so? We have no idea where the main group has retired to."

"If they are anywhere, Armolin, it will be beyond those hillocks to the south. From there they can see the southern extremity of the wood and, if needed, they can attack Julius' right. We do not have the strength to watch there and also occupy the ground we have captured. My guess is that they are just behind those hills."

"I hope you are right! If not, we could be running straight into an ambush."

Cappilius smiled and again wished his brother could have been here with them now, for his expertise in avoiding an ambush would have been useful.

"In war we must all, at one point or another, take a chance. If the sunorcs are to take any active part in this final defence of the wood, then they *must* be there, for anywhere else would be too far off to be of use. Organise your people, Armolin, we go in ten minutes. It is time to find out if I'm right!"

Armolin had known all along that an attack was their best, and now only, defence. All of those still standing could manage just one more charge, but the Cenitarns would still be needed to protect the ground they would vacate. With this in mind, she had already dispatched several hobbits, with a senior dwarf for authenticity, to speak to the Cenitarns.

They would demand loyalty to their brethren, who even now had died in the hundreds to preserve the kingdom, while they had sat in comfort well away from the fighting. As Cappilius finished his speech, she looked to those very same people, who mouthed the figure of seven hundred to her. Seven hundred from three thousand had decided to disobey their officers and join this madcap assault. For them honour had to be satisfied, while in those who remained a slow burning torch of shame began to burn.

It would eventually consume them, but for the moment only those few had decided to join the survivors. Cappilius was thus left with almost one thousand people, of mixed race, to finally secure the broken ground. After casualties, he knew the sunorcs would still number at least double their tiny band.

"Who are they?" Cappilius asked, as he rose with Armolin, eyes betraying his exhaustion.

"The few from the Cenitarn regiments, who have decided to join your little scheme," explained Armolin, pulling her sword free and quickly checking that the bloodstains had not coalesced, causing it to stick in the scabbard.

"Cenitarns?"

"Yes."

"How?"

"Is that important now?"

"No, I guess not. Well, I suppose the more the merrier. How many do you think there are on the far side of this damned valley?"

Armolin looked intensely across the ground they intended to traverse, which ran for only a thousand paces. It had so far been the scene of ten sunorc charges, plus the counter-charges organised by them both, and it was littered with the prone bodies of the unfortunate dead.

She knew the enemy had almost certainly been a full regiment when the fighting had started, and from the corpses it could be calculated that the sunorcs had suffered double their own fatalities. However, there was no real way of knowing whether they had been reinforced.

"Perhaps the same number as us, maybe a few more."

"A little hopeful, but then the number we face will be of little importance. Further delays are pointless. Bring everyone together."

The preparations passed in a blur, as word spread of the impending final charge. If this failed they would all need to survive as best they could in small groups and head straight back towards the warship-bridge. For a few precious minutes, Cappilius repeated this to anyone who stood near, shouting for them to pass the word. If they failed the sunorcs would not stop at the broken ground, but would pursue them to the death, as indeed he would have done to them.

As they gathered on the far side of the slope, they looked at one another with an air of indifference, eyes tired from the day's efforts. Accepting that this was the final effort, while many perhaps knew they would not have had the energy to retreat anyway, so they might as well do this with all the heart and honour possible, they stood in silence, waiting for the order to charge.

It was said that you could look into a dead man's eyes even when he was still alive, knowing the end was only a few moments away. It was of course superstition, but at this point any belief was good. Some of these so-called recognised walking-dead would find themselves ignored, companionship refused.

Cappilius watched a few begin to kneel and offer a few prayers up to Zeus and felt his own belief challenged, as the rage at people being set aside pulsed through his veins.

"This is not what we fight for," he suddenly exclaimed, grabbing one dwarf by the shoulder, thrusting aside another velites of his own people. "This dwarf stands beside us all on this final day. He fears an impending death, so do we all, but some of us can hide this better than others. For this are *we* to allow him no companionship in these last, precious hours? We stand together, or *not* at all! How say *you*!"

Their pride stung, and the stupidity of denying friendship to a colleague exposed, forced them on and a series of cheers echoed across the valley.

"Stand *together*!" they all began to chant.

Cappilius forced his own doubts aside and stepped forward to gather about him all those so earmarked for death, then turned back towards the remainder.

"Here today we will make our final sacrifice, where I intend to sell my life in exchange for ten of the enemy. We are the only people who stand before those who seek to turn the flank and attack from behind the West Hill. We will not let this happen, so we will need everyone to fight hard and with a rage far beyond any already seen today. I therefore throw aside my vows as a Roman officer and pledge to you all that I am honoured to have fought with you on this day. In victory or defeat I will rest in peace, but I will rest easier if we stand *victorious*!"

"Victory *together*! Victory! Victory!" drowned Cappilius' voice for a few seconds, as he patiently waited for the chants to subside.

"Now, across that valley is an enemy who has fought as long and as hard as us. They have watched us retire over this slope and may even consider us already beaten, and that I surely intend to prove incorrect. Now is *our* day. Now is *our* time to shine in the light of Zeus and seek the victory we so richly deserve. Further delays are pointless. Draw swords, link shields, harness your courage and follow *me!*"

With a final nod and with no climatic response the mass began to roll forward at a slow trot. Expecting an arrow at any moment, they moved down the slope, where previously resistance had been swift to appear, but they found no enemy in sight. They began to climb the far slope and still nothing could be seen. No vanguard, no scouts or lookouts, nothing. For a brief moment they hesitated at the summit, suspicious and expecting an elaborate trap.

Still there was nothing.

"Forward," shouted Cappilius, pointing towards the next hill, which looked twice the height of their current position. "We rest on the other slope. Now *move!*"

They now took victory for granted. The sunorcs had retired, yet they could see no reason for such a defeatist attitude. The sunorcs had not been defeated and yet their will to resist had obviously vanished. The enemy had gone and for now Cappilius was happy to accept this at face value, but he knew from experience that they must still proceed cautiously!

Three more valleys followed the next and the position was securely held, while the only sign of the sunorcs had been a small group, which had grunted a few times and then promptly vanished. By the time anyone reached the position where they had been seen, there was not even a set of tracks. Why? What could have made them suddenly turn and run? It was now the Haderian left, not the Alliance's right, that had been turned.

All about Cappilius the fields were clustered with the remains of line upon line of tents and small barricades. They had reached the enemy camp. His small band now stood behind the vast army still fighting at the river to the north, not knowing that their left flank, which was also the most direct route to retire if they were to suffer a reverse, had already been turned. At least seventy percent of the Haderian army had nowhere to retreat to, even though Cappilius' force numbered barely one thousand, and he watched with pride as the Cenitarns made a welcome reappearance.

They all stopped and stared in wonder at the vast amounts of equipment and carts littering the whole area. It was like being in a ghost town. They stood where, only a few hours ago, fifty thousand had slept and had eaten their morning meal; whatever that had been, Cappilius thought with a grimace. Their food was bad enough, never mind what the orcs, hobgoblins, wolves, trolls, goblins or orka considered edible food.

"So what now?" asked Armolin, clearly shocked at how far they had advanced.

"We go back."

"Back? Why?"

"Look around you Armolin," Cappilius said, sweeping a hand across the horizon. "We do not have the necessary forces to hold this position even with the Cenitarns finding their courage, but we can strike at the rear of the woods at the East Hill. If I remember rightly, that is where we will find the Haderian command tent."

"It is, but then what are we waiting for? Let's pay a visit on our erstwhile enemy leaders, and God help their souls when they meet us!"

The laughter rippled through the group as they headed back northeast, but at a more oblique angle, to skirt the southern tip of the woods. On the East Hill they remained oblivious to the danger and Igluk especially was more than irritated by the day's events so far.

It was after all turning into a long day, just when he had especially desired a short one!

⁘⊹⁘

They stood in a small huddle, the trees swaying in the heavy wind that buffeted the entire wood. According to the Mage, control of the elements had remained with them, but one by one they gazed at the sky, where the sun was beginning to break through. Nobody knew what such an ill omen meant, but inside a sudden panic had gripped the heart. For the first time they did not know where they were or what they needed to do.

Indeed this was the first time they had had the use of their own minds in the last two decades, but it was not for them to have known the restrictive nature of their very existence. The power had been as a blanket over their lives, giving them a purpose. Now the purpose had vanished and all that was left to supplant this absolute certainty of purpose was *Igluk*!

This same power had enabled Scipio to control the orka, who had worshipped him as a God, for they knew nothing better: he was to them their creator, their mentor and their father...for want of a better word. Now that security had vanished. Their own leaders were dead, and they now stood on the hill in a confused mass, not truly knowing the reasons for this war. The hatred for the elves remained, but little else, as the dwarves had always been irrelevant to anyone other than the goblins. As for the mortalkind, the Romans, they were of even less interest.

What was the purpose of being here and dying?

They began to draw upon the old hatred, and orcs began to turn on goblins, while the wolves immediately massacred a large portion of the Black Regiments of Gobli. The hobgoblins had vanished once more, while at the command tent Igluk was paralysed by uncertainty. Within a few minutes, the entire Haderian army was on the brink of disintegration and no one had the power to unify them, only the Mage.

Only the Mage!

So where was the Mage, and why did he not appear before them and restore their purpose?

Among the gathering throng at the East Hill, one orka stood taller than most. He too had felt the sudden deep, wrenching sensation inside that had made him stagger and left him uncertain as to where this place was, and why they were standing in this wood. He knew they were in the middle of a battle, which less than an hour ago had claimed the lives of sixty percent of his legion. In addition, after a swift reorganisation, it was established that all the senior officers had perished, leaving him and two other junior leaders to keep the survivors together.

He fought desperately against the urge to run. All about him the sounds of battle echoed across the wood, then from deep within his true nature charged forward! Scipio's training had not been in vain after all!

Pride bordering on blind insanity overwhelmed his mind, as he quickly used his senses to detect everything within visual perception. His eyes settled and the sensation diminished, but a severe hatred of all the goblins burst forth. Looking to either side he knew his people had the same urges, some having already killed the nearest goblins, but with a deep, blood-curdling roar they all stopped to look in his direction.

"Fight *scum*, not goblins!"

He pointed outside the wood, where his small band of orka stood, indicating a few elven regiments that would serve to whet his appetite.

Pride then turned to desperation, as they had reached the edge of the wood only to find that they faced a far greater enemy. Then they began to die in hundreds, and eventually in thousands, as the enemy retreated like a pack of wolves, but continued to strike down a few at a time. They had failed and, even now, as the uncertainty became magnified, he knew his one desire was to go home, but not before he had rectified that dishonour.

Nothing was more important now. Nothing!

His name was Omkanis. He did not intend to insult his ancestors with another defeat until he had regained a victory, as twice this day he had been defeated: once when the legion had advanced, and now at the edge of this wood. Having withdrawn to the East Hill's promontory, he watched the woods before him from this high ground, where a lone rider raced frantically across the back of the advancing Romans.

Something was wrong and that frantic rider's rush was telling him something, but for the moment he could not see it. Off to his left and slightly down the hill, in the nearby bracken, stood Ginnis, now the black goblin leader after all the others had been killed in the wolves' purge scant moments earlier. He had driven off the wolves, but his people were visibly shaken by the sudden assault from allies.

Ginnis sought his aid. He had of course agreed, but somehow this wood did not seem as important as the battle, but now this struggle, between the bracken and the trees, represented his people's freedom.

Yes, freedom was the right word, but he knew little of its true meaning. Duty and honour were all he understood, and after that the sensation that a realisation was coming home to roost in his brain. Somehow he knew the Mage was no more and, if this was true, then he had better take his people away now before more orcs decided to vent their anger on his survivors.

Ginnis' own people were holding the wood and had originally been placed there to reinforce the Great Bridge attack. Now it seemed that Igluk, the Orc-Mage, had defied all logic and left them there with no specific purpose, as the main fighting was currently taking place along the southern and northern banks of the river.

Now the enemy's real deception could be seen, in all its reality. It had been no flanking diversion, but a full-blooded attempt to turn the Haderian army on the left flank. The numbers easily surpassed forty thousand or more, and at least half of the enemy army had been committed.

Ginnis had sent word of this development to the command tent, but the messenger had never returned. He sent another and another, but then there was no further time to waste. He would take his people home and do so now before it was too late.

Omkanis eventually decided that his people must do the same.

Ginnis meanwhile had sent word to the other goblin chieftains, who had swiftly responded and had begun to retire south. This left only the Orcassians at the river defences and the other orka legion in reserve, but they would need time to gain a breathing space to reach the beaches far to the south, where the ships waited. He intended to buy them this time, with his own life if necessary.

Here Omkanis would fight a delaying action, but in truth he could not do so without the aide of the massive orka, for whom a great respect had now developed, after their charge earlier in the day that had failed.

Ginnis had watched this defeat, and had sent a few of his people to help, but it had already gone too far. The orka had broken and run and he knew they sought an opportunity to redeem their lost pride. Here was just such an opportunity, and so he and Omkanis had joined together to form an army within the army. The greater picture no longer existed, for they could easily see that the Great Bridge would fall sooner or later to the Dwarves, which would mean defeat even for the most stubborn of people.

How could it be? They had been so close to victory and then suddenly they now faced utter defeat. More important, why had Scipio abandoned them, the mortalkind-Mage was far more powerful than Igluk! How had the Mage been defeated? Why had he abandoned them in the first place? Then there was that final decisive act of the sun returning.

Ginnis felt his skin crawl as his thoughts turned to Igluk, although Omkanis was indifferent to the new leader of Haderia. A fouler creature could not possibly exist, and Ginnis remembered him from the battle at the river and the subsequent struggle to reach the Noborian River, elven archers hunting them every step of the way.

He had never seen an army disintegrate so fast and so finally. Now it was happening again.

Why?

He turned as Omkanis joined him with an arm raised, pointing towards the far hill.

"They come, Ginnis, below the tree line around the fire," Omkanis said, licking his dripping fangs. "Your people know what to do?"

"They do."

"Then let it begin. They destroyed our people, now we shall destroy them."

Ginnis opened his lungs and bellowed a command and began to trot gently down the hill and through a small ravine, which he had discovered earlier, covered completely in foliage. In fact someone had inadvertently fallen through the broken ground and had found it. It was of course where Valenus had hidden for three days and managed to avoid capture. Now he used it as a secret position where his archers waited for the final stand. It would not be long in coming, as he did not intend for a pitched battle to take many lives.

No, he wanted time.

Time only.

⸻

Neros was of slight build and bulging eyes, with a beard that did nothing to hide his contemptuous outlook on life. He had been Crassus' choice, but it was now Julius who furiously dismissed the fool from command of the legion. A few had argued that the youth had no such authority, while others had flocked to stand by Neros and told Julius to mind his own business, Neros obviously being the more experienced man.

The response had been one of unexpected ferocity, as before them the legion reached the trees, and began to suffer casualties not only from the fire, but also from the well-organised and concealed enemy. Julius' patience had snapped and with a clash of steel the sword landed squarely on Neros' helmet, as indeed it had done on Valenus' skull, all those years ago at the ambush.

Stunned, Neros had immediately retired taking a few loyal retainers, but the majority stayed with the youth. He now ordered a retirement. He managed to hold back half of the commitment, but within a few minutes Omkanis' counterattack was sweeping across their right flank and meeting with immense success.

Ginnis wanted time, Omkanis was taking time, while Julius had run out of time.

At the triangular wood, the moment of crisis had finally arrived...

Cappilius watched the revived orka swing around the southern end of the wood. With a practised ease he kept his own people back, telling them to lie low in the grass and the rolling ravines nearby. With a patience to drive Armolin insane, the Roman waited. He saw Julius strike down Neros, and smiled to think there would be a fine story to hear later, but all the while his eyes were waiting for something else. When Ginnis let fly with his archers and suddenly appeared to Julius' left, he knew the real crisis was almost upon them.

With a nonchalant wave of his sword he pointed towards the orka and began to trot forwards. As before, the orka had forgotten the necessity of supporting their exposed flanks, where heavy soldiers were always vulnerable.

Now, as they had during the morning charge of the original orka legion, Cappilius and Armolin made them pay a high price.

Khazumar watched from the riverbank as the orka charged. For a few seconds he contemplated sending reinforcements to Julius, but knew it would take too long to be of any help, so instead he turned once more back to the Great Bridge. Now in ruins, the bridge barely remained standing, and he was now forcing back the orcs to expose the waterfall crossings, which would trap the enemy on the northern bank, to certain destruction.

If they had tried to use the bridge to escape, it did seem unlikely that it would be able to hold any substantial weight, such had been the sustained damage in several pitched battles over the last few days.

All about him the wounded were hobbling away to the riverbank to try and tend to injuries, as he had earlier ordered that no able-bodied warrior was to assist any of the wounded to retire. The order had been met with anger, but as the goblins and orcs had counterattacked them in an attempt to retake the Great Bridge's southern rampart, his harshness was vindicated. They held, but only just.

Julius was on his own!

There were to be three more hours of fighting and killing, just three more terrifying hours.

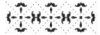

‹-⁘-*-⁘-›

Hadrian looked long and hard at the feet moving towards him. He had no way of looking up, as he had for the past five hours been playing dead, even though he knew he had been pierced twice by orc spears. The feet came closer and for a moment he dreaded they might be the sunorc scouts returning, but something about the fur on those feet made him relax.

Slowly he turned his head onto his chin, being very careful not to open his eyes. After a few more heartbeats, he assumed nobody had seen his movement and he quickly flicked open his right eye. He saw Armolin, but in such a short glance he could not be positive. Was it a hobbit? He had not had much to do with them, so recognising one now after lying here so long was impossible.

Was it a sunorc? No, of that he was certain. No, sunorcs, and even the orcs, had fur on their feet. Massive iron boots they normally wore. Then again the foot had no sandals either.

"Over here," a voice behind him shouted. "I am certain this one moved as well."

"Are you certain?" replied a second voice, which belonged to the feet in front of him.

"I am certain, yes, that one just in front of you."

Hadrian felt fingers seek a pulse on his neck and he stiffened, expecting the final blow. When it did not strike, he opened both of his eyes and gazed up into the most beautiful, hazel eyes of Armolin.

"This one is definitely alive, Cappilius," she called, looking assuringly off to her left. "Do we have any more stretchers?"

"No, we only had materials to make two. Can he talk?"

"He is injured, but the blood does not seem to be all his," Armolin began, tenderly bandaging the forearm, where a gash could be seen by the coagulated bloodline. "I seem to remember this man. He was definitely in Valenus' group that crossed the bridge."

Cappilius moved closer and for a moment held his breath.

"Hadrian! By the Gods, it is a miracle any of you survived!"

"There are others," Hadrian croaked awkwardly, then feverishly drank from Armolin's water bottle.

"Yes. Jarvi reported back to Julius and due to your findings we chose to attack across the river and into those very woods you hid within. Bruti followed soon after and Centurion Neros' legionaries found Tatrius, seconds before he was burnt alive, and only seconds earlier we found Volas and another man whom I do not recognise. More of you managed to survive than we could ever have hoped."

"What of Valenus?"

"Nobody knows where he may have gone, and at least two-thirds of the wood has been burnt to the ground. It does not look too good. Do you know where he was heading? Bruti could not recall. Jarvi mentioned something about a large hill, but we can only find a small stream and a tiny mound to the northeast. Just below the East Hill, where the enemy command tent has been found."

Hadrian thought for a moment, collecting his memories. His head felt as though someone had drained all the fluid out of his brain. He could not think straight, yet slowly he collected his thoughts. Yes, he could remember the mound and the stream, but had Valenus followed the stream? On the map the wood looked relatively small, but once inside it was deceptively large with undulating ridges of bramble bushes and dense undergrowth.

"I have a feeling he is not dead," he mumbled.

"What?"

"I said, I have a feeling he is not dead. If you follow the stream back into the wood, he may be in some of that undergrowth. You have to try, Cappilius, you have to *try*!"

Cappilius knelt beside his colleague and gently removed his forearm from Hadrian's grip.

"I will set off immediately."

"Did we win?" Hadrian called after him.

"I think us just being here answers that question," Armolin confirmed, waving Cappilius on in his search. "We won, but it was so close we are still not sure what to do with our victory. The orka almost broke us again, but this time they surrendered, rather than die, and against all opinion Julius ordered everyone to allow them to live. Now the Haderians are surrendering in droves and we are at a loss as to how to deal with this phenomenon, as it has never happened before. But we can talk further when you have rested. For now, you need only rest and relax. I will find a healer, then you can be moved back across the river."

"Thank you."

Armolin smiled down at the prone legionary and wondered what had made these men, who only a few months earlier had hated Valenus with a passion, decide to follow him into the wood? Not only had most of them perished, but their remains had now been turned to ash. If the fire had caught hold of the grass, then this man would have suffered even greater pain before his death.

Even then, although dehydrated and in severe pain from two serious wounds, his first concern had been for his companions and not his own comfort, especially whether Valenus had been found; and, if not, then to demand they begin to search for him. The more she looked at these men the more she felt confused.

Honour and duty bound her to follow orders, but these people had followed Valenus on the promise of money and other spoils, knowing full well they would never collect anything except perhaps six feet of earth and a headstone. They were a strange people and yet compelling too. She understood how some people called the mortalkind the lesser elves, much to the chagrin of the elves, as their features were similar except for the ears and the shade of the skin.

Her thoughts were disturbed by a great commotion down by the stream. They were a fair distance away, so she could not hear what was being said, but from the whooping and shouting it was clear that they had found Valenus.

"It seems your leader is alive," she said.

"Alive?"

"Valenus, that is the name? Yes, he is alive, if I am reading Cappilius' mad dancing down by the wood's edge correctly."

"That's good news," Hadrian smiled. "A bit of a shame that Volas survived though, he is a right Bas...!"

Armolin grinned and placed a hand gently on the man's mouth. "I see your spirits are returning. Come, if you can walk, we will begin the journey to the healer."

"I can with your aid."

"Then let us be off."

The two journeyed all the way across the battlefield of the West Hill and, by the time they reached the warship-bridge, Cappilius had caught up with them, along with a prone body lying on a new stretcher.

"Alive," he said, motioning to Armolin to move ahead across the bridge first. "But only just."

Hadrian and Valenus simply looked at one another in recognition of a miracle. A miracle! They had survived after all!

<hr />

To all and sundry, the next few hours seemed to blend together, as each movement was no longer acknowledged, exhaustion robbing them of the memory. Instinct was now their fondest ally. No one single event mattered, but all linked together to form part of one long everlasting explosion of destruction, as the headless snake that was the enemy continued to struggle against the inevitable. Some surrendered, following Omkanis' example, believing that to live was better than to be a buried bag of bones, but the majority continued to fight under the direction of Igluk.

The battlefield was now strewn with the dead and the dying, and many of the supporting services had slowly begun to make their presence felt, as they sought to succour the injured and frightened. Nobody embodied better than Kol the anguish of even the most hardened of warriors, where so many had been slain in the name of freedom. If only it had been possible to solve the racial differences another way, and he found his eagerness for battle finally blunted!

He remembered the tear he felt as the enemy swept forward towards the triangular wood, where he had stolen his first kiss. Now this wood was in the throes of burning to the ground. Now a waterfall of anguish had replaced the tear, as the bitter struggle continued, but no longer with any real purpose.

It was then and only then that the General suddenly turned to storm out of the tower and race down to the riverside to implore the orcs to end this useless bloodbath. They had redeemed their honour and fought for reasons best remembered by them, but it was no longer necessary to perish. He knew with absolute certainty, although he did not know how, that the Mage was dead. Igluk now led them, a fool on a fool's errand, a creature who desired power more than he cherished the continuation of life, of their lives!

In his eagerness however, he strayed too close to the orc line, which had been cut off from their rudimentary bridges at the waterfall, by

Khazumar's efforts. Nobody saw who fired the arrow, but it struck with such force that he could not hold his footing on the wet grass and landed heavily on his back.

"No..." came the cry, as the elves and dwarves again closed for the kill, mercy being left far behind this time.

"No, hold them back! End this killing! This must stop!" cried Kol, in desperation.

His cry was lost in the clash of steel, as the final scene on the northern bank was completed and the orcs were either dead or cast down over the waterfall. A fate they did not relish, for they feared that drowning prevented their soul from rejoining the horde in the underworld. Meanwhile Kol was forced to retire, and several people feverishly tried to establish whether the shaft had been poisoned, then sighed with relief when it became clear that no puss could be seen in the wound.

Another scene involved Elvandar, who had earlier charged down the hill with part of the Priesthood Guards, claiming that it was now their true destiny to revenge the Azar-Kad caves insults. Crassus had feared for him, and urged his own people to support the well-trained dwarven elite, but it took too long and they were quickly set upon from all sides.

After the devastation of the scorpions it was a bitter time to desperately try and reach trapped friends, knowing this was an impossible task. The orcs achieved their last victory as they felled the great elf from his horse, but in doing so any semblance of civility ended. Now they would all perish, and without hesitation the orcs charged forward for the last time.

Crassus had brought down numerous scorpions to assist in finally defeating the orcs, but by this time barely a thousand of the fools remained standing, with perhaps the same number lying injured on the ground. Elvandar could not be found and even to this day it remains unknown what happened to his body, but the news travelled fast and this caused the lack of mercy that Kol witnessed. The elves had lost a lord that they esteemed as a king, had then found a new lord in Elvandar, only to have this person also snatched from them in death, so revenge sang sweet in their hearts.

With this last task done they all collapsed where they had come to a stop, and wept. They wept for the injured, for the dead and the lost friends. They wept for the freedom they had finally secured, after it had looked an impossible task. Many even wept for the thousands of the enemy who had also perished, even though their purpose could not be condoned. But, if the truth were known, they truly wept because they were still alive to enjoy the fruits of this freedom, which had cost them all so dear.

So high a price and they had many other losses to consider yet!

After the battle at the great bridge, they had achieved something greater than just a spectacular victory, which was secured by the very isolation of the Haderian survivors. This brilliant success, at its every level—the timing, the concentration of force, and the exploitation of the enemy's weakness, arrogance and over-extension—had all eventually been to their advantage. Indeed it was more, as it achieved a complete reversal in the strategic initiative, where the large mass had failed to defeat the smaller army because of the latter's greater generalship.

From this day forward, Igluk was to remain on the defensive, while Kol pushed onwards, always seeking to prevent the split factions of the Haderian army from mutually supporting each other. The goblins had retired to Sight Fortress, where they were hunted down and executed in droves, their fighting spirit apparently exhausted.

Most of the main hobgoblin force was caught and trapped in northern Dwarmania where, due to their brutality, not a single one of those caught was permitted to live, although later a second faction was left unmolested. Only the orcs, sunorcs, orka and those goblins that remained with Igluk retained any kind of defence, but they were now too few to fight a pitched battle. They were beaten and even the less knowledgeable had no difficulty understanding this fact. More and more began to surrender to the mercies of Dwarmania.

Kol maintained enough pressure to prevent any cohesive resistance, but never sought a final confrontation. Even in victory his people would not have been able to fight such a battle, so Igluk was allowed to leave unmolested. Kol's decision to retire after Holvidar had been vindicated. He was the hero of the day, but to him there were thousands of heroes, not just him. The enemy had left the peninsular, but the war was not officially over.

In the woods, Julius, oblivious to the final victory on the other side of the river, extracted as many of his people as he could before

Omkanis' trap closed, but the loss was apparent, and Cappilius' intervention well thanked. So he, in turn, set the entire wood ablaze, not wishing to risk another life, as news had finally reached him that Khazumar had driven the enemy from the southern bank of the Great Bridge.

From that moment onwards the enemy's will to resist ended but, fearing a trap, they both advanced cautiously towards the East Hill, where, to their great surprise, they found the exhausted Cappilius arm in arm with a youthful hobbit female. The hill was already in their hands, while the enemy leader had used a transportation incantation to leave this place of defeat. For them the day had ended, but for poor Igluk it had only just begun.

After taking Hadrian and Valenus to the healers, the two velites leaders had returned to meet Julius and Khazumar at the East Hill and together all four had continued the advance south.

Moving from one place to the next, Igluk's people were despised and blamed for the defeat by the other factions of Haderia. He had once again ignored the signs, but with hindsight it was always easier to condemn those who commanded. But the real truth was that anyone he now encountered did not really intend to discuss the matter. They intended to cut his head off!

So he ran, after using his incantation, and arrived on the far right where a large portion of Orcassians had fought all day against an enemy that had never numbered more than ten thousand. However, they too had been defeated, while nearby goblins had taken to attacking them in rogue bands, almost as though another power had kept them together as a single entity. A force that no longer existed! Igluk nodded and told his people that he would be their saviour, as the Mage was dead!

He did not of course know this for certain, but then neither did they: if the Mage lived, then Igluk would most assuredly have been dead, due to this defeat. Hence his certainty as regards the claim! A defeat that easily topped all his other defeats, both this day and during the southern campaign. A defeat that ended all cooperation between the Haderian factions, when they had come so close to enslaving the Dwarmanian Kingdom.

The sunorcs had already left, sensing defeat long before it happened. They, in particular, had never been controlled by the

Mage and retained independence. They had come for the sheer joy of killing since the Moravian front had gone quiet during peace talks.

The regiments of doom, goblins all, had quickly regrouped and marched south at a frightening speed to reach their warships. Ginnis was not amongst them as he had been captured, but they fought two skirmishes against the orcs, who were also seeking the same warships to take their people back to Gobli, where Julius and Khazumar shadowed and observed, but did not intervene.

Then, at the right moment, Kommodos arrived with the revived fleet, and destroyed most of the enemy warships in one vast battle that lasted the better part of three days. Even with this final victory, at least fifty percent of the enemy managed to escape.

Igluk, to save his own people, allowed his warships to be boarded by Kommodos, who then escorted them beyond the Gulf of Gobli to their own lands. He too witnessed a sea battle between two factions of goblins and did not intervene, but found it good to watch so many perish with none of his people put at risk. The enemy had been truly broken, and their mutual cooperation completely and utterly shattered.

The second group of hobgoblins continued to ride north and, following orders from the king, was permitted to rejoin the Noborian River, where they finally left their lands. No villages were attacked and not a single life was put in jeopardy, while starvation took many a soul of the wolves and their riders. Of the Black Thorians nothing could be found. Julius and Crassus tried to find out, but Khazumar had simply told them not to investigate further, to avoid friction with the Dwarmanian government. Not unaccustomed to slavery, as a means of punishment, it was assumed this had been their fate, but they never found out. They were never meant to.

Cappa finally found Helin and the two returned north to a hero's welcome. Helin was saddened by the news that her father had perished in the last throws of defeating the enemy, but Issus proudly stated that such a brave soul was surely with his ancestors, where he belonged. Kollis and Komar also returned north and, for the first time, attended Kol's court with a courtesy that shocked one and all. It was over, Sight Fortress was in dwarven hands again and so was the entire southern peninsular.

So ended the struggle of the Gods, who had in their vanity given a special gift to two *very special souls*. It had not been a gift of evil, but more a gift that enabled them to reopen the void if they so desired, the void that had stood for aeons, closed.

One a doorway.

One a key.

One the Mage and the other an Oracle. Names did not matter, but for the moment peace was for all to enjoy.

Peace to enjoy!

But the key and the door still existed and perhaps that was the saddest part of this entire adventure. The door had not been closed entirely and the Gods had again forgotten to bolt it shut!

Hades had but to find another way to open the door! Hades had kept his foot in the doorway in order to make it possible to find another way!

If only Zeus had stayed a few moments longer, he would have known this for sure, but the weak minds of the Gods were soon distracted elsewhere. Although Aarun had tried to maintain a watch his new existence was soon too powerful to ignore, and he had so much to learn.

Meanwhile, Hades began to wait!

Cappa stood at the window of their new home and watched as Helin playfully picked up their newborn son. It was five years since he had run back down those steps at Sight Fortress. Five glorious years of unending happiness, although at first he had felt nothing but guilt. Now everything was different, and he felt more at home in this city of Lo than ever before. He could not recall any time in the past at which he had experienced such happiness.

All of the races of Tannis had grown beyond expectations, while working together for the common good. The enemy had been truly broken and they could settle into their new existence, with relatively little difficulty, once everyone had accepted that there was no going back.

They had also, of course, brought their own brand of social strife, but this too would diminish with time although, as he watched Helin wash a little mud from the child's hands, he felt the first pang of alarm pierce his heart.

Nothing ever lasted forever.

The peace Aarun had spoken of was already beginning to unravel. He also remembered the elf's warning that he must find Igluk, of all people, and become the friend of an orc. What did he have to do with their future? Had he not achieved enough with the death of Khazumar's son?

In his hand, he held a letter from Lord Khazumar from the Azar-Kad caves, where Elvandar, no less, had mysteriously reappeared after his disappearance at the final battle at the bridge. This could hardly be good news, he groaned.

Where had he been these past five years, and why should he suddenly reappear now? Should he tell Helin or should he just leave for Azar-Kad?

Khazumar had mentioned a continued problem with Daxus' rebels, who had started attacking the hobbits from their mountain hideouts. Could Elvandar's reappearance have anything to do with this? Khazumar did not say. All he requested was that Cappa travel immediately from the city of Lo, where he had settled, to the caves. Perhaps Helin should at least know about the raids on her homeland, he thought.

No, I will keep my own counsel for now.

With a resigned look he promptly screwed up the letter and threw it into the open fire. For a moment it delayed, then in a flash the fire quickly consumed the parchment.

Khazumar had also mentioned that Atronius had now taken to calling, nay insisting, his title was *Imperator*, rather than the earlier term of *Primus*. It did not seem much to the dwarf, but to Cappa the significance was profound. The title could only be claimed by a victorious general after a battle, and it implied that further conquests would follow.

What could Atronius possibly be thinking?

This worrying development alone was enough to ruin his day, but there was no reason for Helin to be upset. However, Atronius Sulla had also gone one step further and called their new settlement *Novo Roma*! Did he really think the few survivors of this war could create a new *Republic*?

Cappa felt as though his heart would explode with grief. Enough souls had perished the last time, so why was Atronius trying to start it all over again?

It will have to wait.

I have a new life now and my son is far more important to me.

With a heavy heart, he walked outside to join his son and wife and marvelled at how much she smiled these days. It was a joy to behold and he had no intention of losing that love just yet.

Khazumar, Atronius and Elvandar will just have to wait!

So ended the first tale of the world of Tannis. The second was set to start shortly after the first letter from Khazumar to Cappa, but that is another tale.

(Second book in the trilogy due soon).

Index of main characters and locations

Aarun (Lord) — The elven lord initially assigned by the Gallician court to organise the *arrivals*, due to his knowledge of the lost peoples of Tannis and his understanding of other people's cultures. He was also disliked in Gantran for his constant dabbling in what he called *Healing Powers*, but to other elves this basically meant the forbidden subject of *magic*.

Anka-mork — Second naval port of the Gobli and about half the size of Tula-mork. It was also the only known location where orcs and goblins actually lived in the same region without killing each other. It was here that a necromancer first bred the Hobgoblins of old, and it was believed that they were the mixing of the two races of orcs and goblins.

Armolin — Under-Captain in the maiden regiment commanded by Helin. She was destined to play a major role in the final battle.

Arnim — Marshall of the lost people, commander of their armies and a great orator and politician.

Arrim — A captain of the lost people, bypassed for command of the army by Arnim. He was not trusted by anyone.

Auxillia — Support formation to the legion, usually at the strength of three hundred to five hundred men, each armed with a spear, a circular shield and light leather armour.

Azar-Kad — Azar and Kad were two mountains within the Eastern Mountains in northern Dwarmania. They sat on either side of this range, which was the boundary between Dwarmania and Orcassia to the east. This name was applied to the caves built by an unknown people in ancient times long before any recorded histories, much older than two thousand years. It originally held only four tombs, and the Dwarmanian kings chose it as a final resting-place for all senior officials of the kingdom. The kingdom had been established five hundred years earlier. The number of tombs therefore grew and led to the creation of the Priesthood Guards, given the task of ensuring the security of the King's final resting-place.

Baha Mountains—A range of mountains east of Azar Kad in Orcassia.

Baha'Cha—The only known port of the Orcassians. Whatever was here remained completely unknown, except that vast fleets were sent south to Haderia every year.

Beutis—Known as the southern city of Zeutis, but even less was known of these people, as nobody ever traded with them long enough to learn anything.

Black Thorians—When this term was originally applied it referred to an anti-government organisation, which had at first comprised only *Gretan dwarves*. Set the task of causing the downfall of the Dwarmanian government and the return to the city-state power blocks, they were few in number and derived their name from a plot to assassinate their king in Thoria during a royal visit. After this attempt, one hundred and fifty years earlier, nothing was seen of these people until the *arrival*.

It was felt that they also had every disaffected person in their ranks and were no longer made up solely of Gretans. It was known that even a few elves had joined this force. At the Southern Campaign, for example, over ten thousand joined the Haderian Army alone. How many spies resided elsewhere was not known and probably never will be!

Boss—Heavy circular attachment in the centre of a shield to add weight to any pushing motions.

Bridges of Kallisi—A Moravia construction designed for the people and built by them (although it is not commonly known that Hildar dwarves *actually* designed the bridge itself!). At a time of great unrest, the court decreed that the bridges be built to unite the Northern Provinces and the Southern Provinces of their kingdom. The task did indeed unite the people, and the Island of Modanes— including the city of the same name—was finally joined to the Island of Moravia after one hundred years of toil. To this day it remains one of the greatest achievements of any race on Tannis.

Cappilius Paelignus—Auxiliary commander of the trapped Fort at the Rhodanus Bridge. Tribune Scipio was assigned to relieve this beleaguered force. He eventually rose to prominence in Tannis and to command the Army of Allegiance's scouts.

Cassius Evictus "The Black"—This man had unknown powers from the Underworld, but within the legion was ignored and ridiculed for his membership in the *Brotherhood*, a dark and sinister group of people who practiced human sacrifices.

Cenitarns—(Court Dwarves) The Cenitarns were the upper classes of the dwarven kingdom, and effectively made up the officer grades in the army and in the higher echelon of political posts. Although large regiments were raised they proved immune to training and of little use in battle. Most other dwarves found them arrogant and ill-tempered, while the elves found them intellectual. It was this faction that, one hundred years earlier, began the fashion of going beardless.

Century—Small formation in the legion, generally consisting of between sixty and eighty legionaries, two in each Maniple. Occasionally the first century of each cohort was kept at a double size, so it could in theory contain up to one hundred and sixty men.

Cliffs of Moravia—The sheer height of these cliffs was the reason why Haderia invaded the Dwarmanian peninsular, rather than Moravia. They were a source of protection for the peninsular for the entire known two thousand years of the histories. However, there must have existed ways to ascend as, five hundred years earlier, several sunorc raids on Molanis led this kingdom to create its standing army, although this remained very small and elitist. Until then they had relied on the protection of Gallicia.

Gaius Julius Caesar—Pro-consul of Roma and Governor of the Trans-alpine Gallia and Province, also referred to as Narbonensis. His destiny was heavily linked to the Gods.

Cohort—The working formation of the legion, usually consisting of between three hundred and fifty and six hundred legionaries. The larger force was normally the first cohort of any legion, which was of twice the regular size. There were ten cohorts to a legion.

Decimus Crassus—Centurion of the Tenth Legion and a great wine drinker, but nevertheless an efficient and powerful commander.

Cuirass—Armoured chest guard normally worn by the officers of a legion, but after the *arrival* most legionaries took to using this extra protection.

Danis—The Great Lake City. This city was burnt to the ground by the Orcassians three times in known history and rebuilt by the elves. However, the Iruvian Wall all but ended further attempts to destroy this wondrous city.

Danpuris—The abandoned settlement of the sunorcs. The only example of coexistence between the peoples of the orc, elf and dwarf, and recorded in the lesser scrolls, long since mislaid.

Daxus—Prince of the Helvetii, and of little practical use on a battlefield but, even more crippling than this, he believed in his own right to rule when the Hevetii council elders were unable to oppose his rise to power. Vain and obsessed with power, he had no love for the Romans and made this clear to anyone who would listen, but thankfully most of the tribes ignored his ranting and remained loyal to Atronius Sulla.

Dwalini—Capital of Dwarmania and a vast city that sprawled across a large expanse of flatlands. Founded over two thousand years earlier. The dwarves built the old city of stone, but the new suburbs were of wood and other materials. Known for its towers, which rose to almost five hundred paces in the air, it was regarded as one of the most beautiful places on Tannis, and was entirely free of crime.

Dwarmania—This dwarven kingdom consisted of numerous city-states that had, until five hundred years earlier, existed as separate power bases run by elder councils. However, the kingdom remained heavily divided in its loyalties and priorities.

Dwarmanian Peninsular—The main body of land occupied by the *dwarves*. It was the home of the Hildar, Cenitarn, Northerners, Westonians, Eastonians and Ortovians.

Dwarves—As with all of the races on Tannis, their chronological history was written from year *zero*, although it was known that the races had been on this world for much longer than the lesser scrolls recorded, but in their original writing this was taken as the first year. This was because the ancient scrolls no longer existed and, although the written evidence of the lesser scrolls covered the last two thousand years, nobody was certain of their true origins. To describe a dwarf is also extremely difficult, as general descriptions never really apply.

In stature most of them stood approximately four feet high, whereas the Westonians, Northerners and some Gretans were all known to reach over five feet. They loved building with rocks and hoarding precious jewels. They were the greatest architects of stone ever to exist, and this was a great source of pride to any individual dwarf. Another aspect, which was well known of the dwarf, was the beard, but in later years this became unpopular and most dwarves shaved the greater part of their beards off and kept only a modest moustache, or nothing at all. They all had very quick tempers and they enjoyed fighting immensely, but also had a great capacity for friendship and warmth. The Dwarmanian Kingdom was made up of the following city-states:

Ortovia	Religious
Westonia	Administration and wealth
Northern	Builders and travellers
Thoria	Warriors and nomads
Gretan	Archers and tree dwellers
Cenitarn	Diplomats and military leaders
Hildar	Intellectuals

Lesser provinces, all of which were subject to the administrational control of the named main province:

Eastonia *"Boaters"* (Westonia)
Azar-Kad (*Priesthood Guards* mainly) (Thoria)
East Tower (Ortovia)
Thor's Fingers (Gretan)
Sight Fortress (Hildar)

All the provinces were allocated a provincial-lord who acted as the controlling family. The only exception was in Sight Fortress, where a military leader and a civilian leader resided in tandem. As a sign of status, the ambitious of course fought over and preferred the lordship of one of the main provinces, rather than one of the lesser provinces!

East Tower—Over one thousand years earlier, the trading wars with Gallicia had led the Westonian dwarves to fear invasion. The fear was unfounded, but the building of this fort and high tower increased their security, by closing the eastern approaches to the *mountain crossroads*.

Elvandar—Marshall of the Royal Elven Court Archers, assigned as the direct bodyguard of Lord Aarun.

Elves—The elves were a people that, according to the lesser scrolls, had begun to record their histories two thousand years earlier. They were generally very tall with a slightly greenish/brown tint to their skin, but many also were of a paler shade, which led many dwarves to call men the *lesser elves*. This was seen as rather annoying but, as always with these intelligent and strong people, they tolerated others' deficiencies.

Of all the races, these were the people who still retained a low level of natural magic, and were prone to folly with the greater magic. However, it is believed that no elf had knowledge of the more potent magic, but the obsession remained. With generally long faces and pointed ears, they were easily recognised by the fact that even the smallest rarely stood less than six feet in height.

Flank—This was a military term used to describe the outer sides of an army. North flank, south flank, east flank, west flank or right flank and left flank were the terms normally applied.

Gantran Court—The court was the location, high in the Gantran mountain range to the west of the city itself, of the elven court and the King's palaces. It was rumoured that the walls were painted in gold, but few ever visited. Those who did were required to swear an oath of secrecy.

Gallicia—The High Kingdom of the elven people of Tannis. Founded at year zero, the time that all other races later used for their histories, they had at one stage or another interacted with all the races of the northern hemisphere, even the orcs and goblins. They were superb politicians, and a head for trade led this powerful collection of cities close to war with Dwarmania. On three occasions it also fought a war against Orcassia for the control of the five lakes of Kor.

The wars were bitter and stretched over three centuries. Then, when the Iruvian Wall was constructed to stop further orc raids, a semblance of peace was achieved until this new struggle erupted. It was not until they had signed the Pact of Allegiance with Dwarmania, to reopen trade routes, twenty-five years before this current war, that they were again thrown into the ancient conflict between the races.

Gallician Sea—A body of water that covered the northern coast of Gallicia.

Gantran—Capital of Gallicia and one of the most intricately designed cities ever seen. Built on a hexagonal format, it encompassed two rivers and covered an even larger area than Dwalini.

Gashar—Tower of *Doom* to any orc, it was the largest fortress on Tannis. It housed at least fifty percent of the Gobli population and was a hotbed of internal disruption. It was also here that the Black Regiments of Gobli were formed from the most formidable goblins. The BRG was also trained to fight in daylight and, although they found it extremely uncomfortable, they could tolerate this for ten to twelve hours at a time. In short, they could fight one day in daylight and all the following night, but on the following day some kind of cover would be needed, if they were not to suffer extreme discomfort.

Gashnak — Wall of Towers in the Gobli language. There were literally one hundred and fifty leagues of vast towers, forts and underground tunnels and trenches, designed to keep the dwarves out of Gobli *forever.* They crossed the Gretan forest, far to the east. Fearing further dwarven expansionism, the goblins maintained a constant raiding method to prevent a standing army attacking their defences. So far this had served its purpose. The fortifications were not built with any great skill, but the depth of this defence defied any effort to attack Gobli. At the shallow end it was fifty leagues in depth, while at the deepest levels it ran for over seventy-five leagues. The hatred the Gobli had for the dwarves stemmed from their ancient beliefs that Sight Fortress was built on the *Homeland* mountains. This might have been to some extent true, but their ancestors had been driven from the peninsular many centuries before that.

Gladius — Short sword favoured by the legionary and adopted from the Hispanic blade of similar design. Approximately twenty-two inches in length, its greatest asset was the ability to stab and thrust from behind the rectangular shield favoured by Roma.

Greaves — Shin guards normally worn by officers in a legion but, after the *arrival,* Capparticus suggested that all soldiers be protected.

Gretans (Forest Dwarves) — These people were the most disaffected faction in the entire kingdom. Living in the region facing not only the Orcassion border, but also the Gobli border, they had for the last fifty years or more demanded their own independence. To date it had not been granted.

Gulf of Gobli — A body of water between the dwarven Province of Gretan and the Gobli marshes on the southern end of their lands. It was well known for its intemperate weather, and few people sailed this particular stretch of water.

Gulf of Lopis—Main area where the Gallicians kept their main battle fleet.

Haderia—The accepted original homeland of the orcs. A broad area of land directly south of the Dwarmanian peninsular, in which Haderian was the only known major city, it was readily accepted as a place *not* to visit. It is not known why the Orcassian orcs split away from their origins, but in truth there was little to distinguish one from another, although the Haderian orc generally had a darker tint to the skin, due to a greater exposure to the sun.

Helin Arnim—Commander of the first maiden warrior regiment of the lost people, she was a feared practitioner of the unarmed combat practiced by her people.

Hetra Bay—In the myths of the earlier centuries, this was the breeding ground for the sea creatures of the Underworld, but it was not known why they could not go further than the extremities of this bay. Sea monsters were not uncommon, but the vast numbers supposedly found here is only a deep-rooted fear, amongst the elves especially. In their folklore, a fleet of traders entered this bay on a fool's errand to trade with Haderia. Of the fifty ships, only one returned and on that ship every soul had gone mad. To any elf the *Hetra Expedition* was an example of foolhardy greed.

Hiba—A small town built up around an elven fort designed to close the southern approaches to the *mountain crossroads*. However, it was never really occupied as a military installation and as a result the fort was in serious disrepair.

Hildar (High Dwarves)—The high dwarves, or so they had the rest of the kingdom believe, were the intellectuals of the kingdom who transformed the elven warship designs into the quiremes so readily used by all the races at sea. Innovative and quick to learn, they were also the most racial of all the *dwarves*. To them even some of the dwarven city-states had no right to belong to the kingdom, never mind any other race. These were also generally the smaller types of dwarf and they were proud of their tradition of standing below five spans (feet).

Hobgoblin—Smaller than a goblin, usually about the size of a ten-year-old boy and faster and more intelligent than an orc, but less strong, these creatures tamed the Wolves of the Gobli marshes to ride bareback. Easily recognised by their pointed nose and chin and very wide eyes. They had sharp teeth, but no tusk of any kind. Some races used the term *Gnomes* when speaking of these creatures, but in truth they used both references and delighted in the confusion this created, although it could be argued that a gnome was a small hobgoblin.

Honis—Only one Honis was ever met by an elf in over one thousand years. Taller than most elves, the Honis refused all entreaties to assist the elves in their struggles. Known to have some magical powers and the ability to shield their true form from the naked eye, the Honis would have been an exceptional ally in this Great War, or so many believed.

Since the initial encounter, however, no ambassador sent to the land of the Honis had ever returned and such approaches had ceased centuries earlier. It is not known what kind of relationship the orcs or goblins had with these extremely strange people. When they first met, all the people in the room saw a different representation of the Honis, so once more their true features are unknown! They were never involved in any of the wars on Tannis and so the elves and dwarves normally followed a policy of mutual ignorance.

Igluk—Orcassian orc who had already touched many people's lives prior to the great conflict. He was unique for an orc, in being quick to learn and not suffering from the normal lack of memory of most orcs, whose memory was extremely short. By the time of the great conflict he had risen to the position of *Great Chief* in Orcassia and had actually managed to bring most of the hordes together to create a new army.

Because of his success, the great conflict was devised, as his Orcassians were now able to tie down vast numbers of the dwarven army and allow the Haderian Army an easy conquest of the Dwarmanian peninsular. In time the Mage even taught him some of the lesser magic.

Iknar-mork—The great Haderia seaport, where their fleets were gathered and built. This was the only known entrance into Haderia, as the coastline was notorious for reefs. At the Tatamus Forest, a great marsh covered the entire coast.

Innan-Arrar—The great desert to the west of Haderian and Pitlas and also of the Iknar Mountains.

Innan-Unar—Homeland to the sunorcs. Nomadic by default, the sunorcs were rarely found in the same place from one year to the next, but there had been a considerable change in their society since the *arrivals*, when many had sought refuge within the Haderian city walls. The harshness of living in the wastelands had perhaps become too much for even this very hardy people.

Inner Sea—A name used to refer to a body of water that covered most of the base of the Dwarmanian peninsular. Its real name was Lake Kirkut.

Iruvian Wall—Built along the Iruvian Lake coast and down to the opening of the Noborian River, this wall was constructed literally to stop further orc raids. It was not infallible, but it was extremely effective.

Isle of Sotar—In the ancient texts of the lesser scrolls, the elves believed that a God called Sotar lived on this island. As usual there was no proof, but this was where the name originated. Populated by dwarves and elves, it had at one point also included a sunorc settlement, but when the new hostilities began the sunorcs were driven out by the dwarves.

Isle of Zeutis—An unusual situation, where the island inhabitants were so xenophobic they wore heavy cloaks and had no set size distinction. In truth they were a complete mystery to all the other races, but nothing was known of their origins or what they looked like. Anyone found on the island without a permit was instantly executed. Examples of this extreme form of defence were recorded by the sunorcs and elves, and even a fleet of dwarves, seeking to trade, vanished. To the dwarves, Zeutis Island was just as much a place of evil as Haderia, and they saw no difference between the two.

Issus Cellugda—Leader of the Helvetii scouts, and an elite commander who proved his worth at the caves of Azar-Kad.

Julius Galienus—A youthful legionary who ran away from responsibilities, but also refused the favour of his senatorial uncle Flavius in Roma. A down-to-earth man, he rose to great heights as a Centurion and General in the renewed legion after the *arrivals*.

Khazumar—Lord Commander of the Priesthood Guards. He was the first dwarf to be given such a command without having been a priest. That was the measure of his ability to bring out the full value of any person he met. He was extremely testy, but could also be a great friend, as Marcellus the *Teacher* was to find out.

Kikonos Bridge—This construction was usually referred to as the Great Bridge. It was the only permanent crossing place on the Kikonos River.

Kikonos River—This vast and beautiful natural barrier was commonly called the *Great River* by the dwarves. It literally cut the peninsular in two. As great a river as the Noborian, it marked the edge of their territory until it was decided to expel the goblins to its south.

Kol—General of the new Army of Allegiance during the Southern Campaign and the Great Battle. After a defeat at the Thor's Fingers Campaign, intended to repulse the goblins, he was side-tracked into southern Dwarmania, where everyone hoped he would vanish silently. Indirectly this commander became the saviour of the kingdom.

Kollis—Lord Protector of the Westonian lands and prefect for all the trade in Dwarmania. At first he was an inexperienced bungler, but in time he rose to become one of General Kol's most trusted commanders

Komar—Lord of Sight Fortress, he openly opposed Lord Kol's appointment to command the new Army of Allegiance during the Southern Campaign. He openly believed the army should have made a stand within the walls of the Fortress, but in this he was very wrong.

Kula River—The only source of water within the whole of Gobli.

Kula-mork—Main Gobli port and fleet installation. Every year a fleet was sent to Haderia.

Kunii—These people resembled large creatures of burden, but had developed a high level of civilisation, based on regional villages. However, no one in the free kingdoms ever saw a Kunii, and there is no way of knowing where they stood within the world's politics. It is known that the orcs had attempted to conquer the land hundred years before and had failed, never to try again. It was not known whether they supported the good or evil factions within the struggle, or indeed whether they were even aware of the war itself.

Lakes of Kor—From west to east these were Kor, Loka, Ippa, Danis and Iruvia. These lakes were claimed to be the breeding grounds of the Orcassians but, after conquering them, the elves would not relinquish them. This was the reason for the especially great hatred between the elves and Orcassians.

Legion (Legio)—Major formation of Roma, which at the time of the arrival generally contained between three thousand five hundred and five thousand legionaries.

Lesser Mage—Similar to the elven mystics and healers. The Mages could conjure up basic incantations, but could not tap into the greater power of the Gods.

Leuti—Northern settlement of Zeutis Island situated high in a forest, the only vegetation on the island.

Lo—Settlement in northern Dwarmania classed as the second city of the kingdom, Lord Kollis' seat of power no less. Situated at the base of the Cenitarn Mountain, it was a small citadel with a vast harbour covering an unknown amount of leagues. It was believed that two thousand warships could dock there without straining its resources, but in reality such days never really existed.

Lolis—In times gone by this was the main Moravia port, where one thousand years earlier the first real warships had been built. Wealth from trade enabled the city to grow quickly, but for two hundred years it had been in decline, and vast areas of the city had become wastelands with their houses empty, except for the bandits that terrorised the local mountains. It had the reputation of being the home of all sea pirates, which were, surprisingly, elves.

Lopis—On the northern coast, this was the main Gallician port.

Mage—A powerful medium for the direct implementation of the Gods' powers within Tannis. The void prevented any God from simply throwing forth his powers and so it was that the Mages were found few and far between.

Maniple—The next level up from the Century, this consisted of one hundred and twenty to two hundred legionaries, three in each cohort.

Marcellus Sabinus—"*The Teacher*" Formerly a teacher, this man joined the legion late in life to see the world. His knowledge of the Gods was second to none. He quickly studied the world of Tannis after the Azar-Kad situation, with the aid of Lord Khazumar. Together they developed numerous maps, which Marcellus treasured.

Marius Capparticus—"*Cappa*" Senior Optio within the Maniple commanded by Valenus who rose to prominence due to the men's trust in his character.

Men—Primarily of Helvetii stock and Roman breeding. The maidens were few, but brought from a nearby village of the Helvetii and also from the camp followers within the Roman fort at the Rhodanus River. Generally the Romans were roughly five feet tall and built as any soldier would be when trained to wield a sword and shield for eight hours a day.

The Helvetii peoples were generally taller and of heavier stock, but favoured the broadsword and had less training in tactics on the battlefield. The dwarves and orcs alike saw them as the end of the world, and it is no wonder their arrival was met with hostility.

Modanes—This vast settlement was the capital of the Northern Provinces of Moravia, and was a city completely built of glass, or so rumour had you believe. It was of course only these people's obsession to have open walls of glass, rather than stone or just windows. However, the skills to build such monumental walls of this substance did not travel, and to this day they are the only people to be so motivated in using glass to create large auditoriums where at night you could sit and watch the stars. Their other products, such as vases and plates, were shipped throughout the entire world and could even be found in Haderia, where they arrived, however, by methods other than trade.

Molanis—Capital settlement of Moravia, built at the confluence of two great rivers (Molanis and Mora). It was not a real citadel, as only the palace had a wall and a fort. The city had dwellings constructed only of wood, and although it was exquisite in design, its defences were minimal.

Molisis—Captain within Helin's maiden regiment.

Mora Lake—A body of water south of the Mora River and the Moravia capital, Molanis. Of significant religious importance to the elves, and it was said that a temple had been built there hundreds of years before.

Mora Priests—These priests were the politicians of Moravia and constituted a very deep and kind faction in the entire world of Tannis. It was believed that they were unable to lie and lived a life of purity far beyond any other religions. It was also rumoured that they were an ancient order of warriors, but only the priests were ever permitted to enter their Temple.

Moravia Kingdom—Generally referred to as the *Lower Kingdom* of the elves by the dwarves, orcs and goblins, but in truth this domain of the elves was almost as powerful as the Gallician Kingdom. The people here, however, lived a life far more closely linked to the sunorcs of Innan-Unar than many cared to admit. Some believed that there was an offspring from a carnal knowledge, and most dwarves referred to these elves as the *"Dark Ones"* or *"Dark Elves"*, because they seemed to tolerate the sunorcs and openly traded with them. These ingenious elves built the Bridges of Kallisi, which literally linked all the islands within their kingdom. Stretching for almost one hundred leagues, the construction used three large islands as the main highway. Closed to most outsiders, it was a wonder that few were permitted to see, never mind travel along its full length.

Moravian Sea — Body of water to the north of the Moravia island and bordering the western coast of Gallicia. Many Gallicians disputed this name and referred to this as the Sea of Gantra, but it was not an issue to anyone else.

Mortalkind — This was a phrase applied by the Gods, primarily to the men who experienced the *arrival*. It was also a suitable phrase applied to many of the other races on Tannis, but the other races had a longer life than men, who normally failed to surpass one hundred and ten years. The myth that some of the races were immortal was not true, as even the Gods could not exist forever, but due to our short existence it might seem as though they had done so. In truth any creature that can be mortally injured is of mortalkind, but their cultures did not use this phraseology. Even for men, this term was somewhat inaccurate, as all things are in one way or another mortal.

Mountain Crossroads — Almost two thousand years before the dwarves had found a crossing over their Northern Mountain Range. Although it rose to almost eight thousand paces and was hard on the lungs it was possible to cross over it, but only during the summer. The east side led to Dwarmania, the southern path led to the Southern Province of Gallicia, the northern path led to the open lands nestled between the Northern Mountains and the Gallician Lakes of Kor, while the west side entered the Central Realm of Gallicia and from there ran a direct route to their capital.

Noborian River — This natural watercourse was, by far, the greatest divide between Gallicia, Dwarmania and Orcassia. Fast and deep, it was never bridged successfully and therefore served as a perfect barrier against the orcs. However, in the summer it was less ferocious and could be crossed in boats. This led the dwarves to build the Noborian forts. At the time of this great conflict, eleven had been built, to house up to five thousand people at any one time. In times of great danger, the Thorian Dwarves used them as places of refuge, not always with good results.

Northerners—(Mountain Dwarves) These were the architects of Dwarmania, and the cave at Azar-Kad was their enduring monument. They were generally very wary of strangers and did not contribute to the war at all, seeing it as other people's problem, not theirs. Even more so than others, they chose to ignore the war.

Orcs—These creatures were first bred, by the Gods, in the pits of Haderia. Nobody was certain why they were brought to life, but with so much malice they rarely liked each other, never mind the dwarves or elves. These people first developed the belief that the word *man* or *mortalkind* was a myth lost aeons before by the Gods, never to return. When the lesser scrolls, almost unreadable, were found one thousand years ago, this belief then spread across the whole of Tannis.

To an orc a *mortalkind* was a prediction of destruction and would send it into a battle-frenzy. The belief was perhaps an offshoot of the Gods attempting to educate these creatures, but few orcs would have had the patience to learn the skills of writing, and reading was an absolute impossibility. Unless, of course, they were asked to read a map or plan an attack.

Some within Dwarmania believed, the Ortovians especially, that the orc was a mixture of malice and *mortalkind* emotions created by the Gods of the Underworld but, as might be expected, there was no tangible proof of this belief. There were also those who believed they were fallen elves. Once again this was laughed aside by the elves.

There was further hatred between the orcs and elves due to the understanding that elven maidens had been kidnapped to breed with by the orcs at least two or three thousand years before, hence the origins of the maiden orcs, and possibly also of goblins. This was also an unsubstantiated rumour, but it nevertheless fuelled the hatred between these races.

Orka—Similar in height to the Troll, these creatures were large orcs, but with the added quality of intelligence. They were capable of mastering unified combat manoeuvres and, fighting in formations, they far outstripped any soldiers Haderia possessed. They did not appear, however, until after the *arrival*, leaving no doubt that the mortalkind had been involved in their breeding, along with the Underworld Gods. Some believed they were the Mage's brainchild, but this was never confirmed.

Orkan Mountains—A range of mountains east of the Kor Lakes

Orkan'Cha—The only known city of the Orcassian orcs. These hordes did not generally occupy buildings, but this was the exception.

Orto—City in Ortovia deep in the forest. Few people travelled there and it was a religious retreat for the dwarves.

Ortovians—(Religious Sect Dwarves) These were the conscience of the kingdom and made up seventy percent or more of Khazumar's Priesthood Guards, who protected the tombs at Azar-Kad. Highly superstitious and fearful of many changes, they had an enormous amount of power at the Dwarmania court, but were rarely interested in anything other than their independence. Like Gretans, they did not care much for central government policies.

Outer Sea—A body of water between the eastern coast of the Dwarmanian peninsular and the coast of their Thoria Province, to the east. The Inner Sea on the peninsular was considerably smaller and landlocked. Most of the dwarves in Thoria referred to this span of water as the *Thorian Sea*, but this name was not found on any official maps of the kingdom.

Pila—Also pilum, these were the spears thrown prior to engaging an enemy in close combat. They came in light and heavy varieties.

Pitlas—Here stood a small fortress built around superstition and hatred. Rumour claimed that here the enemy Gods lived and that there was a direct doorway to the Underworld, but this remained unsubstantiated, as no one who entered the fortress ever returned!

Cornelius Porta—Legionary Superbus, the others had placed bets on how long it would be before this disobedient soldier was put to death. He was more trouble than any of them could have believed, or perhaps ever wanted to believe.

Primus Pilum—Atronius Sulla, respected as the most experienced officer in the legion, he eventually rose to command the initial Army of Allegiance at the River Battle. Quick-minded and direct in his tactics, he was rarely caught off guard. An exceptional soldier!

Scorpiones—Scorpion ballistic weapons employed by Elvandar and Crassus in the final battle. Capable of throwing several large arrow projectiles at the enemy in very swift succession, they were able to rip through an entire regiment and leave it devastated.

Scutum—Cylindrical shield used by the legionaries.

Sea of Cha—Little was known of this body of water east of Orcassia and north of Gobli, and nobody ever really tried to find out.

Sea of Innan—Body of water that separated Innan-Unar and Moravia in the west

Sia—Main source of water in Orcassia, which was actually two rivers, but the orcs did not distinguish one river from another. This led people to believe that Sia was their word for water itself. It emerged from the Iruvian Lake and was a constant reminder to the orcs that their homeland was now occupied.

Sight Fortress—Built over one thousand years earlier, the fortress stood at the very tip of the mountains facing Haderia. Although it was not common knowledge, the dwarves actually threw out the goblins that resided in these mountains, now known as the Holvidar Mountains, and initially built the fortress to stop them returning. It then symbolised the very existence of Dwarmania. At first there existed only the citadel, two thousand paces up the mountainside. However, the Hildar realised that, by using glass and metal, it was possible, on a good day, to see the Haderian coast. This led to the second citadel being built three hundred years later, and the third three hundred years after that, with the interconnecting palisades. Finally, walkways were finished another two hundred years later, to connect all three, the latter standing in its uppermost tower at nearly five thousand paces above sea level. From this point it was possible to see Pitlas' outer walls, such was the height and the machinery designed by the Hildar to spy on their enemy.

Sotar Ferry—A vast fleet of ferry merchants existed in these two settlements, but due to their style of life they never even bothered to name their settlements and were known simply as *Ferry*. It was rumoured that sunorcs also settled there, but Gallicia always hotly denied this statement!

Straits of Jupitannis—Body of water heavily crossed by reefs separating Haderia and the southern tip of the Dwarmanian peninsular.

Straits of Sotar—Water surrounding the Isle of Sotar, the stepping-stone between Gallicia and Moravia. Forever a melting pot of piratical warships, it was a no-go area unless you were known to a pirate clan.

Sunorcs—Sunorcs were creatures slightly smaller than the Orcassian or Haderian orc, but they could dwell in open sunlight with little discomfort. Clearly they were bred for this purpose and normally served as fast, light scouts for the Haderian armies. For orcs, they were extremely quick-witted and, although they still relied heavily on their animal instincts, they were brutal in combat and also very skilled at using the bow and concocting poisons.

Tatamus Forest—The only real vegetation in the whole of Haderia, but not the open, beautiful trees as on the main continents; rather a bitter and twisted forest where it was believed even the trees felt a deep malice for anything good or kind. Here it was thought the very use of any word of kindness could cause a ripple to stir through the forest, with malice the reply from everything there within. It was also rumoured that many unknown creatures of the Underworld were bred there, and it was in fact taboo in both elven and dwarven religions. To even mention its name was to bring bad luck.

Thorians—(Border Dwarves) Forever on the border of Orcassia, this region of Dwarmania developed stout and powerful warriors who made up at least sixty percent of the standing army. Excellent tacticians, they also made superior officers, but due to their almost colonial status at court they were normally refused the higher posts in the army. Nevertheless, they occupied the Noborian Fort-line, at the river of the same name, for many years and to them there was no greater honour than to achieve the rank of *Fort Commander*. Due to the orcs, they were also prone to live a more nomadic lifestyle and their encampments tended to move frequently, thus there was no real knowledge of just how many of them there were.

Thor's Fingers—At its base, the Noborian river split into five distinct channels known as Thor's fingers. Thor was the common word applied to Zeus by the dwarves, but it was generally frowned upon by anyone religious.

Titanus Scipio—The ultimate example of a spiteful, callous mortalkind, who was eventually seduced by the powers of the Underworld.

Tovia—The main trading port of Westonia and Ortovia within Dwarmania.

Trolls—Little was known of these creatures other than their sheer size. To what end they were originally bred remains unknown, and indeed the elves believed that they must at some point have been beasts of burden. Strong they were, intelligent they were not. Few survived the great cave war against the Black Thorians, although many stated that the trolls that now fought were not the same as those of old. However, the lesser scrolls gave no insight into Trollian history and therefore all this remained nothing more than conjecture.

Upperis—Dwarven and elven settlement on Sotar, small and dirty and occupied by all the undesirables of every kingdom.

Uxudulum—A lower chieftain assigned to attack the Rhodanus fort as a diversion.

Atia Valenus—Originally a deceitful and ambitious soul, Valenus changed due to the void and eventually became a valued officer within the Army of Allegiance

Velites—Support troops who carried javelins, and indeed archers, were sometimes referred to as velites.

West Tower—Built in response to the dwarven East Tower, to close the western approaches to the mountain crossroads.

Westonians—(Trade Dwarves) These particular dwarves resided in the western region (*Westonia*) of Dwarmania. They originally opened trade routes to Gallicia across the mountain crossroads over the North Mountains. They were also known to prefer elven maidens, this resulting in a considerably larger dwarf than normal. They were completely untrustworthy on any issue involving gold, but they could, however, be trusted with almost anything else.

They had in the past brought Dwarmania and Gallicia to the brink of war due to their piratical trading practices but, on the other side of the gold coin, they were exceptional administrators. Their singular wish for wealth also contributed to the other factions in the kingdom not trusting Westonians. This often clouded their judgement and led to a festering dislike between Westonians and Eastonians.

Wolves—A race of animals similar to a dog but closer to a pony in size, with a reasonable level of intelligence, but no known dialect. The wolf was a fearsome creature, but not exactly evil, just loyal to its rider. Tamed by the hobgoblins many centuries before, there were fifteen or more different breeds. The larger breeds, normally referred to as the *Sadzie*, were sufficiently strong for the smaller hobgoblins to ride to war. Many of the smaller breeds were retained as guard dogs by the goblins within Gobli, but as always there was little proof to confirm or deny these assumptions.

Zeutian Sea—A body of water between the island and the western coast of the Dwarmanian peninsular.

Zeutis—Main port and capital of Zeutis Island.

Made in the USA